Blood Gift

Blood Grace Book VII

VELA ROTH

FIVE THORNS PRESS

This is a work of fiction. Names, characters, places, and incidents either are the product of the author's imagination or are used fictitiously. Any resemblance to actual persons, living or dead, events, or locales is entirely coincidental.

ISBN 978-1-957040-21-9 (Ebook)
ISBN 978-1-957040-22-6 (Paperback)
ISBN 978-1-957040-23-3 (Hardcover)

Cover art by Patcas Illustration
www.instagram.com/patcas_illustration

Book design by Vela Roth

Maps by Vela Roth using Inkarnate
inkarnate.com

Published by Five Thorns Press
www.fivethorns.com

Visit www.velaroth.com

CONTENTS

For all of you who are searching for your magic.
Never doubt your power will grow from the ruins.

CONTENT NOTE

Blood Gift contains low-gore medieval fantasy violence, including imprisonment, torture, decapitations, and human death. Characters deal with trauma from abusive fathers. "All a Game," "Life and Death," and "Anything to Save Her" portray childbirth difficulties and a child in peril. "The Apostate" and "Divining" feature the death of a bird. Sexual content includes biting with blood drinking and light blood play.

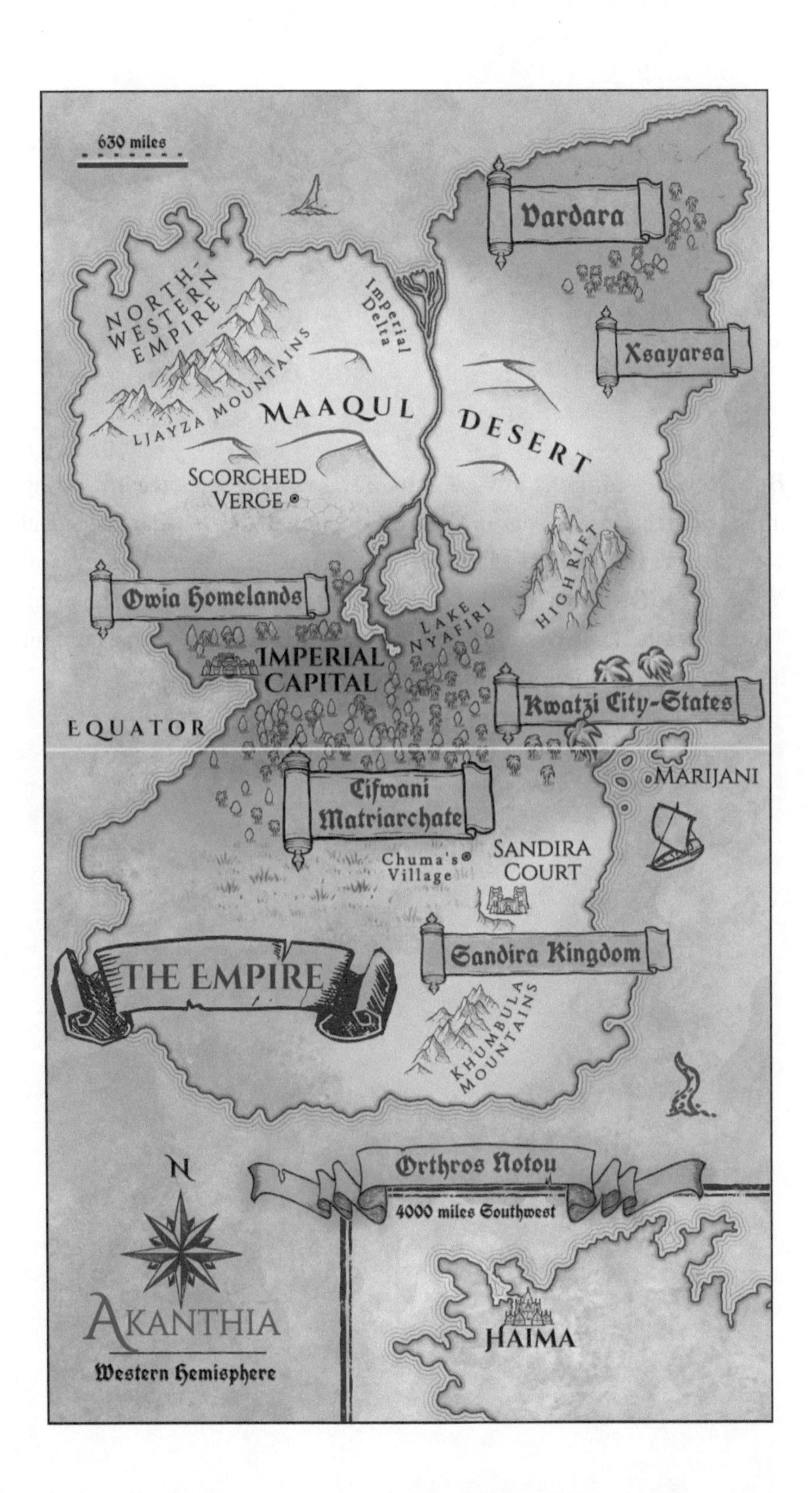

630 miles
Vardara
Xsayarsa
NORTH-WESTERN EMPIRE
Imperial Delta
LJAYZA MOUNTAINS
MAAQUL
DESERT
SCORCHED VERGE
HIGH RIFT
Owia Homelands
LAKE NYAFIRI
IMPERIAL CAPITAL
Kwatzi City-States
EQUATOR
MARIJANI
Cifwani Matriarchate
Chuma's Village
SANDIRA COURT
Sandira Kingdom
THE EMPIRE
KHUMBULA MOUNTAINS
N
Orthros Notou
4000 miles Southwest
AKANTHIA
Western Hemisphere
HAIMA

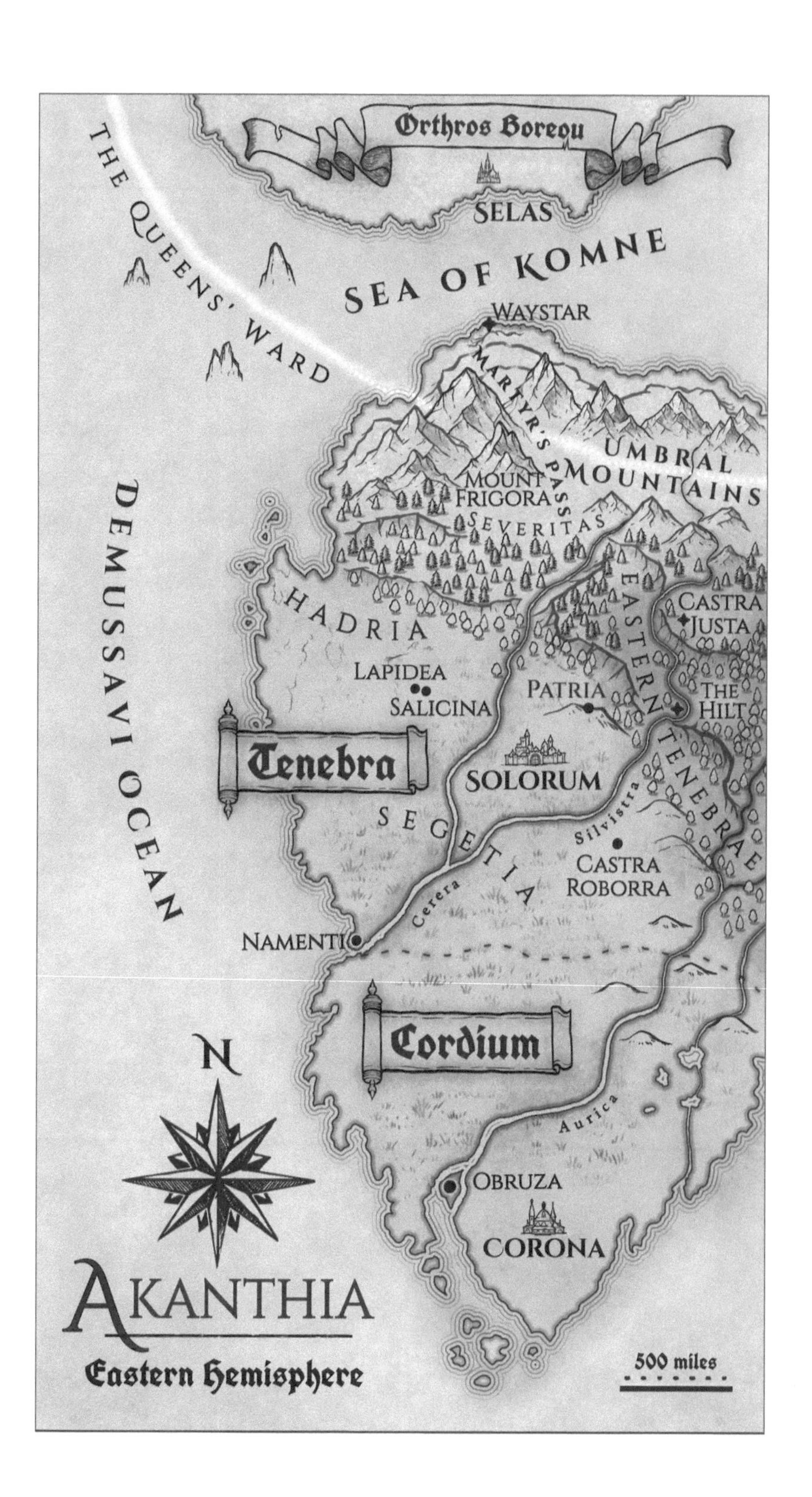

Orthros Boreou
SELAS
THE QUEENS' WARD
SEA OF KOMNE
WAYSTAR
MARTYR'S PASS
UMBRAL MOUNTAINS
MOUNT FRIGORA
SEVERITAS
DEMUSSAVI OCEAN
HADRIA
EASTERN
CASTRA JUSTA
LAPIDEA
SALICINA
PATRIA
THE HILT
Tenebra
SOLORUM
TENEBRAE
SEGETIA
Silvistra
CASTRA ROBORRA
Cerera
NAMENTI
Cordium
N
Aurica
OBRUZA
CORONA
AKANTHIA
Eastern Hemisphere
500 miles

43

nights until

NOTIAN WINTER SOLSTICE

13th Night of the Month of Ourania
1,597th Year In Sanctuary (IS)

AMBASSADOR CASSIA KOMNENA

IT WAS TIME FOR Cassia to appear before the most powerful woman in the world and tell her no.

She drew a shaking breath of humid night air and stared down the path through the Empress's cassia trees. Any moment now, she and Lio would receive their summons to appear before Her Imperial Majesty. This grove had witnessed so much history. It seemed a fated place for Cassia to change the future.

She ran her hand over her new medallion of office, comforted by the weight of the cool silver disk around her neck. Its blood magic emanated into her, faint but certain to her budding arcane senses.

She might still be human for the time being, but she was officially an ambassador for the Hesperines now, an advocate for her immortal family and friends, in service to the Queens of Orthros. *I earned this,* she reminded herself. *I deserve it.*

"And you wear it beautifully," Lio said in answer to her thoughts, which he had surely heard with his mind magic. "No need to be nervous, my rose."

As always, he understood. Her beloved Lio, all fangs and unconditional support. She ran her fingers down his fair face and dark, close-cut beard, her hand coming to rest on his medallion. It was a dream come true to be his partner not only in love, but also in their careers as diplomats.

But her heart pounded for all the wrong reasons. "I never imagined my first official appearance as an ambassador would be a private audience with the Empress herself."

He rested his hands over hers, holding them to his chest. "You have already foiled the plots of the mightiest mages and all but dethroned the

King of Tenebra. With such accomplishments to your name, where else would your career begin but in high places?"

"The Empress's greatness far outshines those men."

"You have also negotiated before the very brightest lights—our immortal Queens."

"If I were to make a mistake before our Queens, their only reply would be forgiving smiles, the only consequence my own mortification. In an encounter with the Empress, not only is her dynasty's sixteen-hundred-year-old alliance with Orthros at stake, but..." Cassia's feet seemed fixed to the ground, unable to take another step. "The next few moments could alter the fate of the entire world. Because of my decision."

Lio touched her shoulders and drew her closer. "Your choices always transform Tenebra and Orthros for the better. This will be no different."

"Now my actions will also have consequences for the Empire, our ally. The homeland of so many of our family and friends. My sister's adopted land, which kept Solia safe when she had to flee Tenebra. I could never forgive myself if I brought harm upon the Empire."

"We do have a deep bond of gratitude with the Empress." Lio ran his hands up and down Cassia's arms. "All the more reason not to fear. We are about to appear before a just monarch who will hear our words with sympathetic ears."

"You're right." The anxiety fizzing through Cassia at this moment was so different from the panic she had once battled when facing the tyrant king who had sired her. "I am equal to this."

"You were made for it." Lio's dark blue gaze swept from her head to her toes.

Under such admiration, it was impossible not to feel emboldened. "And you, my love? Are you proud to have your first private appearance before Her Imperial Majesty?"

"It feels right because we're together."

Cassia traced the high collar of his black formal robe, feeling the braid of her hair hidden underneath. Her tie around him. The reminder that he was her Grace, bound to her for eternity by Hespera, the Goddess of Night. "No matter what the Empress may try to persuade me to do, you have nothing to fear from this audience. Nothing can separate us."

He slid two fingers under her chin. When he opened his mouth to speak the simple words, his fangs were unsheathed. "I know."

He was armored only in silk, wielding nothing sharper than an ambassador's medallion. But Cassia knew he was the most dangerous person who would ever love her.

From her guest room in the Imperial Palace, they had been waging their campaign of research, strategy, and persuasion. It was meticulous. It was slow. And he was enjoying every minute of once again rearranging the world so that no one would ever take her from him.

"I've made my decision," she said, "and I know it's the right one. Not even the Empress has the power to change my future."

But Cassia's decision would change the Empire, Orthros, and Tenebra. She had command of her own destiny, as well as responsibility for the consequences.

Most difficult of all, she must help her sister understand her choice, after Solia had sacrificed everything for her.

"Her Imperial Majesty will see you now," came a woman's eerie, metallic voice.

They turned to see one of the Golden Shield nearby. These women gave their all to protect the Empress. Yet Cassia resented the golden armor concealing the warrior, especially her helmet, forged with the same face as every member of the elite guard. Cassia couldn't tell if this was Solia or another of her comrades in the Empress's service. Knight had leapt to attention, but if his canine senses could discern their familiar Soli under the armor, he gave no sign.

"Your liegehound may accompany you in Her Imperial Majesty's presence." The Golden Shield spoke with none of the affection Soli might have shown Knight.

"Thank you." Cassia took Lio's offered arm and the encouragement he sent into her thoughts. At her murmured command, Knight paraded beside them, and she was as glad for his reassuring presence as she was proud of his gait.

The Golden Shield escorted them under the showers of yellow blossoms toward the center of the fragrant orchard. Toward the tree where Cassia had reunited with Solia after fifteen years apart. The same tree an ancient Empress had planted with her sister, before bidding her farewell forever so she could live on as a Hesperine.

That would not be her and Solia's fate, Cassia vowed. When she became immortal, she would not let it separate them. She must find a way for them to have the futures they wanted and each other.

On the bench beneath the ancient cassia tree sat a woman who was undoubtedly the Empress. A thrill traveled through Cassia from standing in the presence of a mortal woman who held so much power.

Her Imperial Majesty, the shining Eldest Sister, daughter of the Queen Mothers, anointed by the ancestors and pleasing to Zalele, Goddess of the Sun, wore her might as easily as her simple wrap dress of yellow cotton. Her deep brown skin was luminous with gold dust in the spell light, and her tight steel-and-black braids were woven around an ornate golden circlet.

Tasteful but glittering reminders that her lands stretched far and wide, her treasuries ran deep, and more people lived loyal to her than to any other monarch in the known world. She smiled at Cassia with full, beautiful lips, crows' feet deepening at the corners of her eyes.

No one could ever come close to the place the Queens of Orthros held in Cassia's heart. There was room for her to be enamored of the Empress, though.

This Empress sought to make Cassia a queen.

There was a time, not so long ago, when Cassia would have coveted such power. She would have emulated the Empress and relished teaching the lords of Tenebra a lesson with a gold-dusted, female hand.

But at this moment, Cassia's greatest desire was to go home, hug Lio's little sister Zoe, and water her house plants.

She almost laughed with relief as one of her greatest fears drained away. She was not tempted.

"Your Imperial Majesty," Lio said with great respect, "allow me to present Ambassador Cassia Komnena of the Diplomatic Service of the Queens of Orthros, my partner for eternity."

His words sparkled through Cassia, little shards of joy, sharp and real and wondrous. She gave a deep bow befitting a Hesperine diplomat, and as she straightened, her medallion landed against her chest with a satisfying thump.

Knight lowered his bulk into a graceful down-stay, rewarding Cassia's efforts to prepare him for this audience. The grooming she had given his masses of shaggy fur would not last long, but it was worth the benevolent smile he won from the Empress.

"Ambassador Cassia." The Empress's regal voice rested upon her like a strong and gracious hand. "How glad we are to see you safe and well after your capture by our enemies."

Cassia found this to be the easy part, for expressing thanks was central to the Hesperine way of life—her way, now. "Your Imperial Majesty, for all you have done to rescue me from the Rezayal and for your generous hospitality since, you have my deepest gratitude and that of our bloodline. For your treatment of my sister during her years at your side, I have no words to thank you. I hope my deeds will soon speak clearly."

"What joy it has brought us to reunite you and Princess Solia after so long. I am sure you are eager to see her again, but at present, she is enjoying some well-deserved hours of sleep while her sister-in-arms attends us."

Calculations took shape in Cassia's thoughts. The Empress had planned this audience for Solia's off-duty hours and told Cassia as much. What did Her Imperial Majesty wish to say that was not for Solia's ears? What did the Empress hope to hear from Cassia that she might be less likely to confess in front of her sister? Assuming what the Empress said was true, and Solia was not hidden in that armor.

Lio touched his medallion, one of their private signals during negotiations. That meant he was confident. He must agree with Cassia that the Empress was telling the truth.

"Thank you for granting my sister a reprieve, Your Imperial Majesty," Cassia said.

The Empress made a generous gesture. "Are you well, Ambassador Cassia? We know how you suffered as the Rezayal's prisoner. We will gladly have a chair brought for you, should you need to rest."

Cassia bowed again, her head spinning at the suggestion that she might sit in the Empress's presence. "You honor me, Your Imperial Majesty, but I have never felt better, thanks to the expert care of your personal physician."

The Empress gave a nod, clearly pleased with Cassia's manners. When Cassia had learned politics in the dung heap that was the kingdom of

Tenebra, she had never imagined she would use those skills on the other side of the world in the Empire, for the sake of the Hesperines. All those years under the king's tyranny now seemed like something solid in her hand that she could wield, rather than a dreadful specter haunting her.

Solia might not be present, but her words were on Cassia's mind. *I have made my power my own, and I wield it with pride. My legacy may be ill-gotten, but I have freed it from the king, as surely as I have freed myself.*

It was time for Cassia to wield her power. "We come before you representing the Hesperines, your faithful allies, to propose a new course of action for the Empire and Orthros to undertake together for the benefit of all our people. I'm afraid this plan may not be what my sister has anticipated, but we assure you that our alternative gives no less consideration to the best interests of your Empire."

The Empress considered Cassia. "Princess Solia tells me that you spent your life believing she was the rightful heir to the throne of Tenebra because she is King Lucis's eldest daughter."

"Yes, Your Imperial Majesty."

"It must have come as a great surprise to you when she revealed that you are, in fact, the crown princess through your mother."

"I confess, I never imagined that I am the only surviving descendant of the Mage King and the Changing Queen."

"In our Empire, we inherit through our foremothers. We have listened with great interest to accounts of the ancient Changing Queen, who was the past matriarch of your clan. It is said she ruled with wisdom, long before the crown fell to warlords like the present king. It would please us to see Tenebra once more in the hands of such a queen."

Lio addressed the Empress. "We appreciate what an unprecedented moment this is, when you are willing to bestow your concern upon Tenebra, although you have previously kept that land isolated from your people for the protection of your Empire."

"We do not imagine that isolation will last forever," the Empress replied. "If it is to end in our time, we will end it with our own axe rather than allow the spear to strike us."

"There is no spear that can take you by surprise, Your Imperial Majesty," said Lio.

The Empress's gaze flicked between the two of them. "But perhaps a surprise is in store for us."

Cassia, for all her acumen at reading every minute clue a courtier might betray, could not interpret the Empress's expression. Lio had warned her that the Empress was a light mage who used her magic during audiences to illuminate or conceal. Everything she allowed others to see—or hid from them—was not only deliberate, but expertly crafted.

Cassia could not guess if the Empress would let the axe fall once she learned of their intentions.

Tension was a stone in Cassia's belly as she spoke. "Your Imperial Majesty, I am honored that you would devote your resources to aiding me in seizing my birthright." *Take another breath,* she reminded herself. "But my bloodright is to remain at Lio's side as a Hesperine. I have already given my allegiance to the Queens of Orthros. I cannot break my oaths to them, to my immortal clan, or to Lio, whose life depends on my blood."

The Empress flexed her fingers, her gold rings catching the spell light.

One more breath. "The next ruler of Tenebra will be the one who guides that kingdom's first steps toward your Empire. But as the two sides of the world cleave together, there is much more at stake than one queen's policies. There are threats no human is prepared to face. I can best safeguard your lands and people not as a mortal monarch, but as a Hesperine diplomat."

Still the Empress said nothing.

Cassia must make her see. "My inheritance is more than a crown. I am also the heir to the Changing Queen's rare magic, passed down through the women of my line. I must keep my ancestors' power alive by awakening my own dormant magic. Once I understand my abilities, it will be safe for me to transform into a Hesperine. I vow to honor both my mortal and immortal matriarchs."

The moment was upon her. She must say the words and let the consequences fall.

"With the utmost respect," Cassia declared, "I can never take the throne of Tenebra."

She had done it. Once more, she had refused that destiny, this time before the highest authority in the human world.

Lio rested a hand upon hers, his touch a reassurance and a claim. That hand held her in the Hesperine world, never to return to life as a mortal.

He spoke with pure confidence. "Orthros is sensitive to the fact that we have deprived Your Imperial Majesty of your preferred candidate for the Tenebran throne. As a result, the Hesperines are prepared to support your aims in every other way possible. Ambassador Cassia and I would be pleased to present Orthros's plan for your consideration."

The Empress was silent for a moment that seemed to last forever.

Had Cassia just made an enemy of Her Imperial Majesty?

She gave Cassia a faint smile. "You were in Orthros for months before you arrived in our Empire, and yet your sister did not know you had escaped Tenebra and found safety among the Hesperines."

Cassia swallowed, her tongue dry. "She has told me that the Rezayal intercepted that information."

"No," the Empress said. "I did."

Before Cassia could feel anger at the Empress for keeping her and Solia apart that much longer, the pieces fell into place. And she understood that the Empress had been her ally all along, in ways she had never imagined.

"Your Imperial Majesty," Cassia inquired, "may I ask if you were planning to conceal that information from my sister until after my Gifting?"

"Naturally. I wished to spare you any delays so you could secure your bloodright in peace. Alas, you met with an interruption in any case and remain mortal against your wishes."

The moment Cassia gained her fangs, her sister's plan to put her on the throne would be impossible. It was out of the question for any Hesperine to hold political power in Tenebra, where they were called heretics and monsters. If Solia had known how close Cassia had come to her Gifting, she would have done everything in her power to stop the transformation.

The Empress had not wanted that to happen.

Cassia could only conclude from this that she was not the Empress's intended candidate for the throne, after all.

"It is not I whom you spent five years grooming for the throne," Cassia said.

The Empress's smile deepened. "Solia will be a queen after my own heart."

Cassia felt one destiny lift off of her, even as she sensed another waiting to ambush Solia.

No. No, they could not let this happen.

"Your Imperial Majesty," Cassia said carefully, "I left Tenebra in the hands of Lord Flavian, a more honorable man than the present king. I have ensured he will take the throne in a matter of weeks by peaceful means."

"Of course you would take such pains to care for your people in your absence. Not knowing that your sister lived, you would do the best you could for Tenebra under the circumstances." The Empress waved a dismissive hand. "How fortunate that a poor substitute like Flavian will no longer be necessary, do you not agree?"

With those pleasant, implacable words, Her Imperial Majesty made her position clear on Cassia and Lio's master plan for the future of Tenebra.

But Lio persevered. "As you are aware, Your Imperial Majesty, we Hesperines must uphold our new treaty with the nobles of Tenebra who visited Orthros during the recent Solstice Summit. These Allied Lords favor Flavian, one of their own, for the throne. The Hesperines are in a position to negotiate with him and ensure he deals fairly with the Empire. With him as king, we can prevent any danger to your people that might arise from ending isolation. Orthros can act as both your portal and your ward while the Empire establishes contact on your terms."

"We appreciate that our Empire was never far from the Hesperines' thoughts while Orthros faced the prospect of Flavian's kingship. How glad we are that you will find yourselves in a much improved position under Solia's reign. With a Hesperine's sister ruling Tenebra, are not the possibilities marvelous?"

"A circumstance Orthros never dreamed of in our long history with Tenebra," Lio said smoothly, but Cassia felt his tension, a silent protest.

"I am under the impression Solia has not imagined this outcome, either," said Cassia.

"She is devoted to you," the Empress replied. "She would never place herself above you, the sister she regards as her queen. But we know that your greatest desire is to be removed from the line of succession, and in this, we can assist you. We trust that we have Orthros's full support in return."

Cassia's next argument died in her throat. If they told the Empress no again, it would be a refusal Her Imperial Majesty did not wish to hear.

Cassia had once more escaped becoming the Queen of Tenebra. But she had failed to realize how deeply her sister was in danger of meeting that fate.

"WHAT HAVE I DONE?" The words slipped from Cassia's mouth as soon as she was alone with Lio.

He closed the doors of their guest room behind them, shutting out the Golden Shield on the terrace and all that had happened in the orchard beyond.

When he said nothing, she looked up. His reflective eyes caught the light, glowing at her like blue jewels. Moving with the grace only an immortal possessed, he spun her around and pressed her against the door.

He brought his mouth down on hers. His lips scathed her, his beard raking her skin as his tongue stroked rough and warm into her. His magic, his presence, hummed all around her and within her.

Her thoughts melted away. She wrapped her arms around his neck, sagging between his long, firm body and the wood carvings at her back.

Then he was lifting his head, and she was drawing a breath, blinking up at the sight of his sharp, extended fangs.

"This is what you've done," he said. "You've chosen us."

She pulled his mouth back to hers. Her blood pounded with only one truth. *My Grace. Mine.*

For that moment, she let herself forget everything beyond the grip of his hand on her hip and the trail of heat his mouth made down her neck.

"Cassia." His voice was velvet against her throat and in her mind. "You've chosen me. Over a throne. Not once, but twice. Do you have any idea what that does to me?"

She ran her hand through his hair, holding him closer to feel the tips of his fangs prick her. "Show me."

"I will. Every night for the rest of eternity." He placed a slow bite upon the surface of her skin, a foretaste.

She shivered, longing to stay here against this door for an hour with no concern in the world but satisfying their Craving.

Lio pulled his mouth away, although he held her there with his body for one moment more. "As long as we're together, we can find a solution to everything else."

"We have to. If the Empress sent Solia to Tenebra, it would be little better than exiling her from her friends and family in the Empire and Orthros. I just got her back. I cannot lose her again."

"We won't allow that to happen." Lio stood back and drew Cassia further into their room. "I'm sorry the Empress took us by surprise tonight. I confess, I was so preoccupied with protecting you from her plans, I didn't predict that she would try to pull your sister away from you."

"Neither did I, but I should have." Gripping Lio's hand, Cassia slid her other one through Knight's ruff. "Solia is the woman she has mentored, whose loyalty is proven. Of course the Empress would favor her for the throne over me, and there's certainly nothing about Flavian that would impress her."

"The Empress and Tenebra will simply have to make do with him." Lio took a seat in one of the luxurious carved chairs, his hand lingering in Cassia's.

But she began to pace. "How will we ever persuade the Empress of that?"

He let her go, his gaze tracking her as she moved. "Indeed. In this era, when isolation is ending, fate has offered her an unprecedented contender for her enemy's throne."

"And she has spent years perfecting her. A queen born of Tenebra but shaped by the Empire. Why would the Empress give up such an opportunity?"

"She never will." Despite Lio's grim words, his tone held anticipation.

"You're right," Cassia said, following his train of thought. "We cannot change the Empress's mind. We will have to convince Solia."

"Yes. An appeal to your sister's heart will be more effective than negotiating with one of the greatest politicians of our time."

Cassia tracked toward the windows and the glimpses of the orchard outside. "And yet, my sister has her heart set on me becoming queen. I hate how bitterly we argued when she told me I'm the heir. It was…not what I wished for our first conversation after fifteen years."

"I know. But you have spent much happier hours with her since."

"She still doesn't understand that the world needs me as a diplomat, not a queen. That my mother's magic is all that matters, not her right to the throne."

Solia still did not understand Cassia and Lio's bond.

Cassia paced back toward the bed where she had been convalescing. "We completely avoid these topics every time she comes to see me. That is hardly a solution."

"I know." Lio's usually candid face was too neutral.

In that absence of expression, Cassia read the entire conflict between him and her sister.

What Solia had also avoided was visiting anytime Lio was awake. Cassia did not accept her sister's excuses about being assigned night shifts, any more than she accepted Lio's silence about her sister's disapproval of him.

Cassia paused. That was when she realized Knight was not shadowing her, as he was wont to do when she paced. He had posted himself beside Lio's chair, sitting there in stoic solidarity. If only humans had such keen instincts as dogs about who was a rightful member of the pack.

"Do you want to talk about what you and Solia said to each other that night?" Cassia asked, not for the first time.

Lio rested a hand on the liegehound, an immortal sitting easily with his natural predator. "When it comes to Solia, actions speak louder than words. You know I am determined to win her approval, but that cannot begin until her dream for your future ends. She must accept that you will, in fact, spend eternity in Orthros with me. I have an idea, a way we can demonstrate to her once and for all that you will never be queen."

Once again, Cassia gave into her restless need to move, to think on her feet. "What do you have in mind?"

"A display the Empress will appreciate. It must take place before her entire court."

"Making a show of removing me from the line of succession will keep us in her favor. But we must go into that encounter with a plan for how to remove Solia as well."

"Yes, we must give her a compelling reason to resist the Empress's plan." Lio stretched his long legs out in front of him.

Cassia halted her furious strides, lest she trip over the very tall Hesperine in her path.

He gave a quiet laugh. "That is a beautiful scowl, my rose. Do not be cross with me. I know that sometimes, my Lady of Schemes needs to pace. Other times, you need to sit on my lap."

"How can you be so cheerful when we've just learned that the Empress herself stands in the way of our plans?"

"Whenever we find ourselves facing a terrible threat, I will always offer my lap as a solution. Or any other part of me you might find helpful under the circumstances."

Her hands unknotted.

"I also confess," he added, his voice deep and soft, "very little could dim my spirits at the moment. You've made me too happy."

This was what she had done tonight. Secured her Grace's happiness. And her own. It made her feel more powerful than any monarch.

Powerful enough to solve anything, even this impossible situation.

She slid into Lio's embrace, curling against his body. "Your lap is an excellent place for scheming."

"But also a place to rest when you've been out of bed too long."

"Ah, I see how it is. This was all a plot to get me off my feet."

"I will compensate you with both cuddling and diplomatic insights."

"I deem this a fair bargain, Sir Diplomat. What insights do you have on my sister? For I must confess, you are better suited to judge her character than I am at present. I am nothing close to objective."

"Your sister is driven by duty and loyalty. It will be no easy task to motivate her to rebel. But she will, I am sure—for a more personal loyalty." Lio gave Cassia a wicked half smile. "It worked on her sister."

"Love." Cassia wound her hand in the braided silk cords that held Lio's medallion. "You think we are not the ones who should appeal to her heart."

"That is Tendo's case to make," Lio said.

"Do you think he is willing," Cassia asked, "even though Solia broke his heart five years ago?"

"I know he is," Lio answered. "Are you certain she still loves him the way he loves her?"

"I am convinced that if they were Hesperines, she would be dying of Craving for him."

"Then if forced to choose between him and the Empress, I think your sister will not be able to subdue her inner fire with discipline any longer."

"But how will we arrange for them to meet in secret? He's Prince Tendeso of the Sandira Kingdom, the most public figure he could be. Solia always makes a point to visit me when he's tied up at a court event. She is forbidden to reveal her identity to anyone but you and me until discharged from service in the Golden Shield. Going against that decree would risk our alliance with the Empress."

"That is our first challenge," Lio said. "Convincing Solia to unmask herself to him in spite of the Empress's command."

"Can you extricate Tendo from a royal ceremony at a moment's notice the next time Solia comes to see me?"

Lio gave her a wry smile. "I think he and I will both find that entertaining."

"Then I will take it upon myself to persuade Solia."

Lio nuzzled her nose. "We are fitting champions for them."

Cassia sampled his lips, fighting the temptation to do more. "I'm so grateful for what we have. I want it for them, too. Is that too much to ask?"

"We have always been told our love is too much to ask. And yet, look where you are now." He gathered her closer on his lap. "Using diplomacy to enable seemingly impossible love—while protecting the common good—has become our area of expertise."

42

nights until

NOTIAN WINTER SOLSTICE

14 Ourania, 1597 IS

BATTLE OF HEARTS

THE FOLLOWING NIGHT, THE Golden Shield who stood guard on the terrace abandoned her post. Watching her shut the door behind her and draw the curtains, Cassia felt a flutter of anticipation.

In the closed room, Solia lifted off her helmet, revealing her cropped blond hair and piercing, sky-blue eyes.

Cassia was suddenly seven again, and after a long day of her nurse's rebukes in her dismal room, the moment she had looked forward to and clung to had arrived. She would get to spend time with her sister.

She wasn't sure this feeling would ever fade, no matter how many times she beheld the sister she'd thought lost to her forever. No matter how different Solia the fierce warrior was from Solia the gentle princess.

Knight bounded up to her, and her face softened. She gave his ears a good rub and said to Cassia, "Good evening, Pup."

The childhood nickname brought a lump to Cassia's throat. She wrapped her sister in a hug. It was still a shock for Solia to be here and real and touchable.

Solia held her tightly for a long moment before drawing back. The timeless moment ended, and the demands of the present fell upon them once more. When one of them was Orthros's ambassador, the other the Empress's bodyguard, and both candidates for a throne, there was no such thing as a simple sisterly visit.

"I have something for you." Cassia beckoned and crossed to the bed, where she had laid out a bright blue wrap dress. The lavish Imperial style left one shoulder bare and glittered with gold geometric embroidery. It was remarkable how easy it was to get anything she asked for, when she was the Empress's honored guest.

Fond surprise crossed Solia's face, and she looked so much like her seventeen-year-old self for a moment. "It's beautiful. Thank you. I'm sure I'll have occasion to wear it when the Empress decommissions me from the Golden Shield."

"Why don't you try it on now?"

Solia gestured to her armor. "I must return to my post right after our visit."

"It will only take a moment, and this room is shut tight. Where's the harm?"

"I should not disarm while on duty."

"Remember when we used to play dress-up?" Cassia put on an impish smile. "Your royal gowns hung off of me, but you let me try on all your pretty clothes just the same."

Solia crossed her arms over her smooth gold breastplate. "You deserved royal finery of your own."

Cassia let the reference to her lineage pass and smoothed her hands down the elegant Hesperine robe she wore. "I want for nothing now. Let me return the generosity you showed me then."

Solia sighed. "Very well. You know I'd do anything to please you, Pup."

Cassia could only hope her sister would say the same when she made her next request.

Solia disappeared behind Cassia's dressing screen, and there came the clank of metal. When she stepped out again wearing the dress and matching golden sandals, she turned in a circle with her arms out.

Cassia put a hand to her mouth. She took in her sister's lovely face, now chiseled by life; her curves now honed to muscle; her royal grace turned into martial poise. "You are more beautiful now than you have ever been."

Solia huffed. "You might be a bit prejudiced in my favor."

"Of course," Cassia replied, "but I know someone else who will think the same when he sees you."

Solia went still, her face suddenly as blank as a mask. "Goddesses above. What are you up to, Cassia?"

Cassia gestured to the other door leading from the interior of the palace. "Lio is bringing Tendo to meet you."

She could see Solia taking refuge in a warrior's discipline to withstand the emotions overwhelming her. But when Cassia took her hands, Solia's skin was hot with her volatile fire magic.

It happened every time Cassia mentioned Tendo. The man Solia had almost married. The love she had given up to put Cassia on the throne.

A small blue flame darted across Solia's eyelid. "The Empress could have my head for this."

"She'll never know."

"I will."

"Solia, when will she release you from her service?"

"Soon. But I don't know precisely when."

"And when she does, is that how you want Tendo to learn the truth about where you've been for the past five years? You want him to find out with the rest of the court that you were safe at the Empress's side while he believed you to be in prison?"

Solia grimaced and looked away.

"This is your opportunity to tell him what he needs to hear. This is Lio's and my gift to both of you. Hespera's darkness will safeguard this secret from the Empress. For a good cause."

Solia swallowed.

Cassia rubbed Solia's sun-tanned arms. "Would you like to rehearse what you'll say to him with me? Would that help?"

"That persuasive tactic is unfair. You're reminding me I have a sister to talk to after all these years of keeping my own counsel."

"That is no tactic, Soli. It's the truth, and it won't change, no matter what the future holds for either of us."

Solia cupped Cassia's head and planted a kiss on her hair, then had to rub her blond brow to douse an orange spark of flame. "I'll do it. I owe it to him."

Cassia slowly let out the breath she'd been holding. That was all it had taken to convince her dutiful sister to agree to thwart the Empress.

Lio had been right. Solia felt a deeper sense of duty to Tendo.

"May I stay with you for a moment?" Cassia asked. "I promise we'll leave you two to talk in privacy afterward."

"In fact…I would appreciate having you at my side very much."

That admission filled Cassia with warmth. Solia had been her whole world for the first seven years of her life. Now she had a chance to support her sister in return, and Solia was willing to let her.

Solia sighed. "Am I the only one who finds a conversation like this more terrifying than a battlefield?"

"Imagine how he'll feel when he walks in."

"Does he know I'm here?"

Cassia shook her head. "Everything is yours to explain to him, as you see fit."

Lio appeared through the closed door. "He's waiting outside."

Cassia held her breath, hoping the appearance of her own love would not prod Solia's wounds. But apparently Solia decided now was not the time to voice her disapproval of Cassia's bond with Lio.

Solia gave Lio the least hostile look she had yet bestowed on him. "I know you are his friend. Thank you for trying to make this easier for him."

Lio inclined his head, and Cassia could tell how much her sister's words meant to him.

"Why don't we wait behind the dressing screen so no one sees you from the corridor?" Cassia suggested.

Solia nodded and hooked her arm in Cassia's. She was rigid with tension as they concealed themselves.

Cassia heard the door open, then Tendo's voice. "All right, Silkfoot. What do you and Freckles need me for so urgently that you staged that dramatic rescue from a small army of Queen Mothers? Not that I'm complaining, mind you. If one more person tries to arrange a marriage for me today, I swear I will fly up to the highest tower and not come down."

Solia pressed a hand to her mouth, and a quiet sound escaped her, halfway between laughter and tears.

Cassia gave her a questioning look. Ready?

Solia straightened and, head held high, strode out from behind the screen with Cassia at her side.

And then Solia halted in her tracks, as if she'd stumbled into a dream. Tendo was the dream of many women in the Empire. His deep brown skin was adored with scars from his victorious battles as the mercenary

Monsoon. Now he wore the royal finery of Prince Tendeso of the Sandira Kingdom, his sash adorned with ceremonial feathers and bones.

But only Solia was his dream. His black-and-tawny wings unfurled from his back, and he ran both hands down his face to cover his mouth. He held out his arms and whispered something, an endearment Cassia did not understand.

Solia crossed the distance, a whorl of flame eddying around her. And then she was in his arms. His wings wrapped around them both, soothing her fire, cocooning them in a world all their own.

Cassia blinked hard to clear the tears blurring her vision. Lio's arms and magic wrapped around her, her own dream, her own world. With a magical Hesperine step, he transported them away.

DIPLOMACY WAS NOT THE art of bringing warring factions to the negotiation table, as Lio had once imagined. Kingdoms were simply collections of people, who were much more likely to be broken than alliances. To be an ambassador was to practice the delicate craft of piecing hearts together.

Lio knew that Tendo and Solia's hearts would decide their fate. All he and Cassia could do now was sit here in Mak and Lyros's guest room and wait.

Knight rested his head on Lio's knee and looked up at him with speaking eyes. Lio's empathy with animals stopped at the liegehound's mental defenses against Hesperines, but mundane dog communication was remarkably straightforward. Lio found himself running a hand through Knight's ruff, as Cassia was wont to do for reassurance.

Lio's cousin Mak fidgeted in his seat across the coffee table, his muscular frame seeming too big for the pretty chair. "Thorns, I want to know what they're saying to each other."

Lyros leaned over and put an affectionate hand on Mak's knee to still him. "I want to know if they've punched each other yet."

Lio shook his head. "No prying. I've put so many veils over that room that no mage or Hesperine in the Imperial city would hear someone scream in there."

Cassia choked on a laugh. "Well, that's probably for the best, considering their tempers."

And their passions, Lio thought. "Some negotiations are best carried out without words. If I were Tendo, I wouldn't plan to do much talking."

"That's a surprisingly sensible comment, coming from a scrollworm like you," Mak teased.

"This from the warrior who, mere seconds ago, wanted to know what they're *talking* about," Lio returned.

"What can I say?" Mak caught Lyros's hand and gave his Grace's knuckles a gallant kiss. "I can be a Hesperine of action and a romantic at the same time."

Lyros's eyes narrowed with amusement. "Who said my reference to punching wasn't romantic?"

"Oh, it was." Mak's brown eyes glinted. "It makes me want to drag you into the arena right now."

"That's what Solia and Tendo should do." Lyros nodded sagely. "Fight it out."

"Always ends in kissing," Mak agreed.

Goddess bless, Lio was grateful his best friends had requested reassignment from border patrol to bodyguard duty. He and Cassia had barely survived their last journey without Mak and Lyros, and he had sorely missed their company.

Despite their Trial brothers' levity, Cassia wore a frown as she reshuffled the diplomatic paperwork spread out before them.

Lio put his arm around her. "We've accounted for every upheaval that might occur from pairing a presumed-dead foreign princess with a sometimes-mercenary Imperial prince and leaving the dubiously qualified Tenebran king to deal with ancient and deadly necromancers."

Cassia stared at the pile with pursed lips. "We'd best start planning for the upheavals caused by those upheavals, though."

Lio pulled her back against the couch. "Perhaps we should spare further efforts until we determine whether the aforementioned princess and prince intend to kiss or kill each other."

She sighed. "Fair point."

At last they heard a door slam open. Lio and his Trial brothers winced.

Emotions buffeted the Blood Union, inundating their empathic Hesperine awareness. Tendo's aura emerged from within the veil spells Lio had placed next door. Then came the beat of wings flying away from the palace.

Cassia darted to the window and peered out into the night, her aura pulsing with worry. "He's leaving!"

Lio had already stepped to the door. "I'll go after him."

"I'll see if Solia is all right," Cassia replied.

"We'll be waiting," Mak promised. "Tendo might need to punch something when he gets back."

Lyros nodded. "Tell him we'll be ready to spar."

"Thank you." Lio sent them a wave of gratitude through the Blood Union.

An eagle shifter could lead even a levitating Hesperine on quite the chase, and robes would only get in the way. At Hesperine speed, Lio pulled off his formal attire, wrapped his medallion in the silk, and levitated off the terrace wearing only a pair of loose Imperial trousers.

He had to step to Tendo's position midair to catch up, then steady himself with levitation. He shadowed his friend, but said nothing. It was best to let Tendo know he had reinforcements, but wait for him to speak.

Not that speech would be easy. This high, the wind assaulted Lio's sensitive ears and buffeted him so much that levitation was a struggle.

But Tendo flew like the air was his kingdom. The wind itself roared with his anger and pain. He pumped his wings as if punishing the realm below.

The glory of the Imperial Capital swept past beneath them. The whitewashed clay walls of the Imperial Palace's oldest wings. Then the newer additions, grander renditions of the same style, rising higher, sprawling broader, their foundations decorated with red-orange bas reliefs that glowed with magic.

And then the city. The largest human metropolis in Akanthia, the entire world. The collage of contrasting architectures fit together in perfect coordination. This testament to mortal glory was busy with spell lights and the tiny, sparkling auras of people, even at this hour of the night.

Lio could see the boundaries of the city ahead when he finally shouted, "Are you planning to fly halfway across the Empire? Tell me you're not heading back home to the Sandira Court right now."

Tendo didn't answer. But he spiraled into a descent toward the vast arena below.

He landed atop a pillar, breathing hard from his flight. The flat top was broad enough that Lio could set himself down beside his friend without getting knocked off by Tendo's wings.

Lio didn't have to ask where they were. He recognized it from the stories. The Battle of Souls, the most prestigious tournament in the Empire, took place here. Five years ago, this was where Solia had defeated Tendo in battle and broken his heart.

Lio doubted Tendo wanted the concerned, kind words that were the language of love at House Komnena. "You'd better not be considering deserting me," Lio said instead. "We have that council tomorrow evening with the Empress's bankers. I'll never get through their droning without your dirty mercenary jokes to keep me entertained."

Tendo gave his characteristic snort and crouched on the pillar.

Lio took that as an invitation to sit beside him and pointed down at the arena below. "So tell me, would things have turned out better if Cassia and I had tossed you two in there instead? If we were wrong to reunite you in a luxurious palace bedchamber, our apologies."

Lio didn't wish to cross the veil by prying further, but it didn't escape him that Tendo smelled like fire magic and woman. Promising. What had gone wrong?

"This would have turned out better," Tendo gritted, "if she had not let me believe a lie for five years."

Lio grimaced.

Tendo's aura vibrated with magic and fury and anguish, his feathers riled. "I watched the Golden Shield arrest her in this arena. I believed she was locked away in the Empress's most secret prison, suffering Mweya knows what."

Lio gave a nod of encouragement, listening in silence.

"I devoted years of my life to trying to find her and break her out." A bitter laugh escaped Tendo. "But I was looking in the wrong place. I didn't think to check the Empress's right hand." His voice rose. "Don't tell me I ought to be grateful she was safe all this time. Of course I am. The things I imagined she went through—" He broke off, his voice cracking. "I would have done anything to see her free and unharmed. I *did* do anything. I gave more than just years to the cause of rescuing her."

There it was. The most poisonous wound inside of Tendo. A stain on his honor.

That would be a very difficult one to heal.

"I set aside the good of my subjects," Tendo cried. "I broke all my bonds of loyalty to our mercenary band. I, a Sandira royal, a gold roster warrior, crawled through the grime of the Empire's worst dungeons with no regard for the law, just for the hope of finding her. And she let me do it."

Tendo surged to his feet again, standing with his toes on the very edge of the pillar, looking down at the arena as if into his grave.

"Don't tell me she had her reasons. I don't want to hear her excuses about duty and the greater good and protecting my freedom. While she was upholding all those pretty things, I was throwing them all to the winds for her sake."

"I'm so sorry, Tendo."

The shifter rubbed his face again, snapping his wings. "You have nothing to be sorry for, my friend."

Lio rose to his feet and joined Tendo on the brink. "I understand what you're experiencing, and not because Hesperine Blood Union lets me feel your emotions as if they're my own. Did you know that Cassia once told me she could never stay with me? She decided to give up Orthros and return to Tenebra to become queen."

Tendo's gaze snapped to Lio. "She left out that part when waxing poetic about your love."

"It was highly unpoetic."

"You would have died without her blood."

"She didn't know that at the time, but that was little comfort. I wanted her to choose me freely, without needing the threat of my impending death for motivation."

"Those two sisters really are the most dangerous shadowlanders ever to reach Orthros or the Empire's shores."

"That's what makes them so irresistible."

Tendo muttered a string of curses under his breath. "How did you convince Cassia to stay?"

"She changed her mind because she realized she could have a better life with me than as the Queen of Tenebra."

"She chose you in the end. That made forgiveness rather easy, didn't it?"

"I'm the forgiving sort. I don't judge you for not being so, Tendo. But there's something you should know. Something Cassia and I learned from the Empress."

Tendo's eagle eyes sharpened on Lio. "Is a Hesperine ambassador about to tell a Sandira prince a state secret that the Empress has not authorized him to reveal?"

"Of course not. We're simply a couple of former mercenary comrades drinking at the arena. I'm sure the Empress does not concern herself with what Sunshine and Monsoon of the Ashes say to one another when commiserating about women."

"That's camel shit, but let's try to add as much authenticity to it as we can." Tendo pulled out his flask and took a swig before handing it to Lio.

Lio braced himself and sipped. His Hesperines senses screamed at the strong spirits. "Bleeding thorns."

Tendo laughed. "That's the good stuff—ora from the Sandira Kingdom."

Lio handed it back to Tendo. He would need it. "Cassia is not the Empress's preferred candidate for the throne of Tenebra."

Tendo said nothing for an instant, then, "Oh, gods." He tossed back the flask.

"Solia doesn't know," Lio continued. "The Empress is about to tear away the goal she has lived for all these years, her grand cause of putting Cassia on the throne."

"And she'll put Solia on the throne instead."

"Unless Solia refuses."

"Why in Zalele's name would she refuse?"

"Give her a reason to, Tendo."

The shifter's laugh was bitter. "She didn't choose me over her royal duty to Tenebra, remember?"

"That was for Cassia's sake. Solia never wanted a throne for herself. This is your chance to show her she could have a different life. With you."

"I told you once before. There is no changing her course once she has set it."

"Did you give her a chance to change course tonight? Did you ask her one more time to choose you?"

"We didn't get that far." Solia slammed a fist into the face of a cotton practice dummy, and sawdust puffed into the air.

"Tendo didn't suggest you two try again?" Cassia asked gently.

With her other hand, Solia punched the dummy in the gut. "Not after I told him the truth."

After finding her guest room deserted, Cassia had come looking for her sister in the Golden Shield barracks without much hope of being admitted into their private compound. To her surprise, the guards had waved her through as a family member and even allowed her to bring Knight. Now here they were in a tidy courtyard, watching her sister beat her undeserving target to a pulp.

Solia was back in the golden cotton wrap the guards wore under their armor. She landed punch after punch, utterly focused on the vaguely human-shaped dummy. Until it suddenly burst into flames.

Solia swore and whirled away from it, her fists aflame. Knight's hackles rose, and he stood on alert in front of Cassia, his ears tilted in confusion.

"*Hama*," Cassia soothed him.

Solia lifted her hands slowly and backed away.

"*Toaa.*" Cassia stroked Knight's head until he sat down beside her, though he was poised to leap up again at any moment.

Solia wrapped one hand around her other fist, shutting her eyes. But the fire didn't douse. It climbed up her arms.

A thought came over Cassia, as it often did lately whenever she saw someone cast a spell. She would soon take part in this. Would she struggle as Solia did? What dangers did Cassia's powerful and mysterious magic have in store for her?

Cassia bit her lip. "Is there anything I can do to help?"

Solia's eyes opened a sliver. "Actually...perhaps there is. Come a bit closer."

"All right." Cassia patted Knight again. "*Het Baat.*"

Once he was in a down-stay, she ignored his whine and stepped away from him to approach Solia.

"That's close enough." Solia's voice was firm.

Cassia halted.

Now Solia shrank the distance between them. The air grew hotter. Slowly, Solia opened her hands. Fire roiled in her palms.

"Don't be afraid," she said.

"I'm not." Cassia's trust in her sister had been formed before she could remember. She felt only expectant fascination as she watched Solia's hands come nearer. Nearer.

The fire faded. By the time Solia touched Cassia's arms, her palms were merely warm.

She pulled Cassia into a hug and sighed. "See there. I would never hurt you, and the fire knows it."

Cassia wrapped her arms around Solia in return. "Your instinct to protect me is stronger than your magic."

"It wasn't always. But I have taught the flame that lesson. My heart rules it."

Cassia didn't let go. "How has your heart fared tonight?"

"We have more important concerns."

"I don't. I haven't seen you in fifteen years, and I waited all this time to be your sister again. At this moment, nothing is more important to me than whether you are all right."

Solia rested her head on Cassia's shoulder. "I love you. Have I told you that since we met again?"

"I love you too," Cassia said fiercely. "Even when you don't say it, you show it."

Knight, excluded from the display of affection, gave another whine, impatient this time. Cassia called to him, and he nudged his head under Solia's hands in the hope of being petted.

Relief crossed Solia's face. "See there, Sir Knight. I was protecting our Pup long before you were."

Cassia swallowed. "But I suppose that's the problem with Tendo, isn't it?"

"I've always put you first," Solia said. "He shouldn't expect me to do otherwise. I wouldn't ask him to put me before his brother. Anesu is his family—his king."

"You don't have to choose between Tendo and me anymore."

"But I did in the past. And Tendo hasn't forgiven me for the choice I made then."

"He may not be ready to forgive you tonight, but that doesn't mean he won't in the future."

Solia drew back, now calm and dignified. "I don't need his forgiveness. I need him to understand that I did the right thing. But it's not enough for him that I regret what he suffered for my sake. He wants me to regret my choice. To feel shame for behaving with honor." Her calm broke, her voice thickening. "And he has the gall to tell me I compromised his honor. I never asked him to put his subjects at risk or abandon our comrades. I did everything I could so he wouldn't have to."

Cassia nodded. "You wanted him to have the life you both loved—which you couldn't have anymore. You were trying to give him a parting gift."

"Why doesn't he understand that?"

"I don't think he wanted that life if he couldn't live it with you."

"Well. I am certainly the last thing he wants now."

"And what do you want, Soli? If he had asked you to choose him tonight, would you have said yes?"

Solia did not answer. But that was better than a no.

Tonight had been a disaster. But Cassia would not let it end like this for the two people who had lost so much for her sake.

She and Lio would keep trying to bring Soli and Tendo together, Cassia vowed. This negotiation was not over.

41

nights until

NOTIAN WINTER SOLSTICE

15 Ourania, 1597 IS

BY ANCIENT LAW

At last, Lio stood in the Imperial throne room with his partner. He and Cassia waited before the dais where the Empress would soon take her seat. Their Trial brothers were at their sides, along with the unlikeliest of diplomatic bodyguards, a Tenebran liegehound.

The auras of the courtiers were more dazzling than the gold that bedecked the chamber. Every murmur was an exchange of power. The air was thick with countless layers of emotions and perfumes from all over the Empress's vast lands—intrigue and jasmine, honor and sandalwood, calculation and patchouli.

Lio, as an immortal, was unable to hear the ancestors speak, but the ceremonial wooden masks on the walls seemed to communicate their presence to him. He felt the urge to offer them a bow for admitting this young diplomat from far away into their presence.

Somehow, despite his twisting path, Lio had restored his career as an ambassador. This was what he was meant to be. A champion of peace, even when no one would listen, in the center of this tangle of people whose choices would determine the world's fate.

"Are you glad you didn't resign from the diplomatic service?" Cassia's breath was warm upon his ear, her voice soft beneath the veil spell he held around them.

He rested a hand on her lower back, breathing in her scent—courage and roses. "I would not have missed this for the world."

Everything was changing. The Empire and the shadowlands were on the brink of contact; Blood Komnena was on the brink of gaining—or losing—Solia. Lio did not know what was to come, but he was certain of one thing.

Cassia would be his through it all. Tonight, he would make that clear before the great powers gathered in this room.

"You are still willing to go through with it?" he asked her.

She didn't hesitate. "Of course."

The certainty in her voice fed his Craving for her, and yet he still sensed her despair. Their plan to secure Solia's future with Tendo before this moment of reckoning had failed. "I'm so sorry, my rose."

"We must simply do our best to pick up the pieces afterward," she said.

"Perhaps the pieces will come together now," Mak encouraged from Cassia's other side. "What's about to happen could help knock some sense into Tendo."

Lyros sighed. "Since our efforts to do that were unsuccessful."

"Solia may even have a change of heart when she sees who's waiting for her," Mak said. "Although the Empress's throne room is an uncommon place for a family reunion."

Cassia arched a brow. "Not at all an unusual setting for our family's dramas, it seems."

Mak shook his head. "This is why Lyros and I had the good sense to become warriors and avoid our loved ones' political nonsense."

"It's a shame you two have gotten yourselves attached to Cassia and me," Lio said. "There will be many throne rooms in your future now."

Mak chuckled. "Small price to pay if it means we're close enough to punch a jinn the next time one tries to toss you into a magical jail cell."

"That won't happen again." Lio shuddered and wove his arm tighter in Cassia's.

"These court affairs aren't such a hardship." Lyros's green gaze drifted over Mak. They both wore the formal regalia of all Stewards in Orthros's small army, Hippolyta's Stand: short black battle robes with the constellation Aegis embroidered in silver on the chest.

Mak brushed his fingers across Lyros's temple. His brown Grace braid could be seen against Lyros's darker brown hair, tied back with his speires, the ceremonial hair ties of Hesperine warriors. "I'll put up with any stuffy negotiations for that look. Not to mention getting to admire you while we spar with the Ashes."

The famous mercenaries known as the Ashes were gathered at the forefront of the crowd. The five of them had important political ties to their respective homelands within the Empire, but also personal ties to Solia. They had been her and Tendo's family for eight years, before she had given up her freedom to serve the Empress in secret.

A dozen of the Golden Shield flanked the Empress as she entered, while one of her woman advisers recited her praises. Her Imperial Majesty, now in her full finery, was a moving masterpiece with heavy gold jewelry and an ornate headdress. Lio, Cassia, and their Trial brothers bowed, while the Empress's subjects knelt, only rising when she had settled on her solid gold throne.

Lio's gaze went to the Golden Shield behind the Empress's right shoulder. That was where Solia had stood the night he had, unknowingly, first met his Grace-sister and announced his and Cassia's bond to her before the entire Imperial court. Not how he had planned to tell Solia that he was a potential cause of death for her sister.

The Empress spoke. "For centuries, justice has flowed down from the Supreme Goddess Zalele to our people through the hands of our foremothers. Tonight, we shall deliver another judgment which upholds rightness and law in our Empire."

The Empress gestured to her left. There was Ukocha, the now-retired leader of the Ashes. The small, muscular woman looked dignified and deadly, even with her arm in a sling. She stood with her old friend, the notorious Captain Ziara of the Empress's privateers, whose beaded locks swayed in the invisible breeze of her wind magic. Behind them were a number of graying Imperials who all wore the same sign somewhere on their embroidered wraps or jeweled brooches: an acacia branch.

"Every surviving Victor of Souls honors us with their presence tonight." The Empress paused as cheers for the famous winners of the Battle of Souls went up throughout the hall.

"Sisters and brothers," she said, invoking the symbolic clan bond between her and the rulers of the sister states that comprised her Empire. "Recall the momentous Battle of Souls that took place five years ago. Perhaps my trusted adviser can remind us of those events." Her gaze slid to the Diviner of the High Court.

She must choose her words with care, for she had once been a member of the Rezayal. She had chosen the Empress's side in the end, but only remained at court on her sufferance, and everyone knew it. "Alas, the winner that year was not deemed qualified to be declared the Victor of Souls."

"And why was that?" the Empress inquired.

The Diviner cleared her throat. "She was not a citizen of the Empire, and therefore could not receive the acacia."

It was possibly the most polite way the Diviner could state that the Rezayal had been out for Solia's blood because she was a foreigner.

"And what did we do?" the Empress pressed.

The Diviner paused. "Under the policy of isolation, she was not permitted to reside in your Empire. Your Imperial Majesty, always upholding the rule of law and the safety of your people, had her arrested."

"So we allowed everyone to believe," the Empress replied.

"Your Imperial Majesty?" the Diviner queried uncertainly. Her courtier's mask slipped, betraying her surprise.

The Empress smiled like a cat who had caught her prey. "We placed this honorable warrior under our protection, where the Rezayal could not persecute a most noble defender of our Empire. Although she was born in faraway lands, she has proved her unwavering loyalty to us for many years. Let it be known she is a welcome guest in our lands."

The Empress lifted a hand. Solia, who usually leapt at the command, now paused. Her fleeting hesitation was the only sign that she'd had no idea this would happen tonight.

When she left her place at the Empress's side to kneel before the throne, stifled gasps and murmurs went up around the room.

"Sunburn of the Gold Roster," the Empress declared, "Victor of Souls, Sister Commander in the Golden Shield, we thank you for your deeds on behalf of our people and your decorated service at our right hand. We hereby decommission you from the Golden Shield. Disarm, rise, and once again wear your own name: Princess Solia of Tenebra."

Emotion swelled in the Blood Union, and the overflow of human hearts was enough to make Lio rock on his feet. There was the glee of those who lived for court drama; the outrage of the Diviner's sympathizers; and the worry of the Empress's advisers, who must now recalculate.

But the Ashes were a nova. Among them, only Tendo's conflicting emotions betrayed no shock. Only Solia was opaque, her mind concealed from Lio's magic by her enchanted armor.

She unbuckled her sword. She laid the blade of the Golden Shield at the Empress's feet, but her hand lingered on the hilt for a long moment. At last, she released it and rose.

Piece by piece, she removed her armor and her many hidden weapons. Finally she stood before them in nothing but fabric and the golden defensive spells that clung to her skin like molten metal, her face still hidden by her helmet.

Now she removed her mask to reveal her guarded blue gaze and golden hair. Her spell-armor receded over her sun-tanned skin. The magic guarding her thoughts and emotions deserted her, and Lio could sense her clearly in the Blood Union for the first time.

Hello, Grace-sister, he thought. *There you are.*

She appeared as composed as if a sudden beheading wouldn't cause her to twitch. But underneath, she was so vulnerable that Lio thought she might shatter before their eyes.

After five years of absolute discipline, everything certain in her world had just been stripped away from her. It was difficult to be angry about her disapproval when she was reeling.

But the family of her heart was here to catch her, as Lio and his Hesperine family had always tried to do for Cassia.

Kella broke the stalemate that gripped the court. The princess of nomads and new leader of the Ashes was not an emotional woman, after devastating battles, desert survival, and bonding to the vicious sand cat that served as her mount. But she looked at Solia with tears in her eyes.

"Eldest Sister," Kella addressed the Empress, "may I approach your throne?"

"Come forward and welcome your sister-in-arms once more among you."

Kella's cat stalked forward, her broad paws silent on the tiled floor. Solia stood still, as if she half-expected Tilili to pounce on her instead of simply carry Kella to her side.

As soon as Kella came within arm's reach, she wrapped Solia in a fierce embrace. At last, Solia's true mask fell away, and she came to life. She held her friend, squeezing her eyes shut over her own tears. Solia's words were too quiet for the humans to hear, but Lio's ears picked them up.

"Can you forgive me?" Solia asked.

"What is there to forgive?" Kella replied. "Loyalty and freedom are all that matter in this life. You answered to one and gave us the other."

The rest of the Ashes soon surrounded Solia. Karege grinned with all his fangs, his affectionate words booming through the court. Tuura fussed over her, her mere presence as a mind healer soothing the fraught encounter. Hoyefe, charming as ever, managed to make Solia laugh even without conjuring a single illusion.

Lio felt an unexpected pang. The Ashes had accepted him. When would Solia?

Ukocha's daughter broke into the knot to throw her arms around Solia. The Empress observed young Chuma with an indulgent smile.

Solia looked at the top of Chuma's head. "I can scarcely believe how you've grown, First Bladelet."

"I missed you so much, Sunburn! When the Golden Shield searched our village, it was you, wasn't it?"

"I'm so sorry if I frightened you."

"Me, frightened? Ha. Never. I was *angry.* But now I realize you must have been there to protect us." Chuma beamed, her bright spirit lighting up the room as always.

Her mother stood behind her. Ukocha, Solia's mentor. Her gaze went from the sword on the floor to Solia's embrace around Chuma. "You turned out well."

Solia bowed her head. "You honor me."

"You have brought great honor to me as well. My trainee, a Victor of Souls and Golden Shield. That will be a fine tale to tell around the village fire to keep retirement interesting."

Tendo watched the reunion unfold. When Solia's gaze lifted to his, Lio sensed the ache of hope in her aura.

Tendo gave the woman he loved a faultless bow. "Princess Solia of Tenebra, greetings from the monarchs of the Empire. How momentous, to have a royal from that faraway land among us."

Lio felt the urge to drag Tendo into the fighting ring himself. There were any number of romantic or at least conciliatory things he might have said to Solia, cloaked in courtly discourse. But he had chosen to draw his line in the sand here: she was a foreign monarch to him.

Solia bowed to Tendo in return. "I rejoice to be welcomed by Her Imperial Majesty's brothers and sisters. I am blessed to walk in her Empire freely."

Lio had to credit her. It was an excellent reply. She twisted Tendo's words into a welcome, reminding him the Empress had granted her the right to be here. Was that reference to freedom an invitation or a taunt? With Solia and Tendo, one never knew.

The Empress turned her gaze upon Lio's Grace. "Cassia, Crown Princess of Tenebra, we restore your sister to you."

Crown Princess Cassia. That title would once have struck horror in Lio's heart, but it had no power over him now. He had her promise. And she had his strategy, which she was about to enact. It was her turn to play her role in the spectacle she and Lio had promised the Empress. The one he had devised not only to protect their alliance with Her Imperial Majesty, but to send a message to his Grace-sister.

Cassia came forward with Knight shadowing her. She and Solia embraced in front of the excited court. Solia clung to her a bit longer than necessary, and Cassia leaned in, as if they drew strength from each other.

Then Cassia rested her small hand on Knight's powerful shoulder, reminding Lio of the first time he had seen her, a petite mortal with hidden strengths. They were not hidden now. "Your Imperial Majesty, you have my gratitude for sheltering my sister and me. We have fled the kingdom of Tenebra, where your light has yet to shine. We beseech you for your guidance regarding the future of the land of our foremothers."

The Empress, who had spent years moving everyone in this room into position, not least by having Captain Ziara steal her a Tenebran princess, now answered Cassia's petition with a benevolent smile. "How fortunate that you and your sister arrived safely on our shores. The ancestors empower us to speak their wisdom. How can we advise the shadowlands?"

"We face a succession crisis, Your Imperial Majesty. A wicked king holds the throne, while the rightful queen goes unacknowledged. For I am the only descendant of our greatest matriarch."

Solia's heart swelled with emotion. This was the moment she had fought for. She knelt before Cassia. "My Queen. I am now free to swear my fealty to you."

Cassia placed her hand on Solia's head. Lio could only pray that what he and his Grace were about to set in motion would not damage the newly restored bond between her and her sister.

Lio felt a twinge of sympathy for Solia, but even more, an exhilarating sense of victory as he watched Cassia destroy everyone else's plans for her life with a few words.

"Before Your Imperial Majesty, Empress over queens; before your sisters and brothers who rule the states of the Empire; before my royal kin from the Kingdom of Tenebra; and before the delegation from Orthros, let it be known. The only inheritance from my Tenebran ancestors that I claim is this: the magic of the Changing Queen. Here where Orthros's matriarch Kassandra once stood before her sister the Empress, I make the same choice: I and all my descendants will be Hesperines, forever removed from the lines of mortal succession. I hereby abdicate from my throne."

Solia surged to her feet. Fire churned in her aura, and her hand went to her belt, where there was no longer a sword for her to grasp. "Your Imperial Majesty—!" She stopped herself, seeming to fight for control, to search for words, when they had not been her weapon for a long time. "Tenebra is in dire need, and only our rightful queen can save us. My queen only needs time to adjust to her new role. I beseech you not to acknowledge her declaration."

"Alas," the Empress said gently, "it is done."

"With respect, Your Imperial Majesty," Solia said fiercely, "she has not abdicated before Tenebra's Council of Free Lords. Tenebra has not relinquished her."

The Empress beckoned to Lio. "Ambassador Deukalion, as a scholar and ally from Orthros, remind our court of the ancient law just invoked."

He came to Cassia's side and took her arm. "This precedent was established sixteen hundred years ago when Your Imperial Majesty's ancestor reigned. The Empress at that time had a half-sister, whom her enemies sought to use to challenge her rule. For the good of all, her sister chose to gracefully withdraw to Orthros, where she is now Elder Firstblood Kassandra."

"A peaceful solution to a dark time in our history," the Empress agreed.

"Alas," Lio went on, "Vardara, the land of Kassandra's forefathers, would not acknowledge her renunciation of power. To prevent a violent succession crisis, Orthros and the Empire codified in their laws an alternative way for abdications to become legally recognized."

The Empress nodded. "It was decreed that our friends from Orthros would play the honored role of neutral mediators in such times of tension. With Orthros and the Empire united in favor of Kassandra's renunciation, Vardara had no choice but to accept it. I am certain Tenebra will find themselves in a similar position. Remind our court what is required for Princess Cassia's abdication to be legal."

Lio lifted a hand to indicate the gathering before the dais. "She must declare her intent before these witnesses: the Empress, a quorum of officials from other sister states, a Hesperine delegation, and a royal family member."

Solia's gaze burned a path from the Empress to the Ashes, from Cassia to Lio, and finally her own empty hands, which tightened into fists.

The Empress's adviser struck her staff upon the floor. "Let it be known across the lands under Her Imperial Majesty's rule and foreign kingdoms that bow before her might. She who was once Crown Princess Cassia has no further claim on the throne of Tenebra and shall henceforth be welcomed in this court as Ambassador Cassia Komnena of Orthros."

"Let it be known," Mak echoed, "the defenders of Orthros's laws will uphold this decision within our borders..."

"...and beyond," Lyros finished, "everywhere that Hesperines roam."

Cassia bowed to the Empress. "You have my gratitude."

Relief ran deep in Lio. It was over. No one could ever try to put Cassia on the throne again. Not even her sister.

"Pup." Solia's tone lost all decorum, a naked plea. "Don't let go of everything your mother wanted for you."

"I haven't, Soli. I will not shy from the difficult path of learning my magic. But that is a journey I must take in Orthros, with my Hesperines. Please, try to understand."

"I do understand," Solia replied, but there was no empathy in her words. Her anger felt like a carefully aimed fire spell, and her cherished sister was not her target. Her gaze fixed on Lio. "I see very clearly why you had to do this. Since Ambassador Deukalion is such an expert on the precedents Kassandra has set, I am sure he will appreciate it if I invoke another ancient tradition. Like Kassandra's husband, I expect him to prove himself worthy by performing the Labors for the Matriarch."

Lio had known Solia must be a brilliant strategist, but this confirmed it. She was trying to lay a trap for him. He would indeed have appreciated her asking him to perform the labors, if the matriarch in question were not a fire mage with a grudge against him.

Cassia cut in, her wariness sharp as thorns. "For those of us who do not have such expertise in Imperial tradition, perhaps my fellow ambassador can explain to us what these labors entail."

Solia answered for him, a challenge in her eyes. "It is a ceremony in which a man who wishes for a union with a woman requests the blessing of the matriarch of her clan. I am your only surviving female relative. That means Ambassador Deukalion must petition me."

Lio did not look away. Let Solia see he was willing to face any challenge for his Grace. "Your sister will set a series of tasks for me. When I succeed at the labors, she will grant us her blessing."

Cassia's aura flared with protest, but the Empress spoke first. "The two motherless daughters before us and their queenless kingdom have our protection, and it would please us to see Blood Komnena honor Cassia's mortal matriarchs. But Ambassador Cassia is already a citizen of Orthros. We cannot require Ambassador Deukalion to perform the labors."

"Your Imperial Majesty," said Solia, "he wishes to take Tenebra's rightful queen from the mortal world, to take my only kinswoman into his bloodline. Should he not be expected to earn that right?"

"Her bloodright as his partner is well known. Should he wish to fulfill your request, it must be his choice."

Lio did not hesitate. He had promised Cassia and himself he would win her sister's blessing. If he had to turn Solia's trials into his negotiation table, so be it. "I welcome this opportunity to show my respect for Princess Solia and her adopted land through a time-honored Imperial tradition. I will gladly perform the labors for Cassia's matriarch."

Solia's expression reminded him of the Empress a moment ago, that of a predator cornering her prey. Cassia's unspoken objections sounded an alarm in Lio's blood.

"A gracious gesture," the Empress approved, "but one matter of the greatest import remains in question. Who is to wear Cassia's crown?"

Lio looked at Tendo, willing him to say something, anything to tempt Solia away from the destiny the Empress had in store for her.

Tendo folded his wings tightly against his back, his face like stone.

"Your Imperial Majesty," Solia said, "there are no other candidates for the throne but my sister."

"Are you not the daughter of the ruling king?" the Empress asked.

"He seized the throne with violence and dishonor," Solia protested. "His rule is not legitimate."

"Is there not another path to the throne for you besides war? One paved by the love of your people?"

"In fifteen years, they have surely forgotten me."

The Empress looked to Cassia. "Have they?"

Cassia hesitated. Lio knew how she hated to play along with this part of the game. But they had no choice.

"No," Cassia finally answered. "Tenebra still mourns Solia's loss. I have no doubt they would rejoice at her return."

Silence reigned in the court, while Solia's aura was in chaos. Lio caught Tendo's gaze and glared at him. He had never been so tempted to give another person's mind a push with his thelemancy.

The Empress rose from her throne. By magic, there appeared in her hands a long, slender object wrapped in golden fabric. The scarf levitated to Solia and draped over her cropped hair, the delicate Imperial silk flowing long down her back.

The fabric had concealed a sword. The golden hilt was engraved with the acacia, but it was a gladius forged in the ancient Tenebran style.

The Empress held out the weapon to Solia. "This is my gift to you."

Lio made his last, desperate move. "As the Empire's ally and mediator, Orthros asks if any sister states object to Princess Solia being declared the future Queen of Tenebra."

No one spoke. Until Tendo bowed first to Solia, then the Empress. "The Sandira Court wishes Princess Solia well in her new endeavor."

Solia did not look at him. She reached out and took hold of her new sword.

THE GREATEST AMBASSADOR

By the time she and Lio returned to their rooms, Cassia's legs ached from standing in court, and her belly was sour from the Empress's celebration feast. Worse still were the unsaid words she had for Lio.

Someone had opened the terrace doors in their absence. She felt an instinctive jolt of warning. Then she spotted the note fluttering in the breeze, pinned to one door by a dagger she recognized.

Cassia stared. "I thought he gave it to his brother."

"I saw him surrender it." With a frown, Lio pulled the long dagger out of the wood and laid it across Cassia's palms. "It seems he wasn't quite ready to let it go after all."

There was no mistaking the wickedly pointed Sandira blade with its carved wooden grip. She had seen Monsoon fight for their lives with this. It was his fortune blade, the emblem of his life as a mercenary before he had given into his royal duties as Tendeso once more.

Lio read the note aloud.

Dear Shadow and Sunshine,

The Sandira expect their prodigal prince to return, just as the Tenebrans require their new queen.

It's time for me to extricate my wings from all these grasping courtiers and go home. It may take a few more duels in the Court of Claws for my brother and me to finish working out our differences, but he needs me.

Thank you for the many repeated invitations to visit you in Orthros. I would be honored to be a guest in your home. But you will be surprised how small House Komnena feels if Cassia manages to convince a fire mage to visit. Let me know when you have room for me at a later time.

Silkfoot, I wish I could be there to watch you perform the Labors for the Matriarch. Remember everything you learned from me and try not to get burned, all right?

Regardless of who Freckles is related to, I crossed the Maaqul with you two. We're tangled up in plenty of life debts of our own, so don't imagine you can get rid of me easily.

- Tendo

Lio rested his hand on the dagger. "We'll keep Solia and this blade safe for him until he has a change of heart."

Cassia hesitated, unwilling to ask the next question, needing to know the answer. "You do think he'll have a change of heart?"

"How long did I manage to stay away from you?"

"Half a year, before you gathered an entire diplomatic summit just to reunite us."

"Mark my words. Tendo won't last any longer than I did. Although I shudder to imagine what his version of calling the Solstice Summit will look like. I do hope he doesn't start a war."

"Tonight was not the Solstice Summit, Lio." The words she'd been saving for when they were alone finally boiled out of her. "I was standing right there, but you didn't even discuss the Labors for the Matriarch with me before agreeing to my sister's demands. That was a decision we should have made together."

He did not appear surprised at her protest. She knew he had sensed her seething all night. "The Empress made her preferences clear. It would have been difficult to say no."

"More difficult than all the other times we've stood up to a great power together? No. Even the Empress agreed it was your choice."

"Yes, Cassia. My choice. I want to do this."

"Solia should never have asked this of you! It is unjust."

Lio pulled her closer, despite the very large dagger she held between them. "Give Solia and me this chance to resolve matters between us. She and I must take responsibility for our differences and make our peace."

"Making peace is not her motivation for the labors."

"I have withstood sabotage by fire mages with evil intent. Solia, on the other hand, is only trying to protect you. She and I are completely aligned in that goal, and I intend to prove it to her."

"Yes, I am what you have in common. I can mediate between you and bring you closer. But not if the two of you are locked in some kind of battle of wills!"

"You are a magnificent diplomat, my rose. But this is one alliance you should not have to work for. I never want you to feel you must negotiate between your own Grace and sister. I will not allow you to be caught between us."

Sunbind her, she wanted to kiss that sweet, persuasive mouth of his. But she had a point to make, and she couldn't let her Craving for Lio cost her this debate. "You expect me to stand aside like a spectator while she puts you through who knows how many tasks?"

"Five tasks for an ambassador," he replied. "It varies depending on the woman's status. For a princess, it is eight. Kassandra told me her husband had to perform ten tasks for her mother because she was the daughter of the Empress."

Trust her scrollworm to know such things. He was so calm that it only made Cassia angrier. "Knowing Solia, she'll claim I'm still a princess and ask for eight instead of five. But she has no right to demand any. You're my Grace. You have nothing to prove. I shall go to her right now and tell her she must set a more reasonable condition for giving us her blessing."

"You do need to speak with her. But it's more important to change her mind about returning with us to Orthros than about the labors. When our family arrives tomorrow, wouldn't you rather tell them they aren't here to visit her, but to bring her home?"

Cassia fisted her hands at her sides, her fingers closing around the hilt of the dagger. "If she were being fair to you, she could meet your parents and Zoe tomorrow night with open arms, and I wouldn't have to convince her Orthros is her home."

"Another reason I agreed to the labors. I hope my goodwill gesture will endear her to the idea of at least visiting House Komnena. If nothing else, she will need to oversee my tasks for her."

This was not how Cassia imagined it would be when she introduced Solia to her Hesperine family. Zoe was looking forward to it so much. Cassia could only pray her little Grace-sister would not be disappointed.

Lio stroked Cassia's arms. "Try to look forward to tomorrow night, if you can. We'll finally get to see Zoe. Now that you're well enough for her to come see you, she'll give you no rest."

His comfort seemed to wrap around her, and her traitorous senses reached for his magic before she could control the impulse. She felt her aura bloom and tug at his power, her surrogate for blood until she could feast on his vein.

The next thing she knew, he was kissing her, and she could not have stopped him for all the debates in the world. He fed her the sensation of his lips, the flavor of his tongue, the prick of his fangs while he held her to him with a firm, gentle hand behind her head. With his other hand, he slid the dagger from her grasp.

When she found the coherence to pull back, he let her go. Her chin high, she backed away through the open doors. "I will table the matter of the labors—for now. Under protest."

"Understood," he said seriously, but the smile in his eyes reminded her how much he enjoyed the flavor of her temper.

She descended from the terrace with Knight, trying not to think of this as a retreat. The fresh air offered her some relief from the flush of her Craving. She would walk off her hunger on her way to the Golden Shield barracks.

Knight wandered to and fro on the path, sniffing at the cassia trees' fragrant bark. After he had been on his best behavior all night, she let him roam. Suddenly he lifted his head, then trotted off like a dog who knew where he was headed.

"Where are you going?" She shook her head, following him.

Cassia found him with his head on Solia's lap. She sat on the bench under Kassandra and her sister's tree. The sight gave Cassia hope. Why would Solia be here if she did not want to see Cassia? If she blamed her beyond the hope of reconciliation?

Solia scratched Knight's chest, not looking up. "They're moving my things out of the barracks. My guest room is right next to yours."

What a mundane thing to remark on. What a monumental upheaval in Solia's life.

Cassia sat down beside her. Perhaps her sister would let her be supportive, as she had when facing Tendo. "What do you need to do first?"

Solia rubbed Knight's ears. "The Empress didn't tell me. I stood there like a fool, waiting for orders. But she gave me none. All the decisions are mine to make now."

A specter of grief passed across Solia's face. Was she thinking of Lady Iris? How she must wish for the advice of her handmaiden, friend, and co-conspirator. But Iris's wisdom had died with her when she had sacrificed her life so Solia could escape Tenebra.

"Why don't you stop thinking about it for the rest of the night and start fresh tomorrow?" Cassia ventured.

"That is an unfairly sensible thing to suggest at a time like this."

It's all right to hate all of this, you know, Cassia wanted to say. *It's all right to be angry.* But the words that came out of her mouth were, "Are you angry with me?"

Excruciating emotion welled up inside her. She had been a destroyer of kingdoms today, but curse it, right at this moment, she felt like a little child again. It seemed her life would be over if Solia disapproved of her.

Now she had Solia's full attention. "Angry with you?"

"I just got you back. If this causes me to lose you again—"

Solia grabbed her close and held on tight. "You are too precious for me to waste a moment blaming you. Angry? Of course. At you? Never."

Cassia heaved a sigh, aborted tears slipping from the corners of her eyes.

"I would still die for you," Solia said.

"I will not let you become a martyr!" Cassia drew back. "Now it's your turn to refuse the crown. I told her no. So can you."

"She liked hearing no from you, I now realize." Solia got to her feet, pacing under the tree. "I have been so blind. All this time…it was me she planned to put on the throne."

Cassia slid a hand into Knight's ruff. If she was to be guilty of tarnishing Solia's view of the Empress, so be it. Without Tendo to persuade Solia, it fell to Cassia to give her sister reasons to rebel against her destiny. "She manipulated us. It was the Empress, not the Rezayal, who hid my presence in Orthros from you to further her plans for us."

"Goddesses above and below. I should not be surprised." Solia gave a humorless laugh. "After I boasted of forging myself into your perfect general, how neatly I have allowed myself to be outmaneuvered by the royals. And the diplomats."

Her gaze was not on Cassia as she said it. Solia paused, looking back toward the guest wing where Lio waited. "I could never be angry at you. I know you had no choice."

Cassia got to her feet. "What? You cannot think Lio somehow forced me into this."

"He didn't have to." Solia turned back to Cassia. "I am the one who brought you back from the Maaqul after you'd been apart from him. No one needs to tell me what your bond means. I held you in my arms while you were dying of the Craving."

Cassia took a step forward. "I'm so sorry you had to see me like that, Soli. But I'm safe now. You and Lio rescued me."

Solia's face hardened. "You did not pay with your life that time, but what a price you paid tonight. You had to give up your mother's legacy because of him."

That was when Cassia realized that although her sister didn't blame her for her decision, Solia did not understand it at all.

Solia's eyes were full of anguish. "I considered every possible solution. Ever since I learned he is your Grace, I tried to adapt our plan. A marriage to a heretic, a Hesperine king consort—all of that was out of the question, of course. You would have had to conceal your bond with the utmost secrecy."

"How can you imagine I would want that life?"

"I was lying to myself, thinking we could manage it. All it would take to destroy you and your reign would be separating you from him. If your enemies ever discovered what he is to you, they would have held the ultimate power over you. And with your life dependent on him, you could never put your kingdom and your subjects first. He is your weakness. Strategically, there is no answer. You cannot be queen with the Craving for a Hesperine."

Cassia opened her mouth to protest how her heart would have broken long before her body died. She had kept her love for Lio a secret before, and she could never endure that again.

Explanations would do no good. Solia was thinking only in terms of death, not love.

But she was acting out of love.

"Everything I have done," Solia said. "I have done for you. But if I must choose between protecting your legacy and your life, I will defend your life at any cost. Even if I must take the throne myself."

"No, don't you dare. Don't imagine this is the next sacrifice you must make for my sake."

"I have done harder things for you, Pup."

"Then do the hardest thing of all," Cassia challenged her. "Tell the Empress no."

"Tell Her Imperial Majesty no? After she has handed me a sword, a treasury, and a plot to take over a kingdom. Do you realize what you're suggesting?"

"Yes. I am suggesting the greatest heresy of all: that you put happiness ahead of duty. Don't be a general or a queen. Be my sister. Imagine it, Soli. No more politics. No more sacrifices. Just you and me and the chance to make up for all the time we lost. We can have that."

In answer to this, the appeal to her sister's heart Tendo had failed to make, the appeal only Pup could make, Solia's face did not soften with love. Her eyes did not fill with longing. If anything, she only looked harder. Heat emanated off her in waves.

That was how Cassia knew there was hope of changing Solia's mind.

Cassia recognized that anger. She had felt the same bitterness when she had believed she could never have the life she wanted. Until the Hesperines had proved to her that it was within her grasp.

"Come home to Orthros with me," Cassia said. "Let me show you what it can be like. You can have any life you want. Be with anyone you love."

"There is no time. In little more than a month, the Council of Free Lords will vote to revoke their mandate from King Lucis. When that happens, a queen must be in position, ready to claim their favor."

Cassia tried a different argument. She would play along with Solia's plan if she must, long enough to get her to Orthros. "What role are the Hesperines to play as you take over Tenebra with the Empire's support? We can help you. You need to negotiate with our Queens."

Solia's eyes narrowed.

Cassia raised a brow at her. "Can you refute this?"

"No. But I'm afraid I'll have to send a representative to Orthros to settle that. I must go to Tenebra."

"After all these years…" Cassia shook her head. "You're going to leave me?"

"Not if you come with me."

Cassia swallowed. "But I must go back to Orthros."

They faced each other under the tree as they had the night of their reunion, in the very same stalemate, despite the weight of the crown resting on a different head.

Cassia had failed.

After everything they had been through trying to save each other, she was losing her sister.

She thought desperately for another strategy, anything to throw her sister a rope to save her from this fate.

In the dreadful silence between them, a voice called across the orchard, "Cassia!"

She could scarcely believe her ears. "Zoe?"

Cassia turned toward the sound to see a small form darting toward her at immortal speed. The purple blur ran into Cassia and clung to her.

Cassia went down on her knees and threw her arms around Zoe. The suckling was skinny and tense and wrapped in the softest silk. She felt so real. She felt so dear. "Oh, how I missed you."

Zoe's breath came in gasps between her words. "You said we would see each other again after your journey, and you were right!"

Cassia hid her tears in Zoe's hair, smelling her sweet betony-and-rimelace scent. "Zoe flower. I'm so happy to see you."

"I couldn't wait any longer, and Mama said we could come a night early, so as soon as we came through the gate, I found you with my spyglass and stepped here."

Zoe's long, light brown hair was uncovered, a good sign that she wasn't hiding her head in anxiety, but she was shaking with emotion. Cassia tucked Zoe's favorite mantle, embroidered with dancing goats, closer around the suckling's shoulders. Knight busied himself sniffing and nuzzling his smallest responsibility from her head to her toes. As Zoe petted him, her trembling began to subside.

The air around them grew warmer. Cassia felt Solia's hand rest on her hair. And she knew in her veins that she would cross the Maaqul again for this.

"It looks like you have someone very important to introduce me to," Solia said.

Zoe's eyes were wide as she looked up, speechless, at her hero.

Cassia sought her elder sister's gaze, willing her to understand how deeply this child connected them. "Solia, this is Zosime Komnena—my Grace-sister. She's been longing to meet you."

"Cassia told me everything about you!" Zoe burst out. "She's the best sister in the world because you showed her how."

Solia, Victor of Souls, knelt on the ground in the Empress's orchard, and Cassia's mind flashed to Princess Solia kneeling in a garden in her Tenebran finery. "How old are you, Zoe?"

"I just turned eight."

Solia's eyes flicked to Cassia's again, and the memory passed unspoken between them. Solia had left just before Cassia's eighth temple day.

"Where did you come from?" Solia wondered, as if querying the mysterious gods how this unpredicted child had become part of Cassia's life.

But Zoe answered, looking at her feet. "Tenebra. I didn't like it there. Cassia and Lio brought me to Orthros so I could be their sister."

Solia paused. "Well, we have much in common, then. We both had to run away from Tenebra, and we agree that Cassia is the best sister in the world. I can see we'll be great friends."

Zoe blushed and reached into her pocket for three canvas pouches tied with garden twine. "I have a welcome gift for you! They're just seeds because we can't plant them yet—it's too cold at home and Cassia's greenhouse isn't done—but when Papa and Mak and Lio build it, we can plant daisies and goldenrods and delphiniums, just like Cassia did for you."

Solia fingered the seed pouches. "Cassia told you about our first garden, did she?"

"She told me all the stories! About lessons and the swimming pond and why you had to leave." Zoe's brow furrowed. "I know not everyone can come back, even if they want to. My human parents can't come back. But you coming back is one of the best things I could ever imagine!"

Cassia watched the first fissure open in her sister's armor. An expression of pure, vulnerable emotion appeared on Solia's face. Cassia knew that look. She had seen it often as a motherless child, when Solia had been determined to fix unfixable hurts.

Solia held out her arms to Zoe in wordless invitation. For once, the shy child didn't hesitate. She went into Solia's arms, smiling with all her baby fangs and half of a new front tooth.

Solia held Zoe and stroked her hair. "I look forward to going to Orthros with you so we can plant your welcome gift."

Cassia let out a sigh of wonder. No matter the unresolved questions between her and her sister, Solia did not have the heart to disappoint this innocent child.

There came a swell in the air, like an unseen crest of the ocean pressing on Cassia's arcane senses. Magic, familiar, Hesperine. Then Komnena appeared in the orchard, dressed to impress the Imperial court, but with her fangs out as if ready to tear apart any threat to her children. Apollon and Lio stepped into sight in her wake. When their gazes landed on Zoe and Solia together, the magic eased, and their expressions of panic drained away.

"Oh," Komnena said softly, putting a hand to her mouth. Behind her, Apollon smiled, resting his hands on her shoulders.

"Lio!" Zoe reached out to him, her other arm still around Solia.

He went to her, a sheen of tears in his eyes. "I've been so worried about you."

She clutched him close. He and Solia ignored each other in a momentary truce for Zoe's sake.

The next thing Cassia knew, Zoe was introducing Solia to Komnena and Apollon with a ceaseless commentary about how wonderful they and Lio and Orthros were. Cassia could not have gotten in a word about her Grace-family, and she need not try.

Komnena held Solia's hands in both of hers. Solia glanced between

Komnena and Lio, as if noticing the family resemblance between him and his mother by both Hesperine blood and birth.

"You are Cassia's kin," Komnena said, "which makes you ours. You are not to feel like a guest. I'm the Queens' Chamberlain, so helping newcomers make themselves at home is what I do. There are no requests too large or small and no such thing as a foolish question."

"Thank you." Solia's tone was gracious, but she wore her mask of discipline, a sure sign she was feeling overwhelmed. So much like the court mask that had once been Cassia's own daily armor, before the Hesperines had made it unnecessary.

Let Solia be overwhelmed. Let the Hesperines' otherworldly beauty and breathtaking kindness break down all her defenses.

Apollon seemed like a nocturnal sun with his golden hair and robe and magnanimous aura. Cassia no longer shrank from his powerful presence. She sought his gaze, and he winked at her.

He extended his hand to her sister. "Well met, Solia. I've waited sixteen hundred years to have a fellow warrior in the family."

She didn't take the offered wrist clasp. "I confess..." She made a seemingly deliberate pause, a strategist buying herself time to choose her words. "...when Karege regaled me with tales of the Lion of Orthros, I never imagined we would meet under these circumstances."

How well Cassia understood what Solia must be thinking. Her sister did not know what to do with someone like Apollon. Not after the name *Father* had been dead to them for so long.

Apollon smiled at the flames dancing over Solia's hands. Stone appeared on his palms, coating them like armor. He clasped her wrist, patting her fiery knuckles with his other hand. "Our bloodline is notorious for defying expectations. I hope you'll feel right at home."

Komnena pulled Lio and Cassia into an embrace then, pressing a tearful kiss to Cassia's hair and Lio's cheek.

"We're all right, Mother," he reassured her. "I'm so sor—"

"Now, now. Don't apologize. Not when a mother's worry is as natural as the rising of the moons. But do try to stay home for a while."

When Cassia wrapped her arms around Apollon, he gave a delighted laugh of surprise.

He held her gently, and she felt engulfed in his steadiness. His words rumbled with deadly protectiveness that felt bigger than the desert. "I wish I had been with you in the Maaqul."

"You were, Papa. Your kind words saw me through a very dark hour."

He pulled Lio close. "Well, perhaps I have learned something from my son, if my words have become as helpful as my hammer."

"No," Lio replied, "I first learned kind words from you."

"But I hear you have been letting your magic out, too." Apollon grinned. "You must tell me all about your adventures."

When their family turned Lio loose for a moment, he put his arms around Cassia. She could feel the relief in his body.

"Zoe had proved to be the greatest ambassador of us all," Cassia said.

Oh, Goddess. Everyone Cassia loved would be together at last.

Solia was coming home.

40

nights until

NOTIAN WINTER SOLSTICE

16 Ourania, 1597 IS

COMING HOME

CASSIA COULD SCARCELY BELIEVE that Orthros was just on the other side of the spirit gate in front of her. The portal sparkled in the air like starlight on water, surrounded by fig trees in the Empress's gate courtyard. After traversing the lands of the Empire, both dangerous and wondrous, the end of their journey would only take a few more steps.

Lio tucked her cloak around her. "Are you ready?"

"Let's go home." She burrowed in the bespelled silk, longing for Orthros's frozen beauty.

Mak bumped her shoulder with his. "This time, your sister is coming with us."

Cassia smiled at him. "We've done it. Both of our sisters are safe, just as we swore."

Knight wagged his tail, interested in all the activity. Palace servants bustled past with their trunks, taking instructions from Komnena. Amid so many strangers, Zoe clung to Apollon, who kept whispering things that made her grin and giggle.

Solia strode into the commotion wearing in tall boots, Imperial trousers, and a long, high-collared Vardaran tunic. Her new sword was at her waist, the golden silk scarf fastened around her shoulders with an acacia brooch. With her came Kella, Hoyefe, Tuura, and Karege.

Cassia's heart lifted. "Dare I hope you've all decided to accept our invitation?"

There was a spark in Solia's gaze. "Since I am to negotiate with the Queens of Orthros on matters affecting both Tenebra and the Empire, an Imperial delegation will accompany me. My allies represent the Azarqi nomads, the Owia aristocracy, the diviners of the Empire, and Imperial Hesperines errant."

Solia might think she was bringing the Ashes to help with the Empress's plans, but this only played into Cassia and Lio's plot. With Solia's mercenary family accompanying her, she would be all the more tempted by a life of freedom with the people she loved.

Lio offered an official bow and a roguish grin to the mercenaries. "We will be delighted to host the Ashes. We hope you'll find Orthros's snows refreshing after the sands of the Maaqul."

"You'd better give me a nice room, Sunshine," Kella warned, "considering how you and Cassia borrowed my tent."

A faint blush warmed Lio's pale skin. "To be sure, First Blade, you shall have the best chambers in our residence."

Mak snickered. "You didn't tell Lyros and me about that part of your adventure. You've been holding out on us."

"It was a lovely tent." Cassia brought her memories of that night to the surface of her thoughts just to watch Lio's blush deepen. "We're so glad for the chance to return your hospitality, Kella. But you said you couldn't leave the Empire because you have so many new contracts."

Kella's indigo-stained lips curved in a sly smile at Solia. "A new client recently offered to buy out all our other contracts. She has deep pockets, compliments of the Empress. We've signed on to accompany her wherever she may go, however long she may need elite reinforcements."

"We would have gone with her anyway, but she insisted on paying us." Tuura patted Solia's hand. The Ashes' diviner might look motherly, with her kind smile and round figure, but she had indeed gone to the most dangerous places in the world to fight alongside her mercenary comrades.

Mak clasped Karege's wrist. "You didn't get enough of Orthros's politics on your last visit?"

The elder Hesperine, whose cloud of hair was as impressive as his prowess in battle, gave Mak a mighty clap on the shoulder. "Oh, that was more than enough oratory for me. This time, I'm coming for the sparring matches. And I'll get paid to put up with the elders."

"Solia knows the way to mercenaries' hearts." Hoyefe pressed both his hands to his breast. The handsome master fencer and illusionist never had trouble winning hearts himself. "Fame, fortune, and an invitation to a land full of gorgeous, hungry immortals."

Lio laughed. "It seems you'll finally have the opportunity to find some Hesperines of your own, Lonesome."

"I wouldn't miss this for the world!" Hoyefe put a hand on his hip, puffing out his chest. "Not least because you are in need of my expert romantic guidance. I understand you are to perform the Labors for the Matriarch."

Not if Cassia could talk Lio out of it. She let him feel her disagreement loud and clear in her thoughts.

"I certainly am," he said, unrepentant. "I should have known you have experience in that area."

Hoyefe stroked his artfully groomed mustache. "I have indeed performed the labors for many a lovely woman—and lived to tell the tale."

Kella rolled her eyes. "Sometimes you go through the entire ritual to shack up with another actress. You just like an excuse for the drama."

"You wound me, Standstill!" Hoyefe declared. "The labors are a time-honored tradition to consecrate a union. Or several."

"Well, I suppose it's a good thing you can give Sunshine a few pointers." Kella looked Lio over. "He'll need them, going up against Sunburn."

Hearing the fortune name she had borne as a mercenary, Solia smirked.

"Now, now, you're worrying Shadow." Hoyefe conjured a rose out of thin air and twirled it before Cassia until she couldn't help but smile. "Don't be alarmed, my dear."

"I'm very grateful you'll be there to help Lio," she admitted.

Hoyefe leaned closer. "If you feel inspired to thank me, you can introduce me to any Hesperines you know who are as handsome as yours."

"None are as handsome as Lio," Cassia said, "but I'm sure we can find you plenty of good-looking possibilities on the docks."

Lyros slung an arm around Hoyefe's shoulder and led him toward the gate. "Wait until Mak and I take you to Hyacinth's Ambrosia. No coffeehouse offers finer male company."

"Tell them to bring an appetite," Hoyefe said. "Once those lovely fellows are done with me, they won't have room for coffee."

Cassia squeezed Lio's hand, and he nodded, joining their family and friends at the gate, where Komnena was handing around more bespelled silk cloaks. Cassia waited with Solia.

Her sister scanned the courtyard as if seeing more than this pocket of the Imperial Palace, as if trying to gather up all the years and memories hidden within these walls and beyond.

"You'll come back," Cassia reassured her.

"Yes. But it will never be the same."

"Perhaps it will be better."

Solia's gaze returned to her. "My pragmatic Pup. When did you become an optimist?"

"Not when. Where. Come through this gate with me, and I'll show you."

Zoe chose that moment to run over to Solia for one more hug. "Mama says we must wait for you at home. I'll make sure Bosko doesn't eat all the mince pies before you get there."

"Thank you," Solia said solemnly, a hidden smile in her eyes.

Apollon gave Komnena a kiss before she took Zoe through a neighboring gate. Then he turned to Lio and Cassia, Mak and Lyros, Solia and the Ashes. Suddenly he looked very much like an elder firstblood and warrior who had led the Blood Errant in countless battles.

"Kin by blood and battle," her Grace-father said, "enter Orthros as my family and guests. Know that my house will always be your Sanctuary."

Cassia hooked her arm in her sister's, and together, they followed Apollon through the portal.

This time, Cassia was ready for the whispers of the ancestors, which mortals always heard when passing through spirit gates. She ached for one more message from her foremothers before leaving this land where she had first heard their voices. And this time, unlike every time she had gated before, she understood their words.

Well done, daughter.

Return home now.

Go with blessings.

Lio's hand found hers, warm and smooth, his thelemancy ever entwined with her. And on her other side was a different warmth, a crackle of fire magic—her sister.

Cassia blinked back tears and passed through into the land of her living bloodline.

They arrived in a broad chamber carved from Haima's deep red bedrock. Thick, intricately carved pillars rose high above their heads. Spell light gleamed upon the wealth of weapons on display and on the immortals who waited there.

Hippolyta, Guardian of Orthros, had assembled her Stand. Arkadia, who had once shared Cassia's pain over lost sisters. Alkaios and Nephalea, who had given Iris the dignity a hero deserved in death. And Nike, who had saved Cassia's life that fateful night when Solia had been forced to flee. Mak and Lyros went to join the line of Stewards, and Aunt Lyta looked upon them with pride.

This was the first time Cassia had seen Nike in regalia and speires since the long-lost First Master Steward had rejoined the Stand. She stood with her Trial brother. Rudhira wore no princely finery, only a short red battle robe and sandals, his long red braid tied with his own speires.

The warriors of Orthros were ready to make the opening argument for why Solia belonged in their family. Petite, powerful Aunt Lyta made the introductions with all the ceremony of announcing contestants at the arena.

Rudhira gave Solia a royal nod. "Welcome to Orthros, Princess."

"Blood-Red Prince." She gave him a deep nod as well. Her gaze went from him to Nike to Apollon, the three surviving members of the most notorious errant circle in Hesperine history. "I have competed against the best mortal warriors in Akanthia, yet never stood in the presence of the Blood Errant. It is an honor."

"You must join us at the arena, Victor of Souls." Nike offered Solia a salute to the victor.

"With pleasure, Victory Star." Solia returned the salute, then made one of her studied pauses. "I am deeply aware of my bond of gratitude to you, Alkaios, and Nephalea."

"It is remarkable to meet you in the flesh at last." Alkaios ran a hand over the stubble of his light-brown hair, which was slowly growing back after a near-fatal battle with fire mages.

Solia bowed her head. "We must discuss how I can honor what you did for Cassia and Iris."

Nephalea's smile was gentle, although her slender frame was honed by the Hesperine battle arts. "It is reward enough to see you two here together."

The night that had shattered Cassia's world had, all these years later, brought her and her sister and these three Hesperines together again. Iris had not made it to Sanctuary, but Cassia and Solia were living in the world she had shaped, the reality her sacrifice had made possible. Just when Cassia needed a reminder that she was not dreaming, Lio gave her hand a squeeze.

"Before we continue into Orthros," Aunt Lyta said, gesturing to a row of empty weapon racks, "I'm afraid everyone must disarm. This is the Armory of Akofo, named in honor of a great warrior of the Owia—Kassandra's husband, father of Prometheus. We ask all our Imperial guests to entrust their weapons to the Stewards' care here."

Mak held out both hands to Solia. "We will show your blade the same respect we give the Blood Errant's own armaments."

Rudhira and Nike's famous weapons levitated nearby in a bespelled display. His massive two-handed sword, Thorn, hovered next to the Chalice of Stars, her round shield. There were empty spaces for Apollon's absent Hammer of the Sun and Prometheus's long-lost twin swords, the Fangs. All had been crafted of the Hesperine alloy adamas, the hardest metal in the world.

Solia laid her sword across Mak's palms. "Her nights in this armory will become part of her legend."

Lyros bowed to Tuura. "Your staff will remain with you, of course, for a divining rod is a sacred ancestral artifact that should not be parted from its wielder."

"That's very thoughtful of you, young man," the mind healer replied.

While Solia and the Ashes turned their arsenals over to the Stewards, Rudhira clasped Lio's wrist and pulled him in for a hard embrace. "The Maaqul, Lio? Bleeding thorns. My attempts to prevent my only Ritual son from going errant too young have utterly failed."

"He's my son," Apollon said. "It was a losing battle."

"Thank Hespera you two made it home safely." Rudhira's healing magic cocooned Cassia like a quiet night in the depth of winter. "I see the Empress's physician has been very thorough, but even so, I would like you to come by the Healing Sanctuary."

"Of course I will." Cassia swallowed a chuckle. For a heroic and deadly warrior, her Ritual father could be such a mother hen. But she shouldn't be surprised. He was a healer at heart.

He even gave in to Knight's begging eyes and adoring tail-wagging and scratched the hound's back. "I'm glad you're safe, too, you smelly mongrel. I hope you bit off some of the jinn's hands, and that they take even longer than Hesperine appendages to grow back."

Once the weapons were stored, the Stewards escorted everyone up the spiral stairs, past clerestory windows to a gallery, where double doors opened onto the small island dedicated to the armory.

The frigid air of Orthros filled Cassia's lungs, and magic soared into her. Goddess bless. She could feel the power here more clearly than ever, as abundant as the dark sea lapping at the shore, as bright as the two stars reflecting on the waves. The lights of Sisters' Port twinkled across the water, where Haima rose atop the ice cliffs of Orthros Notou, an elaborate silhouette against the blue-black sky.

Uncle Argyros stood waiting by the pier. His silver-blond braid and silver silk formal robes wavered in the polar breeze, the only motion about the still immortal.

"Ah," said Silvertongue in his legendary voice, "my beloved warriors and wayward diplomats."

The dignified, intimidating Queens' Master Ambassador pulled Lio and Cassia into his arms, betraying a secret only his family knew—he gave excellent hugs.

"I thought I'd lost you two." His voice emanated mind magic, saying much more than simple words.

Lio held onto their mentor for a long moment. "It would take more than the Maaqul to put an end to your students, Uncle."

Cassia lifted her medallion. "It was well worth crossing the desert to find this waiting for me on my return. I am honored to officially be your newest ambassador."

Uncle Argyros shook his head. "Let us pray your lessons are more peaceful from now on."

Cassia glanced at the stately banners decorating the pier and the boats moored there. "Are we expected at a welcoming ceremony?"

"Indeed," Uncle Argyros replied, "the firstbloods have assembled to celebrate our returning diplomats and Stewards and to greet the presumptive monarch of Tenebra, along with her Imperial delegation. I'm sure they will enjoy themselves while we are all at House Komnena eating mince pies with the sucklings."

Cassia's eyes widened. "May we do that? Skip the ceremony and go home?"

"Yes." Uncle Argyros's eyes glinted with thelemancy that had overcome armies. "I am entitled to inconvenience important people."

Lio put an arm around Cassia as their powerful immortal family stepped everyone into warmth and light.

They arrived in the Ritual hall of the Notian House Komnena. White rose petals were strewn across the vibrant tiles, and garlands of fat white blooms trailed up the ornate pillars. Cassia lifted her gaze to the dome, a honeycomb of geometric mosaics depicting Hespera's Rose and the constellation of Anastasios, the founder of their bloodline.

He had been quite the rebel, helping discover the secret of immortality and defying the Mage Orders. She hoped Apollon's Gifter was rejoicing from the heavens at the fiery new member of the family she and Lio had brought home.

Their Trial sisters flocked around them. If it was possible for a veil spell to scowl, Kia's did. "I'm furious at both of you, and you can expect terrible lectures on how not to get lost in the Maaqul."

"Oh, we were so worried." Nodora breathed a great sigh of relief. "But lectures have to wait, Kia. Solia seems a little overwhelmed, doesn't she?"

"Of course she is," Kia muttered. "Too many stuffy elders. She needs a proper welcome from the Eighth Circle."

Xandra gave Solia a little wave, flames dancing between her pale fingers. "Oh, it's so lovely to meet you! There's never anyone in Orthros to talk with about fire magic."

Solia's brows rose. "I wasn't aware there are Hesperines with fire magic."

Xandra made a face. "I'm the only one. But I trained in the same Imperial practice as you—minus the killing part."

"Do you blend blood magic and fire magic, as the Cifwani people do?" Solia asked with obvious fascination.

"Yes, exactly," Xandra replied. "One of my mothers is of Cifwani origin, just like your mentor, Ukocha."

"May I ask when she came to Orthros? I wonder if I know her kin."

Xandra chuckled. "No, she's been here since the beginning."

"You have something else in common with Princess Alexandra," Cassia said.

"Oh, don't give me away," Xandra scolded cheerfully, although Knight was already betraying her secret, cutting in front of everyone in the hope of pets from her. "It's so nice to simply be a Trial sister sometimes, instead of the Queens' daughter."

"Well met, Royal Firstblood." Solia gave her a remarkably dignified nod for a royal encounter taking place over a shedding liegehound.

Xandra pushed at the tousled strands of dark hair escaping from her coronet braid. "None of that official title nonsense, not tonight. Let's have some fun around the Ritual circle."

"I'm Kia." She gave Solia a wrist clasp. "Eudokia Hypatia, if you really want to know."

"Hypatia, as in the author of *New Cosmology*?" Solia asked.

"You've read it?" Kia brightened, straightening her favorite turquoise mantle. She might have bitter differences with her mother, but she was proud of Hypatia's place in the scholarly canon.

Solia nodded. "Tuura would never leave such an essential text out of my education."

"I'm Nodora," their sweetest Trial sister introduced herself. "I'm from the Archipelagos, so the shamisen is my specialty, but one of my fathers is from the Empire." She held up the drum she carried. "If you wish for some Imperial music to make you feel at home, you have but to ask."

"That's a kind thought, thank you," Solia said.

Zoe was soon clinging to Solia again, with Bosko not far behind. Arkadia and Javed's eleven-year-old son wasted no time peppering Solia with questions.

"What was it like, riding your horse across the desert?" he asked. "Will you tell us stories about the Golden Shield? And the Battle of Souls?"

Zoe clutched a squirming goat under each arm so they wouldn't nibble Solia's boots. "Bosko! You have to say 'please!' "

He swallowed and collected himself. "Please, Cousin Solia, if you have time, would you mind talking to us about when you were in the Empire?"

Solia smiled and pointed to the speires binding his mop of dusty brown curls. "You appear to be a Steward-in-training."

Bosko nodded, straightening his shoulders.

"I'm happy to tell you about my experiences in battle, but only if your mother Arkadia says I may."

Bosko raced off to ask for her permission, but it sounded as if Kadi was already swapping her own battle stories with Nike and Kella, who had unharnessed herself from her mount and levered herself into a chair. Tilili stretched out on the floor at their feet, batting one of the sucklings' wooden horses with a lazy paw. From the other side of the circle, Apollon's lion familiar made eyes at the sand cat.

Karege and Mak were laughing with Rudhira and Apollon, while Hoyefe asked Lyros about the famous artists in his bloodline. Javed had his and Kadi's three-year-old daughter Thenie on his lap as he talked with Tuura about medicinal poultices.

With Komnena to smooth the way, all their friends and family were taking their seats around the wide, round coffee table at the center of the Ritual circle. Yet Solia lingered on the edge of the gathering. She drew in a breath, as if bracing herself against a threat.

Then Kassandra stepped into sight. She had arrived last, but Cassia knew the Oracle's timing was always perfect in her mysterious way. The elder firstblood was always selective about how she flaunted her past, but tonight, she looked like the Imperial princess she had once been, wearing stripweave of purple and gold, her floor-length locks heavy with solid gold adornments.

"Ah, Kassandra," Uncle Argyros greeted her with a gleam in his aura. "I see you escaped the ceremony. Did you manage to leave without causing a stir?"

She gave a rich laugh. "When have I ever squandered an opportunity to cause a stir?"

Apollon laughed with her. "Never."

Solia gave her a deep bow. "Princess Efiriye."

"Well, Sister Commander," Kassandra mused, "it has been a long while since anyone has called me by that name. I take it you have studied my sister's time as Empress."

Solia glanced at Lio. "I have recently been reminded that her reign has particular relevance for the present day."

"And how fares my niece-by-many-greats who presently rules the Empire?"

"Her Imperial Majesty sends their most admiring regards."

With a rush of gratitude, Cassia realized what Kassandra was doing. Solia was much more comfortable with Imperial royals than Hesperine elders.

Lio's slow smile told her he was thinking the same. He gave Kassandra a kiss on the cheek. "Thank you so much for being here tonight, Ritual mother."

"It is good to see you, my little bloodborn," she said, although he towered over her and everyone else in Orthros, typical of the few who were born Hesperines instead of transformed after birth. She held him to her for a long moment, perhaps thinking of her lost bloodborn son. "My visions of your time in the Maaqul were enough to concern even me, and I have seen everything."

Cassia embraced her, suddenly enfolded in the scent of Imperial spices and a magical aura so powerful that she almost gasped. "I hope you approve of our decisions on our journey."

"You did marvelously well." A mischievous smile banished the sadness in Kassandra's eyes. "I won all my bets with Ziara and Huru."

"You know the privateers who saved my life?" Solia's formality wavered at the mention of her friends.

Kassandra chuckled. "I manage Orthros's trading fleet. The queen of privateers and her first mate are two of my most respected colleagues and, I confess, two of my favorite women to gamble with. Such a charming couple."

Solia gave her head a shake. "Akanthia seems smaller and smaller."

"Orthros is the gateway to the entire world, my dear," Kassandra replied.

The words, coming from the Oracle, rang with significance for Cassia. *The gate in our time.* That was how Cassia thought of Orthros since escaping Btana Ayal, the ruins where a shattered portal marked humankind's tragic attempt to unite the Imperial and Tenebran sides of the world. There had been no Hesperines then. Orthros could succeed where Btana Ayal had failed.

Solia put her hands behind her back. "I appreciate more and more why Cassia recommended I pay Orthros a visit. It would be an honor to hear your wisdom on the Hesperines' position between Tenebra and the Empire."

Kassandra said, "You will hear plenty of my opinions when you meet with my Ritual sisters, the Queens."

"Do you know when that will be, Elder Firstblood?"

"Tonight, we are gathered for more personal reasons, are we not? Come, sit with me."

At Kassandra's invitation, Solia joined Cassia's Hesperine family in the Ritual circle.

All the tension drained out of Cassia. They had made it.

Lio put a steadying arm around her, and she couldn't deny she needed it. "Do you need to lie down?"

She shook her head. "Everything I need is right here within reach. At last."

He pressed a tender kiss to her hair. "You also need to lie down."

She was rather too exhausted and happy to resist. He coaxed her to recline at the low table. She found herself in a cozy pile of floor cushions, two sucklings, a pair of goats, and one liegehound, with her Grace and her sister nearby. Kassandra had somehow gotten Lio and Solia to sit next to each other between her and Komnena.

"Will you tell us a story about the Empire?" Zoe asked.

The secrets of the desert no longer seemed so enormous, here in the bright spell lights of home, with the voices of her family all around her. And she knew what Zoe's bedtime story would be tonight. "Let me tell you about the first time I used magic."

"You used magic?" Zoe squealed.

Bosko's eyes lit with excitement. "You found out what your affinity is?"

Cassia looked around at the expectant faces of loved ones ready to be happy for her. That made it all feel more like delivering good news to her family, rather than spilling the heavy magical secrets of the ages.

She took a deep breath. "They're not quite awake yet, but once they fully come to me, I'll have three affinities. I will be a Silvicultrix."

The sudden silence told her that the ancient Hesperines around her, who had witnessed and wielded the wonders of the divine, were in awe.

"Sil-vi-cul-trix?" Zoe sounded out the complicated word. "What's that?"

"A Silvicultrix has a very old kind of nature magic from Tenebra called Lustra magic," Cassia explained. "It gives me three different kinds of power: plant magic, beast magic, and soothsaying."

"Plant magic!" Zoe's face lit up. "Just like you wanted so you can make your garden grow better! Does beast magic mean you can talk to my goats?"

"I hope so." Cassia stroked one of Midnight Moonbeam's little horns, and the black-and-white goat bleated. Not to be left out, Zoe's brown-and-white kid, Rainbow Aurora, squirmed closer to demand affection, too.

"What's soothsaying?" Bosko asked.

"It means I can influence people with my words," Cassia told him. "I must be very responsible about it, because it's not right to make someone act against their Will."

In words the children of Orthros could understand, Cassia explained how she had discovered the truth of her magic. She spoke of how the spirits of her ancestors had appeared to her in Btana Ayal, the ruined city in the Maaqul Desert where the fabric of reality was torn. She brought her matriarchs into the Ritual circle with her.

The elders were as riveted as the sucklings by her account of the forgotten city, all that remained of a lost civilization ruled by the powerful, benevolent Diviner Queen. Judging by Kia's face, there would be an explosion among Orthros's scholars before the night was through, as Cassia's revelations altered their understanding of world history.

When Cassia came to the end of her tale, Uncle Argyros gave a wondering laugh. "Now I understand why you reminded us of the Changing Queen when you arrived."

Cassia felt her eyes widen. "I did?"

"Yes," Uncle Argyros said. "Apollon and I remarked on it to each other at the time. You have a certain presence about you."

"Not to mention her freckles." Apollon smiled.

They had seen Tenebra's greatest queen in the tyrant king's bastard who had arrived on their doorstep in need of Sanctuary?

Well, when she thought of everything she had done to secretly steer the kingdom and protect her Hesperines, she supposed the resemblance was not impossible.

Cassia glanced down at her freckled hands. "You saw her in me before I did."

"But we met her sixteen hundred years ago," Apollon said. "After all this time, we never suspected you were her direct descendant."

Cassia wondered at the twists of destiny that had brought her into this family, whose history was as ancient as her mysterious ancestor. "I have so many questions about her. About all the Lustra mages you might have met. You know everyone in Orthros. Are there any Hesperines who have my affinities?"

Her Grace-father shook his head. "In all our centuries, we have never known one of the Changing Queen's people to accept Hespera's Gift of immortality."

Cassia's mouth dropped open. "You mean I'm the only one? In sixteen hundred years?"

"Do not fear," Rudhira said.

Cassia was sure there would be times of fear on the path to mastering her magic. But this moment, when she was surrounded by her Hesperines, was not one of them.

MAGIC LESSONS

CASSIA FLUFFED THE PILLOWS on Solia's bed one more time. "Are you certain you have everything you need?"

Her sister gave her a wry smile, her gaze drifting around the room where Cassia was getting her settled. "Only four chambers and a private courtyard. I am disappointed. I insist on twice as many tassels on the silk cushions and three more baskets of luxury soap."

Cassia chuckled and gave Solia a hug. "I want you to have the best of everything."

"I know. I've always wanted that for you, too." She held Cassia for a moment before pulling back. "But I've been sleeping in a barracks for five years, and I was always on the road as a mercenary before that. You'll find my needs are basic."

"Well, you will simply have to endure me spoiling you a little."

"We don't have much time for spoiling, I'm afraid," Solia said, gentle but firm. "When is my audience with the Queens? Nothing was said of it tonight, not even by the Blood-Red Prince or Princess Xandra."

"You'll find that the nights seem to move slowly here in Orthros. Immortals have a different perception of time. No one hurries."

"The Hesperines may move at their eternal pace, but the changing of the seasons does not. Summer Solstice will take place in Tenebra in only forty days, and with it, the council that will choose the new monarch. How often do the Queens hold audiences?"

"Often. But Lio and I wish to attend with you. Alas, we must reassure a few dozen relatives that we are not dead before they will let go of us long enough for us to do any politicking." And if they happened to slow Solia down with family bliss until she forgot about taking over a kingdom, all the better.

Solia's brow knit with regret. "Of course."

"You weren't in such haste when we were tucking Zoe in just now. I seem to recall it was you who gave in to her pleas for one more bedtime story."

Solia's lips twitched. "Yes, well, bedtime rituals must continue, even when one is busy trying to overthrow a king."

"You always made time for me that way." Cassia paused, choosing her words with care. "Are you feeling all right? Lio's family can be overwhelming. I didn't know what to do with all their kindness when I first arrived."

"I can imagine. It would have been a difficult adjustment for you after leaving your dangerous life in Tenebra."

That hadn't answered Cassia's question. Solia was too calm as she sat down and pulled off her boots. Cassia saw right through the composed elder-sister expression on her face.

Solia might have embraced her mercenary family in the Empire, but she was still off balance when confronted with a Hesperine family who had already chosen to adopt her, whether or not that was her plan.

"Kella is next door," Cassia offered.

"I hope you did give her the best rooms," Solia said.

"Lio and I are just a corridor away as well, if you need anything."

"I'll be fine, Pup."

Solia had always been an excellent liar, especially when she was trying to protect her little sister from herself.

Cassia hated this. She wanted to be her sister's confidant in all things. Lio and all the family that came with him should not be one of the topics of conversation that felt like walking on shards of glass.

Cassia's gaze fell to the hairbrush on the dressing table, and an idea came to her. She picked up the brush and stepped behind Solia's chair. "May I?"

"You're much taller now than you were the last time," Solia said fondly.

"You were always so patient about the flowers I tried to put in your hair, no matter how I tangled it." Cassia began brushing her sister's cropped hair.

"It's much easier to untangle now."

Solia sat back and let Cassia revive the treasured ritual from long ago. With quiet brush strokes, Cassia created a moment of calm between them.

"Apollon told me something," she said eventually, "the night I first arrived at House Komnena. 'This house is strong enough to weather all your worries and your fears with you. Take as much time as you need letting them run their course.'"

Solia paused before answering. "I hate that you had any fears, Pup."

"Every person who comes to Orthros brings their own fears. This is a very safe place to have them."

"I'm glad you are no longer afraid." How expertly she turned the subject back to Cassia at every turn.

"It would be easy for my fears to return because of what Dakkoul did," Cassia confessed. "I had barely learned to trust. I gave my newfound openness room to grow and made friends with him. Then he proved to be the leader of the Rezayal and took me prisoner. It was a terrible failure of judgment on my part."

"It wasn't your fault," Solia said fiercely. "He is a mind healer. He exploited his ability to make people trust him and used that against you. Even someone as careful as you is not immune."

"Even so, that would make me put on all my armor again, if I let it. But simply being back in Orthros has reminded me why trust is so very worth the risk. Everyone who was around the Ritual circle tonight deserves trust. Sometimes I can scarcely believe the list of trustworthy people in my life has grown so long."

"I'm sorry you had so few allies in Tenebra." Another evasion.

Do you see? Cassia wanted to ask her. *Do you understand now why this place healed me? Won't you admit* your *fear—that you will want to stay enough to tell the Empress no?*

"If I hadn't had to leave you," Solia said, "there were things I would have told you. Things I believed Iris would tell you in my stead. Everything your mother entrusted to us."

It was unfair of Solia to raise the subject of their human loved ones when Cassia was trying so hard to talk about their Hesperine family. But she could not resist the bait. Her hands stilled. "There's more than what you've already told me?"

"While you were convalescing, I didn't want to burden you. But there is much more."

Cassia set the brush down carefully, her hands unsteady with a sudden rush of apprehension and anticipation. She circled her sister's chair to sit on the edge of the bed across from her.

Solia began, "Wisdom about your magic has been passed down orally from mother to daughter through every generation of your line. Thalia hoped to do the same with you, but she also imparted her knowledge to me, so I could tell you in case anything happened to her."

Cassia wrapped her arms around herself, remembering the tangible embrace of her mother's spirit in Btana Ayal. "She said you would explain the rest to me."

"Your magic isn't like other affinities. Each of the powers of the Silvicultrix awaken at different times over the course of her life."

"Do they arrive in a certain order?"

"No, it's individual for each woman, and sometimes more than one can awaken at the same time, or very close together."

Cassia blew out a breath. That sounded overwhelming. But if Lio could manage multiple affinities at once, so could she, surely. "All right. When do they usually arrive?"

"Each magic is a response to events in your life," Solia explained, "like an instinct that comes to you when you most need it."

"What events?"

"The magic of plants grows in a season of purpose. The magic of beasts comes to life in a struggle for survival. The magic of soothsaying finds voice in a life of openness toward others."

"That's so vague! What caused my mother's affinities to awaken?"

"Her plant magic arrived first. She began her life as a so-called orphan in a Temple of Kyria…a common situation for a child born out of wedlock to a mage."

"My grandmother was a mage of the Harvest Goddess as well?"

Solia nodded. "She chose to have Thalia in secret and raise her as one of the orphans. As soon as your mother was old enough, your grandmother put her to work in the temple garden. Your mother's plant magic awoke, just as your grandmother had hoped, and Thalia became her apprentice."

"It sounds as if the women of my line have often outsmarted the Orders to make their own life paths." Cassia's smile faded. "What danger brought on my mother's beast magic?"

"A plague. She and the other mages labored day and night in the temple infirmary to mix medicines. She caught the illness from their patients and had to fight for her own life."

The more Cassia learned about her mother, the more she admired Thalia. "She risked her life for others."

"She was a dedicated mage. Her soothsaying awoke when she was made Prisma."

"I didn't know she was the leader of her Temple of Kyria." The unfairness of it made Cassia's eyes burn. "She was so important to her temple sisters, only for that to awaken her soothsaying—the very magic that caused the Mage Orders to take her away from them."

"The Orders always try—and often fail—to control the women they fear. That's why they force soothsayers to live shrouded in the Temple of Chera like female necromancers and oracles. That life is not much better than the death sentence they give female fire mages like me."

"Serving the Mourning Goddess must be a truly terrible life, for her to choose to become the king's concubine to escape it. Why didn't she wield her soothsaying against Lucis?"

"He took magical precautions to protect himself from her voice. But she found ways. She gradually brought the court under her spell. She was planning to make her move to seize the throne after you were born."

Until Lucis had murdered her with his magefire.

Cassia took a shaky breath. Meeting Thalia had turned an old ache into fresh, powerful pain. "She said she wanted me. She suffered all of that so she could have me."

"Nothing was more important to her than you. And now she lives on in you."

"I must create the right conditions in my own life to awaken her magic in myself."

"Perhaps, together, we can understand what those conditions are for you. What gives you confidence and purpose that might awaken your plant magic? What makes you feel that your deeds matter?"

Cassia's hand went to her medallion. "I've felt that way ever since I became a diplomat."

Solia crossed to sit on the bed beside Cassia. "I hate to ask you when you have fought for survival. I don't need to."

"That has been every moment of my life." Cassia decided not to mention that she had nearly died of a fever when she was fourteen. It would only cause Solia to wish she had been there.

That was by far the closest to death Cassia had ever come. But clearly, that had not brought on her beast magic. If that battle for survival had not been dangerous enough, what about her more recent scrapes with death?

"If I had to point to a moment of extreme danger," Cassia said, "it would be Lio's and my battle with the Collector."

"Tell me who the Collector is," Solia demanded, "and whether he is still alive so I can use him to whet my new blade."

"When you were spying on the king years ago, did you ever see him hold secret meetings with a sorcerer?"

"Oh, gods," Solia swore.

"You do know him," said Cassia.

"I still remember his voice."

Cassia rubbed her arms. "Yes. His true voice speaks through his guises. Do you know who he is?"

"To my knowledge, an apostate necromancer, merely another rogue who practices magic without the Orders' sanction. He and the king have been using each other for years."

"He's more than just a necromancer."

Solia frowned. "He has more than one affinity?"

"Well, yes. He's a mage of dreams as well. But that isn't all."

"A necromancer and a mind mage of Hypnos?" Solia shook her head. "That is too much power from the god of death and dreams."

"The Collector has amassed his power with essential displacement—a necromantic ritual that allows him to rip magic out of one person and put it in another. Or keep it for himself."

"I know what essential displacement is," Solia said grimly. "That's how he hides the king's magic from the Mage Orders, so they won't force

Lucis off the throne and into a temple. They made a bargain. The sorcerer removes Lucis's magic temporarily anytime there is a risk he might be discovered."

Cassia did not wish to imagine the torture of having one's magic ripped out and put back in over and over…or the human sacrifice required each time. "A bargain? What did Lucis promise him in return?"

"I was never able to find out. Cassia, I know that look on your face. You suspect something."

"I think what the king promised him…was me."

"What does that graveshit want with you?"

"The king is the smaller spider, caught in a more deadly spider's web. This sorcerer is the Collector, the Master of Dreams—one of the six Old Masters. They are the necromancers whom the Rezayal fear will reach the Empire. In this, Dakkoul was not wrong. Tenebra and Cordium are the shadowlands, existing under the pall of the Old Masters. And we must never, ever let them reach this side of Akanthia."

"It seems I will need more than my sword to make him pay. But make no mistake. He will pay." Solia put her arm around Cassia's shoulders. "Tell me about his attack on you."

"He manifested during the Solstice Summit and tried to capture me. Lio and I defeated him together." It was by no means the first time Cassia had spoken of the duel aloud, but it was the first time she had told Solia. When she was done with her account, she felt another layer of her terror from that night had peeled away.

"Why you?" Solia asked. "What was his plan?"

"It doesn't matter any longer. I'm safe from him here."

"I can keep you safe from all our enemies now."

Cassia didn't want to go on. These moments of trust were so precious to her that she could hardly bear to disrupt them by reminding her sister of their unresolved conflicts.

But Solia needed to know what was at stake. And if anything could motivate her to stay in Orthros, it might be this.

Cassia put a hand over her sister's. "If I ever venture into Tenebra again, the Master of Dreams will not let me escape him a second time. I have to stay inside the Queens' ward over Orthros. If you return to Tenebra, I cannot go with you. We'll never see each other, except when you can get away to visit me here."

Cassia let silence fall between them and allowed her sister to consider the consequences.

"Cassia—" Solia began at last, but then broke off, closing her hand around a fistful of fire. "For now, we need to focus on the conditions for awakening your magic."

Cassia bit her tongue. If her sister wanted to keep avoiding the question of Tenebra, so be it. Cassia had given her the truth to ponder.

"What about your soothsaying?" Solia prompted.

"The Hesperines have opened my heart so wide that I cannot seem to close it again. If anyone can awaken my soothsaying, it is them."

"Have you seen any signs of your magic awakening? Thalia said you might notice an even better season in your garden than expected, animals willing to behave against their instincts for you, or sudden aptitude for a new tongue."

Cassia's heart beat faster. She found it hard to get her words out. She wanted their implications too much. "I was able to revive Roses of Hespera that had been dead for hundreds of years." But Lio had helped.

"Lio's uncle could talk of nothing but how you made a coffee tree grow in Orthros for the first time in history."

"I also persuaded my liegehound to protect Hesperines instead of eating them." Perhaps it was only a sign of Knight's loyalty to her, nothing more.

"I notice you're already fluent in the Divine Tongue."

"I can read lips in Divine, too, and thanks to our journey in the Empire, I'm learning Tradewinds quickly." But the Hesperines were good teachers.

"It has already begun." There was no doubt in Solia's tone. "Congratulations, Cassia. Thalia would be so happy. It won't be long now before you are in full possession of your power."

In the depth of veil hours, hearts beat throughout Lio and Cassia's once-empty residence. As the two of them retreated through the sleepy halls to their own chambers, he savored his awareness of the auras in their home. The Ashes seemed to be settling in, but Solia's pulse pattered with restlessness.

"I don't suppose I should check on her again," Cassia fretted.

"Zoe or Solia?" Lio asked.

"Both. But Zoe has Knight staying with her in the main house to help her regain her calm. Perhaps I should stop by Solia's room one more time."

"I think what she might need now is time with her own thoughts."

Cassia sighed. "You're right. But Goddess—Solia is *here*. It's difficult to let her out of my sight."

"I know, my rose. Your aura is all difficulty at the moment." Lio Willed open the door of their bedchamber for her.

She went inside ahead of him, her words spoken to the shadows in their Sanctuary. "It was good to see you and Solia sitting together."

Lio cursed silently, raising the spell lights so she wouldn't trip over the trunks they had yet to unpack. It should not be a momentous occasion for her Grace and sister to take chairs next to each other without conflict. He could do better than this.

He would make Solia accept his and Cassia's life together, one labor at a time, no matter what his Grace-sister demanded of him.

Cassia turned to him, sliding close. "It looks like you're already making progress with her. Why don't you simply give it a little time before you two embark on these labors? Perhaps you won't need them, after all." She ran a hand down his chest.

He felt the pressure of his fangs ready to unsheathe at this display of soothing sweetness from his prickly Grace. With all her softest places pressed against him, he could not deny this method of persuasion was highly effective. But he would wager he could be more persuasive still.

"Cassia, stop worrying about everyone else for just one moment and look where we are." He caressed her cheek, lifting her face toward the ceiling.

She gazed up at the mosaics of her favorite flowers. "We're home."

He wrapped his arms around her. "We're home."

She rested her face on his chest, and he sighed into her hair. They stood there together, and he felt as if they were truly still for the first time in a very long while. Their Grace Union seemed to calm all the noise of the world.

"I wasn't sure I would ever make it back here," she whispered.

He shut his eyes to soak up the feeling of her in his arms. "I know."

She gave a pained laugh. "Do you know what I kept thinking while I was the Rezayal's prisoner in Btana Ayal? How much I hated to die filthy. I wanted a bath so desperately. It was a foolish regret to harbor in what I thought might be my final hours, but there you have it. I agonized over not getting to enjoy our bathing pool one more time."

He said her name, gripping her against him. He hated that Dakkoul still walked free. The night would come when Lio would find him and enact justice for Cassia. But tonight, Lio could do this. "Can we set this matter of the labors aside long enough to take a bath together?"

"I cannot promise that. But I am not against negotiating in the bath."

He swept her up in his arms. As he carried her past their bed, she reached out to caress the juvenile roses growing in the latticed alcove. The green vines gave a gentle shiver, as if in greeting. Along the back wall of their room, stone panels slid open before his magic, and moonlight shone through their lacy openwork to play across the carpets.

"Orthros never grows less wondrous to me," Cassia said.

He carried her out to the courtyard, where their private bathing pool was hidden by high walls. Through the bespelled glass roof, the Blood Moon and the Light Moon shone down, Hespera's Eyes looking on their homecoming in welcome.

"Oh!" Cassia took in the pots of seedlings that left hardly any room to walk around the bathing pool. "All the plants I ordered at the Moon Market have been delivered! Komnena placed them here in the warmth and humidity, just as I asked."

Lio spun Cassia in a circle so she could see the tropical bounty. The damp warmth rising off the bath made her silk robes cling to her. She gave a happy laugh and kicked off her shoes, enticing him with a glimpse of her bare, freckled toes. His worry for her eased under the certainty that they had made good memories in the Empire, too.

He set her on her feet by the rim of the pool. "Wait right here."

He levitated over the plants to a nearby cabinet where they kept bathing necessities. A bar of the rose-scented soap she had taken to crafting would be just right for tonight. When he turned back to her, he found her kneeling among her new plants.

"I can't wait to start properly potting them." She stuck a finger in the soil of one small coconut-fiber container. "The bath will be a good place for them until the greenhouse is finished. They'll keep us in suspense for their first blooms, but they'll be worth the wait."

"How long do you think that one will take to flower?" he asked.

"A month or so." She glanced up, as if realizing he was standing there with soap and towels in his arms, just watching her. She blushed.

He stalked toward her. "Do you have any idea how adorable you are when you're doting on your plants? Your happiness is one of my favorite delicacies."

The way her gaze fixed on him told him her plants were forgotten. He dropped the towels and pulled her to her feet. The roof grew foggier as they stripped each other with demanding, reassuring touches.

They had finally made it back to their Sanctuary, where her mortality had no sting.

Holding her slick, bare body against his, he levitated the soap into his hand. He trailed a corner of the bar softly down her spine. "Let me bathe you, My Queen."

Her back stiffened at his words. "I am your Ambassador, Sir Diplomat."

"Of course. And most of all, my Grace." He placed a kiss upon her hand that was too intimate to be courtly. "But you are also the queen of my heart."

She narrowed her eyes at him, but a smile tugged at her lips. "Only you could get away with saying such a thing, Glasstongue."

Lifting her hand as if in a dance, he turned her to face the bath. "Does the kingdom you have chosen please you, Your Majesty?"

She wasn't looking at the promising seedlings or the comforts of the bath. She gave him a long, slow look over her shoulder, and his body tightened everywhere her gaze touched him.

He handed his petite, naked Grace down into the crimson marble bath as if she wore a festival gown. Her ankle, ringed by his braid, slid into the red-tinted mineral water of Haima's hot springs. She settled onto the bench carved into the side of the bath, while he sat on the edge of the pool behind her. Sliding his feet into the water on either side of her, he folded a soft towel behind her head.

She looked up at him through her lashes. "Your queen insists you join her immediately."

"Always so impatient to destroy kingdoms." If she intended to soften him toward her argument, it would not work. He began teasing the braids out of her long hair, savoring the intimacy of running her promises through his fingers.

"*Mmm.* You did mention you enjoy my kingdom-destroying tendencies. Come closer, and I shall be as destructive as you like."

He grinned, showing her his fangs. "As an immortal, I tend to respond to commands in my own good time."

"Such a heretic!"

"I do my best."

He used a pitcher to dampen her head, then began to wash her hair with her rose soap. She didn't protest his attentions, as she once might have. At last, he had accustomed her to letting him take care of her. As he scrubbed her scalp in deep, slow strokes, she sank a little further into the water and closed her eyes.

But a furrow appeared between her brows. There it was again, the frown he had glimpsed on her face throughout the night.

He rubbed her neck with his soapy fingers. "What is it, Cassia?"

"I doubt it's anything."

He trailed suds over her shoulders as he began to knead knots of tension out of her. "You've had something on your mind ever since we got home."

"I still suspect it's wishful thinking." She tilted her head, nuzzling his leg, and placed a slow bite on the inside of his knee.

"Patience, Your Majesty," he chided. He slid his hands downward to soap her breasts, teasing his slippery palms over her nipples.

She bit him again, harder. His fangs lengthened.

"I will not be swayed from my quest." He cupped warm water in his hands and let it trail over her breasts to rinse them. "You know I will tease out your each and every thought."

"I have my pride. When I'm trying to avoid a topic, I cannot simply wilt at the first touch of your magic. I must mount resistance."

"You have never in your life wilted, my rose. But I can coax you to bloom for me." He let his thelemancy prowl the edges of her mind ward. The spell she had allowed him to fuse to her thoughts was for her protection. But having his magic forever bound to her mind offered intimate benefits as well.

At his arcane caress, she moaned. "Oh—oh, perhaps it isn't wishful thinking at all."

"You know I specialize in making your wishes come true." He poured another pitcher of water over her hair to rinse it, letting his magic flow deeper into the ward.

She let her head fall back. "I—I think I can feel the magic better since we came home. Especially yours."

"You can? That's an excellent sign! Your brief experience with your power seems to have permanently heightened your senses. Is the effect getting stronger over time, do you think?"

"It's difficult to tell. All of Orthros feels like a bright blur to me, as if I'm surrounded by countless spell lights that are too close together to tell apart. I'm not sure if my senses are stronger, or if there's simply so much magic here that it's more obvious."

Lathering a soft cloth on the soap bar, he levitated down to join her in the water. "Well, we can do some experiments to determine the acuity of your new awareness."

Her laugh turned into a gasp as he trailed the cloth up the inside of her thigh. "Only you could be so academic while...while..."

"Stimulation of the physical senses can sometimes cause a correlating increase in magical sensitivity."

"It can? Well..." She trailed off for a moment while he massaged her between her legs. "...I begin to understand what you meant when you said something about spells and...pleasure rituals..."

Her brow knit in concentration while he washed every edge and curve of her. He stoked her desire, luring out all her senses. The steam rose around them, heady with the fragrance of roses. Splashes echoed from the fountainhead in the center of the bath as it carried away the suds on gentle currents.

"Close your eyes," he murmured, dipping the cloth between each of her toes.

Her eyes slid shut. He conjured a faint spell light in her blind spot, where no glow would shine through her eyelids.

Her brows rose. "Did you just cast a spell?"

"Can you tell where it is?"

"It's hard to say with so much magic everywhere."

"Keep your eyes closed." He pulled her off the bench to float in the water before him. "Stop thinking. Just feel."

He slipped the cloth between her buttocks, and she drew in a breath. "The spell…it's behind my left ear."

"Very good," he said. "That's impressive precision, Cassia."

"Clearly, I have an excellent teacher."

He let the cloth drift away in the water, teasing his fingers along the lips of her krana. "Does Her Majesty enjoy her magic tutor's methods of instruction?"

"This is certainly my preferred way to learn."

He dipped two fingers into her channel, finding her as slick inside as out. "If you complete one more challenge, I'll give you a reward. But you must not open your eyes."

She parted her thighs to sink into his touch. "Would your thelemancy enhance my awareness?"

"Yes, but we don't want my magic to affect your perception. We want to test your own abilities."

This time he conjured a spell light inside their bedchamber, in the alcove where their roses grew. Hooking his fingers, he pulled them slowly out of her.

She canted her hips, chasing his retreating hand. "It's over our bed. It's easier—to sense—even though it's…farther away."

"Why do you think that is?" He plunged his fingers inside her again.

"Your magical hands," she groaned.

"That's only part of the reason." He increased the pace of his hand, penetration and retreat.

She shook her head. "Wishful thinking."

"Tell me what you're thinking." He teased her kalux with his thumb.

At his touch on her most sensitive place, she clamped her knees on either side of his hips. "Our roses. Could I sense it better—because it's near them?"

"That's my theory," he said with satisfaction.

"Ohh. My garden magic." A smile flitted across her mouth. She rested her face in the crook of his neck, her fingers digging into his shoulders.

The flow of pleasure in her aura crested, ready to crash. He let his thelemancy rise at the boundaries of her mind like a tide. "Now, are you ready for your reward?"

"I'm ready." Her husky voice echoed through his senses, her aura swimming with eagerness for his magic.

He was beyond ready, his postponed hunger making his fangs prick his lips. "Keep your eyes closed."

He dragged his fingers out of her again, pulling her along the edge without sending her over. Turning them in the water, he sank back onto the bench and parted her knees so she straddled him.

She licked her lips. "I get the idea I earned the highest reward you offer, Sir Scholar."

"Tell me if you find it satisfactory." He grasped her hips in both hands and pulled her onto his hard, aching length, letting his magic plunge into her mind.

Deep, as deep as he could go in one move. Her low cry echoed around them. So good. Her body was hot in the warm bath, her hunger the tight grip he needed.

Her eyes had flown open. She tried to move, sending water lapping at his chest and torturous sensations along his shaft. He eased his hold, breathing deeply for control as she began to circle her hips.

"I want you to know just how much I prefer this seat to the throne of Tenebra." She flexed her hips again.

He shuddered up into her. "You will find me much easier to conquer, My Queen."

"Oh? You are not planning to resist?" She nibbled her way up his neck, pulsing her inner muscles to the same rhythm.

He bared his throat to her. "Why would I, when you rule me so well?"

She bit his earlobe, her tongue teasing his enchanted sapphire earring. Thank the Goddess for Lyros's creation, which prevented her from breaking Lio's skin. She could bite him anywhere they pleased without fear of drinking his blood before her Gifting.

"Any grievances I need to address?" she asked.

"I need you to bite harder, Your Majesty."

Her teeth clamped onto his throat, tantalizing, almost enough.

"More," he demanded.

Her canines dug into his warded skin, and she closed her mouth over his vein to suck him hard. He bucked under her, and she rode his instinctive thrusts.

More? her thought-voice invited.

I want your vein.

Take.

He matched her, mouth to vein, and sank his fangs into the other side of her neck. The grasp of her teeth became a vise as she cried out in the back of her throat.

My Queen has demands in return?

She gripped him inside her and rocked at an insistent pace. But with each of his long pulls at her vein, she surrendered a little more to his grasp on her hips and the slower, harder drives of his rhabdos. He drank the rich flavor of her power and tasted it sweetening into thoughtless need until she was pliant on his shaft, letting him move her. Her Craving now ruled her.

How blessed he was to be the one holding all her appetites in his arms. He braced his feet on the floor of the bath to thrust into her Craving. His magic poured out of him in rhythmic surges, a heated tide that drew agonizing pleasure through him, building delicious pressure where he was buried inside her. The water slapped against them as she feasted on him, soft and wet and ravenous.

He angled his hips. Goddess. Yes. Just there. She whimpered, and a new trace of spice threaded through her blood. He gritted his teeth to stop himself from letting go.

At the deepening bite, she exploded like a spell. And he lost himself. The Craving left him mindless in the flow of her blood. He consumed her with rapid pumps up into her giving body.

She found her voice first. "You have dethroned me."

He arched a brow at her, unwilling to budge from his exquisite situation. "You still seem well seated to me."

"Yes, well, look who is holding me there."

He gave her buttocks an unrepentant squeeze. "I've told you I have a taste for powerful women."

"I want my magic so much I could weep. I want to please you with it."

He ran his hands softly over her hips. "Then why hesitate to tell me what you were sensing earlier?"

Her gaze dropped. "What if I had been wrong?"

"You will be wrong sometimes, and that's all right. Magic is complex, and making mistakes is part of learning. But in this case, you were correct."

"I suppose I'm still afraid to get my hopes up sometimes. It seems too easy. After everything I've endured...how can my magic simply *appear*?"

"You've suffered enough! You've fought so hard and come so far."

"Perhaps that's true. There have been signs...it's possible my magic is very close to fully manifesting."

"What signs? I want to know everything."

Lio gathered Cassia more comfortably across his lap and listened, riveted, while she shared with him the wisdom Thalia had passed down to her through Solia.

"Kyria and Hespera bless your mother," he said when she finished. "Our understanding of your magic may still be incomplete, but thanks to her, we are no longer without knowledge. And what we do know makes it clear that you are coming into your full power even now. I can hardly wait."

Cassia's pulse picked up, betraying her anxiety. "Lio, I will need your help. A great deal of help, I suspect. It is...so much power. And I understand so little. If I make even a small mistake, the consequences could be devastating, couldn't they?"

Holding his naked Grace in his arms, along with all the latent magic contained within her, he was keenly aware of his role as her guide on the arcane path set out before her.

It was terrifying and marvelous, and he would have done anything to secure this calling if Hespera had not appointed him.

"I want to help you," he said. "I want to be the one you come to with questions, the one who holds you after every failed spell. I want to taste every drop of your new power in your veins as your magic surges through you for the first time." He slid his finger up the freshly healed skin of her jugular, and she shivered.

He brought his fingers higher, tilting her chin up. "This is your journey to take with me. Many will support you along the way, but I am your Grace. I will share this experience with you in a way no one else ever could. And you will find me unusually possessive of the privilege."

"Oh, Lio. I'm so glad it's you." She rested her forehead on his.

The gesture of trust made him place a tender kiss on her mouth. "Don't worry, my rose. It's common to lose control of your power, especially during the Gifting. But I have plenty of experience with difficult magic."

"What sort of disasters do you think we should be prepared for?" Cassia asked.

Lio sighed. "I would prefer not to air a list of worst-case scenarios, but I know you find it more reassuring to be forewarned."

"Always," Cassia agreed. "That way, it cannot take me by surprise, and that gives me the upper hand."

It struck him how defensive she still was at times, even in intimate moments like this. "Keep in mind that all of this is theoretical. It might not even happen. And if it does, by the time we attempt your Gift Night again, we will have a plan for any challenges that arise."

She nodded for him to continue.

"Very well," he said. "Imagine if you changed into a hawk while your transformation was incomplete, and you couldn't change back. We don't know what effect Hesperine blood has on Lustra shape changers in their animal forms. Would it complete your transformation as if you were human? Or would your body react as an animal's does—receiving healing and longevity, but not the Gift?"

"I see." Cassia spoke with the pragmatism to which she always resorted to protect herself from unpleasant truths. "So I might be trapped in bird form, somewhere between mortal and immortal. How inconvenient to spend eternity as your familiar."

"Nonsense. I would have to find a spell to transform me into a hawk so we could mate for life."

"Let us try to avoid any situation that inspires you to martyr yourself. But I suppose plant magic might be equally disastrous for you. What if I made roses grow out of your nose? That could be terribly painful, even if you do heal fast."

Lio choked on a laugh. It was good to hear her making jests as a defense as well. "I will gladly endure your thorns, my rose. But yes, it would be a problem if, for example, I found myself bound to the ceiling by vines and unable to reach you to finish giving you my blood."

"You know how averse I am to the notion of being tied up in bed. I have no intention of exploring that particular application of my power."

"I never said I minded you tying me up." He raised a brow at her. "But perhaps we can save that particular experiment for a more opportune time."

Her face flushed. "I would want my magic to be firmly under control for that, yes."

"But I'm afraid shape changing and plant magic are not my gravest concerns." He stroked the inside of her wrist. "Your soothsaying is arguably your most dangerous gift of all. I'm a thelemancer. I know what it's like to have power over someone's Will."

"Oh," she said softly, and he could taste her apprehension in their Union. "I could actually impair your Will with my words?"

"I have never met a soothsayer, much less had practical training in resisting their power. So the fact is, I don't know. But if the tales—and the Orders' fears—are any indication, you could talk me into a state in which I am no longer coherent enough to properly care for you during your transformation. I wouldn't have the Will to finish Gifting you, and if you didn't get enough of my blood quickly enough, you would die."

"I never want to do that to you. To master your Will without meaning to."

"I never want you to know what that's like."

A moment of silence passed between them.

"Research," she said at last. "We must devote ourselves to research, beginning tomorrow."

"Yes. We will leave no stone unturned." He tucked a wet strand of her hair behind her ear. "But it will have to be after midmoon."

She frowned. "Do we have a commitment I've forgotten?"

"No. Solia and I have agreed I will begin the labors tomorrow."

Cassia sat up straighter. "That's what you two were taking about when you were sitting together?"

He hated feeling her disappointment. "It's tradition for the man's eldest female relative to negotiate with his prospective bride's matriarch. My mother asked Kassandra if she would do us the honor, since she's older, and these are her Imperial traditions."

"And Kassandra agreed?" Cassia's voice rose.

"Yes. The oracle herself is in favor of it. Doesn't that reassure you it's meant to be?"

"No. For all we know, she is intervening to prevent disaster!"

"Cassia, all will be well. I don't need protection from your sister."

"I'm very much afraid you might."

Her anger might have hurt him and left him doubting her confidence in him, if not for this truth, which he sensed roaring up from deep within her. She was worried about him, again, after so many nights of fear and worry during their ordeals.

He slid his hands into her wet, tangled hair and kissed her again. Deep and hard, impressing upon her that he was here. They were safe. She made a frustrated noise in the back of her throat and kissed him back with ferocity.

Their Union carried his words into her thoughts. *You seem ready for your second course, my Grace.*

She bit his tongue.

I want to serve it in our bed with you under me this time, he said.

She wrapped her arms around his neck and moaned. He levitated them out of the bath, shedding water onto the tiles and a few of the nearby plants.

She came up for air, but she gave a gasp of surprise, not lust. Her face was frozen in astonishment. He followed her gaze.

Where there had been a green seedling in a coconut fiber container, there was now a cluster of leaves and a single moonflower, unfurled and reaching toward the Goddess's Eyes.

"It shouldn't..." she whispered, as if she might frighten the miracle away. "It shouldn't have bloomed for at least a month."

With care, Lio levitated the plant into her hands. She cradled it close, its fresh, verdant scent filling the air.

"There is your evidence, Cassia. A greeting from your plant magic, letting you know you needn't wait long."

"I'd best study fast."

39

nights until

NOTIAN WINTER SOLSTICE

17 Ourania, 1597 IS

A DISPLAY OF STRENGTH

LIO HAD NEVER SEEN the Owia luxuries that now filled the rooftop pavilion where Kassandra awaited him and Solia. They joined his Ritual mother under a purple canopy, and Solia draped her cloak over her arm in the bespelled warmth. The table and chairs were wood, a rare sight in Orthros, but classic for the Owia. They might have been visiting the Empress's palace, if not for the stunning view of Haima's vibrant, snow-topped domes below. And the ancestral masks hanging from the pavilion poles. They all had fangs.

Kassandra's gold bangles caught the spell light as she gestured for them to join her. Solia sat down across from her while Lio took a seat between them. Kassandra poured coffee from a solid gold pot and offered them a plate of delicacies that might have graced any table in the Imperial Capital.

Solia accepted the hospitality as if it were second nature. Lio surmised that her interactions with the Empress had not consisted solely of standing silently in a suit of armor. Solia might still be adjusting to the notion, but the Empress had forged her into as much a politician as a warrior.

Lio was more apprehensive than he had admitted to Cassia about what tasks a woman like Solia would set for him. Kassandra had most likely foreseen Solia's demands and whether he would succeed at them. His Ritual mother wouldn't let him go into this if he was doomed to fail. Would she?

She patted his hand. "It brings me joy to act as your matriarch."

"You have my gratitude," he said.

Her words took on a tone of ritual. "I, Elder Firstblood Kassandra, bring before you my son by Ritual: Deukalion, Firstgift Komnenos."

"I, Solia, first of my dynasty, will hear his petition."

So this was how Solia saw her clan. She invoked neither Lucis's hated blood nor that of her mother, who had been too broken to care for her. He and Cassia must convince her to adopt the name Solia Komnena. Tonight, their entire family's efforts at persuasion were in his hands.

A dreaded voice in the back of his mind warned him of the consequences of failure. If he could not sway Solia from her plan to build her dynasty, she would return to Tenebra. Cassia would once again be parted from her sister, except for rare visits when the new queen could escape her duties to visit Orthros.

For Cassia could never set foot in Tenebra again.

"Lio." Kassandra brought Lio back from the brink of his thoughts. "You may now state your intent."

"I, Deukalion, Firstgift Komnenos, intend to give the Gift of immortality to your sister Cassia and to avow her before all those we love, Hesperine and human. Most importantly, I intend to keep her safe and happy for all time."

Above all, safe from the Old Master who had tried to take her from Lio.

Solia listened, her face composed. He could not discern if his words made a good impression on her or not.

And he should have been able to tell. After she had taken off her armor before the Empress, her aura had been unshielded by spells for a brief time. So why had she once again become opaque to him?

His gaze flicked to the scarf draped over her shoulders. Her lips curved in a victor's smile.

He gave her a slight bow. She had indeed won this round.

The golden silk from the Empress must offer Solia some of the magical protection that her armor had once granted. Spells that blocked thelemancy and Hesperine empathy were among the rarest, most powerful enchantments that only someone with the Empress's resources could provide.

The Blood Union would be of no use to him in his efforts to win Solia's blessing, and neither would his mind magic.

"We must, as a formality, agree on the number of tasks." Kassandra looked at Solia expectantly. "Five for an ambassador."

It took a strong mortal to look Kassandra in the eye and disagree with her. "For my sister, it should be no less than eight for a princess."

"Cassia is no more a princess than I," Kassandra replied, "and she came a long way for her ambassador's medallion, as I did for the title of elder firstblood. The greatest honor you can do her is to agree to five tasks."

"She is my sister, and I am the future Queen of Tenebra. That makes her a princess in my eyes, no matter what side of the border with Orthros she stands on."

Lio made a calculated gamble. "Solia, I have a proposal for you."

She glared at him. "You ask a great deal. Not just a lifetime with my sister, but eternity. For a request of this magnitude, I intend to set you tasks accordingly."

This was a round he had already won. He had overcome much more difficult ordeals than this for his Grace. "She is well worth any challenge. Assign me five tasks to begin. By the time I complete the fifth labor, if you hold the throne, I will perform three more. But if you are not yet crowned Queen by then, you must accept only five."

He could see in her eyes that he had awoken her thirst for competition. "I will take this bargain."

"Is that amenable to you, Ritual mother?" Lio asked.

Kassandra lounged back in her chair, looking pleased. "Very much so."

Lio was not sure whether to be encouraged or apprehensive that this fit with her preferred vision of the future.

"Very well," Kassandra said. "Matriarch Solia, first of her dynasty, proposes five labors for the privilege of Gifting and avowing her sister Cassia, to be increased to eight should she be crowned queen by the time the fifth labor is complete. Deukalion, my Ritual son, will you undertake this challenge?"

"I will."

"Solia," Kassandra continued, "will you pledge to grant your blessing upon their Union, should he complete the tasks set before him?"

"You have my word."

Thank the Goddess for that. Despite the distance between them, of this Lio had no doubt—Solia was a woman of her word. She had just promised him her blessing. It was not an impossibility.

As long as he didn't fail.

Kassandra refilled their coffee cups, breaking the tension. "The first labor is a test of the man's strength, and it falls to him to offer a suitable service to his bride's matriarch. Lio, you will now propose a task for Solia's approval. If Solia is dissatisfied with your suggestion, you forfeit your choice, and she will assign you a labor herself."

Thankfully, his mother and Kassandra had warned him about this the night before, and he'd had many hours to ponder it as he had lain awake, holding his sleeping Grace.

"Matriarch Solia," Lio said, "I offer you my greatest strengths: my intellect and my magic. I propose that for the first labor, I help Cassia learn her magic. I will assist her in researching her affinities and give her practical instruction in spell casting. As her power awakens, I will guide her through any challenges based on my own experiences with my dual affinity."

Solia observed him, the image of calm. "You do have a reputation as a scholar and sorcerer. And thelemancy is notoriously difficult to control. These are skills that would benefit Cassia."

Solia was considering it. Progress. Lio had feared she might try to prevent his involvement in Cassia's arcane legacy. Not that he would let that stop him. And not that she needed to know some of her little sister's magic lessons involved erotic baths.

He took a sip of the strong Imperial roast, letting her deliberate, showing he was confident.

"I am inclined to accept," she said, "on one condition."

"How do you wish to modify the task?" Kassandra inquired.

"There is one expert I require Lio to collaborate with during this labor. The only person who can tell Cassia what Thalia wanted her to know about their magic. Me."

This was no gesture of peace and harmony. Solia intended to keep an eye on him. Working closely with her might go about as well as any encounter between a Hesperine and open flame.

But as Lio had told Cassia, he would jealously guard his privileges as her Grace.

He raised his cup to Solia. "I look forward to the opportunity for us to support Cassia—together."

"See to it that you put all that thelemantic mind of yours to the problem," Solia said, "and theory isn't enough. Keep up the training."

"Of course. I would also like to call in other experts to advise Cassia when necessary. Will you still consider my labor fulfilled if I do so?"

"Cassia's best interests are all that concern me," Solia said. "Consult whoever you must, as long as you don't let them do your work for you."

The barb didn't sting Lio, although Solia sounded like a sophia reminding sucklings not to shirk their lessons. There was no one who could do his work for him. Only Cassia's Grace could fully aid her in this.

Kassandra pursed her lips. "I deem it necessary to agree on a duration for this task."

Solia arched a brow in an expression that reminded him of Cassia. "I should be prepared for you to drive hard bargains, I see."

"Of course. Cassia is indeed worth any challenge, but so is Lio. As his matriarch, it is for me to negotiate to his advantage."

"How can we possibly set a duration on the task?" Solia protested. "We cannot predict precisely when Cassia's magic will manifest."

"That is what concerns me," Kassandra replied. "If her magic takes more time than expected to appear, due to circumstances beyond Lio's control, he should not be deprived of your blessing."

"We have every reason to believe all three of her magics are on the verge of manifesting."

"Matters of magic can often prove to be what you least expect."

"Allow me to make another proposal," Lio said. "As Cassia and I have already discussed, we must not undertake her Gifting until we have a proper understanding of her magic. Solia, would you consider my task fulfilled if we learn enough to be confident her magic will not pose any danger during her transformation?"

Solia shook her head. "I cannot agree to those terms. I don't want her Gifted until she is in full possession of her magic."

"I cannot agree to that." Lio strove to keep his tone civil, despite how everything in him rebelled at Solia's demand. "Her Gifting is likely to help her magic arrive."

"Do you have evidence of any Hesperines with Lustra magic?" Solia countered. "Who is to say the Gifting wouldn't prevent her affinities from awakening?"

Hespera's Mercy, let that not be the case. Surely Solia was looking for excuses to delay. "Of course, we intend to research all of this before we make a decision. But I am not able to promise you I will not Gift her. I will not make that choice for Cassia. It is her decision when she will become a Hesperine."

"A sacred decision," Kassandra agreed.

Solia's jaw tensed. "I will counsel her not to rush into anything."

Lio bit back his urge to remind Solia that Cassia was a grown woman capable of—and entitled to—her own choices.

Solia still remembered Cassia as a seven-year-old child. When Zoe was grown, Lio would feel no less protective of her than Solia was of Cassia now.

"This calls for a compromise," Kassandra said. "Cassia must choose the best time for her Gifting—before or after her magic arrives. I suggest you consider Lio's task fulfilled when he has helped Cassia gather enough evidence to make an informed decision."

Solia sighed. "Very well. I can agree to that. As long as the choice is entirely Cassia's own."

"I would never allow anyone to interfere with her right to make that decision for herself," Lio promised. And if Solia chose to take it as a warning instead, so be it.

If his Grace-sister thought he would meekly carry out her tasks without challenging her in return, she was mistaken. Meekness wouldn't win respect from a woman like her. But testing how far he could push her would be a dangerous endeavor.

Lio walked Solia back to House Komnena. She strode restlessly along Founders' Way, past the residences of the elder firstbloods and cedars just as old. It seemed the walk had been a good suggestion on his part to help her work off some tension. Besides, they needed to spend more time together without Cassia to mediate. Even if that time consisted of silence colder than the polar wind.

He led Solia under a four-pointed arch, the side entrance to his and Cassia's residence, through one of the red stone courtyards. A few potted plants stood about like cheerful heralds of his Grace's ambitions to turn every nook into a garden paradise.

The voices of the Eighth Circle drifted from the coffee room. Lio and Solia entered to find Cassia ensconced on a sofa between Kia and Nodora, with Knight at their feet. Xandra, Mak, and Lyros sat on the couch across from them. They faced each other over coffee cups, pie crumbs, and a Prince and Diplomat board. The game, known as Kings and Mages in the shadowlands, demanded intense focus, but they appeared to be laughing more than strategizing. Solia halted on the warriors' side of the table and tilted her head at the chaotic playing pieces.

Lio crossed to Cassia's side and leaned on the back of the sofa to give her a kiss. "Princes versus diplomats? Who's winning?"

"No one has any idea, but it's great fun." She took his hand, worry lurking under her cheer. The glance she cast between him and Solia appeared casual, but his Grace missed nothing with her keen observations. "Did you two have a pleasant visit with Kassandra?"

Lio hoped she would see that she need not fear the labors after all. "Your sister has approved my offer to be your magic teacher."

"With me as an adviser throughout the process," Solia added.

Cassia's face was neutral, but there was a hint of hope in her voice. "You two intend to work together to help me with my magic?"

"Yes, my rose. We will also consult with experts along the way, starting with these five right here." He swept a hand out to indicate their Trial circle.

Xandra blew out a breath. "We're all more expert than we'd like on living with magic that doesn't behave itself."

Kia straightened her favorite turquoise mantle. "I've collected all of Orthros's extant written sources on Lustra magic for us to begin analyzing. We have a pile of scrolls to get through."

"One good swing of my fist ought to get through them fairly quickly," Mak said.

"I'll make you read twice as many just for suggesting it, you lunkhead," Kia griped with affection.

Smiling, Lyros sat back on the couch. "I'll help with reading. When we're not casting wards to prevent accidents during spell casting practice."

"Is it very many scrolls, Kia?" Cassia asked, trepidation in her aura.

That was Lio's question too, although he was worried about there being too few, rather than too many.

"It's a new frontier in magical research, shall we say," Kia replied.

"That's what I was afraid of, but we'll make the most of what we have." Lio rested his hands on Cassia's shoulders. "With all of us reading through them, they will be manageable."

Solia gave Cassia a considering look. "Does reading give you headaches?"

"She remembers every word she hears and can read lips in multiple languages." Lio knew Cassia's struggles with literacy were the last thing she wanted to admit to the sister she admired.

"It's no fault of your attempts to teach me as a girl," Cassia hastened to say. "Unfortunately...completing my education is proving more challenging than I expected. But I am making every effort."

Solia shook her head. "Your mother had headaches, too."

"She did?" Cassia frowned. "But she was a temple-educated woman. She wouldn't have had any trouble reading."

"When her soothsaying began to awaken," Solia explained, "she could barely read for months, she said. Even when her magic settled and she could tolerate texts again, she always learned better from listening than she did from reading."

"Oh." Cassia was quiet for an instant. "Then...I'm not a slow learner."

Solia sat down next to her on the sofa. "You've never been a slow learner, Pup. You simply learn in your own way. Why do you think we relied so much on recitation when I was giving you lessons?"

Cassia let out a breath, her aura nearly sagging with relief.

Lio ran his hands over her shoulders. "Cassia, did you really think yourself incapable of scholarship?"

"I've had my doubts," she admitted, "but this encourages me. Perhaps you all can read the most important portions of the scrolls aloud for me?"

"Of course," Lio said.

"I've also found a number of songs with references to Lustra magic," Nodora offered. "We can learn so much from listening to sagas and ballads."

"And there are some things you can only learn to do by, well, doing," Xandra added. "Book learning isn't very helpful with certain affinities. Fire magic takes quite a bit of practical training, doesn't it, Solia?"

"That's true," Solia agreed.

"Thank you for going to such lengths for me," Cassia said.

Nodora touched Cassia's arm. "You may not have been through Trial with us, but this is our opportunity to see you through your own sort of initiation."

Solia gave Lio a look that, while not exactly approving, no longer made him feel as if she wished to set him on fire. "You have carefully considered which peers to consult in our research, I see."

"Only the best for Cassia."

She was about to have three of the most powerful and poorly understood magics tearing through her. She needed her Trial circle. She needed her sister. And most of all, she needed her Grace.

23

nights until

NOTIAN WINTER SOLSTICE

33 Ourania, 1597 IS

OPPOSING MAGICS

LIO HAD INTENDED FOR their research to lead them to Hippolyta's Arena eventually, but not after two weeks in Orthros's libraries. It had taken only sixteen nights to go through every scrap of written evidence they had about Lustra magic. And he had thought he appreciated how little they knew about Cassia's magic.

"What answers do you expect to find among the warriors?" Cassia asked with a puzzled expression.

Lio kissed the furrow between her brows. "Since we exhausted the scrolls, it's time to turn to other sources."

They stood with Solia and their Trial circle at the edge of the arena. Wild gusts of snow obscured the sky, but here within the Stewards' wards, the air was still and merely cool. Solia's gaze traveled down the tiered, carved benches to the ring of sand below, where generations of Orthros's warriors had practiced the Hesperine battle arts. Although Lio couldn't sense how she felt about setting foot here, he knew a look of reverence when he saw one.

"Welcome to Hippolyta's Arena, Victor of Souls," Mak said.

"It is an honor to have you here." Lyros, like his Grace, already wore his black battle robe, ready to support Lio's plan.

"The honor is mine," Solia replied.

Aunt Lyta waved to them from the arena floor, where she and Kadi appeared to be demonstrating advanced tactics for Alkaios and Nephalea. Knight wagged his tail, his ears perked, as if hoping for another game of chase in the ring with Kadi.

"Which sources are we here to consult?" Solia turned to Lio, and he took heart that there was no doubt in her tone.

"Eyewitnesses to Lustra magic," Lio explained. "The Blood Errant. After that, Uncle Argyros is expecting us in his library to tell us about the Changing Queen firsthand."

"Ah. All of them will certainly have insightful accounts." Coming from Solia, that was practically a glowing endorsement of Lio's idea.

Xandra's aura sparked with anticipation. "I wonder what Rudhira will reveal about his adventures. He doesn't talk about his past very often."

"Why does everyone call the First Prince 'Rudhira'?" asked Solia. "I thought his name was Ioustinianos."

Xandra explained, "Methu—Prometheus—gave my brother the name 'Rudhira' on their adventures, and his admirers adopted it."

Kia patted the travel desk under her arm. "I'll make note of tonight's findings about his past."

"Oh yes, please do." Nodora's smile was unusually mischievous. "I'll want to refer to them as I compose. Every bard in Orthros will be jealous when I write a ballad about previously unknown deeds of the Blood-Red Prince."

At that moment, Zoe popped into sight, wearing her new red-and-white courier's sash. "I delivered all the notes you gave me in nine minutes!"

"Only nine?" Lio traded her a tin of gumsweets for the message she carried. "You've almost reached Ajia's speed! And it's only your first official night as a courier."

At the mention of her new friend, Zoe brightened even more. "I can't wait to tell her!"

Cassia smiled. "You're helping Lio gather everyone for my magic research?"

Zoe nodded. "But my first summons was from Princess Konstantina. She told me I'm serving the Queens with honor, and she tipped me with a new storybook!"

Solia straightened Zoe's sash. "You deserve it after training with such dedication."

Zoe clutched her hands together around her candy. "I'm so glad you got to be here to watch me at tryouts."

Solia smiled. "I had no doubt you would be chosen."

"We're so proud of you," said Cassia.

"I'll finish these in eight-and-a-half minutes!" the emboldened suckling promised before stepping away again.

Lio scanned the note she had brought. At last, a solid lead after scrolls full of dead ends. "Nike and my father are on their way, but Rudhira stepped back to Tenebra."

Xandra's face fell. "He promised a longer visit. But I suppose we should be glad he's spending more time at home at all."

Lio shook his head. "He says he'll return shortly with another expert."

"Oh, who is it?" Cassia peered at the message.

"He doesn't say, but if there are any other Hesperines errant who have battled Lustra mages, perhaps they can give us more recent information."

"Battled them?" Solia echoed. "The Blood Errant gained their knowledge of Lustra magic from enemies?"

"Yes," came a voice from amid a flurry of snow and darkness beyond the edge of the wards. Nike crossed into the calm of the arena, her ginger braid and black fighting robe billowing around her. "We once battled a Lustra changer who could take the form of a forest lynx. His wife needed some help to get away from him."

Lio's father appeared beside her, brushing marble dust off his hands, but he had already changed from work robes into his golden athletic tunic. "You should tell the tale, Nike. You're the one who made her a very relieved widow."

Nike's mouth tilted in a fanged half-grin. "But it was Rudhira who made her a happy widow."

"Oh," said Xandra, "we *must* pry this story out of him."

As they all descended to the front row together, Cassia said, "It sounds as if the matriarchs of the Lustra would not be pleased with how this changer used our magic."

"He was a possessive, bitter Tenebran male," Nike replied. "You know the type all too well. I sent him to his ancestors with apologies to the Changing Queen, although I regretted the loss of his magic."

Nodora drew her long, straight black hair over her shoulder with a pensive frown. "It's sad to think of his traditions being lost. He shouldn't have squandered his rare gift."

Lio sat down beside Cassia, while Solia took the seat on her other side, now their custom by unspoken agreement. Their truce in pursuit of their shared goal gave him hope, despite how little they had actually learned so far. Solia seemed more and more comfortable at family events, like Zoe's courier tryouts.

Lio dared anyone, even a Victor of Souls, to resist the fierce love of Blood Komnena. In fact, that was precisely the challenge he would issue Solia tonight, with some help from the warriors.

Nike leaned back against the railing that separated them from the arena. "What would you like to know about the changer?"

"Did you try using thelemancy on him while he was in lynx form?" Lio asked.

"I was able to reach his human mind within the cat. He lost hold of his lynx form and became a man again."

Lio let out a sigh of relief. "That means I can help Cassia if she ever struggles to return to human form."

Cassia slid her feet under Knight's fur and leaned against Lio, less tense than she had been in several nights. "Thank you, Nike. You just allayed one of our greatest fears."

"We now know that Cassia's beast magic will not pose a threat during her Gifting." Lio looked to Solia, waiting for her to acknowledge that this was a milestone toward his completion of the first labor.

"There are still two more affinities to account for before she can make a decision," was her only reply.

"But this is a great breakthrough," Cassia said. "What else do you think we can learn about my magic from the battle, Nike?"

Nike gestured to her neck. "The changer had an amulet imbued with Lustra magic."

Solia had been sneaking glances at Aunt Lyta's demonstration, but now her gaze sharpened on Nike. "Like the ivy pendant passed down to Cassia by Thalia?"

"Yes and no," Nike answered. "The magical signature I sensed on Cassia's pendant was much stronger."

"Well," Solia said, "Cassia's pendant is an artifact of the Changing Queen's. I would expect it to be far more powerful."

"What happened to the amulet?" Lio could think of at least twelve different probing spells to try on it to assess the nature of its power.

"I destroyed it," his father said from beside him.

Lio tried not to groan aloud. "Father, you, ah...destroyed an extraordinarily rare artifact of one of the most poorly understood forms of magic?"

"My stone magic was sufficient to reduce it to dust," he said without remorse. "Sorry to break your scholarly heart, Son, but we couldn't risk it holding some evil power over the man's wife."

Lio rubbed his beard. "Well, I can hardly argue with that."

"I can tell you about its magical signature, though," Nike said. "Cassia's pendant feels...purer. As if the lynx changer's magic was corrupt."

"Fascinating!" Kia's quill scratched behind Lio's head where she sat in the second row. "That suggests that Lustra magic in recent centuries has been abused, or perhaps simply weakened because the Orders suppress it, which leads to the loss of Lustra mages' teachings and traditions. How thrilling to imagine that Cassia could access undiluted magic through the pendant."

Cassia said nothing. Neither did Solia. The pendant was also a symbol of the Queen of Tenebra. It did not escape Lio that Cassia had not worn the artifact since Solia had tried to force her to take the throne.

Nike observed Lio and the tense sisters. "When the changer talked about his wife, he called her his 'mate.' He believed they had an unbreakable bond stronger than marriage. I sensed no magical connection between them, so whatever he was referring to, those two did not have it. But I do wonder if there might still have been credence to his ravings."

"What do you mean?" Cassia asked Nike. "Do you think Lustra mages experience some kind of Union akin to Grace?"

"It is not outside the realm of possibility." Nike crossed her arms. "It would be interesting to discover how a Lustra mate bond might strengthen a Grace bond, don't you think?"

Something possessive and female uncurled from Cassia, and Lio liked the feeling of it in their Union very, very much.

"But there's something else you should know," Nike said. "The cats he controlled were able to deal damage to my wards with their claws. Not unlike liegehounds."

"Cup and thorns," Lio swore.

Kia's quill halted mid-scrawl. "Are you suggesting Lustra magic might be one of the anti-haimatic magics?"

"Someone define that for me, please," Cassia said.

"Affinities that oppose blood magic," Xandra explained ruefully. "Like fire magic."

Outrage flashed in Cassia's eyes. "You're saying my affinity could be a Hesperine weakness?"

"Don't worry, Cassia." Xandra reached forward to pat her shoulder. "If that's the case, you'll manage, just as I do."

"The expert Rudhira is bringing with him is the one to ask about that," Nike said. "But I can tell you there was no love lost between the lynx changer and Hesperines, and I didn't get the impression he had learned his prejudice from the Mage Orders."

Cassia glanced at Lio's father. "Could that explain why there are no Hesperine Lustra mages?"

His father nodded. "The Changing Queen herself was never hostile to us, but none of her people ever sought Sanctuary in Orthros, even after they could no longer practice their magic freely in Tenebra."

"It might not be prejudice," Nodora offered. "Perhaps they simply don't want to give up their own ways."

Nike said wryly, "He called us abominations of the natural order. Seemed to feel quite superior that his affinity had more ancient roots than our immortality."

There were complex cultural and magical implications here that they were missing. Lio could only hope that information existed somewhere and was not completely lost to time.

His fruitless ruminations were interrupted by Karege, who appeared holding Zoe's little hand in his big, strong one. The rest of the Ashes were with them.

Pleasant surprise slipped through Solia's composure. "You're joining us too?"

Lio congratulated himself on another successful maneuver.

"Zoe invited us. I would go anywhere such a charming messenger bade me." Karege patted his robes and let out a huff. "I've been away from Orthros for so long, I forgot I should always carry gumsweets for the Queens' Couriers! Let me see if I can find something even better…" He dug in a purse at his belt and withdrew a shiny coin. "How about pirate gold?"

Zoe's eyes went as round as the coin. "Do you think it ever crossed Captain Ziara's palm?"

"I know it did, for I won it from her the last time we played cards with Ukocha."

Zoe held her prize in both hands. "I can't wait to show Ajia! After our last deliveries of the night, we're going to play privateers at Bosko's house."

"Bosko and Ajia are great admirers of Captain Ziara as well," Solia hinted.

Karege chuckled and produced two more coins. "For your friends."

"Oh!" Zoe's aura sparkled with glee. "You have our gratitude, Karege!"

"You have our gratitude for your help tonight, Zoe." Lio kissed his little sister on the cheek before she disappeared to answer her next summons.

Cassia shook her head. "I am astonished anyone could pry the sucklings away from an arena event like this, especially Bosko."

"I told him we would be doing very boring research. I don't think Aunt Lyta wishes for the children to witness what she has in mind tonight." Lio nodded toward Solia.

She had joined Kella and Tilili at the railing. "Well, Standstill, did you ever imagine we'd stand in Hippolyta's Arena?"

"Of course I did." Kella reached forward to scratch Tilili's cheek, and the cat rubbed against her hand. "I always knew we'd climb as high as we liked. We're Ukocha's girls, after all."

Hoyefe lounged against the railing beside them, watching the Stewards. "If I were not so excited to spar, I would feel compelled to capture all this muscular beauty in a sketch."

"Magic and swords aren't allowed in this arena, Lonesome," said Solia. "Good luck keeping up with the Hesperines."

He gave her a cocky grin. "I had no trouble keeping up with them at the coffeehouse last night."

Solia laughed. "I hope you're not too tired to spar after all that exertion."

She and her mercenary family had slipped back into their friendships as if no time had gone by. Lio had no idea how long it would take her to be so relaxed with him, if she ever was.

Tendo was a good listener about all of this, if only via letters. In their next correspondence, Lio would mention that Solia never joined her heart-free comrades for their romantic adventures on the docks. Even if Tendo had said he didn't want to know.

"Victor of Souls," Aunt Lyta called out, "for such a gathering as this, I am willing to make an exception for magic."

An audible gasp went up around them.

Solia's heartbeat picked up. "You do us a great honor. But I do not wish to disturb the sacred, unbroken tradition in this arena."

"Sacred, yes, but not unbroken." Aunt Lyta released her tousled braid from her speires, then began to bind her long hair again, Uncle Argyros's Grace braid a gleam of silver-blond amid her auburn. "I allow magic at times for the sake of my Stewards' training, to give them real experience in battling spells. I see no harm in it tonight for a friendly match between warriors with mutual respect. What do you say, First Blade Kella? My Stewards against your Ashes, with boasting rights for the winner's prize."

Tilili's tail swished, as if the cat were responding to her rider's excitement. "Which Stewards?" Kella inquired.

"Kadi, Alkaios, Nephalea, Mak, and Lyros," Aunt Lyta proposed. "I will judge the match."

Kella looked to Solia. "I find myself one mercenary short. Have a go with us? For old time's sake?"

Solia gave a wicked smile. "I dare anyone to try to stop me."

Scrollworm though he was, Lio felt a rush of anticipation as he watched Solia and the Ashes stride out onto the sand with Mak and Lyros. Their small audience sent up a loud round of applause for the contestants.

The Stewards stood in a line of orderly black robes, their hair tamed with their speires. Across from them, the Ashes formed up around Kella, each one unique and ferocious. Solia stood at the First Blade's right hand.

Cassia leaned closer to Lio, her voice low. "You asked Aunt Lyta to do this."

"Ah," he replied, "perceptive as always, my Grace."

"Someone should tell Solia you gave her this gift."

"I think the gift will feel less complicated to her if her benefactor remains anonymous."

"You ought to have credit for such a goodwill gesture," Cassia protested.

With a shake of his head, he smiled. "Tonight is an opportunity to warm Solia's heart toward someone else. Research is not the only reason I invited the Blood Errant."

The Lion of Orthros got to his feet. "Lyta, what do you say to six against six?"

Lio let out a sharp whistle and cheered for his father's suggestion. As Cassia applauded, she sent him an admiring glance that said, *Excellent move, my Grace.*

"The Blood Errant raises the stakes!" Aunt Lyta cried. "I will permit a six-versus-six melee...but only if my First Master Steward fights with the Stand."

Nike grinned and trotted over to take her place at the center of the Stewards.

Lio's father stalked out onto the sand, stretching as he went. Lio couldn't remember the last time he had actually seen his father spar, much less wield magic against an opponent. How rarely Apollon reminded Orthros that he was untamed.

Father halted in front of Solia. His voice was a quiet rumble, only for the ears of those he let into his veil spell. "May I fight at your side for your first match in this arena?"

She looked up at him. "Of course. It is the opportunity of a lifetime to spar as your ally."

His eyes crinkled at the corners. "How about a little wager?"

Solia gave a surprised laugh. "I suspect betting with the Lion of Orthros is dangerous."

"Oh, certainly. But not dangerous for you."

She hesitated. "Well, then, what stakes do you propose?"

"If our side is victorious, you will call me Papa."

Beside Lio, Cassia gasped. "Oh. He knows the way to her heart. Just as he knew mine."

Lio twined his fingers in Cassia's. "Do you think she'll take the bet?"

"I can hope."

They waited, while Solia gazed back at Apollon in tense silence.

"You know I don't believe in losing," Solia finally said.

"Or in backing down from a challenge," Father replied.

She extended a hand. "Very well, but you must promise me something as well, if we win."

He clasped her wrist. "Name your stakes."

"I want a statue of Iris fit for a queen's capital."

Father's face softened. "I would craft that for you without a fight. But I know it will mean more to you as a prize well won. I will make Iris a memorial as fine as any Hesperine martyr's."

Together, Sunburn and the Lion of Orthros faced their opponents. She looked small next to him, but her aura, too, was larger than life. She and Lio's father had never seemed more like family than at this moment.

Aunt Lyta bit her hand and cupped her blood in her palm, raising it high. Then she let it fall. Red stained the sand, and the match was on.

Even Lio's immortal gaze struggled to follow the melee. The Stewards were blurs of white fangs and black robes. The Ashes flowed in and out of the chaos, fluid and yet in perfect rhythm. The mortals might be slow, but they fought like veterans who had many years of practice sparring with Karege.

Lio had seen both the Stand and the Ashes in battle and even fought at their sides. But he had never seen them like this.

In the midst of it all, Lio's father and Solia were two streaks of gold.

Cassia gripped Lio's hand, turning her head to and fro as she tried to track the match. He kept up a commentary as best he could, but as soon as he pointed toward a duel, the fighters had already repositioned.

A powerful body wrestled Tilili to the ground. Kadi, using her weight against Kella. But Kella flattened herself against her mount, and the lithe pair rolled as one, slithering out of Kadi's grasp. Mist snapped into Kella's grasp and became water, then hardened into frost. A volley of razor-sharp icicles flew at Kadi. She stood her ground, raising a wall of shadow that shattered Kella's arcane blades.

Mak and Karege were locked in a brutal wrestling match, laughing all the while. Beside them, Lyros danced across the sand, using agility to evade Hoyefe's fists and Tuura's staff. He retreated toward Alkaios to fight back-to-back with his fellow Steward.

When Alkaios grabbed Lyros in a headlock, Lio gasped. Light magic sparkled, and Lio saw that it was no Steward holding his Trial brother, but Hoyefe. The figures Lio had thought to be Hoyefe and Tuura resolved into Alkaios and Nephalea. Both halted in their tracks and shook their heads, as if realizing Lyros was not the enemy. The real Tuura, suddenly visible, closed in from behind them. Her staff swept through the air, and with it, a current of magic that knocked both Stewards off their feet.

At the heart of the battle, Lio's father and Solia faced each other on either side of the whorl of shadow wards who was Nike. He sank back on his heels, his knees bent, and raised his arms. His muscles flexed as if he lifted a great weight.

Magic surged beneath Lio's feet, pounding through their shared blood, and his heart roared. This was nothing like Father in his workshop, and yet so like him. The spell was an artist's attack, a warrior's creation.

The floor shuddered. Massive chunks of stone tore up through the ground to hover in the air around his father.

Then magefire roared to life in Hippolyta's Arena.

THE ONLY LUSTRA MAGE

FLAME ROLLED OUT OF Solia's hands. The hands of his Grace-sister. A primal shudder went through Lio before he could stop it.

Cassia wrapped her cool hands around his, no judgment in her touch, only reassurance. He tasted no acrid Anthrian magic in the back of his mouth. The arena filled with pure heat and light.

Solia's flame never touched a Hesperine. The fire poured from her hands and collided midair with the rocks at his father's command. Molten stone spiraled down around Nike, pressing in on her wards.

All Lio could see of her were her fangs in a pulsing orb of shadow. Then the darkness exploded outward. Stone shattered.

Solia's fire flared to life once more; his father clapped, raising his broken rocks back to life. They began the cycle again, weaving a new cage around Nike to test her wards.

"Why can't she step out of it?" Cassia cried.

Lio raised his voice over the noise. "Something about their spell—magefire and blood magic, combined. I've never seen the like."

The entire battle orbited around the clash of darkness and light at its center. At last Nike's shadows flared out again. But this time, the cage blazed orange, and fluid stone flexed away from her wards. As her blast of power faded, Solia and his father's combined magic wrapped tighter around Nike.

Lio's father lowered his hands. Solia kept moving, her gestures of command their own beautiful, deadly fighting moves, pouring heat into the stone his father had given her.

With Nike and Solia locked in magical combat, Lio's father plunged into the melee at Karege's side. The two elder warriors fought their way through the young Stewards, leaving defeated immortals in their wake.

Through the waves of heat rippling in the air around Solia, Aunt Lyta's black handkerchief drifted down to land at the feet of the Victor of Souls.

As if fighting a mighty current, Solia wrenched her arms to her and crossed them over her chest. The heat curled back in on her. The stone cage cooled, fading from white-hot to the deep red of Haima's bedrock. Lio sensed his father's magic sinking back into the ground, going deep to its rest. And the cage was simply stone again.

Aunt Lyta's voice rang across the arena. "This match goes to First Blade Kella and her Ashes; to Solia, Victor of Souls; and to the Lion of Orthros."

Lio, Cassia, and their Trial circle sent up their most deafening applause and cheers.

Nike disappeared, then reappeared outside her cell. She gave Solia a salute to the victor. "By the Goddess, that was well fought."

The Ashes helped the defeated Stewards up, everyone exchanging taunts, compliments, and claps on the shoulder. Aunt Lyta was right behind them, going to each of her trainees with generous praise. Cassia leapt from her seat to congratulate her sister, Knight dashing off with her, and their Trial sisters went to console Mak and Lyros about their defeat.

Lio followed and pulled his father in for an embrace. "It was good to see you spar."

"Was it?" His father kept an arm around his shoulder. "I tried not to do it too often when you were younger. I never wanted violence to touch your life, least of all through me."

"Is that why? I thought you were...content."

"Oh, I am, Son. I would take a dance with your mother over a fight anytime. But I must admit, I enjoyed myself tonight."

Nike stood back, admiring the cage of stone. "It's rather beautiful, in its way. You should keep this one, Uncle."

He tilted his head. "The sculptors' circles would be scandalized if I tried to pass this off as art."

"In that case," Nike said, "you must certainly display it where I can see their faces."

When Mak and Lyros joined them in front of the stone cage, Lyros enthused like an initiate at the Hippolytan Games. "Brilliant strategy! Disabling Nike was the only way your side could have won against the Stewards."

Affection warmed Nike's aura. "Uncle Apollon is one of the few people alive who can give me a real challenge, I admit."

"The way he and Karege plowed through us!" Mak shook his head. "Uncle, you should fight with us more often."

"Yes, you should," Lio agreed.

When Solia and Cassia broke away from the Ashes, Cassia slid into Lio's hold, while her sister came to stand by his father. There was not a drop of sweat on Solia, the air around her parched and warm. She seemed more at ease than Lio had ever seen her. She looked...calm.

They shared this plight, he realized. Peace was elusive when you carried so much magic in you. There was no feeling quite like those fleeting moments after you had poured enough power out of you to give you rest.

Cassia would face the same struggle in her future. But he and Solia would both understand.

Nike held out a hand to Solia. "Never in my existence have I enjoyed fighting against magefire until tonight."

Solia took the offered wrist clasp. "It was a privilege, Victory Star."

A silence fell, one that had the chance to be comfortable, but still held the possibility of pain. Lio could hear that Cassia was holding her breath.

Father slid an arm around Solia's shoulders.

She didn't flinch. She relaxed. "I'm looking forward to that statue, Papa."

CASSIA KNEW RUDHIRA HAD entered the arena when Knight ran away from her, his tail wagging. But when she turned, she saw that her hound had bypassed the Blood-Red Prince himself to drool upon a different Hesperine errant.

Kalos knelt so Knight could lick his face. "That's a good boy."

With his wagging tail smacking the Blood-Red Prince and Kalos rubbing his ears, Knight wore the smile of a hound who had died a hero and ascended to Sanctuary.

Rudhira gave the dog hair on his battle robes a dark look. But then his grim expression dissolved into a rueful laugh, and he began to pet Knight.

Apollon's shoulders shook with silent laughter. Nike, on the other hand, laughed aloud and couldn't seem to stop.

Rudhira held up his free hand. "Not a word."

"It's only your most humiliating surrender to the enemy of all time. I wouldn't dream of rubbing it in." Nike's fanged grin promised she had every intention of doing so.

"Knight is not the enemy anymore, are you, good sir?" Kalos seemed oblivious to the liegehound slobber on his dark green travel robes.

Lio tried to reach around Knight to give Kalos a wrist clasp, then with a laugh, gave up. Cassia wanted to hug the shy Hesperine, but she let Knight show physical affection on her behalf.

Kalos's kind green gaze met hers briefly. "Glad to see you found Solia."

"All thanks to you." Cassia touched her sister's arm, inviting her forward.

Solia pushed her tousled hair out of her face. "This is the Hesperine scout who tracked my movements over the last fifteen years? You're the one who managed to find me after I evaded the king and the Mage Orders and absconded with privateers."

Always more comfortable on his own in the wilderness than in a crowd of people, Kalos looked at Knight as he spoke. "Finding people for my prince is my duty."

"He is too modest," Cassia said. "He is the best scout and tracker in the Prince's Charge."

Solia gave Rudhira an assessing look. "May I ask what the Prince's Charge is?"

He answered with an amused tilt to his red brows. "A force of Hesperines errant under my command, dedicated to the cause of alleviating mortal suffering in Tenebra."

"With respect, First Prince, do you mean to say there is a fanged army roaming my kingdom with an immortal royal at its head?"

"There have always been Hesperines errant roaming your kingdom, Princess."

So much more hung unsaid, a discordant note of secrecy.

Rudhira could have told Cassia's sister of his secret identity in the

Tenebran nobility as Hold Lord Justinian, and of Castra Justa, his fortress hidden in the harsh wilderness of the eastern Tenebrae. There would be no harm in Solia Komnena knowing that the First Prince was the guardian of the Hesperite settlement, the last community of human Hespera worshipers, which would be destroyed if the Mage Orders ever discovered it.

But if Rudhira revealed any of that to the would-be future Queen of Tenebra, it would place her in a complicated political position with her own lords and the Mage Orders.

Cassia gritted her teeth. Once they convinced Solia to stay, these moments of politics would no longer intrude.

Solia did not press further, saying to Kalos, "You have my gratitude for helping Cassia find me when powerful forces were trying to keep us apart."

"Cassia helped us find Nike," Kalos answered. "I was honoring that bond of gratitude."

"A word to the wise," Nike said. "Don't ever try to hide from this one. He makes liegehounds look lazy."

"He is also the most qualified of us to advise Cassia about Lustra magic," Rudhira informed them.

"I had no idea," Lio said. "Thank you for coming all the way here to help us yet again, Kalos."

Kalos's pale complexion reddened under the attention.

"I have so many questions," Cassia said. "Shall we go somewhere quieter where we can talk?"

She held a location clearly in her thoughts. When Lio squeezed her hand, she knew he understood.

Rudhira threw an arm around Nike's shoulders, then Apollon's. "I'll be here tossing my Trial sister into the dirt if anyone needs me."

"You can try!" Nike taunted. "If I win, you must tell everyone the romantic tale of you and the lynx changer's widow."

"Since you'll lose," Rudhira returned, "you'd better be prepared to tell everyone what you were up to with a certain strapping town guardsman around that time."

"Challenge accepted."

"Mak," Lio said, "we won't mind if everyone else would rather watch Rudhira's match instead of sitting through boring research discussions."

Trust Mak to catch on to their intent. With a touch of his usual good humor, their Trial brother coaxed everyone to their seats.

Lio stepped with Cassia, Solia, and Kalos back to the residence. When they set foot at the construction site of Cassia's greenhouse, magic enveloped her.

Something deep and strong slept in the stone foundation Apollon had built. The cheerful shadows of Mak's wards blanketed the iron frame he had forged, which rose around them in graceful arches like the sketch of a work of art that was yet to be. All the greenhouse lacked were the glass panes Lio would install and imbue with light magic. As soon as he was not so occupied trying to win her sister's blessing.

The structure had overtaken the entirety of their largest courtyard, and she felt a bit giddy when she thought of everything she could grow here. She had already set out the plants that would be safe enough under Mak's spells for the time being.

In this little pocket of wildness, with fewer people surrounding him, Kalos relaxed as she had hoped. He sat down on one of the iron benches and obliged Knight with more attention. "Now it makes sense, Cassia. That's why you were able to make a liegehound accept Hesperines. Your liege bond with him helped, of course, but it was also your sleeping magic, I suspect."

Lio took one of the iron chairs and drew Cassia near him. "Have you had many encounters with Lustra mages, then?"

"Well," Kalos began, "you know what my former profession was."

Solia propped her hip against a stack of stone blocks Apollon had yet to haul away. "I'm afraid I don't. Would it be intrusive of me to ask?"

Kalos hesitated. "I was a heart hunter."

"I haven't been in Tenebra in years," Solia replied without censure in her tone, "so correct me if I misremember. Don't the heart hunters live in warbands on the border with Orthros to hunt down Hesperines?"

"That's right." Kalos sighed.

"How you became a Hesperine must be quite the tale." Solia sounded impressed.

"Now I use everything I knew as an enemy to teach our Hesperines errant how to fight heart hunters. And their magic...Lustra magic."

Cassia needed to sit down. Fortunately, Lio's lap was very close. "Kalos, are you saying you are a Lustra mage yourself? The only Hesperine in existence who shares my magic?"

Within the shelter of the greenhouse's spells, a new flavor of magic rose and stretched. It felt like a howl, solitary and yet so familiar, a cry from the wilderness that made her ache to answer.

This was Kalos's aura unconcealed by Hesperine veil spells.

"I won't be so alone with my magic after all," she breathed.

"I've only got one of your three," Kalos said, as if that were something he ought to apologize for. "My tracking abilities are a form of beast magic, you see."

Cassia truly wanted to throw her arms around him. "You're a changer?"

"Nothing so important as that. It's not like what it used to be when the Silvicultrixes reigned. Heart hunters only have remnants, and I can't say our ancestors would be proud of us. But what we practice is indeed a surviving form of Lustra magic."

"Why isn't this documented?" Lio asked. "The implications are incredible. I cannot believe we had no knowledge of this."

"That's my fault," Kalos murmured. "I, ah…rather prefer to keep my origins and my magic to myself, and my comrades are kind enough to respect that. I never thought that would cause trouble for anyone."

Cassia had been shamed her whole life in the Tenebran court. She hated that Kalos believed anyone here in Orthros would treat him that way because of his past. "I shall be the one who causes a great deal of trouble for anyone who dares complain."

Kalos blushed again. "Thank you. You know I'll tell you anything you wish to know."

"Would you consider giving me magic lessons once my affinities awaken?"

Kalos blew out a breath. "That's rather like asking a mountain mutt to show a royal liegehound how to sit."

Cassia couldn't help but laugh. "You do yourself far too little credit. I'm a mutt myself, remember."

He gave her a half grin. "I suppose. Even so, I know so little about your other affinities."

"It sounds as if you know a great deal," Lio countered. "You're able to channel animal abilities in human form?"

"That's right."

"A specific animal?" Lio inquired.

Kalos looked sheepish. "Well, yes. This one right here." He patted Knight.

"Oh, Kalos," Cassia cried, "if only you were a changer! How marvelous it would be to turn into a liegehound."

"I'll settle for having my opposable thumbs and their uncanny tracking skills. But if you think I can help, I'll teach you what I can."

"Did you have to meet certain conditions for your affinity to manifest?" Cassia asked.

A shadow passed behind Kalos's eyes. "Heart hunters have initiation rites. I'll spare you the details. Suffice it to say, your warband wakes your magic for you when you join."

Cassia was glad Kalos's former warband could never hurt him, or anyone else, again. Rudhira had made sure of that.

She bit her lip. She wanted to ask about Kalos's Gifting, but how could she pry into such a sacred event? The best she could do was give him an invitation. "Lio and I fear my magic will be dangerous during my Gifting."

Kalos rubbed the back of his head, leaving his dark brown horsetail more tousled than it had been before. "It was my past, not my magic, that made my Gifting difficult. But I can tell you that blood magic changes Lustra magic."

Cassia's heart was sinking as fast as it had risen. "So it's true? Lustra magic is anti-haimatic?"

"I'm afraid so. But when my beast magic and Hespera faced off, she won that contest. I'm nowhere near as powerful as you'll become, though, so I can't say how your affinities and blood magic might combine."

Why could nothing be easy, just once in Cassia's life? She wanted her own magic. She wanted her Gift. How could these two integral parts of her stand in opposition?

Lio wrapped his arm around her waist. "Against all odds, you are here in my arms. We are on a winning streak against the world."

"You're right." She would have her magic and her fangs, Goddess help her.

"In your opinion," Solia broke in, "should Cassia wait until after her magic awakens to be Gifted?"

Kalos grimaced. "Now that's the most important question, isn't it?"

The fact that his answer was not a wholehearted *no* made Cassia's gut clench.

"I don't know." There was so much regret in his voice. "As I explained, I already had my Lustra magic, but my Gifting altered it. If I'd become a Hesperine first, I'm not certain my affinity would have manifested in the same way. Perhaps it could have…but perhaps it would be repelled by the blood magic." He met Cassia's gaze. "Is that a risk you're really willing to take? To miss the chance to have your magic…forever?"

Cassia knew her answer to that question, although she didn't want to say it.

But Lio did. "This is not even a decision. There is no choice between the Gift and your power, Cassia. Out of the question. You must have both."

"Of course Cassia must have her magic." Solia's tone was all but threatening. "She already gave up her crown. I will not allow anything or anyone to rob her of this, too."

"Do you know the conditions for awakening her affinities?" Kalos asked.

Solia nodded. "Cassia's mother explained them to me so I could guide Cassia."

"That's good news," Kalos said. "Have you met them, then?"

Cassia knotted her hands. "It seems so."

"Yes," Solia agreed, "it's only a matter of time before Cassia's magic arrives."

"She has already experienced signs of it manifesting," said Lio.

"What about a letting site?" Kalos asked.

Cassia exchanged glances with her Grace and sister. Neither of them seemed to have an explanation to offer.

"Did your mother tell you about those?" Kalos asked Cassia.

She shook her head. "If a letting site were important, surely she would have mentioned it to Solia."

Kalos frowned in thought. "I'm quite sure this is required even for

Silvicultrixes. It's why they used to lead the ancient rites. The old religion has been rather warped over the centuries, but this has never changed..."

"Letting...letting of what?" Cassia suppressed a shudder. She knew animal sacrifices were part of old Tenebran rituals. They weren't talking about bloodletting, were they?

"Letting of magic," Kalos clarified, "from the Lustra. The wilds. Our magic doesn't work like temple magic, you see. Plenty of us end up in temples, passing as regular mages, but we're something other. We have to..." He made a frustrated sound. "Sorry, I'm not a man of words."

He looked around at Cassia's pots of evergreens. "Well, it's like being a Hesperine. We need blood. Lustra mages need the wilds. One of the difficulties of being a Hesperine Lustra mage is that I need both. My power is at its best when I'm in the wilderness. But that isn't enough for the first awakening of your magic. You need a letting site."

Cassia felt so much more encouraged than she had mere hours ago. They were finally learning something that could truly get her closer to her goal. She could taste it within reach.

Excitement seemed to vibrate out of Lio. "This suggests that Lustra mages draw on a power source greater than themselves. So unlike temple mages, who pull from their innate affinities within, Lustra mages must have an innate channeling ability instead."

Kalos's tone was hushed, reverent. "The Silvicultrixes were the ones who could withstand channeling the most power. They were the priestess-queens of the letting sites. If there's any truth to the old stories heart hunters still tell around the campfire...those sorceresses were like nothing we can imagine in this epoch."

"If what they channel is nature itself...then..." Lio fell silent for an instant. When he spoke again, his words were full of wonder. "We've found the lost paradigm of magic."

"This sounds like an important discovery," Cassia said.

"Let me show you." Reaching around her, he lifted his hands, tracing light and color in the air in front of them with his long, elegant fingers. "There are three known paradigms of magic, each one following its own rules and affecting related aspects of reality."

He conjured the illusion of a deep blue sphere that rotated before her eyes. "*Manteia* is sorcery, such as mind magic or necromancy. It affects that which you cannot see and touch, including thought, emotion, and life force—in other words, the spirit phase."

With a twist of his wrist, he spun a whorl of red-gold into another sphere. It hovered opposite the blue one.

Solia said, "*Mageia* is magery, the paradigm of magic that affects the natural phase, which is the physical world. All elemental magics fall into this paradigm—fire, water, and stone, for example."

"I see," Cassia said. "Hence thele*mancer* but pyro*magus*."

"What did I tell you?" Lio said near her ear. "You remember everything you hear."

He flicked his fingers back and forth, and a trail of arcane symbols and Divine script ran between the spheres. "Mageia and manteia are opposites, yet operate on the same principle: resonance."

Cassia studied the patterns and connections between them. "So manteia resonates with spirit, and mageia with nature?"

"Precisely! Affinities are simply specific resonances with, for example, the mind or fire." He raised his palm, and a purple sphere manifested to form a third body in mystical orbit. "This is *progonaia,* ancestral magic. It is not based on resonance, but on channeling."

"Channeling from the spirit phase," said Cassia.

"Yes." Lio traced symbols and letters to connect the blue and purple spheres. "Do you see what's missing?"

"There is no paradigm that channels the natural phase," Cassia concluded.

He took her hand in his and held her palm up in the empty air. Then green spell light rose from their joined hands. The paths of connection with mageia and progonaia twisted into place like a new vine.

"*Hulaia.*" He rested his face against hers. "That is what it should be called, after the Hulaic Epochs, the time before recorded history when magic was untamed. We have found the lost paradigm. It was Lustra magic all along."

Her skin pebbled, and a chill of excitement went down her spine. She was no scholar, but in that moment, seeing intangible mysteries drawn in Hesperine spell light, she could feel it. Something great and old had finally been unveiled. Within her.

Lio gave an elated laugh. "This is the answer to a mystery that has gone unsolved by mages and scholars since before the Great Temple Epoch, when the organized study of magic began."

Cassia shook her head. "That's thousands of years."

"Lustra magic is older than that," Kalos said, "and we've kept our secrets."

Lio sat back. "Kalos, if you prefer for me not to commit these arcane secrets to paper..." It sounded as if he had to drag his words out of himself. "...as much as it pains me, I will honor your silence. This need never enter the canon of magical theory in the libraries of Orthros."

"I don't mind what you write, as long as you keep my name out of it. It's Cassia's magic, too. I dare say you two will have many great things to contribute to Hesperines' magical knowledge in the centuries to come."

"In that case...Goddess bless! We may be the first to write a treatise on the Hulaic paradigm."

Cassia was still staring at Lio's diagram. "But what about blood magic? To which paradigm does it belong?"

"Ah." Lio pricked his finger on his fang and conjured a crimson sphere. It sank into the center of the diagram, sending out tendrils that snaked to the other four lights. "It is called *haima*. Is it a blend of mageia and manteia? Or the fifth paradigm? Those questions remain unanswered. Perhaps one night, we will find the answers for them, too."

She studied the pulse between haima and hulaia, between red lifeblood and the green forces of the wilds. Something stirred in Cassia, a hungry thing that had never shown an appetite for thrones or riches.

This was the only power she had ever coveted.

She wanted magic so vast that she could protect her Hesperines from anything and teach even an ancient necromancer to fear her.

"How do I find a letting site?" she asked.

"Some are hidden," said Kalos, "some lost or forgotten, others protected. They've been there since ancient times. It's believed that the Silvicultrixes made them."

Cassia recalled the words of one of her ancestors, the first mage of her line, who had spoken to her in Btana Ayal. *...magic had been like the trees of the untamed forests or the wolves that roamed the wilds. A force of nature* *we feared and respected, but could not control. The Diviner Queen taught us to make magic into our garden, to befriend it like the dogs that guard the homestead.*

Could that ancestor, the original Silvicultrix in Cassia's bloodline, have been one such sorceress who opened the letting sites? Could the Diviner Queen have taught her how?

Cassia's wonder gave way to horror. Lio stiffened, and she knew the same thought had occurred to him.

"No Silvicultrixes ever came to Orthros," she said.

Kalos met her gaze. "I'm so sorry, Cassia."

"There cannot be any letting sites within the Queens' ward, can there?" The words were so bitter on her tongue.

Kalos shook his head.

Lio said nothing. Cassia could not bring herself to say it, either.

Trust Solia to speak the words. "The only way for Cassia to awaken her magic is for her to return to Tenebra."

THE LOST PARADIGM

Everything around Cassia seemed suddenly vivid and clear. The voices of her loved ones. The constellations above, bright against the deep darkness of the sky. The fragrance of her rimelace flowers, like fresh snow and verdant spring all at once.

It was all so precious and so ephemeral.

Somehow, she had thought she could hold on to this with both hands and still reach for her magic.

"Cassia cannot ever return to Tenebra." That voice was the most familiar of all. Lio's, rumbling with mind magic that was threatening to slip from his control.

Solia's voice answered. "Her legacy has always been in Tenebra. Where else would she seek it?"

Lio's arm tightened around Cassia's waist. "Anywhere there is not an Old Master lying in wait."

"I am not afraid of the Collector," Solia told him.

Lio's magic grew darker. "All that proves is that you have never battled him."

Cassia realized she had no time for despair. Not when her Grace and her sister were about to undo the fragile progress they had made with each other.

She got to her feet and stood between Lio and Solia. Knight leapt to her side with his hackles up and his chest out. The look on Cassia's face must have been effective, for both Lio and Solia stopped speaking.

"We need more information," Cassia told them. "We must consider everything we've learned and make a plan."

"The need to return to Tenebra has been clear from the beginning," Solia replied.

"Not without a strategy," Cassia said.

"I love you and your strategies." The pain in Lio's voice cut through her. "But plans don't matter to an Old Master."

His words cut her deeper. She could feel his dread, like a Craving chill, like a murmur of the Collector's voice in their ears.

"Tenebra is out of the question." Lio turned to Kalos again. "Have you ever scouted Orthros for a letting site?"

Kalos was now standing at the edge of their small gathering, as if ready to bolt when anyone lost their temper. He shook his head.

"How can we be certain they don't exist anywhere inside the ward if we haven't searched?" Lio's question was more like a plea.

Cassia wanted to cling to denial, too. But her past in Tenebra had taught her how fruitless that was. Better to face horrifying truths before they could ambush you. "They aren't natural occurrences, are they, Kalos? They're something the Silvicultrixes must create."

Now he nodded. "They're like the First Ritual that gave the original Hesperines immortality. A magical feat. A lost art. You can't make new ones. That's why the sites that remain are jealously guarded."

"By whom?" Cassia asked.

"Surviving Lustra practitioners." Kalos grimaced. "All the sites I know of are deep in heart hunter territory, fought over by the warbands. It would take an expedition with the Charge to get you there, and it wouldn't be easy."

"There must be another way." Lio sounded ready to tear apart every library and interrogate every expert until they found it.

"There is a letting site that's relatively easy to reach," Solia said quietly.

Cassia stared at her sister. "Where?"

Solia leaned against an iron column, her arms crossed, wearing her hard warrior face. "You won't like the answer, but here it is: Patria."

"Goddess," was all Lio said.

Kalos took a step nearer. "The place where the free lords are meeting to choose a king to replace Lucis?"

"Yes," Solia answered. "The Mage King established it as the traditional location for the Full Council to gather each time they must grant their mandate to a new king. I'm sure he and the Changing Queen had their reasons for convening near a letting site."

"You knew about this?" Lio demanded.

"Thalia told me which letting site I should take Cassia to. She knew we couldn't reach the one at her temple in Cordium. She felt the one in the vicinity of Patria would be most strategic."

Cassia shook her head. "Soli, why didn't you say anything?"

Her gaze dropped. "I almost did. In the grove when Zoe found us… again in my room on our first night here. But you were so happy to be back in Orthros, with me. I wanted to let you enjoy it a bit longer without this hanging over your head."

A lump formed in Cassia's throat. With the days until the Full Council slipping through their fingers, her sister had been giving her time.

Solia pushed away from the column and crossed to Kalos's side. "If you'll kindly step me to House Argyros? Cassia and Lio can join us there when they're ready."

As soon as Kalos and Solia were gone, Lio pulled Cassia into his arms. His aura seemed to swallow her, an unseen roil of shadows enveloping them both. She realized they weren't in the greenhouse anymore, but standing before their bed. Their surroundings plunged into inky darkness, as if his anguish had sucked the light from the room. As if all his power was concentrated on tucking her away in the safest place he could find.

"This isn't happening," he said into her hair.

"We shouldn't panic yet. We have options." Such a meaningless attempt to comfort him.

They both knew the Old Master wanted to add her to his collection, another tool to be used in his plots. And once he considered someone his, he never let them go.

Cassia pulled back to look into Lio's eyes. She forgot her next words of reassurance at the sight of his bared canines. And she knew he was on the verge of sinking his fangs into her right then and there, just to remind them both that no one had taken her from him yet.

His magic pounded through her with her pulse. "The moment you leave the safety of the Queens' ward over Orthros, the Collector will come for you. I will not allow that to happen."

She kissed him, not caring that his unsheathed fangs sliced her tongue. No, needing to give him that sharp reminder that the present moment was real, and they were here in Orthros together. The ground disappeared from under her feet; he had swept her into his arms. She felt cool air on her mouth, saw the flash of his fangs above her.

Goddess, yes, was all she could think. He needed this connection with her, now. Needed his bite to bind him to her.

He struck her throat, and she cried out, locking her arms around his neck to hold him to her vein. He cradled her in his arms while his fangs speared her. Long, hot surges of her blood flowed out of her, leaving an ache of unfulfilled pleasure in their wake.

Even as his magic rose to feed her hunger for him, she felt it. The deep emptiness inside her where her own magic had been for that brief, miraculous time in Btana Ayal.

Through the dizzying rush of his bite, the truth confronted her. Her magic was a piece of her. Without it, she would never be whole.

Lio's arms tightened around her, but the grip of his teeth gentled. The fragrance of their roses washed over her, somehow more powerful than ever before, laced with the scent of the blooming moonflower she had set on the shelf above their bed. She felt the softness of their blankets under her back, and the tiny spell lights in the alcove danced above her.

Then a wave of darkness broke over her. His magic. Untamed, endless, so much of it that it filled her deepest hollows. A moan of raw hunger tore out of her. Her body bowed off the bed, riding the crest of his power. Her krana convulsed, and nourishing pleasure pulsed through her every vein.

When she collapsed back onto the bed, gasping, he kissed her throat until his bite healed, and she caught her breath.

"What are the consequences?" Her voice came out hushed and hoarse. "If I must do without my magic? Is it…treatable?"

He rested his face in the crook of her neck, his hand tightening into a fist in the blankets. "Magic is inseparable from a mage's life force. If you were deprived of your power while human…that would be fatal."

"The Gift would save me."

He raised his head. She saw the answer in his eyes. "You would live forever with part of yourself missing. I can't bear to consider it."

"But we must consider it."

He brushed her hair back from her face. "No, my Grace. You must never suffer that. Not for me. Not for anyone."

"If it comes down to a choice between my birthright and my blo-odright, blood always comes first, Lio."

"No." His word rattled every piece of glass in the room. "I would sooner rip my own magic out of my soul than see you make that sacrifice."

Despite all her resolve to be strong and pragmatic, she started to cry. "I love you."

Lio stroked her cheek, rubbing her tears away. "I won't let him take you, Cassia. It doesn't matter what I must do. I will destroy him with my own two hands if I have to. You will be safe."

She lay there with him and let him hold her as close and as tightly as he needed. She felt sick that all she could do was console him.

She could not protect her Grace from what was inside of her.

She didn't want to put him through this. But she feared that this time, they could not reshape the world for their love, not in the face of magic whose rules had been written epochs before.

CASSIA WAS SURE THAT if she had already been a Hesperine, she would have sensed the worry in Uncle Argyros's library like a crushing hug.

Everyone who had been at the arena was waiting for her and Lio around the coffee table or on the nearby couches. Kassandra had joined them, sitting apart in a chair, twirling her spindle in her fingers over and over to turn something raw into a fine thread between her fingers.

Uncle Argyros was grave. "Solia and Kalos have explained the situation."

"You found the *lost paradigm*." Kia's glowing expression faded at the sight of Lio's face. "Right. Not the time for scholarly celebration."

Mak made a frustrated sound and leapt up to give Cassia an actual crushing hug. "Stop worrying. Lyros and I will keep you two squishy dip-lomats safe. Do you understand?"

She hugged him back. "Oh, Mak."

Lio held up a hand. From a nearby stone shelf, a long scroll levitated into his grasp. As he spread it out on the table, the coffee cups rattled. It proved to be a map of Tenebra.

He pointed to Patria. "This is our goal. We must get Cassia safely to Patria, remain long enough to discover how to awaken her magic, then get out."

Cassia, Mak, and Lyros joined Lio at the table to look at the map. Solia came to stand on Cassia's other side, her presence warm.

Lio gave Solia a look. "We have determined that Cassia must awaken her magic before I can Gift her. Are you satisfied?"

"Yes," she said. "I consider your first labor complete."

Kassandra gave her spindle a twist. "Are you ready to assign Lio his second labor? Traditionally, the matriarch asks him to perform a task that probes his weaknesses."

There was no challenge in Solia's voice. "I believe we can both agree that escorting Cassia to the letting site should be your sole focus now."

"No one is better prepared to protect her from the Collector than I am," Lio said.

It was true. And yet, this would twist the knife in Lio's weaknesses. His fear for Cassia. His nightmares from their last duel with the Old Master. He had never entirely healed from that battle.

"All I ask is that you don't hesitate to accept help," Solia said. "We are all prepared to rally around Cassia to keep her safe."

"Will you take on this labor?" Kassandra asked.

Lio leaned his fists on the table. "Of course."

"I bear witness," said the Oracle.

Rudhira appeared not to have touched the coffee in front of him. "This means that some of our youngest Hesperines and a newgift are to go errant into a tense mortal political situation—while our people are far away in the southern hemisphere."

"That's right, Rudhira," Lyros said. "Hesperines, plural. Lio, Cassia, and Solia are not setting foot in Tenebra without Mak and me."

Rudhira did not smile. "With everyone in residence here in Orthros Notou, the only other Hesperines anywhere near Tenebra are the Charge. I want you to wait until after Migration, when everyone returns to the north. You will be safer with your families just over the border in Orthros Boreou. Is it possible to delay?"

Lio bowed his head over the map. "I wish it were, but waiting could be dangerous for Cassia. Her magic is trying to awaken, but needs a letting site to fully manifest. We don't know what risks she might face if we stall the process."

"Yes, we do," said Cassia. "We should explain the specific dangers to everyone."

His jaw clenched. "I know what happens to humans who are deprived of their magic. It's the fate of the Collector's victims when he ends his possession of them and leaves—taking their magic with him. They die."

"That isn't going to happen to me," Cassia soothed him.

"Never," he vowed.

"I wish I were surprised," Rudhira said, "but this is consistent with Imperial magical theories about necromancy and life force, according to my knowledge as both a theramancer and a healer. Do not fear, Cassia. We will see you through this. But such an endeavor will require my permission as Prince Regent of Orthros Abroad. Present the specifics of your plan to me before the Queens tomorrow night."

Solia would finally get her audience with the Queens. But all she said was, "I'm sorry, Cassia."

Cassia gripped her hand.

Uncle Argyros beckoned to Cassia. "Come. There is something I wish to show you."

She glanced at Lio, but he nodded for her to go ahead. It seemed their mentor wanted a moment with her alone.

She accompanied Uncle Argyros up the curving staircase hewn into the gray stone walls of the library. They walked along the gallery under the dome. He must have veil spells here, for the voices from below faded away, and all she could hear were their silk shoes on the carpets.

"I know how you and Lio must be feeling at present," said Uncle Argyros. "I feel the same way myself, every time I have to return to Tenebra to renew our Equinox Oath with another mortal king."

Cassia glanced at him in surprise. "It never occurred to me that you would dread your journeys to Tenebra. You're the diplomat who assisted the Queens at the first Equinox Summit...who negotiated the original Equinox Oath."

"It is true that I embrace my calling as the defender of Orthros's original treaty with the kings of Tenebra. But that doesn't mean I look forward to going back each time. Leaving our loved ones here at home...worrying about the safety of those who accompany me...facing my own memories."

"Of course you understand," Cassia realized.

During his mortal life in Tenebra, he had lived through the horrors of the Last War, when Hespera's Great Temples had been razed, and the Mage Orders had hunted down so many people he loved.

"Do the memories get easier after sixteen hundred years?" she asked.

"Yes and no," he said. "The memories get easier after many hours with the mind healers. The journeys to Tenebra get easier with good company." He smiled. "Despite the hazards of the last Equinox Summit, I will always remember it as Lio's first with me—and the one where we met you."

"I cannot imagine my life if you had not made that journey."

"Then there was the Equinox Summit when Lyta and I Solaced Kadi. And many more besides that, which gave us great gifts in spite of great danger."

He halted in front of a spell-lit display, which was flanked by half-moon stained glass windows and inlaid with a pattern of the moonflowers that represented the diplomatic service. At the sight of the scrolls levitating there, Cassia's lips parted.

One of the documents, she recognized. That was her hand print on it from when she had saved it from the Collector. The Solstice Oath, the new treaty with the allied lords of Tenebra. But the other...

"Is this what I think it is?" she asked.

"The Equinox Oath," Uncle Argyros answered. "The very paper signed in blood and magic by our Queens, the Mage King of Tenebra, and your ancestor, the Changing Queen."

Cassia folded her hands in front of her and leaned forward to study the seals on the treaty. The Queens' glyph of Hespera pulsed red beside the Mage King's glowing golden emblem. The Changing Queen's seal was a gleaming green ivy leaf. Cassia could tell there was still magic in them after all these centuries, little mysterious whispers she couldn't fully grasp.

"You may touch," Uncle Argyros said.

"Oh, surely I shouldn't!"

"It is very well protected with spells," he reassured her, adding, "I think we can make an exception for the Changing Queen's direct descendant."

She reached out one finger and touched the ivy. She gasped at the strength of the aura she sensed in that tiny sign of her distant ancestor. She could almost understand it, like a familiar voice just out of earshot. She listened harder, but it was still too far away.

With a finger on her ancestor's pulse, Cassia reached out and fitted her hand to the mark she had left on the Solstice Oath.

She withdrew her hands, only to reach into her pocket for the Changing Queen's ivy pendant. The power in the wooden disk was so much stronger to Cassia now that her senses were awakening. It was a hawk's cry, a louder echo of the seal on the treaty.

She slipped it over her head and tucked it under her robes to rest hidden beneath her medallion of office. "Perhaps it's not impossible after all."

Uncle Argyros smiled, as if she had just given him the right answer to a challenging question.

22

nights until

NOTIAN WINTER SOLSTICE

34 Ourania, 1597 IS

CIRCLE OF QUEENS

LIO'S WORST NIGHTMARE WAS coming true in the rooftop garden of House Annassa. The bowers of white roses promised Sanctuary, but he couldn't keep his Grace hidden away here. Every step they took through the eternal blooms carried them toward their fears.

Their Trial circle and the Ashes walked in silence with them, Knight's and Tilili's paws padding softly. But somehow, Solia's gilded sandals seemed loud on the glittering black marble floor. Her ambitions were clear tonight. In her golden wrap dress, she looked like a queen already.

She cast a wondering glance around her. "I had heard that House Annassa is the Queens' only palace."

"Yes," Cassia said, "their home is open to their people."

Solia watched red water fall into the basin of a fountain. "And they have no throne room save this garden?"

"They are too powerful to need thrones," Cassia replied.

"I can see that," Solia murmured.

The Queens sat hand-in-hand amid silk cushions on the raised section of floor that served as their sofa. Queen Alea's white hair pooled long and thick around her, intertwining with Queen Soteira's countless centuries of braids. The first Graces were divine love incarnate.

All Lio could think was, *Goddess, let Cassia and me survive long enough to enjoy even a taste of what they have.* The Ashes' formal introduction to the Queens passed him by in a blur.

Cassia took his hand, bringing him back to reality. If only he could hold her in his protection as easily as her small hand fit in his.

"Annassa," Cassia addressed the Queens by their honorific, "it is with great joy that I bring before you my sister, Solia."

"It is an honor, Annassa," Solia said. "Her Imperial Majesty asked me to convey her admiration."

Queen Soteira replied to this greeting from the ruler of her mortal homeland. "How glad we are that you have been under her wing."

"As Cassia has been under yours," Solia acknowledged. "For giving my sister Sanctuary, you have my gratitude."

"She is dear to us." Queen Soteira's voice was rich with theramancy.

"And so are you," said Queen Alea with one of her ancient, yet youthful smiles. "As the kin of one of Orthros's bloodlines, you will always have a home here, no matter where your future path may lead."

Solia seemed to find no words in response to this. Lio found it comforting, somehow, that even she could be so struck by this offer of unconditional Sanctuary from the Queens.

And yet the most powerful Hesperines alive did not make the world feel safe tonight.

"Annassa," Lio said, "I fear all our paths lead to Tenebra."

Queen Alea's pale, round face furrowed with concern. "Ioustin has told us of your plight, my dears. Under other circumstances, we would never allow you to go Abroad when such threats await you. But it is clear an exception must be made in this case."

Queen Soteira gave a heavy sigh. "We pray your venture into Tenebra will hold unexpected blessings, even as your journey through the Empire subjected you to unexpected dangers."

If Kassandra had any insights to share on what surprises their travels had in store, she said nothing. The oracle sat silently on the Queens' left.

"Every precaution must be taken," Queen Alea said. "We will grant our blessing only when our prince regent is satisfied that your plan will not cause needless danger to you or any of those under his protection Abroad."

Rudhira sat to his mothers' right, dressed in formal silks with his braid draped forward over his shoulder. Lio's Ritual father had seldom appeared so much like the Queens' heir.

It was his sister Konstantina who handled the affairs of government on the home front while Rudhira was in the field, which did not always promote harmony between them. She and Rudhira had once been like Zoe and Lio, but now the Second Princess was one of the most powerful elders in Orthros, her centuries-long hair draping behind her chair in heavy coils. But tonight, she sat at her brother's side and touched her dark hand to his pale one in a gesture of solidarity.

Lio gave them a deep bow with his hand over his heart, the honor Hesperines reserved for their immortal royals. "Thank you for your support, Aunt Kona. We know our further involvement in Tenebran affairs does not align with your vision for Orthros's future."

"As my mothers have said, there are times when exceptions must be made."

"I'm sorry, Master Kona." Cassia's aura ached with genuine regret. "You've barely begun mentoring me in rose gardening, and I must already take leave from my lessons."

Aunt Kona raised her majestic brows. "By no means should you apologize. A great future awaits you among my students, but to fulfill your potential, you must be in possession of your full power."

They knew the future she had in mind for Cassia did not only involve gardening, not when Orthros's rose expert was also a political mastermind.

Aunt Kona's smile was rather smug. "Go and claim these gifts for your people. It is high time we inducted a Lustra mage into Orthros's Circle of Rosarians. I can hardly wait to see what you do in our gardens."

"I look forward to the plans you have for me," Cassia said.

Then Aunt Kona beckoned to Xandra. "Come sit with me, Sister."

Surprise flashed in Xandra's aura, but she took the seat at Aunt Kona's right. To the Queens' left, Lio's parents stood with Uncle Argyros, Aunt Lyta, and Nike. At an encouraging gesture from Nike, Kia and Nodora joined them, while Mak and Lyros closed ranks around Cassia and Lio.

A part of Lio's mind, which remembered to think like a diplomat instead of Cassia's angry Grace, noted the significance. His parents, aunt, and uncle were the only elder firstbloods in attendance.

The Queens were not interested in the opinions of the entire Firstblood Circle tonight. But they did want to involve their heirs. The Eighth Circle was in the thick of Hesperine politics now—and all the dangers it brought. There was no turning back.

Lio had prepared for this his entire life. But could anything truly have prepared him for an Old Master to target his Grace?

"First Prince," Lio formally addressed Rudhira, "we come before you with two proposals for your consideration. This is my request: give Cassia and me your blessing to go errant. We will go secretly to Patria, making every effort to avoid the Collector's attention, and remain only long enough to awaken her magic before returning to the safety of Orthros."

Before speaking, Mak saluted Rudhira with a fist to his heart. "We take full responsibility for ensuring not only their safety, but mitigating any danger to others that might arise if the Collector makes an attempt on Cassia."

Lyros was next to offer a salute. "We are ready to work with the Charge to ensure our strategy satisfies your concerns."

"I deem this the approach that carries the least risk," Rudhira said.

Cassia looked at her sister. "We hope Solia will accompany us there—and back to Orthros once we have achieved our goal."

There was sympathy in Rudhira's eyes. He knew they were fighting an uphill battle against another plan already in motion. "And the second proposal?"

Solia answered him. "There is no need to enter Tenebra like thieves in the night. My sister's days of treading carefully there are over. She and the Hesperine delegation can officially accompany me to Patria, where I will attend the Full Council of Free Lords and proclaim my right to rule."

Rudhira rested his hands on the ornate arms of his chair. "That is a proposal my mothers must consider. While our Hesperines errant are my purview, Orthros's position on a potential change of government in Tenebra must be the Queens' decision."

"We are aware of the opportunity before you, Solia." Queen Alea gazed at her with eyes that had seen sixteen hundred years' of Tenebra's history. "But you also have a right to the queendom of Orthros. There is freedom and glory for you here. An eternity of anything you choose."

Praise Hespera for the Queens, who had the most silver of all tongues. Perhaps they could sway Solia in a way Lio and Cassia could not.

"Three lands would welcome you with open arms," said Queen Soteira. "Tenebra. Orthros. Or the Empire. Yes, even your beloved Empire, and even if you throw off the destiny Her Imperial Majesty has in mind for you. You would be surprised how open her borders would be to you with a little persuasion from us."

"I appreciate the magnitude of what you are offering me," Solia said.

"Do you? I think Cassia must show you." The Second Princess waved a gracious hand. The small table by her chair, draped in a cloth, levitated to stand before the Queens.

Cassia faced her sister across the table. "Soli, last time I was here with the Queens, before we went to the Empire to find you, I made a promise: that I wouldn't rest until I offered you this with my own hand."

Cassia pulled back the cloth. Lio's Grace could still take him by surprise. He had thought this relic tucked away at their residence, where she fussed over it with ongoing frustration. The mosaic pot of soil might not have impressed anyone who didn't know its significance. But Lio did.

It was the only Sanctuary Rose that had survived the Collector's attack. Aunt Kona and Cassia said the roots under the soil still held life. What were they planning?

Cassia rested her hands on her pot, her chin set. Lio knew that look. She was determined to prove a point, and Goddess help anyone who tried to stop her.

"Lio, please come stand behind me."

"Certainly." He did as she asked, resting his hands on her slender shoulders.

Cassia reached into her frayed, stained gardening satchel, which she wore with her formal silks, and pulled out her hand spade. She set the sharp edge of it to her hand, where she had cut herself time and time again to bleed power into Hesperine spells.

The fragrance of his Grace's blood filled the Queens' garden, and he watched the red drops sink into the barren soil inside the pot. He sensed her focus her Will as he had helped her learn to do during their practice sessions.

When a surge of magic flowed out of him, he bit back a gasp. He could feel her drawing on his power to strengthen her own nascent magic. It was as intuitive as their Union. He fed more magic into her focus, letting her aura's demand measure how much he gave her. His heart pounded with the exhilarating rush of power, and he gritted his teeth so he wouldn't show his unsheathed fangs to his Queens.

Cassia's hands tightened on the rim of the pot, one trailing more blood into the soil, her knuckles white. He felt her, them, flowing deep into that little piece of the ruins the Collector had left behind.

And he realized she had been right. He felt it through her. Life.

The soil burst open. Fresh green canes sprang up before their eyes, formed buds at their ends, and unfurled into three blooms as fat and thriving as the surrounding garden.

Cassia heaved a breath and began to crumple.

Lio caught her close against him before she fell. "Goddess bless. That was brilliant."

Aunt Kona began to clap, and the entire circle joined her in a round of applause for Cassia's first display of magic. Knight whined in concern, pressing against Cassia's robes, and she slid a hand through his ruff to reassure him.

Lio's Grace leaned her head back against him, triumphant. He realized that her display had not only been for her sister. He could hear her promise in her thoughts: they would not let the Collector win.

Lio lifted her bleeding hand to his mouth and placed a tender kiss upon the cut. His intention was only to heal her, but he tasted new flavors in her blood. Verdant. Wild. Her magic, growing stronger. When they did not have an audience, he would take the time to savor that.

Across from them, Solia reached out to trace one white rose petal with her finger.

"My power belongs in Orthros," Cassia said, "as do I. This can be the place where you belong too, Solia. All you need to do is choose it for yourself. It is my honor to speak on behalf of the Queens. With this white rose, the Hesperine symbol of welcome, I hereby offer you Sanctuary."

"Pup," Solia murmured, her eyes fraught with emotion her spells concealed.

"Please, Soli. Don't let go of everything we want for ourselves." Cassia held out her hands.

Her sister gripped them. "I am not letting go. I'm holding on tight."

Then Solia faced the Queens. "I know I will always have refuge here, and for that, my sister's adopted people have my gratitude and my love. But whether Tenebra will have me or not, I will have it, for the good of all."

Lio felt Cassia's pain in his own blood. Certainty passed between them. Solia had already made her choice before she set foot here. Just as Cassia had known what she would do before she abdicated in the Empress's court.

There had never been any hope of changing Solia's mind. These two sisters might as well be stars set on their paths in the heavens. Lio wished Tendo were here, for he was the only other person who understood.

Solia's voice echoed, unwavering, across the Queens' rooftop. "I will take the throne of Tenebra. I ask for the support of everyone here. If you cannot in good conscience aid me, then I hope for your blessing. If even that is too much to expect, I pray only that you will not seek to sway me from my cause."

A soft wind chased her words, only the fountains speaking as she awaited Queens' response. The ancient monarchs exchanged a glance, a sign that they must be silently consulting via their Grace Union.

Queen Alea's aura was wrapped in her rare Sanctuary magic, a beautiful secret to Lio's senses. "For Hesperines to intervene in the politics of Tenebra, after the Equinox Oath forbade us to do so for sixteen hundred years, is a decision that must be weighed with the utmost care."

"I understand," Solia said. "Shall we discuss my strategy so you may take it into consideration?"

Cassia leaned into Lio. He understood her need for that physical anchor to each other. Tenebran affairs were a storm rising around them—Solia's firestorm. They were watching it begin, and there was nothing they could do to stop it.

"You intend to secure the queenship by peaceful means?" Queen Alea asked.

Solia answered, "I will claim the throne not my might, but by law. When the Council of Free Lords revokes their mandate from King Lucis, I will win their support and become the rightful queen."

Uncle Argyros raised his open palm in the circle petition to join in the discussion. "What is your plan for gaining their favor?"

"Cassia assures me the people remember me. I will give them the queen they have always wanted, but thought they lost."

Aunt Lyta extended her hand next. "How will you ensure that the deposed king does not retaliate?"

"Is Lord Hadrian still as honorable as I remember him to be?" Solia asked Cassia.

Cassia's aura balked at being drawn into her sister's plot, but she answered. "Honorable to his bones. He hates serving Lucis, but continues to do so for the greater good of the kingdom. As a veteran of the feuds that once tore Tenebra apart, he knows only a strong monarch can keep the free lords in check."

"How likely is he to transfer his loyalty to me?" Solia asked.

Cassia swallowed. "The night we thought you died, he—the most powerful lord in all of Tenebra—begged until he was hoarse. But the king would not let him save you. He has held you in his heart as his true queen all these years."

"I regret his needless grief," Solia murmured. "When he follows me, his men will follow him. Lucis will be left with a weak force that obeys him out of personal loyalty—or fear. He will not have the might to oppose me."

"He has a mighty ally," Queen Alea pointed out. "Cordium supports his reign. They have already sent war mages to aid him. When you challenge him, you know how they will respond."

But Solia smiled. "Indeed, I am well aware how the Mage Orders will react to a woman like me. A walking abomination against their religious laws." She counted them off on her fingers. "No one may wield magic outside a temple. No man may wield both spell and sword. Oh, and women are not to wield the sword at all."

"As much as that needs to change," Kia said, "it will be incredibly difficult to uproot those ideas from people's minds."

"They don't even believe women *can* be fire mages," Xandra reminded her. "They still kill girls with our affinity, thinking it a mercy because our magic will only drive us mad and destroy us."

"Not during my reign." Solia's tone could have left a man with burn scars. "I have devoted my life to putting a woman with magic on the throne. But when I revealed my plan for Cassia to my allies, it was my downfall, the reason I lost their support and had to flee. The reason she and I were separated for fifteen years. It was the most harrowing lesson I have ever learned. Do not imagine I will make the same mistake twice. This time, I will choose my moment wisely, and when I finally demand they accept their queen's magic, I will be ready."

Queen Alea's voice was gentle. "I was alive during the Ordering. I lived through the Last War and all the persecutions the mages unleashed on women like us, who wield power against their doctrines. Are you certain you can be ready for such a reality?"

Solia raised her chin. "I don't expect change to happen overnight. Not all of it will be accomplished in my lifetime. But I will be the beginning of the end of the Ordering."

Lio remembered how lofty his own goals had been on his first journey to Tenebra for the Equinox Summit. How he and Cassia had clung to those ideals during the Solstice Summit when she came to Orthros. Solia might believe in her cause, and she might have been honed by politics and war at the Empress's side, but she had been in the Empire too long. He and Cassia had been here, fighting the Mage Orders with every diplomatic word and act of sabotage.

Solia had no idea what she would face. But Lio said nothing, for she would find out, and he did not wish that moment of reckoning on her.

"I can rally Tenebra to stand with me against the Cordium," Solia promised.

"If you miscalculate," Queen Alea cautioned her, "you could provoke the Mage Orders to retaliate as they have not done since the Last War."

"If it comes to that, the Empress will provide me with military aid," Solia said. "Even Cordium's mages, princes, and mercenaries are a pitiable force compared to the Imperial Army."

Hespera's Mercy, how calmly Solia described the Empire and Cordium marching to war against one another.

"But Her Imperial Majesty and I regard that as a last resort," Solia continued. "She wishes to introduce herself to the Tenebrans as their patroness, not a foreign invader. She will provide me with support in the form of money, arms, and supplies that I can use to outfit my own forces. Only her elite mercenaries will render direct aid."

Kella offered a bow from Tilili's back. "Our sister states are united in the Empress's cause. Tenebra and the Empire will move forward as allies. It is our hope that Orthros will stand with us."

Karege put a hand to his heart. "And that Hesperines errant will be free to fight with our comrades, whatever official course you set for our people, My Queens."

Queen Soteira shared another look with her Grace. "Our power is great, and thus any use of it has the potential to incite further harm."

Annassa Alea nodded. "Hesperines have not been called upon to take sides in a conflict since the Last War—and even then, we sought only to protect innocents from the Orders' onslaught. We chose to withdraw to Orthros rather than fight for our right to exist in Tenebra. This is a long precedent to overturn."

"If Lucis remains on the throne," Solia said, "war is inevitable. Cassia and Lio have told me that Lucis has already opened Tenebra to Orders. Their persecution of Hespera worshipers has already begun. Only I can prevent the Next War."

"So can Flavian," Cassia insisted.

"Do you truly believe he is equal to this?" Solia returned.

"He will maintain a united Tenebra," said Cassia, "which can prevent the feuds and Cordian incursion."

"Maintain, yes," Solia replied. "He will maintain the Tenebra we have always known. Unless I reforge it into a new kingdom, history will repeat itself. As long as the Mage Orders control magic and worship, an entire continent will always be at their mercy. As long as corrupt men hold everyone else's power hostage to their doctrines, war will only be a matter of time. Only real change can secure peace."

Solia spoke the truth. Although she sought to drive change with sword and fire, Lio with diplomacy, their cause was the same. He wanted to believe she could achieve everything she promised. But he could not find it in himself to rejoice at the prospect of such a future, when it would cost Cassia her sister.

Aunt Kona made the circle petition. "Solia, you should be informed of the measure Orthros has in place in case violence should break out. Thanks to your sister, I have tabled this vote until we see the outcome of the Full Council. But if that outcome is the Next War, Orthros will invoke the Departure, withdrawing all Hesperines from Tenebra and sealing the ward forever."

Shock reverberated in Karege's aura. "My Princess, I have been gone from the Firstblood Circle for too long. I can scarcely imagine you would consider this."

"It gives me no joy, dear Karege," she replied. "But we will do what we must to ensure the Mage Orders do not threaten our existence—or subject Tenebrans to needless harm due to our presence."

"With all respect," Cassia spoke up, "the outcome of that vote is not a foregone conclusion. Many in Orthros are committed to keeping our borders open."

"That's right," Xandra said. "The Eighth Circle has many partisans who will support my vote against the Departure."

"The Charge has no intention of withdrawing," Rudhira reminded them.

Nike crossed her arms. "Orthros has no reason to abandon Tenebra and cower behind the ward. We have the strength to stand firm in our purpose."

"I welcome the debate we shall have, should that night arrive," Aunt Kona replied. "You have allies on both sides of this discussion, Solia."

"I can see that, Second Princess," Solia responded, cool as steel, "but know that the Empress and I are united in our efforts to end isolation. It would grieve us for Orthros to abandon that principle. And I will not allow anyone, human or immortal, to lock my sister away from me. That is not up for debate."

"There is an easy solution to that," Aunt Kona said graciously. "You need only join us on this side of the ward."

"I am offering you a far superior outcome." Solia turned to the Queens again. "A queen who will turn the hostile land south of your border into an enduring ally. I am not asking for Hesperine intervention in a war—I ask for your help in preventing it. To do that, I must secure the throne. I request only that Orthros send official representatives to support my claim at the Council."

Xandra made the circle petition. "Mother, *Bamaayo*, these proposals are sure to cause an upheaval in the Firstblood Circle. Should you wish to call a vote, my Trial sisters and I are prepared to rally our partisans."

"We will need all our royal firstbloods to guide Orthros in the aftermath of our decision," Queen Soteira said, "but Hesperines' role in Solia's campaign will not come to a vote. This is a choice we must make for our people."

Lio felt the relief and trepidation that passed among all the Hesperines there. The Queens seldom enforced their Will on Orthros. They never would, unless their people faced a risk so enormous.

Aunt Lyta bowed to the Queens with her hand on her heart, the traditional heart bow. "No matter your decision, Annassa, the Stand is ready. With Nike home to reinforce us, there is no threat we cannot meet."

Nike bowed alongside her. "We will shield Orthros from every new danger."

"We will need our Stewards as well." Queen Soteira's words struck Lio as ominous.

She bent her head nearer Queen Alea. The two Graces were clearly in deep, private conversation. Like all parents in Orthros, the Queens spoke unheard with each other about their children. But the thoughts shared by their two minds held the power to alter lives and kingdoms.

Finally, Queen Soteira tucked a strand of hair behind Queen Alea's ear, brushing her fingertips along the black Grace braid that Queen Alea wore like a circlet.

Queen Alea spoke for them. "Solia, Princess and aspiring Queen, do not imagine that the Hesperines have forgotten our ideals. We have held out for centuries, offering a Sanctuary of freedom even when all hope was lost. We cherish your vision of a future that many have believed impossible. For this reason, we will send the foremost defenders of our ideals with you to Tenebra: our diplomats."

Lio and Cassia's gazes met. Their Grace Union was still a soft, elusive strain, but they had talked for hours the night before. Words spoken aloud, openly and honestly, had made them of one mind.

They knew what they must do. Even when all hope was lost.

"Annassa, if I may." Cassia turned to Kassandra.

The Oracle offered her a long, rolled bundle of fabric. Lio sensed his Grace steeling herself and realized what Kassandra must have brought with her.

Cassia took it slowly. "You were right. The white rose is not a choice, if it is the only one offered."

"You've done well," Kassandra approved.

Cassia took the bundle to her sister and, holding in both hands, unfurled it before the would-be queen.

The historical banner did not bear King Lucis's coat-of-arms, a sword pointed downward in obedience under the Mage Orders' fire. This was the Mage King's emblem from over a millennium ago, a blade and fire spell held high under the shining rays of the sun.

"How is this possible?" Solia stared at the worn, but still brilliant banner and touched a burn hole in the fabric. "This isn't merely a banner… it is *the* banner." Her voice thickened. "The one Thalia gave me. The one Iris and I guarded in secret and took with us to Castra Roborra, where the lords betrayed us."

"Yours?" Cassia said. "I knew it was a banner from the Mage King's time, but yours? My mother's?"

"It is one of the three artifacts your family has preserved in secret for generations."

"The other is the Changing Queen's pendant?" Cassia asked.

"Yes," Solia answered, "and the third is their flesh and blood—you."

"Well, I'm glad they passed it down to me so I can give it to the rightful queen."

"I cannot say that I am worthy of it. I took it all the way to the Empire with me, to protect it." She glanced away. "But I am ashamed to tell you that there came a time when I…did not keep it."

Lio mourned that distant moment in Solia's life, when she had perhaps been willing to rebel against her destiny. He was glad she had tried to throw this burden away. He wished it had never returned to haunt them all.

"I found it," was the only explanation the Oracle offered.

"I didn't want to keep it, either," said Cassia, "but now I know I must offer it to you, along with something else. My wisdom, such as it is. You need an adviser, someone who can give you insight into current affairs in Tenebra. I know I can never replace Iris, but in her honor, I will do my best."

Solia shut her eyes for a moment. Then she accepted the banner from Cassia and pulled her sister into her arms. "I need you at my side."

Lio drew a deep breath, bracing himself for what would come next.

Queen Alea beckoned to Uncle Argyros. "It is time to finish our discussion regarding the Ambassador for Tenebran Affairs."

Lio and Cassia's mentor came to stand with them. He put a hand on each of their shoulders. "I will tell you both what I told Lio before your departure for the Empire. I will always be proud of you, whether or not you accept what I am about to offer you."

Lio swallowed. "Thank you, Uncle."

"We needed to hear that," Cassia said.

"Before I was the Queens' Master Ambassador," Uncle Argyros told them, "before we had a queendom called Orthros with a diplomatic service, I was simply the mind mage who offered my skills when our people negotiated with the Mage King for our survival. In that sense, I was Ambassador for Tenebran Affairs before I was anything else. And when you, Nephew, became my first and only student to take an interest in the broken kingdom we left behind, I imagined for the first time that I might have a successor."

"No one will ever fill your shoes," Lio said.

"I wouldn't wish for you to," his uncle said with a gleam in his eye. "Your own shoes are quite suitable for the role and will carry you in directions I would never think of. And how much better that you do not walk this path alone."

"No," Cassia said, "and he never will."

"Two new experts on Tenebran affairs have risen in our sky," Uncle Argyros said. "As much as I grieve to place such a weight of responsibility upon you, I have never felt more reassured that our relations with Tenebra are in good hands. If you will have it, I will pass this title on to you two with my whole heart."

"I still have so much to learn," Cassia said, "and I look forward to our studies—but my past in Tenebra has prepared me, too."

Lio put his hand over his uncle's. "You have taught me well for this night."

Silvertongue's legendary gaze rested upon them, full of centuries of memory, but it was the years of love that shone brightest in his aura. "You are ready."

"And so are we, Father," said Mak.

Lyros nodded. "Where Lio and Cassia go, we go as their official protectors."

"With my blessing," Aunt Lyta told them.

"We'll be here," Xandra promised from beside her illustrious elder siblings. "Kia and Nodora and I will not stop fighting in the Firstblood Circle. Orthros will need us to vote in support of our new role in Solia's reign."

Lio's father embraced him and Cassia. "A momentous night, Eighth Circle. May the Goddess's Eyes light your path."

"And her darkness keep you in Sanctuary." Lio's mother held onto them for a long moment, the family's Union aching with her pride and worry.

Aunt Lyta reached out her hands to Uncle Argyros. He took them, and they said nothing aloud. But if anyone knew what Uncle Argyros needed to hear on this occasion, it was Aunt Lyta, speaking through their Grace Union. She caressed his cheek, and he shut his eyes for a moment. A sigh escaped him, anguish and relief all at once.

Nike embraced him. "It is hard to lay down a quest."

"Ah, my shooting star," he said. "You know."

Lio's father clasped his uncle's wrist, then threw an arm around him. "It's about time, Brother."

"Argyros," Queen Alea called to him gently.

He turned to her, and instead of giving the heart bow, he did what Lio had never beheld. He knelt before Queen Alea and kissed her hand.

"Sixteen hundred years, my friend." She held his hand in both of hers. "You have stood between us and destruction. Your words have been mightier than swords. And yet I find myself at a loss for words now. How can we express our people's gratitude to you?"

"I need none, My Queen. It has been the greatest honor of my life."

"You have done all that you promised us you would."

Uncle Argyros let out a sigh. "With that blessing, my heart will rest."

Lio blinked hard, his throat aching. His mentor had waited an epoch to lay down this burden.

That epoch was over. The world had just shifted. His uncle was no longer the ambassador who would make or break peace between Hesperines and their mortal enemies.

It was now Lio and Cassia who stood between Orthros and destruction.

3

nights until

NOTIAN WINTER SOLSTICE

5 Eukairia, 1597 IS

ANYTHING FOR ORTHROS

"Do you like the idea of putting the vegetables in their own section here?" Cassia marked a space on the paper in front of her and glanced at Zoe.

The child hugged Knight, her face forlorn. "I suppose so."

Cassia sighed and put down her charcoal. She had hoped spending time with Zoe at the greenhouse site would bring the suckling some comfort, but to no avail.

Cassia pushed everything else from her mind: the strategy sessions with Mak and Lyros, the last-minute lessons with Uncle Argyros, the speeches before the Firstblood Circle, more councils with the royal family, and the endless packing. She wrapped her arms around Zoe and focused on the thought that there was nowhere in the world she would rather be than here.

"I wish you didn't have to go," Zoe cried.

"I know, Zoe flower. I wish I could stay home, too. Just remember we'll come back safely, as we did from our journey to the Empire."

"You barely got home, and you already have to go again!"

"It will be much easier this time. We'll step home often to spend time with you." Cassia stroked Zoe's hair. "Then, once we've found my magic, we can come home for good."

"You're ambassadors. You'll have to travel all the time forever."

"We will always, always come home. And we will be home much more often than we're away."

"I wish you didn't have to be diplomats." Zoe started to cry.

And then Cassia's tears escaped too, and she felt useless instead of like an elder sister with the strength to protect Zoe from her fears.

Goddess, this must have been how Solia had felt all the time. How had she borne it?

Cassia rocked Zoe, murmuring reassurances that comforted neither of them, and prayed Solia would join them as Cassia had asked.

When the horns of Haima called out half moon, Solia strode into the courtyard right on time. She took one look at Cassia and Zoe and Knight in a miserable heap, then came to join them at the center of the greenhouse. On her way, she picked up the two unsupervised goats, who were trying to nibble the potted plants Cassia had placed out of their reach.

What do I do? Cassia mouthed to her sister over Zoe's head.

"Whatever has happened?" Solia handed Zoe her goats to hold, then retrieved a handkerchief from the nearby picnic supplies and began to dry Zoe's face. "I have never seen such terrible tears in Orthros, where there is seldom any reason to cry."

"You just got here," Zoe wailed, "and now you have to go."

Solia pulled Zoe, goats and all, onto her lap now. "It's just like your Ritual father. He goes to Tenebra to help others, but he always comes home to visit."

"But he's safer than you and Cassia and Lio. Rudhira is really old and has lots of magic and a big sword."

Solia's mouth twitched. "Well, the rest of us are not elders like him, to be sure. But Lio and I have lots of magic, and so will Cassia." Solia refrained from mentioning her sword in front of Zoe, for which Cassia was grateful. "Besides, Rudhira and the Charge will be there to help us, and Mak and Lyros won't leave our sides."

"Why do you have to help those other people? They're not your sister like me."

Solia shut her eyes and rested her cheek on Zoe's hair. She let out a deep, quiet sigh, regret creasing her brow. "It is very hard to answer the call of duty when we long to be home with those we love. But I want you to understand why I'm making this decision. It's not because you aren't important to me. It's because you are so very important."

Solia sat back, looking into Zoe's face. "I know how many sad and frightening things happened to all of us in Tenebra. But instead of never going there again, I want to return and become queen so I can change

Tenebra. I'll make it a safe place, so that anytime the people you love must travel there, you won't have to be afraid."

Zoe sniffed and listened more quietly now.

"If I make Tenebra safe," Solia asked, "is that at least second best after staying in Orthros?"

"That depends." Zoe gnawed at her lip. "How often will you come back to visit?"

"Often enough to enjoy your present with you."

"You got me a present?" Zoe asked.

Solia gave Cassia a conspiratorial look. "Do you have the box I gave you in the Empress's orchard?"

"Of course." Cassia reached into her nearby gardening satchel for the treasure.

Together, the three of them gathered around the beautiful inlaid wooden box. Solia and Cassia lifted the lid to show Zoe what was inside.

"Seeds?" Zoe asked, a note of hope returning to her voice.

"Yes," Solia answered. "Whenever I used to go away, I would always bring back a present for Cassia—something new for our garden. I've been saving these while I was in the Empire. I collected them from all the exciting places I traveled over fifteen years. Now they can grow in Cassia's greenhouse. I hope you'll share in this gift and help us plant them."

Zoe twisted her hands together, looking into the box with wide eyes. "You'll come home so we can plant them together? All three of us?"

"I promise," Solia said.

Solia had never broken a promise. Not even her promise that she and Cassia would see each other again, which had taken fifteen years to fulfill.

Cassia realized Solia was not saying this only for Zoe's benefit. It was a promise to Cassia, too, one she had so desperately needed to hear.

Cassia put her arm around both her sisters. "Thank you, Soli."

Blood magic pulsed beneath Cassia's feet as she stood within the Ritual circle at House Argyros. For an instant, she allowed herself to shut her eyes before the firstbloods and family who had gathered for the delegation's sendoff. She focused, as Lio was teaching her to do, and let her awareness of their traveling companions fade.

She drank in the powerful feeling of Hesperine magic. Just one more moment on home ground. One more long draught of Orthros before she must somehow find the strength to cross the border in the wrong direction.

Lio seemed woven into the magic that breathed under them, braided into her heartache.

The fragrance of moonflowers brought her back to her responsibilities. Uncle Argyros draped garlands around their necks, reciting the traditional blessing for departing diplomats.

"The wisdom of the firstbloods is with you, the blessing of the Queens is upon you, and the Goddess's truths are in your veins. Walk lightly in the land of our enemies; deal gently with the mortals we once were; wield your words before your fangs. Go forth and rebuild another piece of Hespera's Sanctuary in the land we left in ashes."

Lio offered her his arm, palm up, and she laid her hand in his. Together, they responded, "We will walk the path of our martyrs; we will reach with the hands of our Queens; we will speak with the voice of our Goddess."

Aunt Lyta placed wreaths of blackthorn upon Mak and Lyros's heads. "The might of the firstbloods is with you, and the Goddess's justice is in your veins. Bear the burden of violence for your Queens. Protect our people in the land of our enemies; show Mercy to the mortals we once were; wield only your fists and your fangs. Go forth and defend the gates of our Sanctuary."

Mak and Lyros joined hands, lifting them like one fist above their heads.

When Apollon and Komnena stepped forward to stand before Solia, she appeared surprised. They each held out a hand to her, and she took the invitation.

"The love of your firstbloods is with you," Apollon said, "the Queens' refuge remains for you, and our prayers to the Goddess shadow you. Walk safely in the land of our past, Daughter. Hespera's Sanctuary is always open to you."

Then four of Orthros's diplomats for Imperial affairs said a blessing for each of the Ashes. More Hesperine farewells and prayers rose around them in the countless tongues of their people. So many had found a home here in spite of past suffering, because Orthros was a land of peace. Their words washed over Cassia as powerfully as the blood magic on which she stood, and she felt homesick already.

She was leaving for her magic. For her sister. But for her people, too.

That was what becoming a diplomat meant. She would do anything for Hespera's Sanctuary, even go back to Tenebra.

Uncle Argyros and Aunt Lyta pierced their palms with their fangs, then pressed them together to mingle their blood. Their libation fell into the Ritual circle. An arcane tremor seemed to emanate through the floor, and Cassia rocked on her feet. As if he had been prepared for that, Lio steadied her.

As soon as the ceremony ended, Zoe dashed into the circle with Knight. She clung to Lio, Cassia, and Solia until the last possible moment, while they reassured her over and over. Their Trial sisters gathered around with jests to ward off tears.

Rudhira paused before the Queens, who exchanged veiled words with him before he approached the Ritual circle. "Let us retrieve our weapons."

Mak and Lyros stepped everyone to the Armory of Akofo. Solia and the Ashes strapped on their glittering array of deadly blades with the efficiency of professionals. Cassia stood aside with Lio and Knight and checked her gardening satchel one more time. It had carried her treasures and weapons through every danger.

She closed her fingers around her spade and drew a deep breath. It had once been a mundane gardening tool, but she had used it in so many blood rituals by now that she could feel the magic emanating out of it.

"You have a small army of protectors," Lio reminded her.

She brushed her fingers across his temple. "But the protection that reassures me the most is right here."

He placed a kiss on her forehead.

Finally, without a sound, Rudhira's two-hander levitated from its stand beside Nike's shield. Spell-light gleamed along the blade as it slid into the scabbard on his back. He might look his most un-Hesperine, wearing a Tenebran tunic and breeches under a light coal of mail, with Thorn at the ready. But it was his sacrifices in Tenebra that made him the most

Hesperine of all princes. He beckoned, and Cassia, Lio, Mak, and Lyros came to stand before him.

"As long as you are in Tenebra," he said, "you are under my care as Prince Regent of Orthros Abroad, and you are bound by Charge Law. You have my protection and that of all Hesperines errant. You also have the responsibility to support us in return and take no action that could increase the danger to any of our own."

They all nodded their understanding.

Rudhira's gray eyes softened. "You are so young, and yet none of you are unprepared for what you will face. Even so, when I give you advice, I expect you to listen. Understood?"

"Yes, Ritual father," Cassia said, as the others murmured their assent.

"Good," Rudhira replied. "The first thing you must be prepared for is the sun. With only three days until the Summer Solstice, you're in for long Dawn Slumbers, I'm afraid. In the part of Tenebra where we're headed, the day lasts for seventeen mortal hours. There is no nightfall, only seven hours of twilight. Prepare to be sluggish at all times."

Cassia's heart sank. She must do without Lio for seventeen hours a day.

"We've trained for high sunlight conditions," Mak assured the prince.

"And we know training is no substitute for experience," Lyros added.

"Solia and the Ashes will be with Cassia while we sleep," Lio said, in the tone of someone announcing his own prison sentence.

Rudhira paced in front of them. "You know the royal family of Orthros seldom issues commands. We strive to earn your love, rather than demand your obedience. But in life or death situations in hostile territory, there is not always time for gentle guidance. If I ask you to do something, you must not hesitate. Even if I ask you to abandon your quest and return home immediately."

"Of course, My Prince," Mak and Lyros told him without hesitation.

Rudhira paused before Cassia, looking at her with the steely eyes of a mind healer. She felt he could see into her soul, to the wild, possessive creature inside her that would rather die than come home without her magic. It was a proud beast that knew she deserved her power and would fight for what was rightfully hers.

Rudhira held her gaze with his ancient eyes. His aura of command stirred something in Cassia's blood, although she was not yet bound to Orthros's royal family by the Gift. Her heart knew. She was a traitor to mortal kings, but her immortal prince would have her loyalty for eternity.

"Yes, My Prince," she told him.

He gave a solemn nod, then subjected Lio to his scrutiny. The swell of magic in the air, theramancy and thelemancy, sent a frisson over Cassia's skin.

Rudhira said, "Your father has dragged me out of situations when he was wiser than I. Do not resist and make the same mistake I have in the past."

Lio was silent for an instant longer, then, "I find myself unable to promise I will obey, if it means leaving Cassia's side."

"Do you not trust me to refrain from making unjust requests?" Rudhira asked.

Lio's jaw relaxed. "Of course, Ritual father."

"Then you must promise to heed me, and to let the Charge do our duty—which includes helping you protect Cassia."

Lio bowed his head. "You have my word, My Prince."

Rudhira turned to the Ashes.

Karege spoke up. "Have no doubt, My Prince. I may like my sharp knives and shiny gold, but I have never forgotten I am a Hesperine."

"Carrying a blade does not make you forget," Rudhira said. "I know I can rely on you. As for the mortal veterans of the Ashes, the Charge looks forward to having such esteemed warriors of the gold roster among us. May our battles prosper Orthros's alliance with the Empire, First Blade Kella."

Kella gave him a salute with her silver filigreed fortune blade. "It will be an honor to fight with the Charge. Braving Tenebra is an adventure worthy of the Ashes."

Finally Rudhira stood before Solia. "Princess, I cannot command you. But I urge you to trust that Orthros has your best interests at heart, and to take my counsel into consideration."

"I can promise to consider it," she said, which was hardly a promise at all.

Rudhira's brow raised slightly. "I may be a prince who will never become a king, but I do have considerable experience as a royal and a warrior. I suggest that you make use of all valuable assets at your disposal, including my advice."

Considerable was one way to describe sixteen hundred years of life.

"I appreciate how fortunate I am to have your support," Solia replied, "but I am sure you understand that mortal interests must be my first concern, and mortal advisers may be somewhat closer to the problems facing my subjects."

"As your mortal adviser," Cassia broke in, "I think you will find Hesperines errant more invested in human concerns than other humans. They are kinder to your subjects than your subjects are to one another. Or so I found them to be, the night they saved my life."

Solia paused, surely thinking of Iris's death. "I never disputed that."

Rudhira appeared satisfied with this concession and stepped back. "If you are all ready, I will escort you to the Charge's base of operations near Patria."

It was really happening. They were going back to Tenebra.

Cassia had been preparing herself for this moment all week. Or trying to. But now, none of the visits to the mind healers seemed to matter. Her belly knotted. Her heart raced like a frightened rabbit's. Her skin felt hot under her travel robes, and sweat made Knight's fur stick to her palm as she held onto him.

By the Goddess, she wanted to return to this forsaken kingdom triumphant, unafraid of the specters that had once tormented her. But apparently old, instinctual fears could still rear their ugly heads.

Lio's voice was soothing in her ear. "We don't have to go gracefully. We just have to get ourselves there and back. That's feat enough, don't you think?"

Lio always knew what to say. Even when he was as terrified as she was. But why couldn't *she* be strong for *him* in this moment, instead of standing here in a mess of nerves?

Memories roared in her mind. The crash of an avalanche. The sneers of heart hunters. The flash of magefire. And countless moments kneeling before the king, grinding her down.

His hand came to rest at the base of her neck, his touch cool on her hot skin. "May I help?"

She knew his mind magic could chase her haunted thoughts away. But she refused to need someone else to conquer them for her.

She knew the other Hesperines could smell her fear. The Ashes would recognize the look in her eye from the moment before battle. Rudhira's theramancy could detect her terror from miles away.

She could not fail them. She could do this. She must do this.

Anything for her people. Even Tenebra.

"Please let me help." Lio put his fingers to her racing pulse.

She tried to forgive herself for clinging to his hand. "You are helping. You are at my side every step of the way."

"I will not leave you. Even when I fall into the Dawn Slumber, the mind ward will not."

His power swept into her thoughts, tracing the shape of his ward inside her mind. A reminder to them both of the powerful defenses they had created for her together, wrought not only of his magic, but also her own strength of Will.

She straightened her spine and lifted her chin. She would go with her head high, even if she was on the verge of being sick.

"I'm ready," she declared, and hoped the king felt her words all the way to his royal palace in Solorum.

He should be much more afraid than she was.

"Very well." Rudhira gave a nod of what seemed like approval. "Each Hesperine, please step with one mortal. Follow me carefully."

They paired off, Lio pulling Cassia gently against his side, while Knight pressed against her robes.

Then, with a mere step, home slipped away. They whispered over the border she had fought tooth and nail to cross.

Too easily, too fast, she was standing in Tenebra again.

3

days until

SUMMER SOLSTICE

31th Day of the Month of Chera's Coin
1597 Ordered Time

ON THE CUSP

The scents struck her first. Steel. Wood. Even the dirt smelled different.

But there was still a lingering fragrance of roses, as if they clung to her. She thought she could feel an echo of Sanctuary magic. But that was impossible, wasn't it?

She opened her eyes. Spell light shone through the deep twilight. She glimpsed a broad, open pavilion and a long table. Beyond that, tidy crimson tents. Hesperines going to and fro with silent grace. Chargers approaching Rudhira to welcome their prince back to the field.

Solia was beside Cassia, leaning heavily on her sword, lifting a hand to Mak in thanks. "Still better than a traversal, I admit."

Cassia shut her eyes again. Changing hemispheres in one step was always miserable. If Lio hadn't been holding on to her, she would have suffered a wave of dizziness. He took her hand and set something silky smooth on her palm.

"Look where we are." A hint of wonder had lifted the dread from his voice.

She forced her eyes open once more. In her hand was a scarlet rose with an abundance of petals. She lifted it to her nose, desperate to breathe in its sweet, wild scent.

The vibrant blooms climbed up the stone columns all around them. The pavilion's foundations looked ancient, as did the statue before them. The woman in white temple robes must be Hespera, for she had one eye of red stone. She held a scroll pointing up toward the sky, with her bare foot treading on a fallen sword.

Cassia was safe here. She knew it, because although Knight sniffed the air with perked ears, he did not perform a patrol of the area to check if there was any danger.

Lio touched Cassia's hair. "This is the Summit Sanctuary."

Rudhira pricked his thumb on his fang and made a libation on Hespera's open palm, stroking his hand lovingly over hers. "This is where the Hesperine founders and refugees made camp during the original Equinox Summit."

"I thought that took place at Solorum," Cassia said, "like all the Equinox Summits since."

"Solorum was a construction site at the time," Lio explained. "The Mage King was still cleaning up the debris of war and building his capital. Most of the actual negotiation during the first Equinox Summit was held at Patria, after the Full Council confirmed the Mage King's reign. He guaranteed our people protection here until everything was agreed upon."

"My mother Alea placed the Sanctuary ward on this place herself," Rudhira told them. "Of course they are weaker in her absence, but this place still gives Hesperines errant refuge, after all these centuries."

"This is one of my father's statues," Lio said.

"Of course," Rudhira replied. "He built the pavilion, too."

Cassia held out her hand to Lio. He pricked both their fingers, then rested his hand over hers as she smeared their combined blood onto Hespera's palm. Familiar power pulsed up her arm, straight to her heart.

There was still Hesperine-built stone under her feet. Roses still thrived here. The Goddess watched over this place.

They stood on the last cusp of safety. Tenebra loomed beyond.

Mak and Lyros made their libation next, but Karege didn't join them at the statue. He was guiding Tuura to a chair, and she sank down into it as if about to topple.

"Does our healer need a healer?" Hoyefe asked in dismay.

Tuura shook her head. "No, I only need a moment to adjust."

Solia gathered around her with the Ashes. "Are you all right?"

"Oh, I am." Tuura drew a deep, shaky breath. "But this side of Akanthia most certainly is not."

Kella looked grave. "The magic that cuts the shadowlands off from the spirit phase must be affecting you."

"I cannot describe the Silence." Tuura reached out and took Cassia and Solia's hands as if there had just been a death in the family. "I'm so very sorry you had to grow up here where you cannot hear the voices of your foremothers."

Cassia hated the Old Masters for this. If not for their evil, the Diviner Queen would never have had to close off this continent from the spirit phase and all communication with the ancestors. The Collector and his hex of necromancers had ruined so much in the shadowlands. They had stolen the chance for Cassia to ever speak to her mother's spirit again.

Worst of all, the Collector had put that haunted look in her Grace's eyes.

"I am sorry for your discomfort, diviner," Rudhira said respectfully. "I have it on good authority that you will still be able to use your ancestral magic, although your spells must be adjusted."

Tuura nodded with a thoughtful expression, her breath coming steadier now. "I won't be able to directly channel from the spirit phase, of course, but my soul's connection to my own ancestors should sustain me from within."

"If I can assist in any way, you have but to ask," Rudhira promised.

"I know. But enough fussing over me. We have work to do."

Rudhira pointed out into the camp, where Chargers were stepping in and out of sight with horse-drawn carts. "Your supplies from the Empress will move through here."

Solia's gaze followed the trunks and crates that were levitating and stacking themselves neatly in a supply tent. "I miss spirit gates already."

"I don't blame you for being uneasy that your supply line relies on personal delivery by fanged heretics," Rudhira said without a twitch of his lips.

Solia gave a faint snort. "And I can hardly blame your firstbloods for disliking that Orthros is directly involved in outfitting a human army."

"What army?" Cassia asked innocently. "Orthros's official involvement is purely diplomatic. We are merely fostering trade between our Imperial and Tenebran allies."

"And we have gifts for our allies, as well," Rudhira said. "If you will accompany me."

He led them out of the pavilion and through orderly clusters of vibrant red tents. The paths were marked by low stone walls and time-worn archways, all overgrown with the scarlet roses. At the edge of the camp, the vines gave way to a clearing.

Beyond lay the verge of the Tenebran woods. Cassia drifted to a halt, her robes snagging on thorns, and looked into the shadows between the oak trees. All her senses seemed to follow her gaze, reaching deep into the wild gloom.

"Cassia?" Lio's soft query brought her back. "What do you sense?"

"The forest has...a presence now. Well, I suppose it always has. But now I know it's there." She shook her head.

"That's a promising sign," Lio said, but Cassia did not miss the slight frown on his face as he gently disengaged the thorns from her robes.

She had scarcely noticed that a small herd of the Charge's horses grazed in the clearing. She put Knight in a sit-stay, since the Hesperines' breed of horse, the Orthros Warmblood, did not take kindly to liegehounds.

One of the powerful, elegant warhorses trotted over to Rudhira. The gray mare gazed at him with doe eyes while he stroked her nose. It seemed of all Rudhira's many admirers, here was one lady who held his heart in return.

"Is this your famous familiar, Veil?" Cassia asked.

"Do you hear that, girl?" Rudhira asked the mare. "Your legend precedes you."

Then another image from legend manifested in the clearing. Nike rode into sight out of thin air on Blackthorn, her own warhorse and familiar. A number of other horses followed Blackthorn's lead without a tether.

Rudhira raised a brow at Nike. "Your mother let you leave Orthros?"

"She knows I'm coming back within an hour, not a century." Nike dismounted, straightening her Stand regalia.

"She made me promise I wouldn't try to recruit you into the Charge," Rudhira said. "Your family is determined to keep you on Aunt Nike duty and have you babysit sucklings instead of Hesperines errant."

"That was an easy promise for you to make," Nike returned. "I know you don't want me here, beating you in front of the youngbloods as I did in the arena the other night."

Rudhira's eyes glinted. "On the contrary, I insist on a rematch in front of my Chargers. They'll learn so much watching me defeat the Victory Star."

Blackthorn had trotted over to Veil to exchange greetings. Orthros

Warmbloods had long lifespans and uncanny intelligence. No doubt Rudhira and Nike's familiars had missed each other, too.

Among the other horses, Cassia recognized Mak and Lyros's black familiars and Lio's tall white horse, Moonflower. When she saw who else Nike had brought, her throat grew tight.

The golden warhorse had carried Solia across the Empire, even through the Maaqul to find Cassia. Cassia suspected the mare had been one of her sister's few friends and confidants during her silent years in the Golden Shield.

The horse nudged her head against Solia's chest. Solia murmured to her, running her hand down the mare's neck.

"How did you manage this?" she asked Nike, her voice thick. "She belongs to the Golden Shield. They wouldn't let me take her."

Nike smiled. "Mother breeds all the Golden Shield's horses. She called in a favor to get your girl decommissioned."

Solia rested her face on the mare's forehead. "You have my gratitude."

Karege, Tuura, and Hoyefe had already claimed three other horses. Kella rubbed Tilili's cheek. "I may have no need of a set of hooves myself, but you have my thanks for bringing my Ashes' mounts to them."

There was one horse left. She looked as if she'd danced through a wagon load of cinnamon and emerged with dusted legs, mane, and tail and little spots all over her white body. Unlike the massive Warmbloods bred for tall Hesperines, she was as petite as a woman's palfrey, but too spirited to be a lady's horse, judging by the cross look in her eye.

Lio rested a hand on Moonflower's shoulder. "As much as I enjoy you riding double with me, that mare looks like the right size for you."

"I'm not sure I can handle her," Cassia said, "but I dare hope that little rebel is for me."

"She is," Nike replied. "Mother has been saving her for someone who's a match for her."

"I'll do my best. I'm afraid my only experience is sitting like a display piece on the back of docile creatures." Usually while riding beside Flavian, unfortunately.

And Lio knew it. His tone perfectly innocent, he said, "You do very well on our rides. You have an excellent seat."

She tried not to blush, thinking of how their wild rides on Moonflower usually took them to a secluded place for an entirely different sort of ride.

"A woman needs her own horse," Nike said firmly. "First, let her sniff you. Then, once she's had a chance to smell who you are, get acquainted by blowing in each other's nostrils."

Sniff. Share breath. Cassia could do this. She was excellent with dogs. She could learn the ways of horses, too.

Cassia held out her hand. The mare put her ears back and snorted.

"Not so easily impressed, are you?" Cassia mused.

"She's self-reliant," Nike said.

"I can understand that." Cassia met the mare's gaze. Her eyes were startling. Rather than the solid brown eyes of most horses, she had white irises like a human.

Cassia reached for the feeling she had when she was speaking the training tongue to Knight. A moment of connection, when it seemed as if he might speak right back to her. "I'm looking for a horse who isn't intimidated by evil kings and necromancers. You seem like just the one."

The mare twitched her tail, then stretched out her neck and gave Cassia's hand a sniff.

Cassia leaned forward. A little more. She blew gently in the mare's nose. Her nostrils flared, and she puffed back. Her breaths warmed Cassia outside and in.

"I'm Cassia," she said. "Who are you?"

"Celeris's baby," Nike answered.

"Celeris?" Solia asked. "Isn't she the founding mare of the Orthros Warmblood breed?"

Nike nodded. "My mother's familiar, who carried her across Tenebra to evacuate Hesperite villages during the Last War. Mother doesn't breed her anymore, but Celeris has a mind of her own. When Mother secured breeding rights to an Imperial stud with rare red leopard markings, she was planning to pair him with one of the warhorses. Imagine her surprise when she realized Celeris was in foal. When this filly dropped, it was obvious who her papa was. It's no secret she can get in and out of any gate she pleases, but she really pulled the veil over our eyes that time."

Cassia gasped at the mare and covered her mouth. "Why, you are the lovechild of a forbidden tryst. How delightful."

Nike gestured to Knight. "Let's see how well she tolerates a liegehound."

With a hand on the mare's neck, Nike led her away from the other horses. Cassia called Knight over. At the sight of a liegehound racing toward her, the spotted mare merely looked bored.

"Not afraid of liegehounds," Lio said with approval. "A necessary skill for anyone who intends to be part of your life."

Cassia slid her fingers through the mare's mane. Knight nudged his head under her other hand, jealous for pets. She hugged him against her. The three of them might make a fine company...except... "I'm not much of a horsewoman."

"Good," was Solia's unexpected response. "It will be easier for you to unlearn Tenebran riding and adopt Imperial or Hesperine styles."

Cassia started to protest that the daughter of Celeris was too special a steed for someone like her, but then stopped herself.

She was Cassia Komnena. She needed a truly Hesperine horse for her own.

"I love her," she confessed. "Does she have a name?"

Nike explained, "A Warmblood takes her name when she and her rider begin their new life together."

Elegant flower names ran through Cassia's mind, but none suited such a defiant girl. Cassia smirked and patted her horse's speckled side. "I'll call her Freckles, and I dare anyone to underestimate either of us."

She managed to put a smile on Lio's face with that.

"She'll carry you through whatever this quest demands of you." Nike rested her hands on Cassia's arms. "I'm sorry we've traded places. I'd hoped we could both stay on the same side of the border."

"So did I. But I feel better knowing you have our backs, and that Orthros has you." It might not be official until after her Gifting, but in Cassia's heart, Nike was already her Ritual mother. She knew she could trust her with her life. And probably embarrassing questions, too. Cassia mustered her dignity. "I find myself in need of advice on a rather personal matter."

Nike's veil spell rose immediately. "The horse paddock is an excellent place for female confidences, in my experience."

With Freckles nosing at her pockets in search of treats, Cassia couldn't disagree. "I, ah, have concerns about mages being able to sense…how close Lio and I are. When we first met, he assured me our secret meetings weren't enough to alert anyone. Then, when we spent more time together during the Solstice Summit, I had a pendant imbued with Sanctuary magic that concealed any Hesperine magic on me. But that was destroyed in the duel with the Collector."

"You're wise to take this into consideration."

Cassia hesitated, but decided that what she was about to reveal was probably no secret to Nike. "You are one of the few who can sense Lio's mind ward on me, aren't you?"

"Yes. Possibly the only one, aside from my father and Ioustin. Lio did excellent work. Far too subtle for most Hesperines to notice, much less clumsy Tenebran mages."

"Could war mages tell the ward is there with their specialized anti-Hesperine spells?"

"Not even them," Nike assured her. "A mind mage that serves Hypnos is another matter. But I know you are already on alert against the mage of dreams."

Cassia suppressed a shudder. "Will war mages be able to sense…anything else?" She felt a blush rise to her cheeks. "In my blood?"

Seldom had such a teasing smile appeared on Nike's face. "Worried they'll notice Lio's magical handprints all over you?"

Cassia's blush intensified. "Yes!"

"They do have spells for detecting if someone has been bitten by a Hesperine. Those are some of the most difficult for us to avoid and combat."

Cassia's heart sank.

"However," Nike went on, "there's one Hesperine errant who has been working on experimental thelemancy to conceal the magical signature of the Drink, or even the Feast. It's rather dangerous research, only possible where there are war mages about for testing purposes."

Cassia felt her eyes widen. "That Hesperine errant wouldn't happen to be my Ritual mother, would she?"

"You're in luck." Amusement lightened Nike's gray eyes. "I've spent a great deal of time in Cordium under the war mages' noses, and I have to eat."

"I'd love to hear tales of your experiments, especially if they were romantic."

"Ioustin will have to beat those out of me in the arena. But I'll stay here for another hour or two and show Lio how to cast the spells I've developed."

"Thank you. I hate that he must endure all of this for the sake of my magic. But at least your spells will allay one of his fears."

Nike might still harbor doubts about her stalled quest for her lost Trial brother, but none of that showed in her now. "Do not regret your quest. Do not feel guilty, even when it burdens those we love. If I have learned anything in sixteen hundred years of life, it's that the most important things are the hardest won."

UNDER TENEBRAN LAW

CASSIA TRAILED HER FINGERS over the roses for reassurance as she reentered the pavilion, her other hand in Lio's. Now that Nike had departed, it somehow felt as if home were truly far away.

Rudhira strode around the table, his Tenebran riding boots making a distinctive thud on the stone floor. Organized maps, correspondence, and sketches were spread across the timber tabletop, and an empty wooden notice board stood to one side, ready to be hung with key documents.

Lio paused to skim a scroll, then glanced at Cassia. She picked out enough words to recognize it. They had read a longer version of this dispatch in Uncle Argyros's library during a strategy session where Solia had not been present.

The authors of the dispatch were also notably absent. Basir and Kumeta, the Queens' Master Envoys. It seemed Orthros's spymasters had no intention of introducing themselves to the presumptive Queen of Tenebra. Cassia, Lio, and Rudhira would have to selectively relate the spies' findings to Solia.

Cassia picked up a dish of pins with colorful glass heads and stood before the largest map, which showed Orthros Boreou, Tenebra, and Cordium. Now that she had been to the Empire, the shadowlands seemed smaller to her than ever. So why did Tenebra feel enormous, like some behemoth breathing down her neck from the other side of the ward over this Sanctuary?

She moved her hand past Solorum, Tenebra's capital at the center of the map. Between Solorum and the eastern forests, where Patria was marked, she placed a green pin. "Here is the letting site."

Solia winced. "Yes, but it may be too much to hope that it's conveniently underfoot at the council location. Patria is a fairly large domain. Do you recall what else is there? Grounds with game? The king used to hunt there, didn't he?"

Cassia paused to think, scratching Knight's ears with her free hand. The fact that she must pause at all made her frown. The answer to Solia's question should have come instantly to her mind. She had once hoarded such details, never knowing what slice of information might be of use, or even save her life.

"I suppose he didn't send me there often, if at all, not if he hunted there." The king had always preferred to keep the bastard out of sight, which thankfully meant she did not need to tolerate his presence often.

Lyros put a reassuring hand on her arm. "We'll be there to help you locate it. The search will go quickly with Hesperine aid."

Mak waved a hand over the green pin. "I can't imagine a great heap of leaking magic will be too difficult to find. You'll be able to sense it, won't you, Cassia?"

"I'm not sure," she admitted. "Kalos mentioned that some letting sites are carefully hidden."

"You can ask him when he joins us," Rudhira said.

Solia plucked a pin from the dish in Cassia's hand and offered the red marker to Rudhira. "May I ask where we are now?"

He did not take the pin, only circled a finger over a swath of forest to the east of Patria. "Somewhere in this vicinity. I suggest not wandering out of the camp unless you have a Hesperine with you to assist with your return. This place is rather difficult to find from the outside."

"Hmm." Solia placed the red pin in the forest. "We must be at least a day's ride from Patria."

"A polite distance," Rudhira said. "Regretfully, the Charge is not welcome too near the Council. The Allied Lords are still cautious about showing open friendship with Hesperines, lest they frighten Tenebrans less sympathetic to our cause."

Lio sighed. "There is a great deal of work to be done persuading the rest of the kingdom to take the Allied Lords' view."

"Meanwhile," said Rudhira, "we support them from here, and Flavian sends his intermediaries to consult us. To get near the letting site, you will have to secure an invitation for the Hesperine delegation to attend the Council in a diplomatic role."

As they studied the map, Chargers came in and out of the pavilion, saluting Rudhira before conferring with him under veils. They smiled at Lio, Cassia, Mak, and Lyros. She recognized the Hesperines errant from the Solstice Summit, when they had guarded the guest houses. She wondered if they would not have concealed their conversations if Solia had not been present. Then again, Rudhira kept plenty of secrets from his own youngbloods.

Cassia selected a brown pin and positioned it next to the green one at Patria. "Flavian has been camped here for over a month."

Rudhira said, "We received news he has taken up residence in Castra Patria, the castle that overlooks the council grounds."

"Bold," Lio said, "but by right, the most powerful free lords may claim chambers in the castle for the duration of the Council."

Solia pursed her lips. "How many of the other free lords have joined him at Patria?"

"A quorum," Cassia answered, "enough to convene the Full Council without the king's approval. Flavian has told Lucis this is merely an effort to unite the lords against threats facing Tenebra, for the peace and stability of the kingdom. Officially, choosing a new king has never entered anyone's thoughts."

Solia rolled her eyes. "Flavian always did have a pretty excuse for his misbehavior. But Lucis will never believe that."

"He is too suspicious of everything and everyone," Cassia agreed, "but he underestimates Flavian, who has always done his bidding. Lucis will never suspect Flavian of being the mastermind behind an overthrow."

"That's because he isn't." Lio narrowed his eyes. A sketch of the lord in question levitated off the table and flattened itself onto the board. A few pins shot into it with unnecessary force, narrowly missing Flavian's charming face.

To Cassia's dismay, Knight growled at the sketch. He had become more attuned to Lio's emotions than she had realized.

"Lord Flavian of Segetia," Lio said, "is a mediocre man who has been handed a plot by an extraordinary woman. Don't give him credit for your brilliance, Cassia."

"That is something we can agree on," Solia said.

Lyros attempted and failed to pry one of the pins out of Flavian's hair. "Easy there, Ambassador. Fool though he may be, Flavian is still necessary to our strategy for the time being."

Mak patted Lio on the shoulder. "Don't make me haul your ass out of a jinn prison again."

"Flavian is no jinn," was Lio's icy reply.

"For such a peaceful fellow," Hoyefe mused, "you must have a compelling reason for this grudge."

"Lyros is right," Cassia cut in, "we need to focus on Flavian's role in our plans."

Hoyefe crossed his arms, standing back to admire the sketch. "He's rather appealing, for a Tenebran barbarian. I dare say his sword skills and roguish dimple win hearts all across the kingdom. I can tell there's a story here."

Cassia steered them back to the subject. "Flavian doesn't lack political acumen. His flaw is his desire to please everyone. But we can use that to your advantage, Solia. If he were a more ambitious man, it would be harder to persuade him to give up the plot I constructed for him."

Solia glanced between the sketch and Lio, but seemed to decide she had more pressing concerns. She plucked a sky-blue pin out of the dish and twirled it between her fingers with quiet menace. "And where is the king?"

"Still inside Solorum Palace," Lio said, "as far as we know."

Cassia swallowed. Solorum might be hundreds of miles away, but it didn't feel far enough. She was on the same continent as the king again.

Yes, she was. And so was Solia. *They* were closing in on *him,* she reminded herself.

Solia pinned the capital. "Coward. I look forward to my reunion with my father after all these years. I have such surprises in store for him."

Cassia was not ready to think that far ahead. If all went according to plan, there would come a moment of reckoning when the king's fate would be decided. She feared if she delved into her heart too closely, she would find vengeful wishes not befitting a Hesperine peacemaker.

She put a hand on her sister's. "You must not reveal yourself to Lucis until we are fully prepared to confront him. We must conceal your presence in the kingdom from him and his spies at all costs."

"Don't worry," Solia replied. "I know when to hold my fire. I must first secure the Council's mandate and win Lord Hadrian away from Lucis. Then I will have the legitimacy and the forces to quell any retaliation he attempts."

"Lio..." Cassia brought him into the conversation, knowing that Solia would not, although they needed his insights. "How do you think the Mage Orders will respond at that point?"

Solia interjected, "I am keeping my magic a secret for the time being. They will have no grounds to object to me."

"True," Lio replied, "and they may decide it is in their best interests to discard the deposed king. It's possible they will officially recognize the Council's decision and start courting your favor. They may regard a woman as easier to control, and you can use that miscalculation to your advantage."

"That mistake will be very dangerous for them," Solia mused.

Lio hesitated. "It is also possible they will decide that keeping Lucis on the throne is more favorable to their ambitions. We must prevent the Mage Orders from fighting at Lucis's side in a civil war against you and the Allied Lords."

"Yes." On this, Solia did not hesitate to voice her agreement with Lio. "That is not how I want my reign to begin."

"We can provide you with the bargaining power you will need, if it comes to that." Lio fixed an orange pin beside the brown and green ones. "Chrysanthos, Dexion of the Aithourian Circle. For his acts of sabotage during the Solstice Summit, we sent him to Tenebra as the Allied Lords' hostage."

Solia gave a low whistle.

"What makes this man a valuable prisoner?" Kella asked.

Lio explained, "The Order of Anthros rules supreme over all other Mage Orders, and the Aithourian Circle is a small group within it that holds the greatest power. They control all war mages in the shadowlands. Men with the affinity for fire, lightning, or other magic with battle applications are forced to join the Aithourians in Corona, capital of Cordium."

Cassia stabbed a pin into Corona, the so-called Divine City. "The Dexion is second-in-command and future successor to the Aithrourians' leader. But also, secretly, his bastard son."

Hoyefe shook his head. "Tracing one's parentage through one's mother is so much more sensible. But the Tenebrans' preoccupation with sires and shame is useful to us in this case, I suppose."

"You have a prize hostage for me, along with secrets I can use to blackmail him?" Solia arched a brow. "This will certainly improve my position if the mages support Lucis…and when it is time to reckon with them about my magic. Have the Orders made any official response to the Council yet?"

Rudhira crossed his arms. "They have quietly provided a war circle of Aithourian mages to reinforce Lord Hadrian's soldiers."

When had the envoys brought this bad news? Cassia bit back a curse. "At least we can rely on Lord Hadrian to be unhappy that they've been foisted on him."

"We will have to plan our approach to him carefully." Lio grimaced.

"Very carefully," Rudhira warned. "Those Aithourians may well be able to detect you through your veil spells, and they will certainly alert the king to any Hesperine presence."

"Would you show me where Lord Hadrian's army is?" Solia handed him a blue pin.

Rudhira placed the pin to the west of Patria, between there and Solorum. "He is entrenched here, a buffer between the lords and the king."

Solia nodded. "Despite the Aithourians, Lord Hadrian's presence should discourage open conflict, and not only because of his military might. He is in favor with both the king and a large faction of the lords."

"Yes," Cassia said, "he is still the only man in Tenebra whose loyalty Lucis does not question, and the Hadrian side of the feuds is still a powerful force in the nobility."

Solia shook her head at Flavian's brown pin and Lord Hadrian's dark blue one facing off on the map. "Segetia and Hadria still have not laid down their rivalry?"

"I have seen it nearly ruin my friends' lives," Cassia said. "Flavian's and Lord Hadrian's families have not engaged in open conflict since Lucis became king, but the hatred between Segetia and Hadria endures."

Solia turned to her. "If I antagonize one side or the other, it will be disastrous not only for my campaign, but could plunge the entire kingdom back into the chaos of the feuds. In your opinion, whom should I approach first? Flavian or Lord Hadrian?"

"Possibly the most crucial political decision we will face," Cassia said. "Thank you for trusting me with this question."

"Of course." Her sister raised a brow. "As Lio said, you are the one who spoon-fed Flavian his strategy. We are both princesses who have aspired to the Tenebran throne. We will combine my plan with yours—and build upon the plot Thalia left for us."

Solia's confidence was dangerously contagious. But it was Cassia's duty, as her adviser and a diplomat for Orthros, to remain cautious. "I believe you are already assured of Hadrian's loyalty. He will not hold it against you if you approach Flavian first. On the other hand, if you approach Lord Hadrian first, Segetia might think you favor their enemy. Worse, it might also align you with Lucis. That is the very last message you wish to send to the lords upon your triumphant return. Lio, would you agree?"

"Yes," he replied. "It is in your best interests to focus on courting the lords who are assembling in resistance to Lucis's rule. You live in Tenebra's memory as the hope of rescue from the king. You have only to step into that role. Your cult is strong."

Solia stood back from the map. "My 'cult'?"

"I don't think you realize," Cassia said. "The way Tenebra has mourned you is a kind of worship. You're more than merely a beloved, fallen princess. You are a symbol of a future that died with you."

"But the lords still have no inkling that I'm alive."

Cassia placed a golden pin at Solorum, where the royal crypt lay. "No, they believe it was you, not Iris, who perished. But when I told them the truth—that the Hesperines collected the remains of the fallen that night—they opened the royal crypt to find there was no body in your tomb. They know the king abandoned you to be desecrated, then held a mockery of a funeral. Next, we must convince them your death was a lie, too."

Solia picked up a sketch of Lord Hadrian. The envoys had captured the strength of character in his lined face. "Do you think Lord Hadrian will recognize his lost princess in a woman who could best him on the battlefield?"

Karege scratched his head through his legendary cloud of hair. "One who bunks with foreign heretics."

"And reads highly subversive literature," Tuura said with a rueful expression.

"And loves where she will," Hoyefe put in.

Kella snickered. "Don't forget she swears like a mercenary."

"You're one to talk, Princess Kella," Solia shot back.

"This is why we must be thoughtful about how we present you to your people," Cassia said. "Leave that to me. When I'm done with you, Lord Hadrian will know in his heart that you are his true queen."

Solia pinned Lord Hadrian's portrait next to Flavian. "Very well. Once we have secured Flavian's cooperation, we will approach Lord Hadrian in secret."

"Oh, yes, I fully intend to secure Flavian's cooperation," Lio said, but he was looking at Cassia, and she knew he was not talking about Flavian's support for her sister.

"I'm sure that will be the least of the obstacles facing us," she tried to reassure him.

Solia's eyes narrowed. "What obstacle?"

Lio's tone was as frigid as a deadly blizzard in Martyr's Pass. "Under Tenebran law, Cassia is still betrothed to Flavian."

LIO FOUGHT THE URGE to tear the envoys' sketch of Flavian from the board and obliterate it with a spell.

He could do better than such an act of petty vengeance. He had reunited with his medallion and his training in steering kingdoms out of wars. He would find an intelligent, civilized way to crush this mortal's designs on his Grace.

Solia rounded on Cassia. "Betrothed? To Flavian of all people?"

Cassia waved a hand too deliberately. "An inconvenient detail."

"A crown isn't enough for him?" Solia demanded.

"He presumes to claim Cassia's hand as well." Lio's fangs were ready to unsheathe.

Hoyefe studied Flavian's portrait again. "I don't see the problem. He looks like a fun choice for a threesome."

Solia pinched the bridge of her nose, dousing a small flame. "And it's already legalized? Kyria's tits."

"Language, Princess!" Kella scolded her with a wicked grin.

The more strongly Solia reacted, Cassia only became more composed. Lio recognized the telltale signs of his Grace going on the defense. The rigid spine. The cool tone.

They had just set foot in Tenebra, and she was already transforming back into Lady Circumspect.

Lio hated this place.

Cassia ran a hand calmly over Knights' back. "It was hardly my idea, but when the king and Flavian's father betrothed us, I was handed nettles and did my best to make nettle tea."

Nettle tea. That was how she described her onetime plan to actually marry Flavian and become Queen of Tenebra.

Cassia set aside the map pins. "We can use this to our advantage."

Her words put Lio back in a courtyard of white roses in Orthros, where he had offered her everything, and she had told him she would doom them to her political union with Flavian.

"Nothing about Flavian is an 'advantage,'" Lio bit out.

Cassia's hand slid into his then, small and strong and dear. "I think releasing him from the betrothal will be a prospect we can use to tempt him."

Lio tightened his hand around hers. "Last time you spoke to him, he had every intention of marrying you."

"So much has changed. I fear the greatest threat now will be a betrothal between him and Solia. Many will see such a marriage as the ideal solution to the contested succession."

Solia laughed out loud. "As if I would ever take a lapdog like him for a husband."

Lio wanted to suggest an eagle instead, but he doubted reminders of Tendo would endear him to his Grace-sister at the moment.

"There is some hope he has come to his senses," Cassia said. "If we can persuade him to marry the woman he loves, it would be extremely useful."

"Which woman?" Solia asked. "I dare say he has loved half the females in Tenebra. Although love has little to do with what's in his breeches."

Hoyefe sighed. "He's no fun after all."

"He stopped chasing skirts a few years ago," Cassia said, "when Lady Sabina of Hadria made him her conquest."

"This Sabina sounds like a capable woman," Kella mused.

"She is," Cassia assured them. "Unfortunately, she's Lord Hadrian's daughter."

"Sabina and Flavian?" Solia was laughing again. "She can do better. But I suppose I can see my old friend making him *her* lapdog."

"If they offer to solve the feud for you," Cassia said, "I suggest you encourage it."

"I'm more interested in encouraging alliance marriages with Imperial noblemen," Solia said. "We shall see if any Tenebran lady's fascination with Flavian survives their encounters with more civilized men. In any case, Flavian will have to do without the crown, your hand, and mine."

"It is no trivial task to dissolve a betrothal." Lio had no illusions this was a minor inconvenience when they were trying not to antagonize Flavian, who was nearly king. If he could think of half a dozen ways it could cause political problems, he was sure Cassia could think of a dozen.

She said nothing, but she also had no clever reply. A silent admission he was right.

"I cannot disagree." Rudhira gripped Lio's shoulder in sympathy. "Do not misunderstand me. Cassia's betrothal is an injustice in Hesperine eyes. But Tenebran morals being what they are, if Orthros's ambassador romances a mortal lord's betrothed, it could cause retaliation against our Hesperines errant. You two will need to be discreet until the betrothal is resolved."

Lio could not have borne the admonition from anyone else. But he could not argue with this wisdom coming from Rudhira, who had thoroughly disregarded Tenebran morals in mortal women's arms for centuries.

"I know," Lio said.

Rudhira gave a nod and released him.

"Lio and I are done with secrecy," Cassia protested.

It was a consolation that she was willing to advocate for something so impossible, when she knew the political delicacy of the situation better than anyone.

But it was still impossible.

He touched her medallion, and for the first time, the disc around her neck felt heavy. "We must not do anything to harm Hesperines' reputation in Tenebra, which could bring harm on our people."

Her aura burned with a sense of injustice, but then her gaze dropped. "I would never do anything to put them at risk."

Lio hated the words, but he said them. "You still need your reputation among the Tenebrans, as well, if you are to have a place at your sister's side."

That earned him a rare concession from Solia. "Lio is right. Don't do anything to endanger your position here. Rest assured that once I take the throne, I will have the power to dissolve the betrothal."

"We need a faster solution," Cassia insisted.

Lio rested a hand on her lower back, and he was satisfied with the little shiver that went through her body at his touch. "You nearly died for the treaty with the Allied Lords. We will not do anything that places that victory at risk. But we will make it clear to Flavian that his claim is null. I will find a way."

Solia fixed her gaze on him. "Do not do anything rash."

He put a hand on his medallion. "I, a Hesperine diplomat? I would never."

Her eyes narrowed.

"Lio will not need to do anything." Cassia's aura tightened with anger. "I dare that betrothal to survive my first conversation with Flavian."

Kalos's arrival interrupted her. While he paused to greet Knight, she pressed her lips together for a moment. When she turned to him, she gave him a smile and tapped the green pin. "Any inkling where the letting site at Patria might be?"

"I'm afraid not," Kalos said. "I'd go scouting for you, but my intrusion would break our agreement with the Allied Lords."

Lio said, "Not if they never knew you were there."

"Oh, I could dance on the council table without the lords noticing,"

Kalos agreed. "It's the Cordian war mage who gives me pause. I've gotten in and out of the Magelands and lived to tell the tale, so I wouldn't mind a secret scouting trip to Patria under the Dexion's nose, except that the consequences could be far worse."

Cassia's aura sharpened with protectiveness. "What could be worse than you being taken prisoner by the Mage Orders for being a heretic trespassing in their territory?"

"Mortal politics," Kalos said. "I don't want to ruin all our diplomats' hard work, or Solia's overthrow, or start a civil war."

"And we don't want to put you in that position." Cassia sighed. "Surely it won't be too difficult for me to find the letting site. Won't I sense it?"

Kalos tilted his head. "It's hard to say. It depends on how your ancestors hid it. But if the Changing Queen intended you to find it one day, I think you'll know it when you're near. It will draw you."

"We're grateful for everything you've done," Lio said, his heart heavy. "Our delegation, with Solia's help, will have to search for the letting site."

Lio could not leave Cassia in the protection of the Summit Sanctuary while someone else faced danger for her. Not only did politics make that impossible, but she would never stand for it.

"The Hesperine delegation will find welcome at Patria," Lio continued. "When the allied lords departed Orthros after the Solstice Summit, they invited Cassia and me to return to Tenebra with them. I believe now is when we should take them up on their offer."

Mak smirked. "And they'll have to tolerate a couple of warriors in the bargain."

Lyros nodded. "I don't think they will object to our presence. We earned their respect in the gymnasium during the Summit."

"Tilili is an excellent hunter," Kella spoke up, "and quite sensitive to magic. She and I can assist with the search too."

"I also wonder," said Tuura, "if channeling the natural phase has anything in common with channeling the spirit phase, perhaps I could adapt my spells for detecting spirit tears."

Cassia took a deep breath. "We can do this."

Solia hung the map on the board and turned to Rudhira. "How soon can we speak with Flavian's intermediaries?"

Rudhira gestured to the long table piled high with threats and unsolved problems. "Their next visit is tomorrow night. You have until then to prepare."

Lio shook his head, staring once more at the map. "We're not ready."

Solia frowned at the map pins. "We've accounted for everyone."

Cassia offered the pins to Lio. "What are we missing?"

"The one enemy we can never pin down." Lio swept a hand across the map. "The Collector could be anywhere. He already is everywhere. He could speak to us through anyone, at any time."

Solia's tone was calm. "We spent our last week in Orthros planning how we will keep Cassia safe. She will never be without our protection."

Rudhira offered a slight blow in Tuura's direction. "You could ask for no better expert on necromancy than an Imperial mind healer. Combined with your knowledge from battling him, Lio, you and Tuura have the magic you need to detect possessions. And I am only a step away."

"And the Stand is right here." Mak crossed his arms. "If that leech tries to pull something dramatic at the Council the way he did at the Solstice Summit, this time Lyros's and my wards will shield everyone from his tantrums."

Perhaps they were right. Was Lio simply giving into his fears for his Grace? Or was this sneaking dread a reliable intuition, born of his experience with his enemy?

The Collector was the opposite of Lucis. He would not choose the most practical or efficient route to victory. He enjoyed toying with his prey. He lived for complicated games of deception. He'd had epochs to perfect the plots he spun in his intelligent, corrupt mind.

Whatever he had in store, Lio feared it would take them completely by surprise.

Perhaps they could not plan for it at all. They could only do their best to react when the blow came.

2

days until

SUMMER SOLSTICE

32 Chera's Coin, 1597 OT

SCION ANGARA

CASSIA WOKE LONG BEFORE she was rested, the pit of her stomach burning. Her pulse pounded, a frenzied contrast to Lio's Slumbering heart. She wrapped her arms and legs around him, as if his unbreathing body could somehow still her own gasping.

Eventually she remembered to breathe as the mind healers had taught her. She recited their kind advice in her mind like prayers. At last, her body calmed, and her thoughts were once again her own.

She clung to him a moment longer in the bespelled darkness, hiding from the day beyond their tent. She was glad he was oblivious to her battle with her fears.

At last she dragged herself from their cot, exhausted. Knight leapt up from the floor and wallowed into the space she had vacated. The cot shook, hardly intended for a Hesperine of bloodborn height and a liegehound. He whined, resting his head on his paws, his tail draping over Lio's sleeping face.

Wearily, she laughed. "How I would like to stay in bed, too, dearest. I know we don't want to leave Lio. But I'm afraid Flavian's emissaries are coming in a few hours. We must be ready. I need my Knight with me today."

She didn't even have to give him a command. He abandoned the cot and stayed with her as she dressed and gathered the pack of what she would need to help Solia prepare.

At the door of the tent, the familiar tether pulled at her heart. A fear far more instinctual than any induced by the king. Her blood was telling her not to leave her Grace, that the Craving was waiting for her when she let him out of her sight.

She practiced her breathing again, giving herself that time. They needn't do this gracefully, as Lio had said. She was here, and she was trying, wasn't she?

She managed to leave the tent. Evening light shone in her eyes, and she squinted in disgust. She enjoyed the luxurious sun of the Empire. Orthros's rare sunlight glittering on fresh snow was beautiful. But this was Tenebran sun, the chariot of Anthros, supreme god of war and order. Cassia cursed him and made a rude gesture at the sky.

There were no Hesperines awake to mock the god of war with her. A shiver of loneliness skittered down her spine. She walked past Mak and Lyros's silent tent, toward the only sound in the Sanctuary. Human voices. Light and a curl of fragrant smoke spilled out of the open flap of Solia's tent.

Her voice sounded different when she spoke Tradewinds. Freer, richer somehow. Then there came a peal of her laughter. "I've never seen a man throw down his spear so fast."

"I think he pissed himself after taking one look at you." That was Kella.

"It was the most unsatisfying battle of our career!" Hoyefe scoffed. "Sunburn scared them all away before I even drew my sword."

"They stole her books!" Tuura exclaimed. "What did you expect?"

"And my books weren't all they left behind," Solia said with satisfaction. "You must admit, their abandoned gold was a beautiful sight."

Just out of their view, Cassia hesitated, holding Knight back. She didn't want to bring Solia's responsibilities into this rare moment of uncomplicated happiness with her mercenary family.

But Tuura must have sensed her, for the mind healer called, "Shadow! Come join us. We just brewed a fresh pot of coffee."

Cassia could not say no to coffee. She went inside, and Solia patted an empty floor cushion beside her. Cassia set down her pack and joined her sister.

Kella poured her a cup of coffee from the pot brewing over the fire. Tilili lounged beside her, resting her chin on one of Kella's residual limbs above where her knee had once been. The cat opened her eyes to slits and deigned to purr at Knight.

After three cups of coffee and another tale of her sister's deeds had revived Cassia, Kella and Tuura sent Hoyefe on his way.

"This strategy session is for women only," Kella told him.

"But I am an expert on fashion," he protested. "Sunburn needs the advice of a cultured aristocrat from the Imperial capital more than that of a feral desert princess and a scrollworm from a peanut village."

Throwing playful insults right back at him, they banished him.

Kella sat Solia down on a camp stool and ran her indigo-stained hands through Solia's golden hair. "Let us see what we can do to turn you back into a princess."

Solia made a face. "Only if I get to be a princess who's as deadly as you are."

Cassia handed Solia a large hand mirror of the clearest Orthros glass, and Kella looked at their reflections in it over Solia's shoulder, pressing her brown cheek to Solia's fair one. The image struck Cassia, so similar and yet so different from the times when Iris had sat Solia down at her dressing table to assist her before formal events.

Iris would have loved Kella. She would be happy Solia had a true friend now.

Tuura set out a collection of pots on her travel desk. "My alchemy is still something of an experimental process as I adjust my ancestral spells for the Silence, but these should suffice."

Cassia eyed a hint of razor burn on Tuura's cheeks. The diviner had a shaving cream she swore by to help her with the inconveniences of the male body her female spirit inhabited. It seemed that mixture needed adjusting as well. "I think Tenebran and Imperial alchemy can strengthen each other, judging by some of the concoctions we brew in Orthros. Have you thought about adding some northern lavender and honey to your aloe cream?"

"Oh, what an excellent idea," Tuura said. "We should mix it together and see if ancestral channeling and Lustra channeling play nicely."

"I would love to." Cassia glanced at Kella, who was joking about skinning snakes while braiding Solia's hair, and lowered her voice. "I wonder if you might also help me with another potion."

Tuura looked at her with concern. "Of course, Shadow. Are you well?"

"I will manage. But it would be easier to manage with alchemy." Cassia rarely confessed her episodes to anyone except Lio and the Hesperine mind healers, but today, she was determined. She tried to describe the symptoms of her fear as factually as possible. "I need something for the daylight hours when Lio can't help me."

Tuura embraced her, her plump arms soft and strong. "I'm so glad you asked me, Shadow. After we help your sister get dressed, we'll mix a batch of shaving cream and my tonic for battle survivors."

Cassia hugged her back fiercely.

"What do you think?" Kella asked, gesturing to Solia's hair.

She had tamed Solia's plain thatch of cropped hair into elaborate braids against her head, woven with silver Azarqi charms shaped like feathers.

"Oh, marvelous," Cassia exclaimed. "You can carry a bit of the Empire with you, Soli."

Solia touched the silver filigreed charms. "Always."

"And they're imbued with Azarqi quiet spells," Kella explained, "to obscure our conversations when the Hesperines can't help us along with veils."

Tuura transformed Solia's face next, and when she was done, one would never know Solia wore cosmetics at all. But the potions softened her sun-spotted complexion with a healthy glow, brought out the blue of her eyes, and turned her chapped lips smooth and rosy.

Finally, Cassia brought out the treasures stored in her pack. She held up a sky-blue gown of fine linen, embroidered in silver. "This would be appropriate for your first encounter with Flavian's representatives."

Solia raised her brows. "How did you find me a wardrobe fit for an aspiring queen, in the latest Tenebran fashions, in only a few days?"

"I asked Kassandra. The Oracle already had a trove of gowns ready for you. I think much of what comes off her loom begins in her visions of the future. And it's a good thing, too, because I saw what you packed. Were you really planning to make your first impression on the lords of Tenebra in battle gear?"

"The thought had admittedly crossed my mind," Solia answered.

Cassia mentally apologized to Uncle Argyros for using violent analogies, but she needed to speak Solia's language right now. "This meeting with Flavian's emissaries is only the opening skirmish, but the impression you make on them now will set the tone for what is to come."

Kella was shaking her head. "Cassia is right. You must dress for the occasion."

"You wear armor in your mother's tent all the time," Solia groused.

"But when the royals of the Azarqi camps assemble, I dress like a princess, not a mercenary. My blades are still there, even when I am wearing silk. Ukocha taught us to fight in dresses, full armor, or nothing at all. It's not as if you can't behead someone while wearing a skirt."

"Indeed," Cassia said, "but the lords don't know that. If they underestimate your skirts, your sword will have a greater advantage of surprise when you finally draw it."

Solia rose from the camp stool. "Very well. Armor me for a princess's battle."

"It will be my honor." Cassia began to unfasten Solia's Vardaran tunic, while Kella and Tuura set aside her blades for the time being. "Allow me to give you some information on Flavian's intermediaries."

Solia's expression lightened. "Excellent. Do we know whom he's sending, then?"

"And what languages they speak?" Kella asked. "All the Ashes learned Divine from Karege."

Kella left the rest unsaid. Tendo had been the only one to learn Vulgus, the language of Tenebra, Solia's mother tongue.

"Both of Flavian's intermediaries are fluent in Divine," Cassia assured her. "We won't need anyone to translate from the vulgar tongue."

"They're not mages, are they?" Solia asked warily.

"One of them is, but he's an ally. Eudias is a former member of the Aithourian Circle who defected to the Allied Lords' side in protest against the war mages' abuses."

"Ah," Tuura said, "is he the young mage whom Lio freed from the Collector?"

"Yes, Lio saved his life." Cassia helped her sister slip into a fine cream-colored tunica.

"Does he know about you and Lio?" Solia asked.

"Well, I don't trust anyone outside of Orthros that much." Cassia lifted the gown, Tuura and Kella guiding it so it didn't disturb Solia's braids and cosmetics.

"And the other emissary?" Solia asked, smoothing the embroidery along her chest with one hand.

Cassia adjusted the laces of the gown. "He was eight when you last saw him. Iris was distressed about a spider in your hearth room. He caught it for her, and I helped him let it out in the garden. You gave us figs from the king's prize Cordian trees, which we were never allowed to eat."

"Benedict?" Solia sounded as surprised as Cassia had expected.

Cassia nodded. "I thought you would remember him well."

"He was a sweet boy," Solia murmured. "Tell me, did Tenebra warp him into a monster like his father?"

"Who was his father?" Kella asked.

"Lord Bellator," Solia answered, "who betrayed Iris and me."

Tuura *tsked* with regret. "How did the poor boy fare after that?"

"His life might have been very short," Cassia said, "but Flavian's father took him in, promising to raise him loyal to the king. Ben is now the First Knight of Segetia and a member of the Knightly Order of Andragathos, a respected group of holy knights. He does his best to live down the shame of his father's treason."

Solia's gaze was distant. "He didn't know my betrothal to his father was a ruse. He asked me if he could call me 'Mother.'"

"He carries such guilt over your death," Cassia said. "He will rejoice to learn the truth."

"I once thought I could trust Bellator," Solia pointed out.

"Ben is not like his father, any more than you and I are like the king. Ben and I both lost everything that night. He has been a faithful friend to me."

At last Solia's Tenebran gown was arranged to perfection, but she shook her head. She picked up her scarf from the Empress and held it out to Cassia. "We must find a way for me to wear this at all times. It will conceal my affinity from other mages, so I can reveal my power only when I am ready."

"I already have a plan for that." Cassia wove the scarf from the Empress around Solia's head, attaching it to the Azarqi charms. The final result looked like a silk crown—or a golden aura around the head of a goddess. Kella strapped on Solia's sword.

Cassia held up the mirror in front of Solia again. "What do you think?"

Solia looked into the glass, her face stony. But then she smiled slowly. "Oh, my clever Pup. There is one woman in the Tenebran imagination who wears both a gown and a sword, isn't there? The goddess Angara."

"One of the Fourteen Scions, eldest daughter of Kyria and Anthros," Cassia said. "Men will tell you her sword is a symbol. But I say, let Tenebra see her mythical blade manifest as real steel."

LIO SHOULD HAVE BEEN tense and alert, waiting in the pavilion for their first diplomatic encounter on this journey. Instead, he felt as if his head were full of syrup. It was going to be a long summer.

His only consolation was that Cassia was as sleepy as he was . Her yawns were a great improvement over her agitation of the night before. It seemed her time with Solia, Tuura, and Kella had done her good, as had Tuura's tonic.

"I haven't seen you in this robe before," Lio murmured in her ear under a veil. It was a simple, elegant affair of blue that made him think of the cousin of moonflowers that bloomed during the day.

She cast him a sly glance. "You sound distracted from the task at hand, Ambassador."

He slid his arm around her waist while he still could. "I admit to some preoccupation with taking you back to bed and removing that silk veil over your hair in much less time than it took you to put it on."

She pressed a kiss to the corner of his mouth, resting her hand on his chest. He drank up the little signs of affection that they must hide only moments from now.

Cassia touched her braid through the collar of his robe. "I hate that we had no time for a proper feast after you had such a long Slumber."

Lio sighed. "I think Rudhira would have woken me with a Night Call if I'd spent another minute in the tent. It seems the mortals are determined to arrive as soon after twilight as possible."

"Eudias and Ben should know better than to be afraid of the dark."

There came the sound of hoofbeats. It was already time.

Lio checked the concealment spells Nike had helped him place upon Cassia. The experimental magic was an alloy of blood magic and thelemancy that demanded attention to maintain, but it was a brilliant innovation.

"I don't know when I became the sort of Ritual father who advises you on propriety," Rudhira muttered. "I hope you all go out for your wildest night on the docks after all of this is over. In the meantime, try not to look like you want to take a bite out of Cassia, hmm?"

Mak and Lyros laughed, while Lio sighed and put more distance between himself and his Grace. Every inch felt wrong.

But Cassia still stood at his shoulder in her medallion, his partner on the Hesperine side of the gathering. The Ashes were assembled beside them, with Solia to arrive at the appointed moment.

Two Chargers escorted Eudias and Sir Benedict into the pavilion. Lio smiled at the transformation in the mage. The cowering apprentice was gone. Eudias's olive complexion and curly black hair showed his Cordian background, but he now wore the red-gold robes of a Tenebran mage of full rank. The wiry seventeen-year-old stood tall, carrying his magic like a friend, not an enemy.

Shy Eudias was the first to speak. "Ambassador!"

Lio clasped Eudias's arm. "I thought we were past titles, my friend."

"I suppose we are, Lio."

"Tenebra seems to agree with you," Lio said.

"Much better than Corona," Eudias replied with feeling.

"Hullo, Ben," Cassia said to the knight with a kind smile.

Considering the shared tragedies in her and Ben's past, Lio should not begrudge the man her smiles, but he did. The Allied Lords still believed Cassia had stayed behind in Orthros to preach the Goddess Kyria's teachings to the heretics, not fornicate with one on a nightly basis. And Benedict might as well have been the high priest of the Cult of Maiden Cassia, memorializing her for her great sacrifice.

Lio also did not take kindly to Benedict appearing in the camp in the gold and white surcoat of the Knightly Order of Andragathos, which was known for shining its holy light on Hespera worshipers at sword point.

Benedict gave Cassia a reverent bow and kissed her hand. "Your Ladyship, I never imagined I would see you again."

"It is Ambassador Cassia now." She touched her medallion. "I've come as a diplomat."

Confusion flickered in Benedict's gaze, but then he took in her blue robe, and his expression cleared. "You are so devoted to your calling as the Goddess Kyria's peacemaker."

Lio *was* thick-headed this twilight. If he had been properly awake, he would have realized what Cassia was doing. Her hair was covered, a concession to Tenebran standards of modesty. Her robe was Kyrian blue. She was playing into Benedict's image of her.

Goddess bless Mak for greeting Benedict with a wrist clasp, which effectively detached the man from Cassia. He still looked starry-eyed from Cassia's nearness, but he greeted Mak and Lyros as if he were genuinely glad to see them.

"You have met our delegation from Orthros," Rudhira said. "Allow me to present you to our allies from the Empire, led by Kella, First Blade of the Ashes and Princess of the Azarqi."

Benedict was too courteous to stare, but Lio sensed that it was an effort for him this time. The Ashes were unlike anyone he had ever seen. He gave Kella a gracious bow, but did not attempt to kiss her hand with Tilili's sharp teeth between them. "Your Highness, we regret that we did not have the opportunity to meet you and your companions among the Imperial guests when we were in Orthros."

"We are here with the Empress's blessing," Kella responded in Divine, "to extend her hand of friendship to Tenebra during troubled times."

"We appreciate how unprecedented this is," Eudias said, "given the Empress's policy of isolation. We are honored to have you in Tenebra."

Lio wanted to cheer for Eudias. He was becoming quite the diplomat himself. Lio asked, "Is the offer that Allied Lords extended to us after the Solstice Summit still on the table?"

"I should hope so," Eudias said.

"That is a decision we are not empowered to make," Benedict explained, "but we will bring word to the lords that our allies from Orthros and the Empire wish to attend."

"And encourage them to honor the invitation," Eudias added.

Rudhira said, "We, in turn, will continue to honor their request that the Charge remain at a distance. However, our terms are that Stewards Telemakhos and Lysandros accompany our delegation to Patria for protection. Before our ambassadors arrive, their bodyguards must be allowed to patrol the Council site for dangers and cast wards for protection."

Eudias and Benedict conferred quietly for a moment, then Eudias said, "We will recommend that the lords accommodate these reasonable requests."

Cassia shared a glance with Lio. This was going well. Except for the fact that Flavian was waiting for them at their destination.

"Ben," Cassia said, "it is our hope that we can meet with Flavian to discuss his endeavors. But we would prefer that news of our arrival reach his ears only for the time being. I'm sure you understand."

"We will proceed with the utmost discretion, Your Ladyship. You must be reunited with my lord as soon as possible."

Lio cut in, "Ambassador Cassia and I have urgent diplomatic matters to address with him."

"You can rely on me, of course," said Eudias. "Whatever has brought you all this way at such a volatile time, it must be of the greatest importance."

Lio steeled himself as Cassia reached out and took Benedict's hands. "I must prepare you for who you are about to see. Know that we have the Hesperines and the Ashes to thank for this miracle. They helped me find the truth—and someone we thought lost."

Benedict's brow knitted. "What can you mean?"

The joy shining through Cassia now was no act. "Ben, we were wrong about the Siege of Sovereigns. My sister escaped."

Silence fell over the pavilion. Eudias turned an astonished gaze on Lio, and he nodded.

"Solia is alive," Cassia declared. "The Empire harbored her all these years. And now she is ready to return to us."

Benedict let out a breath, almost a groan. "I don't understand."

"I know," Cassia said. "It seems impossible. But it's true."

"How can you be sure—" Benedict cut himself off.

"Because she's here." Cassia paused while Benedict took that in. But not too long, Lio noted. Before Benedict had time to wonder what this would mean for Flavian's ambitions, she asked, "Are you ready to welcome our princess home?"

Benedict went pale. "Me, Your Ladyship? I am the least worthy man in all of Tenebra to be the first to behold her."

Cassia shook her head. "No, Ben. You are the best choice. No one's welcome could be more powerful than yours, don't you see?"

The knight drew in a shaking breath, then drew himself to attention. "Yes. Yes, I understand. And I will thank the gods for this opportunity to atone."

"You have nothing to atone for. All you need to do is show her who you really are."

Benedict was still reeling, his aura a clash of shock and guilt and courage, when Solia appeared in the pavilion.

Her traversal was one of the most subtle Lio had ever seen. The difficult spell left no sign of strain on her face. She was suddenly standing between the Hesperines and the Ashes, her fire magic banked just under her skin, emanating warmth and a faint glow.

Benedict staggered backwards, a prayer flying from his lips.

"Do not be afraid, Ben." Solia extended a hand, giving him a gentle smile.

He fell to his knees before her. "Your Highness. What act of the gods is this? Are you—?"

"I am no apparition." She took his hand.

At her physical touch, he startled. "You're alive."

"Basilinna." Eudias spoke the age-old title, which the Mage-King's daughter had first borne, the epithet of a princess of the royal line. The mage slid his hands into his sleeves and inclined his head.

"I thought..." Benedict's voice was thick. "All these years. I believed my father had slain you."

"Iris made that sacrifice in my place."

He gasped as if someone had dealt him a blow to the gut. "Words can never express my regret, Your Highness."

"Cassia tells me you are a man who speaks through your deeds and lives with honor."

"Her Ladyship does me too much credit, but I assure you, I would sooner die than break my oaths."

"A time is coming when you must choose which oaths you will keep and which must be sacrificed."

Eudias took a deep breath. "I understand that. Princess Solia, let it be known that I do not condone the Aithourian Circle's involvement in the Siege of Sovereigns. There are mages who will not tolerate the abuses the Orders commit as King Lucis's ally."

"Thank you, Mage Eudias," Solia replied. "Ambassador Deukalion has told me much of your bravery on Tenebra's behalf."

His ears reddened.

"Rise, Ben," Solia bade him. "I ask no promise of you tonight beyond this: tell your liege lord I am here, and attest to the truth of my return. We have no time for doubts. Decisions must be made that will affect the future of the kingdom."

He hesitated. But then Solia showed him what was in her other hand. A fig.

A kindness to her friend. A political masterstroke. The lines between friendship and schemes were already blurring, even as the divide between Ambassador Cassia and Lady Circumspect widened.

Solia wrapped Benedict's fingers around the fig.

He rose to his feet, his head bowed. "Yes, Your Highness."

KYRIA'S HANDMAIDEN

Cassia's first chance to get Ben alone came near midnight. He had sat at the table for hours, talking with Solia as if confessing to Angara herself, listening to everything she patiently explained to him about her escape and her life since. It was a heavily edited narrative. Solia breathed no word of Cassia's claim on the throne, as they had agreed.

The hours were long, with Lio within reach but untouchable. She needed to feel his hand in hers. To smile without reservation at his and Eudias's clever conversation. To simply look into his eyes without feeling as if they were being watched. The slight distance between their bodies left her parched.

She would destroy this betrothal, starting tonight.

Ben would not leave Solia's side until she released him, saying, "You have been steadfast in your protection of my sister. Walk with her and let her ease your concerns about how she has fared since taking up residence in Orthros."

Cassia felt Lio's gaze on her as the knight offered her his arm. She tried to send Lio reassurance in her thoughts, but all she managed was a flare of bitter frustration. She schooled her face as she and Ben strolled through the spell-lit camp, staying within sight of the women in the pavilion.

"Your Ladyship, the wards on my holy amulet of Andragathos protect us from prying Hesperine ears. You can tell me the truth."

She doubted anything about that amulet would prevent Lio from knowing what they spoke of, but if it loosened Ben's tongue, all the better.

"Are you all right?" he asked with such sincerity.

She patted his arm in reassurance. "You saw what the Hesperines are like during the Solstice Summit. You know you don't need to worry about me."

"I respect them as our allies, but their ways are not ours. It must be lonely for you, living in such a foreign place, with only your prayers to remind you of home."

"I am not lonely. I have many friends there, Hesperines and Imperial mortals."

Ben's eyes narrowed. "Have they given you proper living arrangements befitting an emissary of Kyria?"

Cassia choked down a laugh. Lio's bed was the last place one would expect to find Kyria's handmaiden. "I am well provided for."

Ben looked at her intently. "Ambassador Deukalion behaves honorably around you? None of us begrudge him his admiration for you—as long as he remembers it must remain unrequited."

"Lio is my partner," Cassia said carefully. "We work well together as diplomats."

"My lord and I worry about you. If he has taken liberties, I swear we'll—"

"Ben, what have you been telling Flavian about Lio?" Cassia stopped herself and tried for a calmer tone of voice. "The ambassador has been nothing but a friend and ally to us. He does not deserve for his honor to be questioned."

"He is still a heretic, and you are still betrothed to my lord. When he learns the Hesperines have paired you with a male partner, he will not take kindly to it."

Cassia could not entirely dismiss this as Ben's propriety. Flavian had a nuanced sense of honor. He had been genuinely anguished when she had gone into perceived danger in Orthros. Even as he remorselessly sinned in bed with Sabina, he would persist in his foolish notion that he was honorbound to protect Cassia because of their betrothal promise.

She felt the urge to shake Flavian and Ben. But she and Lio would have to tread very carefully indeed.

"You have an escort whenever you are in the ambassador's presence, don't you?" Ben pressed.

Ha. When she was with Lio, their only companion was their mutual Craving. "You see that I am traveling with my sister, and we also have Diviner Tuura and Princess Kella with us."

"But the Hesperine delegation is only the ambassador and the two Stewards."

Cassia swallowed a laugh. "My virtue could not be safer with Mak and Lyros, I assure you."

Ben looked uncomfortable. "I am aware of their...understanding... but Orthros should at least send female Hesperines along with you. It isn't appropriate for you to spend so much time with males."

"These are unprecedented times, Ben. All of us must be prepared to take unprecedented action for our cause. Which is why I must find a way to release Flavian from his obligation to me."

Ben's steps slowed, and he turned to her under one of the stained glass lanterns that reminded her of her real home. "But you've come back to Tenebra. Surely that means there is hope you can remain with us."

She squeezed his arm gently. "No. I will always return to Orthros."

"Your place is at your sister's side," Ben protested.

"Nothing will ever separate me from my sister again. But Orthros is where I belong."

The red lantern-light made the lines of pain on his face look deep. "How can Princess Solia's return not change your decision?"

"It is not a decision. I cannot fight what binds me there—nor would I wish to." Cassia bit her tongue before her angry words tumbled out. *I belong with Lio. None of your foolish human discomfort matters.*

She must do better than this. But Hespera help her, it was so much harder to go back to lying through her teeth, now that she had spent all these months living the truth.

"Forgive me," Ben said, instead of debating as she had expected. "It is selfish of me to question your devotion to the Mother Goddess."

She didn't want to lie to him. This journey, however unwanted, was granting her one final word with the Tenebran world before her Gifting, and she wanted that word to be honest. This was her chance to say farewell to her few friends—and perhaps make amends with enemies, so she could go into her Gifting with a clear conscience.

She was committed to Hespera's path. She knew she was worthy. But no matter how she tried to explain this to Ben, he would never understand.

So Cassia let him believe what made all of this easy for him. What kept him comfortable.

"I cannot marry Flavian," Cassia said. "It does not befit my calling, and it is unfair for him to be tied to me."

He started to walk again, his head bowed in thought. "You wish to take the path of a mage, then?"

There was a sliver of truth she could cling to. "Yes. Yes, Ben. My mother was not a handmaiden from a Temple of Hedon."

His gaze snapped up. "What?"

"She was a powerful mage of Kyria."

Benedict's face flushed with outrage. "The king took a mage of Kyria for his concubine? He defiled a temple virgin? If I had not already disavowed him for his broken oaths to the lords of Tenebra, I would repudiate him for this."

"He murdered her."

Ben halted in his tracks.

Cassia had not intended to tell him. But it made her too angry for him to be more outraged over Thalia's maidenhead than her life. "The king killed her and blamed it on an assassin. Solia was old enough to remember."

Ben put his hand over hers where she still gripped his arm. "I am so sorry, Cassia."

There. Finally. He spoke to her, not some vision of her that he imagined.

"I want to follow in her footsteps," she explained. "Please try to understand. I know this isn't what you hoped for, but it's so important to me. To her memory."

Ben's face was grave. "As a Knight of Andragathos, I am perhaps one of the few who understands. It is difficult to walk a holy path outside of a temple, but the gods need warriors in the field. Or diplomats, in this case."

She tried not to let her gaze drift to the nearby shrine of Hespera. The ancient stone basin was filled with rose petals and centuries of reverent bloodstains. Her Grace-father had crafted it. Her Queens had anointed it. Her Hesperines errant had worshiped here for ages.

Benedict's sympathy would disappear if he realized Hespera was the Goddess who called to Cassia. He would see it as a betrayal of everything he believed in.

Her old life in Tenebra felt like weeds, tangling her up and trying to choke her.

She forced the words out. "Thank you for trying to understand."

"You remain strong in your convictions, truer than I." He gave her a sad smile. "It is wrong of me to want something different for you than Kyria has ordained. I see now that what I imagined for you and my lord cannot be."

"You'll help me convince him to end the betrothal?"

Ben nodded. "I will help him understand you must remain unwed in Kyria's name."

The lies wound tighter and tighter around her. But oh, how effective they were.

Lio almost wished Benedict's amulet did ward off Hesperine hearing, for then he wouldn't have to listen to Cassia playing along with the knight's assumptions.

All of this was temporary, he reminded himself. The final dues they must pay to Tenebra. But for this price, it was not enough for Flavian to merely release her. Lio would have him acknowledge that her rightful place was at her Grace's side.

Torturing himself eavesdropping would accomplish nothing. He needed to talk to Eudias.

Lio poured the mage a cup of wine from a flagon. "You can speak freely now."

Rudhira gestured to the Stewards, Solia, and the Ashes. "Everyone at this table knows the truth about the Collector."

Eudias looked to Solia. "You are aware of the Old Master, Basilinna?"

"And your role in helping Lio defeat him," Solia said. "Thank you for fighting alongside him and my sister."

"I am glad you know where I stand."

"I applaud the Hesperines' decision to keep the Old Master's presence quiet. Informing Tenebrans that he is among us would only incite witch hunts."

A faint shudder went through Eudias. "Yes, I'm afraid Tenebrans' fears and superstitions would get the better of them if they knew a rogue necromancer could be possessing any one of their neighbors. Instead of relying on evidence to find those the Old Master is exploiting, they would persecute anyone who fell under suspicion."

"Too many innocent people would suffer," Solia agreed.

"But we have safety measures in place here at the Sanctuary," Eudias explained, "Before Sir Benedict and I cross the ward, two mind healers examine each of us to ensure neither of us is possessed. Sir Benedict is unaware their spells include him and believes it is a precaution against allowing me, a war mage, into a Hesperine Sanctuary."

"And we're grateful to Eudias for going to these lengths," Rudhira said.

"It is a reassurance to me, as well," Eudias replied.

Rudhira continued, "We also have Chargers under veil spells shadowing all parties traveling in for the Council. Our mind healers check each one for the Collector's presence. But once they arrive at Patria, there is nothing more we can do."

Eudias's aura crackled with frustration. "If only I could have convinced the Allied Lords to allow a Charge presence at Patria. But if we can get your delegation in, there is hope. We need a thelemancer who has fought the Collector and Hesperine warders who can cast protections like those that saved us all at the Summit."

"We have someone even better." Lio nodded to Tuura. "Diviner Tuura is an esteemed Imperial mind healer. Much of Hesperine knowledge of necromancy comes from the traditions in which she is an expert."

Relief filled Eudias's aura. "I thank all our gods that we will have a theramancer at Patria at last. I will tell you anything I can that will help you protect others from him."

Tuura smiled at him. "One reassurance I can offer you is that it is rare for a necromancer to possess the same person twice. Now that you have thrown off his yoke, your resistance to him is stronger. And your bravery is apparent."

A breath escaped Eudias. "Thank you for your wisdom, diviner."

"Have there been any signs of the Collector's presence?" Lio asked.

"None that I can perceive," Eudias answered, "but without Hesperine expertise, how can we be certain? The Tenebran mages of Anthros and Kyria have delegations at Patria to ensure the Council proceeds peacefully and fairly. But they are not prepared for an Old Master. Lords and their retinues arrive every day. The Collector could be hiding anywhere."

Solia did not look pleased. "So could the king's spies."

"Once they enter Lord Flavian's perimeter," Eudias explained, "none are permitted to leave, lest they carry tales to King Lucis. But..."

Lio shook his head. "If the Old Master has already possessed someone among them, then we have no secrets from him or the king."

The lords at Patria were like lambs trapped in a pen with the wolf. The thought of taking Cassia into that made Lio's magic roil.

After Eudias and Benedict left, Lio followed the fragrance of Cassia's blood. He found her standing by the shrine with Knight, her spade in her bleeding hand. She stared into the basin at her fresh libation, as if waiting for Hespera's Cup to pour forth answers to the conflict inside her.

As soon as he drew near, she turned to him and pulled him to her. "I need to kiss you. Now."

He lowered his head. "Finally."

Her kiss was ravenous. With a groan, he opened his mouth to her, letting her ravish his fangs and tongue. He heard her spade fall to the grass; her hand cupped his cheek, trailing warm blood over his skin. When she came up for air, he took a long, hungry lick from her cut.

"I can't do this," she said. "I can't sit next to you and lie. I don't have it in me anymore."

He stroked her hair. "Shh, it's all right, my rose. We made it through tonight. You'll feel better once I take care of your Craving."

She drew in a sharp breath, resting her forehead on his chest. "You're right. Yes. My Craving. It's dulling my skills. I must learn to keep my wits about me in spite of it." She lifted her head, her eyes focusing on him. "Tell me, what did you learn from Eudias?"

"We cannot be sure that Patria is safe." Lio explained the situation, rubbing small circles on her lower back.

She melted against him, her aura all but purring as he fed her his little touches. "I wish I could say I'm surprised, but the lords were always fools."

Lio knew she would hate what he had to say next. "Tuura and I need to make sure the Collector has not infiltrated the Council. We should go ahead with Karege and Lyros. Mak will stay here to communicate with Lyros through their Grace Union. Once we're sure it's safe, he can bring you, Solia, and the other Ashes to Patria."

Fury tore through her aura, although she kept her voice factual. "You're right. There is no sense in walking into what might be a trap. We must be sure the Collector isn't lying in wait for me—or watching when Solia reveals her presence. If he found out she had returned, then he would tell Lucis before we're ready."

"You know I wouldn't step out of your sight unless it was absolutely necessary. You'll be safe here with Rudhira."

Her hands curled into fists on his chest. "But I won't be there to keep you safe. We defeated him together last time. What if he comes for you, and I'm not there?"

"I will have our allies with me and our Grace Union within me."

"I know. I *know* this is the wise course of action. But all I *feel* is that I should be at your side."

He tangled his fingers in her hair, tugging a little. Her eyes slid shut. He tilted her head back, speaking against her throat. "I understand, my Grace. There's no wisdom in the Craving. Just need."

"I hate him. We should be doing this together every step of the way."

"We are. I will only be gone for a few hours at most."

"I should be there, shedding blood into your spells."

The scent of her blood curled around them, carrying on it a pulse of the shrine's timeless power. He guided her hand to his throat and let her feel how his own pulse was racing. "I can think of much more pleasant ways for you to shed your blood for me. Right now."

Hunger glazed her eyes. His fangs slid out. He could see she was done with wisdom for tonight. She would not be able to think clearly until he fed her.

But then she went still and snapped her head around, as if something had captured her attention in the woods beyond the camp. Knight pricked his ears in the same direction.

"What is it?" Lio followed her gaze. His night vision revealed nothing but trees.

"I'm not sure." She looked into the verdant darkness, just like she had the night before. As if she sensed something he could not.

Did this have anything to do with what Kalos had said about drawing power from the wilds? Lio should ask Cassia for more details about what she sensed. This could be an opportunity to study what effect returning to Tenebra had on her awakening magic.

But the thought filled him with inexplicable frustration, and he found himself saying, "We shouldn't leave the safety of the Sanctuary to investigate."

"No, you're right, of course." Her aura reached. Not for his magic, but into the wilds to the east.

His fangs lengthened. He wanted her eyes on him. He needed her aura reaching for his magic.

His own Craving boiled his thoughts down to a very simple realization. He couldn't bear for Cassia to need anything from Tenebra that she couldn't find in Orthros. In him.

This goddessforsaken kingdom had kept his Grace from him before. How dare it hold her magic hostage now, too? He knew he was being a jealous fool, but all his Craving wanted was her Craving in return.

He called to her mind with his power. She gasped, and her wide hazel eyes focused on him again.

He stroked her cheek. "Did you like that, my Grace?"

She took hold of his collar and pulled him closer. He stroked her thoughts again.

She yanked his collar open and bit his throat. "Take me to our tent. Hurry."

Yes. That was what he wanted to hear. Her demands. For him.

He stepped them to their tent, and the total darkness of veil spells closed around them. Hesperine magic seemed to cut them off from the world, and for a moment, he could forget they were in Tenebra.

The scent of her freshly shed blood filled the small space. He plucked at that thread of life and conjured a spell light. She watched the glow rise from her hand, then ran her bloodstained palm down her cheek, her eyes sliding shut. "Your magic feels so good."

"Do you want more?"

"I want to feast on your power all night."

She wanted to forget Tenebra, too. He could do this for her. Banish all the conflict inside her with their pure, basic need for each other.

He let his thelemancy wash through the mind ward, worshiping her unbroken Will. She tore at the front fasteners of his robe and nipped her way down his chest. Goddess, yes, this was right. Her need to devour him. He stood there and let her strip him, urging her on with pulses of magic into her thoughts. His robes and medallion landed on the ground, then his underlinens.

He pulled her against him, grunting as her soft belly pressed into his erection. He lifted his other hand to her head and, one by one, plucked out the pins holding her veil.

She shook out her hair, her aura stretching, eager for his magic. At her invitation, his power responded like his fangs at the smell of her blood. His magic strained toward her. He held it in check, letting it out in a measured wave.

She ran her nails down his back, sending a cascade of sensation over his skin. "Come deeper."

"As deep as you want," he promised. "Will you lie down for me?"

She slid from his arms with a sultry smile. "They say it's dangerous to lie with a Hesperine."

He grinned, letting his fangs out. "I'm not dangerous at all, I promise."

"I know better, my mind mage. But I love to live dangerously with you."

She stretched out on their bedroll, her ash-brown hair falling in a tousle around her. With one teasing finger, she lifted the hem of her robes to show him her ankle.

He levitated down over her at immortal speed and framed her between his arms. She jumped, her heart pattering with excitement.

His grin widened. "That is not a proper Kyrian response to a naked Hesperine threatening your virtue."

Her gaze raked his body. "I am a very bad handmaiden."

"How bad?" He hiked her robes up to her waist to expose her slim, freckled legs and demure underlinens.

"Not a maiden at all."

Kneeling before her, he spread her legs and propped her feet apart on the wool army blanket. "I believe I had something to do with that on this very blanket."

"You had a remarkable amount of virtue to lose, for a heretic."

"And none of it left, after one taste of you."

He stripped off her underlinens with a flick of levitation. Holding her ankles, he flared his nostrils, taking in the scent of her desire. He gazed down at her, half bared to him, half wrapped in linen. Her pretty blue robe would not look Kyrian at all when he stained it with the blood of the Feast.

She rose up on her elbows. "Bring those fangs of yours closer."

"You asked to feast on my magic. I must fulfill that request first." He let his power ripple through her mind.

Her lips parted, and her eyes slid shut.

"No," he said, "look at me."

Her lashes rose, a dusky flush spreading across her face.

"Do you want more of that, my Grace?"

"Always."

Holding her gaze, he let his thelemancy roll out of him in soft currents. Her hands fisted in the blankets, and she began to pant. This time, he didn't need to ask her if she wanted more. Her essence pulled hard on his, just like the time in the Maaqul Desert when they had discovered she could feast on his raw magic.

Anxiety flared in her aura. He ran his hands up the inside of her thighs to soothe her. "It's all right. You know it's natural to want my magic in place of my blood."

"But my pull on you hasn't felt this strong in a long time. Not since my Craving was dangerous."

"You're safe, my rose. It's all right if you need me more tonight. Let me chase the specters of Tenebra away."

She let out a sigh, and her aura sucked at him like a newborn Hesperine at her lover's vein. They groaned together.

The musk of her lust filled the tent, but she didn't reach for his body, as if the flow of his magic held her riveted to the blanket. She shifted her hips, her breaths coming heavier. And all along, her eyes were on him, as if nothing else in her world existed.

His back tightened with the need to thrust into her restless body. He let all of that desire take over his magic, and it plunged inside her hungry aura.

She tossed her head, her lips moving as if she were drinking him. With her feet braced on the blanket, she arched toward him, open and ready for him. The unmaidenly view of her wet krana was divine.

"Lio," she pleaded, her body and aura straining toward him.

"I want to fill you, Cassia. So full there won't be room in your thoughts for Tenebra. Would you like that?"

"Yes. I just want you."

He let go of the layers of complex self-control that he maintained, every moment of every day, to keep his dangerous magic in check. All his power fled toward his Grace, knowing where it belonged. He flooded her mind and body.

Memories of her past and fears of her future faded, eclipsed by their Union. He felt every countless brush of her thoughts against his as a physical touch on his skin. In those intimate caresses, he found nothing but her and him.

Her pupils dilated. He gazed into her soul as she cried out his name. He watched every grimace that crossed her face and every spasm that curled her toes. She twisted and tossed on the blanket, and his fangs and erection throbbed with the echoes of her climax.

She collapsed back onto the blanket. The jealous fool inside him basked in the knowledge that his magic alone could satisfy her.

But so could his fangs. "Do you want my bite?"

Her hand flew to her throat, and she tugged down the neckline of her robes.

With an effort of Will, he untangled his thelemancy from her thoughts. Pleasure and frustration scoured him as he withdrew his magic from inside her. She whimpered in protest.

He lowered his mouth to her throat and kissed her vein. "I want to bite you like I did the first time, when you wouldn't let me touch you. All it took was my fangs to make you climax, and I dined on your first pleasure."

Her hands roamed over his shoulders. "But I can't make myself stop touching you."

He smiled against her throat. "I never said you had to."

He licked and sucked at her throat, a little foreplay for her vein. She dragged her hands down his back. Her greed felt so good.

With one firm, gentle motion, he sank his fangs in. She dug her fingers into his shoulders as the first rush of her blood flowed into his mouth.

At the explosion of flavor on his tongue, his jaw clenched. He was the connoisseur of all her flavors, and yet he had never tasted her like this. The earthy, woody notes of her magic were stronger than ever.

Returning to Tenebra had done this to her blood.

"Let my blood fill you," she rasped. "Let me chase your specters away, too."

His Grace sensed his inner conflicts in return. His instinct to hide his feelings overcame him, but he threw it off. Tonight, he wanted nothing between them, least of all his own inhibitions.

He lifted his head. Her gaze followed the trail of her blood down his chin. Crimson splashed onto her robes. Beneath the stain, her nipples peaked against the fabric.

"Cassia...I need you to need me tonight."

She sucked in a breath. "Lio, I need you every night. Every moment. Every century. And I will always make sure you have everything you need from me."

He swept down and pierced her throat, fast and hard. She gave a wordless cry of welcome and dug her fingers into his hair. With long, urgent pulls on her vein, he flooded himself with her.

The new flavors of her magic were inebriating. But he held back his body and magic, a pleasing torture, allowing only the Drink to consume his senses. He forgot everything except her promise that she would never leave him thirsting for her again.

Her arms and legs twined around him, her sharp lust pricking his aura. Then her blood released the purely natural power of her climax into his veins. She squirmed softly under him, rubbing her bony hips and small breasts against him. He fisted his hands on the blanket with the effort of not touching her.

Their Grace Union flickered open, and she cried out in his mind. *I want your touch.*

Laving at his bite to heal her, he sent his intent into her thoughts. *Now I want to pleasure you without my fangs. Only with my mouth.*

I'm your feast. Dine on any part of me that you want.

Moving with Hesperine quickness again, he slipped down her body and pressed his mouth to the tempting banquet between her thighs. At the sudden touch of his lips, she startled again, mewing with approval.

She held her saintly robes out of his way and let him devour the most intimate part of her body. She watched him ravish her, just like the first time she had let him take her into this forbidden territory, never to return.

Like the heretic she now was, she canted her hips, serving her soft, wet folds up to him. With his tongue, he teased out her most sensitive bud of nerves. When she gave another husky moan of encouragement, he fastened onto her kalux and suckled her.

He felt all her senses fix on that point, on what he was doing to her, on him. He kept her knees spread, driving her wilder with his tongue. She was stunning, her hands fisting in her robes, her body quivering toward another inevitable loss of control in his hands.

Just before her aura broke apart, he pulled away.

She gasped, half sitting up. "Lio—!"

He rolled onto his back beside her, rubbing a hand across his damp mouth. "Still hungry?"

She bared her canines and straddled him. Her tangled hair fell around him, and she dug her nails into his pectorals as if to hold him down. All he saw in her eyes was hunger now, and oh, how it satisfied his own.

Her hot, tight core came down on his erection. He lay back and let her have him. Breathing hard, she took him with fast, urgent shoves of her hips, as if she would die if she didn't get him inside her. The vision of her in her bloodstained robes hazed before his eyes.

When she had worked herself fully onto his shaft, she stretched out over him to bite his chest. Holding him between her knees, she squeezed his burgeoning erection with her inner muscles, rubbing her kalux against him with little swivels of her hips. His chest bruised and healed under the grazing pressure of her bites.

Their Union was a torrent of Craving, all-consuming. Her hunger tore his magic out of him, and he let go. The pressure in his soul released, and his body spilled inside her in rough pulses. All he could hear was his heart pounding in his ears and her moans as she rode him.

When they came to their senses, she didn't move. She cuddled against him as if she never wanted to unseal her body from his. He wrapped his arms around her at last.

This was where she belonged. In natural union with his body and Grace Union with his heart. Untethered from the mortal world.

By their Goddess, he would free her and her magic from this kingdom once and for all.

1

day until

SUMMER SOLSTICE

33 Chera's Coin, 1597 OT

THE ONCOMING STORM

LIO CAUGHT THE WARM, metallic scent of a storm on the air when Eudias traversed into the pavilion the following night. The weary mage sank into the chair Lio pulled out for him, and Cassia offered him a cup of water.

They waited in silence with the others while Eudias drank deeply. He set down the empty cup and heaved a breath. "The Allied Lords will welcome the delegations from Orthros and the Empire. They have agreed to hold the Council meetings at twilight so Hesperines can attend."

Triumph rose in the Blood Union among everyone in the pavilion. Except Cassia. Lio sensed the weight of her dread. He fought the powerful instinct to reach for her hand. He mustn't, not in front of the mage.

As much as Lio hated to make her wait here and fear for his safety, he had no remorse. He would do what he must to keep her safe.

"Do we have permission to check Patria for danger?" Lio asked.

"Yes, you can come ahead." Eudias gave him a wry smile. "I promised the lords I would stop you if you try any dangerous spells. But you'll find my definition of what qualifies as 'dangerous' to be quite different from theirs."

"Thank you," Lio told him.

Eudias grimaced. "I'm afraid Lord Flavian has one more request. He would like Princess Solia and Ambassador Cassia to follow in the morning."

"Out of the question," Lio and Cassia said at the same time.

"We know the Collector is targeting Cassia," Lio continued. "She must have Hesperine protection when she arrives at Patria."

"We discussed this," Solia said. "Cassia will be safe with me."

Tuura patted Lio's arm. "I will be there during the day, too."

Lio knew, intellectually, that an Imperial mind healer and a fire mage with sisterly devotion were excellent protection. But he needed to protect his Grace himself.

"Does Flavian accept the truth of my identity?" Solia asked.

Eudias gave her a solemn nod. "He takes Sir Benedict at his word."

"In that case, we accept his terms," Solia announced. "I hoped to go a day early and discuss matters with Flavian before the Council commences, but so be it. I shall simply have to make a grand entrance on Summer Solstice."

Lio unclenched his teeth. "When do the rest of us leave?"

Eudias answered, "As soon as I catch my breath."

Solia looked at the mage with concern. "Two traversals in as many nights. Do you need to rest?"

Eudias shook his head. "Thank you for your consideration, Basilinna, but I'm all right. I have no objection to the Hesperines stepping us to Patria, however. I left an uncharged elemental heptagram behind that we can use as a focus."

"That was good thinking," Lio said, impressed.

Eudias's gaze dropped. It seemed he was still learning how to accept praise.

Lyros and Karege brought the horses, the Orthros Warmbloods sporting the light fabric saddles Hesperines preferred, with mortal saddles for Tuura's and Eudias's mounts. Lio wore Imperial travel attire tonight, the loose trousers suitable for horseback riding. But if they ran into anyone important, his medallion and Vardaran tunic of silver and blue would not fail to impress.

Cassia stood in silence, her hand in Knight's ruff, but her thoughts spoke loud and clear. She was tolerating this under protest. Lio gave the mind ward a reassuring touch with his magic and felt her shiver.

Then Lio focused on the magical imprint of Eudias's heptagram and stepped them, with Lyros, Karege, and Tuura's auras slipping along after them. The Sanctuary ward peeled away, and they arrived on the bank of a small river. Eudias's spell gleamed among the rushes, a seven-pointed star waiting for a touch of lightning magic to awaken it.

Lio felt exposed without Hesperine magic around him. He followed Lyros's gaze, surveying their surroundings. Across the river, the countryside was lightly wooded. On this side, the terrain rose gradually into rolling fields.

A sea of tents covered the hills, filled with the tense presences of mortals trying to sleep. On the highest rise stood Castra Patria, the fortress even older than the Mage King's palace. Its heavy towers and eroded parapets had been built with no thought for beauty, only for the protection of the small lives clustered around it, uncertain of their future.

Eudias showed them a parchment map of the region. "This small tributary of the River Silvistra forms the boundary of Patria to the south and east. That makes it easier for Lord Flavian's sentries to control who enters from this side. To the north and west, he had his men erect guard posts at intervals, and their patrols are vigilant. Master Gorgos and the other warders among the mages of Anthros maintain defensive spells, as well."

Marvelous. Their defenses relied on Master Gorgos, the incompetent bigot who had attended the Solstice Summit. Lio gave Eudias a rueful look. "In your professional opinion, are Master Gorgos's wards effective?"

Eudias sighed. "They're sufficient to deter non-mages, and if war mages tried to break through, at least we would sense their attack on the wards in time to respond. But these spells are nothing to an Old Master."

"A Gift Collector would still be able to slip in," Lyros predicted.

"Dare I ask what a Gift Collector is?" Tuura inquired.

Karege shook his head grimly. "Battle mages who serve Hypnos, the god of death worshiped here. They specialize in assassinating Hesperines."

"That's what their name means?" Tuura sounded outraged. "No wonder you prefer to go errant in the Empire."

Lio could not disagree. "They've been bounty hunters for the Order of Hypnos for centuries, but we recently learned that their true master is the Collector himself."

Eudias pointed to the vulnerable points on the map. "I would feel more reassured if you check the defenses, Steward Lyros."

"Of course."

"I will begin my divination on that side, too," Tuura said. "Lio, you begin your thelemancy here. Between the two of us, we will perform a magical sweep from opposite directions and leave no stone unturned."

"An excellent plan, diviner," said Lio.

Eudias handed her the map. "I'll act as the ambassador's guide."

"I'm going with Tuura," Karege said. "Will you two be all right by yourselves?"

"Eudias and I have survived this battle before," Lio reminded him. "But I will send Tuura a mental distress signal if we need reinforcements."

"And I'll do the same if we run into any trouble," Tuura promised.

Lyros pulled his horse alongside Lio's. "Cassia told Mak to tell me to tell you: 'This isn't the Maaqul. You don't have to do anything without help.'"

"Please ask Mak to tell Cassia that I have no intention of engaging in misguided heroics."

"Good." Lyros clapped him on the shoulder before he, Karege, and Tuura rode away.

A fairly comfortable silence fell between Lio and Eudias. Then the young mage gestured to the river. "With the help of my magic, the water could improve the reach of your spell. If you have no objection to collaborative casting, that is."

"Far from it." Lio dismounted and left Moonflower to graze on the bank. "Our magic defeated the Collector last time. We should cast together to try to detect his presence."

Eudias tethered his horse under a nearby tree, his face grim. "Are you worried he will be able to hide even from us?"

"Yes," Lio confessed. "Although we are wise to many of his tricks now, he always seems to have another one up his sleeve. But my hope is that you and I will be able to detect him more easily because of our past... encounters."

"I've been thinking about what Diviner Tuura said," Eudias said. "If my resistance to him is greater, I should also be more alert to his presence."

The mage pulled off his shoes and sat down on the bank, sliding his bare feet into the water. A reminder of a pool in his memories where his life would have ended, if not for Lio. An invitation to return to that moment when their survival had demanded complete trust.

Lio set his own shoes aside and joined Eudias. The water didn't feel as cold as Lio had expected. Eudias's water magic flowed through the river like a friendly greeting to his element, while the lightning magic that made him a war mage was quiet.

Lio said, "I've been meaning to congratulate you on your promotion from apprentice."

"Thank you. The Tenebran mages of Anthros have rather taken me under their wing."

"You're doing well," Lio observed.

Eudias blew out a breath. "I never thought I would be free of the Aithourian Circle…or the Collector. Now I have the hope of a life here in Tenebra. The future won't be easy for a war mage who refuses to serve the Aithourian Circle, but I will not let anyone drag me back to Cordium."

"If you ever need Sanctuary, you know we will welcome you in Orthros."

"I am grateful for that. But I am…needed…here. Tenebra reminds me of the rural village I came from. It's been a long time since I didn't regret having to leave." He made a face. "I do miss proper libraries, though."

Lio groaned. "I can imagine. Will it get you into trouble with the Tenebran mages if a Hesperine smuggles you scrolls from Orthros?"

Eudias laughed. "By all means, let us try."

Lio raised a brow. "And your study partner among the mages of Kyria?"

A blush darkened Eudias's cheeks. "Mage Ariadne is also at Patria as part of the Kyrian delegation. We have…an understanding."

"I'm glad to hear it. You know I am the last to judge if you two do more than practice together."

Eudias trailed his feet in the water. "She needs someone patient."

"It sounds like you are needed here, indeed."

The young mage turned to Lio. "You know I suffer from a case of overeducated openmindedness. And that our duel with the Collector drew my lines of loyalty in unusual places. It is perhaps presumptuous of me to ask the person who saved my life to spill his secrets, so all I will say is this. You can trust me as surely as I trusted you."

Eudias's olive branch felt more like a lifeline to Lio than he would have expected. "I am in need of an ally."

"Hm, I think we can do better than that. What do you say to a friend?"

Lio stopped to wonder if a Hesperine diplomat and a war mage could ever be friends. But he already knew the answer. He had seen into Eudias's mind.

Lio extended his hand. "Thank you, my friend."

Eudias gave him a Hesperine wrist clasp. "I hope you don't regret it once you realize how full of presumptuous questions I am."

"I would expect nothing less from a fellow overeducated, open-minded scrollworm."

"Very well. Do you and Ambassador Cassia have an understanding, then?"

Oh Goddess, had Lio made a mistake with Nike's spells? An equally troubling question was, why was he so tempted to tell Eudias the truth? He could never reveal what Grace was to any Tenebran or Cordian. There was too much risk of Orthros's enemies using Grace bonds against Hesperines.

Eudias interrupted his internal debate. "I heard her, you see. When you and I were in the Collector's mind game. Her voice was around every corner, helping us. I think the two of you must have a very deep understanding, indeed."

Lio breathed a sigh of relief. Eudias already knew a version of the truth. And judging by the thriving cult of Sacrificial Maiden Cassia, he had also been keeping their secret safe for them. "She isn't staying in Orthros for the treaty. She's staying for me. Forever."

"Well, I can hardly blame her," Eudias said lightly. "Your library is much more tempting than the horses or hunting dogs or whatever it was that Lord Flavian offered for her bride price."

Lio laughed. "Ah, I think it was the greenhouse that won her over, in fact."

"Ah. Yes, that would make Ariadne almost as jealous as the books."

Lio rubbed his face. "I have to get Cassia out of this betrothal. I was hoping you would be willing to help."

"Marriages, or in this case, unmarriages are one of my areas of expertise as a mage of Anthros."

"Are there any grounds on which a woman may break her betrothal? If not, what can a..." He grimaced. This was all so Tenebran. "...rival suitor do to...extricate her?"

"I'll need to familiarize myself with the differences between Tenebran and Cordian law. I'll do some research for you."

"You have my gratitude."

"Once you've freed Cassia from her promise to Flavian, are you hoping for a legal marriage to her?"

The words took Lio completely aback. "Is that…even an option?"

"One would think an Anthrian marriage to a Hesperine heretic would be impossible, but there are a surprising number of loopholes in sacred law and tradition. I can try to find one for you, if you wish for your union to be respectable in Tenebra."

Lio had never even considered the possibility. Marriage was a mortal institution that had given a cruelly neglectful man power over his mother. Wedding vows had only ever threatened to take his Grace from him.

He had never thought of them as something that could bind Cassia to him.

If a marriage could help win Solia's blessing…if it could wipe that smile off of Flavian's face…

"I will speak with Cassia about it," Lio said.

"Of course." Now Eudias tugged on a leather thong around his neck, pulling his lightning charm out from under his robes. He closed his palm over the wooden artifact. "As for tonight's spell, I had in mind a third-level aerial synthesis. What do you think?"

"I think if you can already cast a third level synthesis, it's surprising they didn't promote you sooner."

Eudias seemed to hide from the compliment by concentrating on his casting. Lio let his thelemancy flow into the current of the river and the patterns of the magic. The structure of the spell was impressive. When not under duress, Eudias was a precise and intuitive caster.

Eudias's magic carried Lio's along, racing to circle all the mortal minds gathered at Patria. Lio heard Tuura's casting in the distance, rising and falling with the rhythm of an Imperial chant, drawing nearer. Then a gust of wind snapped his magic aloft, and his stomach dipped as his power sailed up into the storm clouds.

Lio rolled over the tents and the castle and the tiny human lights within. Hundreds of unguarded minds, their ramparts and swords useless against either a benevolent Hesperine thelemancer or an abusive mage of dreams.

Lio would never forgive the Collector for making it necessary to trespass on so many Wills. He could only pray he had gotten to them first.

He would have to hold all of them at once to be sure the Collector had nowhere to hide. He let his power build in the storm.

Eudias opened the clouds, and their combined magic poured down over Patria. They swept among the mortals with the wind, whispering through each mind. Wakeful humans ran for cover, casting furtive glances into the stormy darkness. Lio let their memories, dreams, and secrets scurry past him to safety while he searched their fearful corners for the taint of the Collector's presence.

All he found were mundane nightmares. Could it really be true that the Collector had no spies at Patria?

Lio was not reassured, not yet. He churned more thelemancy into the storm. He sensed Eudias guiding the latent charge of power.

The clouds ignited. Lio's heart arced down out of the sky on a burning path and struck deep into the ground. Lightning lit up the twilight, and for that instant, every mind for miles was illuminated by his mind magic.

That was when he saw the one mind that remained dark.

"There!" he shouted over the wind. "Did you see him?"

"Go!" Eudias called back.

With Eudias stabilizing their spell, Lio pulled his mind out of the storm and focused all his power on that single mind that was shadowed by evil.

Lio's thelemancy spun into a void. He tasted death, and bile rose in his mouth.

He had already stepped before he realized it. He found himself atop a wooden guard tower, hovering over a fallen human.

"No. No, no." Lio sank to his knees beside the mortal, chasing deep into the man's mind, reaching for his fleeting life.

It was too late. The man breathed once, and his last words emerged in a voice Lio knew from all his nightmares. Deep, sophisticated, utterly in control.

"Give Cassia my greetings," the Collector said.

"You will never touch her!"

Lio's declaration fell on the ears of a dead man. He knelt there, staring down at the Collector's victim. The man looked about Solia's age. He wore

Segetian colors, now darkened with rain. There was not a mark on him, except for the arcane stain of necromancy.

Lio dragged a hand over his face to wipe away tears and rain. Then he closed the man's eyes.

Lio didn't know this man's name, but he knew who he was. Another mortal bystander caught up in a conflict he could not understand, who had never stood a chance of fighting back. He was just like the frightened father slaughtered in front of Lio on his first night in Tenebra. Just like the innocent man Cassia had seen sacrificed for necromancy while the king looked on.

Did this Segetian sentry have a lover waiting for his shift to end? Children asleep now, who would wake to learn he was gone?

His entire life had been cut short in an instant so the Collector could have the pleasure of taunting Lio. Threatening Cassia.

Lio became aware of Lyros's hand on his shoulder. They shared a moment of silence, the Blood Union throbbing with their instinctive horror. Death felt wrong when you were immortal. Empathizing with death was sickening when you were a Hesperine.

"We found the Collector's spy," Lio finally said, "but not in time to save him."

"I'm so sorry." Lyros gave his shoulder a squeeze. "Cassia says, don't you dare blame yourself."

"He threatened her," Lio snarled around his fangs.

Alarm filled Lyros's aura. "The Collector spoke to you?"

"Do not tell Cassia that." Lio rubbed his face again. "Not yet. I should tell her myself."

They were dealing with vast, ancient, unknown magic. And the cost of how unprepared they were was this man's life.

"Is there anything I can do for him?" Tuura called from the base of the tower.

Lio gathered the man's body in his arms and levitated down to where Tuura waited with Karege and Eudias. "I'm afraid he's beyond our reach, diviner."

She ran a hand over the man's hair as if he were a dear child. Eudias stared at the Collector's victim and swallowed hard.

"It's just like Martyr's Pass," Lio said. "When I found the Collector in this man, he cut his losses rather than confront me. I wasn't fast enough. I must learn to find him without warning him I'm coming. To drive him out before he kills."

Before he came close enough to even speak Cassia's name. Tonight, his victim had merely delivered a message. Next time, they might try to take Cassia captive.

"No, Lio." Lyros shook his head. "This is the fault of the lords. If they had allowed the Charge a presence here, this man would never have been possessed, much less murdered."

"And they should know it." Lio's jaw clenched. "I want Lord Flavian to look this man in the eye and think about his responsibilities."

"Lord Flavian?" Eudias dug his fingers through his hair. "You want to meet him now? Like this?"

Lio realized how far his fangs had unsheathed. He supposed his Vardaran tunic didn't look so fine plastered to him by the rain, and he smelled like scorched earth. Such irrelevant things, compared to the destroyed life he carried.

"Yes," Lio said. "Tell Lord Flavian the Hesperine ambassador is here."

AMBASSADOR DEUKALION'S BLUFF

LIO LISTENED TO THE water dripping off of him onto the castle floor in front of Flavian's door. The scents of rain and suffering filled the stone corridor. It was almost impossible to keep holding death so close to him, but he refused to let go of the shell of this man whose name he hadn't even known.

Lyros gripped Lio's arm. "You don't need me to tell you that Cassia is not in favor of this. It's a good thing Mak is not easily persuaded, or she would have had him step her here by now."

"It's not safe enough for her here. Not yet. But it will be when I'm done."

"Tuura and Karege are still out there patrolling the perimeter. Don't you think we can bring Cassia now?"

"Absolutely not. The Collector was here mere moments ago."

Lyros sighed and nodded. "She is furious that she won't be with you for your first confrontation with Flavian."

"Tell her she should not be expected to manage us. I won't put her in that position, and I certainly won't let him do so. We must take responsibility for our own conduct."

"That's not how she sees it, and you know it. She's afraid this will turn into a 'mortal pissing contest.'"

"Hesperines don't piss. If Flavian wets himself, that's his own deficiency."

"Stop to think strategically, Lio," Lyros insisted. "Are you sure this is the first impression you want to make on Flavian?"

"Yes. Trust me."

Lyros sighed. "You know I do. I will stand with you."

"Thank you, Trial Brother."

"What will you tell Flavian about the man's death?"

"Since we cannot mention the Collector, I intend to blame a Gift Collector for this instead. Ask Cassia if she agrees we should tell Flavian that Skleros was here."

Lyros sighed and was quiet for a long moment. Then he gave a nod. "She can't deny it's the best we can do under the circumstances. Ben has surely told Flavian about Skleros's sabotage during the Solstice Summit, so they will find it believable."

"And since Skleros's whereabouts have been a mystery since then, there is no evidence to the contrary."

All that kept Lio from barging through the door was Eudias's voice on the other side of it. The young mage had worked hard for the trust the lords placed in him. Only out of respect for him would Lio wait to be invited in.

"There's been a murder." Eudias's words were too quiet for a mortal to hear through the stone walls and thick wooden door, but easy for Hesperine ears to detect.

There came the whisper of a sword being drawn, then Benedict's urgent murmur. "Who? Where?"

Eudias answered, "I'm afraid swords will not avail in this case. Ambassador Deukalion and I found him. The ambassador wishes to see you, Lord Flavian."

Then came another voice, low and hoarse. He sounded exactly as Lio had imagined, like a noble son who had been out debauching himself and hadn't slept in a week. "Pack the Hesperines' silk-assed light mage back to their Sanctuary. I trust you to do it diplomatically."

Eudias cleared his throat. "Ambassador Deukalion is rather difficult to sway from his course, once he has set it."

"I wasn't supposed to formally receive him until after Princess Solia's arrival tomorrow."

"I'm afraid it cannot wait."

"Hadria is breathing down my neck and Severitas is shouting in my face. I cannot afford for a Hesperine to step out of line. And if violence has erupted in the camp, I certainly don't have time for diplomatic blather. Ben, go find out what happened."

Eudias said nothing more. The door swung open to reveal Benedict, about to charge out to meet the threat. He stopped short, his eyes widening.

Lio must have made precisely the right impression for this diplomatic encounter, because Benedict backed out of Lio's way in haste.

Lio did not send the door slamming back against the wall. He did not announce his epithets or offices. He was above such posturing. He strode into Flavian's solar in complete silence.

But the feral Craving in him was still gratified when Flavian jumped to his feet and staggered back, keeping his desk between them.

Flavian's solar was an ancient room, more drafty than stately, appointed with impressive furniture and an unimpressive man. Tenebra's paragon of manhood looked as he had in Cassia's memories, well-dressed and athletic, with the chestnut hair of the Segetian line. But his cocky charm was nowhere to be seen now. He stared at Lio with bloodshot eyes and ran a nervous hand over his unshaven chin.

With Lyros a quiet threat at his side, Lio laid Flavian's fallen soldier out before him on the large desk. "What was his name?"

Flavian's gaze dropped to the sentry, and a grimace of regret crossed his face. "Aw, gods. Hamon."

"Did he have a family?" Lio asked.

Flavian heaved a sigh. "My men were his family. He's one of our best. Was."

Eudias rested an unsteady hand on Hamon's brow and said a blessing in the Divine Tongue. A glyph of Anthros gleamed to life on the man's pallid skin.

Benedict echoed with a prayer to Andragathos, but did not sheath his sword. "Who did this? I don't see a wound on him."

"It was necromancy," Lio stated.

Flavian looked to Eudias for confirmation, and the mage nodded.

"How is that possible?" Flavian protested. "The necromancers the Temple of Hypnos sent to attend the Council are all trusted Tenebran mages. They're village undertakers, not assassins."

"This was the work of a Gift Collector," Lio said. "Skleros, the same master necromancer who tried to undermine our negotiations with the Allied Lords."

Flavian's expression hardened. "And what is a Gift Collector doing at Patria? Is it a coincidence that he appeared the same night as a Hesperine, and that one of my men got caught in the middle?"

It seemed Flavian was working on finding his spine, but his men deserved a better defense than their lord blaming someone else for this tragedy.

Lio said, "The Gift Collector has been here all along. He strolled through your perimeter days, perhaps weeks ago. I am the reason he is gone."

Flavian rested his hands on the desk and leaned forward over Hamon's remains. "I ask again, what was an assassin of Hesperines doing in my camp?"

Lio stood calmly. "The same thing he was doing at the Solstice Summit in Orthros. Sabotaging King Lucis's enemies for the Orders."

Lyros asked, "What information might Skleros have extracted from Hamon that he could report to the king and Cordium?"

Flavian shook his head. "I find it doubtful that an expert necromancer from the Magelands would attack my sentry when his Hesperine prey is within reach."

"With respect, Lord Flavian," Lyros continued, "would not Hamon have known everyone who entered Patria from his checkpoint? That information would be tempting to the king and his allies. It could help them determine which lords are siding with you, or how many of their allies have joined the Full Council to vote in Lucis's favor."

"What else did Hamon know?" Lio pressed. "Was he privy to any of your meetings with the Allied Lords?"

"No," Flavian snapped. "He was a foot soldier, not a commander. But a loyal one. That's why I entrusted him with the task of overseeing who entered that part of the perimeter."

It was as Lio had suspected. This had been a warning shot from the Collector. He had not yet infiltrated Flavian's inner circle, but he would not stop at perimeter sentries.

"Gods." Flavian's gaze dropped to his soldier once more. "He should have died in battle, not been hunted for sport by a Gift Collector lying in wait for Hesperines."

"If there were not a single Hesperine in Tenebra," Lio said, "you would still have Cordium's assassins at your throat. Lucis's mage allies would interfere to aid him, regardless of whether Orthros involves ourselves. But if we had a presence at Patria, no Gift Collector would have set foot here."

Silence was more effective than diplomatic blather. Lio left the rest of his point unspoken and let Flavian think it for himself. If Hesperines had been here, Hamon would still be alive.

Flavian straightened to his full height. Lio looked down at him.

The man's aura flashed with anger. "And here I was expecting diplomacy from you, *Ambassador*. Are you implying that I cannot protect my own men?"

"It won't help Hamon for either of us to nurse our pride, Lord Flavian. And it won't help you to have an ally who is all diplomatic blather. Steward Lyros and I are here on behalf of Orthros to offer you something that is actually of use to you while Hadria is breathing down your neck and Severitas is shouting in your face. Protection."

At last it appeared to dawn on Flavian that he had made an apprentice-level mistake when dealing with Hesperines: he had not taken their preternatural hearing into consideration.

"I am a light mage," Lio said, "but I am also one of the most powerful Hesperine thelemancers, next to Silvertongue and the Victory Star. Mage Eudias and I dueled this necromancer before. Let me help him protect Patria."

"Ah, there are the pretty words I was told to expect from Glasstongue," Flavian said lightly. "I'm afraid they won't work on me, Ambassador. I know that when you told the Allied Lords you're a mind mage, it was merely a bluff during a crucial point in negotiations. And I know you revealed to them afterwards how harmless you are."

Taking care not to frighten the mortals had been necessary at the time. But Lio could not afford to hide his magic now. After everything he and Cassia had survived, he knew when to keep his power in reserve—and when to use it to the fullest.

"Allowing them to deem me harmless was a kindness," Lio said. "But now I will let them fear me, if it means keeping them alive. The bluff was that I am merely a light mage."

Flavian scoffed. "You expect me to believe you, when you change your version of the truth to suit yourself?"

Whether Lio made an enemy or ally of Flavian tonight, he must make a believer of him. "It seems an exercise in truth is in order. With your permission, I will provide you with evidence of my power."

"Ambassador," Benedict broke in, courteous but firm, "is this really necessary?"

"With respect, Sir Benedict, I believe it is. The Allied Lords returned home in a cloud of rumors about the events of the Summit. Lord Flavian, as the man in command here at Patria, should have the facts to inform his decisions."

"What magical exercise do you suggest?" Eudias asked.

"Lord Flavian should hold a thought in his mind—something I have no way of knowing. For example, something that no one who came to Orthros for the Summit could have told me. If I can tell him what he is thinking, that should be demonstration enough of my power."

"This is your idea of proof?" Flavian demanded. "You want to use your magic on me?"

"No, I will not perform any active castings. If you focus on a thought, I will be able to hear it without applying my magic to your mind or trespassing on your Will in any way."

Flavian's eyes narrowed. "I don't have time to play games."

Lio let a trace of his power infuse his voice. "This is no game, I assure you. I do not play with people's lives."

A subtle shiver went through Flavian, and the determination in his aura faltered. Words flashed across the surface of his thoughts, too unguarded for any mind mage to miss. *Uncanny bastard...should have believed the tales about the size of his fangs...*

The man's discomfort sent satisfaction running through Lio's veins. But he had made his point and should not indulge himself. Flavian had no personal aversion to Hesperines, and Lio had best not give him a reason to harbor such prejudices now.

Waiting for Flavian to make up his mind, Lio closed his mouth and gave his fangs an opportunity to recede.

Finally Flavian looked Lio in the eye. "Very well. Prove to me whether you're as powerful as you claim."

Closing his eyes, Flavian crossed his arms and leaned against the wall behind his desk. His own bluff of easy confidence would have been convincing, if his aura had not been teetering on the edge of doubt and fear.

With some caution, Lio attuned himself to Flavian's thoughts, wary of what he would see. After all, the man was part of the Brotherhood of Hedon. No telling what unsavory things he had done in the name of the god of pleasure and chance.

But what Lio saw in his mind's eye was a familiar scene. He had witnessed it in Cassia's memories. A bonfire on the greensward of Solorum palace, a gathering of nobles. This time from Flavian's point of view.

Lio's gut clenched as Flavian recalled sneaking away to meet Cassia in the woods, alone. When Flavian remembered the kiss he had planned to give her, all the helpless rage Lio had felt that night came flooding back to him.

Flavian's eyes had come open. He was watching Lio for a reaction, and a sense of outraged satisfaction flared in his aura, as if Lio had just proved him right about something.

He had turned this into a test of Lio's honor, not his magical power.

Lio had walked in here unveiled, determined to deal straightly with Flavian. Now he realized his own critical misstep. He snapped a veil spell around himself, but it was too late. He must have betrayed his reaction.

Lio arranged his thoughts in an arcane pattern his uncle had taught him to use for controlling his thelemancy. It worked on his Grace instincts, too. Sometimes.

"That is not a secret, Lord Flavian." Lio managed to keep his voice dignified. "We are all aware you danced the Autumn Greeting with Ambassador Cassia."

"Is that the only conclusion you drew from my thoughts about Lady Cassia?" Flavian returned.

The title of *lady* grated on Lio's ears. "It seems I should have specified that you focus on a secret that is fit to repeat in front of Sir Benedict and Mage Eudias. I will not announce any behavior of yours that could reflect badly on Ambassador Cassia."

"In case you are not familiar with Tenebran law, a betrothal is legally binding and all but a marriage. There is nothing dishonorable about me spending time alone with my betrothed."

He left the rest unsaid. But Lio heard the words loud and clear in the man's thoughts. *It is entirely dishonorable for another male to spend so much time with her, especially a Hesperine.*

Flavian followed the warning with a challenge. "I am not ashamed to admit Lady Cassia and I shared a private dance after the ceremony."

Benedict crossed his arms. "I helped them leave the crowd myself."

Bleeding thorns, not even Benedict's sense of propriety could avert conflict in this situation.

Lio knew there had been no private dance. Cassia had gotten Flavian alone in order to inform him in no uncertain terms that she would never share a kiss, much less a bed with him. But if Lio revealed he knew that, it would make it all too clear how open Cassia was with him.

Lio cleared his throat. "Ambassador Cassia is now a valued member of Orthros's diplomatic service, and her conduct, both public and private, has our respect and discretion. I cannot say the same for the mortal drunkards who gossiped so much about your promise dance that their lewd rumors even reached Hesperine ears. It doesn't take a mind mage to know what happened that night. Shall we try again with something that is actually a secret?"

"That won't be necessary." Flavian's tone was dangerous. "I'm convinced of your affinity. It is clear to me that your diplomatic service has assigned Lady Cassia a mind mage for a partner. Know that she is still a valued member of the Tenebran nobility—and still my betrothed."

Lio's Grace instincts demanded that he declare now, to Flavian's face, that his little human pretensions toward Cassia would die, while Lio's bond with her would endure the test of eternity.

Lio drew in a deep breath. Holding onto the vestiges of his control over his fangs and his magic, he said, "Cassia's path is her own to decide. She is who she chooses to be. And she has all of Orthros standing in defense of her Will over her own future."

Flavian straightened. "She has her Tenebran allies standing ready to rescue her, should her future not turn out as she deserves."

Any man who thought Cassia needed rescuing was a fool. But Lio need not tell Flavian so. Cassia required no help to show him that herself.

Lyros broke the standoff. "Lord Flavian, now that you are aware of the magic available to you, let us discuss what precautions we can take to strengthen your defenses. Steward Telemakhos and I would like to place wards at the perimeter. Ambassador Deukalion can enhance them with mind magic."

"What of the Equinox Oath?" Lord Flavian replied. "It stipulates that Hesperines not take sides in Tenebran political conflicts. Do you still revere that treaty or not?"

"We do," Lio said, "but protecting innocent mortals from unjust harm is well within the purview of Hesperines. The Equinox Oath permits us to shield your citizens from criminals. King Lucis has broken his oaths and the law. We do not consider warding a political act."

"There are plenty on King Lucis's and my side who won't see it that way."

"Hesperines are well accustomed to the chasm between the truth of the Oath and Tenebran perception of our actions. We assure you, we will do nothing to jeopardize your position with the lords who are skittish about your alliance with Orthros."

"The Tenebran mages will notice blood magic, Ambassador. Then they will talk. Then those skittish lords will feel like lambs trapped in a pen of Hesperine making. No. I will not agree to these wards."

Lio knew then that this fool had found his backbone at the worst possible hour of history. Flavian would not release Cassia's hand or Solia's crown without a fight.

AMBASSADOR CASSIA'S HAND

"Mak, I cannot stay here!" Cassia dug her nails into her palms.

Her Trial brother was a solid wall of immovable, musclebound Hesperine. "Lio is right, Cassia. The Collector was just there. They need more time to make it safe for you."

Knight stood at attention beside Mak, clearly in agreement with him.

With magic of her own, Cassia would have stepped herself out of the Sanctuary then and there. As it was, she stood at the edge of the pavilion with Mak, trying fiercely to persuade the most stubborn Steward in Akanthia to budge. "How do you feel, knowing Lyros has just confronted death without you?"

"I feel he's capable of handling the situation. And so is Lio." Mak's tone was reassuring.

But Cassia felt chastened. "This is not a lack of faith in Lio."

"No," Mak agreed, "it's the fact that you can't take your hands off politics for five minutes. Stop trying to control everything."

"This is Tenebra. If we let a single piece slip from our control, it will be disastrous."

"*Our* control, Cassia. You're part of a delegation now. You don't have to manage all of this alone."

"And what is Lio doing?" Cassia demanded. "He decided without us that he will have his first audience with Flavian."

"As long as Flavian survives the encounter, I'll deem it a success," Mak muttered. "Don't worry. Lyros won't let Lio do anything stupid."

That should have mollified Cassia, but it didn't. Her panic was pushing its way to the surface. She mustn't let it out. She must regain the control that had saved her life in this kingdom over and over.

Solia had been standing at the table with Kella and Hoyefe, in consultation with Rudhira. Now Cassia's sister beckoned to her and Mak.

Cassia made to rejoin the others, but Knight refused to budge. She had to command him three times before he would allow her past him. Mak followed them with obvious reluctance.

"I am going to Patria now," Solia announced. "I need to be present for our delegations' first audience with Flavian. Lio should not have taken such action without us."

Cassia clung to frustration as an antidote to fear. Her own protest against Lio's decision was one matter. They were partners. But her sister's disapproval of her Grace was unacceptable.

With brisk hands, Cassia checked the pins in Solia's scarf-coronet. "What are you planning to say to Flavian?"

Solia smoothed her golden gown, then adjusted her sword belt. "I was planning to let the diplomats coddle him while I make him uncomfortable. It seems we must reverse roles."

Rudhira did not look pleased. "This is your decision, Solia. But I do not advise you to set foot at Patria until Lio and Lyros give us the all clear."

Kella checked a silver fastener on Tilili's saddle. "We understand if you prefer not to offer a Hesperine escort. Solia, Hoyefe, and I can traverse."

"Speak for yourself." Hoyefe conjured a spell-mirror in front of himself and gave one of his curls a twist. "I always prefer a Hesperine escort, especially handsome Chargers."

"If I had my way," Rudhira rumbled, "the Charge would be all over Patria."

Solia looked at Cassia. "Will you come with us?"

"That is not our decision," Mak replied.

He was right. Cassia was not an obedient person, but she was a loyal Hesperine. She had promised her Ritual father she would heed him.

She gave Rudhira the heart bow. "My Prince, I ask that you let me go with Solia. I need to be at Lio's side."

Rudhira studied her for a moment. "You'll be surrounded by Mak, Lyros, your sister, and the Ashes. I suppose I can allow it without Komnena having my head for letting you go into unnecessary danger, or Apollon charging out here to knock some heads together in your defense."

That made her smile.

"Mak," Rudhira said, "step Cassia back here if necessary. Understood?"

"Of course, My Prince." Mak had his eye on her. She knew he would pluck her off her feet and carry her to safety, if his orders called for it.

Cassia silently cursed the Collector for making her his target. It was his fault she must be treated like she was fragile. When she got her magic, she would show him just how fragile *he* was.

"I'll step us," Mak said. "Might as well spare you all the traversal."

"Mak, would you…veil me?" Cassia knew she must ask, although she winced at the admission. "I don't want my expression to betray anything in front of Flavian."

"I can do that," he assured her. "My veils aren't as subtle as Lio's, but they'll do the trick."

Mak's spell enfolded them, her last comfort before the pavilion disappeared. Her panic gained the upper hand again.

They were leaving the Sanctuary.

Dark stone closed around her. Damp, chilly air sank into her bones. Voices filled her ears with the Vulgar Tongue.

Knight broke away from her, muscling through the crowded room to sniff every corner for potential dangers. Cassia drew a shaking breath into her tight throat and tried to calm her pounding heart, but to no avail. Orthros was so, so far away.

But Lio was right here. Their gazes found each other across the solar, across the lifeless body of the first casualty. She searched her Grace's gaze, Willing him to hear her thoughts. *I know you're not all right. But I'm here now.*

She felt him touch the mind ward, but it was not a reassuring caress. It was a declaration. *My Grace.*

That was when she remembered Flavian. She took in his tense posture and the way he glared at Lio. Bleeding thorns. Lio had not made a conciliatory first impression. At all.

Flavian did not quite hide his astonishment at the sight of Hoyefe, Kella, and Tilili. But when he looked at Solia, he seemed to forget everyone else in the room. Despite whatever Benedict had said to prepare him, Flavian looked as if he'd seen a ghost.

"Your Highness." He came out from behind the desk. The bow he gave her was faultless, despite his disheveled appearance.

Flavian could usually manage to look dashing after a stroll through a dung heap. Not tonight. The only time Cassia had seen him like this, he'd been deep in his cups. But there wasn't a whiff of alcohol in the room now, and he no longer wore his amulet of Hedon. It was duty, not pleasure, that had reduced him to this.

"Flavian." Solia's omission of his title made his name sound gentle, a reminder of their sweet princess from years ago. "It's been a long time."

"A lifetime." He put a hand to his chest. "I regret pouring syrup in your shoes when we were ten. You don't know how often I have thought of it, since..."

"Ah, yes. The infamous night when I danced through the king's entire ball with my shoes stuck to my feet."

Pain, fleeting but genuine, flashed across Flavian's face. "You loved those shoes. Because Iris embroidered them for you. I am so sorry."

A moment of silence passed between them.

Then Flavian was turning to Cassia. Approaching her. He said her name.

He had addressed her as "my lady" when she had left. When had she become Cassia to him?

"My lord," she replied.

He reached for her hand. She felt Lio's response like a quake in their Union. This small gathering of onlookers was a powerful deterrent that kept her Grace frozen across the short length of the room.

But before Flavian could touch her, Knight pushed in front of her and gave a quiet, warning growl.

Flavian lifted his hands in surrender, looking a bit hurt. "Easy there, boy. Have you forgotten me already?"

She made herself give Flavian a conciliatory smile. A few minutes in his presence, and she was already plastering brittle, false smiles on her face for him again.

"I feared I would never see you again," Flavian said. "Thank the gods you're safe."

"Of course I am. Our Hesperine allies would allow no harm to come to me." She hesitated, studying the weary man whom she had groomed to take the throne. "Are you all right?"

He gave a slight laugh. There was an edge to it. "We have much to discuss, you and your sister and I."

He reached for Solia's hand next, as if intending to kiss it, but too late. She was pressing her fingers to the dead sentry's throat.

Watching her touch a corpse without hesitation, Flavian protested, "Eudias, let us entrust Hamon to the undertakers now that the ladies are here."

"Give me a moment," Solia requested.

Flavian opened his mouth to protest, then dropped his hand. "Of course."

Ben bowed his head. "You are as kind as Tenebra remembers, Your Highness."

It must appear to them that Solia was merely showing compassion for a fallen subject, but Cassia suspected her sister was using some kind of spell. Cassia could feel something *wrong* about the man's remains. Like a foul odor, but not one she could smell with her nose.

"I'm sorry," Lio said. "His name was Hamon."

Cassia longed to wrap her arms around her Grace and tell him this was not his fault. But all she could do for now was stand here and remember this man with him. She studied Hamon's face, and her heart tightened.

She had seen death often. And she had not cared. Now she cared so much, she felt as if she might break. But she knew she wouldn't. Caring as much as Hesperines did only made her stronger.

Solia sighed and stepped back from the remains. "Go ahead."

"I'll help you move him," Benedict offered.

Eudias shook his head. "No, thank you. I will take Hamon myself."

He rolled up his sleeves, drawing a deep breath, then placed his hands almost reverently on Hamon. It seemed Eudias felt the need to do this for the man who had not been fortunate enough to survive the Collector. The determined young mage performed yet another traversal, disappearing with the body. Cassia hoped Eudias would accept a tonic from Tuura after all of this, before he ended up bedridden.

That sickening arcane scent left the room, but the specter of death in Lio's eyes remained. "I have suggested to Lord Flavian that he allow Hesperine wards around Patria."

"And I have respectfully declined," Flavian returned.

Their exchange sounded as respectful as mutual swords in the gut. Goddess, how had this gotten so far out of hand, so quickly? She had thought Lio had fully recommitted to the conciliatory path.

Then again, Flavian was the one exception who made her gentle Grace see red. She sent Lio a questioning glance, but there was not a shred of remorse in him. The look in his eyes thrilled her traitorous Craving.

Solia took charge of the conversation, and Cassia deemed it wise to let her. "I am sure we can all come to an agreement on the best way to ensure the safety of everyone gathered at Patria."

"You can trust Segetia to shield you, Your Highness," Flavian said with some of his characteristic gallantry. "Patria is under my protection."

"We will not allow the lords or the king to retaliate against you," Benedict promised.

"And I am here to offer my protection to my subjects." Solia gestured to Kella and Hoyefe. "As are my Imperial and Hesperine allies."

"Your Highness, you can understand my caution. Imagine the outcry among the lords and mages if we allow foreign spells to be cast unchecked."

"Your men cannot be expected to defend themselves without magic from an enemy they cannot see. My allies are equipped to face these adversaries."

"I can allow you to perform your own patrols," Flavian replied. "That's the best I can do."

"I would agree to that, provided you'll permit joint checks of all parties entering the perimeter. My allies must be allowed to magically examine all new arrivals."

"Only if Mage Eudias is present to ensure their spells are within agreed upon limits."

Solia looked to Kella. "Is this acceptable to the Ashes?"

Kella nodded. "Our Diviner can ensure no evil passes the checkpoints, as well as advise Lord Flavian's men on how to be prepared for necromancy."

Then Solia turned to Lyros. "As the Hesperines' strategist, do you find this sufficient?"

"Only wards would offer complete safety," Lyros replied, "but it is clear a compromise is necessary. The Stewards are prepared to do our best with cooperative patrols—if we are permitted to cast wards over our delegations' own chambers."

"Very well," Flavian said. "As a courtesy, I will not question any spells you cast over your own rooms. Princess, I have prepared accommodations for you all in my wing of the fortress. You will be safe here while we discuss your plans."

She inclined her head. "I value your loyalty. You have accomplished a great feat by gathering allies and enemies here and keeping peace so the Council can commence."

Oh, she was coddling him indeed. Cassia knew how it grated on Solia to give Flavian that much credit. To be treated like a guest in her own kingdom.

Flavian met Solia's gaze. "Are you here for the Full Council, Your Highness?"

She looked back at him, unwavering. "I did not survive the last fifteen years and cross the world for anything less than my crown."

For once, Flavian's expression and body language were opaque. "I would like a private word with my betrothed."

Lio's power was a tide pressing against the confines of the room. Cassia felt herself flush in response to her Grace's magic, and she was more grateful than ever for Mak's veil spell. "There is nothing you cannot say in front of my sister, my lord."

"I haven't seen you in months, my dear. Would you begrudge your betrothed a moment alone with you?"

What was he playing at? Whatever it was, two could join in this game. A conversation alone was the opportunity she needed to convince him to break their betrothal.

"If my sister can spare me," she agreed.

When Solia did not hesitate, Cassia took that as a vote of confidence in her plan. Solia gave Flavian a stern look. "Do not go far."

"Of course." Flavian opened a door at the back of the room, letting in the night air, and gestured for Cassia to precede him.

Mak blocked the doorway and inspected what lay outside. Then he posted himself just inside the solar. "Call to me if you need me. I'll hear you."

"Thank you," Cassia said. "Would you veil our conversation from everyone else, please?"

Mak hesitated. "As long as you remember what I said about being part of a delegation."

"I promise."

Lyros was standing beside Lio. To keep him in check, Cassia knew. She hated to put her Grace through this, but she would do what she must to free them from this mess.

She joined Flavian outside on a small parapet. With her hound between them, he didn't try to hold her hand again.

A lone torch sputtered in the gloomy twilight. Rain misted her hair, but the surrounding towers mostly blocked the weather—and enemy archers. Well designed, if one wanted a breath of air without the risk of assassination. Poorly thought out, if one wanted a vantage point.

Even so, she took the opportunity to reach out with her new, awkward magical senses. She could feel Mak's veil spell, but nothing out of the ordinary. She had known the letting site was unlikely to be at the castle, but she couldn't help a wave of disappointment.

But what was that crackle, somewhere in one of the high towers? It left a burnt taste in the back of her mouth. Well, well. After all the times she had worried about an Aithourian fire mage sensing Hesperine magic on her, could she sense Dexion Chrysanthos now?

"Cassia..." Flavian began, pulling her back to their confrontation. "What happened in Orthros after Ben came home?"

"I made a life for myself there," she said.

"Why?" he asked, a simple, but dangerous question.

"I'm sure Ben has told you of my intentions."

Flavian gave her a look as if she had made a clumsy bluff at cards. "The night of our promise dance, you told me we should not share a marriage bed so I can pursue my illicit affair with Sabina. You are no Kyrian missionary."

Thorns. She really had shown her hand that night. "Very well. You know a holy calling isn't my reason for wanting to dissolve our betrothal. Sabina is. I will not be an obstacle to your happiness. Considering that we are in the process of deposing King Lucis, I think it's about time we did away with his arranged betrothal for us, don't you?"

"I have come to know you through your plot much better than I ever did during those inane horseback rides while I was supposedly courting you. The woman who positioned me to take over the kingdom is no romantic. What is your real reason for wanting out of the betrothal?"

It was both gratifying and dangerous that Flavian no longer underestimated her. But it sounded as if he still did not suspect her darkest secret—that love was indeed her reason for everything.

"You stayed in Orthros with a plan," he said. "Was it about finding your sister all along?"

A safe assumption. One that would deflect suspicion from her and Lio. Cassia was tempted to allow Flavian to persist in this notion. But then he would believe she had used him. At least, used him worse than she actually had.

"No," she said. "When I made it possible for you to pursue the kingship, I had no idea Solia was alive. I never would have laid this upon you if I had thought she was returning."

"Right. All that time I thought I was romancing you, and you were actually polishing me up to become king. I was merely the most convenient potential monarch, since you couldn't find a better one."

"Flavian—"

"First you agreed to a betrothal when you had no intention of being my wife. Then you ran off to Orthros and left me to manage the king. Then Ben comes back with all but a diagram of how to take over Tenebra, and you expect me to rise to the occasion. Well, I have. I've done everything you asked of me for the sake of the kingdom—and now you wish to discard our promises. And you expect me to simply throw away all my blood, sweat, and tears and let your sister parade into the palace."

"I thought it might come as a relief to you."

"Is that all I am to you? A willing lackey? A reluctant king?" Flavian leaned a fist on a crenel, his face hard with determination she had never seen, but always suspected was hiding in him.

"No," she said. "I always knew you had courage and strength of will, if only you would decide you'd had enough of doing what others wished of you."

"Well, I've had enough now." He gave her an angry smile. "I will not release you from our betrothal. I find it as useful to me at present as you apparently found me useful to you. What is a little manipulation between friends?"

Goddess help her. She had known he could become a politician, a leader, if he would ever step out of his father's shadow and cut the king's leash. She had never imagined he would prove her right in the worst possible way.

"How dare you," she shot back. "I never toyed with your heart. I never came between you and Sabina."

"No, but you certainly used our betrothal as a stepping stone to your ambitions. Pardon me if I do the same."

"I have no ambitions now."

"If finding your sister was not your reason for going to Orthros in the first place, then something else was. It's clear you have Ambassador Deukalion wrapped around your finger, as surely as you did me. I might feel some sympathy for him, if it weren't so wrong for him to slaver after you. Even I have never stooped so low as to lust after another man's betrothed."

Hespera's Mercy. Flavian didn't suspect she was in love with Lio. But he knew Lio wanted her. They were one wrong word away from him discovering the rest of the truth.

"I assure you," she hastened to say, "Ambassador Deukalion has never behaved immorally with me."

"Not with a liegehound to fend off unwanted advances, I can see. But until I know what you're plotting with the Hesperines, I will not let go of such an advantageous card in my hand as our betrothal. I am nothing if not an excellent gambler, Cassia."

Would she relive this moment during her Gifting, confronted with all the ways her choices had come back to punish her?

She focused on the cold rain, not her boiling blood. Control. She must be the Lady of Ice, as Flavian had always called her. "I will not marry you, Flavian. Whatever you intend for our betrothal, it will not end in a wedding. Sabina would have both our heads, and you know it."

He made an exasperated sound. "Anthros strike me, this would be so much easier if I didn't like you."

She gave him a cold smile. "Yes, I once thought we might have been friends. I see I was wrong."

In silence, he opened the door for her. She marched past him back into the solar, burning with humiliation.

She had miscalculated. Her plan was a disaster.

Everything was spinning out of control.

She couldn't look at Lio. Couldn't bear Mak and Lyros's concern. She posed herself by her sister like a statue of a lady with a liegehound for a shadow, gathering the shreds of her self-mastery.

Flavian strolled behind the desk. "Your Highness, we rejoice at your safety. We will always welcome you as our beloved former princess. But if you wish to be welcomed as our future queen, you will need to secure the Council's mandate."

Her face betrayed no concern. "I am confident the lords will acknowledge the fact that the throne is rightfully mine."

"I have labored to earn the throne," Flavian replied. "If the lords deem me worthy, I will take it. If you wish to claim it instead, you will have to earn it as well."

The air around Solia heated. Although Kella and Hoyefe didn't reach for their weapons, Cassia saw the tense readiness in them. Tilili switched her tail, and Knight's hackles rose.

"Lord Flavian," Solia said, "are you declaring yourself my challenger at the Full Council?"

"No, Your Highness. I have spent weeks gaining support among the lords. You have come here challenging me."

"This is madness!" Solia barked. "Lives depend on us acting quickly and decisively to crown a new monarch. Having two contenders at the Council will only mire us in lengthy negotiations. It will expose our true purpose and give King Lucis time to act."

Flavian was undeterred. "Anyone who intends to claim the throne must be able to hold it in the face of those challenges."

"Tenebra needs clear leadership," Solia protested, "a single figure to rally around, if we are to ensure a peaceful transfer of power. We must waste no time uniting behind the rightful monarch, if we are to withstand Lucis's retaliation."

"Many will hesitate to rally around a woman or unite behind a stranger who has spent half her life in foreign lands. Can you protect your lords from the king who sent you fleeing? Are you strong enough to stand between us and his Cordian allies?"

Solia took a step forward with fire in her eyes. "When you break before those threats, I will still be standing."

Flavian stood his ground. "Prove it."

SUMMER SOLSTICE

1 Anthros's Sword, 1597 OT

THE LONGEST DAY OF THE YEAR

Cassia should have woken slowly with Lio in their bed at home, looking forward to the Notian Winter Solstice celebrations. Instead, there would be no time for sleep before the Tenebran Summer Solstice began at dawn. Her Grace would spend Anthros's accursed festival Slumbering apart from her in this goddessforsaken fortress.

She, Solia, Kella, and Tuura stood amid their travel trunks and surveyed the chambers allotted to them, while Knight sniffed every stately but faded tapestry, chair, and candlestick. The only Hesperine comfort was the ward Mak and Lyros had cast over the rooms.

Kella raised an eyebrow. "The Tenebran version of luxurious accommodations is one bedchamber for us all to share, and an entire room wasted on a loom?"

"The weaving room," Solia grumbled. "The all-important gateway to a lady's domain, where I'm to receive my petitioners."

Kella guided Tilili over to the decrepit loom and repurposed it as a weapon rack.

Tuura waved the cobwebs out of one corner with her staff and began setting up an ancestral shrine using charms from her medicine bag. "The boys' ward is very good, but my shrine will make this place a haven from necromancy."

"Thank you," Solia said. "I'm sorry this is all my kingdom has to offer you for the time being."

Tuura chuckled. "Dear Sunburn, think how well we've all made do with rougher accommodations than this."

Solia scowled. "Any patch of hard ground under an Imperial sky is superior to this pile of stones."

Cassia had to agree. "An antiquated fortress in Tenebra, in the summer, packed with humans vying to get close to Flavian, is certain to be sweltering, odorous, and utterly lacking in privacy."

Of course, Flavian had banished Lio and the other males to a chamber in a far-flung corridor. Every gray wall and moldering tapestry between Cassia and her Grace infuriated her.

But a cowardly part of her was relieved. She was not looking forward to her next conversation with Lio. Facing him after her catastrophic failure would be harder than whispering advice in Solia's ear about lords who might or might not want her dead.

Solia nudged her trunk of elegant gowns open with the tip of her sword. "Well, adviser, I must appear for Dawn Rites within the hour and make an impression on my Council. What can we do to make Flavian hate every moment of it?"

Cassia's mind raced through all the Summer Solstice traditions. "He'll have a full array of festival events planned to bribe, distract, and ingratiate himself to allies and opponents alike. Our goal must be to steal his thunder."

Cassia helped Solia, Kella, and Tuura get ready. Her work was almost done when a knock came at the door.

They found Hoyefe waiting in the hall in a blinding ensemble of gold Owia finery. "Oh, well done, Cassia. The costumers at Imperial University Theater couldn't have done better."

"I'm so glad you approve," Cassia said. "How would you feel about engaging in a bit of theater with us today?"

He stroked his mustache. "That depends on the role."

"We need to discourage rumors of Flavian marrying Solia." Cassia leaned close and whispered in Hoyefe's ear. "And perhaps encourage some gossip about an eventual match with an Imperial king?"

"I don't have the wings for that part, but I'll see what I can do," he whispered back with a wink. Then, loud enough for the others to hear, "I love any excuse to flirt and spawn gossip. Count me in."

Solia took his arm with an affectionate swat. "Don't forget it's theater."

"And I intend to make the most of it." He tweaked her chin. "This might be my only chance to romance you without a bloodthirsty shifter threatening to dismember me."

Perhaps because she could pretend it was all an act, Solia let that pass with a suppressed smile and a roll of her eyes.

When Ben arrived, the stars in his eyes confirmed that Cassia had achieved her goal with everyone's appearances. He offered her his arm. "In case you need deflection from those who haven't relinquished you to Kyria."

"Thank you, Ben." She might truly wish for them to relinquish her to her Hesperine, but she would gladly let Ben shield her from Flavian while Lio slept.

As he escorted them through the Castra, the gossip began. The corridors were busy with lords and the few of their ladies who had braved Patria—everyone important, trusted, or mistrusted enough for Flavian to keep them close instead of relegating them to the camp.

Cassia knew the character of such courtiers well. Theirs were the cutting tongues that had abused the king's bastard her whole life. That was how she had learned to feed them the rumors she wished them to spread for her.

They parted to make way for Solia, their whispers following her. Who was the mysterious lady with the sword and royal purple gown, her face and hair hidden in a golden veil? Who was the foreign suitor radiating charm at her side?

Who was the visiting princess riding a mythical cat, bedecked in indigo and silver? Who was the priestess from afar, wielding her staff with dignity, resplendent in her vibrant robe and headwrap?

The only thing any of them could say with certainty was that Lady Cassia had returned from Orthros. How different their whispers were now. *Returned alive…noble mission…Kyria's maiden emissary…* Cassia suppressed a bitter laugh. She had gone from whore's daughter to divine virgin in their eyes.

Little did they know she was neither, but a proud heretic. She reached for Lio's presence, but the feeling of him so near and yet out of reach made her mouth go dry with thirst.

The greatest challenge of the day would not be hiding her sister's identity until the right moment. It would be hiding her own Craving.

THE SUN BLAZED DOWN on the tournament field from a cloudless blue sky, sending a prickle of sweat over Cassia's skin. When Ben showed Solia's party to her box, Cassia was grateful to take her seat. The knight joined Flavian, who took the presiding place across the field from them, his box bedecked in the blue and gold of Tenebra, rather than the darker Segetian gold.

Cassia bristled at the sight. That was one of her suggestions, that he downplay his side of the feud and align himself with Tenebra as a whole. Seeing her glare, he gave her a bow. She returned a cold smile and unfurled Solia's banner, letting it drape over the railing in front of her sister. Gasps and wild theories traveled through the crowd that was filling the wooden stands.

Cassia held her breath, waiting to see if Flavian would seize control and unmask her sister. But he said nothing, apparently willing to play along for the time being, if only to keep his unopposed status for as long as he could.

Trumpets sounded, and Flavian stood to say a few rousing words. It took very little to stir the excited crowd into a frenzy. Boots pounded in the stands, Tenebrans' form of applause. Cassia played her role and stamped along with them, the rhythm making her own tension pound higher.

But Solia sat forward in her seat, her posture alive with interest. Cassia should have known. Solia had never cared for tournaments when Cassia had been a girl, but that had been a lifetime ago—before Solia was a Victor of Souls.

"You live for this sort of thing, don't you?" Cassia tried not to let her apprehension through in her voice.

"You have no idea how tempted I am!" Solia exclaimed. "I could humiliate every man who competes today."

"That, dear sister, is precisely what I am afraid of. Do not get any ideas."

Solia held up a hand. "I know. They must crown me in skirts before I can spring my sword on them. What is the prize, though? It's sure to be generous on such a sacred day, when the political stakes are so high."

"According to Ben, an estate and the privilege of lighting the festival bonfire. The lands are small, within Lord Flavian's father's power to grant without the king's permission. But they come with a title."

Solia cursed. "I'd love to pluck that plum off of Segetia and revert it to the crown. But even more, I would relish the looks on everyone's faces if I lit the bonfire with my bare hands."

"*You* may not. But I fully intend for that prize to be ours today."

"Hmm," said Tuura from Cassia's left, "as entertaining as it would be to make an impression on these louts with my staff, I think it would send the wrong message about my intentions as a mind healer."

Kella leaned around Solia and Hoyefe to look at Cassia. "Please tell me cats are allowed during the mounted combat."

"I'm afraid not." Cassia glanced across to Hoyefe. "Fencing, however, is most certainly allowed."

Hoyefe put a hand to the hilt of his curved sword. "I would be delighted—if my First Blade approves."

"Your First Blade insists!" Kella clapped her hands. "I hereby appoint you to show the shadowlanders what the Ashes are made of."

Solia withdrew a purple handkerchief from her sleeve and cast Cassia a quizzical glance. "I take it that's what this is for?"

"Care to make Hoyefe your champion today?" Cassia asked.

With a flourish, Solia presented Hoyefe with the handkerchief. "Lonesome, go forth and humiliate them on my behalf and become the first Imperial with a title and land in Tenebra."

"I make no promises to revert it to the crown. I have a new theater production to fund, after all."

"I wouldn't dream of robbing you of your prize," Solia promised.

"In that case, it will be my pleasure." He gestured to the first challengers. "Shadow, whom do you recommend I start with?"

Cassia eyed the warriors entering the field with a variety of weapons. "Best wait for the first few waves of contenders to weed themselves out, then challenge the winner."

Hoyefe sat back to watch. "Excellent. I'll observe their fighting styles in the meantime."

The opening melees gave way to mounted challenges and duels, shedding defeated contenders with each passing hour. Noise and dust rose from the sweaty spectacle. The sun grew higher, and Cassia envisioned herself sitting naked in the snows of Orthros in an attempt to cool herself.

When a lean, flaxen-haired lord was the last on the field, awaiting his final challengers, Solia asked Cassia, "Who is that? He looks like a northerner."

"Yes, that's Lord Severin, from the border," Cassia replied. "A strong ally during the Solstice Summit. He will support the contender for the throne who can promise him his people won't starve."

"If only every lord had such sensible priorities." Kella's gaze scanned the stands again, surely missing not a single blade or bladed look.

"It's his father we should worry about," Cassia warned. "Free Lord Severinus hates Hesperines and may have supported the heart hunter attack that nearly killed us all on our way to the Solstice Summit. Then he decided his son was more useful alive and voting on his behalf to overthrow Lucis. Fear of losing the old lord's support is one reason Flavian will not allow a greater Hesperine presence at Patria."

"Well," Solia said, "you and Severin and I have something in common, then. Our fathers tried to murder us."

Hoyefe considered Severin. "He looks like he needs someone to ease his burdens at the end of a long day. Do you know what flavor of comfort he prefers?"

Cassia petted Knight, who was panting in the warmth. "I'm not sure, but if anyone can find out, it is you, Hoyefe."

"Drawing him out will be fun," Hoyefe mused. "Time for me to begin the next act of our play, in which I play the conquering hero."

"Remember, dear Lonesome," Tuura added, "we are here to make allies, not make the shadowlanders fear an Imperial invasion."

"I will make it clear I have no intention of invading Tenebra. As to not invading Lord Severin's breeches, well, I make no such promises."

Hoyefe made a show of kissing Solia's handkerchief before striding onto the field to the crowd's *oohs* and *ahhs*. He handed his luxurious Owia wrap to one of the squires, his linen under-robe displaying his muscular arms and legs. He whipped out his curved sword with a flourish, its golden hilt glinting in the sunlight. Solia gave an affectionate laugh at his display.

He paused to advise Flavian's herald of his titles, and then the man announced, "Hoyefe of the Ashes, Gold Roster Master Fencer, Graduate with Honors from Imperial University's School of Fine Arts, Lord of the Owia Homelands, shall fight as the champion of the mysterious lady in purple."

He and Severin bowed to each other. There came a hush. Then Hoyefe made the first move, lightning-fast. Severin leapt to parry just in time, but Cassia knew he was already fighting a losing battle.

Hoyefe danced around the young lord, relentless and yet somehow teasing with his quick, nimble attacks. He got under Severin's guard, murmuring in his ear. Then Severin danced back, fending him off.

Cassia studied Severin's body language. There was anger there, but also interest. When the men's swords locked, Severin let Hoyefe lean in a little too close, linger a little too long. She had never known this about her friend, but now suspected Hoyefe would be one of the best things that had ever happened to Severin.

At last, Hoyefe disarmed Severn and sent his Tenebran knightly sword spinning out of reach. Hoyefe held the point of his Owia blade up to Severin's heart with an even more disarming smile. Severin looked back with drawn brows, his face ruddy and hair tousled, more animated than Cassia had ever seen him.

"Lord Hoyefe is the victor!" the herald declared.

Flavian rose from his seat. Cassia was already savoring the vision of Flavian on his ass in the dirt with Hoyefe laughing over him.

But Flavian gave her a sardonic smile. "Sir Benedict, First Knight of Segetia, will fight as my champion today."

Cassia cursed under her breath. Flavian hadn't taken the bait, only her advice. She was the one who had instructed him to remain neutral in royal tournaments. Her own rebellion played out before her eyes, mocking her.

Ben joined Hoyefe on the field and saluted, his face grim with determination. This was a far different battle than Flavian fighting to keep one small piece of his family's vast lands. This was a knight fighting to become a lord—a knight who harbored a secret love for a lady above his station.

Ben was ready for Hoyefe's first move, but even so, the Ashes' fencer soon put the knight on the defensive. But Ben didn't stay there. He pushed back with steady force.

Cassia barely understood and never enjoyed sword fights, and thought of tournaments as nothing more than an opportunity for men to stroke their own blades in public. But today was different. Solia, Kella, and Tuura's commentary made the entire affair both understandable and entertaining.

Cassia wrapped her hand around her medallion, resisting the Ashes' infections enthusiasm. Solia looked happier in this moment than she had at any of their family events in Orthros. Well, except her duels in the arena, of course.

When Ben's sword landed in the dirt, the stands echoed with Tenebra's groans of defeat. Cassia rose to her feet with her sister and the other Ashes, cheering in spite of her spinning head.

This was the part of the tournament that sent a thrill through her. The scandalized cries of the crowd. Flavian's forced smile, his posture restless with suppressed anger. The knowledge that her moves on the board had helped Hoyefe steal a playing piece.

She had beaten Flavian today.

Ben stood still for a long moment, as if stunned. Then he gave Hoyefe a stiff bow. Cassia's hand went to her medallion, her cheer fading. She knew what that little estate and title might have meant to Ben. The first step toward turning his hopeless love for Lady Eugenia into the hope of being worthy of her.

This empathy with all sides was Hespera's greatest blessing and curse.

Hoyefe hurled his torch into the tower of logs. In the celebrants' cheers, Cassia heard layers of politics. Whatever their feelings about a foreigner taking the prize today, they were eager to stay on this new lord's good side.

Heat wafted off of Solia and the bonfire as it caught. Cassia pressed a hand to her sister's arm. She knew how hard it was for Solia to let others fight her battles for her.

Cassia's battle had shrunk to her fight with her own body. Leaning on Knight, she fought to keep down what little she'd eaten at the feast. Although her head felt barely attached, she tried to find insights to offer

Solia. That lord there could be bribed to support her, as long as she outbid Flavian. This lord here might side with her against Cordium if she restored Tenebran religious autonomy. There were some nobles aligned with the Hadrian faction, testament to the fact that the Allied Lords bridged the feud.

When an overfed cleric in red-gold robes stepped forward to bless the bonfire, Eudias trailing him with dark circles under his eyes, Cassia suppressed a groan. "That's Master Gorgos, Tenebran mage of Anthros. Went to Orthros with us, hoping to earn a promotion. Now angling to become the royal mage of whomever wins the crown. Supports the treaty, but sees it as his sacred duty to keep the Hesperines in check. Fond of overeating while preaching about self-denial."

"In other words, a typical royal mage of Tenebra," Solia said in disgust. "Why do our kings always choose men full of more hot air and prejudice than common sense?"

"They want stupid mages they can control," Cassia replied.

"I will want a clever mage I can rely on," Solia muttered. "If he can't cast spells at least half as well as I can, he can go back to blessing babes on temple days."

Master Gorgos gawped at the unexpected additions to his congregation, his gaze going from Hoyefe to the torch now burning away amid the bonfire's kindling. He drew himself up, as if about to launch into a sermon, and Cassia prayed it wouldn't be about foreigners.

Quickly, Eudias said, "Master, the fire is rising quickly. We cannot allow unexpected events to delay the blessing from going up at precisely the appointed time, can we?"

Master Gorgos released the gusty breath drawn to power his aborted admonitions. "Right you are. Such a devout lad."

Solia murmured, "Eudias excels at managing that idiot."

Cassia scowled. "I will ask him to manage Master Gorgos right out of Patria if that windbag insults any of our Ashes. That man's head is full of ignorant notions about the Empire."

Hoyefe chuckled. "Whenever this dreary place is lacking in entertainment, I intend to make a sport of provoking Master Gorgos."

Kella smirked. "Once you're done with him, we'll feed what's left to Tilili."

The Mage of Anthros droned his way through the Solstice prayers in the Divine Tongue, but Cassia knew the crowd was meditating more on her and her mystery guests than the gods. Barely contained excitement built in the crowd until Master Gorgos signed a glowing glyph of Anthros in the air to mark the end of rites. Cassia suppressed a shudder at the sensation of pinpricks that traveled over her skin.

Tuura peered into Cassia's face with concern. "Are you feeling all right?

All of Solia's attention honed on Cassia, as if she were ready to slay any sniffle that threatened. "What's wrong?"

Cassia waved a dismissive hand. "Tenebra does not agree with me, but I will manage."

Kella said in a low, firm tone, "Now is not the time for us to hide our weaknesses from each other, Shadow."

She knew there was no arguing with Solia or the First Blade. "I feel wretched. But as I said, I will manage."

Solia's eyes narrowed. "Is it a mundane illness…or a Hesperine one?"

Cassia was in no mood for Solia to find another reason to be angry at Lio. "This is not his fault."

"But is he the reason?" Solia pressed.

"It seems too soon for Craving," Kella observed. "It took days for you to become ill in the desert."

"In truth, I don't know," Cassia admitted. "My separation from Lio set me back. Perhaps it is Craving. But it could simply be Tenebra. I never had a strong constitution until I went to Orthros."

"You were ill often when you lived in Tenebra?" Tuura asked.

Solia frowned. "She was never ill as a child."

"That was thanks to your care, Sister." She buried a hand in Knight's ruff.

She did not have the luxury of feeling this ill. Not here, now. The worst challenge awaited. The Fire Dance.

Kyria's Autumn Greeting was for betrothal promises, Chera's Spring Equinox dance for weddings. But Anthros's summer Fire Dance was the dance all warriors looked forward to sharing with their wives.

The lords and ladies waited with bated breath while Flavian cut a direct path through the crowd toward Cassia. He held out his hand to her.

Knight bared his teeth. If he tried to bite Flavian, Cassia was not sure she would stop him. "We are not wed, my lord."

"We missed our spring dance," he replied. "Will you not make it up to me tonight?"

"I will dance with no one tonight."

"I'm afraid I must insist on a dance to remind Ambassador Deukalion how things stand between us. He may not be here to see it, but he is sure to hear about it after twilight."

Conniving coward! If he danced with her when Lio was powerless to stop him, it would only torture Lio more to hear about it after the fact. "I have made it clear that he does not deserve your ire. I will not participate in your petty taunts."

"Perhaps I haven't made myself clear. I am a man of my word—I will welcome a Hesperine delegation at the Full Council in honor of the treaty. But I am a man. I do not have to welcome Ambassador Deukalion."

"You wouldn't dare."

"Oh, I assure you, I would. If you don't open the Fire Dance with me, I will request that Orthros send a different ambassador."

The world spun around Cassia. She couldn't be separated from Lio. He would have to stay here in secret. And if he were discovered, the political consequences…

"I have a more competitive offer for you," Solia said.

Cassia looked at her sister, startled.

"I will dance share the Fire Dance with you." Coming from Solia, the invitation sounded more like a battle challenge. "In return, you will guarantee Ambassador Deukalion's seat at the negotiations for the duration of the Full Council."

Cassia could scarcely believe her ears. Solia was defending Lio? Was it a callous move, merely to protect Cassia from her Craving? Or dare she hope it meant Solia's sympathy for Lio was growing?

Flavian's brows rose. "You do realize what sort of gossip you will encourage tonight, once they realize who you are?"

Solia offered Flavian her hand. "Wouldn't that gossip be of some use to you, as well?"

"I never turn down another useful card in my hand, and that is a valuable one indeed." He took her hand.

The crowd gasped, and the minstrels' drums, lutes, and horns filled the night with the traditional song. The beat pounded in Cassia's head.

No, no. She mustn't let this dance undo all the ground they'd gained from Hoyefe posing as a suitor. She couldn't let this rumor reach Tendo's ears in the Empire.

But Cassia let it happen. For her Grace.

Her sister and Flavian stood silhouetted against the bonfire. Then they began the ancient dance, twirling, clapping and leaping around the flames. The images swam before Cassia's eyes, burned onto her vision.

Tuura took her arm. "I'd like to meet the Kyrian mages. Why don't you introduce me, and we can sit with them for a little while?"

"That's an order, Shadow," Kella said.

"Will you keep an eye on Solia?" Cassia pleaded.

"If Flavian puts one finger in the wrong place, I'll cut it off," Kella promised.

"And I shall dance with Sunburn afterward," Hoyefe assured her, "once for myself, and twice for Monsoon."

Tuura guided Cassia to where the Kyrian mages sat at the edge of the festivities. The Semna, the retired Prisma of the Temple of Kyria, clasped Cassia's hands. Her wizened face creased with delight under her white hood. "How we rejoice to see you returned from Orthros, my dear! You must tell me all about your progress guiding the Hesperines back to Kyria's teachings."

Cassia's guilt twinged. The venerable mage was one of the few people in all of Tenebra with pure intentions and sincere faith. She did not deserve lies. But the Hesperines also did not deserve to be told they needed to change. Cassia dodged the question by introducing Tuura.

"I would love to discuss healing techniques with you, Semna," Tuura said. "I hope I can contribute knowledge from the Empire that will benefit Tenebra."

"What a blessed opportunity." The Semna gestured to the seat beside her. "I hope we will learn much from each other as sisters in healing."

Tuura joined her, and Cassia sank onto the bench beside them, grateful not to move a muscle for a few minutes, except to pet her concerned dog.

The Semna's attendant turned a smiling pair of brown eyes on Cassia and Knight. That was all that could be seen of Ariadne above her veil. "This explains why Lord Flavian suddenly moved the Council to twilight. I take it our Hesperine allies will attend?"

"Ambassador Deukalion sends his warmest greetings." Cassia resisted the urge to glance at the sky again. The longest day of the year indeed.

Ariadne scooted closer, lowering her voice. "I won't ask about your mysterious guest in purple, for I know she will reveal herself to us when it's time. But I would love to know the Eriphite children are fairing in Orthros."

Cassia could have wept with relief for this little moment to talk about Zoe. Ariadne was not only Eudias's young sweetheart, but one of the mages who had helped Lio smuggle the children out of Tenebra to safety. "They're thriving. Do you remember the eldest girl? I'm teaching her gardening."

"Don't tell the other children, but when we were hiding them in our temple, she was my favorite."

"A bias I well understand," Cassia replied with a smile.

"What is it like in Orthros?" Ariadne asked her. "Do you get to enjoy the libraries often?"

"Oh, I do. I strive to be diligent in my studies. The residence where I stay has an excellent library." Cassia left out the fact that the library window seat was one of her and Lio's favorite places to break religious laws.

Ariadne sighed with evident longing. "I wish there were more texts in our temple. Pakhne and I have already read every one."

Cassia looked around for the Semna's other attendant. "But where is Pakhne? Is she not with you, as she was in Orthros during the Summit?"

"We have divided the Mother Goddess's forces," Ariadne said. "Pakhne represents us in Lord Hadrian's camp, because she came from a family of his action before giving up her status to serve the goddess."

"I remember." Cassia recalled very well indeed that Pakhne and her sister had not liked her very much, for both political reasons and the stain of her illegitimate birth. But Cassia and Pakhne had come to respect each other in Orthros. "Does her sister still frequent Lady Hadrian's weaving room?"

"She does." Ariadne gave Cassia a significant look.

Many of the kingdom's important negotiations took place in the weaving rooms, whether men acknowledged it or not. Solia would need the support of women like Pakhne and her sister.

When the Semna and Tuura concluded their animated discussion of healing herbs, the elderly Kyrian mage turned to Cassia again. "Now then, tell us of your mission. Have you made many converts among the Hesperines?"

"It will take more time," Cassia hedged. "To change things as I hope to, I must remain in Orthros longer. I must ask for your help, Semna. Lord Flavian still wishes to marry me, but it cannot be."

She frowned. "He has not released you from your betrothal?"

Cassia shook her head. "Sir Benedict has helped me explain to him that I must remain faithful to Kyria, but Lord Flavian does not understand."

"I will have a word with him about this," the Semna promised.

Cassia had seen the Semna scold the Dexion of the Aithourian circle. If anyone could shame Flavian into giving up their betrothal, it was her.

This was Cassia's great triumph of the day. She must look her Grace in the eye and tell him that her brilliant schemes had gotten her trapped in this betrothal, and her only solution was to let her sister dance with Flavian instead, while she begged the Semna to bail her out and lied every step of the way.

She longed for twilight. She dreaded it.

"You're unwell," Ariadne said with the kindness and confidence of a healer.

"Merely tired from travel." Cassia hugged Knight to her and willed her belly to settle.

Tuura gave her a look that indicated she was not fooled by Cassia's excuses.

The Semna took Cassia's hand. "You have a fever. All this to and fro between Orthros and Tenebra is trying on the constitution. There now. Borrow a little of Mother Kyria's strength."

The Semna's healing magic trickled into Cassia, but she still felt like a thirsty plant in dry soil. This was something that could not be cured with Kyrian healing. Not mere exhaustion, then. It *was* Craving, already. It seemed her separation from Lio when she'd been a prisoner had left her unable to last more than a night without him.

Her heart began to pound with instinctive fear. What if they were separated again? So many things could go wrong in Tenebra…

She pushed the dread back down. She must not let Craving reduce her to this incapable creature. She would learn to carry on in spite of it.

It took all of Cassia's strength to concentrate on her conversation with the Semna. The mage spoke of Kyria's teachings of forgiveness and paths for Hesperine redemption, while in the back of Cassia's mind, she thought of how much she needed Lio's kiss on her parched mouth, how she needed his magic touching her in places no mortal man could reach…

By seemingly tiny measures, the brilliant afternoon light softened to dusk. The fire burned, and the dancers spun.

Lio's power washed over her like a dark tide, and she knew he had awoken.

She bit back a gasp, her cheeks hot. He felt like a shadow reaching out of the fortress, growling in frustration at finding her so distant from him.

But she couldn't go to him. They must meet in the great hall for the commencement of the Full Council of Free Lords. With the eyes of the Tenebran nobility looking on, she must not betray that she was no Kyrian virgin, but a Hesperine's Grace.

THE TRUE QUEEN

IF THE ANCESTORS COULD speak in the shadowlands, Cassia thought the great hall of Castra Patria would be full of whispers. Although it wasn't the grandest she had seen, it held history larger than the confines of its walls. But the smoke that drifted up from the fire pit toward the shadowed ceiling offered no visions. The bare stones held no presences.

The presence Cassia could feel was Lio's. His magic seemed to stalk the halls, drawing nearer.

At the head of the room, the dais stood empty, the Mage King's stone chair vacant. No contender was to ascend the dais until all the votes were cast. Not to say ambitious lords had not stormed it and tried to force the outcome of a Council.

Flavian attempted no such crime. He took a seat in one of the carved wooden chairs that faced each other in tiers across the central aisle. Solia claimed the front row directly across from him for their party, which he had intended, judging by the chair missing to Solia's right, a clear invitation to Kella and Tilili. Her chin high, Cassia sat at her sister's left, Knight sitting at attention by her knee.

No matter how Flavian upheld the rule of law, Cassia would never forgive him for his villainy at the Fire Dance. He had threatened her Grace. There was no greater crime under the law of her bond with Lio.

Lio might not know the cause of her anger, but there was no hiding it from him in their Grace Union. His magic was restless in the mind ward, a mirror for her fury.

The free lords of Tenebra filed into the chamber. Each bore his Council

Shield emblazoned with his crest, the ceremonial armament reverently passed down through the generations of his line. The raucous men who had beaten each other bloody on the tournament field, engaged in gluttony at the Solstice feast, and done the Fire Dance with their women now took their seats with dignity. They placed their shields at their feet. Lesser lords, knights, and ladies filed into the back rows behind the voting lords' chairs of office.

Cassia felt all their stares at the mysterious lady in purple and her entourage, who dared occupy the front row.

Flavian's guards shut and barred the doors, closing them all in with the history-altering decisions that would be made in this room.

"Are you ready?" Cassia asked her sister.

"Yes." Solia put her hand on Cassia's. "But will you be all right through the rest of the Council?"

"Of course."

"Can you manage until he gets here—and *after* he gets here?"

Cassia squeezed Solia's hand, unwilling to admit the truth. She was terrified she would not be able to manage at all.

When Lio's presence loomed just outside the great hall, her breath caught. The other mages must have sensed him too, for Eudias cast an expectant look at the doors.

"Oh, well done," Hoyefe murmured. "Lio is about to win the prize for the most theatrical performance of the day."

The panels the mortals had sealed now swung open before a crest of Hesperine magic and thudded back against the walls. Lio stood in the doorway flanked by Mak, Lyros, and Karege.

Hespera's Mercy, her Grace was so beautiful. Taller than any man in the room, all elegance among the rough Tenebrans, with his innocent face and deadly magic. His gaze found hers, glowing at her with reflected torchlight.

Of its own accord, her aura reached for him and took a long draught of his magic. Her fingers dug into the arm of her chair. Goddess, she couldn't let herself do this here, now. She had to make it stop.

Lio strode forward, his black robes sweeping around him. His sapphire earring glittered at her. She thought she would go up in flames.

She dropped her gaze, scrambling for control of her magical senses. Then suddenly Lio was standing over her, a blessedly cool, impossibly tall shadow.

Flavian was announcing something about Hesperines and delegations, Cassia was not sure what. She didn't trust herself to look at Lio when he was this close. But then his veil spell wrapped around her, and she dared lift her gaze.

Oh Goddess, she wanted to drag her fingers through his perfectly groomed hair, yank open his formal collar, and dig her teeth into the pale skin of his throat.

When he took her hand, his familiar touch felt like a shock through her entire body. He kissed the air above her knuckles, and she felt the caress of his breath. But his voice was dangerous. "What did Flavian do?"

"Nothing. We must compose ourselves."

"Did he touch you?" Lio asked, his voice quiet, his anger rolling into her aura with his magic.

Her toes curled in her slippers. "No, my love. I'm all right. I'll tell you after the Council."

She glimpsed the tips of his fangs between his lips, but he released her hand and took his seat. Beside her. She had to sit beside him and resist the urge to climb onto his lap.

Mak, Lyros, and Karege took their seats on Lio's other side. All the players in their game were on the board. And they were relying on Cassia's strategy.

She felt Lio's deft touch in her mind. Her belly calmed, and her anxiety faded. Now was not the time to resist direct help from his thelemancy. If he kept doing that, she might make it through the Council.

Flavian's chair creaked as he stood. "Lords and knights of Tenebra, delegates from afar, of the forty-nine Free Lords of Tenebra, forty-six are here assembled or have sent their representatives, who are empowered to vote on their behalf. On behalf of my father, Free Lord Titus of Segetia, I bear witness."

Severin replied, "On behalf of Free Lord Severinus, I bear witness."

One by one, the free lords or their representatives identified themselves and swore to a quorum.

Lio murmured, "I'm keeping count of how many of these men hold their seats thanks to your schemes."

"Why stop at free lords?" she said with false confidence. "Next, I shall install a queen."

"You have already done that, My Queen, and told me you're pleased with your throne."

Her aura tried to spin his magic into her again. Oh, no. She must not think about being seated on him. Did he want to torture her?

"Not at all," he said in answer to her thoughts. "I want to tide you over during the proceedings."

Flavian glared at them. Although he couldn't hear them, he seemed to object to Lio leaning even a hair's breadth her way. Lio looked back at him with a chilling gaze.

Flavian began to pace the central aisle. "My lords, I have gathered you here in the name of uniting against the threats facing our kingdom. I thank you for leaving home and hearth to answer this call. I thank you for braving what we have not spoken aloud, but all fear—the king's wrath."

Flavian halted at the foot of the dais and faced the Council. "I will speak it aloud now. Make no mistake. We are here to revoke our mandate from Lucis, forsworn King of Tenebra, and place a just monarch on the throne."

The silence in the room seemed to grow heavier. If Lucis had any allies here, none spoke.

"Over the past weeks," Flavian continued, "I have quietly presented each of you with evidence of Lucis's crimes. I hope I have also demonstrated to you that there is one man among us who would make a worthier king. My lords, do you need me to make my case against Lucis? Do you need further proof?"

"Nay!" went up throughout the room, and boots pounded. Cassia heard the words *traitor, betrayer, assassin* on the lips of Lucis's once-cowed Council.

"Are you ready to vote?" Lord Flavian asked.

"Long live the new king!" his supporters called.

Flavian reached up and planted his banner on the dais. At the sight of his new crest, Cassia longed for a fire spell. He had adapted the royal coat of arms, removing the fire that symbolized the Orders so the sun and the sword stood on their own. It was the design she had created for him.

"I hereby ask that the Full Council of Free Lords crown me King of Tenebra."

Cheers went up throughout the hall. Without waiting for Flavian to finish, the free lords began to raise their Council Shields and affix them to the high backs of their chairs over their heads. The signal that they had made their decisions and were ready to vote.

Flavian had executed Cassia's plan well. Too well. It was thrilling and sickening. If she and Lio and Solia had not come here tonight to intervene, her plot would have worked. Flavian would have been king by the end of the night.

"Of course he would," said Lio. "Your plan always works. Unfortunately for him, he has lost the most important mandate. Yours."

"He is supposed to accept challengers before they hang their shields," Cassia hissed. "If he fails to do so, he will not like how I remind him."

But Flavian drew his sword and raised it above his head. "Is there any man here who will make the same demand?"

A few arrogant laughs. More shields went up.

Cassia met her sister's gaze. Solia nodded. It was time.

"Orthros is ready," Lio promised.

"The Empire is at your side," Kella said.

Solia drew a breath, too quiet for anyone but Cassia to hear. Then she rose to her feet.

"No man dares oppose you," Solia declared, "but I do."

Gasps and shocked murmurs greeted her words. The shields faltered.

Her purple train swept behind her as she lifted her banner with one strong arm and planted the Mage King's emblem on the dais. Turning to face the assembly, she pulled away her veil. For the first time in fifteen years, the lords of Tenebra beheld their lost princess. Cassia felt as if she were seeing Solia for the first time all over again.

"I, Solia Basilinna, heir to the throne, demand that the Full Council of Free Lords acknowledge my right to rule."

The room erupted. Shouts, prayers, people leaping to their feet. Flavian called for order, but they ignored him.

"My lords," Solia cried above the din, in a voice that would surely reach the highest row of seats in the Empress's arena. "I will hear your questions about my return—but ask with decorum befitting this exalted hall."

Silence fell.

A lord with wavy blond hair rose from one of the back rows. Trust Lord Adrogan to present the first irreverent question. The bitter second son only cared about lining his pockets. "With all due respect, no one has seen Princess Solia in fifteen years. How do we know this is even her?"

Cassia surged to her feet. It was a mistake. She would have toppled over, if not for Lio's levitation spell and his thelemancy calming her dizziness. She felt his power hum through her, bracing.

"I know my own sister!" Cassia cried. "Show some respect to your queen."

Another chair creaked. Aging but fit, Lord Gaius rose to his feet. The gray-haired lord had been Lord Hadrian's representative at the Solstice Summit—and dislocated Lord Adrogan's shoulder for dishonoring Solia's memory. "My sons died at Castra Roborra trying to rescue our princess. I know her." Though a hardened warrior, his voice grew thick with emotion. "Their sacrifices were not in vain."

Lord Severin rose from his chair. "I was there the night we opened the royal crypt and found Princess Solia's tomb empty, although we never dared hope it meant she was alive."

"Do more than hope now," Solia said. "See with your own eyes. Hear the testament of my Imperial allies who harbored me, the Hesperines who brought me back to you—and my beloved sister, who did not rest until she found me."

With Lio and Kella, Cassia gave her account to the Council. Once, she had revealed what she believed about Solia's murder to them and secured their faith in her sister's legend. Now she amended the record and prayed they would trust the truth.

Lord Gaius was the first to bow. Then Severin. Then the gesture swept through the hall, until every person there bowed or curtsied before Solia.

And then the shields came down, one by one, as quickly as they had been raised. Flavian's face was hard, although not surprised.

Solia had won tonight. But this was only the first round. They were in for a long battle.

The edges of Cassia's vision hazed. Oh, no. She could not collapse. Not now. Her control over her own senses began to slip, even as Lio's power surged into her again.

She was losing her grip on everything. Especially herself.

Would the mages sense the current of magic between them? Would her physical response to Lio's nearness betray their secret?

They had to escape. Now.

THE SHORTEST NIGHT OF THE YEAR

TUURA PUT A SUPPORTIVE arm under Cassia's. "Ambassador Cassia is not well. I shall take her back to our chamber."

"No." Cassia was alarmed at how weak her voice sounded. "The rest of the Council..."

Solia touched her cheek. "You've done your part. Go."

Cassia had no choice but to let Tuura guide her toward the doors. The cord of magic between her and Lio stretched and kept flowing. She glanced over her shoulder.

He was following them out. No, no. What was he thinking? He couldn't be seen leaving with her.

But a perfect image of him remained in his Council seat. Hoyefe winked at her, and she could have collapsed with gratitude. Trust a romantic like Lonesome to help them along by maintaining Lio's illusion.

Arm in arm with Tuura, her other hand on Knight, Cassia made it out of the great hall without stumbling or giving into the temptation to reach for Lio.

It seemed an eternity before they turned into a deserted corridor. But the instant they were out of sight of Flavian's guards, Lio caught her close. She almost whimpered with relief just from being able to touch him.

"I'll leave you two to misbehave." Tuura's staff tapped the floor as she ambled away.

Cassia couldn't tear herself away from Lio's anguished gaze. "My Craving...it's worse than I thought. I can't last as long without you."

"You're still recovering from when you were captured," he said. "You need to lie down and let me give you what you need."

It was a good thing he was holding her up, because the protectiveness in his voice weakened her knees. "No. Take me to the place I'm thinking of. Now."

His eyes widened for an instant, but then his fangs lengthened, and she knew she had devised an excellent plan for her apology.

She barely felt him step them to the parapet outside Flavian's solar. Inside the room, a piece of furniture scraped across the floor and slammed against the door. Knight growled and posted himself on guard at the exit.

Layers of Hesperine veil spells wrapped around them with the twilight mist. Cassia's heart began to race. With each beat, another flash of his magic sang through her every nerve.

"Flavian will regret this," Lio said.

"Mak told you." Cassia was thankful for that small mercy from their Trial brother.

"He told me Flavian refuses to release you from your betrothal. What else has he done? What happened today?"

"He threatened to have you replaced as Orthros's ambassador. You must be careful around him."

Lio only laughed. "I'd like to see him try. He is the one who should be careful."

Cassia must try to explain how sorry she was, how she would fix this. She searched for words.

Lio nipped her neck, scattering her thoughts and sending a jolt of need between her legs. "Flavian should thank his gods I have more honor than he does. You don't know how much I want to raid his mind and tear out all his thoughts of you until he forgets how to say your name."

Cassia took Lio's hand and pressed it to her throat, letting him feel her pulse against his palm, savoring the caress of his long fingers. "Your name flows in my veins. Remember what you told me the night the betrothal was finalized. That agreement is nothing but puffs of air."

"Puffs of air for which I will never forgive him."

"But can you forgive me?"

He raised his head, his fangs long and dangerous and tempting. "Forgive you, my rose? For what?"

"For getting myself into this mess! For completely miscalculating how difficult it would be to convince Flavian to release me."

"This is not your fault. How dare he trap you? How dare he use the petty bargains of men to trespass on your Will? He has given you no choice. And that, Cassia, is the transgression that makes me want to teach him a lesson the Apollonian way."

"But I went through with the promise dance."

"You were alone at that dance. Fighting so hard to keep us all safe. And I couldn't get to you."

Amid all the worst seasons of her life, it had been the worst of all. "I didn't know if I'd ever see you again."

"I will accept no apologies from you. And I will never let our feast be some kind of atonement." He cupped her face in his hand, lifting her chin. "You come to our bed with your head held high."

It was so very Hesperine of him to say. So very Lio. "I love you. Feast on me. Here, now. Not so I can apologize."

"Then for what reason?" He backed her slowly toward the wall behind her. "Tell me why you want my fangs inside you."

"Make me forget everything Flavian said to me here. All I want to remember is what you say in my ear when you push my legs apart and pin me to this wall."

She watched his fangs drop further at her words, and she pressed her thighs together.

"Remind me I'm your Grace," she said breathlessly.

The wall came up against her back. The hard ridge of his desire pressed into her belly. He slid both his hands behind her head and tilted her face up to him.

When his mouth took hold of hers, the current of magic between them became a flood. Warmth and energy surged into her chest and groin. She moaned and arched into him, rubbing against his erection in time to the pulse of his magic.

He left her dining on this mere taste while he kissed her senseless. She needed more than his kisses. But she never wanted them to end.

He let her up for air. The magic didn't stop. Her hips twisted between him and the wall, seeking to ride the current. Needing to ride him.

This was who she really was. Her free, true self did not fit behind her old mask of control anymore.

He trailed his fangs delicately up her neck, not yet breaking the skin. Then he murmured in her ear, "Are you cold?"

Trust Lio to think of her comfort when all she wanted was for him to pound into her until she couldn't stand up. Goddess, his sweetness only made her want his fangs more. "I feel like I'm on fire."

"That confirms another of my theories. The magic *is* keeping you warm."

His hand came to her collar, and his nimble fingers did away with the fasteners of her robe as only an immortal could. Cool, damp air washed over her breasts, and she gasped with relief from the heat. He watched her chest rise and fall, and her nipples tightened under his gaze.

He barely moved, but the rest of her fasteners gave way. Her silk robe slid open all the way to her ankles. He moved back to look at her, his hands propped on either side of her. She leaned there, bared to him in the night air. Exposed on the parapet of a castle full of men who thought they controlled her.

A wild laugh flew out of her. They had no idea.

"You're so beautiful," Lio said. "I love seeing you like this."

"Let me see you." There it was, the voice she now recognized as her own, bold and sensual.

He was a blur of Hesperine grace before her eyes. Then his robes were at his feet, and he stood naked before her, like some new god Hespera had sent to her in the night. His power pumped into her, a sensate heat in her chest and between her legs. Cassia's nails dug into the stone behind her, and she squeezed her legs tighter.

"Let go," he said. "Stop trying not to pull on my magic."

Was she still trying not to? She hadn't realized it. But yes, within her, there remained a deep hesitation.

"No one will find us here." His voice echoed through the mind ward. "Our secrets are safe."

Oh, that close call in the great hall *had* affected her. Fear of discovery—just *fear* was what kept a tight grip on the current of magic now trying to overwhelm her.

He braced his hands on either side of her again, leaning closer. She could feel the heat coming off of him. The magic was warming him, too. "Ever since we returned to Tenebra, you've been holding back. Don't let this kingdom do that to you."

She gasped. "You're right. Why am I doing this to myself?"

"Self control was once your only self defense. But you're a heretic now, my Grace. No matter the little ruse we keep up in front of the mortals, you are not Lady Cassia Basilis any longer. Your old fears are no match for you."

The evening mist was gathering on his pale skin, a sheen on every line of light muscle along his chest and torso. Her gaze drifted downward to his waiting erection, and she licked her lips, biting back a moan. As if in response to her appetite, a little crest of his power washed over her.

His erection leapt, and he gave a short groan. "Oh, *yes*, Cassia. Feast on me just like that."

She stretched her new senses, trying to release her inhibitions. Like fists curled tight inside her, they throttled her pull on his magic. "But something terrible could happen to you—to us—to the kingdom if they find out about us too soon."

"You're safe with me. You always have been."

Those words undid her. The tension deep within her released, and she surrendered to the pulse of the magic.

A wave of power and pleasure crashed into her, pushing her back against the wall. She heard a distant cry. Hers? She spoke; she didn't know what she said. She only knew she wanted all of him.

What she heard clearly was his triumphant growl in her ear. "*Yes.*"

His ethereal darkness spun through her. She felt like she was floating on the current of his magic. But his grip on her thighs was firm, real, lifting and spreading her open. His body was solid, bracing her against the stone.

As the next wave of his magic flooded her, his hard length drove inside her with all his physical power. Amid the vast haze of pleasure in her body, her awareness narrowed to that vivid point of their joining. His head gliding into her wetness as naturally as his magic coursed through her veins. His thickness stretching her, pushing through her resistance, turning painful tightness to exquisite pressure.

She let her head fall back with a wanton moan, reveling in the feeling of him embedded in her, so deep, holding her to the wall. "You've ruined me. No mortal could fill me like this."

He smiled down at her, his fangs at their fullest. "No one but my Grace could devour me like this."

"Remind me I'm a heretic," she said. "Remind me I'll be a Hesperine."

"You're already one of us," he rasped. "You feast on me so well."

He bared his throat to her. Her channel tightened around his shaft in reflex. Goddess, yes, she was so far from human anymore.

She struck his throat. Oh, *Goddess*, it felt so good to bite. So right. She canted her hips to welcome his reflexive thrust. They ground against the wall together as she dragged wave after wave of magic out of him, sucking on his throat.

His power came more easily to her each time, surging harder into her. This was the greatest temptation of all, this satisfaction she knew she could give him. This power she had over him.

His fingers dug into her thighs, and he pumped faster between her legs. Pushing her higher. She felt the sharp, teasing edge just before her release. But he was even closer. She knew his body. She heard the way he was panting like a mortal.

She felt boneless in his grip, held up by his penetration and the current of his magic. She couldn't concentrate enough to harness that current to drive him over the edge. So she surrendered to it even more, giving her body over to his hold, giving her senses over to her hunger.

The floodgates of his magic opened wider. He said her name, a surprised groan, and drove into her one more time, his whole body rigid with effort. Yes, yes, he was about to lose control first.

But then his fangs sank into the sensitive flesh of her throat. She cried out at the shock of pleasure that made her core clench around him.

The quiver of her near-release broke into climax. She dissolved into shameless moans. An instant later, he pulsed inside her, and his uncontrolled power shattered into her. She writhed on his shaft, shuddering between him and the wall, and glutted herself on him.

She wasn't sure how long it took for her senses to surface from the flood of sensation and magic. She returned to awareness with her face resting on his shoulder, cradled on his lap. "Did I...faint?"

He was sitting on the parapet with his back propped against the crenelations. He caressed her face, his hand stroking all the way down to her breast and her too-sensitive nipple. "No. You were just…lost in the moment."

If she'd had a scrap of energy left in her, the sight of him grinning like that, with his hair disheveled and her blood smeared through his beard, would have made her want to eat him again.

"Yes, do please eat me like that again," he said, and she knew her thoughts were an open book to him in this state.

She let him see what she had in mind for her next feast on him. The thought of having him taut and silken in her mouth made her wish her knees weren't jelly, so she could kneel right now. "Next time, I will succeed in making you lose control first."

His long lashes dipped, hooding his gleaming eyes. "I look forward to you trying."

"Challenge accepted."

He raised a brow at her. "Do you feel less betrothed to Flavian at the moment?"

Laughter erupted out of her, and it took her a few moments to stop. "What betrothal? All I remember is you growling in my ear."

His brows drew together. "Growling? I would never growl at you."

"It was definitely a growl."

He appeared quite taken aback, as if he were having a philosophical debate with himself. "I associate growling with predatory behavior."

"In this case, it was only associated with a hungry Hesperine." She put her mouth to his ear. "I liked it."

When she pulled back to look at his face again, his troubled expression had been replaced by something else. She had put the most endearing blush on her Hesperine's cheeks.

She stroked one fine, rosy cheekbone, and her humor faded. The urge to protect him rose up in her. She knew he was powerful and dangerous, and that he had survived Tenebra's ugliness before. But her sudden protective instincts toward her Grace were not interested in such logic.

He smiled. "I'm all right, my rose."

"Of course you're not. A Hesperine is never all right when someone dies. And you are never all right when you can't save someone. Do you want to talk about last night?"

He stroked her hair. "Eudias knows about us."

The unexpected reply startled Cassia. "What? How did we give ourselves away?"

"We didn't," Lio assured her. "He realized when we were all fighting the Collector."

She relaxed. "Oh. In that case…I'm glad, actually."

Lio appeared relieved, too. "It's good to know you feel that way. There was no chance for us to talk and agree on what I should or shouldn't say to him."

She ran a hand down his chest. "I'm sure you chose the right words in the moment. Just like you trusted me when I had to tell Perita about us."

Cassia wondered where her former handmaiden was right now. Her dearest mortal friend and confidant was one of the few people from this kingdom she would miss. By now, Perita would be due to give birth anytime.

She was probably safe in Hadria for her lying in. Would her devoted husband, Callen, get to be with her for the arrival of their first child? Or was he even now serving in his lord's army in the camp between Patria and the capital?

"You and Eudias faced life and death together, just as Perita and I did. I'm glad you have someone you can talk to about me. You need more friends here. And we need more people we don't have to hide from."

"Especially a person who can advise us on how to dissolve betrothals."

If that advice did not involve storming into Flavian's solar and antagonizing him, Cassia would be glad for Eudias to give it to Lio. But she was not going to debate with her Grace over what he had done last night, not when she knew he was still hurting from Hamon's death.

Lio's gaze darkened. "I heard that, too. Debate with me all you like, my Grace. I have no remorse."

"But now Flavian knows. He realizes that you want me."

"Let him."

"He believes you're dishonorable and I'm up to something."

"You are up to something," Lio said, "and he should be very worried."

"But this only makes it harder to persuade him to dissolve the betrothal."

"I have no intention of persuading him. Leaving the decision to him gives him too much power. We will force his hand."

"Force will only risk turning our allies into enemies."

"The lords expect me to be a silkfoot buttering Flavian up with diplomatic words. They won't respect me for that. But they will respect me for standing up to him."

"Of course they will. They respect male posturing!"

"I can play their games—on the Goddess's terms," Lio said.

"Does Eudias have a less provocative suggestion?"

"I am not sure you will find it less provocative. He thinks it might be possible for us to marry."

She drew back. "Why in Hespera's name would we do that?"

"It would make the Tenebrans less disapproving of our relationship."

"We don't need a wedding to prove anything to them! We don't need mages of Anthros and Kyria to mutter over us to make an honest woman out of me. Our Union has always been the most honest thing in my life."

"Of course." He ran a reassuring hand down her arm. "It would merely be a formality. A gesture. So I would have to strangle fewer mortals for uncouth whispers behind your back, and I could put my hand on your elbow in public without risking immolation."

"That is not funny. Have you heard Tenebran marriage vows, Lio? You would hate them. All that nonsense about a wife obeying her husband."

"I can ask Eudias if we can modify the vows and the marriage still be legal. I'm perfectly happy to swear to obey you instead."

"You know I would never let you do such a thing."

"It could be fun in bed."

At last, an exasperated smile tugged at her mouth. "We don't need marriage vows for that sort of fun, my Grace."

"But we do need elbow touches to last us between feasts." Lio enfolded her in his arms again, slowly.

She let him, soaking up this closeness to last her through the long hours when she would have to distance herself from him.

"Come Autumn Equinox," Lio said, "wouldn't you like to dance the

Autumn Greeting with a Hesperine? Can you envision the look on Flavian's face if he watched you share a promise dance with me?"

"Well, I must admit that is a very satisfying image."

"Just imagine it," he murmured. "Everyone in Tenebra would acknowledge our right to be together."

"I doubt it would work out that way in practice. Is a marriage between a human and a Hesperine even legal here?"

"Eudias is willing to find out for us. Don't you agree it's at least worth discovering what our options are?"

"We don't need that option. When all of this is over, we will go home to Orthros and avow each other before our people."

"Of course we will. And I will do as many labors as I must to make sure your sister is there, congratulating us. But what about when we are here in Tenebra with her? We're trying to build a future that is somehow in Tenebra and Orthros at the same time."

He touched the pendants around her neck. She had been so wrapped up in him, she had not been thinking about them. But bared to him as she was, her ambassador's medallion and the Changing Queen's pendant were still around her neck.

"We wouldn't have to hide," Lio said. "We wouldn't have to be afraid."

Glasstongue was using his most dangerous power on her—his compelling, alluring words.

"All I'm asking," Lio said, "is whether you are in agreement about Eudias researching it for us."

It was not the demands of Tenebra, but pure Hesperine temptation that finally made her say, "Very well. I will consider whatever information he finds for us. This does not mean I am agreeing to go through with any of it."

"That will be the subject of our next debate, Ambassador," he promised.

THEIR OLDEST ENEMY

CASSIA'S EXHAUSTION WAS GONE. Energy now coursed through her body, and she could easily forget she hadn't slept. "There's one more thing I want to do while we're here."

"I can think of more than one thing I'd like to do with you on this parapet before we rejoin the others."

She took a greedy kiss from him, but then disentangled herself from his lap to search for her underlinens. "I'm rather in need of a cleaning spell."

His magic tingled over her body. He snatched her underlinens before they blew over the parapet, then handed them to her.

"Thank you for defending my illusion of modesty," she said.

"I'll never let your underlinens fall into the wrong hands. Unless it's my own heretical hands when I take them off of you."

"Those are the right hands." She tidied her clothing, astonished to find she wasn't sore anywhere. Between the healing properties of Lio's bite and the exhilaration of his magic, she felt like she could conquer the world. "Now then, what do you say we infiltrate Flavian's solar and rifle through his important documents?"

"Ambassador Cassia, are you suggesting espionage?"

"And perhaps some theft."

"That is almost as enjoyable as the other things I was imagining. Let's move quickly, while everyone is still in Council."

Lio touched the door, and she heard its lock grind open again and the door bar creak up. She wrapped an arm around Knight briefly, giving his head a rub, then sent him in first to sniff the room for danger. She felt Lio's power flare in the darkness.

"How interesting," Lio said.

"What? Is there magic in the room?"

"An Aithourian spell designed to repel Hesperines," he explained, "but it isn't cast properly."

Cassia took his arm and pulled him back from the door. "Did the Dexion cast it?"

"No. Eudias did. A mage of his skill would never cast such a malformed spell—unless he intended to. I suspect Flavian asked him to keep me out of the solar, and Eudias decided to make sure I had access."

"Oh, clever Eudias."

They slipped inside the dark room, and Lio conjured a faint glow so Cassia could see. "Anything in particular we should keep an eye out for?"

She glanced around the chamber, looking for places she would hide her secrets. "Flavian has something that is mine, and I want it back."

"Your papers," Lio guessed, "the documents you sent him outlining your plan for the overthrow."

"I know he's already used them—and perhaps destroyed them. But if they're still here, I want them back."

"Anything else he might have from your courtship?" Lio asked, his voice taut. "If he has a romantic token of you somewhere, I refuse to leave that with him, either."

Cassia snorted. "He gives tokens of his affection to all the ladies he flirts with, but never accepts them in return."

Lio began rifling through the correspondence on Flavian's desk. "Lucky him. I won't have to break his hand for cutting off a lock of your hair."

Cassia went from chair to chair, feeling the seats for slits or hidden compartments. "I would not object to you breaking something more essential to his romantic pursuits than his hand. Secretly. So it won't disrupt negotiations."

"Don't tempt me," Lio warned.

While Lio read the documents on the desk at Hesperine speed, Cassia sent Knight on the hunt for her scent, on the slim chance that her papers still smelled like her after all this time. She searched behind furniture, inside wine bottles, and under rugs.

"Who is he writing to?" Cassia asked.

"A significant number of influential lords and religious leaders. This stack of letters is essentially a catalog of his supporters."

Cassia cursed. "Anything we can use to sway them to Solia's side?"

"I'll note any detail that could help us." From an inner pocket of his robes, Lio pulled out a sheaf of paper the size of his hand, tied with string, and a small stick of charcoal.

Cassia couldn't suppress a smile. "You bring writing supplies to forbidden trysts with wanton damsels on hidden parapets."

"Wanton damsel, in the singular. No one else tolerates my scrollworm tendencies the way she does." He began jotting notes, his charcoal dashing across the small slips of paper so fast it blurred before Cassia's eyes.

She began running her hands along the walls to feel for loose stonework that might conceal a niche or latch. "I will be disappointed if there isn't a secret door or compartment of some kind. If Patria is anything like Solorum, the Mage King filled it with secrets."

Lio set down the letter he was reading. "Do you think the Changing Queen did, as well?"

"What a fool I am." Cassia pulled the ivy pendant out from under her robes. "Why didn't that occur to me?"

"Becoming a mage is a profound change of mindset," Lio said. "But it is time for yours to change, Cassia. This is one of the most important lessons every mage must learn. Stop thinking like someone who lives by mundane rules. Start thinking like someone who is powerful."

The energy of their feast made her so aware of her new senses, of the new presence in her own veins—her magic, sleepy though it might be. She held the Changing Queen's talisman in both hands. The ancient wood felt different. More awake, somehow, like a hawk that had opened its eye to look right into hers.

"Well, I can start with what worked at Solorum and see if the pendant will let me walk through the walls into a hidden passage." She said the Changing Queen's first name, the one given to her by her own people, the Lustri. "Ebah."

She put a hand to the wall in front of her. Her palm met solid stone.

"Very well," she dared the wall, "I will try something not so simple."

Lio came to stand behind her. When he rested his hands lightly on her shoulders, his soft touch sent another thrill of energy through her body. It seemed her lustful aura was not above taking another sip from him so soon after their banquet.

"We really must stop spontaneously feasting like this," he murmured in her ear, in a tone that told her he had no interest in stopping. "If you're not satisfied with our revenge against Flavian on the parapet, his desk is right there."

At the mental image of Lio bending her over that desk, she bit her lip hard. "I am trying to concentrate on my spell. You are a terrible magic tutor."

With a low laugh, Lio kissed the sensitive skin under her ear, then stood quietly behind her.

She focused on the magic she sensed in the pendant, and on the kindred power within her. She Willed the wall open.

The stone endured, silent and unyielding.

She dropped the pendant, and it clacked against her medallion. "Whatever secrets this fortress's walls hold, they don't seem as willing to reveal them."

"Yet," Lio said.

LIO WISHED HE HAD more ideas, but his knowledge of Lustra magic was full of gaps. It didn't help that his thoughts seemed unwilling to make connections at their usual speed. The effect of constant twilight.

And they had only six more hours of that almost-night, such as it was. "We can experiment more later. We need to save time to start searching for the letting site tonight."

Cassia winced. "You're right. We must make the most of the shortest night of the year."

"The others are meeting us in the courtyard after the Council ends."

She muttered, "I'm glad one of us had the presence of mind to make such arrangements while I was losing my mind from Craving."

"It's safe to lose your mind with this thelemancer." Lio tucked his notes into his pocket again. "Now then, where else might Flavian have hidden your papers?"

"His bedchamber, perhaps."

"By all means, let us ransack the scene of his conquests." Lio pointed at a door adjoining the solar. "I smell him that way."

Cassia made a face and sent Knight through the door ahead of them once again.

He bounded toward one corner of the room and began circling a portion of empty air, sniffing with great excitement. At the presence Lio sensed within the invisibility spell, he relaxed. Knight never failed to sniff out members of their own pack.

"Fancy meeting you here," came Hoyefe's disembodied voice.

"Oh, I'm sorry, Lonesome." Cassia called off Knight.

Hoyefe popped into sight, waving a reassuring hand. "I'm only glad it was Shadow's shadow who discovered me. Now I'll know to watch out for liegehounds when sneaking about. Their senses truly are impressive."

Lio gestured around the room. "It looks as if we all had the same idea about spying on Flavian."

Hoyefe wrinkled his nose at a half-finished slice of bread on a side table. "I couldn't resist prying into the intimate affairs of Tenebra's famous lover. I cannot say I am impressed."

The antiquated room did sport a four-poster bed of impressive proportions with rumpled bedclothes, but it stank of the sweat of sleeplessness, not copulation. Travel trunks were scattered about, half unpacked. A shaving kit and bathing oils lay abandoned by the wash stand. It was the private space of an exhausted, overworked, unmarried man. Lio took far too much pleasure in this evidence that Flavian was not thriving in the plot Cassia had designed for him.

"Have you found anything?" he asked Hoyefe.

"Only this, so far." The illusionist held out a small square of tapestry depicting a fox with a sprig of blue flowers in its mouth. "He keeps it under his pillow."

Cassia's bubbling laughter filled the room.

Lio raised a brow at her. "I thought you said he doesn't take tokens from his flirts."

She put a hand to her belly, trying to catch her breath between laughs. "Cup and thorns, what a sentimental idiot. I would recognize that color of thread anywhere. It's Hadrian blue."

"The romantic plot thickens," Hoyefe said. "We find evidence of Sabina, but no Sabina. Where could she be?"

"And what offense did he commit that explains why he's sleeping alone?" Lio wondered.

"It's a long list, I suspect," said Cassia, "and staying betrothed to me is at the top."

Lio gave a humorless smile. "If Sabina is done with him, I will make good on my threats to break important parts of him."

"Alas, he still has a younger sister at home who would mourn him," Cassia replied. "Let's do some damage to his room instead."

The four of them made quick work of the chamber, despite the challenge of finding anything in the disarray. Fortunately, Flavian was unlikely to notice if they made a further mess of it. Lio and Cassia were still searching, and Knight still sniffing, when Hoyefe stretched out in Flavian's chair by the fireplace, holding up a familiar packet of papers. "Is this what you're looking for?"

Cassia accepted the packet from him and clutched it in her hands. "Thank you, Hoyefe. Lio and I have risked so much for these."

Lio put a hand on her back, looking down at what had once been a guarantee of her escape from Tenebra, which now entrapped them in a tangle of politics. "Where were they?"

"At the bottom of his chamber pot, in an enchanted box." Hoyefe twirled his lock picks in the air. "My tools make quick work of the spells. What you've all told me about incompetent Tenebran mages is entirely true."

Lio wanted to break even more parts of Flavian for hiding Cassia's masterwork in such an undignified location. "I'm glad to see these restored to the brilliant politician who dictated them to me. I look forward to watching Flavian flounder without them."

"He has gotten his use out of them, I suspect." Regrets swirled in Cassia's aura.

"Not at all." Lio looked down his nose in disdain. "He kept them instead of burning them. As if he couldn't even follow through on the overthrow without referring back to your instruction manual."

"There's another reason he might have kept them." Hoyefe's drawl held a note of warning. "They're written in a Hesperine ambassador's hand."

Goddess. Now who was the fool? When Cassia had dictated these to Lio, he had never considered Flavian might use them to cast blame upon Hesperines.

"This is my fault," Cassia said. "You trusted my judgment about Flavian. But I promise you, you can trust me to undo what I've wrought."

Lio shook his head. "This is equally my responsibility. I was so eager to foist the kingdom off on him so you could stay with me that I didn't think through the implications."

"I found something else in the chamber pot," Hoyefe said.

"Do we want to know what it is?" Cassia asked.

"Besides this?" Hoyefe dangled Flavian's amulet of Hedon from his fingers, studying the god of pleasure's aggressively phallic glyph. "If this is what Tenebrans consider godlike, they will be easier to impress than I thought."

Apparently Lio was pettier than he realized when it came to Flavian, because he snickered just as hard as Hoyefe did.

Cassia's smile was wicked. "Well, I can say that a Hesperine has already impressed Flavian's betrothed."

Lio didn't usually allow his bloodborn proportions to inflate his pride, but at the moment, he returned Cassia's smile with a fanged one of his own. "If I steal his betrothed, Hoyefe, will you work on dethroning him in the eyes of the rest of the ladies of Tenebra?"

"Challenge accepted. But I'm afraid I found something more concerning than the disappointing proportions of Tenebran manhood." From the bottom of the box, he withdrew more documents. On the small slips of parchment, a series of letters were written in a tiny, nondescript hand.

Lio frowned. "Is that a cipher?"

Hoyefe nodded. "Someone has been gathering information on the happenings here at Patria and trying to sneak it out of the perimeter. It appears Flavian intercepted these."

"You're certain he isn't smuggling information out himself?" Lio asked.

Hoyefe shook his head. "This information could be very damaging to his attempt to take the throne."

"You've already decoded them?" Cassia asked.

"My dear, this little code is no match for one of the Empire's most accomplished spies. I'll read the rest of the notes and tell you when I know more. But based on what I've already seen, I can tell you who would find this information most valuable."

Cassia shook her head. "I can think of too many."

"Indeed," Hoyefe said, "but we have here a list of lords who have declared their willingness to vote on a new king. Who would be most interested in a catalog of traitors?"

Lio was not surprised, but he did hate the chill that came over Cassia's aura.

"Our oldest enemy," she said with a bitter smile. "Naturally, the king has spies inside Patria."

"The question is," said Lio, "has Flavian caught them already—or are they still here?"

OUT OF THE FORTRESS

CASSIA HAD TO FORCE herself to release Lio when they stepped down to the main courtyard of Castra Patria. It was deserted except for their waiting companions, but she could feel the gazes of Flavian's sentries on the wall above.

Reluctantly, she let Knight walk between them. She hated letting Lio go when there was so much tension in him. Even without touching him, she could feel the wary hum of his magic.

"We have no cause to fear leaving the keep," she reminded him. "You've already checked the area, and I'm surrounded by protectors."

"Even so, I do not intend to let my guard down."

Their Trial brothers, Solia, and Kella waited by torchlight in front of the stables with everyone's horses saddled and ready. Lio extended his hand to Solia. "Thank you."

Instead of clasping his wrist, she waved a hand. "It was nothing."

"Hardly. I regret that you had to dance with Flavian in Cassia's and my defense. But you have my gratitude."

"Enduring a turn around the bonfire with that fool was one of the easier challenges I've faced for Cassia's sake."

Cassia bristled inwardly. Her sister might as well have said *I didn't do it for you.*

"You have my gratitude nonetheless," was Lio's diplomatic reply as he lowered his hand.

Cassia smoothed the moment of tension by smiling at the others. "Good moon. Isn't Karege joining us?"

Kella stroked Tilili's flank, the cat switching her tail as if restless to be on the hunt. "I asked him to stay here with Tuura. I don't want her without an ally in this den of barbarians, but she needs a good night's sleep. If she's to protect us from the necromancer during the day, she can't burn her candle at both ends."

"Good." Lio sighed. "Since I'm only of help at twilight."

Cassia looked from Kella to Solia. "Will you two be all right without sleep tonight?"

Kella offered Cassia a flask from her saddlebags. "I brought Caravaner's Milk. It's an enchanted draught we Azarqi use on long journeys when it isn't safe to stop and rest."

"You should save it for you and Solia," Cassia said.

Solia studied Cassia. "You seem to be feeling better."

"Of course she is," Mak said with a grin.

"Lio has restored me." Cassia kept her voice low, but she didn't care if she was blushing, or if her sister saw the self-satisfied expression on his face. There was no shame in admitting her Grace took good care of her.

"So it was Craving." Solia's tone was neutral, but Cassia didn't miss the implied accusation.

Before Cassia could come to Lio's defense, Mak did. "No one should go into battle hungry."

"Every strategist knows you need to keep your troops fed." Lyros's smile suggested he had certainly seen to Mak's provisions.

"Romance before a fight is too much of a distraction in my opinion," Kella put in, "but you've always sworn by it, haven't you, Sunburn? What's that you used to say? Something about a round or two with his sword to warm up?"

Solia shot Kella an outraged elder-sister look, and Cassia covered a laugh with her hand. Kella gave Cassia a conspiratorial grin.

"I certainly find such things too much of a distraction now." Solia unrolled their map with unnecessary force.

Lio's eyes gleamed with amusement in the spell light he conjured. They all gathered closer to study the map.

The keep stood in the center, surrounded by the camp and, beyond that, the wider circle of Flavian's guard perimeter. But to Cassia's alarm, much of the domain of Patria lay beyond the checkpoints. That region was marked with symbols indicating what kind of game could be hunted there, but she also saw farms, villages, and a few lesser castles.

Cassia looked at Lio. "And you sensed no hint at all of a magic source during your spell casting last night?"

He shook his head. "If it's inside the perimeter, it is not something I can detect. We must see if your senses reveal it to us."

Solia shook her head. "I'm sorry Thalia didn't tell me more about where the letting site might be. She didn't even disclose how she got her information."

"That suggests her source was not for a ten-year-old's ears," said Kella.

"As was often the case," Solia agreed. "She only told me that when it was time, we would bring Cassia to Patria, that there was a 'safe place' here where we could let her magic manifest."

Lyros said, "It will take many nights to cover this much territory without exhausting Cassia."

"I am not that poor a horsewoman." She gestured to the Imperial trousers and Charge-issue riding boots hidden under her cloak. "I even changed into the proper attire."

"You'll be an excellent rider in no time," Lyros hastened to assure her, "but sensing for the letting site will take magical effort on your part, which can be tiring. We'll divide the domain into strategic searchable areas, and as we cover each one, we can then step past those to new areas to save time."

Lio did not look pleased. "Let us hope we find the letting site inside the safety of the perimeter."

"If we don't," Mak said, "we'll be prepared for any threats we meet out there."

Cassia found Mak's confidence reassuring. But she could tell Lio did not. Hamon's death had left him feeling utterly unprepared.

But it was time to go. As everyone else mounted up, Lio held Cassia's stirrup for her.

She raised a brow. "You don't plan to levitate me into the saddle this time?"

"I am told Ambassador Cassia prefers not to be toted around like a breakable treasure. Besides, I would prefer not to earn the disapproval of the Victory Star and the Guardian of Orthros. Nike and Aunt Lyta want you to be an independent horsewoman."

"It's Freckles' disapproval we might need to worry about the most." Cassia's mare was giving Lio an unimpressed look.

"Hmm, yes," he replied. "She's not at all in awe of us Hesperines, is she?"

"If you'll put up with me," Cassia told Freckles, "we'll have a nice, long ride somewhere interesting you've never been before."

Freckles's ears twitched forward, and she stood still. With everyone making helpful suggestions, Cassia managed to mount without embarrassing herself, settling her gardening satchel across her saddle. She paused to appreciate Lio's Hesperine healing properties, which had left her able to sit in a saddle without discomfort, even after he had thoroughly ravished her against a wall.

With Lyros in the lead, they set off at a walk across the courtyard. Knight trotted alongside Freckles, and she did not deign to notice him. Before they reached the gate, a Hesperine step slipped them out of the keep. The guards on the walls above appeared startled, but waved them on. At least Flavian's permission to perform patrols gave them an excuse for this venture.

Solia wrapped her scarf around her head, leaving only her eyes visible. A sheen like the Golden Shield's armor spread across her face. "I'd rather no one recognize me and halt our progress to bow and scrape."

"I'm glad we don't need veil spells," Cassia murmured. "I have enough difficulty telling spells apart as it is."

Lio nodded. "The less magical interference right now, the better. As we ride, open your senses as we've been practicing."

"Will you guide me through the exercise again?" She knew Lio needed to feel that he was taking action to help her.

His words in Divine were soothing, the cadence almost mesmerizing. "Feel the Blood Moon's light upon your head."

She glanced up at the waning half moon, the Goddess's heavy-lidded red eye.

"Envision its current flowing into you," he said. "Feel its warmth in your brow."

It was easy. All the paths inside her felt open from the infusion of his magic.

"The current flows to your heart."

Her heart picked up pace.

"Envision the veins that run between you and the world. Now find the vein that flows from you to what you seek. Let the current run forth from your head and your heart. Follow it outward."

She let her eyes slide shut. Her sense of connection to her mount strengthened, and she trusted her horse to understand where she needed to go.

Cassia's senses expanded outward, past the messy glow of magic right around her—her powerful companions. Beyond their auras, the world was disappointingly barren. Not like Orthros, where spells grew like roadside flowers.

"There's so little magic here," she said. "All the mages are in the keep, aren't they?"

"Well done," Solia said.

"Can you tell how many?" Lio asked.

"I'm afraid not," Cassia said. "But there are different…flavors…of mage?"

Mak chuckled. "What a Hesperine analogy."

"This is a very Hesperine exercise," Solia muttered, "but it will do as a focus aid."

"What do you use for focus aids instead?" Mak asked.

"Sharp objects," Kella put in.

"I was trained by a spellsword, after all," Solia said.

Despite Solia's remarks, Lio sounded as if he were enjoying this exercise. "How many affinities can you sense in the keep, Cassia?"

"Hmm." Cassia tilted her head. "That strain of a comforting song is surely Tuura, and I'd know Hesperine magic anywhere—Karege. The sparkly one is Hoyefe?"

Kella laughed. "An excellent description."

Cassia concentrated, then wrinkled her nose. "There's the one with the burnt aftertaste—that must be the Dexion."

"Disgusting excuse for a fire mage," Solia said.

"There's the scent of a storm that I associate with Eudias," Cassia went on, "then cool water that seems Kyrian to me."

"That's right," Kella confirmed.

Cassia was trying to detect the arcane, not mundane, but she felt the urge to taste the air. She tried moving her tongue in her mouth, then felt foolish.

"No, that's a good idea," Lio said. "Using physical movements to focus your magical senses is a proven strategy for humans. And once you're a Hesperine, your mundane and arcane senses will actually be in Union, which will make it easier."

"Oh. That's helpful." She sniffed the air. "That incense smell is what I associate with undertakers."

"It covers up the stench of death," Mak said with displeasure. "Those are the necromancers who are allowed to be here."

"Then there are a few others I can't identify...they're too faint."

Lyros said dryly, "That's Master Gorgos's contingent. Not powerful enough to make an impression."

"You're getting better at distinguishing different affinities." Lio's praise warmed her. "You just identified progonaia, haima, mageia, and manteia in the area, without allowing the powerful concentration of magic around you to distract you. I'm confident you will sense hulaia when we find it."

Cassia opened her eyes. She was startled to find them surrounded by tents, with the keep some distance away. She hadn't realized how long she'd been lost in the exercise or how far they had ridden. "I can still sense the magic in the keep from here."

Lio gave her a knowing, pleased look. "I had a suspicion your range was increasing, too. We just tested and proved my theory."

"Clever, my love."

"Now, keep your senses open. Maintain a resting current, as we've discussed, so you don't overextend and exhaust yourself too quickly."

She tried to relax into the state of openness without reaching, which Lio called a resting current. But now that she was once again aware of their surroundings, tension crept up her spine, and Freckles' tail twitched in response. Knight darted ahead and behind their party, circling the horses, as if anxious that he could not be everywhere at once.

Now that they were out in the camp, she was too wary to close her eyes again. They wove between the grand pavilions of visiting lords, draped in heraldic banners, and past the humbler tents of their retainers. Many were quiet, their occupants sleeping, but others were open, spilling light and slurred voices into the night. They needn't have worried about waking anyone.

The drunken parties hushed as they rode past, and mortals gave them hard, wary looks. Cassia glanced at the flag over that group and saw the emblem of a lord who had not come to Orthros for the Summit. But they were here. That meant an opportunity to win them over, as they had the Allied Lords.

Cassia's sustained tension left her jumping at shadows, which usually proved to be nothing more dangerous than a drunk stumbling into the dark for a piss. At the sight of Hesperines, he startled and scurried off with his breeches half undone.

Cassia tried to maintain her resting current, but eventually her senses became fuzzy, and there seemed to be magic everywhere, a blur reflecting back at her no matter where she reached.

When Hesperine levitation righted her in the saddle, she realized she was swaying on her horse.

"Time for a rest," Lio announced.

Cassia shook her head, trying to clear it. "How can I be this tired after such a short time?" And after such a thorough dose of Lio's power a mere hour past.

"Magic takes a tremendous amount of energy," Solia said.

Cassia tried to relax her death grip on poor Freckles' mane. "You all cast spells all the time without falling over."

"Your stamina will improve over time," Kella promised.

"Has anyone spotted any trees?" Lio asked.

"Woods that escaped being cleared for the camp?" Lyros sounded doubtful.

"Follow me," Kella said. "Tilili and I can find you a sprig of green in the Maaqul."

She and her cat led everyone unerringly to a small copse of willows that had been spared.

"How do you suppose these survived?" Mak asked.

"The Kyrians." Cassia bit back a yawn. "Willow has medicinal properties."

The moment they rode under the cover of the trees, she felt as if she'd downed a willow bark tonic.

"Better?" Lio asked.

She blinked in surprise and drew a deep breath. "Much."

"Per Kalos's suggestions, I thought a higher concentration of wildness might restore some of your energy." Lio did not sound pleased to be right.

"What's wrong?" she asked.

His expression cleared. "Nothing. I'm glad we proved another theory."

Anyone else would have been fooled by his pleasant smile. But not Cassia.

"Let's wait here until you feel ready to continue." He dismounted and stood by her horse, reaching up to help her down.

This time, she let him. "Are we covering enough ground, Lyros?"

"Another hour," Lyros answered, "and I'll be satisfied with how far we've searched tonight—but only if you feel able."

"We can ride back to the keep after this rest if you need to," Mak said.

"You needn't fuss over me so. I can make it another hour, certainly." But she couldn't deny that when Lio seated her at the base of one of the willows, she was quite glad to be still for a moment.

She tried not to begrudge her mortal body the respite. She had pushed it through murder holes, bled it into Hesperine spells, and dragged it across the Maaqul. And presently, it was her link to her mother's magic.

When all of this was over, she would reward her weary body with the Gift.

She leaned her head back against the willow's trunk. But she didn't close her eyes. She contemplated her Grace, puzzling over his facade of confidence. He seemed…disappointed, somehow.

Regret drained away what little energy she had regained. He was disappointed in their progress, surely. Disappointed in how long it would take them to find her magic, so he could finally transform her.

"Lio—" she began.

She had no chance to finish. She saw the threat too late to move. She could only sit there and realize that an arrow was flying her way, and it was going to strike her.

THE KNIFE

LIO HURLED A LEVITATION spell at the arrow, ready to fire a volley of mind magic at the archer.

But the arrow did not stray from its path.

The horror of that realization cost him a precious instant. Then he lunged for Cassia at Hesperine speed and carried her down to the ground, covering her with his body. He braced himself for the impact of the arrow. But what if it went through him?

No pain came. He lifted his head. The arrow was an inch from his eye, grasped in Mak's fist.

Lio didn't move, holding Cassia's trembling form under him. He felt her heart pounding. Who had dared shoot at his Grace? Who had dared make her pulse race with fear?

Lio held back the instinctive blast of thelemancy straining to escape him. If he waved a flag at the Collector, nothing good would come of it. Lio had learned that lesson, and it had cost Hamon's life.

Forcing himself to focus, Lio structured his power into a veiled seeking spell. He swept the concealed magical probe through the trees.

Mak and Lyros's wards were everywhere. The air rippled with the fire spells Solia held at the ready. But Lio sensed no unfamiliar auras in the direction the arrow had come.

Knight circled the copse, his nose to the ground. At the base of one willow, he let out a howl. Sinking back on his haunches, he made a mighty leap, snapping his jaws at a branch above. Not quite high enough. He landed again with a snarl.

Tilili shimmied up the tree, Kella clinging nimbly to her back all the way. Lio heard a hiss and the sound of claws rending fabric and flesh. Then a body fell from the branch and hit the ground hard.

Solia stood over the man, her sword drawn. Kella and Tilili dropped to join her without a sound, the cat poised to pounce on her prey again. His legs were a mess of claw marks. He should be alive, but unable to run anywhere.

He stirred. The emptiness inside the moving body disoriented Lio. He couldn't sense the man's mind. Couldn't hear his heartbeat. His wounds weren't bleeding.

Lio's stomach turned over, and he swallowed hard.

"Lio, let me up." Cassia pushed against him. "I need to see what's happening."

"We're not sure it's the only one." Lio said.

"It?" Cassia echoed.

"It's bloodless. Undead." Lio was looking at the first reanimated corpse he had ever encountered outside of a tale.

The creature who had once been a person suddenly slid to its feet with uncanny coordination, its joints bending at impossible angles. Oblivious to the painful wounds on its legs, it sprinted away.

Solia's sword flashed, missing the bloodless by a hair. Tilili bounded after it, but Mak and Lyros were faster still, a blur even to Lio's eyes. Bones cracked. Flesh tore. It had never occurred to Lio what a beheading sounded like in reality to sensitive Hesperine ears.

When Mak and Lyros were still, Lio made himself look at the results of their work. Lyros had its body on the ground, controlling its struggling limbs with a complicated grip. Mak held the creature's detached head.

It blinked, scanning its surroundings, then met Lio's gaze. Not with the hollow eyes he expected. It looked at him with cunning perception. This was no clumsy minion, but the carefully crafted tool of a master necromancer.

Of course. In his arrogance, the Collector would make even his bloodless pawns the highest quality.

Mak's saddle bag flew open, and a canvas bag imbued with warding magic levitated into his hand. He stuffed the severed head inside. "There. Now the thing can't see or hear us and carry information back to its master."

"I'll burn it when we're done with it." Solia held out her hands to Mak, and he surrendered the head to her.

"We could use some help from Tuura to disanimate this," Lyros said through gritted teeth.

"Let her sleep," Kella said, her fortune blade in hand. Tilili launched herself at the undead, and Lyros let her have it. The cat pinned the writhing, headless corpse to the ground with her razor-sharp claws.

Lio showed himself some mercy and looked away from the creature. He stopped breathing so he wouldn't smell the odor of rot wafting off its body.

His father had dealt with such things for hundreds of years. Rudhira and Nike had survived it, too. Methu had died for it.

Lio would learn to bear the horrors of going errant for the sake of the irreplaceable woman in his arms.

Cassia shifted under him, squeezing a hand over her nose. He didn't let her up, but gave her more room and handed her a handkerchief. She covered her mouth and nose with the Orthros silk, tilting her head to meet his gaze.

Her hazel eyes were so full of life, her aura so vibrant in the shelter of his body. That could change in an instant. She was so mortal.

"I've got you," he said.

Her scent gave her away. Salty fear at what had just happened, but mixed with a warm musk, her body's instinctive response to his nearness, to his protection.

"Don't forget I've got you, too." Her words were bold. "If there are more undead, Knight will find them. *Seckkaa!*"

Knight headed into the shadows, sniffing. Several minutes later, he returned to Cassia. There were no dismembered pieces of an enemy in his jaws, only a knife.

"No more bloodless in the area," Cassia concluded, "but what has he found?"

"Don't touch it." At last Lio rolled to the side to let Cassia up. Mak offered him a hand, while Solia helped Cassia to her feet.

Lio cast a magical probe over the weapon Knight had retrieved. "I don't sense any curses on it."

Kella fiddled with a silver pendant hanging from Tilili's saddle. "My Azarqi charms aren't warning me of any curses, either."

"Let me take it, just in case," Mak said.

"We'll keep our wards up," Lyros agreed.

"And I will melt it if anything unpleasant happens," Solia promised.

Lio rarely regretted his affinity, but at the moment, he wondered if he would have been more use to his Grace if he had inherited his mother's mind healing, rather than mind magic. He gritted his teeth and let everyone else protect her.

At Cassia's command, Knight dropped the knife into Mak's warded hands. He turned it over, studying it, and his magic deepened. "It's an ordinary kitchen knife, as far as I can tell. Rather dull, in fact, and now with liegehound teeth marks all over the grip."

A silent, collective sigh of relief gusted through the Blood Union.

Solia pulled Cassia into her arms. "You're all right."

Cassia's anger was already overtaking the fear in her aura, but she held Solia, perhaps more for her sister's sake. Every instinct in Lio screamed that he should not let Cassia out of his arms, but he stood back and let the sisters reassure each other.

"Good reaction time." Mak clapped him on the back.

"Would it have been better to levitate her out of the arrow's path? Or step her to safety?"

"No," Mak answered. "We didn't know how many archers there were. You might have levitated her into the path of another arrow. And stepping away from your bodyguards is never a good idea. Don't you forget that."

"I won't." Lio swallowed. "Good catch."

"I didn't fancy prying a poisoned heart hunter arrow out of you."

"What?"

Mak motioned them over to the headless corpse. He was right. The man had been a heart hunter, judging by his all-white gear of wool and fur—and the anti-Hesperine charms strapped to his chest. But he was armed with a Tenebran soldier's bow.

"That's why we couldn't smell him," Mak said. "The anti-haimatic Lustra magic covered up the necromancy and made it possible for him to ambush us."

Kella cursed. "That could explain why Knight was able to track it better than Tilili."

Lyros's gaze fell, and he rubbed the back of his neck. "And why his arrow went through our wards. I'm so sorry."

"I will not accept apologies from any of you." Cassia embraced Lyros, then Mak. "Why would you cast your wards with heart hunters in mind, this far from the border?"

"Now we will," Mak said.

Solia nudged the bloodless with her boot. "If the Collector wants to give us a challenge, he'll have to send something much more dangerous than a single undead."

"He knows that," Lio said.

"Yes." Cassia slid her arm around him. "We know he wants to take me alive, not kill me. So why the arrow?"

He gave into his need to hold her close. "I think this is another message. All of it is personal."

Lyros pointed at the anti-Hesperine charms. "You think using a heart hunter against us is a reference to our battle with him in Martyr's Pass?"

"But this one isn't wielding a crossbow," Lio said.

The color drained from Cassia's face. "The arrow is just like the one that almost killed me the night Nike saved my life."

Mak's gaze fell to the arrow in his hand. "It's as if he knew I would catch it."

"This goes back even farther than that," Lio said. "A necromancer's undead concealed with Lustra magic is exactly what the Blood Errant faced when they battled that lynx changer eight hundred years ago."

"That's right," Mak said. "When they were telling us stories in the arena, they explained that the changer had a necromancer ally."

"How would the Collector know all this about your past?" Kella asked.

"He was there at Martyr's Pass," Lyros pointed out.

"And in the past," Mak said slowly. "When the Blood Errant defeated the lynx changer and the necromancer, there was a Gift Collector roaming the area. Perhaps he heard some tales at the local inn."

Lio nodded. "Anything the Gift Collectors see or hear most likely becomes their master's knowledge. And he has a very long memory."

"But how did he know about the arrow?" Cassia's voice was rigidly matter-of-fact, but she could not hide how deeply this unnerved her, not from him. "I thought there was no one there except Nike, Alkaios, Nephalea, and me."

"Are you certain the arrow is a message?" Kella asked. "It doesn't seem specific enough to me. All of this could merely be a strategic choice. He wasn't sure how close his bloodless could get to you, so he armed him with a weapon that has greater range."

"I agree with Kella," Solia said. "We should not read too much into the Collector's taunts."

Lio hated to admit it, but Solia had a point. And if it would make Cassia less frightened, he would swallow his pride. "We know he likes to play with our thoughts. We won't give him that power."

Mak drove the arrow in the bloodless's chest to help keep it pinned to the ground. "One thing's for certain. The Collector showed us another of the tricks up his sleeve. It won't work a second time."

"That's what worries me," Lyros said. "He's parading all his tactics in front of us."

"Yes," Cassia replied. "He would never do that unless he had even more tactics in reserve."

"Or all of this is merely a distraction," Lyros went on, "and we have yet to understand what his main strategy could be."

An orb of fire flared to life in Solia's hand. "Well, let's send him a little message. This is what I think of his strategy."

"Wait," Lio said, before she could destroy what remained of the undead. "Let us try a strategy of our own."

"I know what you're thinking." Mak's aura lit with eagerness.

That made Lio wonder if he had thought his suggestion through. But it had worked for the Blood Errant. "If we let the damaged bloodless go, it should return to its master to be repaired."

"And we can follow it." Lyros did not sound displeased by the idea, either.

"Excellent," Kella said. "Why wait for your enemy to ambush you again when you can confront him?"

"Do you think this will actually lead us to the Collector himself?" Solia asked.

Cassia shook her head. "Doubtful, don't you think, Lio? He has never appeared in person… I must confess, I shudder to imagine his true form."

After feeling his power, Lio could scarcely envision the mage at the center of that void. "I think the undead will lead us to whatever necromancer he is currently using as his Overseer."

"Overseer?" Kella asked.

"One of his commanders," Lio explained. "Hypnos is the god of death and dreams in this part of the world. Mortals who are to be punished in the afterlife are sent to his realm, where his Overseers are the taskmasters of the unfortunate dead. In life, the Collector's commanders call themselves his Overseers. We battled one, a Gift Collector called Skleros."

A shiver went through Cassia's aura, her thoughts buried too deep for Lio to read without effort. But he could guess. She was remembering when the Collector had offered to make her one of his Overseers.

"That's what the kitchen knife means," she said suddenly. "Gift Collectors have to obey the Mage Orders' rules against mages wielding weapons. So they improvise. Kitchen knives are one of their favorites. Perhaps it belongs to this creature's master."

Lio tried not to think of how many painful ways a Gift Collector could harm someone with a dull kitchen knife. "Of course. We should expect this bloodless to lead us to a Gift Collector. We'll take you back to the keep now. You can stay with Hoyefe, Karege, and Tuura while we—"

"No," Cassia said before he finished. "I have to come with you."

Lio turned to face her, putting his hands on her shoulders. "We have no idea what we're heading into, or how far out of the perimeter it will take us. It would be madness to bring you along."

"All of that is true," she said, "but Knight is the only one who can track the undead with it covered in Lustra magic."

Lio's magic rose, demanding an outlet for his fury. Cassia was right. And Lio was willing to wager, in this twisted game, that the Collector had planned it this way. "This could be a trap, luring you to follow the undead back to whomever the Collector has sent to capture you."

"That's likely, but I agree with Kella. Better to face it than wait for it to find me."

"She has fought in battles in the Maaqul," Kella said, "and even against this very foe. Any member of the Ashes, even an honorary one, need not be treated as a non-combatant."

Solia took a step nearer to Lio. "I think that tucking a woman away from danger does not actually keep her safe. I am in favor of bringing her with us, and you know how much that costs me."

Lio looked down at his Grace and stroked her cheek. "You know what this costs me, too. But it is Cassia's decision."

"Decide quickly," Lyros advised, "before dawn makes all of us Hesperines useless against the enemy."

Cassia covered Lio's hand with hers. "Hear out my precautions and tell me if you are not reassured."

"I doubt any precautions will reassure me," he said, but listened.

"Mak and Lyros can cover me in wards, taking heart hunter arrows into consideration this time. If we encounter any enemies, I'll keep Knight on guard at my side instead of sending him on the offensive. Assuming any enemies survive a few minutes with Solia and Kella."

"We'll go under veils," Solia said. "Patrols might be allowed, but an undead hunting party is the last thing we want the mortals in the camp to witness."

Lyros nodded. "Lio, your thelemantic veils could conceal our minds and auras from the Collector. This time, we could hope to take him by surprise and protect any innocent bystanders."

"We can cast thelemantic wards, too," Mak said. "That will take time, but you can prevent the Collector from possessing anyone while Lyros and I prepare the wards. Then you can infuse our spell with mind magic."

But it would not be a Sanctuary ward. Could the spells of three youngbloods hold against the full force of the Collector's attacks? Lio seldom had cause to doubt the great magic he, Mak, and Lyros had inherited from the elder firstbloods. But he had felt how much magic the Collector had to throw at them.

Cassia shot a concerned glance at her sister and Kella. "Can you cast thelemantic wards on Solia and Kella before we go?"

"We won't need them." Solia patted her scarf. "Imperial theramancy protects us."

Kella held up her wrist and shook a silver bangle she wore. "Tuura enchanted mine. Before we go, we'll warn her and Karege that we may leave the perimeter. That way, she can keep watch over Patria in your stead, Lio."

Cassia looked up at Lio again. "See there? We are well prepared for this enemy. And if anything goes wrong, you can step me back to the keep to stay with Tuura and Karege."

He frowned down at her raised chin and the stubborn set of her mouth. "You will not protest if I step you back?"

"Not for an instant. I'm not a fool. You know I never go into danger without cause—and a plan."

"You are the least foolish person I know. But you are also the most determined when you have a cause, even if it means putting your safety second to your goal."

"But I won't put your safety second, Lio." She leaned into him. "And my safety is your safety."

Cassia also knew what this cost him. And he knew she would never put him through this, unless they had no choice. She was right. Knight was the only way to find who had sent the undead.

They could leave their enemy in the wind and wait for him to strike. Or they could hunt him down. There were no safe ways forward. All they could do was spring the trap.

INTO THE TRAP

WHEN THEY WERE ALL mounted around the bloodless, Lio reached over and gripped Cassia's hand. "Ready."

She squeezed back, then took firm hold of Freckles' mane. "*Ckuundat.*"

Knight perked his ears. The moment Kella pulled Tilili off the bloodless, the headless body sprang to its feet. Solia yanked the head out of the bag and hurled it away from them. The bloodless raced after it with uncanny speed. Before the head landed, the creature caught it from the air.

They all held their breaths, waiting to see which way it would go. And then it disappeared.

Lio had an instant to feel both relieved and frustrated, before Cassia called out, "*Seckaa!*"

And Knight was off, bounding in the direction the bloodless had gone.

Moonflower sprang forward in response to Lio's Will, the horse's long legs keeping them close to Cassia and Freckles. Knight raced between tents and past campfires, sure of his hunt. Tilili wove after him, Mak and Lyros's Warmbloods following with the agility of immortal equines.

Under the crackle of burning logs and the murmurs of wakeful humans, Knight's panting breaths guided them onward toward the prey Lio could neither see nor feel. No anticipation came over him, no thrill of the hunt like Tendo had sometimes described. Lio had been born without that human instinct. But whatever they met at the end of the hunt, his Hesperine instincts would make sure it was no threat to his Grace.

He felt Cassia's aura sharpen. Her presence expanded in the night as she reached with her arcane senses.

"What do you feel?" he asked over the pounding of the horse's hooves.

"I have an idea," she called back. "Join our minds."

"How deep?"

"As deep as you need to sense what I'm sensing."

He swept into the tense patterns of focus she held in her mind. Amid the rush of their ride, she felt as close as if she pressed her cheek to his.

Not close enough. He recalled the first night his mind had joined to hers on pure instinct, and he had looked at the world through her eyes. He surrendered a bit more of his control to their bond.

His need to protect her overcame all inhibition, and their consciousness blended. His heart sped up to match her mortal pulse. Scents dulled, sounds grew quieter, and when he looked out over Freckles' auburn ears, he could not see nearly so far.

He was so close to Cassia that he didn't even hear her words, but knew her question. Could he sense the bloodless? He peered ahead, past Knight, letting their bond carry him out to the full reach of Cassia's senses. Nothing.

She grasped his hand, sending him a flash of awareness of his own body. Warm blood smeared across his palm before she released him. He lifted his hand to his mouth and tasted her lush new flavor again, stronger now. Biting his palm, he mingled their blood. Power infused their Union, tangling him tighter with her senses.

There. He felt the bloodless like the changing patterns of a chameleon's skin. The spell was unlike any he had encountered before. He still couldn't see or smell the undead, but now he could detect the natural disguise the unnatural creature wore.

A sense of victory passed between him and Cassia, and a hint of wonder came through his fear for her. They were working magic together. Her magic.

But when the tents fell away behind them and a guard post loomed ahead, Lio's dread regained the upper hand. They were leaving the perimeter.

Another surge of thelemancy rose in him, and he let it. He felt air fill his lungs as Cassia gasped. Her aura pulled him closer. Whatever lay ahead, they would face it together.

Unseen shadows rose, Mak and Lyros strengthening their wards. The air warmed with Solia's readied fire spells. A dagger appeared in Kella's hand.

They slipped past Flavian's sentries. The men shuddered as if a chill breeze had slid under their collars, then went back to staring into the trees.

At the edge of the river, Knight faltered, sniffing the bank with urgency. The Lustra spell seemed to melt into their surroundings like an animal slinking into the grass. No, they could not afford to lose it now!

But there it was again on the other side of the river. Through Cassia's mind, Lio reached out with his own magic and stepped them all across the water. She let out a surprised, elated sound. Knight bayed, finding the trail again, and they rode on.

Her hound led them past fields and through patches of forest. Each time the bloodless seemed to disappear, Lio and Cassia sensed for it again and stepped their party ahead to wherever it reemerged.

The moons sank lower in the sky. Step after step, they covered miles, Lio knew not how many. He could no longer care what lay in wait for them at the end of the chase. He would face it again if he could ride toward it joined so deeply to her mind, their magic wound together.

When more tents came into sight ahead, they shared an instant of confusion, then understanding. They had not circled back to Patria. It was not Flavian's banner that waved in the night wind, illuminated by torchlight. The blue flag bore a castle on a cliff over the sea, the emblem of Hadria.

Cassia turned her head and called out to Solia. "You're not ready to meet Lord Hadrian. Should we stop?"

A beat of silence. Then Solia answered, "No. Ready or not, we must find out where the necromancer is hiding in his camp. Keep the veils up."

They slipped between patrols of sentries wearing Hadrian blue. Into the precise rows of military tents where the day watch slept. Past the carefully banked embers of fires and racks of well-polished weapons.

The question crept up his and Cassia's spine. Just how deeply had the Collector embedded himself here, where there was no Hesperine presence at all? Here, where his ally Lucis still reigned?

At last the Lustra magic fell away from the bloodless, and it slipped into a long infirmary tent. Then it disappeared completely from their senses, as if behind a grave shroud. Disgust and a question rose in Cassia, and Lio shared his knowledge with her. They were sensing necromantic concealment spells that covered the entire tent. The undead's master must be inside.

"*Hama! Barda!*" Lio said with Cassia.

Knight halted at the edge of the tent and went into guard stance. They were at the end of their hunt. Lio heard a voice, Solia's, he thought. But the voice of Cassia's thoughts was nearer. *Whatever lies within, we face it together.*

Together. So close. He had no desire to stop listening to her. Her aura pulled him deeper, like an ocean current dragging him into her irresistible embrace. He was hers. Forever.

A sharp pain in his arm jolted him back into his body. He gasped like a mortal surfacing from the sea. Colors, sounds, and smells struck him. He managed to focus his vision on his forearm in time to see a fang mark heal.

"Back with us?" Lyros asked. "Thought you might need some help."

"Thank you." Rubbing the tear in his sleeve, Lio turned to see Cassia swaying in the saddle and Mak helping her down.

He had no time to ask if she was all right before Solia pointed to them in twos and gestured around the tent. "Spread out! Surround it, leave no exits unguarded. We go in on my signal."

She was ordering Lio away from Cassia. His veins burned with protest.

Lyros guided his horse around Lio's, herding him and Moonflower toward one side of the tent. "Cassia will be safe with Mak. You're with me."

Lio took a deep breath and heeded his Trial brother. They dismounted, Lyros sending their mounts off to join the other horses nearby, then took their post at the side flap.

"Try to master the necromancer's mind and prevent any more violence," Lyros said. "I'll protect you while you cast. Trust Mak to keep Cassia out of the way if the enemy targets you."

Lio tried to see the logic in that plan, despite how his Grace's heart hammered on the other side of the tent. Mak's presence beside her was Lio's only hope of sanity. Auras of fire and water flanked the front entrance as Solia and Kella took their positions.

A cry tore through the night, coming from inside the tent. A human child, wailing as if its world were coming to an end.

Lio had an instant to feel a sickening sense of rage at the necromancer, before Solia signaled them with a tongue of fire. They charged into whatever the Collector had in store for them.

ALL A GAME

Ckabaar. The attack command hovered on Cassia's tongue. She wanted to send Knight into battle and wreak her helpless fury upon the enemy. She needed to act to protect her Grace.

But the crying child could not afford any rash actions. Cassia forced out Knight's guard command. "*Barda!*"

Mak charged into the tent ahead of her, his massive form moving with Hesperine agility. Cassia drew her spade from her satchel and followed with Knight watching her back. The necromancer's shroud spells crawled over her skin and closed around her.

But she felt her Grace locked inside here with her. Lio and Lyros had burst in from the other side, Solia and Kella through the front.

The bloodless heart hunter knelt nearby, resting its shoulders across the lap of a Kyrian mage. Under her midwife's cowl, Cassia recognized her face. Pakhne.

She cradled the undead's severed head and sang a lullaby in the deep, mocking voice of the Collector.

At the sight of the sandy-haired soldier in the center of the tent, horror filled Cassia. Callen fended off half a dozen soldiers in Hadrian blue. His own comrades. His sword flashed in every direction, but they were faster. Stronger. Sweat plastered his sandy hair to his forehead, and blood leaked from a slice across his own blue tunic. Lord Hadrian's men would never attack their own—unless they belonged to the Collector now.

Callen dodged, and Cassia saw through the melee to whom he protected. A young woman cowered at the back of the tent, clutching a baby. And on a cot beside her lay Perita. She was so still, her skin ashen.

No. Not Perita. If the Collector had taken her from Cassia…

"She's alive!" Lio cried. "I feel her mind."

"Has the Collector—?" Cassia asked.

"Pakhne is his only captive," Lio said. "I won't let him take anyone else."

"Change the veils!" Solia's command rang out over the clash of swords. "Reveal us to everyone but Pakhne. And show Kella and me to the Collector's captive, too."

"What?" Cassia cried. "No!"

"She's right." Lyros's tone brooked no argument. "Let Solia and Kella be our diversion."

Lio's magic shifted over Cassia's skin. There was nothing she could do to stop her sister from taking this risk.

Callen let out a shout of surprise, staring at them all with wide eyes. In that instant of distraction, a bloodless snaked under his guard.

Tilili pounced. She and Kella flew past Callen, knocking the bloodless aside. It regained its feet and pointed its sword at Kella instead.

Solia whipped her gladius from her scabbard and traversed into the ring of undead. Putting her back to Callen, she sliced off one undead's hand and sent its sword clanging to the ground. Callen recovered quickly, turned away from her, and faced the enemy again.

"I need to get a ward around Perita." Mak put himself between Cassia and the battle and urged her along the edge of the tent.

It took all her Will to leave Lio and Lyros facing off with Pakhne, out of her reach. *Be safe, my Grace.*

In a crouch, she circled the tent with Mak and Knight. As they went, Mak turned over each empty infirmary cot they passed to form a physical barrier between them and the battle.

From the other side came a cacophony of blades and shouts. A detached arm spun toward Cassia, its fingers flexing. She yelped and ducked. Mak tossed up another cot, and the arm slammed into it. They didn't stop to watch if it clawed its way back to its body.

The whole tent was a haze of magic. Through it all, only Lio's power was clear to Cassia. His pulse pushed back against the grasping spells of death. Mak pulled her along, and they closed the last distance between them and Perita.

But the young woman holding the child—surely Perita and Callen's child—scrambled to her feet and blocked their path. Clutching the baby to her chest, she brandished the broken leg of a cot in a shaking grip. "If you want to hurt them, you'll have to go through me!"

Cassia held up her hands. "We're on your side!"

The woman stood her ground, favoring her left leg. A fresh bruise disfigured her pale cheek. Her gaze darted to Mak.

He ignored her and began to drip a line of his blood onto the floor between them and the battle. Knight took up guard beside him.

"We're here to help," Cassia said. "These are the Hesperines Perita and Callen met in Orthros. Our allies."

Despite the bruise, the woman's heart-shaped face seemed familiar. Dark brown hair. A respectable, but plain gown. Perhaps the handmaiden of a lady Cassia knew? She wracked her mind for information she could use to reassure the young woman, but to no avail.

"I'm Cassia. Did Perita tell you who I am? She is"—her throat tightened—"so dear to me."

The woman's knuckles went white on her makeshift weapon.

"Please," Cassia pleaded. "Let me help. I would never harm her or her child. I cannot lose her."

The woman's lips pressed into a tight line. "She said you're loyal to her."

"Always."

The fight seemed to drain out of her. "I believe you."

Cassia eased the cot leg out of her grip and kept her tone steady, soothing. "What's your name?"

"Miranda."

"Well met, Miranda. You don't have to protect them alone now."

Miranda sank to the ground again and cradled the distraught child in both arms, murmuring soothing nonsense. Mak circled the cot, drawing his line of blood further around Perita, Miranda, and the child. He murmured under his breath, words in Divine that seemed to hang heavy in the air.

Cassia fell to her knees at Perita's side. Her friend was a wan specter under a pile of blankets. Fear left Cassia frozen for an instant, and in that breath, she felt Lio sharing her anguish.

There were more and more friends Cassia feared losing. But Perita had been the first.

Cassia put her hand to Perita's throat. Her pulse was the barest flutter under Cassia's fingers, her blue eyes hazed and distant. Her breath came in fast and shallow.

"What happened?" Cassia asked Miranda.

"The birth was hard. Pakhne has been trying to stop the bleeding since yesterday, but then...I don't understand! She changed. She brought the soldiers in here—they attacked—if Callen hadn't been here..."

"How long has Pakhne been like this?"

"It happened just before you came."

Just before you came. Perita could have birthed her child in peace. Pakhne would have had time to heal her. If the Collector had not used them to lay a trap for Cassia.

Miranda let out a scream, and the child began to cry again. Cassia looked up to see that a bloodless had slipped past Solia's guard. The burly soldier leapt for the gap in Mak's ring of blood, sword outstretched. Cassia's hand tightened on the handle of her spade.

But Mak caught the creature's wrist and twisted. Cassia heard the crunch of fine bones. His other hand closed around its throat, and he hurled it out into Tilili's waiting claws. Kella's mount pinned the bloodless to the ground. As Kella's long dagger slashed down toward its neck, Cassia looked away.

Mak flung droplets of blood onto the ground. The circle was complete. Hesperine magic eddied through the ground under Cassia's knees. But that would not keep Perita's life from slipping through their fingers.

His Grace was just a few paces away from the Old Master.

Lio could not allow himself to watch Cassia's progress through the tent. He focused on their enemy.

Lio looked into Pakhne's once-serene blue eyes and saw the cunning Collector gazing back. The Old Master observed the battle as if he were sitting down to a match of Kings and Mages.

This was all a game to him. One that could destroy any life inside this tent, if Lio made the wrong move.

But the Collector was watching Solia and Kella carve their way through the undead. His gaze was not tracking Cassia and Mak. He gave no sign he knew Lio and Lyros were stalking toward him. Hespera's veils were holding against Hypnos.

Lio had one chance to steal into Pakhne's mind and take her back. Once he made a move to free her, he would betray his presence to the Old Master. Lio couldn't give the Collector the chance to turn this into a duel—or to cut his losses.

A heartbeat passed. Deep within his concealments, Lio spun the mind magic inside him into a precise spell.

The bloodless heart hunter rose to its feet, its head reattached. It turned to join the battle.

Another heartbeat. Lio aimed the thelemantic attack.

Suddenly heat bathed his skin. The arcane heat of a fire spell about to be unleashed.

His gaze snapped to the battle again. Solia knocked Callen's sword aside and took hold of his collar. With a shove that must have magic behind it, she tossed him out of the melee. Out of range of her fire spells.

One strike from Solia was about to make quick work of all these undead.

Then the Collector's pawns would be off the board. And he would bring his better pieces into play.

Who would he possess first? What would he do to the child?

Callen staggered back toward Perita's cot, into Mak's circle of blood. Beside Lio, Lyros chanted one more word with blood-stained lips, and his spell sealed around them.

Lio probed the ward with his mind magic. But the spell structure resisted him. It wasn't ready for thelemancy. If he poured his power into it now, he would only weaken Mak and Lyros's hard-won defenses.

"We need more time!" Lio called to Solia. "Don't destroy the bloodless yet."

"You must be mad!" Solia scoffed over the rising notes of Pakhne's lullaby.

She hacked through the wrist of another bloodless. But behind her, a different soldier rubbed the ragged flesh around its own wrist, adjusting its reattached hand. It made a swing at her with no less strength than before.

Solia parried the blow. "They're too well made! Blades won't be enough." The heat grew in the air.

Goddess, let her understand. Let her trust him, just this once. "Distract them. Disable them. But leave him his pawns!"

Seven fires sprang to life. Her spell consumed each bloodless with beautiful, deadly precision.

With a cry of frustration, Lio cast his own spell deep into Pakhne's mind.

The Collector inhabited her every thought and vein. He was in her memories, bantering with Benedict and discussing books with Ariadne. He was in her tears, trailing down her face at her sister's promise dance.

Death magic spidered through the paths of her spirit that had been made for healing. Threads of necromancy spun out from her, cut strings that had been tugging the bloodless to and fro.

Lio traced every thread, seeking more of the necromancer's victims. Through Pakhne, the Collector and Lio held every soul in Lord Hadrian's camp in the palms of their hands.

The undead were the only stain of death in the camp, this woman the necromancer's only foothold. If Lio could reclaim her, everyone would be safe.

She was strong. A lesser mage would have died already. But she was crumbling. Lio could feel the Old Master eating away at her to feed one more spell.

The Collector's sickening magic reached out of Pakhne, ready to consume the other mortal spirits in the tent. Callen's steadfast heart. Perita's aura, fighting for life. The brave young woman beside her.

Lio spun thelemancy through the mortals and hardened his power into a mind ward.

The Collector's grip closed around their minds and Lio's, three blows at once. Pain erupted in his skull.

But the attack recoiled from his power. The necromancer retreated, chased by the slivers of Lio's shattered ward.

There you are, Deukalion, the Collector said.

LIFE AND DEATH

All Cassia could do was cling to Perita's hand from within Mak's ward, while on the other side of the tent, her Grace dueled the Collector.

Lio's pale skin gleamed with escaping light magic, his hair and robes black with the deep darkness of Lyros's ward. When Pakhne levitated from her chair, Cassia's stomach dropped. Pakhne's head fell back, her arms floating at her sides as if on currents of unseen magic.

Cassia felt the magic around her shift. Like a grave cloth dragged away from her mouth. Necromancy. Goddess help them. If the necromancer had dropped his concealment spells to focus on Lio…

Shouts sounded outside the tent. Cassia called over them, "Mak, we need more veils!"

It was too late. A dozen Hadrian soldiers burst inside, their lord himself in the lead, just as Mak's spells closed around the tent.

Lord Hadrian's gaze swept the scene before him, and Cassia knew how it must look to him. Lio and Lyros, casting magic at Pakhne. Mak looming over Perita in a ring of blood. Solia and Kella standing amid fallen Hadrian swords and embers still flickering with fire magic.

If Lord Hadrian called in the Aithourians, this night would end in even more death. Cassia sprang to her feet, ready to throw herself between the two forces, if that was what it took.

Even before her own instincts stopped her, Mak caught hold of her. "Don't you set foot outside this ward. The Collector is right there!"

He was right. Cassia shouted from where she was, "Lord Hadrian, we're here to defend you!"

"Cassia?" Astonishment flashed across his weathered face. But he didn't lower his sword. At the sight of Mak holding her, his expression hardened.

He made rapid hand signs to his men. One darted for the exit. To get reinforcements?

"Hear me out!" Cassia cried to Lord Hadrian.

But his soldier staggered back from the tent flap, rubbing his head.

"No one leaves the tent until we settle this," Mak said. "The wards come down when the swords do."

"We're trapped," one of the soldiers whispered.

"Stand your ground," Lord Hadrian ordered.

He gestured again, and four soldiers headed for Lio and Lyros, four more for Mak and Cassia. He led the rest at Solia and Kella.

"Stop!" Cassia cried. "We're your allies!"

"Cassia," her sister said in that tone of command, "let me be the one to prove it."

"The warriors are women!" one of Lord Hadrian's soldiers said in astonishment.

A line of fire raced across the ground, blocking the soldiers' path. Solia strode through it and faced Lord Hadrian and his men alone.

"She killed your comrades," Lord Hadrian said. "Don't hesitate."

They descended on her all at once, and Cassia swallowed a scream. Mak tightened his hold on her, this time in reassurance.

"She's a Victor of Souls," he reminded her.

Solia whirled through the soldiers, her scarf rippling around her like a dancing partner. Her gladius slashed, as if an extension of her own body. Her fist met flesh.

No blood spattered. There came no smell of burning skin. But swords clattered to the ground, and men let out grunts of surprise and pain. They fell at her feet, disarmed and groaning.

Kella called something to Solia, and Cassia's sister let out a peal of laughter.

The sheer joy in her stopped Cassia's breath in her chest. Solia had never looked so exhilarated.

At last, only Lord Hadrian was still standing. Solia adjusted her grip on her sword and faced the greatest warrior in Tenebra.

"They should not have underestimated me," she said. "Neither should you."

"Who are you?" he demanded.

"Let me show you."

LIO'S EYES WERE SEALED shut with the force of his power. The battle faded to a distant noise. In his mind's eye, he raced through the ruins of Pakhne's mind.

How are you enjoying this little exercise? The Collector's voice echoed through her head.

I am not here to play, Lio shot back.

You shouldn't take mortal lives so seriously, Deukalion.

You shouldn't underestimate them.

Such effort you expend, the Collector scoffed, *and for what? To extend their fleeting existences by a few moments? A few decades? What matter, when centuries are the blink of our immortal eyes?*

You forget I have the power to make them live forever.

Immortality has always been wasted on Hesperines, the Collector said. *You should learn to enjoy the game.*

They are not my playing pieces. They are my allies, and we will not let you win.

Do not pretend that you fight among the pawns. You knew what you did when you stole my queen. I will take her back, Deukalion.

Never. Cassia is bound to me in ways you cannot break.

I can break anything.

Pakhne's recent memories blasted apart. Little pieces of the birth flew past Lio and blew away like dust. But the Collector gathered other pieces to him. Solia's fighting moves disappeared into his presence. The void he left behind in Pakhne's thoughts collapsed.

Lio raced to shore up her mind. He tossed up thelemantic wards everywhere the Collector turned, pane after pane of crystalline defenses around memories of Kella's words, Tilili's traits, the flavors of the magic she and Solia carried.

You can try to guard your secrets, the Collector said, *but I know Cassia is near.*

But you don't know where she is, Lio replied with a grim smile.

I don't need to find her. It is only a matter of time before she comes to me. I have known her much longer than you have, Deukalion. Do not imagine she is bound to you more deeply than she is to me.

Lio had no time to contemplate the implications of that threat. The Collector's every word shredded precious reserves of Pakhne's life force.

Lio pulled forth all the magic Hespera had given him, mind and light and blood, and let it flow from his immortal veins.

The Collector clung to Pakhne, digging deeper into her bones. *You cannot save anyone from me. Least of all Cassia.*

Cassia and I will not rest until we save every one of your pawns from you.

Very well. The Collector's amused laughter echoed through Pakhne. *You may have this piece. But I doubt you will find my castoffs of any value.*

He released his grasp so suddenly that Lio's magic went tumbling into the reaches of Pakhne's mind. Her unbound thoughts whirled into chaos around him.

Lio wrenched his power back to him and gentled his touch. He snatched at her wild memories and thoughts and emotions before they spun into nothingness.

Piece by piece, he gathered the remnants of who she was and ordered them into the proper places in her mind. He became lost in the precise work, in the impressions of her life. Her sister's fierce embrace. The laughter of her temple friends. The joy of casting her first successful spell.

But that memory led only into scoured paths. Lio stumbled through emptiness.

Where healing magic had once run through her, there was nothing now but decay.

Lio let out a silent cry of denial, but the Collector was no longer there to hear him. The Old Master was gone, and he had taken Pakhne's magic with him.

An impact against his body brought him back to physical awareness. Lio opened his eyes in time to catch Pakhne as she collapsed against him. He caught her in his arms, but staggered.

Lyros reached out to steady him. "Her heart is still beating!"

It seemed impossible. But Lio could hear it too, such a normal sound, pounding in his ears.

"Is the Collector still here?" Lyros asked. "Do you still need thelemantic wards?"

"No." Lio's own voice sounded far away from him. "He's nowhere in Hadrian's camp."

The Collector had left Pakhne alive. But without her magic, what kind of life would it be?

"I want everyone inside one ward," Lyros said.

"Pakhne is too fragile to step."

"We'll have to run, then. Stay close to me!"

The ring of blood around them disappeared in a flash of light, and Lyros urged Lio ahead of him. He raced for the other side of the tent with Pakhne in his arms, Lyros and his wards following.

Heat prickled his skin. They blurred past a ring of fire. Lio let out an astonished curse at what he saw within. Solia and Lord Hadrian were locked in single combat.

He made it into the safety of Mak's ring of blood. Mak plucked Pakhne from his hold.

Then the scent of roses and cinnamon overtook the stench of fire and death. Cassia slid under Lio's arm, supporting him, and pressed her wrist to his lips.

He bit into her tender flesh. The sweetness of her blood chased the taste of necromancy from his mouth. He reached for their Union, and her mind embraced him.

She stroked his face as he drank. "You're back with us."

He wrapped an arm around her waist and held her tightly against him. His surging thelemancy prowled through her mind ward before he could stop it, reassuring him she was still here. Still safe.

"Yes," she gasped. "I'm all right."

Lio dragged in a long draught of her blood, feeling her shiver against him. But their Union dragged at him in return. She didn't want to let him go. His every instinct was to give her what she wanted. Needed.

"One more swallow," Lyros warned, "then I'm prying you off of her."

Lio tore himself from their Union and Willed himself to seal her vein. He raised his head and made himself focus on Pakhne. Mak had placed her on a cot next to Perita's. Callen sat with his wife, rocking her against his chest, while a woman Lio didn't recognize held the child. Knight stood guard, prowling the boundaries of the ward.

"Pakhne is alive," Cassia said. "You saved her."

"No. I didn't." Lio shook his head. He couldn't bear to say the words aloud.

"What's wrong?" Cassia asked.

Mak and Lyros must have sensed the change in Pakhne's aura, judging by their horror pervading the Blood Union.

Lyros said, "Her magic is gone."

"The Collector left her alive...but took her magic?" Mak looked to Lio.

He nodded in silence. The color drained from Cassia's face.

Just then, Pakhne's eyes came open, and she gave a querying moan. Her cowl had fallen back, and Lio could see her clearly. Her fine-boned face, her winged brows. Her tousled hair, the same color as Zoe's. She looked no older than Cassia.

"You're safe," Lio soothed. Such meaningless words, but he would give her what comfort he could. "We're here to help. Just rest."

She put a hand to her head, grimacing. Her thoughts shifted, and her aura stirred. The same way Lio's did every time he awoke, when he stretched his magic as instinctively as his arms or legs.

Pakhne gasped. Then again. Her hand went to her chest, and her fingers closed around the front of her robes like claws.

Her pulse began to race, and her breaths came in rapid, hoarse gasps. Panic blinded her thoughts. Her face crumpled, and she let out a whimper like a cornered animal.

Lio would hear that sound in his memories for the rest of his existence.

He could scarcely bear to look at Cassia. Not when he could feel her horror. They were both thinking the same thing.

This was the fate that awaited her, if she could not claim her magic. This was what not just her life, but her eternity would look like if she was denied her power.

Lio slipped his hand behind Pakhne's head and covered her in a sleep spell. Her thoughts sank into sweet oblivion. The only thing he could do for her now.

"Rudhira will know what to do," Lyros said.

Yes. Lio had another one of the Collector's broken vessels to give to Rudhira now.

"Is it safe to send someone for him?" Cassia asked. "Perita needs healing. Now."

"We've veiled the place," Mak said, "but I'd rather not find out how they hold up against Aithourian revelatory spells."

Lyros shook his head. "Bringing Rudhira here is asking for trouble."

"We'll have to risk it for Perita's sake," Cassia said.

Kella twirled her fortune blade. "Let the war mages come. We'll see how long they keep their fires burning against my water magic."

"Very well," Lyros said. "You go, my Grace. I'll fortify your ward against fire."

Mak gave a nod and disappeared. Lyros began to circle them, adding his blood to the ring on the ground.

Beyond their defenses, Kella and Tilili stood guard over Lord Hadrian's fallen men. None dared try to get through her to interfere in the duel.

Lord Hadrian circled Solia inside her ring of flames, dragging his forearm across his brow. "You could have killed me by now."

"Yes." Solia sounded winded, but her steps were less weary than the old warrior's.

"Grant me the dignity of not toying with me," Lord Hadrian demanded. "If this is to be my final battle, end it!"

The image of his wife and daughters' faces flashed through his thoughts, his final, silent battle cry. With a burst of strength and speed that must have cost him, he lunged.

ANYTHING TO SAVE HER

CASSIA COULD NOT LOOK away from how the battle would end.

Solia gripped her gladius in both hands and met Lord Hadrian's powerful attack with her blade. The clang made Cassia's ears ring.

Then came the slide of steel on steel as her golden sword raced into a counterattack. Lord Hadrian's sword flew from his hands and beyond the ring of fire.

He and Solia stood panting, and he looked without fear into her bespelled, golden gaze. Then he murmured a prayer, a warrior's promise to his god that he was ready.

Solia sheathed her sword. Lord Hadrian let out a hoarse breath.

"This blade will always stand between you and death," Solia said. "Do you understand?"

Lord Hadrian shook his head.

She reached up and pulled her scarf away. The golden mask around her eyes faded. She showed her real face to Lord Hadrian, with her secrets in ashes at her feet.

Cassia knew there would be a cost later. But right now, she could only hope Lord Hadrian would know her sister. He seemed frozen, his face betraying nothing.

"Did you recognize my block?" Solia asked.

His words came out hushed. "So many years ago…I used that very block and counterattack against Lord Gaius…in a demonstration."

"Sabina and her guest begged to watch you train. And you indulged two girls who wished they had been born to the sword."

"I always said, if they'd been boys…"

"You would have trained us. I had to travel far to learn the skills I need. Now my sword is ready, and I have returned."

"My Queen?" Lord Hadrian's voice broke.

Solia smiled. "You know me."

He sank to one knee before her. "My Queen. How can this be?"

She reached out and laid a hand on his shoulder. "Your pleas on the night of the siege were not in vain, and neither were the deaths of your men. You bought me time to escape. I will never forget those sacrifices."

He bowed his head, his shoulders relaxing, as if years of weight had been lifted from him. They seemed to lean into each other.

"You needn't make any more sacrifices," she said. "I will be the queen you always hoped I could become, if you are still willing to give me your loyalty."

"My loyalty has always been yours."

"You must be sure," she said. "I will not rule from the weaving room. In Angara's name, I will lead with my sword, and my fire will never serve the Orders. It will not be easy to follow me."

"Will you let the lords of Tenebra take up arms against each other and slaughter their own brothers?"

"No," Solia vowed. "I will not tolerate the feuds in my reign."

"Will you ask me to choose between the good of this kingdom and my own honor?"

"Never, my lord. Your king has held your honor hostage for too long. Let me restore it to you."

A light came to Lord Hadrian's eyes. "Then show me where your enemies are. I will clear your path to the throne with my own blade."

The circle of fire faded. Solia picked up his fallen sword and placed it in his hand. "Rise, Lord Hadrian."

"I will stand with you, My Queen." Clasping her arm, he let her pull him to his feet.

Cassia knew this was a victory for her sister. But she wondered what the consequences would be, now that they had unleashed two battle-hungry warriors upon the delicate balance of Tenebra.

When Solia looked up from her duel, her gaze met Lio's over Pakhne's cot. He saw no apology in his Grace-sister, only resolve.

He let her see the warning in his own eyes. They would have words about her choices during the battle.

"What happened?" Cassia asked, her tone low and urgent. "I heard you two shouting at each other, but—"

"There will be time to discuss the finer points later," Lio said.

Cassia's aura was sharp with frustration and hurt and worry, but she nodded in agreement.

With Lord Hadrian as their audience, now was not the time. Lio would not discredit Solia's leadership in front of her newly restored ally. He would choose his moment carefully, and Solia had best be ready.

He turned away from her, resting a hand on Cassia's back as she sat at Perita's side. Solia and Kella joined Lord Hadrian in helping up his injured men.

"What happened here, My Queen?" Lord Hadrian asked.

Solia replied, "Can you keep the Aithourians disinterested in this tent long enough for me to tell you?"

"Ah, the guests from Corona whom King Lucis invited into my camp. My lady and her spiced wine are keeping them entertained."

"I do not recall Hadrian spiced wine being able to distract war mages from Hesperines."

"It's a special vintage my lady saves for guests who are inclined to meddle in my battles."

Lio's respect for Lady Hadrian increased yet again. It seemed they had her to thank for drugging their mutual enemies.

Rudhira could heal Perita without fending off fire mages. If he got here in time.

The child was quieter now, whimpering in the other woman's arms. She rocked him gently. "I'm sorry, Callen."

He held Perita against his chest. His aura was numb, as if life was his enemy and had dealt him a blow in battle he had never seen coming. "Thank you for staying by her, Miranda."

"Pakhne and I promised her she didn't have to do this alone," Miranda said.

Lio didn't know her, but he could see she was so loyal to Perita that she didn't flee in the face of liegehounds, Hesperines, and undead. Such an ally of Perita's was an ally of his and Cassia's. Even a friend, one could hope.

Callen lifted his gaze to Cassia. "If this is—the end—I'm glad you're here, my lady."

Cassia gripped Perita's hand. "It's not too late. The First Prince is coming."

Rudhira's aura filled the tent, wrapped in his own veil spells. He stepped in with Thorn drawn, Mak at his side. But Lord Hadrian didn't give any sign he noticed.

"The Aithourians are drunk and drugged," Lio said. "They won't notice your spells."

Rudhira sheathed his sword with levitation and stepped to Perita's bedside. "Master Callen, my mother restored your knee. I have her healing power. I will treat your wife with the utmost respect, I assure you."

"Do anything," Callen rasped. "Anything to save her."

Rudhira sat down on the edge of the cot and rested a hand on Perita's heart. His brow furrowed, and his vast power flowed through the Blood Union.

"Can you—?" Cassia dared ask.

"Yes. We're not too late." The smile that crossed his face was bittersweet. How many memories did he carry of times when he had been too late?

Before their eyes, the color returned to Perita's skin. The alarming smell of blood faded. Her eyes refocused, and she licked her dry lips. "Cal?"

He heaved a sigh, pressing a kiss to her hair. "I'm here, Pet."

Her brow crumpled. "The babe—is he—"

Their son answered her with an ear-splitting squall. Joy shone out of her, and she laughed through her sudden tears. "Bless him, he's got some lungs."

Rudhira gazed at the noisy, messy, squirming little mortal with a soft expression Lio had never seen on his face. This life had existed for no more than a day. And yet Rudhira stopped, amid his sixteen centuries, to marvel. The Collector would never understand. But Lio did.

"He's perfect," Rudhira said. "Well done, Mistress Perita."

Perita looked around her, and her eyes widened. Her hand tightened on Cassia's. "My lady—!"

Cassia beamed at her. "I'm here, my friend."

"I don't need to ask what's going on, then. Clearly it's a scheme of yours." She let out a sigh. "Whatever it is, I'm grateful for it."

"Everything will be all right now," Cassia promised.

Callen helped Perita sit up, and Miranda handed the boy to his mother. With Callen's arm around her, Perita gathered their son to her, and the two lovers finally got to behold the new life they had created, in spite of all this death. The life Pakhne had delivered into this world, in her final act as a healer.

Lio wrapped a veil spell around himself and his Ritual father. "Please—will you see if there's anything you can do for Pakhne?"

"Of course." Rudhira rose to his feet.

He and Lio joined Mak and Lyros around Pakhne's cot, concealed from the mortals. They shared a moment of Hesperine silence. This was one of Hesperines' most sacred duties, laid upon them by Hespera. To be the stewards of broken mortal lives. To bring hope. And when there was no more hope, to give Mercy.

Rudhira's magic reached into Pakhne, and he went still. He, who had seen everything in his long existence, looked sickened. He murmured an ancient Hesperine prayer and rested his hand on Pakhne's head. "I cannot understand how she survived this."

"We didn't think it was possible," Lyros said. "Based on what Eudias told Lio, when the Collector takes his victim's magic, it always kills them."

"Severing her magic from her life force should be impossible," Rudhira replied.

"He did it intentionally," Lio bit out. "I was fighting him for her...and he let me have her. Without her magic."

"Ah, Goddess." Mak hugged Lio around his shoulders. "I'm sorry."

"It's what he does. She was just a tool to him, a way to hurt me. He reduced her entire life to a momentary battle taunt, for the satisfaction of besting me."

"We all know how you tend to blame yourself," Rudhira said. "You know where to find the mind healers when you're ready. And if you do not come find us, I will find you." He looked at the three of them. "All of you."

"We must become stronger in those moments," Lio said.

"We will," Lyros said.

"In time," Mak agreed.

"I wish you didn't have to." Rudhira's gaze fell to Pakhne again. "She was one of the mages who came to Orthros during the Solstice Summit, wasn't she?"

Lio nodded. "She has been representing the Kyrian delegation here in Lord Hadrian's camp, rallying support for the treaty."

Rudhira let out a sigh that seemed to hold centuries of regrets. "Tenebrans who ally with us are precious few, and this world has never been kind to them."

He was right. They were the reason Pakhne had been targeted. Her involvement in the Summit, her personal history with Lio and Cassia—that was why the Collector had chosen her. First, it had been Hamon, an innocent bystander. Tonight it had been Pakhne, an ally. Who would it be next? Which treasured friend? Which family member?

"There must be a way to help her," Lio said. "What about the heart hunter? The one from Martyr's Pass, the only one who survived the Collector during our battle to get the Tenebran embassy safely into Orthros."

"Yes," Rudhira said. "Your presence in the man's mind spared him from the Collector's death strike."

"Are you still trying to heal his mind? Have you learned anything from him that could help Pakhne?"

Rudhira paused. "It may not be possible to ever restore his mind. But thanks to you, he now lives in peace, with good care, and will die a free man."

"Is that the life that awaits Pakhne, then?"

"I'll take her with me and see to her care myself. I can consult my mother Soteira and our Imperial colleagues as well."

"What about the treaty?" Lyros asked. "If Hesperines take a Kyrian mage away without permission, what are the implications?"

"Does Pakhne have time for us to negotiate this?" Mak asked.

Rudhira shook his head. Even now, the flow of his magic was sustaining her fading life. "She won't survive long without the constant care of a Hesperine healer."

"Take her with you," Lio said. "Cassia and I will mitigate the political damage. Hopefully there won't be any, if we can explain this to the Semna." He hesitated. "How long do you think Pakhne has?"

Rudhira's voice was calm. Kind. How often had he used this tone to give terrible news to his patients' loved ones? "Without her magic, it may not be long before she goes to her gods. But we'll make sure she doesn't suffer—and we will not stop trying to heal her."

The implications of those words sank in. They were dealing with necromancy Rudhira had never seen before. He who was trained by Queen Soteira herself in Imperial mind healing, he who had battled Gift Collectors for over a thousand years. This was magic even he did not understand.

What hope did Lio have of protecting anyone from this enemy?

PAKHNE'S FATE

"YOUR HIGHNESS."

When Cassia heard Lord Hadrian's voice beside her, it took her a moment to realize he was speaking to her. She rose from Perita's cot.

He gave Cassia a bow, one befitting his queen's sister. "She says we have you to thank for bringing her back to us."

Cassia doubted she could persuade him not to address her as a princess now. But she knew it was purely a sign of his love for Solia, so she let it pass. "She would have returned to us, no matter what it took, but Ambassador Deukalion and I helped her reach us sooner."

Lord Hadrian lifted Cassia's hand, as if to kiss it, but merely held it. He seemed to find no more words. But they needed none. They had both been there the night they had believed Solia lost forever. They understood what her return meant, as no one else could.

Cassia finally stowed her weapon, sliding her spade back into her satchel. She rested her hand on Lord Hadrian's sinewy, scarred one. "We remained true, and now all shall be well."

He laughed suddenly, an edge of joy in the sound. "So it shall."

With Kella at her side, Solia came to stand at the foot of Perita's cot. Perita's gaze rose from her child, and she stared.

"My lady...?" she asked Cassia, her voice querulous.

A smile spread across Cassia's face. "Allow me to present Perita, once my faithful handmaiden and always my friend. You have already met her husband Callen in battle. Perita, Callen, our true queen has returned."

Callen made to scramble to his feet, but Solia held up a hand. "At ease."

He sank back down next to his wife, clearly at a loss for words.

"Gods above! My lady, how—? You can make anything possible, that's how." Perita seemed to realize this was her first impression on her lost and future queen, and bowed her head. "Your Majesty."

Solia gave Perita and Callen one of her gentle smiles, which was disarming despite the sword at her waist. "Thank you for your devotion to my sister. I too had a handmaiden who sacrificed…everything…for me. Your loyalty to Cassia will never be forgotten in my reign."

"I'd still follow her anywhere," Perita said fiercely.

"And I will still protect you," Cassia vowed.

Solia touched the child's head, and a hush came over the gathering at that royal blessing, a mark of honor that would stay with him his life long. "Have you chosen a name yet?"

Callen found his voice. "After my father, Your Majesty, same as me."

Perita glowed with pride. "Little Callen will be a good man and a fine warrior, just like his papa and grandpapa."

"I lost my father too early." Callen gave Kella a deep nod. "Thanks to your comrade, my son won't suffer the same. May I know her name, so I can honor my life debt?"

Cassia passed Callen's question on to Kella in Divine, and the mercenary sheathed her fortune blade. "Give him my name and tell him I will hold his life debt with fairness."

Cassia repeated this assurance in Vulgus. "You are fortunate, Callen. She holds many life debts in the Empire, and you are the first on these shores. The woman who saved your life is Kella, First Blade of the Ashes, daughter of Queen Hinan of the Azarqi."

"And my trusted friend," Solia added. "Honor her as befits a princess from our ally, the Empire."

"I am at your service, Princess Kella," Callen replied.

"Thank you for protecting my husband, Your Highness," said Perita.

After Cassia translated, Kella's indigo lips curved into a grin. "I wouldn't let those bloodless kill a friend of yours, Shadow. Knocking a few undead off of him was fun. Don't tell him I said that, though."

Solia turned to Miranda. "You bravely defended Perita and her child today. Your courage and loyalty will not be forgotten, either."

Miranda managed a curtsy, leaning on the broken cot leg like a cane. "I am grateful for your consideration, Your Majesty."

Perita held out a hand to Miranda, and her friend reached over to grip it. Cassia's heart tightened with a mix of happiness and envy. She was glad Perita had such a good friend here. But she missed being that friend.

"Is Pakhne all right?" Perita asked.

"Resting from using so much magic," Cassia said smoothly. She would not taint this moment of joy with sad news. There would be time for her friends to confront Pakhne's plight later. But Lord Hadrian needed to know the truth now.

Reluctantly, Cassia left Perita, Callen, and Miranda with the child. She and Solia took Lord Hadrian to join the Hesperines within their veil spells around Pakhne's empty cot.

Rudhira was already gone. Cassia breathed a sigh of relief that he had slipped in and out with the Aithourians and Lord Hadrian none the wiser. Like Cassia, Lord Hadrian had met Rudhira in his guise as Hold Lord Justinian. They couldn't have the most powerful free lord in Tenebra realize Lord Justinian was secretly a Hesperine.

"Where is Pakhne?" Lord Hadrian asked.

Cassia couldn't bear the grief on Lio's face. She wanted to hold him until she talked him out of every bit of self-blame. But she couldn't even risk reaching into their Union. She didn't want him to hear what she was thinking right now.

Alone in her own thoughts, she wondered if Pakhne's fate had been a vision of her own future.

"Our healers have taken her to safety," Lio said.

Lord Hadrian looked to Solia, his hand on his hilt.

She touched his arm. "These Hesperines are our allies. I uphold the new Solstice Oath my sister negotiated with Orthros."

Lord Hadrian gave a nod and released his sword. "Lord Gaius pledged Hadria to that treaty on my behalf, and I keep my oaths—but my vows of fealty to my queen rule them all. As long as you are a friend of Queen Solia, you will be a friend of Hadria."

Lio bowed. "You have Orthros's gratitude for your support, my lord. Rest assured, we are on your side."

"We would all have died today," Cassia said, "if the Hesperines had not defended us. We are facing an enemy too powerful to fight with swords."

She exchanged a glance with Lio and Solia, who both nodded. There were few secrets they could keep from Lord Hadrian now.

Solia turned to Lord Hadrian. "What do you know about the necromancer Lucis calls his ally? You have greater access to the king's solar—and his secrets—than any man in Tenebra."

"I know he consorts with mages of all kinds," Lord Hadrian rumbled in disapproval. "Including a Gift Collector last year."

"Master Skleros," Solia confirmed. "He serves another mage—one even more dangerous—who has been working spells for years to help the king claim and hold the throne."

"His other crimes are not enough?" Lord Hadrian said, with all the anger he had hidden from the king these many years. "He relies on magic to cheat his way to power?"

"I have seen it with my own eyes," Cassia replied. "His secret ally is both a necromancer and a mage of dreams."

Lord Hadrian shook his head. "A father should never allow his daughter to witness such things."

"Cassia and I are the only ones who know of this necromancer's existence," Solia said, "except for the Hesperines who battled him when he tried to sabotage the Solstice Summit. It is safer for our people that way."

"I am as silent a steward of your secrets now as I was when you were girl," Lord Hadrian said.

"Thank you," Solia told him.

"So this necromancer is the one who turned my men against each other?" Lord Hadrian demanded. "What did he do to Mage Pakhne?"

Lio, of course, took it upon himself to answer. Rudhira would have been proud of how he explained Pakhne's condition. "We need to decide what to tell her family. Lord Hadrian, I understand her parents and sister are loyal to you. Will you be the one to break the news to them?"

Lord Hadrian looked weary. "They will have my full support once they receive word. But since Pakhne entered the temple, she is no longer a daughter of Hadria, but of Kyria. It's best if you tell her temple sisters first, then let them decide what her family should know."

Lio gave a nod. "I will tell the Semna and Mage Ariadne upon our return to Patria. We will seek their blessing to keep Pakhne under Hesperine care."

"Can you save her?" Lord Hadrian asked finally.

"We don't know," Lio said. "But we will fight hard for her."

"That is an honest answer." Lord Hadrian looked between Lio and Cassia, his gaze settling on Lio. "Lord Gaius tells me that at the Solstice Summit, you extracted a confession from the Dexion of the Aithourian Circle without laying a hand on him. Anyone who can get a politician from Cordium to spill his guts is no mere light mage."

"Ah, I see my bluff did not fool the insightful Lord Gaius."

"Can your Hesperine mind magic protect my people from the mage of dreams?"

"Yes." Lio's tone held no trace of self-doubt.

Cassia recognized that answer for a diplomat's consummate bluff. She knew Lio was terrified that the answer was no.

"Can you convince the king to remove the Aithourians from your camp?" Lio asked. "Perhaps by allowing them to take the blame for the untimely deaths of your men by friendly fire?"

"Well," Lord Hadrian said, "I begin to see how you got that confession out of Corona's golden boy. I think your plan will work."

"Once they leave," Lio continued, "the Stewards and I can cast a thelemantic ward that blends physical protection and mind magic. In the meantime, if you'll allow it, our Hesperines errant will patrol the area to ensure the necromancer cannot return while you're still undefended."

Lord Hadrian frowned. "I cannot have a ward blocking anyone from entering or leaving the camp."

"No one will ever know it's there," Lio assured him. "You men will be able to ride in and out of it. But if the necromancer or one of his servants tries to cross it, it will repel him."

While Lord Hadrian considered this, Solia said nothing. Cassia wished she would, but she understood her sister's silence. Her duel with Lord Hadrian had been a test of his loyalty. This was a test of hers. She would not command him to accept Hesperines in his camp, as Lucis had commanded him to welcome Aithourians.

Lord Hadrian said, "I remember you from the Equinox Summit, Ambassador Deukalion. You stood between me and a wall of magefire. I believe I owe you a life debt."

Lio gave one of his self-effacing smiles and shook his head. "I would sooner say we have a bond of gratitude, my lord, if you will allow a Hesperine interpretation of that night."

"And how does a man do his duty to a bond of gratitude?"

"If you will allow me to fight with you to protect your people, I will consider our bond honored, and honor it in return."

"Then raise your defenses. Hadria and the Hesperines will stand together against the necromancer—and in support of Queen Solia at the coming vote."

TWILIGHT WAS MELTING INTO dawn by the time they returned to Patria. His thoughts in a haze, Lio let Mak and Lyros step everyone. They landed in the chambers Cassia shared with the other women.

She blinked, and Lio's mind slipped into hers again. Her dull mortal nose brought Lio the scent of the coffee Tuura was brewing at the hearth. Through Cassia's eyes, Lio watched Karege yawn and Hoyefe warm his hands by the fire. Shaking his head, Lio pulled back his power. Cassia helped him with a push. Together, they shoved him back into his own mind. She stumbled a little, and he tightened his arm around her.

"Look what Tilili dragged in." Even light-hearted Hoyefe sounded worried about them.

Karege leapt up from his chair, his fangs unsheathing. "Did we miss a battle?"

Lio focused on the first important question. "Did the Collector try to return here?"

"No," Tuura said, "there's been no sign of him."

"Lio drove him out of Lord Hadrian's camp," Cassia explained. "It's good news that Patria is not where he retreated to."

"But now he could be anywhere." Lio's mind reeled with the possibilities.

Mak threw himself into a chair and pulled Lyros onto his lap. "He's not anywhere near the people under our protection. That's what matters right now."

Lyros settled into Mak's arms. "Agreed. We can't worry about anything outside our perimeter. We have to stay focused."

Tuura was already reaching for her medicine bag. "I see at least three cuts that need a poultice."

Too many people. Lio wanted to drag Cassia into a deep, dark chamber and lose himself in her until he could no longer remember the sound of the Collector's laughter.

But he had no right to seek oblivion. His duty to Pakhne was not done.

"Solia," he said, "a word."

She faced him. "You want to do this now?"

"I'd sooner do it while Pakhne still breathes, which may not be long."

Karege levitated more chairs near the fire. "Why doesn't everyone have a seat? I'm sure we can all sort it out."

Tuura started pouring cups of coffee. "You can all tell us what happened while I patch up Sunburn and Standstill."

Kella kept Tilili at Solia's side. "There's nothing to sort out."

"It's almost dawn." Cassia put a hand on Lio's chest. "You need blood and sleep."

"What I need," Lio said to his Grace-sister, "is for my judgment to be trusted during a battle with the Collector."

"I am a warrior," Solia returned. "You're a diplomat. I know how to make quick decisions in battle."

"I am a mage, and if you don't want more people to meet Pakhne's fate, you must listen to me."

"Would you prefer we be burying Callen right now?"

Lio's voice rose. "We could have saved them all!"

Solia took a step closer to him. "You forget, Lio—I am also a mage, and I know when to use magic over the sword."

"By all means, use your magic," he shot back, "but you didn't have to destroy every single bloodless with one spell."

"If I hadn't, I can't promise Perita and the child would still be alive, either."

"You could have bought us a little more time. Even a few more minutes, and everything would have gone differently! We could have had the thelemantic wards ready. And he wouldn't have tried that attack if he'd still had his bloodless to wield. I could have focused all my power on saving Pakhne."

"He took her magic and left her alive to taunt you. If you'd had hours to battle him with perfectly crafted spells, would it have ended any differently?"

"I'll never know, because you didn't give me a chance!"

Lio dragged his hands through his hair. Dawn was reaching for him. Curse the sun, robbing him of the last word, of the power to change anything.

"We're not done." Lio stepped away before he collapsed in front of Solia.

He fell onto his cot in the other room. All the endings that had not come to pass spun through his thoughts. Was this what it felt like to be an oracle, seeing visions of things you were powerless to change?

97

days until

AUTUMN EQUINOX

2 Anthros's Sword, 1597 OT

WITCH OF THE WILDS

Cassia felt as if she were smothering in the great hall. Knight panted at her feet, just as miserable from the smell of unwashed Tenebran lords and the noise of their arguments. At least he didn't understand their infuriating words.

She hated Flavian's smooth voice as he kept order. Even more, she hated how often Solia had to bite her tongue to avoid antagonizing anyone. It was the lords, not Lio, who deserved to bear the brunt of her anger.

The Semna and Ariadne sat a few chairs away, observing the proceedings. They didn't know. And Cassia would make sure it stayed that way until Lio woke. Telling Pakhne's Kyrian sisters what had befallen her was a grim privilege, but Cassia knew how important it was to her Hesperine to perform that sacred duty.

It wasn't truly the Council that was making Cassia ill. She had braced herself for it, but the longer the day wore on, the more difficult her Craving became.

Tuura shot Cassia worried glances until the diviner finally opened her mouth to speak. But Cassia cut her off with a small shake of her head. In front of Solia, there would be no mention of Cassia's Craving or anything else that would make her sister likely to shout at her Grace again.

"I'm going to the privy." She wasn't; she'd barely eaten or drunk anything all day. But Cassia dared Solia to think otherwise.

"You'll have trouble getting past the door guards before the Council adjourns," Tuura pointed out.

"No," Solia said to Cassia's back, "I already told them she will be leaving early and that the Hesperine delegation will not be joining us this evening."

Cassia looked over her shoulder at her sister, trying to read Solia's face. Was she banishing Lio from the Council for the night? Or was this a peace offering so Lio and Cassia could spend time together? Why was it sometimes so hard for Cassia to understand her own sister?

"I'll go with her." Kella tapped Tilili's shoulder, and the cat rose.

They slipped out of the great hall, and the corridor felt cold in comparison. Cassia took a grateful breath. "Thank you."

"No need to thank me. Tilili wanted out of there, too." Kella kept her seat gracefully as the cat extended her claws, stretching her back and sticking her rump in the air.

Cassia gave her hound's chest a rub. "Knight was getting restless, as well."

"Tilili needs to prowl, and you do not need to wander the halls alone, even with a liegehound. I'll go with you."

"But Solia needs you," Cassia said.

Kella hesitated. "She needs you, as well."

"I should be with Lio tonight."

Kella only nodded. "I'll escort you back to our chambers. I'll talk to Solia, if you can calm down that mind mage of yours."

"Thank you, Standstill."

Kella smiled and started down the corridor. Cassia and Knight fell into step beside her, his ears pricked and hackles up.

In the silence that followed, Cassia asked, "Do you really think the battle could have gone differently?"

"Sometimes there is no wrong answer in battle. And no right one. Hesperines are too preoccupied with changing things they cannot control. But perhaps that's easy for me to say, as an Azarqi. We're taught that it's not our hands that shape the dunes of the Maaqul."

"You've never done something you'll regret forever?"

"I didn't say that."

Cassia wanted to ask Kella why Solia hated Lio so much. But it was unjust to put Kella in a difficult position in between Cassia, her sister, and her Grace. Solia's temper certainly fell into the category of things no one could control, except Solia. Cassia chose to control her own anger tonight.

Despite the knowledge that she was safe with Kella, Cassia's gaze darted around every corner and her ears listened for any footsteps in the halls. She was glad the more useful of her old habits had not entirely died. The hairs on the back of her neck were standing up by the time they reached her door.

Kella said, "I would warn you not to get any ideas about wandering until Lio is awake, but I know you are not the type who takes foolish risks. With a few notable exceptions."

"Yes, I save all my foolishness and risk tolerance for loving Lio."

"I was thinking of the time you wandered around the Sandira City alone and got yourself carried off by a winged menace."

"That was Monsoon's fault!" Cassia protested. "Did he tell you that he kidnapped me?"

"I understand you put up quite a fight and left him with a sore foot. Well done."

"That compliment means a great deal coming from you, First Blade."

"I'll show you how to bruise his wings next time."

Kella left her in the safety of their warded chambers, and Cassia barred the door for good measure. She passed through the weaving room to the bedchamber, where late afternoon light and a whiff of air came in through the small window. Cassia pulled the drape over it. Darkness settled around her, familiar and dear, and her belly calmed.

She sat on the bed, which she and Tuura were sharing, since Solia and Kella preferred bedrolls on the floor. Knight leapt up beside Cassia and stretched out against her leg so she could pet him.

"How grateful I am for an uncomplicated moment with just you and me, Sir Knight."

Her hound whined and rested his head on his paws, looking up at her with questioning eyes.

"I know." She stroked his head and ears. "It feels like Lio should be here, too."

He must be having day terrors about Pakhne. But he had often told Cassia that feeling her presence in his Slumber influenced his dreams. She closed her eyes and reached for their Grace Union.

It was so easy to connect with him this time. The deep Union they had shared during their spell casting had left the arcane pathways between them more open. She could smell his magic, and the tease of moonflower, ink, and blood made her mouth go drier.

She tried to push her hunger away and focus. His magic was roiling, a sure sign he suffered from his dreams. He needed her.

If she entered the chamber where the Hesperines slept, she didn't think Karege, Mak, and Lyros would see it as crossing the veil. But the wagging tongues of Patria would never forgive her if they caught her sneaking into a room full of male immortals alone.

Cassia's eyes sprang open. If there was ever a time when she needed one of the Changing Queen's secret passageways, it was now.

She pulled the Changing Queen's pendant out of her robes as she and Knight returned to the weaving room. Wrapping her hand around the artifact, she stood before the hearth. This fireplace wasn't nearly as large as the one in the royal chambers at Solorum, but ducking, she managed to stand inside it and put her free hand on the sooty stone at its back.

Saying *Ebah* had failed to reveal any entrances in the solar. If that was not the key, could there be another? Perhaps a different name for a different fortress?

Cassia tried the Changing Queen's name in Vulgus. "Hedera."

Nothing. Perhaps the Mage King's name?

"Lucian," she said.

Still nothing. Of course. It would have to be a word in Ebah's mother tongue. What would her people have called Lucian? That meant *light* in Vulgus…

Cassia wracked her limited knowledge of the old garden tongue. All she knew were flower names. But Anthros's fire was called light flower in the old tongue.

"Liohtkar," Cassia said, and her hand passed through the wall.

She cast a glance over her shoulder at Knight. "I'm afraid we're doing this again, darling. Stand guard for me."

He posted himself in front of the hearth as if resigned.

Cassia darted into the passageway. Shadows and dust engulfed her. But she could see. In surprise, she looked down to find her ambassador's medallion glowing, as if with moonlight.

"I didn't know you could do that," she murmured, if only to lift the eerie silence. How many centuries had it been since anyone had set foot here?

Awareness came over her of the powerful advantage she now held over every soul at Patria. But politics quickly fled from her mind. All she could think about was having Lio in her arms again, his magic inside her.

She started forward, trusting the glow of her medallion and the pull of Lio's magic to prevent her from losing her way. She walked with certainty through the twists and turns, her Grace's presence growing stronger.

To her surprise, these halls were not bare like those inside Solorum palace. Ivy vines clung to the walls. How did they grow without light? Could the Changing Queen's power be stronger here…because of the nearness of the letting site?

The ivy grew thicker the deeper Cassia went. Eventually she came to a fork in the corridor that presented her with a decision. Lio's presence was stronger to the left, but the vines led to the right.

Her pulse pounded, demanding she find her Grace. She tried to think. When she had left the great hall, she'd had more than an hour before twilight. She had time to investigate this mystery before Lio woke. And anything that got them closer to her magic got them closer to her Gifting.

She set off down the corridor lined with vines. Their leaves rustled under her feet. Something inside her stirred, a breathless excitement, a fullness within her. Her magic?

When she came out into an open chamber, her breath caught. Ivy covered the walls and ceiling of the round room. But the floor was carpeted in golden flowers that let off a gentle glow. Anthros's fire.

Cassia's jaw hung open. Bits of history wove together in her mind, hinting at the personal tale behind kingdom-changing events. When Lucian had been courting his witch of the wilds, perhaps they had hidden their love from his disapproving lords until he secured their approval. Had Ebah's magic created this haven for them? Cassia's face heated. Had they also done forbidden things on the aspiring king's secret parapet?

"Well, I walk in the footsteps of my rebellious matriarch, but what is my Hesperine to do about Anthros's fire?"

The sun god's flowers were poisonous to Hesperines. It was a shame something so beautiful was anathema to her Grace. Just like her own magic. Frustration rose in her, and that wakeful thing inside her burst out. She lost her balance, falling headfirst into the flowers.

Soft petals cushioned her face. But it wasn't the sharp scent of Anthros's fire that filled her nose. She pushed up on her hands and knees and stared at what her magic had done.

She laughed in wonder. "Not so anti-haimatic now, are you?"

The golden blooms were gone, the room now blanketed in moonflowers.

THE WOMAN IN KYRIAN robes writhed on the cot, clawing at her chest. Lio could feel the hollowness inside her. Anguished cries came from within her hood.

"I'm so sorry." Tears streamed down his face as he reached out to her. "I'll do everything I can to save you, Pakhne."

Her hood fell back. It wasn't the mage who stared at him with judgment.

It was Cassia.

He fell to his knees beside his Grace, his head in his hands.

"Lio," she called.

But her voice wasn't coming from the tortured figure on the cot. She spoke from somewhere behind him.

"Lio!" she called again from far away, and yet so near.

He turned from her weeping form on the bed, toward the hope of her strong voice.

Moonflowers had sprung up on the floor of the tent, lining a pathway. He longed to follow it away.

But he looked back over his shoulder into Cassia's empty eyes.

"Lio," she called for the third time. "Trust yourself."

He turned away from the cot and took the moonflower path.

The tent disappeared, and he stepped into a bower of ivy and blooms.

Lio's first breath of the night filled him with the scent of moonflowers. For an instant, he thought he was home. His heavy eyelids rose.

Cassia looked down at him with a smile. He lay with his head on her lap.

With a gasp, he reached up to press his hand to her chest. Her heartbeat was strong, her aura shining with power. Her magic was still there, nascent, but stronger than ever.

"Goddess, am I dreaming?" Lio asked.

She ran her fingers through his hair. "No, my love. I'm all right. We're both safe."

The sickening truth hit him. Pakhne's suffering was no dream. There was no escape for her.

But he still had a chance to save Cassia, to help her find her magic.

The very magic that was at work here, it seemed. He looked around them. The moonflowers were real. "Where are we?"

She explained how she had found this hidden chamber and transformed the flowers. "So I sat here and focused on you, hoping my Union would influence your dreams."

"It did. You led me here. Did I...Slumber-step? Through walls locked by Lustra magic?"

"That's certainly what it looked like to me."

"How is that even possible?"

She leaned down over him. "No theorizing right now, Sir Scholar. Let me comfort you."

She pressed her lips to his. Pure Sanctuary. He reached up to feel the pulse of life in her neck. She deepened their kiss, parting his lips soft and slow, meeting his tongue with hers in luxurious strokes. Her hand closed around the front of his robes, and his own magic rose to her touch. His power blended with her aura, and her presence blurred around him, until he couldn't feel or taste or smell anything but her.

"What do you need?" she murmured against his mouth. "Tell me how I can ease your grief."

He wanted her to straddle him, ride him, remind him how powerful she was. He wanted to pour his magic into her until she came apart. But he couldn't bring himself to give in to pleasure, not yet. Pakhne's suffering was still too vivid in his mind.

"Grieve for Pakhne," he said, "for her family and friends. Not me."

"I am your Grace. I must do something about your pain."

"Then let me protect you."

"You did," she said. "The Collector didn't hurt me last night, because of you."

Lio rolled them onto their sides, the flowers giving under them, and placed a rough kiss on her throat. He needed to drink the life in her veins, taste that her magic was still there. She stroked his head again, tilting her head back.

"I need this," she gasped. "My Craving is the only thing hurting me."

Her skin tasted of Craving sweat and the musk of her hunger. He sucked at her soft flesh before framing her vein with his teeth and giving her his fangs. Her sigh rasped in his ear.

The taste of her blood burst on his tongue. The verdant flavor of her magic tingled in his mouth more than ever before. Desire tightened his groin, but he pushed his own needs back down.

He focused on her body. The way she clutched at his shoulder and arched closer to him. The new spice in her blood.

"Lio," she moaned. "If you don't want the Feast…you need to stop…"

He tightened his bite. A little jerk went through her hips, and he caught her buttocks in his hand, pulling her closer against him.

"You know I'll lose control," she warned.

He could not accept pleasure tonight, but if she found release from his bite, he would never deny her.

He slowed the rhythm of his swallows, drinking with the deep pulls he knew she enjoyed. She moaned again and melted in his hold. Her aura coaxed his magic into her in gentle rushes, like a caress in the most vulnerable reaches of his power.

"Let me comfort you." She wound her leg around him in a tangle of robes, an invitation to roll over. To lie back.

To stop grieving. He couldn't do that yet.

"I understand," she whispered, and gave him what he needed. She held him close and let him take care of her.

He sank deep into the arcane flow inside her. He traced the new, tender marks of her magic, reassuring himself that she was perfect and powerful and whole.

Her breath came faster. "Oh Goddess. The way you're touching me…I can't stop…"

He cradled her soft, slender frame as she stretched and twisted in his arms. The flavor in her blood rose to pure wildness. It called to him and made his own blood run hot.

He pulled his fangs out of her before he lost his head. But the sight of her was temptation enough. He watched her jaw drop and her eyes slide shut. Her release shuddered through her. He leaned on his fists, braced against the pull of her aura sucking his magic out of his body and into hers.

When she grew still, she heaved a breath and rubbed a hand over her eyes. He caught the gleam of tears on her fingers. Her grief for him washed over him.

He could sense her protest, her desire to touch him, but she respected his wishes. She simply held him until his body cooled.

"Tell me all the messy things," she invited, as she so often did in their intimate moments in the dark.

But tonight, so much of the mess inside him was anger at her sister. If only Solia had listened to him.

And if she had? Would it have changed anything?

Was blaming her the easy way out of this crushing sense of responsibility for the destruction of another person's life?

"I want to make something very clear," Cassia said. "We have often said our Oath of openness and honesty does not come with conditions. That is still true. My sister is not a condition on our Oath. I always want you to speak your mind with me, even about Solia."

"I know, my rose." She would listen to all his fury toward the sister she cherished, but he would not ask that of her. "I'm not ready to talk about what happened."

It was true. But perhaps it was also another easy way out.

He forced himself to sit up. "We should get to the Council."

"We are excused for tonight," Cassia said.

Before Lio asked why, he bit his tongue. He had a feeling that would only lead them into angry words about Solia, as well.

Cassia caressed his face. "I spoke to Eudias in the great hall today. I arranged for us to meet with him after the Council adjourns. He can help us decide how much to tell Ariadne and the Semna about what happened."

Lio heaved a sigh. "That's a good plan."

Cassia brushed a moonflower leaf out of his hair. "I wish we could stay here in the tunnels forever."

"We should come back and explore to see what we can learn about the Lustra magic." He got up and pulled her to her feet. "Your magic is so strong here."

"We agreed it was unlikely for the letting site to be near the fortress… but what if we were wrong? Do you think the power here could lead us to it? Could it even be somewhere inside or under Castra Patria?"

"This could be a real breakthrough in the search for your magic." He felt both their spirits lift.

"I want to test something," she said. "Come with me."

She took his hand and guided him through a maze of ivy-covered passages by the light of her medallion. He conjured another spell light to better illuminate the gray stone walls and verdant green plants. But what pushed back the shadows in his own mind was her.

Lio walked through an enchanted otherworld thanks to his Grace's power. He must be the first Hesperine ever to set foot within this bastion of anti-haimatic magic.

She was out of the Collector's reach here. Her own magic protected her. This might be the only place in Patria where Cassia was truly safe.

She halted him in front of a wall that looked no different to him, but she seemed confident of its significance. In spite of everything, a smile came to his face.

She smiled back. "What?"

"My Queen is about to teach me something about magic."

Her smile widened. "Well, I suppose I am, beloved tutor. We need to test whether you can enter and leave here on your own."

"Now may I theorize about Slumber-stepping?"

"Yes, I will permit academics now that you're properly fed."

"Here is my highly educated guess based on all available research on Lustra magic. That should not have been possible, and I have no idea how it happened, except that you are wondrously powerful."

Her eyes widened. "Truly?"

"Truly. Hesperines can't step in their sleep." He rubbed his chin. "Either you awoke my innate Hesperine abilities while I was unconscious, or you traversed me. Or perhaps you bent some natural phenomenon to your Will?"

Now Lio's own eyes widened. "Spirit walking. Imperial mages spirit walk by channeling the spirit phase. What if you can…nature walk, let us call it, by channeling the natural phase?"

Her excitement turned to dismay. "What if I can't do it intentionally? What if you're trapped here?"

"Don't worry. We'll test all our theories. I'll simply try walking out first." He reached a hand out in front of him, and it hit solid stone.

"Surely you can step out," she said. "The weaving room is through this wall. Mak and Lyros's ward should provide a stepping focus for you."

Lio reached for his Trial brothers' spell, but then raised his brows at Cassia. "Well, as it happens, I cannot step from here. I am at your mercy, Silvicultrix."

Her hazel eyes flashed with indignation. "You are my Grace. I will not stand for my own magic trapping you." She took his hand. "Let me try to escort you."

He watched her walk ahead of him through solid stone. For the first time, he felt some apprehension. He would be able to follow her...wouldn't he?

His hand slipped into the wall after her, and they both breathed a sigh of relief. He followed her through a tangle of magic that pushed him away, even as it twined around him. It was vast enough to make a Hesperine feel small, and yet as familiar as the hand guiding him through it.

"Duck," Cassia warned.

He bent low, but still knocked his head on the mantle of the fireplace on their way out. Knight circled them, scattering soot and licking Lio's hand.

Cassia reached up to rub the spot on Lio's head. "My poor, overtall bloodborn."

He wiped the soot off the tip of her nose. "I will gladly bang my skull on any number of fireplaces to explore secret Lustra passages with you."

"Now it will be so much easier to sneak about without endangering your innocent reputation," she teased. "Let us see if we can find you a more accommodating entrance."

After some exploration, they discovered that the wall behind a tapestry in the bedchamber also worked as a portal. They plunged into the passageways again, this time taking Knight with them. Cassia's steps were sure, her small, silk-slippered feet rustling in the ivy with purpose. She paused occasionally at forks in the passage, her aura reaching, before she guided them onward.

"I am in awe of your sense of direction," Lio said.

"It's much easier to navigate here than at Solorum. I'm not sure if that's because there's more Lustra magic at Patria, or because my own power is awakening."

"How fortunate I am to have such an expert guide. The magic in this place makes me feel like a foreign guest, lost in the domain of a very powerful matriarch who isn't quite sure she likes me yet."

"Well, that makes me her heir, and you my consort, so she had best accept that you're here to stay."

Eventually Cassia halted them before a crumbling archway that was filled in with stonework. She squeezed Lio's hand. "This will take us to the shrine room, where Eudias agreed to meet us."

The outside world demanded their return. Lio found himself frozen on that threshold. Not only because he dreaded telling the mortals what had befallen Pakhne and feeling their pain in the Blood Union.

Until he told them, they still lived in a world where she was safe and whole. He wanted to let them keep her just a moment longer.

But he couldn't wait forever. It was now his duty to tell them the Collector had shattered a piece of their world beyond repair.

Hand in hand with Cassia, he left her domain. They came out in a spacious chamber with shrines to each deity around the edges of the room. Every delegation of mages was represented, including Anthros, Kyria, Hypnos, and Chera. Even the other Twice-Seven Scions like Angara and Andragathos had shrines of their own, despite being lesser gods.

But not Hespera, of course. Beside the shrine of Hypnos, where a shroud hung to represent the god of death, her rightful place was empty. Tenebrans and Cordians always left it so to symbolize their rejection of her.

Eudias stood there with Ariadne. With so many spells in the room, it took Lio a moment to realize what the two young mages were looking at with such apprehension. Knight's growl warned him.

There was a stain of necromancy upon Hespera's empty place. On the floor rested a leather gauntlet with a symbol painted in blood on the palm: an Eye of Hypnos. A Gift Collector's glove, holding a dead rose.

Eudias lifted wide eyes to Lio's. "Can you sense him?"

Lio fought the urge to pull his Grace into his arms. "Cassia, get back inside the tunnels."

"I'll go get Mak and Lyros." She darted back through the wall, one hand on Knight.

Lio's magic honed, ready to destroy the glove with a spell and engulf the entire fortress in a blast of thelemancy that would banish the Collector.

He held his power back and counted to three. Gathered a veil around his magic. Four, five, six. Then cast his concealed seeking spell through Castra Patria.

Lio shook his head. "He isn't here."

Eudias swallowed. "But he was."

"We met him last night," Lio admitted.

Eudias drew himself up, as if coming to a decision, and shared a look with Ariadne. "I believe it's time none of us kept any more secrets."

She nodded firmly and took his hand, despite Lio looking on. "I know about the Collector. Eudias told me what happened to him—and that you saved him. You will always have my gratitude."

Lio bowed his head. "As you have ours, for being such an ally to all of us."

This was one of the Kyrian mages who had given Lio's family his little sister. How was he to tell Ariadne he had failed to protect her temple sister Pakhne?

Lio sent up a prayer to Hespera, hoping Kyria would also hear, and found the words.

THE GAUNTLET

ARIADNE'S WEEPING ECHOED THROUGH the shrine chamber. Lio turned away to give her some privacy in her grief. But the image would live in his mind forever: her kneeling before the shrine of Kyria, her tears for Pakhne staining her veil; Eudias putting his arms around her as she shook with sobs.

Ariadne's anguish inundated the Union, saturating Lio until he felt nothing else. All he could see was a vision of his own family mourning Cassia's magic.

But then Cassia returned, leading their Trial brothers out of the tunnels. She took one look at Ariadne and Eudias, then came straight to Lio's side. "You could have waited. I would have been here while you told them."

"I know. But it was something I needed to do on my own."

She nodded in resignation and put her arms around him.

"You did the right thing to come get us." Mak stood over the gauntlet. "This is a Gift Collector's glove, all right. It reeks of necromancy, and the rose of poison."

"You have no idea how much I want to destroy it." Lio's rage demanded an outlet, and this symbol of the Collector made a tempting one.

Lyros held a warded canvas bag open for Mak. "No, leaving it to us was the best decision."

"It could be covered in magical traps." With his hands emanating magic, Mak picked up the gauntlet and rose and slid them quickly into the bag.

Lyros closed the sack. "This is also our only clue about our enemy's activities at Patria."

Cassia's spine was rigid with composure, but any Hesperine could hear her racing heartbeat. "It's not a clue. It's an invitation. Did you see the size of the glove?"

With a start, Lio realized she was right. It was not the gauntlet of a man like Skleros. It was the perfect size for a woman with small hands.

Cassia held out her own hand. "He told me he wanted me for an Overseer. I don't believe he was merely twisting my thoughts. I think he wants me to use my magic in his game."

Every glass offering at the shrines rattled from Lio's magic. "Hypnos will get nowhere with that ambition. He cannot take you from Hespera."

Her hand closed around her medallion. "Yes. If he thinks he can poison this rose, he's in for a nasty surprise."

Lyros held up a reassuring hand. "We should not respond in fear. This is a valuable discovery. The more we know about his motivations, the better we can protect each other and everyone at Patria."

"Thank you for your level head," Lio said. "All I can see right now is red."

"Understandable," Mak said. "But don't worry. Karege went to get Tuura. She'll be able to tell us more about what sort of necromancy this holds."

When Karege stepped into the chamber, he brought not only Tuura, but all the Ashes. And Solia.

Her gaze fell on Ariadne and Eudias. She went still, in that way she seemed to have learned as the Empress's bodyguard, which covered all pain and uncertainty and decisions. But discipline was also sometimes a way out, not a solution.

She joined Ariadne and Eudias at the shrine, holding up a hand to stave off any bows or curtsies. In silence, she knelt beside them. Ariadne began to murmur a prayer.

Lio rarely felt the effects of being a heretic, but right now, he begrudged Solia the right to pray with them.

Mak poked Lio's chest. "I will give you one night to get over your idiotic self-blame, and if you're not done by then, I'll beat it out of you in the fighting ring."

"I'm not sure it works that way." Lio let Mak collar him in a hug, "But I'll take you up on it in any case."

Tuura took the warded bag from Lyros. "How long has the glove been here?"

Hoyefe answered, "I passed through here this morning—people spill all sorts of secrets to the gods when they don't realize an invisible mage is hiding nearby. I didn't see the glove."

"But that doesn't mean it wasn't here," Lyros pointed out. "It could have been hidden under spells and set to be revealed in response to some kind of magical trigger we don't understand."

Lio gritted his teeth. "This means we have no idea if he placed it here before Tuura and I arrived at Patria, or if he got past our patrols tonight."

"No one could get past Peanut!" Karege protested.

"Tuura," Kella said, "you know I have complete faith in you, but it's my duty to ask. Do you have any reason to believe the Silence is compromising your spells?"

"A fair question, First Blade," Tuura replied with a nod, "but adjusting my spells for this hemisphere doesn't weaken my magic."

"It weakens *her*." Karege put his hands on his hips. "The extra effort her spells take is affecting her health."

"No need to fuss over me, Noon Watch. I don't deny it's tiring, but even so, the Collector should not have been able to sneak in here under my nose. That said, it's best if none of us become overconfident in our abilities where this foe is concerned."

"We should preserve your energy," Kella said. "Will it drain you too much to examine the glove?"

"No, this is an important use of power." Tuura reached into her medicine bag and pulled out a pouch. She sprinkled powder from inside it onto the floor, filling the chamber with the woody and sharp scents of Imperial herbs. Taking her staff in both hands, she used the end of it to spread the powder in a protective circle on the ground.

She set the warded bag inside the ring and raised her staff. An invisible wind seemed to ruffle her wrap dress. She swayed on her feet, murmuring. Whispers swept around the circle.

Cassia gasped, and Lio shared her awe. It seemed that through Tuura, an echo of the ancestors could be heard.

Solia, Eudias, and Ariadne gathered around the casting. They watched the powder float up, shedding light and magic as it swirled around the glove.

Tuura slammed her staff onto the ground once, twice, three times. The presence of death in the room fled, chased away by the whispers of her spell.

The powder dissipated into nothing, and Tuura leaned heavily on Karege's arm. "I've removed the danger."

Mak knelt and took the gauntlet from the bag to hand it to her.

She gestured to the Eye of Hypnos without touching the palm of the glove. "This glyph is more than theatrics, I'm afraid. This blood was drawn here during a magical ritual. A sacrifice."

Mak grimaced. "Gift Collectors often make human sacrifices during their spell casting."

"I've seen them do it." Cassia shuddered.

Tuura shook her head. "The ritual that gave this artifact its power didn't cost a person their life. It cost them their magic. And if that is what this Gift Collector can do to mages, imagine how he can manipulate the life force of those without power of their own."

Cassia rubbed her throat, her anxiety spiking in their Union. Lio slipped his hand behind her neck and sent a trickle of thelemancy into her. She relaxed slightly.

"We cannot let him do that to anyone else," Ariadne said.

She looked at them all with red, swollen eyes, Eudias's arm around her shoulders. Lio longed to ask for forgiveness. But it was selfish to ask her to absolve him to ease his own guilt. She needed time to grieve.

He had told her how sorry he was, but he must show her. "We will cast a thelemantic ward on Lord Hadrian's camp as soon as he gives us the all clear. How else can we help you?"

The petite, seventeen-year-old mage in her delicate veil drew herself up with authority worthy of a Prisma. "I want you to cast wards here at Patria as well. Eudias and I will deal with Master Gorgos and the Semna. Once they agree, Lord Flavian will have no choice but to accept."

"We would be very grateful to you." If she still trusted Lio to take part in warding Patria, perhaps there was hope she could forgive him. "Would you consider leaving Pakhne in the care of the Hesperine healers?"

"She must stay with you," Ariadne said firmly. "No one else understands what the Collector has done to her."

"Will the Semna agree?" Lio asked.

"Leave that to me," Ariadne replied. "We will tell everyone else that she exhausted her magic to save the life of Perita and her child. She's in seclusion with Kyrian elders who are praying for the Mother Goddess to restore her."

"And Pakhne's family?" Lio asked, his heart heavy. "They deserve to know she may not survive. I feel honor bound to break the news to them, but fear that hearing it from a Hesperine would only add to their pain."

"I think it best if the Semna and I speak to them," Ariadne said. "Her father, Free Lord Galanthian, is here for the Full Council, along with her mother. We'll tell them in the morning."

"Where is her sister, Lady Nivalis?" Cassia asked.

A furrow appeared between Ariadne's eyes. "We are rather surprised that she and her husband, Free Lord Deverran, have yet to arrive. He must be coming later for the vote, like Lord Hadrian."

"I'm sure that's the case," Cassia said smoothly.

But Lio knew what she was thinking. Lord Deverran had always had a vital role to play in her plot to overthrow Lucis. After everything that had happened, was he still committed to that dangerous course?

94

days until

AUTUMN EQUINOX

5 Anthros's Sword, 1597 OT

SISTERLY LOVE

Lord and Lady Galanthian's emotions were harder for Lio to bear than the painful pace of negotiations in the great hall. Sitting across from their grief for three nights wore upon him. But he had known the Blood Union would enact justice on him for his failure to save Pakhne.

He was not prepared for the wave of denial and anger that swept into the chamber when Lady Nivalis arrived with Lord Deverran. He bowed to Solia, and Lady Nivalis curtsied, her black gown pooling around her. Against her fair skin and pale blond hair, it made her look ghostly.

Her gaze settled on Lio and Cassia. She had Pakhne's eyes, and they were filled with condemnation.

"That's Pakhne's sister," Cassia whispered.

"I can tell," Lio said.

"You shouldn't blame yourself," Mak reminded him for what seemed the thousandth time, as if repetition would eventually make it sink into Lio's thick skull.

Lyros sat forward in his chair. "No, you shouldn't…but do you get the impression that she does?"

"She knows something," Cassia said.

"She must," Lio agreed, taken aback.

Cassia gave Lady Nivalis a courteous nod. Pakhne's sister turned on her heel and joined her mother in one of the back rows, while her husband took his seat beside her father. Lio would have to look them in the eye all night.

"How could she know you two had anything to do with Pakhne's fate?" Lyros asked.

Mak shook his head. "That makes no sense."

"Eudias and Ariadne would never betray the truth," Lio said.

"Any mortal in Tenebra could ultimately betray us," Cassia reminded him. "Hesperines and the Ashes are the only people we can trust unconditionally."

Lio winced. "I don't mean to sound innocent."

"I don't mean to sound callous," Cassia replied.

"You do not, Lady Circumspect. You sound like a survivor of the Tenebran court."

"And you sound like a Hesperine errant, My Champion. But in this instance, I agree with you—I do not believe Eudias or Ariadne told anyone about our involvement. Nivalis is clever. Perhaps too clever to swallow our story."

Solia nodded and smiled to another lord, who bowed on his way to his seat. "Could her husband's role in your plan be the cause of her ire? It is a great deal to ask of any wife."

"He told me she was in support," Cassia replied calmly, although her aura prickled with defensiveness. "He promised to follow through."

"That was at the Autumn Greeting," said Solia, "when he believed you would make yourself queen. It would be understandable if he felt differently, now that the candidate for the throne has changed not once, but twice."

"I would not toy with him, not about this," Cassia said, but then she sighed. "Not that he has any reason to believe that."

Flavian commenced the Council, welcoming Lord Deverran and his lady. The newly arrived free lord attested to a quorum as the others had, then requested the right to speak. Flavian gave him the floor.

Lio's ire was always close to the surface when Flavian was in the same room as Cassia. Now his unease rose. Was Flavian merely granting the latecomer a courtesy, so he could have his say, as many of the other lords had before his arrival? Or was Flavian involved?

"If Nivalis knows, would she tell Flavian?" Lio asked.

Lyros hesitated. "I hate to say it, Lio, but your judgment isn't clear where Flavian is concerned."

"I know," Lio bit out. "That's why I'm asking."

Cassia shook her head. "No. Deverran and Nivalis will never

support Flavian. They're too loyal to Hadria. If they won't support Solia, they'll abstain."

Lord Deverran rose from his chair. Lio struggled to judge mortal ages sometimes, but Nivalis was Cassia's age, and her husband appeared about twice that. He had a solemn demeanor and an aura that seemed honest. Was that Lio's lack of judgment at play again?

Lord Deverran said, "Lord Galanthian has informed me of the previous proceedings. Princess Solia, allow me to put forth a question that has not been raised. Is it not true that your younger brother, King Lucis's legitimate son Caelum, is in fact the rightful heir to the throne?"

Lio felt the mortals' tension rise at the daring question. But he also sensed that many agreed with Deverran's point.

Solia, however, was unperturbed. "Yes, I understand that in my absence, the king has finally acquired the son he always coveted. But Lucis is a tyrant with no right to rule. I am the rightful heir, for my mother's forebears were honorable kings."

Lord Deverran leveled her with a steady gaze. "What are your intentions toward the boy?"

"Hardly a boy any longer," Lord Adrogan put forth. "He is fourteen and on his way to manhood. Next thing you know, he'll show up and put his banner on the dais."

"Caelum is no threat to anyone here," Solia said smoothly. She didn't look away from Deverran. "And he has no claim upon the throne."

Solia had given him the perfect opening to perform the duty Cassia had assigned him in her plot. But Lio feared that this time, his brilliant Grace might be disappointed in her ally.

He hated that Deverran proved him right and sat down without saying another word.

Frustration and despair sank through Cassia's aura. "He assured me he would stay the course. I know he cares about Caelum. Why does he hesitate?"

"I like his aura," said Karege, confirming Lio's impression. "I think he'll do the right thing in the end."

"You need to speak to him and his wife alone," Kella advised, "away from his peers."

"Any ideas on how to arrange that?" Tuura asked.

"I can always pass secret messages," Hoyefe said.

"Cassia," Solia asked, "can I not simply invite her to my weaving room?"

"Not without also inviting a lady of the Segetian faction," Cassia answered.

"That may not be necessary," said Lyros. "Lady Nivalis is craving a confrontation, I think."

At least Lio was in no danger of reading that wrong.

Throughout the rest of the night's negotiations, Lady Nivalis's determination simmered. What worried Lio most was the sense of injustice radiating from her. The moment the Council adjourned, she made her way forward. Lord Deverran took her arm, and they approached Solia.

"Your Highness," Lord Deverran said, "my lady and I would be honored if we could attend you in your weaving room."

"It has been too many years, my lord." Solia smiled at them. "I will be glad to welcome you and your wife in my weaving room, as Lady Nivalis always welcomed my sister in Lady Hadrian's."

Lady Nivalis's only reply was a curtsy, before she and her husband preceded them all out of the room.

On their way out of the great hall, Eudias pulled Lio aside. "Ariadne and I succeeded in convincing the Semna and Master Gorgos to accept Hesperine wards around Patria. But now we face a new obstacle. Lord Deverran has made it known to Lord Flavian that he will not tolerate more of your magic here."

Lio bit back a curse. "We didn't tell him or Lady Nivalis what happened. How could they know?"

As Ariadne filed past them with the Semna, she shot Lio a concerned glance and shook her head slightly. He gave her a minute nod in return, and she appeared relieved.

"I don't understand," Eudias said. "When Ariadne spoke to Lady Nivalis, she seemed to believe our story about her sister. If there is someone else feeding her and Lord Deverran information, we must stop them. If knowledge of the Collector becomes widespread—"

"I'll find out," Lio promised.

He rejoined Cassia and their companions leaving the great hall. As they made their way to their chambers, Mak said, "We should come with you. This could get dangerous."

"Thank you," Solia replied, "but I dearly hope we'll be safe from one lord and lady, even without the Stand's protection."

Kella cast glances at the courtiers passing them in the corridors. "We Ashes will stay with the Stewards. You'll have a better chance of prying information out of them with fewer people listening."

"I would like Cassia and Lio to join me in my weaving room," Solia said. "Cassia, you can recommend Segetians to invite after this."

Lio was grateful Solia did not seek to exclude him. If there was to be a reckoning with Pakhne's sister, he should be there. "I will step to you in a moment, to avoid gossip."

Solia nodded. "And stay veiled, unless we need you."

They made sure to all be seen returning to their respective chambers, then with some stepping to and fro, Lio found himself alone in the weaving room with Solia and Cassia.

Cassia took the opportunity to wrap her arms around him and give him a quick kiss on the mouth. That sip of her affection warmed him through and through. He rested his hands lightly at her waist, mindful of not antagonizing Solia. She kept her eyes on the door, ignoring the two of them.

Cassia murmured, "We can tell you over and over that you are not to blame, but you must choose to believe it."

"I don't blame myself. But I do take responsibility."

"I worry that you don't know the difference, my Grace."

"Perhaps if I can earn Nivalis's forgiveness, I will be able to find some peace."

The furrow on Cassia's brow suggested she did not think this a likely outcome.

"I hear their footsteps in the corridor." Reluctantly, Lio withdrew from Cassia's arms and drew a veil spell around himself. Cassia and Solia each took a chair by the fire, their shadows reaching long across the room.

Lord Deverran and Lady Nivalis entered, and the door shut behind them, closing out the distant footsteps of the councilors returning to their chambers.

No one attempted pleasantries. Solia gestured to the two other chairs. "We have much to discuss. Will you join us?"

"That remains to be seen," Lord Deverran replied to the double meaning in her words.

"How is Caelum?" Cassia asked.

"Not up for negotiation," Nivalis said fiercely. "Those are our terms. No matter what Lord Adrogan says, Caelum is still a child."

Lio was entirely confident in his instincts on this. What radiated out of Nivalis's aura was clear. Love.

"He may not be my own flesh and blood," she said, "but I intend to be as much of a mother to him as he'll let me. If you attempt to harm him, we'll—"

Deverran rested a hand on her arm. "My men are in place and ready to remove him from Solorum Palace. I will not tell you where I am taking him to safety. However, I will announce before the Council that he is not Lucis's son, but mine. Not for Lord Flavian's sake, nor for yours, Your Highness. For the boy."

"Thank you," Solia said with sincerity. "I will not have him suffer for our father's crimes."

"Won't you?" Deverran asked. "He is a greater threat to you than to Flavian."

"As I indicated before the Council, I do not consider Caelum a threat. I do not base my claim on Lucis's line, therefore the boy he calls his son does not stand in my way. I am not interested in whether Caelum is yours or Lucis's. I only want him not to be a victim, as I was. As his mother was. I am deeply sorry that the king took your betrothed as his second wife. I understand that she met the same end as my own mother trying to give him heirs."

Lord Deverran's face seemed etched in stone. Old grief lingered in him, but a newer anxiety. Lio got the impression he did not wish to discuss this in front of his new wife.

But Nivalis drew closer to him and said softly, "You know I understand."

"Even I do not know if he is my son," Deverran confessed, "but he could be."

"And we will treat him as though he is," Nivalis said.

"Then we are still in accord?" Cassia asked carefully.

Nivalis looked at her with chilly dignity. "As I said, Caelum is not up for negotiation. But my lord's vote is."

Lio watched another thread of their plan unravel before his eyes.

"You would side with Segetia?" Solia asked neutrally.

"Yes, Your Highness," Lord Deverran answered, "unless my wife receives the answers she needs about her sister's fate."

Cassia had been right. Nivalis was too clever.

Lio mentally tallied the votes they thought they could win, those they knew were lost to Flavian, and many more that were still in flux. In every prediction they had made about the outcome of the Council, they had counted on Deverran abstaining or siding with Solia. They could not afford for him to change sides.

Cassia kept her composure. "We heard the news about Pakhne from Mage Ariadne. I'm so sorry, truly. I know the pain of losing a sister. After going to Orthros with Pakhne, I feel her loss."

"Don't you dare," Nivalis snapped. "Do not sit there with your carefully crafted words and twist the truth. Pakhne, exhaust her magic healing one woman in childbirth? Impossible. I was there the night her magic first manifested. She and our mother and I were all worn to the bone from caring for our younger siblings through the frost fever. Mother and I fell ill first. Only Pakhne seemed immune. We were on the brink of death when it happened—her healing rushed out of her upon all of us." Nivalis took a breath to compose herself, and Deverran gave her hand a reassuring squeeze. "She saved our mother's life and mine. She kept our siblings with us long enough for everyone to say goodbye. She wasn't even ill, after doing that for five people."

Lio swallowed, his throat aching. Oh, Goddess. Nivalis had already buried the rest of her siblings. Pakhne had been the only one left.

"I deserve the truth," Nivalis said.

Cassia blinked rapidly. "Your questions are better addressed to Pakhne's temple sisters. Why would we know what befell her?"

That was the piece that didn't fit. Lio had to surface from this empathy and think.

"It is not important how I know," Lady Nivalis replied. "But I do know you were all in Lord Hadrian's camp when it happened."

Who could have told her? Trying to heed Cassia's earlier warning, he thought of which Tenebran mortals had known the truth. Only Lord Hadrian, who had made it clear he was in no position to communicate with Nivalis's family.

The realization struck Lio, horrifying and obvious.

The Collector knew.

Carefully and swiftly, Lio swept a spell over Nivalis and Deverran. He sensed no influence from the Mage of Dreams.

But he didn't need to possess them to whisper in their ears. After the Collector had abandoned Pakhne's body and fled, he could have used any number of his servants to tell Lady Nivalis what had happened. A trusted soldier. A dear handmaiden. A friend, a relative.

What remained of Pakhne's family was ensnared in the Collector's web. Lio owed it to her to do his best to protect them.

He stepped out of the shadows and dropped his veil. Lady Nivalis nearly jumped out of her skin, and Lord Deverran's hand went to his sword.

Solia held up a hand, glowering at Lio. "This is Ambassador Deukalion, our ally from Orthros. He is here to protect us."

"Protect us?" Lady Nivalis faced him. "Nothing has been the same since Pakhne went to your godsforsaken land. What did you do to her?"

Cassia opened her mouth—to defend him, he knew—but then stopped herself. Silently, he thanked her for letting him choose his own words.

"You are right. You deserve the truth." At least, as much of it as Lio could give her. "Did Pakhne tell you of the necromancer who visited Orthros with the other mages?"

"Yes," Nivalis said. "The Gift Collector. The one who sabotaged the negotiations. Lord Flavian says he has killed here already. Does he have something to do with this?"

"Yes."

"It's your fault that he's here. You Hesperines. Why else would he come, if not to hunt you? But why would he hurt Pakhne?" Nivalis dragged a hand across her eyes, as if she hated her own tears. "She truly believed in the treaty. She tried to protect you, didn't she?"

"No," Lio said, "I tried to protect her. You have my word, Lady Nivalis. I did everything in my power to save her."

"Then why didn't you?" she cried.

Why didn't you save her? Lio would hear those words in his dreams. "I am immortal, but not all-powerful. How I wish I were."

"What did he do to her?" Nivalis demanded.

Lio wanted to hold her hand, anything to soften the blow. But there was nothing he could do except tell her the truth. "He took her magic."

Nivalis's lips moved, and she pressed a hand to her belly. "How…how is that even possible?"

Cassia rose and came to her side, reaching out to steady her. "The Gift Collector possesses terrible power that even Hesperines cannot always combat."

Nivalis pulled away. "Why her? She never did anything to hurt anyone. She gave up everything to heal people."

"The Gift Collector is on Lucis's side," Lio tried to explain. "He is manipulating both sides of the feud for the king's benefit."

"I care nothing for your political excuses," Nivalis cried. "Can you tell me that the Gift Collector did not target her because of you?"

Nivalis did not understand the full truth, but she grasped this. That her sister's fate had been sealed when she aligned herself with the Hesperines.

Perhaps the Collector had chosen her because of politics. Lio's mind knew this was possible. But in his heart, he didn't really believe it was true. Pakhne had simply been the most convenient vessel to reach through, to get at him and Cassia.

Nivalis read the truth in his silence. She turned her back on them all and stormed out of the room.

"Lord Flavian has my vote." Lord Deverran followed his wife out.

Solia rose from her chair and stepped toward Lio. "Where is your diplomacy tonight? Couldn't you have found *anything* to say to persuade her you are not the villain?"

"I won't lie to her," Lio said.

"Why do they call you Glasstongue? Do you understand the difference between a lie and persuasion?"

"If you want to persuade them that we are not responsible for what happened to Pakhne, perhaps you would care to explain to them why you destroyed the necromancer's other servants while I was trying to save her!"

Mak and Lyros had stepped in, Lio realized, for his cousin took hold of his shoulder and hauled him a step back from Solia. Lyros put his hands up between them, as if expecting them to come to blows.

Cassia stood by the fire, looking back and forth between them. Knight's hackles were up, the air warming with fire magic.

"I'm assigning you your third labor," Solia barked.

"What?" It took Lio's thoughts a moment to catch up with her abrupt announcement.

"Now is hardly the time!" Cassia cut in.

Solia's jaw was set. "Send a scroll back to Kassandra for her permission, if you like."

"That won't be necessary," Lio said.

"You should listen to whatever she's asking of you before you agree," Lyros advised.

"I know what she's asking," Lio returned. "Traditionally, during the third labor, the bridegroom is expected to learn something from the matriarch. You wish to teach me a lesson, Sister? I'm an excellent student, I assure you."

"You're a scholar," she said. "Clearly, you need a lesson in the battle arts. I'm challenging you to single combat."

"You can't be serious!" Now Cassia stepped between them. "What in the Goddess's name are you two thinking? I will not stand by and watch you two go at it in the fighting ring—over me!"

Lio rested a hand on her back. "It's all right, Cassia."

"It is not all right!" she replied.

"Our family members meet in the ring for friendly matches all the time." Lio's tone was anything but friendly.

Solia lifted her chin. "We'll duel according to the rules of the Battle of Souls. Everything is allowed—fists, blades, magic. Your father didn't hesitate. Are you the Lion of Orthros's son or not?"

"If you have any doubts, then there's a lesson in this for you, too," Lio replied.

"We should seek Kassandra's approval for this," Mak said.

Lio ignored him and whatever words hovered on Cassia's open lips. He looked Solia in the eye. "I accept your challenge. Name the place and time."

Cassia's mouth snapped shut. Her anger stung his senses.

"Tomorrow night," Solia told him. "At the Summit Sanctuary, with the Charge as our spectators. In case you need your Ritual father to put you back together after we're done with our lesson."

"For you to consider the task fulfilled," Lyros asked, "must he spar with you? Or defeat you?"

Solia laughed. "It would hardly be fair to set him an impossible task. He doesn't have to try to win. He only has to finish a match with me. No withdrawal or surrender. We fight until victory or defeat."

"This is madness!" Cassia cried.

No, Lio knew precisely what he was doing. He let his Grace-sister see his fangs. The fire in her eyes didn't falter.

She underestimated him. But not for much longer.

"Enough!" Cassia said. "Both of you, stop. I won't allow either of you to do this, especially not over me."

"He has already accepted my challenge," Solia said. "There's no turning back now. Unless he wants to withdraw and fail the labor—forfeiting my blessing."

Cassia's whole being throbbing with fury and hurt. "Why are you putting him through this? Why are you making me watch?"

There, at last, for the first time. Surprise in Solia's eyes. Hesitation.

Then Cassia spun to face Lio. But the pain in her voice didn't fade. Instead of her glorious temper, it was her hurt that tore at him. "And how could you agree to all of this without even *talking* to me?"

"Cassia—"

She turned her back on him and Solia. "I need a step, please."

"Of course." Mak put an arm around her shoulders.

"Where are you going?" Lio protested.

Mak glared at him. "Away from you two idiots."

Lio reached for Cassia, but it was too late. She and Mak disappeared. Lio rounded on Lyros. How dare his Trial brothers conspire to take his Grace away from him?

Lyros planted a hand in the middle of Lio's chest. "If you or Solia try to follow Cassia, I will cast the Blood Shackles on you to keep you from going anywhere."

"Where is she?" Lio would drag Mak into the arena after he was done with Solia.

"With Mak," Lyros said. "That's all you need to know."

"How long does he plan to keep her?" Flame skittered along Solia's jaw.

Lyros crossed his arms. "If you're worried about the lords noticing her absence during the day, then you'll simply have to think of an explanation to give them."

They had just watched the plan she had risked her life for begin to fall apart. The Collector could be anywhere, lying in wait for her. And without stealing some time for a feast after the Council, her Craving would only grow worse. She should be here, so Lio could hold her and tell her everything would be all right.

But Cassia was gone.

93

days until

AUTUMN EQUINOX

6 Anthros's Sword, 1597 OT

ONE OF THEIR OWN

At twilight, Karege hauled Lio off his cot and stood him up. "On your feet, Sunshine! We don't have much time to prepare you."

Lio's fangs shot out of his gums, and his magic fought against the confines of his body. Where was his Grace?

He tried to think through the instinctive, protective rage coursing through his veins. She was with Mak. Nothing could happen to her.

Lio rubbed his face. "Prepare me?"

"To survive a fight with Sunburn," Karege said, "you'll need at least a year of training with the Ashes. Unfortunately, we only have a couple of hours while she's still in Council."

Lio looked around and saw that Kella and Hoyefe were also waiting for him. They weren't at the Castra any longer, but in a Hesperine tent, and Lio could sense the Summit Sanctuary's ward outside. It seemed Karege had hauled Lio here in his sleep like a sack of turnips.

"Tuura is still at Patria, isn't she?" Lio asked.

"On guard against the Collector." Kella sat astride Tilili, sharpening her fortune blade. "Lyros is with her and Solia."

Hoyefe straightened Lio's robe, which seemed like it was trying to choke him. "Alas, you'll have to solve your romantic woes after the battle."

"But this battle is for Cassia," Lio said. "For us, for Solia's blessing. I need to make Cassia understand."

Kella held her blade up to the spell light. "The time to help her understand would have been before you accepted the challenge. Too late now."

"Is Cassia coming to the match?" Lio asked.

Kella shrugged. "That's anyone's guess. But if she doesn't, you'll simply have to do your best without her blood."

For the first time, Lio felt an inkling of doubt about rushing into this.

Kella's fortune blade suddenly came sailing toward him. He moved to one side, and it flew past his arm on its way to stab a pillow on the cot.

Kella cocked her head. "Decent reaction time for a Hesperine right out of Slumber. You might last a few minutes in the ring."

Lio had endured half a year of Craving, hadn't he? He had bested the Dexion in the gymnasium. And he had survived battles far more dangerous than a sparring match with his Grace-sister. "Oh, I'll last longer than a few minutes, I assure you. Will Solia receive any preparation with Hesperine warriors? I want to ensure our match is fair."

Karege laughed. "She's been fighting with me for years. She doesn't need any preparation."

"On the contrary," Lio said, "I do not believe she's prepared for me."

AFTER A DAY WITHOUT Cassia and an hour of practice with the Ashes, it felt as if Hypnos himself had raked his claws through Lio's veins. But when he stepped out to the Charge's sparring grounds behind the pavilion, the glory of the scene managed to reach him through his misery.

A ring of pennants marked the arena, banners of black and white and red that might have waved here since the first Equinox Summit. Rudhira stood in the center, the night wind stirring his braid. Every Hesperine errant in the camp had gathered around to watch. Lio felt their weary hearts thrilling to the promise of a spectacle to brighten their long, doubtful nights. Their power throbbed around him like applause, ready to cheer on one of their own.

In this match, he was their own.

"Best of luck, Sunshine," Kella said, her tone sincere.

"You all have my gratitude," he told her and her Ashes, before they joined Solia on the opposite side of the ring.

His Grace-sister gave him an almost lazy salute. He bowed. Then Mak and Lyros left her side to join Lio.

Lio glared at Mak. "If you don't tell me where Cassia is, I'll drag it out of you in the ring after I'm done with Solia."

Mak crossed his arms. "She didn't give me permission to tell you where she is. Do I need to toss you in the dirt to remind you to respect her choice?"

At that, the fight drained out of Lio. "She doesn't want me to know?"

Goddess help him, his Grace could still outmaneuver him. It was a brilliant move, and it hurt more than Solia's magefire ever would.

He had insisted Cassia was not responsible for mediating between him and Solia. So she had given him what he asked for. He was on his own with his Grace-sister tonight.

What had he expected? That she would cheer him on as he charged into battle against her sister?

What had she expected him to do? Back down from Solia's challenge and give up any hope of earning her respect?

"You didn't exactly talk things through with her," Mak reminded him. "But if she's feeling generous, she might not leave you in suspense much longer."

Two powerful auras stepped into their midst. Nike appeared on one side of Lio. "A sparring match for your third labor? I'm impressed. Kassandra sent me to bear witness on her behalf."

But it was the ferociously powerful, familiar aura that dawned on Lio's other side that left him nearly speechless. "Father? You—in Tenebra!"

His father pulled him in for a hard embrace. "Only for tonight, within the safety of the Sanctuary, so I can return undamaged to your mother and Zoe."

"I can scarcely believe you've set foot outside of Orthros."

"It's the first time since I took your mother home." His father pulled back and looked around him. "My son is errant at the Summit Sanctuary and about to spar with a fire mage! I couldn't miss this."

"Mother also insisted you come check on me, didn't she?"

"It was a unanimous request from her, Zoe, and Cassia."

Relief made Lio want to lie down in the grass right there. "Cassia went home?"

"She's with Zoe in the greenhouse as we speak."

An arctic breeze, tempered by Mak's wards, drifted through the framework of Cassia's greenhouse. Nearby, the goats were climbing on Knight, who tolerated them with remarkable benevolence. With her spade in her hand and soil running through her fingers, Cassia felt a measure of peace.

But she was still weary to the bone.

"How much new dirt should we put in?" Zoe asked, kneeling next to her.

"Let's start with enough to lift the plant to the level we want it to be inside the pot."

Across from them, Komnena held open the canvas sack they had filled with their potting mix. "How far below the rim of the pot should it be?"

"About two fingers." Cassia put one scoop in the pretty glass container.

Lio had crafted it for her. Had the fight begun? Was he safe? How far would her sister go to prove her point?

Cassia shoved those thoughts out of her mind and offered her spade to Zoe next.

Zoe's face lit up. "I get to use your spade?"

Cassia savored the suckling's happiness. "Of course, Zoe flower. It will give your betony extra magic."

"I can't believe it's already big enough to put in a new pot!" Zoe said.

The betony plant, which Zoe usually kept by her bed to ward off nightmares, was indeed bursting out of its third pot. Cassia now knew its remarkable growth must be due to her magic.

Zoe handed the spade to her mother next, and Komnena added her share of soil. "At this rate, I shall become a competent gardener."

It soothed Cassia's spirit to share this with her Grace-mother and Grace-sister. Komnena's mortal past trying to survive on her barren farm had left her with unimaginable grief and a hatred for trying to grow anything. Until now, when Cassia had turned gardening into a joy the three of them could share.

And a distraction from the knowledge that a fire mage was currently trying to give Lio a beating.

Cassia sat back, too tired to move, and guided Zoe and Komnena through the process. Following her instructions, the suckling and her mother coaxed the plant out of its pot, transferred the root ball to its new home without damage, and filled the remaining space with fresh soil.

When they were done, Zoe slid under Cassia's arm and cuddled against her. "I'm so glad you get to visit more often on this journey."

"I promised you we would." Cassia hugged her close, grateful to let her eyes slide shut.

"I wish Lio and Solia were here too," Zoe said.

"I do too." Her infuriating Grace and sister should be here, allaying Zoe's fears, not stoking Cassia's.

Zoe looked up at her, surprise in her eyes. "Why are you mad? Did someone in Tenebra do something bad?"

With a sigh, Cassia tried to calm her emotions and withstand a wave of lightheadedness. "There are many things in Tenebra that make me mad."

Komnena nodded. "It's all right to be angry about things that are unjust. That is one of the few times when it's good to be mad."

"Tenebra makes me mad, too," Zoe said.

"That's why I wanted to come home and see you." Cassia rested her face on Zoe's hair. Perhaps she would also visit Javed before Mak came to take her back. She needed some Hesperine tonics in addition to Tuura's.

"Will you put your blood on my plant to give it some more magic?" Zoe asked.

"Of course," Cassia replied. "Let's make the libation together."

Cassia cut her palm with her spade, and the two Hesperines bit their hands. Together they gave a little of themselves to the betony plant.

The strength drained out of Cassia so fast she had to swallow hard to keep from retching. Her vision blurred, and she barely caught herself on the heel of her bleeding hand to keep from tumbling over.

"Cassia?" Zoe cried. "What's wrong?"

Komnena's voice was reassuring. "Zoe, step to the Healing Sanctuary and get Annassa Soteira."

Goddess, help me not frighten Zoe. Cassia swallowed hard again, then managed to speak in a calm tone. "We needn't trouble Queen Soteira."

But Zoe was a courier with a speed record. She had already gone.

Komnena guided Cassia to lie down and then pulled a sack of soil under her legs to elevate them. "I want Annassa Soteira to examine you. Your aura feels like that of a mage who has just exhausted herself on a master-level casting. You shouldn't be this depleted from a simple libation."

Cassia closed her eyes and focused on breathing. "You're saying…I used…too much magic?"

Komnena stroked her head. "Do not fear, dear one. Hesperine healers can easily treat magical exhaustion."

Except for Pakhne, who was too far gone. Cassia shuddered.

When Queen Soteira arrived, Cassia didn't have to open her eyes to know one of the Queens was there. Her aura blanketed Cassia's struggling senses, and her panic subsided. Then Queen Soteira's magic touched Cassia. She had felt the great healer's power before, but it never ceased to fill her with wonder. As if the whole night sky suddenly looked at her, and she mattered to the moons and stars.

"Annassa," Cassia said, "thank you for interrupting more important matters to help me."

"Helping any of my children in need of healing is the most important matter."

Cassia was so grateful for this hour away from Tenebra. This was home, where a child could tug on the hand of her Queen, and she would come to anyone in distress. "Where is Zoe?"

"I left her, Knight, and the goats with Javed. She wanted to come back and stay with you, but I think it best we discuss these matters out of her hearing."

"Thank you. I don't wish to scare her."

Komnena explained what had happened, and Queen Soteira pressed a hand to Cassia's heart with an expression as if she were listening. Cassia couldn't bear to watch her face for clues about what was wrong, so she fixed her gaze on the Queen's gold bracelets. Then on the silver ornaments in her crown of braids, where Queen Alea's white braid was interwoven.

"Is this the first time this has happened?" Queen Soteira asked.

"Never this severe," Cassia answered. "But I do get very tired whenever I do magical exercises."

"I agree with Komnena. You should not be this depleted." Queen Soteira adjusted her hand on Cassia's chest and appeared focused once again. "I sense that you have a small reserve of latent magic, which is how you've been making plants grow. That supply of power is currently fully exhausted. Perhaps it acts as a draw for the rest of your power, which you are still expecting."

"But you can restore the power I currently have?"

"Our spells for treating magical exhaustion work by stimulating your own internal magical reserves to replenish themselves. I have been performing that spell as we speak, but your affinity isn't responding. I believe all of this is a symptom of how much you need your full magic to arrive."

"Does that mean I should go somewhere wild? That helped last night."

"Even if you fully restore your current reserve, it will be very difficult for such a small amount of magic to sustain your body."

"What about mages who have small amounts of power? They never become ill from it."

"You are meant to have three powerful affinities. Your body, mind, and spirit are crafted to sustain your triune affinity—and be sustained by it. Have your symptoms been getting worse?"

Cassia's mouth went dry. "Yes."

Was Queen Soteira saying Cassia was running out of time?

"No," Cassia said, "that can't be. All of this is simply my Craving, isn't it?"

"I'm afraid not," said Queen Soteira. "Craving does not make a human this ill."

"But I'm always this ill when I'm away from Lio for too long."

"Cassia," Komnena said in dismay, "you never told us anything about that."

"Lio and I thought it was normal. You said you felt your need for Apollon before you were a Hesperine."

"Certainly. I pined for Apollon, physically and emotionally. But I was never ill like a Hesperine deprived of blood."

Cassia grimaced, thinking of her delayed Gift Night. "It must be because I've remained human for so long. It was pining at first, when Lio returned to Orthros without me. But after I came here and we were together again, I began having physical symptoms. Then, in the Maaqul... that was when we realized it was dangerous."

"What have I told you about not keeping things from me?" Komnena said. "If you and Lio withheld this because you were trying not to worry me..."

Queen Soteira did not look pleased. "I examined her myself after her return from the Empire, and she also said nothing to me. We were admittedly preoccupied with her mental wounds from her imprisonment with that vulture Dakkoul who calls himself a theramancer."

"I didn't mention it because I didn't think I needed healing for my Craving. When I'm with Lio, my symptoms are cured."

"When you're in his presence?" Queen Soteira asked.

Cassia's face flushed. This was far too embarrassing to explain in front of Lio's mother.

Komnena gave her a rueful look. "I know how the Craving works, my dear. But I will stop my ears with veils if it will put you at ease."

"No, it's all right." Cassia mustered her composure. She needn't go into intimate details. "My symptoms go away when I..." Now that she was saying it aloud, she wondered if it sounded strange. "Well, we realized in the desert that this is possible. I drink his magic, so to speak."

The two elders exchanged glances.

"That is not consistent with the Craving," Queen Soteira said with kindness and calm. "In fact, it is unprecedented."

"A phenomenon unique to Lustra magic, perhaps?" Komnena sounded worried. "We now know hulaia is a channeling paradigm. Perhaps that enables Cassia to channel magic from Lio?"

"We can only theorize," the Queen replied.

"We need to consult with Kalos again," Komnena said.

"Evidence is more easily at hand," said Queen Soteira. "Let us fetch Lio so I can gain a sense of this magical channeling that seems to be occurring between him and Cassia."

"We can't," Cassia protested. "Not right now."

"You are ill," Queen Soteira said in gentle warning. "I do not advise waiting."

"No," Komnena agreed, "Lio will be beside himself to get to you once he hears you're ill."

Cassia shook her head as much as she dared. "We mustn't distract him from the match."

"This is the perfect excuse to put a stop to his and Solia's foolishness," Komnena said.

Cassia groaned. Why were her Grace and her sister two of the most stubborn people in all of Akanthia? "I'm furious at both of them for going through with this debacle. But I will not let my need for Lio cost him one of the labors—and my sister's blessing. Solia would take my illness as justification for her anger."

Queen Soteira's lips pressed together in disapproval. "I will agree to this only because Lio's labors have Kassandra's endorsement. Our Oracle has reasons for everything she does. I will place a rejuvenating spell on you to protect your body from damage temporarily. But the moment their sparring match ends, we must bring Lio to you."

"Damage?" Cassia forced herself to ask.

"When a mage is without magic, it harms them on every level—body, mind, and soul. Until we know more, I can only treat your symptoms. But we must soon remedy the cause—the need for magic. Your magic."

"Will it get worse?" Cassia asked.

Queen Soteira placed a reassuring hand on her brow. "The longer you are without your power, yes."

Cassia didn't have to ask how dire it would become. She had already seen what had befallen Pakhne.

THE LION'S SON

FROM THE CENTER OF the fighting ring, Rudhira beckoned to Lio and his father. "Hesperines errant of the Charge, for the first time in ninety years, the Lion of Orthros is among us in mortal lands."

Lio's father chuckled. "Come, let us give the Goddess's forces a tale to tell around the Ritual circle on discouraging nights."

Lio and his father strode out into the arena to the cheers of the Charge. Lio prayed he wasn't about to humiliate himself and his father's legacy by getting burnt to a crisp by his own Grace-sister.

His father raised a hand to the crowd. "The first sparring match in the Summit Sanctuary took place on this very ground sixteen hundred years ago. Between the Guardian of Orthros and myself, in fact. Thank you for welcoming a moldering elder among you!"

This met with laughs and scoffs. As if anyone could mistake Apollon for a stuffy elder.

"Our bloodline was proud the night my Firstgift chose to become a diplomat. He devotes his eternity to preserving the peace we fought so hard for all those centuries ago." Father grinned. "But you'll find he fights hard, as well."

He held out his wrist, and Lio's doubts melted away. His father was right. Lio knew when to negotiate and when to fight. He had learned that lesson in the most powerful courts in Akanthia and the depths of the Maaqul desert.

Before the Charge, Lio accepted the Ritual Drink from his father. Their cheers pounded in his ears. Their Union through the Goddess's blood pounded in his veins. His father's ancient power, the magic that had made Lio immortal, roared through him and restored his strength.

His father lifted their joined hands above their heads, then departed the ring to cheer him on alongside the Stewards.

Rudhira gestured for Solia to enter the ring. "As our challenger, we are honored to welcome Solia, known as Sunburn, once a gold roster mercenary in the Ashes and always a Victor of Souls."

He said nothing about her royal Tenebran heritage. Tonight, it was her history as a warrior that mattered. The Charge gave her a loud welcome with a round of applause. She strode out to face Lio, her bespelled scarf draped around her shoulders as usual. It was so disorienting not to sense her emotions.

"Are you certain you wish to spend a labor on this?" he asked her. "There isn't much I can learn from you. I've sparred with a fire mage before."

"If you mean Xandra, you'll find I don't fight as gently as a Hesperine."

Lio laughed. "No, I defeated the Dexion of the Aithourian Circle in Hippolyta's Gymnasium."

Surprise flashed in her gaze, but then her eyes narrowed. "But neither of you used magic, I take it, for that is seldom permitted in Hippolyta's matches."

"I didn't need magic to make him lose. And in a match at full power, the same strategy will work on you."

"You will find a woman from the Golden Shield a much more challenging opponent than a greased robe from the Magelands."

When it came to fists and magic, yes. But she was just as vulnerable to diplomacy as the Dexion had been.

Rudhira looked from Lio to Solia. "Don't make too much work for the healers. Understood?"

Solia saluted him. "I would never dishonor the battle arts or my opponents with needless harm."

Lio gave his prince the heart bow. "I'll be careful, Ritual father."

Rudhira nodded, then withdrew to stand beside Lio's father. With the Blood Errant watching, Lio felt emboldened.

"I want you to know who I'm fighting for," Lio said, loud enough for their audience to hear, "tonight and always."

"But can you fight well enough to deserve her?" Solia challenged.

"I defeated an Old Master for her sake."

"He will always force you to make difficult choices in battle. One wrong decision could cost Cassia her life. You'll have to make sacrifices. Is your Hesperine heart too tender for that?"

"Test me."

Solia smiled. Then she wrapped her scarf around her eyes. Hespera's Mercy. She intended to fight blindfolded. His light magic would be useless, too.

Solia raised her fists. Lio matched her, but his posture felt wrong, his body strung too tight. He released a long breath, giving himself permission to distance himself from his fears. But the distance from Cassia remained, a deep wrongness, a sense of warning.

She was at home, he reminded himself. Right now, she was in the safest place in the world. Nothing could be wrong, even if his instincts blared at having her out of his reach.

He relaxed into a fighting stance. Rudhira made a libation on the ground, and the match began.

Solia's right fist darted at Lio with precision. Was she using his aura to determine his physical position? That was impressive magical discipline.

She moved fast for a human. But he was still far quicker. He merely leaned at Hesperine speed to avoid her blow. Her left fist came in harder, aiming for his new position with equal accuracy, but the move seemed leisurely to his immortal reflexes.

"Hm," Solia said calmly, "you actually do have technique, I'll grant you."

"Mak and Lyros are excellent teachers."

She tried to get under his guard. It was child's play to dance out of the way of her strike. So this was what it felt like to fight a human as an immortal.

"Are dodges all they taught you?" Solia taunted.

If he unleashed even rudimentary fighting moves on her, he could easily imagine how much damage he could do. In the heat of the fight, that chilled him. He knew how much power over humans his magic gave him. But he had never felt so keenly aware that he could destroy lives with only his hands.

He kept his fists up, but made no move. "We agreed to fight fair."

"You're still playing by Hesperine rules. Your enemies won't. In a battle for Cassia's soul, do you think your pretty principles will serve?"

"My principles are precisely what she needs. As for the rules"—he laughed—"I have left those in tatters for her before."

"Then show me."

He made his first swing, attempting to compensate for Solia's mortal ability. It felt like a slow demonstration for a suckling trainee.

He heard Solia's snort and the slide of her feet in the dirt as she adjusted her position. She didn't dodge. She blocked his blow with her forearm.

"If I can block you," she accused, "you are not fighting hard enough."

She was Solia. It went against everything in him to try to hit her. Even though she was the Victor of Souls, who had defeated Tendo despite his lifetime of battle training and vast ancestral magic.

Lio imagined what Tendo would say to him if he could see him now. *Stop being such a silkfoot and throw a punch.*

Lio pushed through his inhibitions and lunged at Solia, trying one of Mak's favorite tackles.

It was the most perfect Moon Warrior he had ever performed. His move carried them down to the ground at immortal speed for a landing he controlled with levitation. Without giving her time to react, he twisted her into an armlock known for ending matches—Heavy Slumber.

It couldn't be this easy.

"That's more like it," Solia said.

Heat flashed from her skin everywhere their arms were twisted together. Lio gritted his teeth and held the lock. A moment longer, and he could win.

Solia laughed.

The heat seemed to burn into his thoughts, searing them away like the sun. Impossible. This was pure mageia. Fire magic, affecting his body. It couldn't affect his mind. And yet his senses groaned, teaching him the meaning of Hesperine weakness to magefire.

With a hiss, he released Solia and rolled out of her reach before she could use his retreat to her advantage. He was vaguely aware of the gasps of disappointment and calls of encouragement from the Charge.

Both on their feet again, they circled each other.

"Is that all you have to offer, silkfoot?" she demanded.

It was the wrong insult for her to choose. The reminder of Tendo only galvanized him.

Lio let loose. He threw every intermediate move he knew at her, combining rudimentary ones in ways he had never imagined before this moment. He now gave all the Will that controlled his thelemancy over to his body, schooling every muscle as he punched and kicked, blocked and dodged.

Every time he landed a hit, a searing flash of heat punished him. He no longer had to measure the force of his strikes. He couldn't deal her more than glancing blows before her magic repelled him.

"Why Cassia?" Solia's fingers were a burning vice around his wrist. "You could have any Hesperine in Orthros, any woman from the Empire."

"None of them are my Grace." He twisted out of her searing grasp and followed through with a punch.

She stopped his fist with her glowing palm. "That reason is not enough. The fact that you will die without her tells me nothing about why you love her."

Did she think that was a hard question? "I fell in love with her before I knew she was my Grace."

"Why?" She sent a lick of flame nipping at his heels.

He refused to retreat, and evaded to the side instead. Amid the smells of sweat and brimstone, he remembered the first time he had caught Cassia's scent, so full of life on the night he had first witnessed death. "She's a survivor. That inner beauty stunned me when we met. She had fought for every scrap of life, and yet her Will remained unbroken."

"You think you're rescuing her from the cruel human world to carry her around on a silk cushion for the rest of eternity?" Solia hurled a vicious punch at his face.

Lio laughed and evaded the blow. "She only lets me carry her on special occasions. Cassia is always too busy changing the world for me to rescue her from it. And that is more beautiful still. Her cunning. Her anger. Her power."

"Do you appreciate how powerful she is? She always has been. And she will only become greater. What if she grows more powerful than you?" She swung her fist at his jaw again.

Lio levitated out of her reach this time, watching fire spring up where he had stood. "She already is, in many ways. I'm a Hesperine, Solia. Not some Tenebran man who needs women to be weak in order for me to feel strong. I would never hold Cassia back. I will always lift her up, even when that means helping her higher than I can reach."

"How dare you quote Ukocha at me!"

They circled and lunged around the fighting ring. She herded him where she pleased with her magefire.

Lio kept his voice calm. The key was to let her lose her temper while he kept his. "Perhaps it would help if you tell me why you are so angry with me. I will work hard to make amends if I have wronged you."

"You seek to cleave Cassia from mortal existence," she accused.

"Remember what I promised you. I will never, ever take her from you."

"Immortality will always be a veil one of us cannot cross."

"Then stay on this side of it with her. With all of us."

"Are you really fool enough to imagine it's that simple?"

"Simple? When I've had to fight tooth and nail for Cassia's Gifting?" He stepped behind Solia to attempt a Mage's Supplication, the move that had ended his match with the Dexion.

But the ground beneath his feet heated, and a lick of flame chased him across the dirt. He needed his magic.

Lio snatched Solia's arm, twisting it into a Crippled Dove, counting off the seconds until her fire magic would foil his grasp on her.

Before he felt the burn, he abandoned the move. Suddenly released, she recalculated for an instant. Just enough of an instant for an immortal to use.

He made a Sun Strike at her eyes. He felt the blindfold under his fingers.

Then nothing but air. The ground cooled.

And heat flared to life on his arcane senses—on the other side of the ring. He whirled and spotted Solia.

The traversal had left her out of breath, her skin gleaming with sweat, but she smiled. "Two can play your stepping game, Hesperine."

A lick of flame, more tease than threat, raced across the sand. But he would not dance to her fire any longer.

Lio stepped. Where he had stood, he left behind an illusion of himself. Then another. And another. One more for good measure. He poured four streams of thelemancy into the rough specters, then snapped his own magic back behind his mental shields.

He buried his magic deep, until he shook within, his inner defenses rattling with his contained power. But the illusions blazed. He made one blaze brightest of all.

She couldn't see them, but she could sense them.

She stalked at the edge of the ring, her head tilted in concentration. "Well, you aren't a bore after all."

When she drove her fist in his best illusion's gut, oh how gratifying it was to know he had fooled her.

He fortified two of the remaining illusions. Let her try to choose between them. He drifted along the edges of the ring in a whorl of veil spells, as if they played a deadly grown-up version of veil and step.

Solia halted between the two illusions. And then a ring of fire roiled out from her.

It was an almost gentle wave of his greatest weakness. He levitated, raising all his illusions into the air with him. Beneath their feet, three eddies of fire pirouetted up in delicate spirals.

The sparring ring filled with an orange glow, clashing upward toward his formations of white light and black shadow. The Chargers gasped in wonder and held their breaths. He heard the Blood Errant's powerful hearts pounding with exhilaration.

While Solia conjured her magnificent, controlled fire, Lio stepped to her side. Before she could disentangle herself from the spell, he untied her blindfold with quick immortal fingers. Golden silk came free in his hand, and she staggered.

Her emotions raged through the Blood Union. Her anger burned him far more painfully than her magic. She was consumed with it, this sense of injustice.

Holding her only armor in his hand, he unveiled his thelemancy, a silent statement to her arcane senses. He would never trespass on her Will, but in this moment, he could.

She swore at him and swung her fist.

He could have evaded it. But he didn't. He let her flaming knuckles land on his jaw.

The agony was too much for him to scream. Heat more punishing than mere fire exploded through his face and dissolved his thoughts. It didn't stop there. It seemed to sear his every vein.

Magefire.

He crumpled to his knees, disjointed shards of his illusions scattering around him, little flares of light and jolts of shadow whirling on his senses.

"What were you thinking?" The tender question sounded like Cassia for an instant, before his ringing ears registered that it was her sister.

His vision was aglow, as if he'd stared into blinding spell light. He couldn't see her, only feel her now-cold, sweating hands as she gently laid him down with his head on her lap.

If his busted face could have smiled, he would have. He had proved his point. Solia didn't hate him at all.

Then biting frost charged through his senses. He shuddered, first with pain, then relief. The fire fled, banished by magic. Healing. Rudhira. His aura was everywhere, it seemed, as big as the Sanctuary. No, as vast as Orthros.

"What happened?" he asked, deadly calm.

"He evaded that move twice already in this fight." Solia stroked Lio's hair back from his face.

Rudhira sighed. "We all saw it."

"Why in your Goddess's name would he let me do this to him?"

That was the last thing Lio heard before Rudhira's magic swept through him again, banishing him into unconsciousness.

MAGEFIRE WOUNDS

When Apollon arrived in the greenhouse, Cassia could feel his magic rumbling out of him like a protective growl.

Komnena leapt to her feet and went into his arms. "What has happened to Lio?"

"He'll be all right. Ioustin is working on him. We've brought him to your residence, Cassia." Apollon knelt beside her. "But what has happened to you?"

"Take me to him." Cassia tried to sit up, her head spinning. "He must need my blood."

Queen Soteira answered Apollon's question. "And Cassia is in need of his magic, it seems."

"Please, help me up." Cassia hated asking for help. She hated being ill. She hated being *weak*. But all that mattered right now was getting to Lio's side.

Apollon helped her to her feet, and with his strength supporting her, there was no danger of her tumbling over again. Then came the gentlest step Cassia had ever felt, with three powerful Hesperine elders concentrating their power on moving her without discomfort.

But she was not prepared for the sight that awaited her in the coffee room.

Lio lay unconscious on their sofa, surrounded by Rudhira, Mak, and Lyros. A bandage obscured the better part of her Grace's face and head. Where they had cut his robe away from his shoulder and chest, blistering burns covered his skin.

Cassia felt cut to the bone by a sense of betrayal unlike any she'd imagined. Solia had done this.

The sister she cherished and trusted. The sister she had crossed the world to find.

Her sister had done this to her Grace.

Cassia tore her gaze away from Lio to find Solia standing out of the way with Nike and the Ashes. The look of devastation on Solia's face didn't matter. She should be devastated. She should be ashamed.

"How could you do this to him?" Cassia asked.

Nike took a step forward and opened her mouth to speak. But Solia held up a hand.

"Allow her this anger," Solia said, then strode out of the room.

Cassia wanted to run to Lio, but through her horror and nausea, she felt their magical link warming. She tried to control the current, but it only grew stronger. Why was it so hard to let it go when she wanted to, but hold it back when she needed to?

Queen Soteira looked from Cassia to Lio. "I sense the current you described. How remarkable."

"Am I hurting him?" Cassia asked.

Rudhira's brows rose. "No, but I do need an explanation of what's happening—and quickly, if it's anything that will affect my healing spells."

"Cassia has suffered from her lack of magic for some time," his mother answered, "while she and Lio believed it to be Craving. The only reason she is not deathly ill is because her aura is channeling his magic as a surrogate for her own."

"What?" Cassia said. "How is that possible?"

Queen Soteira gestured from Cassia's chest to Lio's. "There seems to be a rare interaction occurring between his bond with you and your condition of being an unawakened Lustra mage. You are not drawing on any other person's magic in this room, and I doubt you could if you tried. Your aura has fastened onto Lio's, so to speak."

No. The magical link between them that had seemed so natural and right was all wrong. She'd taken pleasure in stealing his power. This hunger inside her...was it something that could destroy the one she loved?

"Was any of it Craving?" she asked.

"The grief when you're apart," the Queen answered, "the physical need—yes. But drinking his magic? No."

"What if I weaken him...or deplete him?"

"He has two powerful affinities in eternal supply," Queen Soteira reassured her. "Since this phenomenon is largely unknown to us, we shall keep an eye on the long-term effects. But Hespera knew what she was doing when she matched you to a powerful Hesperine. Our Lio has enough magic even for a Silvicultrix lacking three affinities."

And yet, Cassia could not forget Kalos's awe at the power of the ancient Silvicultrixes. It sounded as if she could channel the magic of the whole world.

Surely sensing her worry, Queen Soteira asked, "Has he experienced any ill effects after you've drawn on his power?"

The pleasure it gave him...the way it energized him in return... "It seemed beneficial to him, if anything, but is that hiding the true harm I've been causing him?"

"I don't believe so," Rudhira answered. "It seems your draw on his magic isn't hurting him any more than his bite hurts you. Based on what I'm sensing, you've formed an arcane symbiosis in which your blood and his magic are a self-sustaining cycle."

But Lio had asked Cassia for her blood. He had never taken a drop until she had wanted him to with her whole heart.

She had been devouring his magic without them even knowing it. It didn't matter how much he had enjoyed it. He hadn't known what she was doing to him and hadn't agreed to it. He'd had no opportunity to choose.

"Can you make it stop?" she asked the Queen.

Queen Soteira rested a hand on Cassia's arm. "Even if I could, I would never attempt it. It would do too much harm to you."

"We have to make it stop until I can speak with him."

"That is out of the question," Komnena said.

Apollon nodded. "Lio would never agree to anything that would be dangerous for you."

"Don't be silly," Mak told Cassia. "Of course Lio wants to give you his magic."

Queen Soteira took Cassia's hands, her healing flowing into Cassia's fingers, up her arms, and pooling in her chest where her heart was pounding.

"If not for Lio," the Queen said, "and this extraordinary way you are able to rely on his magic in place of your own, you would be gravely ill by now. You most likely would not have survived. Do not question this miracle the Goddess has given you."

Cassia's ears roared, and her surroundings seemed distant. But she felt Apollon put his arm around her.

"Everything will be all right," her Grace-father said.

"You give Lio as much as you take." Rudhira's words cut through Cassia's shock. "Right now, he needs your blood to heal. If we wait much longer, he may suffer lasting effects from the magefire."

Cassia sank down on the couch next to Lio. "Is it safe for me to touch him?"

Her Trial brothers each rested a hand on one of her shoulders. Rudhira nodded, and she took Lio's undamaged hand.

She bit back a gasp at the sudden strength of the current between them. Her head cleared, her stomach settled, and energy fizzed through her.

"You're certain I'm not hurting him?" she asked Rudhira.

"Your channeling is not interfering with my healing spells at all." Rudhira handed Cassia a scalpel. "It will aid my magic if we give him doses of your blood throughout the healing process."

"Of course." She held the blade ready.

"I've driven the magefire out of his veins so it can't do further harm. He is stable. But repairing the damage will take time and careful work, especially on his jaw and fangs." Rudhira drew a glass tube from the red healer's satchel at his side.

That made Cassia realize how bad the damage really was. Lio couldn't swallow, much less bite.

Rudhira grimaced. "Magefire is one of the few things that can leave Hesperines with long-term injuries. Fortunately I got to him immediately."

Queen Soteira nodded. "Magefire wounds are Ioustin's specialty. Lio is in the best of hands."

"But it would be wrong of me to promise a perfect outcome," Rudhira said. "It depends on what damage I find as we go deeper."

"How long is long term?" Cassia asked.

"At best, weeks before his jaw is able to properly engage during the drink. In more severe cases, I have seen it take years."

Cassia's hand clenched around the handle of the scalpel. She trailed her other fingers gently over Lio's hand.

Years.

"It doesn't matter how long it takes," she swore. "I will be with him every step of the way."

92

days until

AUTUMN EQUINOX

7 Anthros's Sword, 1597 OT

BURNING SILK

SOMEWHERE IN TENEBRA, IT was dawn again. Cassia could not bring herself to care what chaos the lords might cause. Not while she sat here in the coffee room with polar night outside the door, and her Grace's head in her lap.

Although Lio now slept peacefully, her heart had not stopped racing. She kept her arm around her Grace like a shield, holding a fistful of his veil hours robe. Cassia brushed her fingers along the pale, smooth skin of his jaw, now beardless, compliments of her sister's fist.

Goddess, how had it come to this?

Mak had urged her to let Solia explain, but Cassia didn't want explanations. Even an apology would be too little, too late.

Solia had gone too far. Cassia would never allow her to hurt Lio again.

Cassia's fury felt like some primal beast that knew no reason, ready to tear out of her and rampage in defense of her Grace. The magic flowing into her from Lio only seemed to galvanize her anger.

But what a hypocrite she was, to feel this need to protect him, when she had been stealing his magic all along.

Her sister's footfall at the door announced her arrival. Cassia lifted her gaze from Lio. Solia stood on the threshold, once again wearing her Imperial attire, golden scarf, and mask of discipline.

"Mak suggested now might be a good time for us to talk," Solia said.

When Cassia did not tell her to get out, Solia entered. She took a seat on a floor cushion across the coffee table as if adders might await her amid the tassels.

"Can he bite?" she asked.

Cassia unclenched her teeth. "We'll know when he wakes."

Solia rubbed her face. "Words are insufficient, but I want you to know how sorry I am."

Cassia searched her sister's face, recalling the anger in Solia's gaze every time she looked at Lio, but also the tenderness she had shown Cassia all her life. "I thought you cared about me more than anyone in the world. I thought you would care about Lio for my sake, at least, even if you can't see how deserving he is of your love in his own right. Why do you hate him?"

"Cassia, I don't. I wouldn't deliberately attack any Hesperine with my magic. And I would *never* hurt someone you love. Lio let me hit him."

"He *what*?" Cassia cried.

"Ask Mak and Lyros for their professional opinions. I made a move I knew Lio was capable of evading. The same punch he'd already dodged twice. He had the time, opportunity, and skill to avoid the blow, and I fully expected him to. He chose not to, although he was near victory." She plucked at her scarf. "He removed the artifact that shields my mind. He could have used thelemancy to win."

Cassia gave her sister an incredulous look. "No one saw fit to explain to me that your scarf is a powerful artifact that negates his magic? What in the Goddess's name has given you two the idea that I am to be a clueless spectator in this contest between you?"

Solia opened her mouth, then paused. "We are both trying to protect you."

"'Keeping a woman tucked away from danger is no way to keep her safe.'" Cassia quoted her sister's words back at her. "I've had enough. From both of you. Do not ask me to decide whether I'm angrier at you for putting a burning fist in his face or at him for letting you! He already nearly died for me. Isn't that enough?"

Solia's eyes flashed, although her voice was calm. "All I have seen him do is nearly kill you."

"Is that what this is about? Punishing him for my Craving?"

"I am your elder sister. It is not in me to tolerate any threat to you, even—especially—this."

"Lio didn't choose to inflict the Craving on me!"

"He chose to drink from you. Every Hesperine knows the risk. Why do you think Karege has never acted on his love for Tuura all these years? She could never transform to be with him without giving up her ancestral magic."

Cassia sucked in a breath. "That's why Karege never does more than flirt with Tuura?"

To remain human, never knowing if you were your Hesperine's Grace, was among the worst fates she could imagine. One that had almost been her own.

"Grace has consequences for mortals," Solia said, "and some Hesperines are willing to think about that before they unsheathe their fangs."

Cassia's arm tightened on Lio. "You have no idea, Solia. You cannot imagine how careful Lio was with me. How patiently he waited for me to ask him for that first bite. We didn't think we had a future together. All we knew was that we had that moment. The only time in my life I had ever felt safe letting someone close to me. A Hesperine's bite was the only thing in the world that could have saved me from that isolation."

Solia looked away. "I can imagine, Cassia. How do you think I felt when I met a wind mage who could snuff out my unruly fire spells?"

Cassia had known Tendo was the only person who could spar with Solia without getting burned. But she had never considered the other implications. Now it made sense. He was also the only man Solia could lose control with. "Tendo made you feel safe for the first time."

"But that was...reversible." Solia's voice was toneless. "Unlike Grace."

"You cannot actually believe that the way you and Tendo still love each other is in any way reversible. Are you saying you don't feel as if you're starving every day you must live without him?"

"This is not about Tendo and me!"

"Is it, Solia? No one will blame you if seeing Lio and me together makes you miss the man you love. Goddess knows we're trying to drag that stubborn vulture here to see you."

Solia flattened her hands on the coffee table. "Of course this isn't about that. You think I would let my own past get in the way of your happiness? I want you to have love. I want to be happy for you."

"Then why aren't you?" Cassia wanted that more than anything. And yet it had never felt farther out of reach.

Solia sprang to her feet as if she could not bear to sit still among Orthros's luxuries an instant longer. "I want you to get to decide your own destiny. Not for it to hinge on every twitch of some Hesperine's fangs! Your freedom is worth more than anyone with a cock!"

Cassia glared at her sister. "He isn't just anyone, and he certainly isn't a cock-brained man from Tenebra. He helped me gain my freedom."

"How can you say that, when all your life decisions from now on must depend on him? Your destiny is no longer your own. You are not free to choose your legacy."

"You're still convinced Lio is the reason I abdicated? How can you think that of me—that I would give up all my own desires and goals for a male?"

"I know you would never do that...unless you had no choice. Unless you would die without him."

Cassia shook her head. "You don't understand. Lio nearly died to give me a choice."

"I know he helped you defeat the Collector so the necromancer wouldn't take you from Orthros. All that proves is that Lio wanted to keep you."

"I'm not talking about the battle with the Collector."

The furrows on Solia's brow deepened. "How many times have you been in mortal danger when I was not there to protect you?"

Cassia took a deep breath to steady her anger. Anger, when controlled, was her fuel. Words were her power.

She didn't owe her sister an explanation. But this was an opportunity. Perhaps her last chance to find the right words to change Solia's mind about Lio.

"I understand why the thought of my Craving horrifies you," Cassia said, and it was the truth. "It threatens my life, and you cannot fend it off with your fists. But putting one in Lio's face is not going to solve anything."

"I had no intention of hitting him. I would say he is a fool for letting me...but he is no fool."

"Would you like to sit down and let me explain?" Cassia asked, taking care to let no anger into her tone this time. "Then tell me if you understand why he let you win."

Solia sank back onto the cushion.

"At the end of the Equinox Summit," Cassia began, "I told Lio to leave. I asked him to go back to Orthros and let me stay in Tenebra to plot against the king."

Surprise flashed in Solia's gaze.

"He could have asked the Charge to come get me at any time," Cassia went on, "but instead, he didn't tell a soul about our bond for half a year, lest they interfere in my plans. When I finally arrived in Orthros for the Solstice Summit"—Cassia drew a breath, hating the memory—"he was on the brink of starvation."

Solia's eyes flicked to Lio, then back to Cassia's face. "That was how you found out?"

"Oh, no. He didn't breathe a word about Grace during the entire negotiations. And when I told him I intended to return to Tenebra to make myself queen, he was prepared to let me go."

Solia sucked in a breath. "You planned to go back and take the throne?"

"I suppose you would have loved that. But I could not bear to go through with it."

"You changed your mind because of your Craving."

Cassia shook her head. "I didn't even know I had the Craving. My life was not in danger. My heart was."

"So it was him," Solia murmured. "Love, not death. But no matter which reason, it was him."

"No, Solia. It was me. There was a night when I thought I would lose Lio to Xandra's affections. A very foolish misunderstanding, in hindsight. But in that moment, I knew with all my heart that I would stay in Orthros with or without Lio. I would stay for myself."

Solia appeared taken aback. "Why? Is it the immortality?"

"Not at all. That aspect of it all is rather overwhelming, to own the truth. It's everything else about Orthros. I don't have to watch my back. I can have gardens of my own. People listen when I speak, and they believe I have something valuable to say."

"We could have made Tenebra hang on your every word."

"I would much rather speak at the next symposium of Orthros's Circle of Rosarians. This is the life I want. I'm happy here."

Solia shook her head. "How can growing roses in a garden ever be enough for you, compared to changing the history of a kingdom?"

"Hesperines like Princess Konstantina change history from the rose garden all the time. So can I."

Solia had no reply, and that gave Cassia hope that she had finally made her point.

She ran a hand through Lio's hair. "It was not until I chose Orthros for myself that Lio finally revealed our bond to me. At last, I realized how close he had come to dying for me, without even telling me. The only choice he ever took from me was the choice to save him. I have never been so angry."

Solia hesitated a moment longer. "I didn't know."

"How would you know?" Cassia replied quietly. "You didn't even ask how we met."

Silence fell between them.

"There is something else you should know," Cassia said.

Solia's brow furrowed. "What's wrong?"

"Craving isn't what almost killed me in the Maaqul. This illness I've had for months…it was never Craving at all."

Solia got up and rounded the table to kneel beside Cassia, taking her hand. Her grip was bracing. The kind of touch that made someone feel brave. Cassia was so angry that she didn't want to draw comfort from it. But she did.

"I've been sick from the lack of my magic," Cassia said. "All this time. If not for Lio, I would have become like Pakhne already…or worse. We didn't even realize it, but I've been absorbing his magic. He's not killing me, Solia. He is keeping me alive."

The color had drained from Solia's face. She held Cassia's hand as if she would never let her go. She must be imagining all the possibilities Cassia herself had thought through.

Finally she released Cassia's hand and stood. "I will trouble you no longer. When Lio is able, if he would be willing to speak with me, tell him I would be very grateful for the opportunity to apologize to him."

She traversed out of the room, leaving behind a whiff of burning silk.

ANY SACRIFICE

THE NEXT MOMENTS ALONE with Lio were deceptively peaceful. The flow of his magic into her body settled into a resting current, as soothing as the sight of him sleeping on her lap.

So this appetite of hers wore many guises. A ravenous frenzy. A gentle embrace. It would be so easy to let it fool her into believing it wasn't wrong.

Nothing would ever make it right that she had not shown Lio's Will the same care as he had given hers. All she could do was sit here and continue to commit this crime against the person she loved more than anyone.

When Rudhira returned, Lio's uncle was with him. Argyros took a chair next to Cassia. "We decided I should be here when he wakes."

"Thank you," Cassia said. "That's what he would want."

Uncle Argyros took her hand. She was grateful for that steady hand, but didn't feel deserving of it at the moment.

Here was the philosopher, the thelemancer, the ancient Hesperine who had taught Lio never to break the fragile Will of mortals. Did he know what Cassia had done?

"I sense your inner debate," Uncle Argyros said. "Rudhira told me what you have learned about your magic."

She tried to find words, but it was too difficult to articulate her remorse.

"I will say only this." There was no judgment in Uncle Argyros's voice. "Had I found myself in such a situation with Lyta, I would sacrifice every last drop of my magic for her, if that was what she needed from me. It is the nature of Grace."

"Even if you didn't know?"

"My only regret would be not knowing her life was in danger."

"Thank you." She squeezed his hand. "But I need to know how Lio feels."

"Of course."

"I'll wake him now." Rudhira laid a hand on Lio's head.

Lio stirred. His long, dark lashes rose, and he looked up at Cassia with his beautiful blue eyes.

"How do you feel?" she asked softly.

He frowned. "There are eighty layers of residual emotion in this room for which I have no context. Someone was having yet another important conversation while I was unconscious."

Rudhira gave a wry smile. "This scrollworm's jaw is healed enough for him to speak. That's an excellent sign."

Uncle Argyros breathed a sigh of relief and a prayer.

Lio muttered, "I insist everyone stop discussing momentous topics while I am a useless heap nearby."

Cassia was still too worried to tell him just what an endearing heap of fangs he was. "I insist you stop getting yourself injured."

"Open your mouth," Rudhira instructed.

Lio frowned. "Are you about to cast a stiff-tooth spell on me?"

"I was able to save both your fangs on the side where your jaw broke, but I need to check if they're extending and retracting properly."

"A spell won't be necessary," Lio said with great dignity. He bared his fangs, and they lengthened promptly.

"Good." Rudhira put his fingers on either side of Lio's jaw and felt the joint. "Do you have any pain?"

"No," Lio answered.

"Do not try to hide it." Rudhira's healer tone might be even more authoritative than his princely one.

"I promise, Ritual father. I don't hurt anywhere."

"Do you feel any numbness?" Rudhira asked.

"No."

"Flex your hand and tell me if you feel any weakness in your arm."

Lio opened and closed his fist, and Cassia watched the muscles work under the new skin where he had been burned.

"No," Lio said. "I admit I am rather exhausted, as if several bottles of Sunfire Poison have just gone out of my veins."

Rudhira leaned forward. He wasn't looking at Cassia, but even so, her proximity to his quiet fury sent a shiver down her back. "That was not Sunfire administered by a healer, Lio. You put your face in front of a fire mage's fist."

"Yes, I did," Lio replied calmly.

"What were you thinking?" Rudhira demanded. "You know better! You might have spent years with the healers working on that jaw before you could drink properly again."

"I knew Solia wouldn't hit me that hard."

"That is beside the point," Uncle Argyros cut in.

"On the contrary, Uncle, that is the point, you see? She was holding back."

Now Cassia was beginning to see.

So, it seemed, was Uncle Argyros. He fixed Lio with the infamous gaze that had turned armies out of their path. "Do not try to argue that you just took a magefire blow as an act of diplomacy."

"But it worked, I take it?" Lio looked to Rudhira. "You said I might have spent years. That suggests I won't. How long will it be before I can drink from Cassia again?"

Rudhira made an exasperated noise. "As soon as your Uncle and I leave you to it."

In the face of their combined ire, Lio smiled. Gingerly, as if unsure his mouth would obey. But it was a smile without remorse.

"You're sure he's all right?" Cassia asked.

"Yes. But if he has any pain, stop and send someone for me." Rudhira rose to his full height. "Lio, I will spare you further admonishment until you are back on your feet. But if I have to remind you not to misuse my fighting ring by taking you for a round in it myself, I will."

"Yes, Ritual father," Lio said, still smiling.

Rudhira stepped away, but his aura seemed to leave behind a cold blaze in the air.

Uncle Argyros remained a moment longer. "If you ever scare us like that again, I may consider revoking that medallion of yours. I cannot deny I have seldom seen an ambassador so effectively subvert physical force for diplomatic ends. Just ensure you do not repeat that strategy."

"I only have one fire mage's good opinion to win, so I don't think it will be necessary."

"I will go reassure your mother. I make no promises about mitigating what your father will have to say to you for worrying her." With that, he stepped out and left them alone.

For an instant, Cassia's pure relief eclipsed everything else. "You're going to be all right."

"Of course I am, my rose. Do you think I would ever do anything that would prevent me from feasting on you? That might interfere with me Gifting you?"

"I didn't know what you were planning to do!"

"You left before I could explain."

"You accepted her challenge before I could ask you."

"If I had asked you, would you ever have agreed to my plan?"

"Of course not. I would never endorse you and my sister coming to blows."

"Ambassador Cassia, now that you understand my plan and have seen the results, tell me your professional opinion. Was it effective?"

"I don't care if it was effective, Lio. I never want to see you like that again."

His expression gentled. "I'm sorry I frightened you."

"Surely you could have shown her who you are in some other way than letting her hurt you."

"You truly think anything but a battle would have gotten through to her? She is who she is. I am who I am. We cannot change that. But we can meet halfway—and tonight, the halfway mark was in the fighting ring."

"You could have at least tried every other possibility before resorting to this."

"She challenged me, as one of the labors. If I had refused, it would have cost me all the ground I'd gained."

"If you hadn't taken her bait about the labors to begin with, none of this would have happened."

He put his uninjured hand over hers where she still gripped his robes. "Have you talked to Solia since the match?"

She watched him glide his thumb over her skin. "Yes."

"And how does she feel about me now? Did I succeed in changing her opinion?"

She stroked his hair back from his brow. "In my professional opinion, Glasstongue...you proved more than just the limits of her anger, and the fact that she doesn't want to hurt you."

His smile returned. "What else do you think I demonstrated?"

"You showed her that she should trust your judgment, in battle or out of it."

Ghosts of regret flitted behind his eyes, and she knew he was thinking of Pakhne.

"You also proved to Solia how much you're willing to sacrifice for me. As if everything you've already done for me isn't enough."

"She wasn't here for most of it. I felt a live demonstration was necessary."

Cassia caressed his jaw. "Most of all, you showed her that you're powerful enough to defeat anyone for my sake—including her."

That unabashed smile of his was much too handsome. "This scrollworm beat your sister in a fight. I wish you could have seen my spells."

Goddess, how could he be in such good humor after nearly losing his fangs? "You are quite full of yourself at the moment."

His grin widened. "I managed to fool her with my simulacra."

"Simulacra?"

"Illusions enhanced with mind magery to resemble a living being. My Queen, don't you think your magic tutor deserves a reward for such a feat?"

"I am supposed to give you more blood. Are you certain you don't hurt anywhere?"

"I'm in dreadful pain," he moaned. "I need a willing human to save me from my agony."

She tsked. "You've been spending too much time with Hoyefe."

"He has great success in the romantic arts. Is it working on you?"

She scowled. It was. But she said, "No. Until we are confident the Drink won't cause you pain, all you may have is my wrist."

Lio nibbled up the inside of her forearm. "I can make your wrist very rewarding."

She could not let the sensation of his canines on her skin shred through her resolve so easily. "Rudhira said we would need to be..." A thread of thelemancy teased her thoughts. "...careful. Until we're certain you're not having any trouble s—s—" She drew a steadying breath as the heavy, dark shadow of Lio's power covered her. So close. So tempting.

"Trouble doing what?" he asked, his voice resonating with mind magic.

"Sucking," she breathed.

His tongue darted out to taste the sensitive skin on the inside of her arm. "Clearly the only way to know if I'm having trouble is for me to attempt it. Where shall I conduct this experiment?"

She pressed her vein to his beautiful, persuasive mouth to put a stop to his seductive words. He gripped her wrist, and she found herself compelled by the firmness of that touch.

All he did was give the inside of her wrist a gentle suck, but the resting current came to life and began to pull. His magic washed over her in a soft rush that sent a little jolt through her entire body.

"No," she cried. "Stop."

His power receded from her in a blink and left her as bereft as she was relieved. His flirtatious smile disappeared. "What's wrong?

"There's something I need to tell you." It was so difficult to confess what she had done. One of the hardest things she had ever said.

"Cassia, you're worrying me. What has happened?"

"I found out something about my magic…about us."

His arm tightened over hers where she held him. She could see possibilities, fears running through his mind. Oh Goddess, she was doing a wretched job explaining this.

He seemed to brace himself. "Something that could interfere with your Gifting?"

"No! No, not that. Oh, I'm sorry. I'm so sorry." Bitter tears of shame ran down her cheeks. "Lio, no one in the world is more precious to me than you are . And yet I've wronged you."

"What are you talking about?"

"This illness I've had isn't the Craving. My yearning for you…the lust…all of that was our Grace bond, true. But what happens to your magic when we feast…it isn't natural. It isn't right."

She heard him draw a breath. He was so composed. Too composed, the way he became when he was breaking inside, but still trying to be strong for her. "I think you need to start at the beginning."

Cassia was far more expert at simply facing painful truths than at trying to explain them painlessly. But she told Lio what had happened at the greenhouse as gently as she could.

He pushed off her lap and sat up to put his arms around her. "You were ill—you needed me—and I didn't know. I felt it, but I dismissed it as instinctive worry from being apart from you."

"Lio, your arm." She could feel the tremble in his limb. She gently loosened his hold on her, propping his injured arm across her lap.

"Never mind my arm. Was this fainting spell as serious as that time in the Maaqul?"

"It could have been," she admitted. "But Annassa Soteira came to heal me. When they brought you back, she studied the magical current between us." Cassia felt ill.

Lio stroked her face, lifting her gaze to his. "Whatever is wrong, I'm here now. We'll face it together."

His sympathy was too much. He was so sure of her, so much more concerned for her than for himself. She couldn't bear the guilt a moment longer. "We thought I was drinking your magic as a surrogate for blood. But we were wrong. I've been channeling your magic out of you. *Leeching* off of you to fill the void where my own power should be."

His eyes widened.

"I will not make excuses for myself. It doesn't matter that we didn't know, or that I'm struggling to control it. That doesn't change the fact that you never had the opportunity to consent. I feel such shame knowing that I've done this to you. That I'm still doing it. If it isn't what you want, I *will* find a way to make it stop."

He didn't pull away. In fact, he pulled her closer, stroking her face and hair with a barely contained fierceness in his touch. She searched his face, but for once, she couldn't read the meaning in his tightly drawn brows and the complicated emotion in his eyes.

"Do I have enough magic to sustain you?" he asked.

Her heart broke. That was his first question?

Of course it was.

"Don't think about me," she said. "For just one moment, think about yourself."

He held up a hand. "I need to fully understand the facts. I assume Rudhira and Annassa Soteira want to study the long-term effects?"

She hesitated, then nodded.

"What can they say with confidence as of now?" Lio asked.

"They believe you have more than enough magic. There is little risk that I'll deplete you, and this process is not causing you any physical or magical harm that we can detect."

"Is it hurting you? Are there any side effects of you channeling blood magic through arcane pathways made for Lustra magic?"

"Not that we're aware of."

In the pause that followed, he said, "What aren't you telling me?"

"I don't want you to base your decision on the danger to me, any more than you wanted me to stay with you because of your Craving. But I know how I felt when you didn't tell me I'm your Grace. So I will tell you everything, because you deserve to know."

"How great is the danger to you?" he demanded.

"It seems my magic was due to awaken some time before now. I suppose around the time we first started to notice the magical current during our feasts. If you hadn't been sustaining me...I wouldn't have survived this long without my own power."

He looked as devastated as she had feared. For a long moment, he said nothing, just pulled her face against his chest and held her. He didn't touch her with his magic, but his arms, his presence, felt more powerful than any thelemancy.

"You had to bear this news alone," he said, "when I was out of reach."

"It doesn't matter how much I need you or what the consequences are. Respect your own choice in this, as surely as you respected mine about our bond. Ask yourself—is this all right with you?"

"My Grace. Thank you for being so concerned about my Will."

"Of course I am. What Hesperine principle is more sacred? You've cherished my Will since the moment we met. What can I ever do to make amends for not treating you that way in return?"

"You know I gave you my magic willingly in the Maaqul."

"It was different then. We didn't understand what I was really doing to you. We thought it was because of my Craving."

"How is it any different now?" he asked.

"It isn't something beautiful like Grace. It's some strange warping of the rules of magic. I'm channeling you…feeding on your power. Taking it out of you."

"What could be more natural than feeding on your Grace? All of me. Body. Blood. Magic."

She slid away from him, drawing her feet up on the sofa. She had to put distance between them, or she would give in to how natural the current felt. She would believe his words and forget how wrong it was.

He shook his head, looking so confused. "Why does this trouble you so?"

"Don't you see?" She wrapped her arms around her knees and hugged them to her, as if she could tighten her hold on the void inside her. "It's too much like what the Collector does."

"What?" He slid close to her. "Cassia, no. Nothing about you bears any resemblance to that monster."

"It doesn't make you feel…violated?"

He uncurled her fingers and unwound her arms from around her knees. She should resist. But she couldn't. Lio had always been able to undo her. Before she knew it, he pulled her onto his lap with ease, despite how weak his arm was.

"Let me explain it to you this way," he said. "If I imagined, in my wildest dreams, that my magic could be your surrogate for the entire Lustra, that you could channel me instead… I would search every corner of Akanthia to find that spell. I would uncover any forbidden ritual, make any blood sacrifice—yes, warp any rule of magic to save your life."

"I don't want you to have to do any of that. You've gone through so much for me. Why couldn't my magic be easy for you?"

"Easy?" he scoffed. "You held me after Martyrs' Pass, when I was mad with Craving and afraid I had murdered hundreds of mortals with my magic. You waited for me, suffering at the Rezayal's hands, while I let my power run amok in the Maaqul. My magic was never easy. How could I shy away from anything yours demands?"

"But you cannot do this only for my sake."

"I want it, Cassia. For me."

As long as she had known him, he had never sounded possessive. Until now.

"I'm jealous," he said, his fangs lengthening at the confession. "I know I'm a fool to be jealous of the very laws of nature. But I am your Grace. I feel I should be everything you need."

"Lio, I will always need you. You kept my spirit alive long before my body was in any danger."

"I hate knowing that you need the Lustra—that you need Tenebra or anyone in it."

"That's what was bothering you," she realized. "When we were searching for the letting site, and you took me to the willow copse."

"I didn't want you to know how frustrated I was. How unfair my feelings were."

"You could have told me," she said.

"It would only have made you feel guiltier about everything we're going through for your magic."

She shook her head. "It makes me feel better. I thought you were unhappy with our progress toward my Gifting. Now I understand the real reason for your disappointment."

"That night was evidence that you couldn't find what you need in Orthros. In me." He let out a sigh, as if a weight had lifted from him. "But you can."

"Only you," she said. "I don't seem able to draw from anyone else. The elders said it's a rare magical result of my channeling ability and our Grace bond. I've 'fastened' onto your aura."

"Then it won't stop?" he asked, not with horror, but with hope.

"We're not even sure if it's possible to stop it," she admitted. "I tried to persuade Annassa Soteira to attempt it, but the entire family refused."

His good arm tightened around her. "Why would you ask her to do that? It could have hurt you." He hesitated. "Unless…this isn't what you want. You never had a choice, either, about needing me like this."

"Of course this is what I want. I want it too much. This bottomless hunger inside of me…I'm afraid I'll hurt you."

"Don't be afraid." He kissed her hair.

She tried to calm her instinctive panic. But he knew. He could sense how fragile she felt, as if she might be cut from mortal existence and blown away on a breath.

"You are the cord tying me to this life," she said.

She didn't realize she was shaking until he began to stroke her back.

"I've faced death before," she hissed. "I shouldn't be such a coward."

"You are the bravest person I know. But you have no cause to fear death, my Grace. I will never let him take you."

She wrapped her arms around him, burying her face against his chest, and drew in his scent. For the first time in hours, days even, she felt safe.

But relaxing into his arms also relaxed her hold on the channeling. At the sudden wave of magic, she stiffened.

He ran a hand through her hair. "No, never feel ashamed. I want it, and I want you to enjoy it."

Something inside her released, and a little moan of relief slipped out of her as the channeling flared.

Lio swore. "I can't tell you how good this feels. The respite…"

"What do you mean?"

"Carrying around more than one affinity is never comfortable. Even for a Hesperine. Sometimes I feel like my own skin is too tight."

She leaned into their connection. She felt a wave of tension drain out of him, too.

"Oh my Goddess, Cassia. This is better than wringing myself out into the most exhausting spell I can devise. Don't ever worry about taking too much."

Down to the ravenous, empty core of her, she was grateful for that reassurance.

"I promise I will always make it good for you." She nuzzled his throat. "I'll use this to give you relief and pleasure every time. I'll never take without giving."

She focused her arcane senses, testing the current. It felt like trying to control a river with her bare hands. But there was something intuitive about it. Her hunger knew what to do.

"Always trust your hunger," Lio murmured in her ear.

She stopped fighting the current and let herself slip into its flow. Now she could guide it. She gave it a careful, firm pull.

Lio sucked in a breath, his head falling back against the sofa. "It feels even better, now that I understand what you're doing to me."

"Tell me if you want me to take less."

"No. Take more."

She licked her lips. "How much more?"

He met her gaze, a hint of mischief in his eyes. "As your magic tutor, I need to know how hard you can pull. For research."

She loved him. For that gleam in his eye. For teasing her when, a moment before, they had faced the threat of death.

"I love you," she said, and Willed his magic into her with all her focus.

With a fanged grimace, he gasped.

She pulled back. "Did that hurt you?"

"No." He grabbed her hand and guided her touch to the hard ridge pressing against the front of his robe.

"Oh." She licked her lips and rubbed him through the fabric, giving his magic another pull.

He arched into her hand. "Do not *ever* feel guilty about this."

His eyes slid shut, and he rested his head back against the sofa again. But his face was too flushed for pleasure to be the only cause.

She withdrew her hand from his erection and felt his forehead. "You have a fever, and that is a side effect of magefire, not my channeling."

He caught her hand in his. "My fever is the last thing on my mind."

"We need to cool your body." She peeled what was left of his battle robe off him.

"This is not cooling anything, I assure you."

She left his straining underlinens on. "You need to lie down."

The corners of his elegant mouth twitched. "Is that what you're in the mood for tonight?"

"No exertion for you until you get more of my blood in you."

He let her settle his head on her lap again, but his grin was impudent. "Yes, my Queen."

He wasn't disgusted. He wanted her, strange magic and all. He was even ready to make saving her life fun. She caressed his hair. "Let me give you what you need before I take, my Grace."

His smile softened. "I understand that need."

He sank his fangs into her wrist with delicate precision. Goddess, it was only her wrist, but her loins tightened, and she shifted under him before she could stop herself. He sucked lightly on her vein, once, twice, teasing out her blood. The channeling waxed a little stronger each time. She reached for the arm of the sofa, her fingers closing over the silk damask while she tried to hold her hips still.

Your Will tastes sweetest of all, especially when you're being stubborn.

Grace Union came so quickly and easily this time. She felt the channeling swell, on the brink of crashing over her.

She answered him aloud, trying to resist slipping deeper into their joined minds. "I must learn to control it."

You will. But it doesn't have to be tonight.

"Tonight, you're injured. I refuse to be the one always falling apart for you to put back together. I will be strong for you."

Where is it written that we can't fall apart together?

He took a longer, harder draught from her wrist. Magic pooled between her legs, along with a rush of physical warmth. His nostrils flared, and he rested his head back against her, gripping her wrist more firmly to his mouth.

But his next suck was gentle. Too gentle. His jaw was not locking onto her as it should.

"You are in pain!" she accused.

He pulled her wrist away from his lips with a contented sigh, licking at the trail of her blood. "No. I don't hurt anywhere. Don't you dare make me resort to a tube again when I could have my fangs in you."

"Your jaw is still tender. Don't think I can't tell."

He flexed his jaw, and his tone was more serious this time. "Yes, there is still some weakness in the joint. My muscles are sluggish. But by our Oath, there is no pain. I will be all right, my Grace."

He needed more blood, faster than just her wrist could give him. And the channeling throbbed deep within her, demanding more than just sips of his magic. "You're certain you can bite?"

"Let me show you how certain I am."

She opened her robe to expose her throat. At the heat in his gaze, she found herself pulling it lower to show him her breasts. He rolled over and prowled up her body.

WILLING TO LOSE

Cassia saw the tremble in his shoulder when he let his injured arm bear his weight. She ran her hand over his skin. Much too hot for a Hesperine. She snatched a pillow that was about to tumble off the sofa and slipped it under Lio's arm to support him.

"You take such good care of me, my rose," he said.

She had just been speaking to her sister of the past, when she had cared for no one. She had been the Cassia who had struck fear in Miranda's heart. She had thought channeling Lio's magic might be the most selfish thing she had ever done.

But no, she was still this person who had learned to look after the people she loved. She knew how to take care of her Grace.

"Let me try something," she said.

He arched a suggestive brow. "What do you have in mind?"

"I have a theory of my own. Will you test it with me?"

His smile widened. "Of course. Especially if it involves mutual devouring."

"I didn't know 'mutual devouring' was a documented magical process, Sir Scholar."

"It isn't. I think we're inventing it."

She shut her eyes and sank into their Union, into the channeling, until she could taste the flow of power with her arcane senses. She applied her newly trained magical concentration.

There. She had been right. She could feel the mark the magefire had left on him. That burnt aftertaste ran through his sweet, dark power like a lingering poison.

She concentrated on that portion of his magic, but it was too difficult to separate, too easy to get lost in the whole of him.

He made a low hum in his throat. "This feels so good."

If there was ever a time when physical focus aids would help, surely it was now. She kissed her way along his bicep, his muscle shivering under her tongue. Still his magic eluded her.

She bit his shoulder. There. She had it. She pulled on the damaged magic inside him.

Sparks seemed to fly through her veins, little points of his pain, but they filled her with triumph. She was taking away his hurt.

Is this hurting you? came his voice in her mind.

No more than your Union with my pain hurts you.

The tremor left his limb, and the pillow fell to the floor with a soft rustle. Then he slid his arm under her. He lay her back over the arm of the sofa so her neck was supported, her throat exposed.

His mouth trailed over her vein, his smooth skin caressing hers. His bite did not hold its usual force, but the slow, tentative way he slid his fangs into her flesh sent a curl of pleasure through her. He hesitated. Then his fangs slid out of her, and he bit her once more, more firmly this time.

"Yes," she gasped, stroking his jaw again. "That's better."

With a groan of relief, he braced her against the arm of the couch and drank deeply. The only sounds in their quiet coffee room were her rough breathing and his swallows and her pulse pounding in her ears.

His jaw flexed under her hand, and he withdrew his fangs once more. Then he struck, his bite fastening on her neck, hard and deep.

"Yes," she urged him on. "You need more."

He dragged her farther down onto the couch, pulling her beneath him. His weight came down on her. She cradled him between her thighs, and the intimate contact, even through her robe, stoked the current of magic again. But she was not its puppet. It was her instrument.

She concentrated on the flow of magic through his body. The sharp brilliance under her hands where she tangled her fingers in his hair. The warmth in his chest where his bare skin pressed against her clothes. Down to the heat of his lust.

"How does this feel?" she asked.

His bite tightened, and he shoved her robes out of his way. Her underlinens untangled from around her with a whip of levitation.

A smile came to her face. How rarely she could leave him speechless.

She pulled up her knees and dragged the current of magic down through his body, concentrating on the center of his desire.

He gripped her hips in both hands and pounded home. Stars of pleasure danced on her eyelids, and her concentration slipped. The channeling surged out of her control. A heated flood crashed through them where their bodies joined.

She felt fused to him. She wasn't sure she could part her body from his if she tried. Her hips moved with the current, betraying her, working his magic and his rhabdos for her satisfaction.

She tried to speak, but he pulled back from her vein and looked down at her. Her blood was bright red on his pale chin. A soft glow emanated from him everywhere her skin touched his.

"I want this," he told her.

She breathed a sigh of relief, and he caught it in his mouth with a crushing kiss.

Locked together, their bodies undulated on the flow of magic. The current thrust him into her as it bowed her up to him in arcane tandem. She ran her hands over him, feeling his muscles bunch and flex, her palms making eddies in the patterns of the magic that caused him to shudder.

He pinned her thigh against the back of the couch with his own. Her other heel skidded along the cushions as she sought new leverage. But he hooked his arm under her knee and held her open while he buried himself in her again.

The friction of his shaft and the warmth of his magic built inside her until she thought she would scream. He kissed her whimpers from her mouth, and she tasted his magic on her tongue, lush and smooth. He licked his way along her jaw, sending an arcane tingle over her skin. At last his lips returned to her throat.

His fangs penetrated her fast and hard. Magic coursed deep into her veins. He dragged hard on her vein in time to the current, grinding her into the couch with slow, deep thrusts. Her body hovered on the cusp of climax, as if her hunger would not release her until she ate her fill.

Don't let me go until you get enough, he said.

She wrapped her legs around him and dug her heels into the small of his back. He grunted, altering the angle of his hips in response to her pressure. Oh, Goddess. The current…the rhythm in this position… She bit down on his earlobe, beyond speech or coherent thought.

Yes. At last. His magic saturated her. She couldn't hold any more. She was going to break on his power.

Light and shadow and life exploded into the intimate reaches of her mind, echoing inside the mind ward. His Will met hers, sealed to her for an exultant moment.

Her Grace.

Her cry of recognition gave way to a scream of ecstasy. Through every shudder and swallow and pulse, he was with her, sharing in each visceral instant.

Until the connection shattered, leaving them gasping and limp in a tangle on the couch. She cradled his physical form in her arms, his magic still imprinted on her vision in bright spots.

"Oh my Goddess," he said at last, his voice hoarse.

"How do you feel?" she rasped.

"I have never felt this comfortable in my own skin. Did it help you?"

She shut her eyes, trying to find words for unspeakable gratitude. "I never realized how empty I felt until now. This is the first time in months that I haven't felt hollow."

"Now we know how to give you enough magic." He looked into her eyes. "You will never feel hollow again."

She found his jaw with her fingers and rubbed it again, gently.

He smiled. "Good as new."

She framed his beloved face in her hands. "I'm going to miss your beard."

"Shh," he murmured. "You fell in love with me without a beard."

"Your stubble felt so good on my skin."

"Are you saying you won't enjoy the sensation of my smooth face between your thighs?"

Her thighs tightened around him at the thought. "I never said that, no."

"Your new Hesperine skin will be very sensitive when I Gift you. You'll be glad I shaved."

"I will never be glad you shaved via fire spell. I may be angry about the duel for a very long time."

"That's all right, my Grace. I will feast on your temper, too."

LIO HAD EXPECTED SOLIA to be back in Tenebra, or anywhere she might burn her way through some training dummies, but he found her in his library. When he stepped into the large central chamber of the residence, he sensed her aura tucked away in one of the study alcoves.

This deep into Veil Hours, most of the spell lights were out, but a glow spilled across the blue and turquoise tiles from behind one cedar screen. Lio approached between the thick, round pillars, allowing his footfalls to be audible to human ears. He had surprised Solia enough tonight.

She was waiting for him with two scrolls set aside on the nearby writing desk. Lio saw with surprise that her golden scarf was draped across the back of her chair. That was why he could sense her aura so clearly—and her bitter, genuine remorse.

"How long will it take your jaw to recover?" she asked.

"It's nearly back to normal already."

Her relief felt like a flame settling into embers. But her regret still burned. She was all fire, inside and out. Now that he finally had this opportunity to become acquainted with her in the Blood Union, his first impression was that it was not easy being Solia.

Lio said, "When Mak told me you hadn't left yet, I was glad to hear it."

"Thank you for being willing to see me."

"It would be rather inconsistent of me to not wish to see you, after Cassia and I went to some effort to find you."

"What happened tonight was no way to repay you." Solia stood and squared her shoulders. "Dealing you such an injury was completely unacceptable. I'm sorry, Lio."

"You needn't apologize for the blow, when it wasn't your fault."

She looked away. "Many men are willing to fight and win for the woman they want. But few are willing to lose. Tendo is one of those few. And so are you."

The words took him completely aback. Not only because she finally said Tendo's name aloud, but because she deemed Lio worthy of such a comparison. He would never regret taking a magefire blow to the face to hear this. "I am honored."

"Cassia told me about her dependency on your magic," Solia said. "The healers assure me it isn't doing you any harm, for which I'm thankful. But somehow, if it were hurting you, I think you would still do it for her."

"Of course I would."

"Thalia never told me it could harm Cassia if she waited too long to awaken her magic. Hers came without delay, so I suspect she didn't know about the danger."

"Cassia's magic is such a mystery. How could any of us have guessed?"

"If only I'd known..." Solia's anger heated the air around her. "All these months at the Empress's beck and call, waiting for her permission to return to Tenebra. And the entire time, Cassia was..." Solia seemed unable to say the word. Lio didn't want to hear it aloud, either. "And then she had to find out alone. While I was too occupied throwing my fists at you to be here holding her hand."

Lio dared to reach out. When Solia didn't draw back, he put a hand over hers. The same one that had punched him, he supposed. "I will keep Cassia safe and well. I swear to you. She will lack for nothing, and I will get her to the letting site."

Solia picked up one of the scrolls. "I know from my friendship with Karege that Hesperines apologize with gifts. I want you to have this."

She held the document out to him. It was simple, but beautiful, with wooden scroll ends engraved with flowers. When he unrolled the fine Imperial paper, he found the text written in Vulgus.

His mouth dropped open. "This is Thalia's information on the letting sites. She wrote it down?"

Solia shook her head. "She didn't feel safe committing it to paper. She made me her record and charged me with preserving her wisdom in my memory. But while I was in the Empire, despite her wishes, I wrote down all her teachings for Cassia."

Lio lifted his gaze. "In case anything happened to you."

"Every soldier must be prepared. Karege kept this for me for years. I thought if there was any chance of getting it to Cassia in Tenebra someday, a Hesperine might find a way." Solia cleared her throat. "But the Hesperine who should have this is you."

He could scarcely believe what he was holding. The legacy of Cassia's matriarchs, perhaps the only written record of any Silvicultrix. Meticulously preserved in Solia's precise, practical handwriting.

"Thank you for entrusting this to me," he said.

"It's in good hands." Solia picked up the other scroll.

Lio realized with surprise that it was one he had written. "You're reading my initiation treatise?"

"*The Reign of Lucis Basileus, King of Tenebra, and its Implications for Hesperine Diplomacy,*" she read aloud. "Argyros tells me this is the most advanced and insightful analysis of the king available today."

"You and Cassia know more about him than I ever will."

Solia shook her head. "But we lack your perspective. We are too close." She tapped the scroll against her palm. "Are you willing to continue with the labors? Not because I am trying to punish you."

"I never thought you were punishing me," he said. "If there had never been any hope of winning your approval, you would have simply shaken me from your sandals like the ashes of your enemies. Instead, you've given me an opportunity to prove myself."

"Yes." She threw up her hands. "If only Cassia understood this."

Lio nodded. "This is your way of trying."

"I am trying so hard to like you." Her scowl resembled Cassia's when she was put out.

Lio almost laughed. "I try to be likable."

"It's infuriating. You have no right to be so kind. You make it too difficult to stay angry at you. Especially without your beard, looking like a temple chorus boy."

He raised his brows. "You can't deny you've enjoyed torturing me at least a little."

A half smile came to her face. "During the fourth labor, the bridegroom is supposed to teach the Matriarch something. Don't tell me you won't enjoy that a little, scrollworm."

"That depends on what you want me to teach you. If you're talking about another round in the fighting ring, I doubt I'll enjoy it as much the second time."

"Not to worry, Ambassador. I want you to become one of my advisers."

Lio tried to repress the smile spreading across his face. "You'd like me to assist with politics and diplomacy alongside Cassia?"

"Share all your expertise on Lucis's reign, all your insights gained from decades as Argyros's mentoree and from personal experience during two Summits. I intend to build a Tenebra that is a true ally of Orthros. Your knowledge will shape that future."

This could still go terribly wrong, he reminded himself. "I would welcome this, but before I commit to advising you, I need to know if you will heed me."

"I cannot promise I will always do as you recommend. But I will give everything you say serious consideration, with confidence in your judgment. I hope you will do the same for me, so that even when we disagree—which is sure to be often, scrollworm—we can have a respectful debate."

"And when there is no time for a respectful debate?" he pressed. If reminders of their recent battle would put strain on their newfound trust, better to see the cracks now.

Solia did not bristle, however. "We will adhere to the advice Karege once gave me. Perhaps he mentioned it to you as well. 'If I'm better at something than you are, you listen to me. If you're better at something, I listen to you.'"

"Karege and that very advice saved me in the Maaqul."

"You are better at anything to do with mind magic." To his surprise, her aura gentled. "I am better at carrying the weight of battle decisions. I will listen to you next time we face the Collector—but listen to me now, Lio. Sometimes there are people you cannot save. There is no use in berating yourself. Spend that energy honoring their memory instead."

He felt the wrongness of Pakhne's suffering in his every vein. "I will not shirk my responsibility toward her."

"Neither will I. But I learned the hard way, as Lucis's daughter, not to shoulder the guilt of others' evil. Do not blame yourself, and do not let anyone else place that blame on you. That's one reason I was angry with you last night. Next time, I want to see you defend your honor to the likes of Nivalis."

Suddenly their shouting match took on an entirely different meaning.

One that finally shifted Lio's thoughts, if not his feelings. Intellectually, he knew Solia was right. When would he feel the truth of it?

"I'm afraid we Hesperines tend to feel that we are powerful enough to save everyone."

"I know," Solia said, "but no one is. Don't let what happened to Pakhne distract you. Focus on saving Cassia."

Perhaps his Grace-sister understood him better than he had realized. "That, I can do."

Solia gestured to the two floor cushions in the alcove. "If she can spare you for the moment, I will ask you for your thoughts on a few questions now."

"She's with Zoe," Lio explained, "who is rather in need of reassurance after what happened at the greenhouse."

Solia winced and nodded.

Lio sat on the cushion across from her. "Where shall we begin?"

"How did you and Cassia meet?" Solia asked.

He raised his brows. "I was expecting a question on politics."

"Cassia brought it to my attention that I have neglected some basic rituals when meeting the love of my sister's life."

Lio smiled. "We met because of you."

"Me? I'd been gone for years."

"Yes. Cassia risked the king's wrath to seek out a Hesperine in secret. It took her weeks to feel sure enough of me to finally ask the question she had wanted to know all along." He sighed. "She thought I might know where Nike, Alkaios, and Nephalea had laid you to rest."

Surprise flared in Solia's aura.

"We didn't know it was Iris, of course," Lio explained, "but that does not change the fact that the tragedy of that night led to unexpected blessings. Cassia had never finished grieving for you, or for her mother. I suppose that is something Hesperines specialize in. Helping people mourn."

Solia eyed him. "Mourning does not seem to be what occupied you and Cassia's secret nights at Solorum."

He looked at her innocently. "Mourning was not the only thing she had neglected. Your sister's well being is always my highest goal."

Solia gave a faint snort. "Tell me more about how you two became acquainted—a version appropriate for my ears, mind you. Politics can wait."

91

days until

AUTUMN EQUINOX

8 Anthros's Sword, 1597 OT

TRUCE

AFTER THE VISIT HOME, Lio found stepping back to Tenebra much harder. In Orthros, time's power felt weaker, even for mortals.

He could forget his Grace lived on borrowed time.

But there was one consolation when he and their Trial brothers stepped Cassia and Solia back to Patria. Their guest chamber felt less like a battleground than before. The air no longer simmered with Solia's resentment toward Lio.

Cassia tugged against his arm. "You might occasionally have to release me and let me breathe, my love."

"I have no interest in doing so."

Instead of protesting, she leaned closer to him, her aura full of affection. He was grateful to her for indulging his need to keep her as close as he could.

Kella trotted Tilili over to them. "Thank Ayur you've returned."

"Thank you for holding down the fort." Solia leaned down to embrace her.

Kella sounded more inclined toward violence than usual. "Keeping those lords entertained—and dodging their impertinent questions—is my least favorite sport."

"I rather enjoy it," Hoyefe drawled.

"Rather too much," Kella said.

"There is no such thing as too much," Hoyefe replied with a satisfied smile.

Tuura asked after Lio's jaw, and Karege seemed ready to tell Cassia everything she had missed about Lio and Solia's duel, but Lio held up a hand to interrupt their kind friends. "Time is not on our side. We need to tell you what we learned in Orthros."

Hoyefe sat back, polishing one of his fine Imperial boots. "And I will tell you what I learned on my little forays among the loose-lipped lords of Tenebra. Their breeches are much looser than I was led to believe, too."

Laughing, everyone gathered around the fireplace, which Solia lit for them. She and the Ashes sat close to the warmth, while Cassia joined Lio, Mak, and Lyros a safe distance from the flames. Even so, a sense of camaraderie settled over them all.

Lio and his Grace-sister were no longer at war. Everyone in this room would fight for each other and for Cassia.

After she and Lio explained what they now knew, Kella gripped Cassia's hands. "Have no fear. I do not tolerate any threat to one of my Ashes, whether mundane or arcane."

"You are surrounded by the very best, dear Shadow," Hoyefe assured her. "Trust in our skills."

"We'll find the letting site in no time," Karege promised.

Tuura was already reaching into her medicine bag. "And I'll keep you feeling well until then. Between my tonics and visits to the Hesperine healers, you'll never know you're ill."

As they talked, Lio maintained some physical contact with Cassia at all times, even if only draping his hand lightly on her neck. With each touch, he felt her aura sip at his magic.

"Cassia must have near-constant proximity to me," Lio said. "During the day, she'll need to come to me for brief periods and absorb some of my magic to last her until I wake."

"I still don't like the idea of drawing on you in your Slumber," she said.

He wanted to kiss the concerned frown from her lips. His once-mercenary Cassia, who had insisted she was no philosopher, now cherished every fine point regarding his Will in this situation. When they were alone again, he would reassure her that he found the thought of her drinking his magic in his sleep pleasantly erotic.

For now, he said, "You hold me in your arms while I sleep. How is this any different?"

She was still frowning, but said, "At least Ebah's tunnels will make it easier for me to reach you. I may need help making excuses to slip out of events, though."

"Say no more!" Hoyefe exclaimed. "Sneaking? Forbidden love? My specialties."

"This won't appear in the play you're writing, will it?" Lio asked.

The illusionist gave him a sly grin. "That's the trouble with being friends with a playwright. You never know what I'll use in my next script. And with the money the Empress is paying us for our foray into this land of cutthroats, I can afford to build my own theater when we return home. The goings on at Patria have given me plenty of fodder for tales of court intrigue."

"What have you learned?" Solia asked.

"Many things about Lord Severin," Hoyefe said, "but I'll never tell."

"Ah," Lyros mused, "I had a feeling about why he's dreading his upcoming arranged marriage so much."

"Commitment! Duty!" Hoyefe made a face. "The last things Severin needs right now. Fortunately for him, I have many skills and no expectations."

Mak grinned. "Somehow, I can see that melancholy lord falling for your charms, Lonesome."

Hoyefe's aura was pleased as a cat that had caught a mouse. "If I happen to strengthen his determination to resist his father while we are spending time together, well, that is for his benefit as well."

"I certainly understand how romance can make one rebel against one's father," Cassia said.

Lio rested his hand on her knee. "Any word on the king's informant?"

"They're still here," Hoyefe said, "and Flavian is still intercepting their notes, which makes it easy for me to steal them from him."

"Do you think he knows who they are?" Lio asked.

Hoyefe shook his head. "If he did, I believe he would have apprehended them by now. But he knows their route for smuggling the notes out of Patria."

Solia let out a frustrated huff. "Their route might lead us to their identity. This would be so much simpler if Flavian had not decided to make himself my opponent."

Lio asked, "Has he confronted any of you about the missing papers?"

Kella smirked. "He hasn't dared. If he suspects we're the ones who took them, he isn't drawing attention to the fact that we got the better of him."

"What did the latest notes say?" Cassia asked. "Has the spy tried to report Solia's return?"

"Not yet," Hoyefe said.

Cassia pursed her lips. "That could mean they're not someone Flavian has allowed to meet Solia yet."

"Or that they are," Hoyefe replied, "but they are not ready to give their most valuable information to the king, for reasons of their own."

Solia coaxed the flames higher and set out the coffee pot. "Have you found out anything useful about the Dexion?"

"Oh, yes," Hoyefe answered. "After the layers of silence spells all over the Imperial Palace, eavesdropping at Patria is child's play. Even in that fire mage's chambers."

Lio leaned forward. "You found where Flavian is holding him?"

Cassia put a hand on his, a staying gesture. But she needn't worry. He knew how to handle the Dexion.

"The north tower," Hoyefe revealed. "Flavian is out of his depth with that one, to be sure. He thinks he can appease Cordium and keep them out of his affairs without making them his enemy."

"The situation is too far gone for that," Lio said. "They will never stay out of Tenebran affairs unless the new monarch mounts resistance."

"It sounds as if the Dexion is manipulating Flavian," Solia agreed, "making him believe he has the situation under control. What has the Dexion agreed to?"

"To guarantee Cordium will not interfere in the succession," Hoyefe explained, "in return for safe passage back to Corona."

"That promise will last until he kisses his superiors' jeweled shoes in the Divine City," Lio predicted.

"Surely Flavian is not fool enough to believe him?" Cassia asked.

"He hasn't accepted the bargain," Hoyefe replied, "but he did allow Chrysanthos's apprentice to return to Cordium unharmed as a gesture of goodwill."

Lio swore. "Tychon is back with the Orders? No telling what lies he's telling them about the Solstice Summit."

"What's most important is that they not learn of Solia's return," Cassia said. "Has Flavian told the Dexion that?"

"No," Hoyefe answered, "he doesn't want to admit he has a rival at the Council."

Cassia nodded. "He can get a better deal from Chrysanthos if he appears to be sure of his ascension to the throne."

"Is Chrysanthos allowed contact with anyone else?" Lio asked. "Is he permitted correspondence?"

"He writes letters to his nephew," Hoyefe reported. "Each one is read by Sir Benedict to ensure it contains no secrets."

Cassia laughed. "Chrysanthos must hate having his sentimental nonsense to the little boy examined by Ben. It's a good thing Ben can read Divine."

"What does the Dexion want?" Solia asked. "Besides passage home."

"Revenge," Lio said. "He blames me for my role in his brother's death."

"Ah." Solia nodded. "The mage battle at the Equinox Summit."

Cassia looked from her sister to Lio. "Have you two been swapping battle tales?"

"Lio has some good ones," Solia said, "for a scrollworm."

Cassia tightened her hand on Lio's. "Then you understand why he needs to be careful around the Dexion."

"On the contrary, my rose, he is the one who ought to be careful around me." Lio turned to Hoyefe. "Does he know I'm here?"

"Lord Flavian has not seen fit to reveal that detail to him, either," the illusionist replied.

Lio smiled. "Someone ought to pay him a visit that will inconvenience Flavian. We can do that without revealing Solia is here."

"This is a terrible idea," Cassia said.

"I agree," Lyros said. "We should proceed with caution."

"Fire mages don't respond well to caution," Solia said.

"Lio's idea sounds promising," Hoyefe agreed, "but it will have to wait until another night."

"We've also heard from Lord Hadrian," Karege explained. "The Charge and I are passing messages between his camp and Patria. He has sent his batch of Aithourians packing."

"Already?" Mak grinned. "He's efficient."

Lyros smiled as well. "Excellent strategy, Lio. Your idea of letting them take the blame for the attack seems to have worked."

"How soon can we go and ward the camp?" Lio asked.

"Tonight," Karege said.

Lio shook his head. "We need to search for the letting site again tonight."

"I say we ride," Lyros suggested. "We can search another area for the letting site on the way."

"No," Lio said. "It will take most of the night to cast a proper thelemantic ward over the entire camp. That won't leave us enough time to work on Cassia's quest."

"I tire after an hour or so of searching," she said. "We can go to Lord Hadrian's camp after that. We mustn't leave them without protection."

Everything within him rebelled at one more delay. "The Charge can stay on guard for one more night."

She wound her fingers in his. "You said yourself that wards will keep everyone safer than patrols."

"We'll ask the Charge to cast the ward," Lio said. "Rudhira's Field Masters can do it. Zeno is a mind mage, and Tahmina is a powerful warder. Their Grace bond will strengthen the spell."

"I'm afraid it has to be you three." Karege pointed at Lio, Mak, and Lyros. "Lord Hadrian will allow the Charge patrols, but for casting spells near his soldiers, he wants the Hesperines who proved themselves to his men in battle."

Hespera, grant me patience with these stubborn Tenebrans, Lio thought. "Politics tie our hands in both camps!"

"I could try to persuade Lord Hadrian to let the Charge cast the ward," Solia said.

Cassia shook her head. "Lord Hadrian's trust in you has only recently been restored. You must choose wisely about when to push him. And most of all, Tenebrans' trust in Hesperines is new. The fact that Lord Hadrian and his men will accept Hesperine spells at all is astonishing progress."

Lio knew this better than anyone. But still he wracked his mind for an alternative.

Before he could think of one, Tuura spoke. "You should cast the ward tonight. While you're at Hadria, I'll remain on vigil to ensure the Collector doesn't return here."

"Peanut, you're already keeping Patria safe during the day single-handedly. You need a good night's sleep." Karege looked ready to point his fangs at anything that threatened Tuura's well being.

Lio knew that feeling. He also understood how it felt when the magic of the woman you loved complicated the question of immortality. But after they found the letting site, Lio could look forward to Cassia finally joining him as a Hesperine. Karege must have no hope at all, if he didn't even dare drink from Tuura to find out if she was his Grace.

"I can sleep tomorrow night, when Lio is here," Tuura said.

Karege's frown deepened. "The Silence is tiring you. Adjusting your spells for it takes too much effort. You need rest."

Lio hated this. Dealing with the Silence must only remind Karege how impossible it was for Tuura to sacrifice her connection to the ancestors to live forever with him.

Tuura rested her hand on Karege's, a soft gesture, somehow more powerful than the comforting touches she so easily gave to everyone she cared about. "There are causes more important than my comfort."

Not to me. Karege's thoughts said it loud and clear, although he voiced no further protest.

"What do you advise, Lio?" Solia asked.

They were united in this—neither of them wanted to put anything ahead of finding Cassia's magic. He sensed that Solia regretted putting him in this position. He certainly had not expected his first recommendation to her as an adviser to grind against his every instinct to protect his Grace.

But he knew the Collector. And he was determined Pakhne would be the last innocent the necromancer destroyed in this conflict.

"Yes," Lio said. "We should go to Lord Hadrian's camp tonight."

MIRANDA'S MONSTER

TONIGHT THEY APPROACHED LORD Hadrian's camp at a pace that did not make Cassia fear tumbling off Freckles. She was reassured by the sentry who greeted them. Rudhira himself manifested out of the shadows.

"Any sign of the Collector?" Lio asked.

Rudhira shook his head. "There's not a necromancer or any other mage in this camp."

Lio lowered his gaze. "And how is Pakhne?"

Rudhira sighed heavily. "The same. Any luck finding the letting site?"

"Not tonight."

Cassia hated the discouragement in Lio's voice.

"We've ruled out more locations, at least," Mak said.

"Our search patterns are efficient," said Lyros. "We're covering ground quickly."

"How are your symptoms?" Rudhira asked Cassia.

She reached over to squeeze Lio's hand. "I'm not as tired, now that Lio and I can be more deliberate about the channeling."

"Hm," Rudhira replied. "If you can get rid of the mage at Patria as you did here, Kalos could sneak in to help you search for the letting site."

"I'm working on that," Lio promised.

That was what worried Cassia.

Under veils, they rode past the Charge's line of defense to find Lord Hadrian's mortal sentries waiting. Callen stood in the lead of the other men who had witnessed Solia's duel with their lord. Cassia sensed Lio alter his spells to reveal their party only to Callen and his men.

"My Hesperine allies are ready to ward the camp against necromancy," Solia announced. "While they work, I hope Lady Hadrian will receive me in her tent."

Callen bowed. "His Lordship has told Her Ladyship of your arrival. Allow me to escort you to her tent while the rest of my men accompany the spellcasters around the perimeter."

Solia addressed the soldiers. "The Hesperine and Imperial delegations are here to protect us. Heed any instructions they give you while they cast their spells."

The men bowed deeply.

Cassia pulled Freckles as close as she respectably could to Moonflower and lowered her voice. "I'd best go do some politicking in the weaving room while you cast your spells."

Lio leaned closer, as if it were an effort to refrain from touching her. "If any danger arises, call to me in your mind."

She raised a brow. "And if I did call to you while you were still casting, what would happen to your slow, difficult-to-create thelemantic ward?"

"They would collapse, and I would let them, if you needed me to come protect you."

"We do not have time for your spells to collapse. It will take you most of the night to ward a camp of this size. If you have to start over, you'll have to do it tomorrow night, and then everyone here would be left unprotected for yet another day."

His jaw clenched. "Call me if there is danger. Promise me."

She knew he wouldn't budge from her side until she did. "I promise."

He gave a reluctant nod and set off with their Trial brothers, Karege, and Tuura, escorted by the soldiers. Callen led Solia, Cassia, and Kella toward the center of camp.

As they rode along a deserted path behind a rose of tents, Solia asked, "Any words of advice for my first encounter with Lady Hadrian?"

"Only that she missed you," Cassia said. "Your return will bring her as much joy as it has Lord Hadrian."

"I'm glad one of our matriarchs is still among us," said Solia.

"How true," Cassia agreed. "She was always kind to us two motherless daughters."

Kella and Tilili leapt nimbly over a puddle. "She sounds like a woman worthy of respect. What are her political aims?"

Cassia guided Freckles around the patch of mud. "She is as committed to the good of the kingdom as her husband, and she has made as many sacrifices. Perhaps more. Politics keep her separated from their daughters for most of the year."

"Where are they?" Kella asked.

"In Hadria," Cassia answered, "away from the king and his plots. Lady Hadrian is especially proud of her eldest, Sabina, who manages the domain in her parents' absence."

"Ah," Kella said. "Yes, even mothers who are proud of their daughters' accomplishments miss them."

She must be thinking of her own mother, Queen Hinan, but Cassia refrained from asking. Kella was not the sort of woman who liked having her feelings pried into. So Cassia continued, "Lady Hadrian's greatest pleasure is in surrounding herself with young women whom she can mentor, to remind her of her own girls."

"The way to her heart is through her weaving room?" Solia asked.

The first flare of Hesperine magic at the edge of the camp distracted Cassia. Her aura leapt toward Lio's power as if he had just offered her a treat. She tried to focus on her conversation. "What you can learn at Lady Hadrian's feet will help you in every area of leadership. She can ease you back into Tenebran womanhood...without dulling your blades, so to speak."

"Yes," Solia mused, "I seem to recall her and Sabina's figurative blades being quite sharp."

"They still are," Cassia assured her. "And yet they manage to remain above reproach. You will win a great deal of favor with all the women of the Hadrian faction if you do not demand their lady's respect, but show her yours."

Callen drew to a halt by a large tent, where they dismounted and let him take their horses.

"How are Perita and your son?" Cassia asked him.

He gave her the happiest, most foolish smile. "You can ask her yourself, my lady. She's just inside."

"I'm so glad I'll get to see her."

"So is she. I'll be just here if you ladies need anything." Callen stepped aside to stand guard nearby and busied himself with tethering their mounts.

Solia faced the tent flap. "Why does the weaving room seem more challenging than a duel with Lord Hadrian?"

"Don't worry," Kella said. "Remember that time we had to infiltrate a Queen Mother's court to extricate Hoyefe from her harem? You conducted yourself like a lady."

"Did Hoyefe wish to be extracted?" Cassia asked.

"Not really." Solia snickered. "I don't think Lady Hadrian has any nude male dancers for us tonight, alas."

Kella tsked. "Tenebra is such a boring kingdom."

"But you're right," Solia said. "I didn't do too badly at the Azarqi council whenever I accompanied you, did I?"

Kella's humor faded. "No gaggle of Tenebran ladies could be as much of a challenge as the Azarqi matriarchs."

They slipped inside Lady Hadrian's tent. The woman with the greatest influence in the kingdom sat at her travel loom beside a small fire pit. The tent was appointed with her hand-woven blankets and cushions, an island of ladylike comfort in the ascetic military camp. Perita rested in a quiet corner on a cot, and Miranda and the other handmaidens appeared to be waiting on her and the babe as much as their ladies.

Sabina sat across from her mother at her own loom, looking just as Lady Hadrian must have at that age. Tenebra's most eligible, unattainable lady had a full figure, long, wavy brown hair, and her mother's poise. But also her father's temper.

Cassia had been right. Sabina would not stay at home when she could wage her own battle. The question was, was she fighting for Flavian?

Cassia must find out, for Sabina might be her and Lio's best hope of freeing her from her betrothal.

Upon Solia's entrance, Lady Hadrian pressed a hand to her mouth, and Sabina leapt to her feet. Then with more dignity, the two women fell into deep curtsies before Solia. Behind them, their handmaidens knelt, while Perita bowed her head.

"Your Majesty," Lady Hadrian said.

Your Majesty. Your Majesty. The murmurs moved through the tent on the lips of the women of Tenebra. It became a measure more real to Cassia. Her sister would be queen. If they succeeded.

"Please, Lady Hadrian," Solia said. "Rise and let me embrace you."

"You honor me, My Queen." Lady Hadrian stood and held Solia to her. "When my lord told us the news, I could scarcely believe it...but here you are in my arms again."

When they released each other at last, Solia gave Lady Hadrian a curtsy of her own. "As a girl, I spent so many happy hours in your weaving room, learning from your example. May I join you around your loom once again?"

Lady Hadrian's eyes shone with tears. "It would be my great joy."

Solia held out her hands to Sabina. "I hope we can renew our friendship."

"Of course, My Queen." Sabina took her hands without hesitation, but her gray eyes were shuttered.

Whatever reservations Sabina harbored, overcoming them might prove to be the key to breaking Cassia's betrothal to Flavian.

Lady Hadrian welcomed Kella as warmly as Solia and Cassia, and they all settled around the fire to speak where men couldn't hear. A time-honored tradition, whether among Tenebran ladies in a free lord's camp or Azarqi trader-queens in their nomad tents. They exchanged pleasantries that acknowledged each other's power and paid compliments to rekindle years of respect. They demurred, wearing masks of weakness to conceal their hidden strengths and preserve their advantage of surprise.

When Cassia was satisfied that Kella and Solia were holding their own, she excused herself to sit with Perita. Despite how Cassia hated returning to Tenebra, here was a happiness she had never dared hope for. "Oh, it's so good to see you again."

Her friend beamed, looking more like herself, her light brown curls tucked under a clean kerchief. "I didn't think you'd ever be back in Tenebra, my lady."

"Neither did I."

"I'm so glad you get to meet him." Perita resettled the dozing infant in her arms.

Cassia looked into his small, wrinkly face. His world appeared very simple. He was as close as possible to his mama, and that was all that seemed to matter.

"He is remarkable," Cassia said.

"Say hello to my lady," Perita cooed.

Cassia touched the impossibly soft skin of his tiny hand. He wrapped all his warm little fingers around one of hers and made an endearing nonsense sound.

His first day in this life should never have been so dangerous. Cassia would not let Perita and her family come that close to the Collector again. She must find a way. "I wish you two would go somewhere safer."

"Nowhere is safe," Perita replied. "The king is consorting with all sorts of foul mages. Who knows when a stray spell will fall on the head of a commoner who's in the wrong place at the wrong time? If civil war breaks out, I'm staying as close to Callen as I can."

Cassia wanted to argue, but she couldn't. No one could pry her from Lio's side in the face of danger, either. "I understand."

"Of course you do, always putting yourself in the thick of things. Like the other night." A shudder went through Perita, but then she gathered her composure. "You meant what you said about the Hesperines honoring their life debt to Callen and me. Or bond of gratitude, I suppose they call it. "

"How are you feeling?" Cassia asked.

"Like I want to get off this cot and get to work. That Hesperine healing is something else, my lady. Now I know why Callen wouldn't stop dancing around the room with me after Queen Soteira fixed his knee."

"You are not to put your feet to the floor. I see the other handmaidens are in firm agreement about this," Cassia said, as Lady Miranda approached with a cup of something for Perita to drink. Cassia offered the young woman a smile.

Miranda ducked her head, searching for somewhere to put the cup down as if she were in a hurry to leave.

"I'll take it, if you have duties elsewhere," Cassia offered.

"She doesn't," Perita said, "or if she does, I dare say Lady Sabina will forgive us for delaying her. Sit with us, Miranda."

"I really must return to my duties." Miranda pressed the cup into Cassia's hands as if she feared being burned, then with a hasty curtsy, went to rejoin Sabina by the fire.

"I'm sorry, my lady," Perita said with a frown. "I don't know what's gotten into her. After I've sung your praises to her all this time, I thought she'd be nearly as thrilled as I am to have you here."

"I can hardly blame her," Cassia said. "I have never been well liked among the women of Tenebra. If it isn't my illegitimate birth, it's my betrothal or my political ambitions. If it isn't any of that, it's the fact that I gave her a scare in the company of heretics."

Perita shook her head. "She's more sensible than superstitious. I've told her all about what Orthros is really like, and she believes me."

"So she has no particular animosity toward Hesperines?"

"No," Perita said, "she's better acquainted with monsters of the human sort. You understand."

"All too well. It sounds as if Miranda and I have some things in common."

"She's naturally cautious, like you," Perita said. "Give her some time to make up her mind about you, and she'll come around."

"I take it she's a dear friend of yours."

"Miranda is one of the good ones, my lady. You can trust her."

"I could see that from how bravely she defended you," Cassia replied. "How did you two meet?"

"Well, my lady, since Callen and I began helping you with your schemes, we've been...making friends, shall we say, in lots of places. Folk who see things the way we do, who have no love for the king and the Mage Orders. It's not just lords and ladies who make alliances, you see. And it's not the powerful folk who keep households running. Even if there's a civil war, somebody's got to do the laundry, and you'd best hope the person washing your underlinens hasn't been kissing the king's arse."

Cassia laughed. "Oh, Perita, I missed you so much."

Perita grinned. "Gods know I missed you, too."

"You are the best judge of character," Cassia said. "A friend of yours is a friend of mine. I only hope Miranda will come to see it that way."

"I'm certain she will. She'll have plenty of opportunities. We're Lady Sabina's handmaidens now, so you'll be seeing a great deal of us."

Cassia raised a brow. "Congratulations, my friend. Moving up in the world."

Perita lowered her voice. "There is nowhere higher to go than being your handmaiden."

Cassia still thought a free lord's heiress counted as higher than a bastard, even a king's bastard. But she appreciated her friend's sentiment. "I must admit, I rather like not being your lady anymore. Now we can simply be friends."

"Don't expect me to drop the title. You'll always be my lady." The way Perita said it, it sounded more like an affectionate name than an honorific.

Cassia lifted her medallion to show her friend. "But it is Ambassador Cassia now. Lio and I are partners in the diplomatic service."

"Well, that does suit you!" But Perita looked rather serious now. "And how are you feeling?"

No easy question to answer. *I wish my sister didn't want the throne. I'm going to be a powerful mage, if I survive that long. I want to go home.*

Perita's frown deepened. "Are you as happy in Orthros as you expected to be?"

That was easy to answer, though. "Oh, Perita, I am. I couldn't be happier."

"Ambassador Toothy's shine hasn't worn off now that you're with him all the time?"

Cassia laughed. "Far from it."

She told Perita all about what life was like in Orthros, and how the revelation of Solia's survival had interrupted it. She described the Empire and what they had gone through to bring Solia back.

Perita shook her head. "Well, I suppose Lord Lusty Breeches wouldn't have made a terrible king, but it's a relief we won't have to put up with a Segetian on the throne."

"I only hope everyone else will see it that way," Cassia said.

"My lady, look where you are. There isn't a soul in Lord Hadrian's camp who isn't rejoicing."

Cassia had questions about that, but she didn't wish to place Perita in a difficult position between their friendship and her new loyalty to Sabina. Cassia cast a surreptitious glance at Sabina while she was occupied in conversation with Kella.

"You own your tents?" Sabina asked, clearly fascinated.

Kella swept her braids over her shoulder. "An Azarqi woman's home belongs to her. Granted, our husbands own our camels. But that offers a man little comfort if his wife decides she's done with him, and she packs up her tents and leaves him stranded in the desert with only his camels for company."

The ladies around the fire burst out laughing.

"Azarqi women can do that?" Miranda asked. "Leave their husbands?"

"That's how my marriage ended." Kella had taken up a spare hand loom, and her blue fingers raced across the warp and weft in an Azarqi pattern. "We were divorced the moment I packed up my tents, under Azarqi law. He didn't dare try to follow me, but even if he had, Tilili is faster than a camel."

The handmaidens' scandalized laughter grew louder, and Lady Hadrian's smile suggested she was laughing loudest of all, if silently. But when Miranda caught Cassia looking at her, her laughter rang false. For an instant, their gazes met, and Cassia saw the emotion in the young woman's eyes.

Fear.

Then her demure handmaiden mask was once more in place.

A terrible realization settled over Cassia. If Miranda was not afraid of Hesperines, there could be only one explanation. She was afraid of Cassia.

Cassia knew she had ruined reputations when bartering information for her own gain. She had gotten servants chastised by their lieges for her own indiscretions. In her never-ending battle to escape the king's deadly anger and his many, tiny cruelties, Cassia had committed so many cruelties of her own.

Was she Miranda's monster?

When Cassia's Gifting visions forced her to relive her past, would she experience Miranda's pain? She would not wait to find out on that night. She needed to learn the truth about how she had wronged Miranda while there was still time to make it right.

Cassia knew how difficult it would be to convince Miranda to open up to her. She herself had once been just that untrusting.

There were so many disastrous consequences of her past actions still to solve. Miranda would need time, but right now, Cassia must seize her opportunity to escape her betrothal.

She decided to try asking Perita how things stood between Sabina and Flavian. "How does a certain lady feel about Lord Lusty Breeches' role in all of this?"

Perita lowered her voice. "Those two are more star-crossed than you and your Hesperine ever were. I don't know what to do with them. But I dare say you and I can sort out the mess."

Cassia breathed a sigh of relief. For the first time since seeing Flavian again, she felt real hope. "If anyone can, it's you and I. But it won't be easy. I'm afraid I'm still very much betrothed."

"I know," Perita said darkly.

"Might you have any information that could help get me out of it?"

"Hmm. Give me some time to think. Lady Sabina may have let slip a few things that could be useful. If you think I have irreverent names for people, you should hear what she says about Lord Lusty Breeches when no one but Miranda and I are listening."

Cassia stifled a laugh. "I don't blame her for being furious at him. Do you think she still wants to continue their affair?"

"If she didn't, she wouldn't have a reason to be angry."

"What do you suppose her ideal outcome would be?" Cassia asked.

Perita sighed. "I'm not sure she and that idiot even know. They're trying to make the best of what they can manage."

"Well, I can do better than that."

"Oh, my lady, you have that look in your eye. How can I help?"

"Don't you think Lady Sabina's talents would be better put to use at the Full Council than here in Lord Hadrian's camp?"

"Oh, no doubt. May I make a suggestion, my lady?"

"You never have to ask, my friend. I love your suggestions."

"In that case, I think the first step is reminding her you're on her side. Just as you did the night of the Autumn Greeting, when you told her you didn't mind your husband-to-be dropping his breeches for her instead."

"That I can certainly do." Cassia touched her friend's arm. "I want you with me at Patria too, where the Hesperines can protect you and your family."

Her gaze fell to her son. "I don't deny I'd rather be as close to you and your Hesperines as possible, and if I go with Lady Sabina, it won't be disloyal."

Sabina had retreated to a corner of the tent, apparently to search through a basket of thread. Was she giving herself an opportunity to control her temper?

Cassia crossed the tent toward her. When Miranda took that opportunity to go sit with Perita, Cassia suppressed a wince of regret. She longed to say something now, but she must plan a more careful approach so she did not make Miranda feel threatened.

Cassia picked up a skein of thread that had escaped Sabina's basket and offered it to her. "I thought I might find you outside of Hadria at a time like this."

"It's a rare and exciting opportunity to travel." Sabina dropped the thread into the basket and sorted through the colors.

"Have you considered traveling to Patria?"

Sabina picked at the tangled threads with practiced fingers. "I thought you'd never ask."

"We reserved a seat for you."

"Ah yes, a seat at the long, slow negotiations. Now that there are two contenders for the Council's mandate, you face a painful process. It could be Autumn Equinox before anything is decided."

Cassia woke to that dread each and every day. Autumn Equinox would mean the return of her family to this side of Akanthia—but also Princess Konstantina's plan to bring the Departure up for a vote. If the succession of Tenebra was still uncertain by then, what would Orthros's firstbloods decide to do?

Sabina defeated the knot, smoothing out the separated threads. "I understand you lost Lord Deverran's vote. What a shame."

Cassia's anxiety mounted. "What else did Nivalis tell you?"

"She blames you and Ambassador Deukalion for what happened to Pakhne. But I've spoken to my father, and I know that's not the case."

"Someone from Hadria could help Nivalis understand."

"Yes, you clearly need Hadrian support against Flavian. Someone who can influence everyone in our faction to vote for your sister. But not too much Hadria, or you will scare off your Segetian partisans as well."

"Your father does have that effect."

"He must not set foot at Patria until the moment is right. When he joins the Council, the king will know he has lost. Lucis will intervene. That cannot happen until your sister is ready to face him."

Cassia nodded. "Astute as always."

She was tempted to ask Sabina what she wanted. But no, that was not the right approach with this lady. Some liked to be courted. Sabina liked to do the courting. Cassia waited for her to make her move.

Sabina paused to select another color of thread from the basket. She unwound a Hadrian blue. "You need me. I can quietly accompany you back to Patria. My presence will make it clear to everyone where we stand without inciting a feud."

"We are your allies," Cassia promised. "We will support your goals in return."

"So would that idiot, you know." The spark of anger in Sabina's gaze suggested she was thinking irreverent names again.

"Of course. I have no doubt that you would have him falling at your feet, serving up anything you wish on a golden tray. But I also know you will not join his side against Hadria."

Sabina laughed. "I wouldn't have to. I could sit here and continue weaving, while you and your sister are surrounded by Flavian's supporters, with no reinforcements from Hadria."

Cassia hated how true that was. But she respected that Sabina knew the worth of her favor and would not let Cassia or Solia undervalue it. "My sister is in a position to support Hadria in ways Flavian cannot dream of."

"But is she in a position to support me?"

"If the support you require is of a more personal nature, I assure you, my sister and I are both doing our best to dissolve my betrothal to Flavian."

"Oh, I'm sure you are. But not for my sake."

"Of course for you. I hope my past assurances are proof of that."

Sabina's eyes only flashed with greater anger.

Cassia considered her words. Sabina took after her father, so Cassia risked speaking bluntly. "I gave you my blessing to have an affair with the man I thought I was going to marry. What further proof of my good intentions do you wish for?"

Sabina tugged on two viciously tangled colors and made a little sound of frustration too low for anyone but Cassia to hear.

"I will never marry him," Cassia insisted, "and neither will my sister. I want to make that very clear."

"She shared the Fire Dance with him," Sabina hissed.

Cassia suppressed a groan. She had known they would pay for her failure to prevent that. Once again, she found her own plots backing her into a corner.

"She has shared many more dances with Lord Hoyefe," Cassia said.

"But not the Fire Dance."

It would take more than Hoyefe's flirtation to overcome the cultural significance of that. Solia would not thank Cassia for what she was about to say. But Cassia was not above stirring some rumors in Tendo's favor, whether he and Solia liked it or not.

"My sister has an understanding with an Imperial prince," Cassia murmured. "His brother rules one of the most powerful kingdoms in the Empire."

"Yes, well, whoever he is, he's on the other side of the Demussavi Ocean. Do you expect us to believe Her Majesty will not seize the powerful free lord in the hand instead of the mythical Imperial prince in the bush?"

"I've met him. I promise you, he would never let Flavian marry Solia."

"The lords of Tenebra will never let a foreigner marry their queen and occupy their throne."

The lords of Tenebra had not met Tendeso of the Sandira Kingdom. Cassia knew that if Monsoon decided he wanted something, the oafs of the shadowlands would not stand a chance against him.

But it was clear Cassia would not succeed in persuading anyone of that tonight, least of all Tendo and Soli. Cassia would have to change Sabina's mind some other way.

There was one fact she was certain would alter Sabina's opinion of her forever. But it could also come back on Cassia and everyone she loved more dangerously than any other revelation.

If Sabina chose Flavian's side and told him what Cassia was about to reveal to her… She and Lio could lose everything.

Cassia stood frozen with indecision for a long moment. She had no time to ask Lio if he would agree to this. Just as he'd had no opportunity to discuss it with her before he had confided in Eudias.

She had understood his decision then. Surely he would understand hers now.

Her palms sweating, Cassia said, "I'm in love with someone else."

Sabina went still and stared at her.

Cassia let out a humorless laugh. "You look as if you find this hard to believe. Does everyone truly believe I am so cold?"

Sabina huffed. "Cold? Hardly. You're dangerous when you get that fire in your eyes. But I doubt you have any use for sentimental attachments, except to spin a tale to win my sympathy."

"Did you have any use for sentimental attachments that summer in Saxara when you met Flavian? Did you expect to fall in love with the last person in the world you are supposed to want?"

Sabina hesitated.

Cassia blurted, "My forbidden person and I had a winter in Solorum."

Sabina's hand lowered, her thread forgotten in the basket. "Good Goddess. I think you're telling the truth. Winter…at Solorum…" Her eyes widened.

Sabina glanced over her shoulder and pulled Cassia farther into the corner of the tent, behind a tapestry on a rack. "The Equinox Summit? *The Hesperine ambassador?*"

"Lio's feelings are not one-sided. He is as important to me as I am to him."

It stung a bit, how stunned Sabina looked. "That's why you did all of this? It wasn't some political scheme we can barely understand? It was an affair?"

"It was love." Cassia suspected *we* in this case meant Sabina and Flavian. They had spoken at some point, and Sabina had shared his suspicions about Cassia's motives.

Now Sabina laughed. "Well, you are human, after all."

"Not for much longer," Cassia snapped. "I should be a Hesperine right now, but I came back to help my sister. And no, it's not because I want power and immortality and all that nonsense. I only want to stay with Lio."

"Only a fool would believe that immortality is your reason for going to these lengths. It's not that difficult to get transformed into a Hesperine. But to secure a match with a Hesperine ambassador? Yes. That would require reshaping a kingdom."

"Now do you understand?" Cassia asked. "This is my goodwill gesture. This is something valuable you can use against me, if I don't uphold my end of the bargain. Please, take me at my word. Solia is only interested in her Imperial, and I in my Hesperine. She intends to rule without her power hinging on any man, least of all Flavian."

Sabina's gaze sharpened. "If I joined you at Patria, I trust your sister and I would have the opportunity to speak about what I envision for Tenebra's future—and my own."

"You are precisely the kind of lady she hopes will help her establish that future."

"Very well," Sabina said. "Your sister has my partisanship."

Cassia had best make sure they never lost it, and with it, Sabina's discretion about Lio. Had Cassia done the right thing? She could only hope so as Sabina accompanied her back to the fireside and wove them into her mother's conversation with Solia and Kella.

"Do you remember, my dear?" Lady Hadrian asked with fondness in her eyes. "That visit when we were all at Hadria was one of the happiest times of my life. I still have the tapestry you and Princess Solia wove for me."

"We did so much weaving together." Sabina offered Solia a conspiratorial smile. "When we weren't sneaking out to watch the men at sword training."

"Then your father caught us," Solia said with a laugh, "and we didn't have to sneak any longer."

Sabina reached out and offered her hands to Solia. Solia took them, a hint of vulnerable hope in her eyes. She needed Sabina's political support, of course. But she also wanted a friend.

"Mother," Sabina said, "now that our queen has returned, I do not wish to be parted from her. Will you and father permit me to return to Patria with Her Majesty?"

Lady Hadrian's happiness faded.

"Callen could go as Lady Sabina's bodyguard," Cassia suggested, "and with Hesperine help, it would be safe to bring Perita with us as well. Naturally Lady Sabina will want her handmaiden Miranda with her as well."

Sabina appeared pleased with this idea. "There is no one else I would rather have at my side at a time like this."

"I fear sending my girls into that den of predators," Lady Hadrian said, "although I know you are equal to it."

"I know, Mother, but I cannot in good conscience remain here while our queen faces her Segetian challenger alone."

Solia put a hand on Lady Hadrian's. "And we can all look forward to a future when politics no longer keep us apart."

Lady Hadrian's expression steeled. "We will do anything we must for that day. You have my blessing, Sabina. But you know you must secure your father's."

Sabina's tone was gentle. "I shall ask his permission now."

"You intend to return to Patria with our queen tonight?" Lady Hadrian asked with composure that was surely hiding pain.

"I know it's too soon," her daughter said, "but it will only be for the duration of the negotiations. As soon as the Council comes to a vote, you and Father can join us."

Lady Hadrian found a smile. "I am so proud of you."

Cassia had never seen Sabina near tears, unless they were tears of anger, but now she blinked hard at her mother's praise.

Callen escorted Sabina, Solia, and Cassia to a neighboring tent and ushered them in, remaining outside to stand guard. Upon their entrance, Lord Hadrian looked up from the map on the trestle table before him and bowed to Solia. "How can I serve, My Queen?"

"A personal matter," Solia replied with a smile. "It is your daughter who has a request for you, my lord."

He circled the table to sit against the edge of it. The wry smile he gave Sabina was full of familiar affection. How different a father he was than the king.

"I know that look," he said. "Do you wish to replace my favorite steward again?"

"Something even more disruptive, I'm afraid," Sabina replied. "I wish to accompany Her Majesty to Patria."

Lord Hadrian rubbed his salt and pepper beard. "And what does our queen say to this?"

"I would love nothing better than to have Sabina at my side," Solia replied. "Rightfully, she should be the first lady of Tenebra to join my retinue. But I will not overrule you in this, my lord. Such a decision regarding your own household must be yours to make."

Before he could answer, Callen burst into the tent. At the sight of his sword in his hand, Cassia's heart leapt into her throat. Solia's and Lord Hadrian's hands were already on their hilts.

"The king is coming," Callen announced.

FAMILY REUNION

INSTINCTIVE NAUSEA ROSE IN Cassia's throat. Sweat broke out between her shoulder blades. She wanted to flee like a prey animal.

Then she felt Solia clasp her wrist. Her own hand landed on Solia's wrist in return, and she felt her sister's pulse racing with the same fear.

Their gazes met. She saw courage in Solia's eyes. For the first time in fifteen years, they would face this fear together.

"Where is he?" Lord Hadrian asked.

"Coming down the hill from the west," Callen reported, out of breath.

"Why didn't our scouts spot him sooner?" Lord Hadrian demanded. "Does he have mages with him?"

Callen shook his head. "No robes in his party, my lord. Otherwise I'd swear there's magic at work."

As Cassia's first flash of panic faded, new horror came over her. Lord Hadrian didn't realize.

Cassia and Solia were not the ones in the greatest danger from the king. The Hesperines were. They had rid the camp of Aithourians—only for a fire mage to descend upon them.

She felt Lio in her mind, a glancing touch that told her most of his concentration was still on his spell. But he knew something was wrong.

With an act of Will, she focused all her fear on one thought and pushed it in Lio's direction. *Don't stop casting.*

"He must not find any of you," Lord Hadrian urged. "Sabina will help you escape."

Sabina hastened Solia and Cassia toward the tent flap. "The king believes I'm at Hadria, so I'm coming with you."

Cassia shook her head. "I must get to the Hesperines."

"I'll send someone." Lord Hadrian motioned for her and Solia to hurry.

The plan began to take shape in Cassia's mind. "No. It has to be me. There's no time to explain. Please, Lord Hadrian, ride out to meet the king. Delay his arrival."

"I'm coming with you," Solia said.

"My Queen!" Lord Hadrian protested. "You must go."

"Distract the king," Solia bade him.

His face etched with worry, Lord Hadrian bowed his head. "As you will."

Sabina did not argue. "Miranda and I will have the horses ready and waiting for you outside the camp. Come find us as soon as you can."

Cassia tried not to imagine what might happen if the king discovered the Hadrians were harboring them. "Will you keep Knight with you?"

"I would be glad for his protection," Sabina said.

Cassia commanded her hound to guard Sabina, then ducked out of the tent with her sister.

"This way." Cassia took Solia's hand and guided her toward the northwest, pulling them behind a tent that would hide them from view. "Can you traverse?"

"I don't dare with the king this close. My scarf will hide small spells, but not a traversal. Can the Hesperines veil us?"

"I don't want to risk it. They need to focus on their spells. Time for mundane stealth." Cassia hurried forward along the back of the tent.

"What's your plan?" Solia asked. "Why can't you send Lio a mental warning?"

"I am." Cassia Willed him to heed her. *Don't stop casting.* "I'm telling him not to let the ward collapse."

"You want them to finish the ward under the king's nose? This is madness!"

"They must finish now. What if the king is trying to smuggle in one of the Collector's victims—or worse, an Overseer?"

Solia swore, but followed Cassia between the next two tents. "What can we do to help them with the ward?"

"Does your scarf work on others besides you?"

"Yes, but—"

"We'll need that. And my channeling—if it works the way I believe it will."

At the sound of hoofbeats and voices from beyond the camp, Cassia skidded to a halt at the corner of a tent.

The king was almost here.

She kept her focus on the current of magic leading her to her Grace. "Can you sense the king's aura?"

"Yes," Solia said with disgust. "I've always been sensitive to his aura because of our shared affinity."

Cassia shuddered. "I'm sorry."

"Don't be. He doesn't know about my magic, but I can always feel his. It gives us the advantage."

Cassia was about to dart into an aisle between the tents when a band of Lord Hadrian's soldiers marched into sight, heading toward the commotion at the edge of camp. Cassia caught Solia's hand and pulled her behind a stack of supply crates.

Under the tramping of the soldier's boots, Cassia murmured, "How much like an Aithourian is the king's magic?"

"He was never formally trained," Solia whispered back. "That's why his magic is more unstable than mine. But he has learned some vicious skills from rogue apostates he studied with in secret."

"Spells to detect Hesperines?" Cassia asked.

"I don't know. It's possible."

Cassia sent up a prayer to Hespera before she and her sister ran across the aisle to the shelter of the next row of tents.

They raced through the night, dodging puddles from a summer rain. Ducking away from Lord Hadrian's unsuspecting men, they caught snatches of the worried conversations from inside the tents they passed. The threat of the king loomed around every corner. The fear of losing someone she loved was a vice around Cassia's chest.

It was so much like that night when she had lost her sister.

Cassia clutched Solia's hand. Tonight, they were together. And they would not lose anyone.

Cassia would protect her Hesperines from the king.

Lio's alarm filled mind ward. He knew the king was coming.

Don't. Stop. Casting. She pleaded. *Trust my judgment this time.*

Blood magic throbbed in her arcane senses, growing stronger.

Just ahead, Cassia could see an opening, the central road through the camp. They would have to cross it to reach where the Hesperines were casting.

Lord Hadrian rode through at a gallop leading another band of his men. Every surrounding soldier's eye was on their lord. Cassia and Solia wasted precious instants waiting for them to pass, and for the rest of the army to turn their attention back to preparing for the king's arrival.

"How close is he?" Cassia whispered.

"Almost at the perimeter," Solia warned.

At last Cassia and Solia dared hurry out onto the road in a low crouch. Cassia held her breath. So many eyes. All it took was one pair to see them and tell the approaching king.

The shadows on the other side of the road engulfed them, and she heaved a sigh. Just a few more tents. A few more paces. Almost there.

They burst out of the camp and into the reach of Lio's veil spells. Mak and Lyros stood with blood dripping from their joined hands. Across from them, Lio held his hands outstretched over their line of blood, his casting a silent act of Will. Cassia could not see his magic with her eyes, but it filled her arcane senses. She felt it as heated threads of light and shadow, heard it whirling around him as crystalline echoes. It spun into the ward that was taking shape between him and their Trial brothers.

The resting current throbbed with demand, but Cassia wrestled it back. She careened to a halt before Lio.

He met her gaze, his eyes solid blue and shining with light magic. "The Charge is reinforcing my veils, but if the king knows Aithourian spells..."

"This much magic will be too hard to hide," Cassia finished. "I have an idea. Take a risk with me?"

"Always," he promised.

She spun to face her sister. "Solia, is there a way to get your scarf around you, Mak, and Lyros at the same time?"

"This might actually work." Solia slipped her scarf down from her shoulders to wind it around her wrist.

She closed her fist around Mak and Lyros's joined hands and bound the three of them together, their bright red blood soaking into the golden scarf.

The sense of magic in the air became less overpowering, and Cassia felt hope.

"You're dampening the magic," Lio said in understanding, "trying to reduce it so the veils will be enough to hide it."

She thought he guessed what came next, but she warned him to be sure. "I'm going to try channeling the magic that's coming off your spell. Brace yourself."

When he, Mak and Lyros nodded, Cassia drew a deep breath and took Lio's hand.

A jolt of power shot through their joined hands and rocked her entire body. She felt Mak and Lyros and her sister. Rudhira and his Chargers hidden nearby. Most of all, Lio, her link to them all. She braced her feet, gripping his hand hard, and let herself flow into the current.

The spell was more than the line of shadows and thelemancy Lio and their Trial brothers were building. That was merely the center of the star, which shone far into the night. Cassia must dim that glow without disrupting the spell itself. If she channeled too much, surely she would collapse the ward.

Lord Hadrian and his men rode out of the camp. On the hill above, horses appeared and began to descend. The rider in the lead was a white-haired figure in a cloak of sky blue and gold.

With all the focus she had honed in Lio's arms, Cassia gathered the spell's glow to her and pulled.

Starfire shrank in on her and burst through her veins. She bit her tongue to hold in an exhilarated cry at the power shining through her. The night went dark, the air quiet and calm.

"*Yes,*" came Lio's voice in her ears and her mind, "*it's working, Cassia!*"

He and their Trial brothers poured more magic into their spell, and it overflowed into her.

Through the glare of magic consuming her senses, she watched Lord Hadrian draw rein before the king and give his respectful greetings to the tyrant they all hated.

Her mother's murderer was mere paces away from her and the people she loved.

The king no longer sat in his solar issuing threats. He was astride his warhorse, his armor gleaming in the light of his soldier's torches. His sword was not hanging on the wall, but strapped at his side, his gnarled hand resting on the hilt.

Cassia's gaze landed on the old burn scar on his jaw that marred his white beard. For the first time, she wondered if he had wounded himself on his own uncontrolled magic.

The magic thundering through her felt like a battle cry challenging him, but he didn't look her way.

The voice that had haunted her nightmares now reached her ears for the first time in months. "Imagine my surprise when I was expecting a report that all is well in your camp, and instead I received seven angered Aithourians."

Through the magic connecting them, Cassia sensed Lio's tension. Was his effort to rid them of the mages about to come back on them?

"All is not well," Lord Hadrian said. "Your Majesty requires truthful reports from me. Mages who call themselves our allies caused the deaths of my men."

Blunt and truthful though he might be, Lord Hadrian was still adroit at twisting his words.

The king's voice was gruff as always, but sounded hoarser than she recalled. "Our allies from the Magelands would prefer we handle such accidents with discretion."

"With respect, Your Majesty, there is nothing discreet about lives wasted due to friendly fire."

"And what of lives endangered by Hesperines? We know they are at large in the area. Without the Aithourians, how will you protect my armies from these creatures?"

More power poured through Cassia, and sweat broke out on her skin. Mak and Lyros's line of blood trickled across the grass, as if the magic gave it a life of its own. On the other side of the king and Lord Hadrian, she could see the dark red stain where the Stewards' circle had begun.

Lord Hadrian stood his ground. "Your Majesty knows I am wholly devoted to preserving peace in your kingdom. I cannot do so with those mages in my camp. I have six grieving families to answer to. The Aithourians should consider themselves lucky that I am too loyal to my king to hold them accountable under Hadrian justice."

The king urged his horse alongside Hadrian's until he was staring the lord in the face. "Yes, you have long held the distinction of being the most loyal man in Tenebra. I have never punished you for speaking freely before me. But if you are hiding something, do not imagine you are above my justice."

Cassia gritted her teeth against the force of the spell, against the danger unfolding before her, beyond her control. They could not afford for Lord Hadrian to fall from grace now.

If the king drew his sword, Lord Hadrian would need all their power on his side. This would turn into not only a bloodbath, but a mage duel.

"If Your Majesty is displeased with my performance, I will exile myself to Hadria. I can disband my force this very night and relinquish my camp to our Cordian allies."

A perfect counterattack. The king well knew that Lord Hadrian's army was all that stood between him and the rebellion brewing at Patria, and seven Aithourians would not be enough to protect him.

"I want a tour of your camp," the king demanded. "I must search it for threats and personally ensure that you will be safe without Aithourian assistance."

"We are making ready for you as we speak," Lord Hadrian replied calmly.

"I know your men are always prepared. I'm sure we need not delay. Take me through the camp now." It was not an invitation.

Lord Hadrian had no choice but to turn his horse and ride toward the camp. Toward that last gap in the circle of blood.

The line of blood snaked its crimson, glowing tendrils behind Lord Hadrian's mount. The unseen nip at its heels made the horse dance forward. Lord Hadrian tightened his hand on his reins.

The king looked away from Lord Hadrian, his gaze scanning their surroundings.

And then Cassia felt it. It was so much worse than any Aithourian magic she had ever encountered. The spell that snapped out of the king was wrong. Sick. A twisted, burning thing that smelled of fear and rage.

He was evil to his core. Even his magic was corrupted by his cruelty.

But she had magic of her own, now. Real power to protect her sister and her Grace and their Hesperine family.

She watched the king's magic sweep over them. First Mak and Lyros, who bared their fangs. Then Solia, her knuckles white on the hilt of her sword.

Then it hit Cassia. It burned her skin and made her sweat like every time he forced her to kneel before him. Her stomach flipped, and bile rose in her throat.

Lio tightened his hand in hers, his magic swelling, and she bit back a cry of effort as she held his spell within her shaking frame. Hesperine magic shone, blinding, inside her, her skin and bones the only veil that concealed it from the king's probing curse.

And then the fire banked, and she felt cool air on her skin, and she breathed.

The Hesperines' Wills pushed that line of red in the grass the final distance. Solia focused with them. When blood met blood, the circle fused, and the structure of the spell flashed in Cassia's mind's eye like a shield of glass and adamas.

The magic drained out of her and into the ward, and the strength left her limbs. Lio scooped her up and clutched her close to his chest.

From his arms, she watched the king ride through the thelemantic ward and disappear among the tents.

When the last of Lucis's soldiers crossed the now-invisible barrier, Lio said, "The Collector is not among them."

He hadn't come tonight. But he would. And when he did, their ward would be in place.

Mak and Lyros gathered near, and Solia rubbed Cassia's hand in both of hers, giving no regard to the bloodstains. "Are you all right?"

"I have never been better." Cassia smiled viciously. "I just defeated the king with my magic for the first time."

"That was incredible." Lio's praise was the last thing she heard before she slipped into unconsciousness.

When Cassia came to, the world was moving. No, a horse was moving under her. She was sitting sidesaddle on Solia's big golden steed, and her sister held her close.

"Sorry you can't ride with your sweetheart," Solia murmured. "Too scandalous in front of our audience."

Lio and Kella rode to Solia's left, with Sabina and Miranda on the right, a pack horse trailing behind them. Knight trotted alongside Solia's horse, and at the first sign of movement from Cassia, he licked her shoe.

She gave him an affectionate nudge with her toe. "Don't lie, Soli. You were worried about me and wanted to hold me, as if I'm still seven."

"All right," Solia admitted, "yes. Your Hesperine was gracious enough to relinquish you in the name of elder sister privilege."

Cassia smiled and rested her face against Solia's shoulder. They had just faced the king, and she had spent her strength in an act of magic. She would allow herself some childlike comfort for a moment.

Solia's arms tightened around her. "I'm proud of you."

"Thank you, Soli."

"Ambassador Cassia, how are you feeling?" came Lio's appropriate inquiry, along with a gentle touch in her mind.

She sent him reassuring thoughts. "Better, thank you, Ambassador Deukalion."

"The Hesperine delegation is grateful to you for finding us under our veils to warn us of the king's arrival. Thank you for telling us about the anti-Hesperine charms he secretly carries. They would surely have revealed us to him."

Ah, charms. An excellent way to avoid explaining *by the by, the king is secretly an apostate mage who could have immolated us tonight.* Cassia played along. "Of course. We cannot have him chasing off our Hesperine allies."

"Father didn't realize he had those charms." Sabina looked at Cassia with an expression of concern. "Running to warn the Hesperines must have been exhausting for you. Princess Kella tells me you have been troubled by illness since your return to Tenebra."

"Military camps attract contagion," Kella said. "Little wonder she's been ill from the moment we got to Patria."

"Oh, yes. I'm afraid my health has suffered." It rankled Cassia to imagine gossip about her weak constitution, but if that was the worst rumor that came out of this situation, it would be a triumph.

The structure of her secrets was growing complicated. Nivalis knew a necromancer had stolen Pakhne's magic, but not that it was the Collector; Sabina knew Cassia was in love with Lio, but not that her illness was Craving for him. And although their relationship was no secret to Perita, it was to Miranda. Goddess, how had Cassia let her house of cards become so fragile? Every time one of her carefully placed cards fell, she moved another to prop up the whole, but it only created another instability.

"Don't worry for Mistress Perita's health," Lio said. "The Stewards are stepping her and her son, and Callen is escorting them."

Kella twirled her fortune blade. "We won't tell Lady Sabina's father that she didn't bring her bodyguard for this leg of the journey."

"If he finds out," Solia said lightly, "I will assure him we don't need any extra blades to protect my ladies."

"Of course, My Queen," Sabina answered. "I know I am safe with you and Princess Kella."

Was Cassia too exhausted to read the situation clearly, or did she catch some tension in Sabina? Hiding her temper had always been her greatest challenge. Why would she be angry about Solia protecting her?

Oh. Sabina was still jealous of Solia, even though they had settled the question of Flavian.

Of course. They had both been girls together, watching with envy as the men sparred. But Solia had become a warrior, living a life of adventure with Kella, while Sabina was still trapped in skirts and raising her sisters.

They topped a hill overlooking Patria. Sabina drew rein and took in the tents, festival pavilions, and pile of wood ready for the Summer Solstice bonfire. "I see too many banners from the Segetian faction. You need me even more than I realized."

"My sister promised you I would hear out your demands," Solia said.

"I'm happy to do so here and now. I dare say if I do not give you the answer you want, you will ride for Hadria this very night, and I respect your right to do so."

Sabina turned her horse, facing Solia above the assembly of lords who would decide her fate. "My Queen, as far as I am concerned, you may do as you like with that Segetian peacock. Marry him. Marry him off. Banish him. There are far more important promises I wish to secure from you than his hand in marriage."

Cassia's wariness fought with her admiration. Sabina had managed to surprise her.

"It seems we have similar priorities," Solia said.

"Do we? I don't want to marry and watch my husband inherit Hadria and my father's seat on the Council of Free Lords. I can inherit the lands and the title myself."

Solia nodded. "But the council seat will become vacant, and it will fall to the new monarch to fill it. I have often wondered if this is your father's intention. Does he want Hadria's seat to revert to the crown, to break the power of his own line as a safeguard against future feuds?"

"Yes." Sabina raised her chin. "I will not allow that to happen. Here is my question for you, Your Majesty. Do you intend to rule a kingdom where a woman may hold the throne, but not a Council seat?"

"You want to become the first Free Lady of Tenebra in your own right," Cassia realized.

Solia's horse danced under them. "Lady Sabina, I thought you were asking me to do you a favor. If you're willing to push your way to that table and endure the lords' retaliation, you will have my gratitude and unconditional support. I would love nothing better than to make you the first woman on my Council."

"Don't make promises you can't keep," Sabina said. "I know changing hundreds of years of Tenebran law and tradition will not be quick."

Solia glanced at Lio. "I am working on that with my advisers."

"This is an area where I have been making some suggestions," Lio said. "Free lords are male by tradition, rather than law. Nowhere in the Free Charter did King Lucian codify that one must be a man to inherit a Council seat. It is not specified whether a man or woman should be a

Free Lord. I suspect that was his wife's influence at work, for among the Lustri, women held positions of great influence."

Sabina stared at him. "It's not even in the Free Charter? All these centuries, the lords have pointed to that piece of parchment as if it were written in Anthros's own hand to justify anything they wished their wives to do."

"Transcribing and distributing copies of the original charter is on my list of plans, too," Solia said.

"The rest of Tenebran law assumes a male heir," Lio said, "and varies with incredible inconsistency between domains. Changing those laws will not be trivial, but far easier than changing the Charter. It will be harder still to change minds, but unchanged minds must still obey the new laws."

"You already have your advisers researching this," Sabina said to Solia. "I can see you are committed to fighting for it."

"I have lived in an Empire where it is a reality," Solia replied. "I will devote my reign to making it so in Tenebra. Admittedly, I don't plan to announce this to the free lords while I am still fighting for their mandate. I must get those oafs to offer me the crown first, and once it is too late for them to protest, then I can begin to surprise them."

"What other changes do you envision for the women of this land?" Sabina asked.

Solia sighed. "Many. I fear I may have to leave more than I wish to my heirs. But I will begin with the most important reforms. Inheritance and rape laws."

"And what of the laws that forbid magic use outside of a temple?"

"Those may actually be easier to change because they'll benefit men."

"And women, one hopes. My handmaiden Miranda asks that you hear her petition as well."

Cassia took this as an opportunity to show Miranda she was not the enemy. "I am sure my sister would be glad to hear Miranda's concerns."

"Of course," Solia agreed.

Miranda avoided Cassia's gaze, looking instead at Kella, who gave her a nod of encouragement. "Thank you for hearing me, My Queen. I am inspired by Princess Kella's and your magery. Let us imagine that I knew a woman who was trying to avoid being trapped in a temple due to her magic. A theoretical exercise, you understand, Your Majesty."

Solia smiled. "Of course. We are not suggesting any such women are actually present."

"Indeed. But if they were, would you protect them from impressment into the Orders?"

Cassia's heart squeezed. Was Miranda like Cassia and Solia, also secretly a mage struggling with her own power? What had she suffered while trying to escape the Orders, and what role had Cassia played in it?

Solia's temper came through in her voice. "I would like to set fire to the laws that keep girls ignorant of their own power or confine it to what men consider acceptable in Anthros's eyes. While we wrestle for change, any woman who suffers at the Orders' hands may come to her queen's household for sanctuary."

"That will make you unpopular with the Orders, Your Majesty," Sabina warned.

"They need never know. If I offer a lady or her handmaiden a place in my household, it is purely a domestic matter, yes? Why should it ever reach the clerics' ears?" Solia met Miranda's gaze. "Do you need a place in my household now?"

Her gaze fell. "You honor me, Your Majesty, but I will gladly remain under Lady Sabina's protection, if it pleases you."

"Of course. I would never separate you from your lady." Solia and Sabina exchanged a glance and a nod of silent understanding.

Cassia hated this. Miranda didn't feel safe with Solia—because of Cassia. Had Miranda told Sabina what Cassia had done? It was possible Sabina knew more about Cassia's shared past with Miranda than Cassia herself. How could Cassia not remember, if she had ruined someone's life?

She could think of only one more peace offering. Or war offering, rather. "Sister, perhaps Lady Sabina would also like to know what role your sword will play in the future of Tenebra."

Lady Sabina took this opening, clearly emboldened by Cassia's words. "Is that a privilege you intend to keep for yourself and your Imperial allies—or will you let all the women of your kingdom take up arms?"

A slow smile spread across Solia's face. "Oh, Sabina, you and Kella and I shall be great friends."

"We have a plan for that as well," Cassia explained. "Angara is an exception among the gods. If Solia is careful to align herself with Angara's image, we hope Tenebra will tolerate her as an exception among queens."

"And over the years," Solia said, "I will make new exceptions among my ladies, then among their handmaidens. I will keep making exceptions, and so will my heirs, no matter how many generations it takes for women like me to become the rule."

"And if they will not tolerate such an exceptional queen?" Sabina asked.

"Yes, well, it is always a risk that I will be branded an apostate and the Orders will try to make a martyr of me." Solia waved a dismissive hand that painted a little sweep of fire in the air. "I wish them luck with that."

That fire seemed to take hold of Sabina's eyes, and Cassia knew they had secured the ally they needed.

"Guarantee me my father's seat in the future," Sabina said, "and sword lessons now. We can keep them as secret as we must, for as long as we must. But I will not wait another day for the power to protect my own lands and people. Make me your first exception."

CALCULATIONS

LIO SAVORED THE CONSTERNATION on Flavian's face when Lady Sabina swept into his solar. The rest of the audience seemed to be enjoying it too, judging by Cassia, Mak, and Lyros's auras, and the victorious smile on Solia's face. Lio slid near Cassia in case she needed him, but he couldn't deny he was also twisting the knife by standing closer to her than Flavian would prefer.

Flavian rose from his desk chair, his gaze darting from Sabina to Solia as if he were scrambling to recalculate. "Lady Sabina. What a surprise. I thought we had agreed you would pursue your, ah, goals. From elsewhere."

"Yes, it seemed in my interests to pursue those goals at a distance from the events at Patria." She gave him a cold smile. "But goals change."

"I thought I had made my own goals clear." Flavian's emotions carried his thoughts to the surface of his mind, fair game for any mind mage to overhear. *I thought you knew I'm doing this for us.*

Unwanted sympathy pushed its way into Lio. Perhaps Flavian didn't want any of this, but thought it was the only way he could marry the woman he loved in spite of the feud. Lio understood being in a position like that.

"I'm afraid your goals are quite unclear, my lord," Sabina said. "Felicitations on your continued betrothal to Princess Cassia. Or should I congratulate you on your future with Princess Solia? I admit to some confusion after the Fire Dance."

Lio's sympathy dried up. He had never stooped to manipulating women for his political ends.

Flavian rubbed his face. If looks could kill, they would all at least have been banished from the solar.

"Lady Sabina is here as part of my retinue," Solia said. "I expect her to be welcomed as one of my ladies. I'd like the chambers next to mine prepared for her and her household."

Flavian glared at Sabina. "Those rooms are taken."

Her eyes flashed. "I hear there is an empty bed next door to the solar, but I would sooner sleep in a pigsty."

It took an act of Will for Lio not to laugh. Mak had no such qualms and allowed a snicker to escape. Flavian flushed.

"Empty the rooms next to mine," Solia said. It was not a request. "Shuffle your guests however you need. Pitch someone out into the camp. The Lady of Hadria must be treated as she deserves. Anyone who fails to show her respect will lose mine."

Flavian's jaw clenched. "Whoever fails to support me at the Council also loses my support."

Sabina gave a haughty laugh. "The coppers bearing a king's face won't buy anything at the market once the new queen mints her gold."

"Those who cast aside their coppers in anger may change their minds when the sparkle of gold wears off."

Sabina stalked forward and slammed her hand flat on his desk. "Don't you dare accuse me of poor decision-making in the heat of anger. I would never rest the fate of Hadria on a fit of temper. And I certainly won't rest it on a fickle Segetian." Sabina turned her back on him.

On her way to the door, Solia took her arm. "Lady Nivalis and Lord Deverran will be delighted that you've joined us. I hope you'll all join me in my weaving room tomorrow for some Hadrian spiced wine."

"It will be my pleasure, Your Majesty."

Lio offered Cassia his arm, inviting her to rub it in Flavian's face.

She took his arm and smiled sweetly at Flavian. "We'll see you in Council tomorrow."

Lio paced in his shared room, waiting for Cassia to arrive through the secret passageways. When he sensed her draw near, he levitated the old wardrobe that blocked the portal they had found here. She and Knight slipped out of the wall, and she came into Lio's arms. Her body felt composed, but he could feel in her aura that she was still shaking.

Mak gave Knight a pat, then made a shooing motion. "You head into your hidey-hole so Lyros and I can have the room to ourselves."

Cassia glanced around. "Where has Karege gone?"

Lyros wiggled his eyebrows. "He's somewhere—with Tuura. Now off you go."

Cassia pulled Lio through the portal into the hush of the secret corridor. "I won't keep you too long. I know dawn is coming soon."

He put his arm around her, and they headed for the moonflower chamber. "I don't mind if the Dawn Slumber catches me here."

She looked up at him. "You wouldn't feel trapped?"

"To Slumber under your Grace's magic is one of the pleasures of the bond for any Hesperine. It would also be easier for you to come to me here during the day."

"I'm glad you feel we've made this into our Sanctuary."

"We have your magic to thank for that."

The moonflowers brushed against their ankles as they waded into the flowers. Knight stayed on the edge of the carpet of flowers and sneezed. He shook his head, his ears flopping.

The fresh, overpowering fragrance never failed to make Lio feel as if they were somewhere far from Tenebra, somewhere Goddess-touched. He pulled Cassia into his arms again and ran his hands down her body, molding her to him. But the channeling did not stir.

"I suppose I absorbed enough magic for once," she said.

"What you did tonight, Cassia…it was marvelous."

Her arms tightened around him. "I will never allow the king to hurt you."

"You protected all of us."

"I have power now. I will make him regret threatening the people I love."

"You're right. You are so powerful, My Grace." Lio kept stroking her hair, hoping to coax her thoughts and words to the surface. "That was the first time you've seen him since you left Tenebra."

"It's been a long time, and he has no power over me anymore."

"That is entirely true. But it might still be hard to see him."

She hid her face against Lio's chest. "I refuse to give him any more of my tears."

"Then give them to me, if you need to have a good cry."

A sob squeezed out of her, and at last her body shook with her emotions. Lio sank down to the ground and pulled her onto his lap, rocking her while she wept. All her stale fears washed over him, flowing out of her in cleansing torrents, until she sat boneless in his arms, catching her breath.

"Oh," she murmured. "That did help."

"Your tears are safe in my keeping."

"I know you're about to do something romantic like kiss them off my face, but I'm afraid I need a handkerchief first."

"We have had this conversation. You should not feel self-conscious about human snot."

"Yes, well, I still don't want my immortal to kiss me until I've wiped my nose."

He cast a cleaning spell on her face and kissed her. He gave her soft, comforting brushes of his lips, but she kissed him harder. It was the fierce, protective kiss of a Hesperine who needed to reassure herself her Grace was safe. He opened his mouth to her, reveling in it. When she came up for air, his fangs were throbbing.

"I'm all right," he soothed,

"I'm afraid I put us in more danger tonight," she confessed. "There's something I need to tell you. I didn't have time to talk with you before I had to make a decision."

Lio winced. "Yes, Tenebra seems to have that affect. We are all learning to trust one another's judgment. Or trying to."

"Please try to understand. I had to tell Sabina about us."

It wasn't her declaration, but the worry he sensed in her that gave Lio pause. "You didn't want her to know?"

"No. The number of people who know about us keeps growing and with it, the risk. If we ever lost her support and she chose Flavian's side, then he would find out."

Lio tilted her chin up and kissed her again, until she melted into him and shifted on his lap in ways he enjoyed. "Let him find out."

"Lio, no," she said, breathless, her lips swollen from his kiss. "Flavian must never find out."

"You don't want him to know my love is not one-sided?"

"Of course I want him to know. I want to shout it from the highest tower of this castle. But I mustn't. He doesn't even understand that you love me. He only thinks you want me, and that is dangerous enough. If he knows what we want, what motivates us, he has power over us. Now Sabina does, too."

"What did she do to put you in that position?"

"It was the only way I could convince her to support us at the Council."

Lio drew back. "She returned with us tonight because you told her about us?"

"I had to win her trust. Prove my good intentions. Telling her I'm in love with you was the only way."

"That's why you told her?"

Cassia slid off his lap, kneeling just out of reach. "Oh, no. You don't agree."

A silence fell between them, not one of their comfortable ones.

Lio drew his knee up, resting his arm across it. "Perhaps I'm misinterpreting the encounter, but it seems as if you deliberately gave her that power over us—to produce the desired political outcome."

"No, my reasons weren't that mercenary. Everyone in Tenebra is convinced I'm either a calculating politician or a divine virgin. I humanized myself in her eyes."

Unsure if his feelings were justified, Lio wrestled with his next words. "There are other things you could have told her to change her opinion of you. Tell me if I'm wrong, but...I get the impression you bartered knowledge of our love to her. For her partisanship at the Council."

"How is this different from when Eudias found out? We had no chance to talk about that before you enlisted his help with the betrothal. That just as effectively cultivated his support, and he could just as easily use it against us."

"That's not why I told him. I...confided in him. I feel that it's safe for Eudias to know."

"Telling him for emotional reasons could be even more dangerous."

"I know him, Cassia. He won't betray us."

Her gaze dropped. "I do not disagree that he is less likely to betray us than Sabina."

"That is not why I'm unhappy with her knowing. If you had confided in her as a friend, that would feel different to me. It wouldn't have made our love a piece in the game."

He didn't raise his voice. He tried to be rational about his reaction and keep their Oath by explaining it to her. But the hurt throbbing between them was as powerful as if they were shouting.

"I would never use you that way," Cassia said.

But he knew they were both thinking of a night long ago when she had offered him her blood as an act of revenge against the king.

"I'm not Cassia Basilis anymore." It sounded as if she were trying to convince herself as much as him. "I'm doing my best to find Hesperine solutions for Tenebran problems. But you know how hard it is."

"Yes. I'm not an innocent Initiate Ambassador any longer. Perhaps I should not be so fastidious about the calculations we must make. But it will never be all right with me for our love to become a currency in political bargains."

"That is not what I did tonight." She scrambled to her feet. "Remember what I told you the night you first drank from me. You are sacred."

She pressed a hand to her mouth, turned, and fled, leaving him to his Slumber.

90

days until

AUTUMN EQUINOX

9 Anthros's Sword, 1597 OT

ABSOLUTION

LIO SAT NEXT TO Cassia and watched the lords fill the great hall. The rising tensions in the room were nothing to him, when there was tension between him and his Grace.

He wished he hadn't said anything. It would have been easier to quietly endure his own hurt than endure the hurt in her aura.

But surely silence would only make wounds fester. Keeping their Oath was always the right thing to do, wasn't it?

When Lord Deverran and Lady Nivalis entered, Lio braced himself for her hurt as well. But while he felt her attention on him, her fury had settled into the heavy sadness of acceptance. She took a chair behind their section while her husband approached a seat in the front row near Solia and Sabina.

Lord Deverran raised his Council Shield and hung it on the high back of the chair. Murmurs stirred throughout the great hall.

Mak leaned Lio's way. "That means he's decided which contender to support, right?"

Lio nodded. "Now that one lord has declared, the others will face pressure to make a decision. Once every lord hangs his shield, the vote will take place."

"Does sitting on our side mean he's voting with us?"

"Not always. Some lords keep their choice secret until the vote. But in this case, I believe Lady Nivalis's husband and father have just made it clear we can rely on them for their support." Lio nodded toward Lord Galanthian, who was now hanging his shield on the chair beside Deverran's.

Mak gave Lio a significant look. "So there is no doubt Pakhne's family supports us. Will you stop berating yourself now?"

"I'll try."

This was undeniably a victory. But Cassia's emotions stirred into alarm. Lio followed her gaze to the doors of the great hall.

Lord Tyran was here. Lio recognized the lithe, black-haired lord from the Equinox Summit. But he needn't have relied on his eyes to know an enemy had entered the room. The man carried an aura of cruelty that tainted everything around him, shadowing the frightened, but brave woman trapped on his arm.

"What is he doing here?" Cassia hissed. "I warned Flavian to keep him out of this."

Solia leaned toward Cassia, appearing nonchalant with her elbow on the arm of her chair, but her tone was wary. "Lord Tyran was always popular and charming on the outside, and a ruffian underneath. I take it he hasn't changed?"

"Flavian never should have invited him," Cassia said. "I thought he knew better after everything Tyran has done."

Lio asked, "The woman with him—is that his betrothed, Lady Valentia?"

"Yes," Cassia answered. "We can be grateful she's here. She's skilled at mitigating his crimes. Solia, she is the lady of the Segetian faction you should invite to your weaving room."

Solia nodded in agreement as Lord Tyran headed toward them with Lady Valentia. There was something predatory in the way the man moved, which roused all of Lio's protective instincts.

"Your Highness." Lord Tyran offered Solia an elegant bow. "Allow me to welcome you home on behalf of all your oldest companions. I have such fond memories of our youth."

"Your Highness." Lady Valentia sank into a deep curtsy.

Lio sensed that she carried a heavy weight of grief and had the strength to bear it. Her sober blue gown and the elegant knot that tamed her voluminous dark hair did not diminish her womanly beauty. So many females worthy of respect suffered in this kingdom.

"It's good to see you again," Solia said warmly, but she was looking at Valentia, not Tyran.

Valentia kept her head bowed. "You are generous, Your Highness."

"I'm having a little gathering of ladies in my weaving room after the Council. I would be pleased if you would join us."

"Of course she will, Your Highness," Tyran answered for her. "We are honored by your attentions."

Lord Tyran turned to Cassia, and Lio's fangs lengthened on reflex. He decided not to veil them. The man's gaze went to Lio's face, but his smug smile didn't slip.

"Princess Cassia." Lord Tyran gave her a shallower bow. "I hope we can share that dance you promised me all those seasons ago."

Knight showed Tyran his teeth, as well. Cassia stroked her dog's head and said lightly, "As long as you do not try to buy my liegehound again, my lord."

"Not to worry. I have quite a pack of my own in my kennels now. No offense intended, Ambassador."

"None taken." Lio engaged in an undiplomatic fantasy of raiding the man's thoughts and discovering what truly frightened him. Tyran would not feel secure in his liegehounds after a round with a Hesperine mind mage.

For now, they had no choice but to let him have the last word. Lord Flavian made a show of swearing in Lord Tyran and providing him with Lord Deverran's now-empty seat on that side of the room. Before taking his chair, Lord Tyran raised his shield.

Lady Valentia slid to the back to join Benedict. Lio's Hesperine ears caught their whispers.

"How was Lady Eugenia when you left her?" Benedict held Lady Valentia's chair for her.

She took her seat. "You know how she feels about you and Flavian expecting her to stay home, when she would rather be with you at Patria."

"This pit of vipers is no place for a lady like her."

"Dear Ben…she might surprise you."

Lio's attention returned to his companions when Kella muttered a potent insult in Azarqi. "Where I come from, we leave men like Tyran stranded in the desert to meditate on their crimes. Usually the jinn find them before they die of thirst."

"Let's challenge him to a sparring match," Mak said darkly.

"I wish we could." Lyros's lip curled. "You can feel what a parasite he is."

"He is viciously ambitious," Cassia said to Solia, "and he has an army.

Do not court his favor under any circumstances. You do not want to find yourself indebted to him for his vote. Curtailing his abuses will be a great challenge to you as queen. If he sides with the loser, that will make your task a little less impossible."

"What abuses?" Solia's gaze hardened. "Something personal? Towards you?"

"Towards Perita and Callen." Anger snapped in Cassia's aura. "I never would have brought them here if I'd known Tyran would come."

"They will be safe under my protection," Solia promised. "What has Tyran done?"

"Suffice it to say, his soldiers are notorious for how they mistreat women. When Callen defended Perita from them, Lord Tyran would have had him executed, if I hadn't bribed him and promised him a favor."

Lio's fangs extended further. "Do not think I've forgotten that the 'dance' he was referring to is a favor from you. If he tries to collect, he will regret it."

Solia gave a heavy sigh. "And Valentia ended up betrothed to Tyran after Evander and I made our escape?"

Lio nodded. "Lord Tyran's family's maneuvers before and after the Siege of Sovereigns were some of the most decisive political events of that time."

Solia smiled slightly. "Yes, I saw there's an appendix on them in your initiation treatise, but I haven't gotten that far yet. Care to summarize your findings for me, adviser?"

"Of course," Lio obliged. "When Benedict's and Evander's fathers participated in the rebellion against King Lucis, Valentia's family was not directly involved, but they were so close to Evander's family that they were seen as sympathizers and disgraced."

Solia nodded. "It was understood that as soon as Valentia and Evander were old enough, they would marry. But Tyran's family was just as close to theirs. How did he escape being implicated?"

"They refused to come to the aid of Evander's family, abandoning their former allies to the king's justice."

Solia's brow furrowed with regret. "That was for personal gain. Tyran always hoped to steal Valentia from Evander."

"It worked," Lio said. "Her family had to betroth her to him to save themselves from ruin."

"But if they've been betrothed all these years, why haven't they married?" Solia asked.

"Valentia is cunning about putting Tyran off," Cassia said. "She still loves Evander."

"Can we not tell her he's still alive?" Lio asked. "I can feel how she's still grieving for him."

Cassia hesitated. "That would be sure to win her to our side. But I do not recommend using anyone's love for that purpose."

She lifted her gaze, her eyes beseeching Lio. Her aura ached with apology. An apology that he was now unsure she owed him.

"That is not my secret to tell," Solia decided. "Not until I find out what Evander's wishes are. If I can even make contact with him. I haven't seen him in fifteen years, since he went into hiding in Cordium."

When Lio said nothing, Cassia's gaze dropped again. "Regardless, she is the Segetian lady you should invite to your weaving room. We can find other ways to win her support. Such as helping her dissolve her betrothal."

Before Lio could acknowledge Cassia's peace offering, Solia said, "It's no coincidence that Flavian brought Tyran in now. He needed a strong ally of the Segetian faction, since Sabina has joined us. But how did he get Tyran here so quickly?"

"Tyran was most likely nearby, waiting for his chance," Cassia replied.

Lio kept his eye on Tyran. "I fear we should expect matters to continue to escalate."

Flavian stood to commence the night's negotiations. He strolled the central aisle and paused before his banner on the dais, facing the crowd. "Lords and ladies and guests from afar, at last the entire Council of Free Lords is present. All save one. But even he has sent his representative."

Lio did not appreciate the way Flavian drew attention to Sabina's faction allegiance, rather than letting her transcend it as a respected lady of Tenebra.

She did not appear pleased, either. "I am here with my mother's blessing as one of Princess Solia's ladies. It is an honor to count myself the first among her retinue and to join the lords of Tenebra in this fortress of our shared traditions."

"Ah," Flavian replied, "pardon me, Your Ladyship. You can surely understand the source of my confusion, for ladies sit at the back, while the front row is reserved for voting free lords. We are happy to bring in an extra chair beside Lady Nivalis that better befits your status."

Lio hated to admit it, but Flavian had loaded at least three well-chosen barbs, both personal and political, into that declaration.

"The front row is also reserved for royals," Solia spoke up. "As the princess and future queen of Tenebra, I am entitled to this seat, and I will keep Lady Sabina at my side."

Plenty of male auras in the room bristled at this addition of yet another woman to the four who were already seated in the front row. To Lio's surprise, however, Flavian mounted no further protest.

"Before we commence tonight's discussion," Flavian continued, "let it be known that the resident mages of Kyria and Anthros, as well as the greater part of the lords present, have granted their permission to the Hesperine and Imperial delegations to cast wards around Castra Patria and the surrounding camp."

Lio wanted to count that a victory, but he was too wary that their opponent would somehow twist this to his advantage, too. "We are dedicated to protecting everyone here from the rogue Gift Collector who is allied with King Lucis. We thank you for your forbearance. We will cast wards tonight that will repel necromancy."

"Very well," Flavian said. "Out of respect for those among us with hesitations regarding foreign magic, I would prefer to rely on steel and the wards of Tenebran mages. But I must defer to our temple delegations and the majority of the lords."

And there it was. Flavian had managed to make himself look good, despite handing this boon to Lio. Flavian had effectively established himself as the anti-Hesperine choice for every lord here who would rather crown a new monarch without relying on Orthros's aid.

Flavian bowed in Lio's direction, and Lio did not miss the mockery in it. He could see that the Council negotiations were only just beginning.

As the great hall echoed with the boots of the exiting lords and the soft patters of their ladies' slippers, Lio stood out of the way in veiled consultation with Mak and Lyros, Eudias and Ariadne, and Tuura.

"Yes," Eudias confirmed, "Master Gorgos insists I accompany you while you cast the wards, so I can ensure you don't do anything unholy, et cetera, et cetera."

Ariadne sighed. "It took some convincing, but I managed to persuade the Semna that holy Kyrian oversight is necessary as well. She approved only because Tuura makes an appropriate escort to 'protect my virtue.' As if such things are important when a necromancer threatens us."

Tuura tucked her arm in Ariadne's. "I promise to keep you out of trouble—for the most part. This will be a good learning experience for you."

Lio doubted Ariadne was coming with them to learn about spell casting. She wanted to see with her own eyes that his magic would be enough to protect people from what had happened to her temple sister. He hoped he could prove to her how hard he was trying to keep everyone safe.

"How wide a ward can we cast?" Lio asked his Trial brothers. "We need to encompass at least the camp and the fortress, but that would still leave the surrounding villages and keeps unprotected."

"Hmm," Mak replied, "I doubt we could expand the ward all the way to the next estate."

Lyros put a hand to his chin. "But we might be able to include some of the villages, especially the ones that Flavian is relying on for supplies."

"That would be ideal," Eudias said. "We need to protect the supply line—and make sure the Collector does not use it to infiltrate us. But how can we ride a perimeter that large while keeping your casting stable?"

"There is a type of Hesperine ward we can use," Lyros said.

Eudias's eyes brightened, and he and Ariadne waited expectantly for further information. But Lyros said nothing more.

Lio winced inwardly. Of course. The Stewards were not about to discuss the secrets of Hesperine border defenses with anyone here, not even someone they liked and trusted like Eudias.

Was Cassia right? Was it a mistake for Lio to feel a connection to Eudias?

But how could she expect him not to feel that with Eudias and Pakhne, when he had battled the Collector for their minds?

Solia paused beside them on her way out. "Lio, Lady Nivalis will be joining Sabina and me in my weaving room. She would like to apologize to you."

"I do not feel that she owes me an apology," Lio said.

"I know you don't. But I want you to accept it."

She gave him a look. Not as a queen to her allied ambassador, nor as a disapproving matriarch to an infuriating bridegroom. No, it was a look Lio had seen Nike give Mak. Most definitely the expression of an elder sister who knew what was best for him and would not tolerate any protests.

"Remember what I said," Solia told him. "I want to see you defend yourself this time."

"Very well," Lio replied. "I will try."

He urged his Trial brothers to go on ahead with the other mages while he returned to their room. He was preparing to step from there to the ladies' chamber when Cassia emerged from behind the wardrobe.

She hesitated in front of him. "I thought we might want a chance to talk."

"Yes," he said.

She offered him her hand, as if she were unsure he would take it. That made him want to pull her into his arms. But she was right. They must talk.

He let her lead him behind the wardrobe and through the wall. Knight was waiting for them in the gloom on the other side. Cassia stopped there, her soft breaths and quick heartbeat loud to his ears in the dusty quiet.

"I'm so sorry, Lio. I can scarcely believe I told Sabina about us for a political reason. I will not let myself turn back into that version of myself. I swear it. Can you forgive me?"

"I'm not sure there's anything to forgive," he said. "I'm not sure of anything. That's the problem."

"No, you were right. I crossed a line that I promised you I would never cross again. I want you to know how it horrifies me."

"Are my personal reasons any less ignoble? I enjoy the thought of letting it slip to Sabina, so Flavian will find out. I enjoyed the look on his face when I took your arm in his solar last night."

"You're entitled."

"Am I? Entitled to such petty and personal emotions when there are lives at stake? I'm supposed to be a valuable adviser to Solia, but tonight, I was ready to spill Evander's secrets that don't belong to me. I wanted to ease Valentia's pain—without thinking of the consequences to him if the wrong people found out he's still alive. You still managed to evaluate that decision with your mind, not your heart."

"I don't trust my mind anymore. My heart is what undoes all the twisted thoughts."

"Well, I am not at all sure we should trust my heart. For a mind mage, I am not thinking very clearly."

"If you are not certain of anything, and neither am I, what are we to do?"

He lifted her hand, lacing his fingers with hers. "I don't know. But whatever it is, we must do it together."

She slid close to him, and he enfolded her in his arms. It reminded him of the first time he'd ever held her, when she had been taut with uncertainty and soft with new trust.

"Of all that we might lose while we're here in Tenebra," she said, "this might be what I fear the most. Losing myself. I must never go back to who I was. I must keep myself ready for my Gifting."

"Even Hesperines make mistakes and quarrel, Cassia. Remember what you so often tell me about not trying to be perfect? Hespera doesn't expect perfection of us." He lifted Cassia's face from his chest to look at her. "Our Goddess does not require virtuous Kyrian virgins. She accepts wanton heretics who strive to be kind."

Cassia's laughter bubbled out of her, echoing brightly in the ancient halls. "Feast often. Do no harm. I think I can manage that."

He pulled her against the nearest wall and kissed her until he tasted no more traces of worry and hurt. She had his collar half undone when he reluctantly pulled back.

"Mmm." He licked his lips. "Later. While we're casting the wards, I want you to catch up on sleep."

She sighed. "I suppose I must."

"Yes, you must. I'll need your blood after the spells. You'll need your strength." He let his gaze drift down her.

That promise seemed to satisfy her, for she released him and stepped back. "They're waiting for us in the weaving room."

"Your sister tells me I should stand up for myself with Nivalis. Therefore I shall deign to keep her waiting for a few more minutes. Despite all our uncertainties, you're undoubtedly right about one thing. We must focus on getting you ready for your Gifting. Let's continue searching the tunnels, shall we?"

"Good. I'd rather not wait to show you what I found during the day." She took his hand again. "*Dockk*, Knight."

She guided them swiftly through the corridors and across the room full of moonflowers, halting in front of one of several doorways that led out of the chamber.

"This seems to be a hub," she said, "and all the passages that lead off of it are full of magic for a certain distance. But the magic fades the farther you get from this room—except in one passage, the eastern one."

"How can you tell which way is east?" he asked.

"I'm not sure how, but I'm certain it is. And it makes sense, doesn't it? Wouldn't Lustra magic be stronger in the east, where all of Tenebra's wildest lands are?"

"That's a logical theory."

Lio ducked to follow her down the narrow passageway, which had clearly been designed with mortal height in mind. Knight squeezed ahead of her, while Lio dropped behind. Although the moonflowers only extended a few paces into the corridor, the green ivy grew further, entangled with vines of iridescent red ivy.

"The Lustra magic definitely appears stronger here," he agreed. "How far does this ivy continue?"

"I haven't found the end of it yet." She led him onward for a few minutes, then stopped him in a small chamber where the ivy obscured the walls, floor, and ceiling. "This appears to be a dead end, and I have yet to find a portal. But I'm sure there must be one. We should come back later and find it."

"Yes, and we can tell Lyros to focus our search patterns on the eastern areas of Patria. Perhaps we could find whatever the ivy is leading us to from aboveground."

"We'll work from both sides."

He squeezed her hand. "We are finally making real progress."

After she escorted him back out of the tunnels, they parted. He gave her a few minutes to return to the ladies' chamber, then stepped there on his own. He found Cassia, Solia, and Kella seated around the fire with Sabina and Nivalis. Miranda had a chair behind Sabina's shoulder, and Lio was glad to think that Callen and Perita had some time to themselves with their child in Sabina's neighboring rooms.

A little start went through Nivalis when she saw him. Although she rose smoothly to her feet, her aura was anything but composed.

Before she could speak, however, the door opened to reveal Lady Valentia and another young woman. Lady Valentia urged the girl in ahead of her, casting glances over her shoulder, then shut the door hastily behind them.

"Genie!" Cassia leapt up to pull her further inside.

So this was Eugenia of Segetia. She was just as Cassia had described her, with long, bouncing curls of Segetian chestnut and an aura brimming with boundless enthusiasm for everything. "Oh, Cassia, it's so good to see you, even if you aren't destined to marry into my family."

Cassia, and by extension, Lio were among the few people who knew the secret of Genie's parentage. She was Flavian's half-sister, a child born out of love, but also out of wedlock, to Lord Titus and his cherished concubine Risara. They allowed the world to believe Genie was Flavian's legitimate cousin, the only surviving heir of Lord Titus' late brother, so she could live with privilege instead of the stain of bastardry.

This was the little sister Flavian adored. This was his Zoe. For her sake, Lio supposed he ought to find some sympathy for the man. But all he could think was that he wished Genie had been given a better brother.

She kept sneaking curious, fascinated glances at Lio. He wondered how much of his and Cassia's secrets she knew or suspected.

"What are you doing here?" Cassia asked, shaking her head with a smile.

"Taking years off my life, that's what." Affectionate exasperation disrupted Lady Valentia's composure. But she gathered herself and sank into a curtsy before Solia, and Genie followed her example. "Your Highness, I beg your forgiveness for our intrusion. Allow me to present Lady Eugenia of Segetia."

Solia sat forward in her chair with an amused tilt to her mouth. "I'm happy to meet you, Lady Eugenia, provided you are not here to spy for my opponent."

Genie replied with surprising dignity, "I am here to participate as best I can in these decisive political events. I will not sit at home while my brother and Sir Benedict treat me like a child. And I will not live in a Tenebra where I am treated like a child for the rest of my life."

"Lord Flavian still has the authority to send you back home," Lady Valentia reminded her. "Make your case, but do not try Princess Solia's patience. If you will be so good as to hear out Lady Eugenia, Your Highness."

"My door is open to all women of Tenebra, no matter their family or faction," Solia replied.

Genie's stubborn chin was set. "Your Highness, I am here to plead for a place in your retinue. If you will make me one of your ladies, it will rob Flavian of the power to banish me back to Segetia. And I shall sit with you in Council for all to see."

Solia's brows rose. "Your brother and Sir Benedict should not underestimate you. That is a compelling political bargain."

Cassia returned to her seat. "It will certainly cause speculation that Flavian is less secure in his own domain's support."

Genie's smile widened. "Not to mention make all the lords mock him for failing to control the women of his own house."

Lio leaned against the mantle behind Cassia's chair. Sunbind him, but he liked Genie. He would have a difficult time reminding himself he couldn't trust her any farther than he could trust anyone else here.

"Are you certain?" There was a gentle warning in Solia's tone. "This will put you in a position of conflicted loyalties."

"I assure you, Your Highness, I can help you and my brother at the same time. Becoming king will make him miserable. And I know you are too good to ask me to do anything that would truly harm him. I will gladly strengthen your claim to the throne as much as I can."

"Allow me a word with my advisers," Solia said.

Lio cast a veil around her, Cassia, and himself.

"Well, she's certainly a refreshing surprise," Solia said. "What do you think?"

"We know the secret of her parentage," Lio pointed out. "That may counterbalance any secrets she knows about us."

Solia nodded. "We should be careful what we say in her presence, in case she is tempted to give her brother information. But in truth, this is far more likely to hurt his ambitions than mine."

"I agree," Cassia said. "Genie is clever and should not be underestimated, but I think in this case, her ambition is sincere. I suggest we accept her offer on one condition—that she join forces with Ben in trying to convince Flavian to end our betrothal." Cassia looked to Lio. "If that's all right with you."

Lio hesitated, unwilling to embroil this bright girl in their conflicts with her brother. But he asked himself what Zoe would want, when she reached the Hesperine equivalent of Genie's age. She would want to have her say, both in their family and the Firstblood Circle, and Orthros would never dismiss her voice. "I agree. We will enlist her as one of our allies in breaking the betrothal, like Eudias and Ariadne."

He and Cassia shared a smile. At least this time, they agreed on a solution.

He dissolved his veil, and Solia said, "Lady Eugenia, I am delighted to welcome you into my retinue, if you will agree to support me in this—help us convince your brother to release my sister from their betrothal."

"Oh, with pleasure, Your Highness." Genie looked to Cassia, then Lio. "I'm one of the few people who can persuade him to do things he doesn't wish to."

Lio had no doubt she wielded the power of a little sister who had her doting brother wrapped around her finger. Perhaps this would be their salvation—one girl's sisterly stubbornness.

"Rise," Solia said, "and take your seat."

Genie kissed Solia's hand and all but bounced to her feet. Lio pulled up a chair for her.

She looked him up and down. "Well, Ambassador, you are an unusual rooster to find in the princess's henhouse. I begin to see why my brother and Ben are being so insufferable about you."

Lio suppressed a laugh. "Their concerns are unjustified, I assure you. I am here to keep all of you ladies safe."

She lifted the fan tied at her waist on a ribbon and batted it in front of her face. "I'm sure all the ladies at Patria are most interested in your 'protection.' But one lady in particular, if my brother's fuming is to be believed."

"An honorable champion does not confirm or deny such rumors."

"As a champion of secret romances, neither shall I," she promised, before taking her seat.

"Lady Valentia," Solia continued, "I hope you will join my retinue as well."

Lady Valentia raised her head, her eyes wide. "Your Highness...your generosity astonishes me. I am not certain I am a fitting companion for you. But if you will have me, I will serve you with honor and endeavor to atone for my family's transgressions."

"What transgressions? Allegiance to Evander's family?"

Pain filled Valentia's aura. "Yes, Your Highness."

Solia rested a hand on Valentia's shoulder. "Evander and his father were the only men in Castra Roborra who did not betray me."

Valentia pressed a hand to her mouth, shutting her eyes. As they all watched, Lio felt years of burdens lift from her.

They might not be able to tell her that Evander still lived, but at least Solia had given this back to Valentia—his honor.

"I dared hope," Lady Valentia said, her voice thick. "Thank you. Thank you, Your Highness."

"Under my reign, his family name will be restored, and all of Tenebra will know they were loyal to the true queen. I understand his family estate remains vacant, wasting in possession of the crown. I will see it entrusted to its rightful lord...or lady."

Valentia shook her head. "You will always have my allegiance, but beware of my betrothed. Whatever rewards you give to me will fall into his hands."

"My sister has warned me of the danger."

"I am the only asset I have to offer you. Making me one of your ladies is the only elevation you should give me."

"For now," Solia agreed. "But it seems to me we have two betrothals to dissolve, don't you agree?"

"My Queen. You have given me...all of us...the greatest gift. Hope."

"Rise, Lady Valentia. We will all do great things together."

Sabina caught Lio's eye and gave a slight nod to the empty space beside her. Lio pulled up a chair for Lady Valentia, and the two women whose forefathers had slaughtered each other sat side by side.

Lio put his hands behind his back. "I'm afraid I must excuse myself from this lovely company soon. The night is short, and we must cast wards over Patria. But I am told you wished to have a word with me first, Lady Nivalis."

She still stood on the edge of the gathering, as if now unsure of her place. She gave Lio a curtsy. "Ambassador."

"How are you?" he asked sincerely.

"As well as can be expected."

"I understand."

Her gaze fell. "Lady Sabina has explained the truth of the events in her father's camp. I know now that the Gift Collector is allied with the king, and he targeted my sister due to her involvement with the Allied Lords. It was unjust of me to blame you."

"Sometimes our hearts do not heed our minds."

"I should not have let my anger overrule me," Nivalis said. "Even if my parents can never know the truth, allow me to give you our sincerest apologies. I ask for your forgiveness, and pledge to treat you as befits my queen's ally."

Lio had expected Nivalis to say what Solia required of her, but he was not prepared for the truth in her aura. She truly did not blame him.

Solia gave him that look again.

"I accept your apology," Lio said.

So why did he feel as if he still owed Pakhne's family an apology of his own?

THE APPLE

THE NIGHT INSECTS BUZZED in Lio's ears, as lulling as the lapping of the nearby river. The gloom of twilight felt too bright. He rubbed his face. "I wish Caravaner's Milk worked on Hesperines."

Tuura sighed. "I wish my tonics worked on you, too."

"Where's a good snake when you need it?" Karege waded through the reeds, looking for river serpents. "Nothing like snake blood to sharpen the mind."

Mak tossed each of them a dark glass flask. "This potion from the Charge's alchemists will help."

"Drink up," Lyros advised. "We need to be alert for a casting like this."

Lio drained the concoction. It tasted vile, but sent a fizz of energy through him. While his Trial brothers had one more word with Tuura and Karege about their part of the spell, Eudias beckoned for Lio to join him and Ariadne under a tree.

Eudias looked tired, but alert. "We thought you might like a progress report on our research into betrothal laws."

Ariadne smoothed her veil. "While Eudias has picked Master Gorgos's brain—such as it is—I've been consulting with the Semna."

Lio realized he had his hands behind his back again and let them fall at his sides. "Mage Ariadne...you have Cassia's and my deepest gratitude for aiding us in this. But I do not expect it of you. Not after what happened."

Her brow creased with puzzlement. "What do you mean?"

He didn't want to prod her grief, but it needed to be said. "It would be wrong to ask you to save us, when I could not save your temple sister. I hope one day you can forgive me for what befell Pakhne. Until then, spare your efforts for yourself and for what she would want."

A silence fell between the three of them. It was filled not with judgment, but the mages' surprise.

"Ambassador...may I call you Lio?" Ariadne asked.

"Of course," he replied to her unexpected question. "You may call me whatever you like."

"Lio," she said, "I don't think you understand. You don't need my forgiveness. Everyone who loves Pakhne should thank you for how you fought for her."

"But I failed to save her." Lio looked at Eudias, praying he would understand. "I did everything I could. But it wasn't like our battle against him. I couldn't reach her, couldn't enlist her aid to fight alongside me."

Eudias blinked at him. "What you managed to do for me is by far the exception, not the rule. I know what the Collector has done to the other people he has possessed. He showed me. I believe Pakhne was too far gone, and that no one could have prevented what happened to her. Did you really think we would blame you?"

"It would be perfectly understandable for you to blame me," Lio said.

Ariadne took Eudias's hand. "Of course not. You saved Eudias, and you fought for Pakhne. You have our gratitude."

Lio swallowed. "I am honored to have a bond of gratitude with you two."

Their opinions about that battle mattered more than anyone's. And they were offering Lio something even more than forgiveness—gratitude.

And yet, no weight lifted from his soul. His own bitter guilt remained. What would it take to make him feel absolved of Pakhne's fate?

"Let us help you and Cassia," Ariadne said. "Or at least let us try."

Lio nodded and smiled at her, if only for Cassia's sake. "We're thankful for your aid."

"Well, I'm not sure thanks are warranted yet. Lord Flavian refuses to heed the Semna. The only way the Temple of Kyria could force him to relinquish Cassia is if she officially became a mage and took a vow of celibacy."

"Well, that certainly won't work," Lio said.

"Unfortunately," Ariadne went on, "there are very few situations where a woman can divorce her husband, such as if he brings his concubine into her house."

Lio grimaced. "Ah, so he's supposed to keep his myriad of other companions out of his wife's sight."

Ariadne sighed. "Yes, but that doesn't help with a betrothal. Flavian could keep a troupe of dancing girls in his home for the duration of the betrothal, as long as he gets rid of them before the wedding day."

Lio thought Sabina would have Flavian's head for that long before any wedding occurred. "Are there *any* grounds for a woman to dissolve her own betrothal?"

Ariadne counted them off on her fingers. "He's already married; he's convicted of a crime by her liege, his own, or the king; the Orders want him for apostasy or heresy."

"Marvelous," Lio muttered. "She could more easily break a betrothal to me. Getting Flavian convicted of a crime is tempting."

"Perhaps we should have Lady Sabina marry him at sword point," Ariadne suggested. "I think she'd rather enjoy that."

"You could always turn him into a Hesperine," Eudias added.

"And suffer his presence for eternity?" Lio shuddered. "No, thank you."

"Men have many more options for breaking betrothals," Eudias explained. "For example, competing suitors can try to outbid the bride price the groom gave to the lady's father."

Lio wrinkled his nose at the idea of bidding for Cassia like she was a horse at auction. "As distasteful as that is, outbidding him from House Komnena's treasury would not be a problem—if the lady in question's father were anyone else."

Eudias nodded. "That's the root of the problem. You aren't in a position to persuade Lord Titus or the king to change their minds."

"There must be something I can do!"

"In our professional opinions," Eudias said, "the best option available to you is trial by combat."

Oh, now that was tempting. "I can challenge him to a battle for Cassia's hand?"

"It's a time-honored tradition," said Eudias, "but it has fallen out of favor in recent years, since King Lucis outlawed duels between lords of opposing feudal factions. But you aren't in a faction."

For once, Lio's status as an outcast from Tenebran society had its advantages. He smiled slowly, his fangs lengthening.

"Oh, my." Ariadne's brows rose. "Lord Flavian really should not have underestimated you."

"Alas, it would probably cause a political disaster if I beat Flavian to a pulp. Not to mention Cassia would never agree, nor would Solia." And he had only just won his Grace-sister's trust.

"Give it some consideration," Eudias advised. "I don't think it would be impossible to use it to your advantage, as well as Basilinna's. It might win you the lords' respect."

"Lio, we're ready to start," Mak called.

He thanked the mages again, then rejoined his Trial brothers by the river. Eudias and Ariadne left with Tuura and Karege, who was to step them to another checkpoint.

Once they were gone, Lio tried to focus on the spell instead of fantasizing about putting his fist in Flavian's face. "Explain the ward structure to me."

Lyros pointed at the map. "We only need to step or traverse to key points around the perimeter. Then we can connect them into a complete ward."

"It's one of the Queens' warding innovations," Mak said. "We'll model this on the nodes of their ward over Orthros. All the Queens' spells are designed for blending manteia and mageia, so Annassa Soteira can add her mind healing to Annassa Alea's warding."

Lio nodded in understanding. "So this ward structure will be more receptive to Tuura's theramancy and my thelemancy?"

"Precisely," Lyros said. "Eudias will also lend us the river's power to strengthen the spell. Karege will contribute his blood to Tuura's casting to link her with ours. We'll complete the circle when we all step to the final node."

Mak clapped Lio on the shoulder. "Let's begin. The sooner we finish, the sooner we can all get back to the Castra to replenish ourselves."

Lyros shot Mak a fanged grin.

"Hear, hear," Lio agreed.

They stood in a circle on the shore of the river and made a libation, forming a ring of blood that would serve as the first node. The familiar shadows of Mak and Lyros's power joined with Lio's. Some of his tension unwound. At last, they would be able to fully protect Patria.

He was aware of Eudias's cool water magic enriching the river's current and the distant reservoir of Ariadne's healing affinity. Karege's blood magic resonated in kinship with Lio and his Trial brothers. As on their patrols, the music of Tuura's ancestral magic filled the twilight.

Lio held back his power at first, counting his heartbeats while Mak and Lyros's ward waxed around him.

"Now," Mak said.

Lio spun the first filament of mind magic into their creation. Power emanated from Tuura's node across the miles of fields and villages and tents. The structure of the spell took hold of Lio and locked within his chest, binding him to each of his fellow casters.

Without warning, a tremor of magic went through the link, then slammed into Lio's heart. As he slid to his knees, Mak and Lyros grunted in pain.

Lio caught himself on one hand, clutching his chest with the other, and shot a thelemantic probe through their spell. The whole structure shook, ready to shatter. What was happening?

When his mind magic met Tuura's aura, pain tore through him.

"It's Tuura," he shouted over the roar in his ears. "Should I go to her? Or one of you?"

"You go," Lyros called back. "Mak and I will try to stabilize the spell."

Lio released the power he held in reserve, letting it sink into their ward. The moment he let go, it began to fade from the spell structure. It wouldn't be long before his magic drained from their ward completely.

Leaping to his feet, he stepped to Tuura. He landed on a grassy hillside, where Karege knelt with Tuura's limp form in his arms.

Lio sank down beside them. "What happened?"

"It's the channeling," Karege said. "This is what I was afraid of. She insisted she could last through the spell, but I knew she would pay the price."

Eudias, standing nearby, dug a hand through his hair. "She collapsed as she was pouring her power into the spell."

"I can't wake her." Ariadne rubbed Tuura's hand, healing magic flowing out of the young mage into the diviner.

"This is because of the Silence?" Lio asked.

Karege cradled Tuura to him with one hand on her cheek. "Since she can't channel from the spirit phase, she draws ancestral power through herself. It's almost as if she becomes a spirit gate. And tonight...the gate collapsed."

"I'm collapsing the spell," Lio said.

He pulled his magic out of their carefully crafted ward structure. The spell lock cracked under his ribcage, and he swayed.

Mak and Lyros appeared beside him, Mak bracing Lio before he fell over.

"I'm sorry—" Lio gasped. "I had to."

"Of course," Lyros said, taking in the situation with the speed of a Steward trained for a crisis.

Tuura drew in a breath. But she did not wake.

"What can we do for her?" Lio asked.

"She needs a healer who understands ancestral magic," Karege said.

"We can't bring Rudhira here," said Lyros.

"Is she stable enough for us to step her?" Mak asked.

"I don't know." Karege's aura raged with anger at forces beyond his control.

"I'll get your First Blade," Lyros said. "Lio, stay on the alert. If the Collector has been waiting for his moment to strike, this is it."

"I'll keep my wards ready," Mak said.

Lyros stepped away, and Lio let his thelemantic senses expand to their widest range. He ran his power over mortal minds, and they ruffled under his touch like soft dandelions, ready to puff away in the breeze before a thelemancer's power.

Tuura's heartbeat did not weaken, but the turmoil in her aura grew, as if her magic were an angry wind without direction.

Within moments, Lyros returned with the others. Kella, Hoyefe, and Solia gathered around Tuura and Karege.

Cassia slipped under Lio's arm. "Did the Collector do this?"

"I think the Silence is to blame." The feeling of her petite form, physical and vivid, underlay his amorphous awareness of Patria's minds. "I don't sense him anywhere. Yet. But without Tuura..."

"We are much more vulnerable to him," Cassia finished for him.

Kella stretched Tilili out beside Tuura and pressed a hand to her friend's chest. "The Silence did this. Even Hoyefe and I can feel it."

Solia was pale. "Is this to be the fate of every ancestral practitioner who comes to Tenebra?"

Cassia's arm tightened around Lio. Would a Sandira whose shifter magic came from his ancestors meet the same fate?

"Tuura is a diviner," Kella said firmly. "It's different for her. She needs Imperial healing."

Solia looked from Lio to his Trial brothers. "I want you to bring the First Prince here. I don't care about the political consequences."

Lyros hesitated, then, "I understand. I'll go."

"Thank you," Solia said sincerely.

He stepped away again, Mak and his latent wards remaining. Lio kept his senses open, holding all of Patria in his mind's eye. Amid the fleeting mortal auras, he caught a whiff of death.

"Lio?" Cassia asked. "What is it?"

"I'm not sure, but I need to follow it."

"I'm coming with you," Mak said.

"Cassia will be safe with me," Solia promised. "Focus on the Collector."

Lio stepped, sensing Mak follow him. Together they slipped through the mundane world, chasing that hint of decay. They halted in darkness.

Lio's eyes adjusted quickly, soaking up the meager light that existed here. It appeared to be the remains of a stone cellar, now half collapsed.

"Are we under Castra Patria?" Mak crouched and picked his way through the rubble toward an opening. "There's a tunnel here. Perhaps an old escape route used during sieges?"

Lio crawled forward to join him, the mortar crumbly under his hands. "Can you sense if a human came this way?"

"Whoever they were, they know how to hide their trail. But they left us this."

Mak pointed to a bright, fresh red apple resting in the ruined passageway. An eye of Hypnos was painted on it. The blood was still damp.

Lio's nostrils flared. "A woman's blood."

"I don't recognize her. Do you?"

Lio shook his head. "But we know what he means by it. Another threat to Cassia."

Mak fished a warded bag out of his robe. "We'll take this to the Charge later. I'd wager my horse that it's laden with Gift Collector poison."

Lio swore. "Did he manage to sneak in during the moments after Tuura collapsed?"

"Or did he make it through our defenses earlier, and he chose now to sneak out?"

"We have to finish the wards tonight."

Mak nodded grimly. "There's nothing more we can do here. Let's get back to Tuura."

They returned to the hillside, which was now darker with the moons sinking against the twilight sky. Complex spells thickened the air. At their center, Rudhira knelt beside Tuura, his hands on her temples.

Eudias wore a fierce frown. "If Master Gorgos senses anything, we'll come up with some explanation."

"Once again, we're grateful to you," Lyros said. "Lio, I don't want you trying to cast thelemantic veils. Stay focused on the perimeter."

"I will. But I think the Collector's work here is done."

Cassia put her arm around Lio again, looking from the bag to his face. "Are you all right? Did you find something dangerous?"

"Just another taunt," he tried to reassure her.

Mak held up the bag. "He left us a poisoned apple this time."

"An apple?" Cassia frowned. "Curious. I wish I knew what message he's trying to send with that. It's even stranger than the kitchen knife."

None of them made any more attempts to interpret it. They stood in silence, waiting for Rudhira's verdict, while Solia's aura heated the air.

"I've got her stable now," Rudhira announced at last. "But the only way to heal her is to take her back to the Empire. She needs to reopen her senses to the spirit phase so her ancestors can restore her power. Now that I've healed her, it should be safe to step her to the Summit

Sanctuary, then to Orthros Notou. We'll take her through the spirit gates from there."

"How long will she need to stay in the Empire?" Solia asked.

"It's difficult to say," Rudhira replied. "I'm so sorry. We have no precedent for this. I've never seen anything like this damage to her spirit. I have no doubt she will make a full recovery with the ancestors' help, but it will be slow."

Karege lifted his gaze to Kella. "First Blade, I ask that you relieve me of duty so I can stay with Tuura."

Kella gave him a sad smile. "You offering saves me from having to order you. Escort our fallen comrade home, and send word through the Hesperines as often as you can."

"Three Ashes are still equal to a force of three hundred," Hoyefe said. "We'll fight on in Tuura's name."

Solia squeezed Tuura's hand once, fire dancing up her forearm. "This is my fault. I never should have asked this of her."

Kella touched Solia's arm. "You couldn't have kept her from coming if you had tried."

"She is the best of us," Solia said.

With her scarf on, none of her grief showed in her aura, but Lio wondered if she felt as she had five years ago, when she'd had to tell the Ashes goodbye to join the Golden Shield.

Karege stood, lifting Tuura in his arms. "You'll see us both again, Sunburn. You're not getting rid of us that easily again."

Solia nodded, blinking hard, as Karege and Rudhira disappeared.

"We finish the wards," Lio said. "Tonight. We'll simply have to cast them without our theramancer—and hope they're strong enough."

2

days until

AUTUMN EQUINOX

32 Anthros's Sickle, 1597 OT

THE APOSTATE

CASSIA LEANED FORWARD IN her saddle and urged Freckles over the next rise at a canter, Knight bounding beside them. The fleet little mare kept pace with the larger Warmbloods ahead of them. Cassia was proud that after a season of riding the hills of Patria, she could keep her seat at this speed.

The chill in the air reminded her summer was almost over. The cold seemed to sink into her bones. When they reached the top of the hill and Lyros called a halt, Knight pressed close to her, his fur warming her foot. Cassia rearranged her cloak, trying to be surreptitious. But of course, Lio and Solia both noticed and were upon her like hawks.

"I'm perfectly fine," Cassia said.

Ignoring her assurances, Lio took her hand and sent a pulse of his magic into her, better than a swig of spirits. All Solia did was stand near, and the air around them heated.

Lyros spread their map across his saddle. "We need to keep you in good shape for the search. I won't have any of my troops falling behind."

Cassia was grateful for their care, but she hated needing it. She dreaded the reminders that she was ill...and that her lack of magic affected her more with each passing night. The negotiations were dragging on while her strength was draining away.

Mak drew his horse close to Lyros's to look at the map with him. "We're covering a lot of ground tonight."

That gave Cassia strength. Freezing her arse off in the saddle for another hour was actually helping save her life.

Lio looked to the horizon, the cool air lifting a lock of his dark hair from his furrowed brow. "We're getting close to the eastern boundary of the thelemantic ward."

Lyros pointed at the cluster of cottages below them. "This is Mederi Village, the last settlement inside our protections. Unless we find something here, we'll have to start searching outside the ward tomorrow night."

Lio frowned, Moonflower pawing the ground. "Perhaps we should bring Kella and Hoyefe with us then."

"He wouldn't be pleased to leave his spying—or Severin," Cassia said.

Solia nodded. "We need Hoyefe to keep searching for the king's informant. And we need Kella and Tilili in the keep to tear any enemies apart in case of danger to our allies."

"Don't worry," Mak told Lio. "Lyros and I know how to keep everyone safe. And the rest of you aren't half bad in a fight either."

Solia huffed, peering into the distance. "What lies beyond the fields?"

Lyros consulted his map again. "Looks like heavy woods. The king's hunting grounds."

"That's right," Solia said. "I think he has a hunting estate somewhere east of Mederi Village. What is it called, Cassia? Paradum?"

The name snapped Cassia's drifting thoughts back to attention.

"I don't see that on the map," said Lyros.

"It wouldn't be marked," Solia said, "for the king's safety. It was intended as a place he could get away from the capital and relax."

"Relax by slaughtering animals," Mak muttered. "How often does he go there?"

"Not often, as I recall," Solia replied. "He certainly wouldn't risk it now, while the Council is in session."

"Cassia, what's wrong?" Lio asked.

She rubbed her eyes. She truly wasn't at her best. "How could I have forgotten Paradum is at Patria? I've been there."

Lio rested a hand on her back. "Perhaps you didn't want to remember. I sense your memories of the place aren't particularly pleasant."

"Some of them are. Agata, the cook, was very kind, and I spent a lovely season working in her kitchen garden. Those were the finest peas I ever grew."

She had never gotten to taste them. She had watched her beautiful plants die outside her window while she was ill.

Lio was right. She had most likely shoved Paradum to the back of her mind. Times when her life had been in danger were the last thing she wanted to dwell on right now, when…

But Lio must have seen it in her thoughts, for he asked, "Paradum is where you caught that fever?"

"What fever?" Solia demanded.

Lio glanced between her and Cassia in surprise. "I'm sorry. I thought you two would have talked about it already."

"It was a long time ago," Cassia said, but now she knew there was no avoiding an explanation. "When I was fourteen. While the king had me staying at Paradum, there was a terrible epidemic. Very few people on the estate recovered from the fever. I was one of the lucky ones."

Cassia swallowed. She still missed Agata. Lio touched her mind, sharing in her sadness.

"You could have died," Solia said.

"She almost did," said Lio.

"Well, she didn't." Mak interjected. "It would take more than a stupid fever to defeat Cassia."

Bless Mak. Cassia smiled at him.

Solia did not smile. "Fevers can leave damage."

"No wonder your memories of that place and time are hazy." Lio rubbed her back. "I'm sure the fever left your mind in a blur."

"I lost days…weeks, I suppose, while I was recovering." Cassia shrugged, belying how those blanks in her memory unnerved her. Gaps in her information were holes in her armor.

"That's why your constitution hasn't been the same." Solia's tone was almost accusing, but Cassia knew her anger was directed at the fever and time and distance.

Cassia had once been uncomfortable speaking of the fever's side effects, but now she had a more Hesperine sense of propriety. Lio already knew, and it was the sort of thing one confided in one's sister. Besides, Mak and Lyros were the least concerned about mortal fertility of anyone. "Well, it left me barren, but that has never been a source of grief to me. I'm working very hard to become fanged and even more barren as soon as I can."

Lyros gave a sympathetic laugh. "That's the spirit."

"Clearly Orthros is the place for you," Mak agreed. "Plenty of babies, none of the breeding."

Solia dropped her reins, but her horse stood still under her while she pressed her hands together. She took a deep breath, then reached over to touch Cassia's cheek, her palm still warm. "I'm so sorry I wasn't there, Pup."

"I know. But you're here now."

"Yes." She straightened, turning her horse toward the village. "Let's see what we find in Mederi."

They descended the hill at a slower pace, which Cassia appreciated more than she cared to admit. She leaned back in her saddle, devoting all her attention to keeping her balance. Going downhill was a different beast than going up, especially when she was this tired.

"I can help with levitation," Lio offered.

"No you may not," Solia replied. "That will not help her build muscle or hone her balance. If you ruin her training, I will drag you back into the fighting ring."

"I *will* catch her with levitation if she falls off, Sunburn," Lio threatened.

"If you didn't use it *then*, I would drag you into the fighting ring faster, Sunshine."

"I will get down off my horse and walk if you two mention the fighting ring again," Cassia warned.

"Too soon," Mak agreed.

But Cassia could not deny it was wonderful to hear Lio and Solia teasing each other like proper siblings.

When they reached the bottom of the hill, Cassia felt a moment of apprehension about the low stone wall that circled the village. She might change her mind about levitation if they must jump that. Fortunately, they found a gate, which Lyros Willed open.

At a walk, they rode down Mederi's central lane between rows of thatched cottages. All was quiet at this hour of the night, the farmers sleeping so they could rise with the sun. This part of Tenebra offered fertile land, and the results showed in the well-kept village. Their fields had not been trampled by the feuds during King Lucis's reign.

But these people lived under his shadow. Cassia glanced into the distance, where she could make out wooded hills, the king's hunting grounds.

The villagers might not face the slow agony of starvation, but any one of them could die tomorrow at his whim.

In the village square, there stood a statue carved of the local gray stone. Solia halted her warhorse, one hand resting on her sword, and gazed at the delicate young woman in an elegant gown, who had a crown and a martyr's aura carved around her head. "I don't recognize this goddess. Have I really been in the Empire so long that I've forgotten part of the pantheon?"

"No." Cassia chuckled. "That's you."

"What?" Solia tilted her head, studying the statue again. "Is this what you meant by my 'cult'?"

"Many villages have statues depicting you as a martyr." Cassia gestured at the flowers, grains, and bits of thread at the statue's feet. "Your people leave offerings in your memory."

Solia muttered a curse.

"Why does this make you uncomfortable?" Lio asked. "It helps your cause that they remember you with such love."

"All I've done for them for fifteen years is be a statue. How many of them have suffered at the king's hands while I wasn't here to protect them?"

"Soli," Cassia protested, "you know you did the right thing to escape—and return with the strength Tenebra needs."

"That didn't help you when you lay on the brink of death."

Cassia reached for her sister's hand. "But I knew you loved me."

Solia squeezed her hand hard. "That wouldn't have saved you."

"I understand," Lio said. "Every time Cassia faced danger without me…those moments haunt my dreams, and they always will. But in the words of a wise warrior, we shouldn't waste our energy on things we cannot change. We have work to do now that demands everything we have."

One side of Solia's mouth tilted in a smile. "You did learn something from me, scrollworm."

He gave her a mock-bow from the saddle. "And now I endeavor to be useful as your adviser, Matriarch."

"Stop being philosophical and come look at this," Mak said from the other side of the statue.

They rode around Solia's likeness to join Mak and Lyros. Another statue stood back-to-back with Solia's. This one had an aura engraved with a glyph of Kyria. Knight sniffed the stone liegehound that lay at her feet.

"Oh dear," Cassia said.

Lio looked at her with amusement. "It's not a bad likeness, my Kyrian maiden."

"It's missing one red eye." Mak snickered. "And fangs."

Lyros wrinkled his nose. "The anatomy and perspective are inaccurate. Tenebran sculptors need to take a lesson from the Hesperine masters."

Mak laughed harder. "For someone who insists he can't draw to save his life, you have very specific opinions on art."

"I can't help it," Lyros said mournfully. "My family ruined me. I'm unable to ignore a poorly painted fingernail."

"You won't hear me complain about your appreciation for good anatomy."

That made Lyros grin, one of his fangs showing.

"Well," Solia said, "remind me to commission some statues from Apollon for my new palace, preferably of Cassia with a rose in hand and me with a sword."

Lio smiled at her, as if surprised. "That's a fine image."

Cassia had to agree. Solia might not have endorsed Cassia with fangs, but hearing her sister talk about her with a rose in hand was encouraging.

Lyros looked around. "There's not much else here. Unless you sense anything, Cassia, we can head back to the keep."

Cassia closed her eyes and focused on her resting current. Now practiced at reaching beyond her companions' auras and casting her senses over the land, she expanded her awareness easily. But her magic felt stretched, tired. She tried to ignore the anxiety that gripped her.

The fields beyond the village felt warm and full, ready for the coming harvest. She was beginning to understand that the fertility of the land in this region was no coincidence.

"It feels like most of the eastern villages," she said. "I can definitely tell the Lustra magic is stronger in this direction, just like in the tunnels. But I cannot seem to fix on precisely where it's coming from." Her eyes flew open. "My pea plants."

Lio's eyes widened.

"It was astonishing, how well my garden grew at Paradum." Cassia's skin broke out in gooseflesh at the thought that she might have been so close and never known it. "It must have been because the letting site was near."

"Perhaps that's where Thalia intended to take you." Solia leaned forward in her saddle. "But you arrived too early, when your magic wasn't ready yet."

"Or perhaps when I caught that fever, it delayed me from meeting the conditions for my magic to arrive." Cassia shook her head, tamping down her hopes. "Or perhaps the letting site isn't at Paradum at all, but somewhere farther away. Even so, the magic could be stronger there, pointing us in the right direction."

"Tomorrow, we ride for Paradum," Lyros said.

"I don't remember the way," Cassia lamented. "Do you, Solia?"

She shook her head. "I never went there, only knew of it."

"Then we'll search for it," Lio said. "With the magic at our disposal, it can't be that difficult to find."

"We'll have to approach with caution, though," said Mak. "Even if the king isn't likely to pay us a surprise visit, it's still one of his keeps. The last thing we need is for his steward to alert him that we've been there."

Cassia paused to think. "A lesser lord used to manage the game for him, and his wife kept the household. I spent more time with Agata than my hosts, who preferred not to be in the company of a bastard. Even so, I'm sorry for what happened to the lord and lady. I'm not sure whom he chose to replace them after the epidemic."

"If this is the safe place Thalia mentioned," Solia said, "there must be a way to get you to the letting site there without alerting the king."

Lio rested a hand on the scroll he now always brought on their searches. "She described the arrival of each of her affinities as a vigil that lasted for a night and a day. Perhaps there's a hidden location like the Changing Queen's passageways where you can wait out the awakening of your magic."

Cassia found a smile for him, even though she was afraid to get her own hopes up.

He looked more encouraged than he had in weeks. "We're closer. This could be it. Only a few more d—"

Lio broke off, and Cassia felt what had startled him. A gleam of magic. Everyone turned in the direction of the spell.

"Is that Kyrian healing magic?" Cassia asked.

"Yes," Lio answered, "but Ariadne and the Semna said nothing about visiting any of the villages tonight. There's something odd about the spell. It doesn't feel quite like the Temple of Kyria."

"An apostate?" Solia wondered.

"An apostate healer hardly sounds dangerous," Mak said. "Should we leave them be?"

"Might be best not to meddle in things that don't concern us," Lyros agreed.

Cassia, Lio, and Solia exchanged a glance.

"I think we should at least find out what's happening," Cassia said.

"If someone's life is in danger," said Lio, "the apostate might need help."

Solia nodded. "Let's simply ensure all is well before we return to Patria."

"It's our duty to keep you three safe," Lyros said, "so we advise against this, as the Hesperine delegation's bodyguards."

"But as Hesperines," said Mak, "we feel the same way."

They guided their horses down a side lane toward the spell. It was emanating from a small, tidy cottage at the edge of the village. The shutters were so tight that no light leaked from inside.

"Too close to the edge of the wards for comfort," Lio murmured. "Surely there's no reason for the Collector to target this stranger, or for him to test our wards over one mage, but..."

Solia nodded. "I'm thinking of Pakhne, too. I hate to imagine him adding one more healer's magic to his collection."

Cassia glanced over the village wall and saw a small, dark shape lying on the ground. Knight trotted up to the nearest gate and went into a warning stance. His growl rumbled through the night.

Despite the powerful hum of the Hesperine magic in the ward, a chill went down Cassia's spine. "What is that?"

They rode as close as they dared to the perimeter, and Lio sent a spell light out to hover over the black form. It was the stiff, bedraggled body of a dead crow. Seeing the Eye of Hypnos drawn on its breast in blood,

Cassia tried not to gag. A trail of feathers led from the bird to the gate, halting abruptly at the edge of the ward.

Lio's magic fortified her mind. "He didn't get past the ward."

"But he was here," Cassia said. "Perhaps he still is."

Solia hurled a ball of fire at the crow. Lio shivered, as if he felt her spell pass through the ward. But before the fire hit the bird, it sprang up from the ground and flew off. Solia's fire spell landed on the ground and turned a patch of grass to ash.

"A bloodless crow?" Mak made a face. "Almost as classic as a bloodless vulture."

"We must check on the cottage," Solia urged.

They all dismounted, their intelligent horses waiting obediently while they approached the small house. Knight's hackles were up, and Cassia felt Mak and Lyros's wards at the ready. Amid the rising heat of Solia's magic, Lio's power waxed stronger in Cassia's mind.

"What do you feel in the Blood Union?" Cassia asked.

"Pain," Lio answered. "Someone inside is wounded."

"Lio, your concealing magic is strongest," Lyros said. "You and I will step in first, then bring the others in, depending on what we find."

Solia nodded her approval of this plan. She and Mak flanked Cassia, Knight standing in front of her, and once again she cursed being the weakest mortal in their party.

Lio and Lyros stepped through the wall of the cottage. When they reemerged a moment later, Lio wore an expression of surprise. "Perita and Callen are inside, assisting the healer with an injured villager."

Cassia started toward the door of the cottage. "We have to offer assistance. What are Perita and Callen doing here with an apostate?"

Lio joined her at the door. "The apostate healer is Miranda."

Cassia knocked on the door of the cottage, her palms sweating. If she were engaged in clandestine magic, an interruption was the last thing she would want. "Perita, it's Cassia. We're here to help."

The door popped open, and Perita's pale face appeared in the crack.

"My lady? What are you doing here? Oh, I see." Her gaze went to the Hesperines and Solia, and she dropped a quick curtsy. "Your Majesty."

"If we can sense the magic," Solia said, "so might others. Let us help you complete your task here and hide the evidence."

Perita let out a sigh of relief and hurried them all inside, where a gray-haired farmwife hovered beside her husband's bed. The farmer's weathered face was crumpled with pain. Callen held a flask of spirits ready, while Miranda knelt with her hands on the farmer's knee, her eyes shut in concentration.

The image struck Cassia, so familiar, yet just out of reach. She gritted her teeth. The memory wouldn't come to her.

But a realization did. Could Cassia have lost more than time to that fever? Could she have lost her memories of a person?

Miranda opened her eyes and saw Cassia. The healer went pale.

"You have nothing to fear," Solia said.

The farmwife looked up and gasped. She stared at Solia as if she had seen a goddess. Perita took her arm and guided her forward, murmuring an explanation.

The older woman's eyes overflowed with tears, and she sank stiffly to her knees before Solia, clutching the hem of her long Imperial tunic. "My Queen, My Queen," the woman sobbed, murmured prayers to Kyria.

Solia's clear blue eyes misted with emotion. She touched the woman's gray curls. "Someone fetch a chair for her."

Lio set one by the fire. Solia helped the woman up off her creaking knees and guided her to sit near the warmth.

"You are too good, My Queen," the woman sobbed. "We knew. We always knew you would save us."

"I am here," Solia promised, "and I will not leave you again."

A vice seemed to close over Cassia's heart. Could Solia keep that promise to Cassia and her people at the same time? Could Cassia keep her promises to her sister, when her own heart was also torn in two?

"What has befallen your husband?" Solia asked.

"His knee, Your Majesty. Oh—what are we to do?" The woman drew deep, shuddering breaths, so overwhelmed at the sight of her martyr in the flesh that she could scarcely speak.

"The king's guard did this," Callen said with bitterness.

Cassia shuddered. The king's personal guard, the only soldiers he allowed in his solar, often committed his crimes for him. They were the most brutal men in his service. He chose them for their lack of scruples and kept them loyal by any means necessary.

"Why did they target this family?" Cassia asked.

"What reason does the king require?" Miranda broke in with a panicked look at Perita. "He's vile. That's all anyone here needs to know."

Perita rested a hand on Miranda's shoulder. "It's all right. Our secrets are safe with Her Majesty and those loyal to her."

Miranda trembled, whether with the effort of maintaining her spell, or fear, Cassia couldn't guess. But then the healer bowed her head. "If you're sure, Perita."

"I'm sure. Will you let me tell them what you told us?"

Miranda hesitated once more, but finally nodded.

Perita turned to Cassia and her companions. "Years ago, the king ordered this family to spy for him. He knew Mederi Village was loyal to Queen Solia's memory, and he chose this couple to rat on their neighbors in case of any unrest. He put their only son to work in the royal stables in an attempt to bribe them."

The farmwife lifted her chin. "We never told him anything, My Queen. We fed him lies and hid our neighbors' treason against him."

"But he grew suspicious." Callen's expression hardened. "To keep them in line, he had their son arrested on false charges and threw him in the Western Wing of the royal prison in the capital."

Cassia's belly dropped. No one made it out of the Western Wing alive, except Callen, and only because Cassia, Perita, and the mages of Kyria had fought for his life. "I saw to it that Callen was freed. I will do the same for your son."

The farmwife shut her eyes for a moment, then shook her head. "Kyria bless you, Your Highness, but our boy has already gone to the gods. He didn't survive to his execution. They brought his body back to us on the twenty-second of Kyria's Loom last year. I'll never forget the day."

That date struck Cassia as important. She realized why. She had been in Orthros then. It was the night the Solstice Summit negotiations had finally begun.

She pressed a hand to her belly. She knew why their son had died. Weeks before that day, she had been hiding in the king's solar when the guards had dragged a stable hand out of prison and handed him over to the Skleros to exploit in a necromantic ritual. She had watched the young man suffer as the Dexion's magic was shoved into his body. And on the twenty-second of Kyria's Loom, she and Lio had watched the Dexion reclaim that magic, leaving this couple's son dead.

"They kept feeding the king new and more believable lies," Perita said, "but he's run out of patience."

Callen leaned against the mantle and rubbed his face. "Today, the king's guard smashed his knee so he won't be able to work their fields anymore."

"Yes, he will." Tears escaped Miranda's eyes. "I won't let this happen. I swear to you, he will walk again."

Why did she care so deeply about this family? Enough to risk arrest for using her magic, enough to enlist Perita and Callen's aid, as she had aided them during Perita's difficult birth?

"You were helping Pakhne heal Perita, weren't you?" Cassia asked suddenly.

"Of course I was," Miranda bit back. "I wasn't about to lose another friend."

Her words cut through the haze in Cassia's mind. All the disjointed slivers of memory fit together. Miranda fighting for someone's life. Her familiar face. The garden at Paradum.

"Oh, Goddess." The words slipped out of Cassia's mouth.

Miranda met her gaze. She must have seen the recognition there, for new fear entered her eyes.

"Please," she begged, "don't turn me in. Not this time."

MEMORIES

CASSIA FLED FROM THE cottage just in time to vomit. Lio was at her side in an instant. He kept a reassuring arm lightly around her while she knelt and emptied her stomach at the base of the farmwife's pretty hedges. Yet another way she was making a mess of these people's lives. But there was no way to purge the guilt from inside her.

When nothing came but dry heaves, Lio worked a cleaning spell. He pulled her shaking body into his arms. Hesperines, always trying to cleanse her and pull her closer to her better self. Always seeing her ugly past.

Tears coursed down her cheeks. She had never felt farther from her Hesperine self than in this moment. She didn't want Lio to see her like this, but she couldn't bring herself to push him away.

He ran his hand over her head. "Your mind is all chaos, my Grace. Please tell me what's tearing you apart inside."

"I was a monster, Lio. Before I met you… Never doubt I was the king's daughter."

"You were never his. You were fighting to hold your own against him."

"Do not romanticize me. No matter how much you love me."

He didn't push her away. There was no judgment in his voice. "I have always seen you more clearly than anyone else could. Your petals and your thorns."

"You don't know what I've done," she whispered.

"Will you tell me?" he asked. "You know that nothing you say or do will cost you my love."

"I don't want you to love me for the person you believe me to be… you deserve to know the truth about who I really am."

For a moment, she thought she might be sick again from simply trying to say it aloud, but Lio's power touched her mind, calming her stomach.

"When the king sent me to Paradum," she began, "I thought it would simply be another season to survive in another keep. The lord and lady were glad enough to watch me for him to curry favor, but they treated me like baggage." Cassia swallowed. "That's also how they treated their own daughter. Lady Miranda."

"Now I begin to understand."

"But Agata, the cook, was kind. She put me to work in the garden, and I...I was *happy,* Lio. It was the only time in my life I was happy, after losing Solia and before I met you. And part of the reason why was because Miranda and I became friends. She was my first Perita." Cassia shut her eyes over a fresh wave of tears. "But then I ruined everything."

He stroked her hair, listening in silence.

"She accidentally used magic in front of me. She begged me not to tell anyone, for she dreaded being trapped in a temple. It wasn't the life she wanted, and most of all, she didn't want to lose her inheritance. Everyone living in the vicinity of Paradum...the people in this village...they should have been her dependents. She wanted to become their lady and take better care of them than her parents had."

"What happened?" he asked gently.

"I sold her out." The words emerged from Cassia in a horrified rasp. "I told the mages she had magic."

He listened, giving her time. Why wasn't he angry? Why wouldn't he agree with her that what she had done was wrong?

"Miranda fled rather than succumb to the Orders," Cassia said. "But do you know what she did before she escaped to become an apostate? All these years, I never recalled, until I saw her again. But now I remember her leaning over my bed, working magic. She must have healed me. She must be the reason I survived the fever."

His arms tightened around her.

"I threw away a friend like that," Cassia said.

Lio rocked her in his arms.

"All of this is my fault. I doomed her to a life as a fugitive. I doomed her people to the king's whims, robbing them of a lady who would have tried to shield them from him. Her fear...this family's losses...all of it is because of me."

What had happened to Miranda since then? What hardships had she faced as a woman alone in Tenebra, trying to hide her magic? Cassia shuddered to imagine. "At least she found her way to Sabina, who knows her secret and treats her better than I ever did."

"I do think Miranda has some friends in high places. Someone with resources to help her hide her aura. The first few times I met her, I had no idea she was a mage."

"She's probably the reason Perita is alive, too. She was surely helping Pakhne heal her. That night, you drove the Collector away before he could harm anyone else, including Miranda."

"Then I will consider my bond of gratitude with her honored, and we will continue to watch out for her. Between his attack on the tent and the undead crow, we were right to worry he might target her."

Cassia hung her head. "Now you know. I betrayed a woman that brave and heroic and kind. To save my own skin."

Lio's tone was so reasonable that she could scarcely bear it. "Why did you do it?"

"Because I was selfish and cruel."

"You have never enjoyed being cruel to people. There must have been a pragmatic reason you chose to barter that information to the temple."

Cup and thorns, he knew her so well. His logic went right to the heart of the issue like a razor.

"The king was coming to take me away from Paradum," Cassia said. "He wanted me back at court for reasons I didn't know."

"Whatever his reasons, they couldn't have been good. You had reason to believe you were in mortal danger from your sister's murderer."

How could he be so fair? "I made a desperate bid for the local Temple of Kyria to take me in."

"Resisting the king is risky, even for mages. They would not have been willing to put themselves in that position without powerful motivation. You would have had to win their favor with a gesture of loyalty—such as telling them about an apostate."

"That doesn't justify what I did."

"It helps you understand yourself," he said, "which a necessary step toward making things right."

"How can I ever make this right? I ruined so many lives for my own gain."

"Not for gain—for survival. To protect yourself from your abuser."

"It didn't matter in the end," she said. "My plan didn't work. I fell ill. Miranda escaped the mages. When I survived, the king took me away."

"And you had no happiness for seven more years."

"How can you care about my happiness?" She pressed her face against his chest, taking comfort in his arms that she didn't deserve. She had often feared he was too good for her, and she had been right. "How can you not hate the person I used to be?"

"I love you," he said. "I loved you when you were Cassia Basilis, and I've loved you along every step of your journey to become Cassia Komnena."

"I'm not sure which I am anymore."

"That is obvious, my rose. It was obvious to me the night you pretended not to care about the casualties of epidemics, while helping me sneak life-saving medicine into the Temple of Kyria. But in case you need further evidence, you are someone who is physically ill because you care so much about the people inside this cottage."

She shut her eyes, her tears soaked his robe. This was why she could not stop holding onto him. He always reminded her that hope was not lost. Including hope for herself to transform.

"You already transformed," he said. "We're simply going to make it official on your Gift Night."

"That won't undo the genuinely terrible things I did in the past."

He stroked her hair. "My father has told you how he sought vengeance for his parents' deaths, and later for Methu's. You know Phaedros brutalized countless mortals. Hespera has never been the Goddess of the perfect. She is the Goddess of the broken. That's what Sanctuary and Mercy mean. We come to her as we are. Why do you think we are so determined to mend this world? It's because we know what it takes to mend ourselves."

"You've never done anything cruel in your life."

"But I've done things I regret…failed those who needed me."

She rested her hand on his heart, knowing he was thinking of Pakhne. "Have you figured out how to forgive yourself?"

He shook his head. "I wish I could show you the way. But I still don't know how."

WALKING BACK INSIDE THE cottage to face Miranda was one of the most difficult things Cassia had ever done. The healer was now slumped in a chair by the fire, sweating, while Perita gave her some water. The farmer slept peacefully, his leg in a splint.

Mak and Lyros's worried gazes followed Cassia across the cottage, and Solia opened her mouth as if to speak. Lio shook his head at them and wrapped his veils around Cassia's conversation, as she had asked.

"Miranda," Cassia began, "I would be grateful if you would permit me a word with you. You certainly don't owe it to me, and if you prefer never to speak to me again, I will respect your wishes."

"Of course I'll speak with you, Your Highness," Miranda replied carefully.

Perita glanced between them with a worried expression. "What's going on?"

Miranda squeezed her hand. "Give us a moment."

"I'll explain later," Cassia promised.

Her chin set in protest, Perita joined Callen by the older couple.

"You have my gratitude for saving my life," Cassia began.

Miranda swallowed. "You remembered."

"Not until tonight."

Miranda gave a nod, her lips tight. "Fevers play with the mind."

"I didn't deserve your help after what I did to you."

"You didn't deserve to die. I couldn't let that happen."

She was a healer, through and through, it seemed, unable to do harm even to someone who had wronged her so deeply.

Miranda knotted her hands in her lap. "When I realized the fever had affected your memory, I...I rather hoped you would not recall me. Please, Your Highness, I will not stand in the way of anything you are trying to accomplish here. Perita helped me get this position. Lady Sabina is powerful enough to hide me and kind enough to let me help my people when her duties bring her into this area. I only want to remain at her side. I will cause you no trouble, I assure you."

"You have nothing to fear. I will never betray you again."

Miranda kept her gaze downcast. "You need not try to win me over, Your Highness. I am already in the palm of your hand. Whatever you want in exchange for not telling the Semna about me, I'll give it to you."

Cassia shook her head. What a nightmare for Miranda. The bastard girl who had once ruined her life had now returned as a powerful woman, sister to the future queen. She must think Cassia an even more heartless politician than Sabina and Flavian had imagined her to be.

"After all these years," Cassia said, "after how I treated you, there is no reason for my words to mean anything to you. But I speak the truth. I feel such deep shame."

Miranda did not look up, as if she didn't dare, the firelight casting deep, weary shadows on her still-young face.

"I am so sorry," Cassia said. "If I could go back and change what I did, I would put you and your people ahead of myself. I would never do anything to lose your friendship. I know I can never undo the harm I caused, but I swear to you, here and now, I will do everything in my power to atone."

Miranda lifted her gaze. For the first time, the fear was gone from her eyes. Cassia saw only bitterness, hardened by life.

"You are entitled to your anger," Cassia said. "I do not expect your forgiveness, but I will endeavor to earn it."

Cassia rose and gave Miranda not a Tenebran lady's curtsy, but a Hesperine ambassador's bow. For a moment, Miranda's eyes widened in surprise. Hoping her actions spoke louder than words, Cassia left Miranda to rest from the spell and returned to Lio's side.

"I would like an explanation later," Solia said. "When you're ready."

Cassia was suddenly exhausted. She would have to tell Solia everything, in case any of her past deeds complicated politics. Lio used a bit of levitation to keep her on her feet, and this time, she didn't protest.

Mak changed the subject. "We asked the couple if they know who's trying to send the king encoded notes from inside Patria."

"Unfortunately they weren't able to tell us," Lyros said, "but at least we know he has no spies in the village."

"He'll cultivate new ones," Solia said, "and the next time he punishes this couple for resisting, it will be worse than a broken knee. I want more Hesperine wards around the cottages and fields, and Miranda must have an escort anytime she comes out this far."

"Of course," Mak said. "When the Collector left us that undead crow, he might as well have painted a target on her."

At the thought of the Collector harming Miranda because of Cassia, after everything else Miranda had already suffered, Cassia felt like being sick again.

Solia's hand tightened on the hilt of her sword, her constant reflex. "As of tonight, I am taking this village under my protection. No matter what the king or the Collector try, we will be ready."

"As your adviser," Lio said, "it is my duty to inform you that this could lead the king to suspect you have returned—and it might become your first declaration of war."

The light of the hearth behind Solia glowed around her, looking for all the world like a martyr's aura. "Then it will be the first skirmish of our war."

MIGRATION NIGHT

33 Anthros's Sickle, 1597 OT

CONTINGENCY PLANS

Cassia stumbled through the tunnels, her head roaring and her heart pounding. What if she fainted down here before she reached Lio? She had to keep going. Almost there. Knight whined, staying close for her to lean on.

She staggered into the moonflower chamber. Her vision was going dark by the time she slid down to the ground and threw herself across Lio's Slumbering body.

At the contact, bright magic surged through her and cleared her head. She heaved a sigh of relief.

No harm done. Except perhaps the strange looks she'd gotten, leaving the shrine chamber in such a hurry in the middle of noon rites. Fortunately there were enough rumors about her poor constitution that she was more likely to be deemed sickly than irreverent.

She drew Lio's magic into her with every gasp. Her heart began to calm. She rested her face on his chest, skin to skin in the vee of his open robe.

But she could hear his heart racing. Another day terror.

She wished they were safe at home in Orthros, spending one last Slumber in their beautiful residence in Orthros Notou. At nightfall, all their family and friends would board the ships for Migration Night and leave the southern hemisphere to return to the north. At least everyone they loved would be closer now.

Why didn't that make her feel safer, as she had expected?

Hoping to soothe Lio's tortured dreams, she ran a hand down his chest and opened the channeling wider, like the night she had first summoned him into the passageways. She had learned that deepening their magical connection could reach him in his dreams. As their auras mingled, she heard his heart slow down.

She must return to the day's court events—and make it to her next secret meeting with Eudias and Ariadne. But what if Lio's nightmares returned? She gave into her need to be near him for just a moment longer.

She raised up on one arm and watched him sleep. She had never been a romantic, but he certainly brought out the small amount of fancifulness she possessed. This vision of him sleeping on a bed of magic flowers brought legends to mind. Silly old stories which held that the Mage King had never truly died, but lay somewhere in slumber, ready to return to defend his people.

But a mortal king could not live forever, and if Lucis's atrocities had not been enough to summon him, what good was the legend, in any case? No, in the tale Cassia was living, a young Hesperine ambassador had taken the place of the warrior king as her personal champion.

With an effort, she made herself get up, dust off her robes, and turn back the way she had come. But her fears crept over her, and she hesitated.

She knew she was growing more ill by the day. If Paradum was not the great hope they suspected...if they had to keep searching... She should keep making the most of every foray here in the passageways.

"*Dockk dockk,* dear Knight. The court will have to miss us for a bit longer. Let us try the ivy chamber one more time."

Knight trotted ahead of her through the side passage to the seeming dead end she had showed Lio weeks ago. It was the chamber that still puzzled her. The magic seemed so strong here, so full of potential. She always felt on the verge of a discovery. But none of the magical exercises she and Lio had tried had yielded results.

Even so, she tried again, standing for long moments with the ivy pendant in her hand. She concentrated on that feeling of latent magic. But the sense of possibility did not ignite into a spell.

No more time to experiment today. Cassia hastened back toward the shrine chamber, pausing at the portal to make sure noon rites were in fact over, and it would be safe to meet Eudias and Ariadne. Carefully, she put her ear through the wall.

But it was Ben and Genie's voices that she heard. Cassia wrapped an arm around Knight to hold him back and leaned forward just enough to peer through the stone.

Ben and Genie faced each other at the shrine of Andragathos. She leaned into the distance between them, just a little closer than was appropriate. "You wanted to talk to me alone?"

"Yes," Ben said. "I had to see you before the vote."

"I'm so glad. I miss you." Genie rested her hand on his arm, turning the touch into the slightest caress.

And there it was, the confirmation of what Cassia had suspected. Ben's love was not unrequited at all. She took heart that Ben's cause was not hopeless, if only because Genie tended to get what she wanted.

The knight put a hand over hers, stilling it. But he also did not let go. "You have to leave. Today."

She pulled away. "That's why you arranged a secret meeting? To lecture me again?"

"Trust me. You must get away from Patria."

"Ben, we have had this conversation every day since I arrived. I will *not* go home, and you cannot make me." Genie's words might be those of a petulant child, but her tone held great dignity.

"It's different this time," Ben pleaded.

That plea must have worried Genie as much as it did Cassia, for the girl asked, "What do you mean?"

Ben made a frustrated sound. "I can't say, because I don't know what you'll repeat to Her Highness."

Genie took a step back. "Do you really think that of me? I'm capable of navigating my position better than that."

Ben sighed and rubbed his face. "I know. Believe me, I know how it feels to have divided loyalties."

Genie reached out and touched his arm again. "Have you made up your mind? Is the night of the vote when you will finally act? If so, I want to be there."

Unease prickled Cassia's neck.

Ben shook his head. "No. It's too dangerous. You must be gone before the vote. I don't want you involved in this."

"You need my help."

"I need to know you're safe."

"None of us are safe, Ben. Do you really think I'll abandon everything we've worked for now, at the most important moment?"

Oh, Goddess. What were they planning?

"It's more dangerous than you know," Ben said. "The night of the vote…things will happen that could end very badly."

"If they end badly for you, all the more reason I should be there."

Cold suspicions that belonged to Cassia Basilis tangled with Cassia Komnena's affection for these two. She found it so hard to believe Genie or Ben would do anything that could truly endanger the Council.

But there was no doubt Genie was a new politician in the Segetian mold. And because Ben adhered rigidly to his moral compass, he was capable of desperate action in the name of his convictions. A dangerous characteristic, if his convictions ever misguided him.

He took Genie's hands in his. She drew nearer, tilting her face up toward him. He bowed his head.

"Genie…" he murmured.

"Ben," she whispered back.

"It is not your duty to protect me," he said. "It is my duty to protect you."

Her hands tightened on his, drawing him closer. "I don't want you to treat me like a child. I want you to treat me like a woman."

"You deserve to be treated like a lady."

"Oh!" With a little growl of frustration, she let him go and tossed up her hands.

"What did I say? How have I managed to make you angry again?" He looked as downcast as he had on the tournament field. "Is this about the title I failed to win?"

"Of course not! How can you even ask me that?"

"Genie, I don't understand you half the time. It's as if I can do no wrong, and then I can't do right. What do you want from me?"

"Have you heard nothing I've said to you since I arrived?"

"You made one thing clear." His voice hardened. "My deeds are all that matter to you. I will act, Genie. I'll show you what I'm made of."

"And I will be there—not to watch, but to play my part." She turned on her heel and deserted the room.

Ben knelt before the shrine of his god and bowed his head, murmuring prayers in the tone of a man struggling with his conscience. Then Eudias entered the shrine chamber, and Ben leapt to his feet as if he'd been caught sinning rather than praying. With a nod to the mage, the knight beat a hasty retreat, leaving Eudias staring after him.

Cassia emerged from the wall, and Eudias turned to her with a frown. "Do you have any idea what troubles him?"

Cassia hesitated, recalling her own words to Lio about caution. Her habit of parceling out secrets only to those who needed to know them had returned to her in full force since their return to Tenebra.

Ariadne slipped inside the shrine chamber and joined them before the shrine of Andragathos. "Why do you look so worried, Cassia?"

She decided to take a risk. If something dangerous was about to happen at the vote, it could help for their mage allies to be forewarned. She repeated the conversation between Ben and Genie.

"I can't believe anything wicked of Ben," Ariadne said. "He is so genuinely devout."

"So are many of the cutthroat politicians in the Magelands," Eudias said mournfully. "I hope our suspicions are unfounded, but we'll remain alert."

"Thank you," Cassia said. "Why did you wish to meet with me? Do you have a warning to share as well?"

Ariadne shook her head. "Good news, actually!"

"We wanted to wait until we could tell you and Lio together," Eudias said, "but there are so many rites leading up to the Autumn Equinox that we aren't certain we can get away from prayers after dark."

"No, please tell me now." Goddess knew they could use some good news.

Ariadne's eyes were bright with excitement. "We found a loophole."

Eudias smiled. "It *is* possible for you and Lio to marry under Tenebran law."

Cassia put a grateful expression on her face and tried not to betray the tension spreading through her. This was, objectively, excellent news. But she had not expected it. Part of her had hoped this would prove to be impossible, and thus make the decision for her.

She was deeply uncertain how she felt about this notion of marriage.

Making more vows to Lio could never be a bad idea, could it? But *Tenebran* marriage vows. She had fought so hard to escape them, even as the lack of them had plagued her and her mother's lives.

But one thing was certain—their friends had worked hard to give her and Lio the choice. "Thank you both so much. This is astonishing. How can we manage it?"

Eudias explained, "As you know, per the original Equinox Oath, Hesperines are not permitted to enter temples. Unfortunately, even with the Solstice Oath now taking precedence, this stipulation is deeply embedded in religious law. So we researched marriage rites that can be performed outside a temple."

Ariadne nodded. "There are certain spells that can be cast to consecrate the ground for a wedding. This essentially turns the site into a temple."

"Doesn't that mean Lio would still be forbidden to set foot there?" Cassia asked.

"Yes," Ariadne answered, "but we found precedents for emergency weddings on battlefields or in sickrooms, which only require one of the partners to be standing on divine ground. For example, if a woman's betrothed is mortally wounded, as long as she stands in a Kyrian circle beside his deathbed, he can still marry her before he dies."

"This means I must still be human for the ceremony," Cassia said.

"Yes," Ariadne confirmed.

Well, this was to be a hasty wedding, or none at all, for Cassia had no intention of delaying her Gifting for a moment in the name of Tenebran marriage laws.

Ariadne spread her hands. "The greatest obstacle is finding a mage of Anthros and a mage of Kyria in good standing with the Orders who are willing to perform the ceremony. Fortunately for you, that part will be easy. I would be happy to cast the Kyrian circle for you to stand in."

"Then I can include Lio in the ceremony by casting a glyph over him." Eudias wrinkled his nose. "He won't find it a very pleasant experience, but it won't do him harm."

However Cassia felt about marriage, their friends' efforts meant so much to her. "You both have our gratitude. I'll tell Lio all of this when he wakes."

"One more suggestion," Ariadne said. "There are also some interesting precedents for promise dances. A lord once arrived late to the Autumn Greeting on his way home from war. He wasn't there for the dance by daylight, when most of the other couples made their betrothal promises. But he danced with his lady around the bonfire after nightfall, and the lords and ladies present bore witness, and it was considered by all to hold the same intention and legal weight as if they had danced earlier in the day."

Cassia smiled slowly. Now this was something she would relish—dancing with Lio around the Autumn Equinox bonfire and seeing the look on Flavian's face. "I will put this to good use, I assure you."

"We won't keep you any longer." Eudias glanced up through the clerestory windows, which let in the early afternoon light and last warmth of summer. "Lord Flavian will be expecting you and your sister in the courtyard."

And Cassia would go armed with new schemes.

She thanked the mages again, then led Knight back into the Lustra passageways to return to their chambers. In the weaving room, there was no sign of Genie or anyone else. Solia and Kella's grim voices drew Cassia to the bedchamber, where they were readying themselves for the day's next events and discussing politics. Cassia told them what she had overheard.

"Oh, Ben." Regret crossed Solia's face as she unbuckled her sword. "His guilt over his father is poison. I fear this is some foolish attempt to prove himself a better man. We'll have to keep an eye on him."

Kella, sitting on the bed next to Tilili, squeezed ointment out of a small skin in her hand. "It's good that you accepted Genie into your retinue. Keep your enemies close."

"Possible enemies." Cassia pulled off her slippers.

Kella began rubbing the ointment into one of her residual limbs. "Yes, but with the vote happening any day, we cannot afford to take chances. Every person in the great hall is here not only to vie for their preferred candidate for the throne, but to achieve ends of their own."

Cassia nodded. "And those personal motivations are what will make them the most desperate."

"And the most dangerous," Kella said. "Last-minute changes of heart could cost us everything."

To Cassia's pleasant surprise, Perita interrupted them, bustling in with little Callen strapped to her chest. The cares of the world stopped for a moment while they all indulged their desire to dote on him. Cassia covered a smile with her hand. Had any little boy been hovered over by such a dangerous flock of women?

Perita busied herself dressing Solia and brought Kella her other saddle blanket. Once she had seen to the two royals, she helped Cassia change into her riding gown.

"Just like old times, my lady," Perita said with obvious contentment.

Cassia pressed her friend's hand. "Are you certain Sabina doesn't mind?"

"Not at all." Perita smiled. "Miranda is helping her. She'll meet us down in the courtyard."

Every mention of Miranda still felt like a knife in Cassia's chest. "How is she?"

"Just leave her to me," Perita said. "I'll make her see how you've changed."

"You're too generous to me." Cassia had dreaded revealing her and Miranda's past to Perita. She had expected it to tarnish her in Perita's eyes. She was still astonished that Perita had responded with nothing but understanding.

"We've all done things we don't fancy confessing in the temple," Perita said. "Do you think Miranda is a divine maiden, either? None of us are. I'm not proud of what I told the king about you before I learned to trust you. But the risks you've taken for Callen and me show what you're truly made of, my lady."

"Thank you, my friend." Cassia felt the words were not sufficient.

"Don't thank me yet." Perita smiled with satisfaction. "Not until I tell you the information I learned on laundry day."

"Is someone pregnant?" Solia asked.

"Or perhaps an attempted assassination in the bed sheets?" Kella leaned forward.

Perita giggled. "You all have the best taste in gossip, Your Highnesses, if I may say so. But this concerns a onetime mage of Kyria who was cast from her temple. She was sent home to her brother in disgrace and forbidden to use magic ever again...but she is not content to accept the gift of obscurity."

"Are you talking about Irene?" Cassia asked.

Perita nodded. "The very same."

"You know her?" Solia asked.

"All too well," Cassia said. "When Ariadne's temple was hiding Zoe and the other children, Irene betrayed their secret to the Order of Anthros."

"She sold out children to be punished for heresy?" Kella asked.

Cassia nodded. "Can you guess which free lord's sister she is?"

"Ohh," Solia replied, "didn't Tyran have a younger sister who entered the temple?"

"That's the one," Cassia confirmed. "No doubt she and Tyran are working together—and most likely against each other at the same time. What is she up to now, Perita?"

"She's thrilled to be out of the temple and determined to reclaim her standing among the nobility. She's made a nuisance of herself bringing gifts to Segetia…and ever since her brother arrived at Patria, her letters have also been stacking up on Lord Flavian's desk here."

Solia appeared very interested indeed. "What sort of letters?"

"Flattering ones," Perita answered. "Perhaps even flirtatious. I'm sure that dashing Imperial suitor of yours could find out on one of his nighttime walks."

"I shall certainly ask him," Solia said.

Cassia had not seen much of Hoyefe lately. He faithfully popped in with information, but devoted most of his spare time to Severin.

Perita smoothed the last laces on Cassia's gown, then stepped back to rock the babe, who had begun to squirm and make grumpy noises. "You're all as ready as I can make you. It's a good sign Lord Loose-Breeches invited you all to ride with him today, insufferable as he is."

Cassia sighed. "Yes, I'll grant him that. It is a valuable display of solidarity to show that both sides will uphold the outcome of the vote, no matter what is decided."

"You've never ridden in the Progress of Anthros's Sickle, have you?" Perita asked.

Cassia shook her head. "No, but Solia certainly has. She rode the Progress in the king's stead on more than one occasion, and the people still remember that. This will be another opportunity for her to upstage Flavian."

"Explain this Tenebran tradition to me." Kella slid her oiled thigh over Tilili's back and into the pocket of her saddle. "I find it the least of the evils so far, for it involves riding, and does not specify one must use a horse."

Solia chuckled. "It's a gesture liege lords and ladies are expected to make at the end of each summer. We ride through our domains, making ourselves visible to our people. It's a promise of protection to earn the tithes we'll receive from the autumn harvest."

"Or," Cassia said, "if one's lord is less scrupulous, it's an intimidation tactic reminding you to pay."

"You smile at them, Sunburn," said Kella. "I'll do the intimidating—but only to Flavian if he rides too close to any of us. I'm sick of the smell of his bath oils."

Enjoying a laugh at Flavian's expense, they met Hoyefe in the corridor, while Perita returned next door to get off her feet.

But Hoyefe did not join in their mirth. "Flavian's stash of encoded letters is gone."

"That already happened three times," Kella pointed out. "You always find his new hiding place."

Hoyefe shook his head. "I found where he hid the box this time. But the papers are missing."

Cassia stiffened. "Do you think someone else has been in his chambers?"

"It's possible," Hoyefe said. "Perhaps the spy. Or perhaps Flavian had removed them for purposes of his own."

Kella shook her head. "Why would he ruin his own chances of winning the vote by passing the spy's information to someone?"

"Perhaps it's his contingency plan if he loses," Hoyefe said.

Solia looked to Cassia. "Do you think he is that unscrupulous?"

Another card in Cassia's house slipped out. Flavian had become the man she had always suspected him to be—but in ways she had never predicted. Was he capable of betraying Solia and the law on this level?

Cassia hated to admit that she was no longer confident in her judgment, but she owed Solia the truth. "I am unsure."

"It's all right," Kella said. "We already knew we must be prepared for anything."

Cassia tucked her arm in Hoyefe's. "I imagine you are an excellent forger, Lonesome."

"My dear," Hoyefe replied, "I'm only one of the best in the Empire. Those calligraphy classes at Imperial University were useful for far more than making the scripts of my plays look pretty."

"After reading through so much of Flavian's correspondence, you could write very convincing letters in his hand, I'm sure."

"In my sleep."

"Excellent. I am fond of us having our own contingency plans."

"In that case," Hoyefe said, "you may wish to have a forgery to pull out unexpectedly. What would you like it to say?"

Cassia hesitated, but only for a moment. "A love note. A florid, detailed, filthy love note."

"My favorite kind. I am feeling quite inspired. I shall make you a quick sample and catch up to you resplendent ladies within the hour." With a bow and a smirk, he headed in the direction of the men's chamber.

Flavian was waiting for them in the courtyard astride a chestnut stallion draped in blue and gold barding, Ben at his flank. Sabina faced them on her sturdy, nimble gray mare, with Valentia, Genie, and Nivalis around her on their horses. Cassia's first warning to expect an unpleasant surprise was the unusually angry glower Sabina was directing at Flavian.

"Princess Cassia," Flavian greeted her gallantly, loud enough for all the nobles, mages, and guards in the courtyard to hear. "You look resplendent today, my dear betrothed. Won't you ride next to me during the Progress?"

Cassia's very short patience with him began to shred.

Judging by the heat coming off of Solia, so had hers. "That is not what we agreed. My sister will ride with the Kyrians."

"Oh, what an unfortunate misunderstanding," Flavian replied. "The Kyrians have gone ahead of us into the villages."

"I insist on riding beside you," Solia said.

"That is the place reserved for my liege lady," said Flavian.

"Not today." Solia's voice rang across the courtyard. "The places of lord and lady shall be occupied by the people's two possible future monarchs. We agreed to present a united front."

"I would not ask that of you, Your Highness," Flavian said with mock concern. "The rumors our Fire Dance stirred are already troubling for you. Let us still the wagging tongues and do things properly. Clearly, my betrothed should perform the duties of the liege lady."

Eudias was murmuring to Master Gorgos, as if desperate to talk him out of something. The young mage cringed when his superior boomed, "It is tradition and law. A man should not ride the Progress with a woman to whom he is not married or related. Highly inappropriate. Clearly, Lord Flavian's betrothed should be at his side to set an example of morality and curb the bestial tendencies of the peasantry."

Flavian gave Cassia a false smile. "We are honor bound."

Cassia could feel her bond with Lio pulling her back toward the keep, even as this mortal man expected her to ride away with him. Who did he think he was? When he had once foolishly dubbed her the Lady of Ice, he'd had no inkling whom he was dealing with.

It was already time to put her contingency plan into action.

THE KIND ONE

Cassia pulled Freckles alongside Sabina and whispered, "I have a plan, but I will not go through with it without your approval."

"I've had enough of his games," Sabina hissed. "Tell me what you have in mind, and I'll tell you if it's harsh enough."

If Flavian was alarmed at the sight of his unwilling betrothed and spurned lover conspiring, he didn't show it. Solia kept debating with him about Cassia, and their rising voices covered Cassia and Sabina's conversation.

"Do it," Sabina finally said.

"Are you certain?" Cassia asked.

Sabina gave a tight nod, pale with fury. "If he won't be swayed by that, then I want nothing more to do with him."

Cassia guided Freckles to her sister's side and gave Flavian her sweetest, most menacing smile. "I will ride with you. I value the opportunity for a private conversation."

No roguish, handsome grin on Flavian's face now. He knew she was up to something. Good.

"Are you certain?" Solia asked Cassia. "It will be a long, demanding day, visiting the villages and greeting their elders."

Once again, Cassia wished herself far away, with nothing to worry about but leaving her favorite wool socks in the other hemisphere before migrating. "I must do this."

"Do not exhaust yourself," Solia ordered. "If you need to return to the keep before the Progress ends, we will have someone bring you back to rest."

"I will not overly tax her," Flavian promised.

"To keep that promise," Cassia said, "you would have to put an entire kingdom between yourself and me."

"There was one, until you returned to Tenebra to disrupt my Council."

"The Council you called on my instructions."

Side by side, they led the procession out of the courtyard, with Solia on Cassia's right and her retinue following. Other members of the Council privileged enough to ride in the Progress fell in behind. They continued down the hill in front of the keep to the cheers and, no doubt, gossip of the lesser nobles, servants, and soldiers.

Cassia kept an eye out for Hoyefe, and a glance over her shoulder revealed him guiding his horse seamlessly into the procession. He and Severin, on the other side of the column of riders, did not so much as glance each other's way. Only because Cassia was watching for it did she notice the subtle change in Severin's body language that betrayed his awareness of Hoyefe.

Flavian bestowed manly waves and kingly smiles upon the crowd. She resisted the urge to roll her eyes. Sunbind him and his charisma. While he was occupied charming his potential supporters, he failed to notice the note that passed from Hoyefe's hands, through Kella's and Solia's, to Cassia's.

As the Progress made its slow, showy way between tents decorated in banners and the last garlands of summer, the arcane pull in Cassia's chest became a physical ache. The growing distance between her and her Grace made her angry, too angry to ever regret what she was about to do.

When they reached the fields beyond the tents, Cassia seized her opportunity. She exchanged a glance with her sister, who returned a nod. Solia and her retinue slowed, and as Genie captured Ben in conversation, he too fell back. Flavian was at Cassia's mercy.

"I will give you one more opportunity to release me from our betrothal," Cassia told him.

Flavian had the gall to laugh. "And if I don't? What will you do this time? Send the Semna to lecture me again? You cannot threaten anything meaningful, such as costing me votes. The kingship is within my reach."

"The votes any of us can predict with certainty are split down the middle, and those undecided are anyone's guess. That throne is not yet yours."

"But it will be."

"If you are so confident, why keep me trapped in this promise? You have no intention of marrying me and making me your queen."

"I'm keeping this card in my hand until the final trick. No telling what cards you and your sister have up your sleeves to play in the last hours of the Council."

"And after that? Let us imagine, for a moment, that you have won. Will you finally let me go then?"

"That depends on how much trouble your sister intends to make in my kingdom afterward."

She looked over at him, trying to see in him the man she would once have called a friend. "Don't make me do this, Flavian."

"Making others do as you wish is your specialty, Cassia."

"Is that what this is? You're punishing me?"

"If you think I would punish a woman out of spite, you do not know me as well as you pretend. You think I want to continue parading this mockery of a betrothal in front of Sabina? I would never, if I had any other means of mitigating the damage you're capable of dealing my plans."

"If you do not release me," Cassia said through her teeth, "what I parade in front of Sabina will be far worse than our betrothal."

"You two are thick as thieves. You would never do anything to cause her pain."

"No. But she will thoroughly enjoy the pain I intend to cause you."

His eyes narrowed. "You wouldn't. It would do too much damage to her reputation if you told everyone we..."

Cassia laughed. "You think of all the affairs you've had, we need to choose that one to spawn nasty rumors about you? Certainly not."

"I have been perfectly discreet," he said.

"Yes, everyone knows you keep your fornication within the approved bounds of Tenebran manhood. Widows, traveling players, concubines. But what if all your admirers found out you had deflowered a lady? Worse still, a temple virgin?"

"Unfortunately for your schemes, I haven't."

"That is immaterial." She handed him the note. "There are plenty more where this came from."

One hand on his reins, he held Hoyefe's brief, forged note up to read. Flavian's face flushed red and his brows drew down in anger. "I didn't write this!"

"But everyone will believe you did. Wait until you see the replies from Irene."

Cassia relished the sight of Flavian's incredulous face. "Tyran's sister? She's merely one of the many sycophants begging for Segetia's favor."

"I told you your worst quality is trying to please others. You never should have allowed her letters to enter your solar."

"I received those letters as her liege lord, nothing more!"

"The entire staff knows she's been writing to you, and the entire nobility knows you are showing great favor to her brother. Besides, Irene is a very beautiful woman, and already a little disgraced. It's not a great stretch of the imagination to think you two would disgrace her a little more."

"No one will believe this."

Cassia gave him her most scheming smile. "Are you willing to stake your reputation on that? There are plenty of men who wouldn't care if you defiled a Kyrian maiden. But there are enough. Can you afford to lose their votes?"

His horse pranced under him, and he loosened his hand on his reins as if with an effort. "Think about the effect this will have on Irene."

"I have no sympathy for her."

"This will hurt Sabina far worse than our betrothal!" Flavian protested.

"As I told you, she is quite in favor of the plan."

"Doesn't she understand I'm doing this for her? For us?"

"I fail to see how staying betrothed to another woman and opposing her family's choice for the throne will benefit her."

"Her father doesn't care that I am Segetian—well, at least, he might be willing to forgive it, in the name of peace. The reason he does not respect me is that I have obeyed orders all my life instead of fighting for something. And he will never let a man he does not respect near his daughter."

"Then win his respect. Support Solia. Court Sabina properly."

"Don't you understand the position you've placed me in? If I stand down now and surrender the throne I've fought for, I will look as if I'm giving in to Solia, just as I always have to her father and mine. The only way to win Hadrian's respect is to fight for the crown—and to do that, I have to fight you. The betrothal is the only weapon I have."

Cassia shook her head. "If you think there are no circumstances in which Lord Hadrian would respect you for surrendering, you do not understand the position he's been in with King Lucis all these years."

"Well, he will find himself in a different position with me as king. If the title of queen isn't a worthy bride price for his daughter, I don't know what is."

"A crown does not make you a man of honor, and your honor is all that matters to him. Don't make me destroy it. Release me from my betrothal at the feast tonight, or I will have no choice but to circulate explicit letters between you and Irene. Think of how Sabina's father will feel when he reads those."

She had never seen Flavian so angry. The blacker parts of her heart enjoyed every pulse of the vein in his forehead and the grimace that had wiped the charming smile off of his face.

"No," he said.

"What?" Cassia demanded. She has been so sure this would work.

"I will face your false accusations like a man," Flavian said, "and I will keep you bound to me until I am certain you are no longer a threat."

Cassia's chest felt tight and hot, and sweat broke out between her shoulder blades. She was so angry, she felt a rare urge to strike Flavian. But she would not give him the satisfaction of seeing her lose control.

"You will regret this," she warned him. "In this game of the Cruel Inquisitor and Kind Inquisitor, I am the kind one."

"Oh, I have no doubt. No one knows how to be crueler to me than Sabina."

But Cassia was not talking about Sabina. She was talking about her Grace. She was so angry that the next time Lio suggested a drastic way of getting her out of this betrothal, she would make no attempt to persuade him not to do it.

Her next plan took shape in her mind.

"I will make you an alternative offer," she said.

He looked suspicious, but replied, "I'm listening."

"I will refrain from circulating the letters on the following conditions. First, you will not require me or my sister to dance with you this Autumn Greeting. Second, once our betrothal is eventually dissolved—whenever in the future that finally occurs—you will not stand in the way of me sharing the promise dance with another. If I ever dance with someone else on the Autumn Equinox, you will attest to it being a valid promise of betrothal."

"Well, well. You are showing your hand."

Cassia concealed her tension behind a haughty expression and reached down to scratch Knight's ear. Surely Flavian did not suspect what she was really planning.

"I knew it," he said. "You've always planned to cease this Kyrian maiden act when it suits you. Your sister has a political marriage in mind for you already, doesn't she? Some Imperial, no doubt."

Cassia could have laughed with relief. The extent of Flavian's suspicion was an Imperial prince. Not a Hesperine.

She didn't think Tendo would mind if she referenced his mighty reputation for a little embellishment. "I'll have you know, I am very close friends with Prince Tendeso of the Sandira Kingdom. He has promised me introductions to the many eligible suitors in his extended family. You should see the Sandira warriors fight. One of them could disembowel you in five minutes."

"I hope you and Sabina enjoy your fantasies."

"Well?" Cassia demanded. "What do you say to my offer?"

"Once I have no further use for our betrothal, I won't care if you marry your liegehound. Dance the Greeting with whomever you please. I won't stand in your way."

"It's not enough to refrain from protesting," Cassia insisted. "I want you to acknowledge that the promise is valid."

"I suppose you would want influential Tenebrans to nod and smile to help silence the tongues protesting foreign consorts. Fine. I will support whatever match you make. I intend to be king by then, so I can afford to be generous."

"I want your word."

"You have it—if you will give me your word that you won't drag my reputation through the dung heap with forged letters. And I still expect you to finish the Progress with me today, without making a scene or letting your sister take your place. For now, we are still betrothed."

"That is an unfair demand. You know I've been ill."

"Ha. That's as convenient a part of your reputation as your Kyrian virtue. Do you really think I'm fooled every time you duck out of court events to 'rest'? I have an idea how those papers went missing from my solar."

"This is not a pretense." Cassia hated to admit her weakness in front of him, but if she fainted off her horse, he would find out in any case. "I've been very ill since we returned to Tenebra, and I cannot promise you I'll last all day."

"You're a very good liar, Cassia. I want you right here next to me until sundown. Not back in the keep sabotaging my bid for the throne. You finish the Progress with me, or our deal is off. Do you want me to support your future betrothal or not?"

Cassia swallowed hard. Could she do this?

Yes. She had survived days of Craving in the Maaqul. She could endure one afternoon of riding with Flavian. It would be worth it when he was forced to bless her Greeting dance with Lio.

"We have an agreement," Cassia said.

She would get through this day through sheer force of Will.

THE MORTALS WERE LUCKY they had set the dinner tables with pewter and not glass, or Lio would have shattered every dish in the great hall. He drew a deep, slow breath, willing his magic to stay under his skin. He was a heartbeat away from scaring the humans gathered here, waiting with the Hesperine delegation for the return of the Progress.

Cassia was ill, and he was expected to *wait*.

Mak put a hand on Lio's shoulder and pushed him down into his seat. "Don't do it. Do not step into the middle of the Progress and pluck her off her horse."

"I can feel how sick she is." Her need for his magic was like a knife in his chest. "She never should have been away from me this long. Why didn't someone bring her back early?"

"This day clearly has not gone according to plan," Lyros said, "but you must not charge in blind. We should wait and see what the situation is."

"The situation is that Cassia needs me." Lio's magic strained toward her, seeking their connection, but she wasn't near enough for the channeling to open.

Lyros shook his head. "If she's been working on some kind of strategy today, she won't want you to intervene. You might undo whatever she's accomplished. Solia would have brought Cassia back if she were in danger."

Lio swallowed, his tongue dry from Cassia's Craving. "Not if she's hiding it from everyone."

"They're almost here," Mak reassured him. "Just wait a moment longer."

The lords at the opposite table were giving Lio uneasy looks. With an effort, he veiled his fangs.

The doors of the great hall opened, and the Progress strolled in with as much ceremony mortals could muster after a long day in the saddle. Solia and her companions appeared tired and concerned, but did not seem to share Lio's panic. All of them faded from his awareness as his senses fixed on Cassia.

He could feel her holding herself together by a thread. The channeling snapped into place, and his hands closed over the arms of his chair as he held back the torrent of his power. She stumbled, clutching the arm of the man at her side.

Flavian.

That was who the lords and ladies were gossiping about. As they took their seats, they whispered about Cassia's ride as his lady. It was Flavian who had kept her apart from Lio all day.

Flavian took her toward the table at the foot of the dais. He expected her to remain next to him for the duration of the feast. And Lio was expected to sit here, banished to a side table with the rest of the Hesperine delegation. He wouldn't even be able to sustain Cassia with a subtle brush of the hand under the table.

She would not make it through this.

Lio would have leapt over the table if not for Mak's implacable grip holding him in his seat. As Flavian and Cassia passed in front of them, Lio touched her mind, assuring her of rescue. He felt nothing but determination in her thoughts.

I will make it through this. Just another hour. I will…

He heard the change in her heartbeat as the color drained from her face, and her knees buckled.

Lio stepped before she hit the ground. But he landed against a circle of mortals crowding around her. A hand made impact with his chest and shoved him back. He looked down.

It was Benedict. "Let her own people see to her."

"Get out of my way," Lio snarled.

"You have an audience," Ben hissed. "I will not allow you to harm her reputation."

Lio could hear her heartbeat weakening.

With a flick of his thoughts, he hurled Benedict away from him. The knight fell back against Flavian, and they both staggered. Mak and Lyros held the men back as the other courtiers surrounding Cassia scrambled out of Lio's way.

He knelt and pulled her into his arms, bracing himself for the channeling.

Her aura didn't pull. The contact didn't rouse her.

"She's worse than she was in the Maaqul," Kella said, "but this time it only took hours, not days."

"She didn't say anything!" Solia cried. "I checked on her every half hour…"

Knight whined, pressing close to Cassia's fallen form. Lio heard shouting beyond the roar in his ears. His blood pounded with rage, even as Cassia's heart weakened.

Cassia, I'm here. Come back to me. He sent a pulse of his magic into her.

Her heartbeat picked up. But as soon as that dose of magic faded, so did her pulse.

Lio rose to his feet, lifting Cassia from the floor. He didn't wait for Solia's permission, but she didn't protest, either.

A glint of light on steel caught his eye. Flavian whisked his sword out of his scabbard. "Unhand her!"

Lio rounded on him, baring his fangs. "How dare you. You did this to her."

Guilt twinged in the man's aura, confirming Lio's accusation. He plucked the man's thoughts from the surface of his mind. *Should have believed her when she told me she was ill…*

Flavian stood his ground, his sword at the ready. "She needs the Semna. Put her down!"

With an act of Will, Lio tore the blade from Flavian's hand and sent it clattering across the floor of the great hall. "I challenge you to Trial by Combat. No magic. No swords. Just our fists. I'll take Sunfire Poison and fight you like a man. If I win, you must release Cassia from her betrothal."

Lio didn't care about the cries of dismay or his Grace-sister's anger washing over him in a wave of heat. He didn't even enjoy the fury in Flavian's aura. All that mattered was Cassia's struggling heartbeat, and the imperative that no one ever keep her from his side again.

Wake up, my Grace, he called in her mind. *Please wake up. I may well kill him for this.*

"Will you accept my challenge?" Lio demanded. "Or are you a coward, too afraid to bloody your hands?"

Flavian drew himself up, mustering his dignity. "I insist that the mages administer the potion and ensure a fair fight."

"I'll take two doses of poison, if you wish. I don't need Hesperine strength to defeat you."

"Bold words, *Ambassador*. We'll see how a scholar's fists hold up against mine."

Lio laughed. "Ask the Dexion on your next visit to his cell."

"I agreed to your terms." Flavian held up his hands, as if Lio were a wild animal he sought to calm. "Now release her. Hand her over to the healers."

"She doesn't need healers. She needs me." Lio let his roiling magic out and pumped it into her chest, even as he sent a summons deep into the mind ward.

With a gasp, she roused, opening her eyes. "Lio?"

"I'm here," he said with relief.

Her eyes were glazed with delirium. She wrapped her weak arms around his neck and burrowed closer in his arms.

Benedict stared at her as if his world had suddenly transformed into a place he no longer recognized. "What spell have you put on her?"

"There is no magic at work on her." Eudias's voice carried across the great hall, calm and clear. "I'll cast an Aithourian revelatory spell if you require proof."

Lio shot Eudias a grateful look, then looked Flavian in the eye. "When she is well, I will meet on the tournament field."

With the Full Council of Free Lords looking on, Lio stepped out of the great hall with Cassia in his arms.

THE LUSTRA'S GRACE

LIO STEPPED TO HER bedchamber and tore the tapestry aside with a spell. Knight scratched at the stone.

"Please," Lio said to the portal, "for her sake, let me in."

He braced himself and took a step forward. The toe of his silk shoe passed through the wall.

He didn't know if the spells of her matriarchs had granted him a dispensation, or if holding her was enough to gain him entry, but he silently gave his gratitude to the Lustra. He carried her into the passageways, while Knight stayed behind, on guard.

Cassia slipped in and out of consciousness as Lio raced along, following the tangle of ivy deeper into the Lustra magic. He hoped he wouldn't lose his way, but all he truly cared about was getting her to wherever the magic was strongest. He sensed a faint response in her aura and kept going.

When he arrived at the room full of red ivy that was a dead end, he swore. Where was the moonflower chamber?

He was about to turn around and go back the way he had come when the ivy shivered. Directly in front of him, the red vines parted to reveal an open doorway.

He and Cassia had been here countless times, inspecting every inch of the wall. Why had it opened now? Was it responding to her need?

He sent a spell light into the darkness and beheld a still more wondrous impossibility. A circle of ashes and yews thrived in this netherworld that was so fertile with Lustra magic.

But more Anthros's fire grew at their roots. Lio set his jaw. He could tolerate the poisonous flowers for Cassia's sake. He levitated forward.

The golden glow of Anthros's fire faded. More white moonflowers unfurled where Lio passed, filling the grotto with a gleam as pale as the Goddess's white eye. He sent up a prayer of thanks to Hespera and kissed his Grace's clammy brow.

He lay her down inside the circle of trees on the bed of her magic's making. The blooms around her closed, their petals winding tightly together and pressing against her, as if seeking to give her their strength.

Even as Lio poured his magic into her, he felt the Lustra rising up in answer. He had never encountered magic like this. It was no raw force. It felt *alive*. Almost...sentient.

The power of creation itself.

For a moment, he and that vast, timeless power met within Cassia's small frame.

Her eyes opened again, and this time, her vision was clearer.

"Cassia, stay with me," he said. "I need you to focus. Can you open your aura for me?"

She groaned, and her aura stretched weakly. "What's happening? Why am I not channeling?"

"It's all right," he said, although he didn't know if it was all right at all.

Had she had such a close call...was she so far gone...that she was too weak to channel him? Was her magic giving up?

Oh Goddess, had he done the right thing to bring her here? Should he have taken her to Rudhira? If she slipped away now, when they were alone...

No. Lio knew what she needed. Her Grace.

He fed more of his power into her. The Lustra magic pushed back like a sharp, protective thicket closing her off from him.

No. Lio's shouted it through the passageways with his mind magic. *Do you want to lose your Silvicultrix? Perhaps your last and only one? Let me help her!*

"Reach for me as hard as you can," he said to Cassia.

"I'm trying." Her voice was so faint.

Body contact might stimulate the channeling. He flung off their clothes and stretched out behind her, spooning against her. He pressed a hand over heart, massaging her chest. Her skin was so cold. Her blood quieted, and her mind began to drift toward unconsciousness again.

He was so afraid that if she slipped under, she would not come back.

"No, Cassia, stay with me!"

He stretched his magic, reaching into the roots of the Lustra's ancient power.

She isn't only yours anymore, he cried to that inhuman presence. *She is mine too. She needs us both.*

It flung him away. He wanted to rage at it, but it cared nothing for fleeting emotions. It obeyed only natural laws.

But Grace was the natural law that ruled his and Cassia's blood.

If he bowed to the Lustra's laws, would it acknowledge Hespera's?

Lio bit his wrist and scattered his blood across Cassia's sallow skin and the pale moonflowers.

"Take me," he said, "for her sake."

He stopped wielding his magic. He released it and let it drift unbound, an offering to the Lustra, as he sank his fangs into her throat.

The power reaching up through her seized him and twined him into the arcane pathways inside her. The channeling surged to life. With a heave of breath, she stirred in his arms. She scrambled back against him, as if desperate to mold as much of her body to him as she could.

You're safe, he said deep in her mind, his arm around her. *I've got you. You're safe.*

The cycle of her blood and his magic flowed between them. He tasted the vital flavor of the wilds. That wildness seemed to take hold of him. Energy coursed through his body, and a jolt of lust hit his groin. He grunted in surprise, trying to resist the way her buttocks pressed into him.

A cry sounded from within her aura, echoing through the passageways. The Lustra, calling out. To him.

He stiffened against her. He would not give in. She had almost died. Now was not the time to put any strain on her.

But the demand came again, primal and undeniable. He was her mate. He must obey the natural law.

The law in their blood and bodies was the same, he realized. When she needed him, he would withhold nothing. But no matter what the Lustra asked of them, it was Cassia's Will that he heeded.

Do you need my body? he asked.

She moaned his name, rubbing weakly against him, already wet. *Need you...all of you.*

Hooking his arm under her leg, he parted her. He gave into the need to thrust inside her. As her tight channel enclosed him, another flood of his power opened between them, matched by a surge of Lustra magic from the ground beneath. Her heartbeat strengthened.

She relaxed in his arms, surrendering herself to his body. The act of trust set something afire inside him. Her need was desperate, her strength gone. He would be her strength.

Instinct told him what he must do for her. With a growl, he finished their feast and began their mating.

The soft petals of the flowers crushed under her as he turned her over. When her chest touched the earth, the Lustra magic burst up into her, making her heart race faster.

With a kiss on her temple, he positioned her, pillowing her head on her arms. He held her shoulders, pressing her down into the current from below. Then he shoved her thighs apart with his own so he could penetrate her deeper. She let out a soft cry, arching her back.

He panted with her like a mortal as he pumped into her. Every motion of his body drove more magic inside her and summoned a rush of it from the Lustra. He was not sure who set their rhythm—their bodies or the magic of the wilds. But he built the power higher inside her with every fast, hard stroke into her core.

Her krana convulsed around him. He pinned her shuddering body amid the moonflowers and unleashed his control.

The Will of the wilds pounded through them, grinding them together against the earth. Pleasure, raw and intense, beat through their Union. Their thoughts met, snarling with a possessive sense of rightness.

Mine.

Her blood rushed, and energy shone in her aura. Her scent was full of life. He collapsed on top of her, his magic and body relaxing. The channeling calmed to their resting current, gentle but steady.

The vicious, protective presence of the Lustra receded, once more releasing her into his arms.

He rolled them onto their sides again, curling his body gently around hers. He ran his hands over her shoulders, breasts, and knees, checking to make sure she had no bruises anywhere. She was perfect, whole.

Neither of them spoke, no words necessary or sufficient to capture their shared fear and relief and gratitude.

"I don't want to have another close call like that," she said at last, her voice small.

Those quiet words filled Lio with unspeakable rage. For Cassia, the master of facing her fears, to make such an admission betrayed how frightened she had truly been.

"That will never happen again," he swore. "I will make it possible to find the letting site faster—and until then, I will not allow anyone to separate you from me."

She tucked her head under his chin and cuddled closer to him. He levitated his robe to cover them, and she slid her cold feet between his calves. Running his hand in soothing circles over her belly, he let her hide her moment of vulnerability from the world in his arms.

"Why didn't someone bring you back sooner?" he asked. "How could they let Flavian do this to you?"

"I had to finish the ride."

"Why? Politics? Expectations? Mortal tradition? None of that means anything compared to your safety."

"No. For us. Eudias and Ariadne found our loophole."

He sucked in a breath. "Then it is possible for us to marry?"

She nodded. "And to share a promise dance on the upcoming Autumn Equinox."

A year to the day since she had danced the Autumn Greeting with Flavian, when she and Lio had been trapped on opposite sides of the border, they could have this. They could show Tenebra they belonged together. They could take the first step toward having a future in her sister's kingdom.

"How do you feel about that?" Lio asked.

"I secured Flavian's promise that he will endorse the match."

Lio's eyes widened. "What?"

She looked over her shoulder at him. "If I promised not to blackmail him—and finished the Progress—he agreed to support any match I make after our betrothal is dissolved. I may have allowed, or even encouraged, his very foolish assumption that I was talking about a relative of Tendo's."

"Oh, my Lady of Schemes, I do love how your mind works."

"So now, if only we get me out of the betrothal itself, the way will be clear for us."

Lio plucked a moonflower and held it before her. "Cassia, are you saying you will marry me?"

She wrapped her small hand around his and the flower. "Yes, my Grace. I will avow you before the Hesperines and marry you before the Tenebrans. Our promises to each other always means the same thing, no matter what language we say them in."

He captured her mouth, fighting to be careful with her exhausted body. She parted her lips for him, letting him devour her in small, gentle tastes.

For the first time a long while, he felt less afraid that he would lose her.

"I have a solution for getting you out of the betrothal," he said against her mouth. "I need you to let me do this."

"I don't care what you do to Flavian." There it was, her beautiful anger, once more coming to her defense to chase away the fears. She nipped Lio's lip.

He smiled. "I challenged him to Trial by Combat for your hand."

She smiled back. "I want to watch."

"Don't you think it would be more reassuring to everyone if I walk into the room?" Cassia asked.

Lio paused before the portal and looked down at her in his arms. "I have put your clothes back on and am allowing them to see you, instead of keeping you in here with me, naked. That is all the reassurance they are entitled to expect."

Her lips curved in a smile. "Have I ever told you how handsome you are when you lose your temper?"

He dipped his head toward her, his mind magic slipping his control again. "I'm happy to lose it more often if you like."

Her eyes fluttered shut, and her arms tightened around his neck. "I do like it."

"I am carrying you straight to your bed, and if anyone suggests that you put your feet to the floor before I have given my express permission, I will break their minds. Is that clear?"

"Abundantly, my mind mage."

He swept through the wall with her. Not only Knight, but Mak, Lyros, Solia, Kella, and Hoyefe were all waiting for them in the ladies' bedchamber.

Knight immediately circled them, sniffing every part of Cassia he could reach. She gave him reassuring pats. "There, there, my dearest. You knew Lio would set me to rights, didn't you?"

Without a word, Solia turned down the bedclothes, and Lio set Cassia in the bed. She tsked at both of them as they fluffed her pillows and tucked the blanket around her. Knight leapt up onto the bed to wallow as close to Cassia as he could.

Mak reached over and ruffled Cassia's hair, blinking hard. "We were worried about you."

Lyros let out a sigh, leaning into Mak. "Goddess, I'm sorry your worst enemy in this kingdom is one we can't fight for you. Some bodyguards we are."

"Nonsense," Cassia said. "According to Lio, you held off a crowd of mortals fearful for my reputation. That was very protective, thank you."

Tilili put her front paws on the bed to give Kella a better look at Cassia. "You all right, Shadow?"

Cassia kept hold of Lio's hand. "Now I am."

"It was a close call," Lio said. "Too close."

"Closer than the Maaqul?" Hoyefe asked without a trace of his usual good humor.

Lio nodded. "Between my magic and the Lustra magic inside the passageways, Cassia will be all right, but things must change from now on."

"We have to find the letting site faster," Lyros said.

"Lio and I found a way deeper into the passages," Cassia replied. "If we explore further, perhaps it will lead us there."

"Or we can ride straight for Paradum," Mak said.

"It could still take days to find it, and Cassia isn't well enough for another long ride." Lio decided that now was not the time to discuss his plan for speeding their search. They must remove the lesser obstacles first. "She won't be able to keep her strength up if Flavian separates us again. I will not allow him any more power over her."

Solia reached out a hand, but hesitated, closing her fist for a moment. Then she opened her fingers to brush the hair back from Cassia's brow. "Flavian had no compassion for your health today?"

Cassia's gaze fell. "I tried to tell him, but he thought I was trying to manipulate him. I have embroiled him in my schemes one too many times, it seems. He no longer takes me at my word."

"He will regret this," Solia vowed, but then she turned her hot blue glare on Lio. "But you are the last person who should make him regret it. What in Zalele's name were you thinking?"

"Do you really blame me for doing what I had to do to revive her?" Lio replied.

"A Hesperine just absconded with my sister in front of my entire future court. Do you have any idea what they're saying about her?"

"What is the current state of the rumors circulating among the Council?" Cassia asked calmly. "I will not have anyone saying that Lio kidnapped me."

"It's far too late to characterize you as an innocent victim," Solia returned. "You called him 'Lio' and embraced him before he disappeared with you."

Where another person might have made a self-conscious gesture, Cassia only grew more deliberately composed. "Ah. I remember now. I was not particularly coherent, and it was pure instinct."

Lio could see her taking in the reality of what had happened tonight, as if she were only now feeling a blow that had already landed. He heard her thoughts racing to conclusions.

Oh, Goddess. He had finally done it. He had destroyed her reputation. Could they have done anything differently tonight, with her life in danger? Or had it only been a matter of time before pure Grace instincts betrayed their bond?

Lio braced himself for Cassia's reaction. But he was not prepared for the emotions that surfaced in her aura.

Relief. Defiance. "I'm glad they know."

He sank down onto the bed beside her and kissed her hand. "They will not dare say a word against you once I am done."

"I am not ashamed," Cassia said. "Let them hate me for my true self, rather than love me for living a lie."

"We have your backs," Lyros said, "no matter the consequences for you both."

"For Cassia," Solia corrected. "The lords will be quicker to respect a Hesperine for his conquests than to forgive a mortal woman for her fall from grace."

"I don't care," Cassia said. "I've heard it all before."

"No, you have not yet heard the variations on whore-shaming they save for a Hesperine's lover." Solia stalked away, leaving the floor rug in ashes in her wake. "A few fire spells would silence them! I'd like to hear them gossip after I cauterize their tongues. That would make for a reign without protests." She rounded on Lio. "Where was your diplomacy today? Did you learn nothing in the Imperial court about maintaining your self-control, even when her life is in danger?"

Lio found that the hotter Solia's temper burned, the harder and colder his own grew. "Trial by Combat is sometimes the only type of negotiation that Tenebrans understand."

"We are supposed to be reforming this kingdom, not encouraging its barbaric traditions. You beating my opponent senseless mere days before the Council will not bring about a civilized change of monarch. We all agreed to wear our costumes and play our roles. I will not make an exception for you!"

"This is one of the situations where you must trust my judgment. Remember Karege's advice."

"How dare you suggest you are better than I at ensuring my sister's well being!"

"You're jealous," Lio realized.

"What are you talking about?" Solia scoffed.

Her scarf was secure around her shoulders, but Lio didn't need the Blood Union to be certain of this. He was perhaps the only person who knew what it felt like. "I was jealous of every person who got to breathe the same air as Cassia while she and I were apart. I hate it when someone else has the privilege of protecting her. You feel the same way. That's why it's so difficult for you to like me."

"Do not imagine this is about you," Solia said with disdain.

"Now I get the satisfaction of putting a fist in *your* opponent's face. I'm sorry, Solia. I wish you could draw your sword and humiliate Flavian, and I hope you will get to one day. But I will not apologize for doing whatever I must to free Cassia from him, even if it enrages you."

"You are being selfish," Solia bit out. "You're indulging in this male contest for your own satisfaction while the court tears Cassia to shreds."

"No, Solia. I'm not doing this for me. Cassia and I are doing it for you."

"This is not how I planned to legitimize your relationship!"

"I could take her back to Orthros when all this is over, and to Hypnos with the Tenebrans' opinions. The only reason we need to legitimize anything is because you want to be queen, and Cassia still wants to be your sister."

"And what do you suggest instead?" Solia demanded. "That I hone my skills on training dummies in the peaceful arenas of Orthros while Lucis and the Collector knock Flavian out of their way and destroy this kingdom?"

"Are you two finished?" Cassia asked quietly.

At last remorse dulled Lio's sense of conviction. The last thing she needed was to watch him and Solia break their truce.

"We cannot change any of our past decisions," Cassia said, "no matter how much we want to. We can only act on the situation we find ourselves in now."

"I will not back down from the challenge I issued Flavian," Lio said.

"Cassia, talk some sense into him," Solia fumed.

"I agree with him." Cassia took Lio's hand. "Clearly, there is only one solution to my tattered reputation. The panacea that cures all fits of Tenebran morality. Marriage."

Betrayal flashed in Solia's gaze, and Lio regretted the pain between the sisters. But he still would not regret his actions.

Flavian had been a threat to Cassia long enough. It was time to remove him, and Lio could not deny it would be a pleasure to do it with his bare hands.

AUTUMN EQUINOX

1 Kyria's Bounty, 1597 OT

PRINCESS CASSIA'S HAND

The moment Cassia arrived on the torchlit festival grounds, the censure began. Arm in arm with Solia, she raised her chin and strode through the crowd. The logs for the autumn bonfire were cold and skeletal, the stares of the courtiers colder. Few risked Solia's ire by insulting Cassia to her face, and none came within range of Knight's teeth. But Cassia read their whispered words on their lips. She caught sight of hands signing glyphs to ward off evil.

Plenty made slurs against Lio, but she had to admit, most of their venom was directed at her. They expected a Hesperine to be wicked. But when a mortal woman threw away her virtue, well, that was another matter.

It was like walking through one of her nightmares of their forbidden love being discovered. But this was real. All she had done was speak his name and put her arms around his neck in front of them, and the secrecy she and Lio had fought for all this time was gone.

Having their secrets aired made her feel like someone had wrested her weapons from her grasp. Every person in this crowd now had power over them, and every whisper came at a cost.

Lio could hear their whispers perfectly well. He loomed at her side, his lips tight, as if he were fighting not to flash his fangs at everyone they passed. "I cannot bear for you to endure this because of me."

"You are not to blame," Cassia said. "They are."

"I'd like to warp their minds into a more respectful shape. But if I must use a tournament and a dance to change their opinions, so be it."

Solia did not dignify their onlookers with a glance. She led Lio and Cassia, their Trial brothers, and the remaining Ashes to her box in the tournament stands. Flavian, standing before his seat across the field, acknowledged their arrival with a nod. Ben stood next to him, looking as if someone had died.

"He isn't taking it well?" Cassia muttered. "No surprise."

Lio rubbed his mouth. "I'm sorry. I was not gentle with him."

"He was standing between you and Cassia," Mak said. "You couldn't be expected to stay gentle."

"And I didn't expect Ben to understand," said Cassia.

But what effect would this have on his actions at the vote? She still didn't know what he was planning, or what debate had raged in his heart as he'd prayed. But now that she'd lost his good opinion, she had little hope of pulling him back from the brink of desperate actions.

Lio handed her into her seat. "The walk from the keep tired you."

She knew there was no point in protesting. "I will be all right, as long as I don't try to run any races."

"If you feel ill from sitting up too long, tell me." His fangs showed as he spoke, and she had no doubt he would carry her off a second time, if necessary, no matter who was watching.

"With you near, I am not in danger of collapsing again," she reassured him.

He took the seat next to her. "You know I would feel better if you were in bed."

"Ha," she replied, "as if I would stay in bed at a time like this. I insist on getting to watch."

"I would hate to deny you that satisfaction." He leaned closer to her. "I admit, I'm glad you're here to see this."

"I'll rest after you win," she promised, "so I'll have plenty of strength for our dance."

With Solia and Flavian seated, the attendees of the Council followed them into the stands. Cassia wondered how many seats on Solia's side would be empty. How many supporters would she lose due to Cassia's indiscretion? How much sympathy would Flavian win because his betrothed had betrayed him with a heretic?

Cassia's political mind could predict the tally. It would have left her in despair, if she had a nobler heart. But deep down, she would be relieved if her sister lost. A foolish part of her held out hope they could all go home to Orthros and the Empire together.

The first people to approach them were Eudias and Ariadne. He clasped Lio's wrist, and Lio gave him a grateful clap on the shoulder.

"We have set our preferred rumors in motion," Eudias said. "There are plenty of people asserting the truth that Cassia is not under any spell."

Ariadne took Cassia's hands for all to see. "I've told everyone that Lio took you away to Hesperine healers to save your life."

Cassia squeezed Ariadne's fingers in thanks. "Does the Semna believe that?"

Chagrin entered Ariadne's voice. "She attributes the situation to your success as a missionary. She considers Lio your first convert, inspired by his love for you to turn from the Hesperines' permissive ways and submit himself to a holy marriage."

"She is not against our match?" Lio asked.

"To be a wife is a different calling for Cassia," Ariadne said, "but one the Semna is willing to bless. I'm afraid she may expect you to make a formal renunciation of Hespera, though."

Cassia opened her mouth to say that was out of the question.

Lio held up a hand. "We can decide how to navigate that later. Tonight, I must end Cassia's betrothal."

Eudias and Ariadne sat down nearby, but there was still a swath of empty seats on either side of their party.

Then Sabina and Genie arrived, arm in arm, with Miranda as their attendant and Nivalis and Valentia as their companions. Cassia found her impassive mask suddenly required more effort. There were a few good opinions she had wanted to keep. Too late now. Her handful of hard-won friendships with the ladies of Tenebra were surely over, along with any hope of earning Miranda's trust.

The ladies came to Solia's side of the stands, but did not sit. After giving her their curtsies, they halted before Cassia and Lio. Cassia braced herself. Could they not have made it a quiet cut, instead of a public humiliation?

But to her astonishment, they gave her curtsies befitting a princess. Her surprise must have shown on her face, for Sabina looked rather outraged. "Did you think we would side with that idiot and the common gossips?"

"I would not have blamed you," Cassia replied. "I will shoulder the consequences. I have no wish for others to suffer on my behalf."

"Hadrians do not sit about and suffer. We inflict suffering on our enemies." She held out her hand to Lio.

He bowed and kissed her knuckles. "You honor me, Lady Sabina."

She glanced across the field to observe Flavian's reaction. His stony expression didn't disguise his flush of anger. "It's the least I can do to thank you for knocking some sense into him."

"Do try not to damage him too much, though," Genie requested.

"I will give you no cause for grief tonight," Lio promised.

Genie smiled. "I've grown quite fond of our fanged rooster, haven't you, ladies?"

"Indeed," Sabina said. "If you are the only Hesperine allowed to wed a mortal in Queen Solia's reign, it will be progress. Let us make you our first exception in that regard."

"Let there be no doubt where I stand," said Lady Valentia. "My betrothal to a beast like Tyran should not be lauded while your love is reviled."

Lady Nivalis's eyes flashed. "What did everyone expect you to do last night? Let Princess Cassia die in propriety, rather than save her with Hesperine magic? If they knew where Pakhne is now, the gossips would not spare her, either. This court cares more about a woman's reputation than her life."

Lord Deverran arrived then and joined his wife. "Ambassador Deukalion, do you have a second for the duel yet?"

"I had thought to ask Lord Hoyefe," Lio replied.

Lord Deverran bowed to Hoyefe. "With all respect for our Imperial allies, perhaps a show of Tenebran support would send a message tonight. If you will allow me?"

"Of course." Lio clasped his arm. "You would have my gratitude."

"I'm no spring buck, but I can still throw quite a punch. I somehow doubt you will need my assistance, though."

"I have no illusions that I am a warrior. Sunfire Poison will reduce me to a mortal with more ink stains than callouses."

The hint of amusement in Lord Deverran's gaze suggested he was not convinced by Lio's modest assessment of himself. Indeed, Cassia doubted Flavian would pose much of a challenge to Lio, after he had survived his contests with the Dexion, the Maaqul Desert, and Solia.

But the court could have done so much damage to their cause, if not for this small army of supporters. They filled the vacant seats beside Cassia and Lio.

Only Miranda was left standing before her. "Perita needed to stay with the babe. So I'm here."

Cassia's hands knotted in her lap. "You didn't have to come."

"I did," Miranda said. "Heretics and apostates ought to stand together."

Cassia swallowed, try to compose herself amid a swell of gratitude. "We will stand with you. Always."

"I see that now." All Miranda gave Cassia was a nod, but that simple gesture, those few words...they felt like forgiveness.

"Thank you," Cassia said, her throat tight.

Miranda curtsied to her and Lio, then took her seat behind Sabina.

"Well," Lio said, "we have all the allies that matter, don't we?"

"Yes," said Cassia.

To her surprise, it was Ben who approached next. Dare she hope the show of support from Genie and the Kyrians had opened his mind?

He bowed to Solia. "Your Highness, may I speak with your sister for a moment? We will remain within sight, of course."

Solia drummed her fingers on the arm of her chair with obvious displeasure. "Anything you wish to say to her, you may say in front of me."

"It is of vital importance that I discuss this with her privately." Ben cast a hard glance at Lio.

Lio looked back with the steady gaze of someone who had nothing to apologize for. Ben's tone had Cassia bristling, but this could be an opportunity to reason with him—or find out what he was plotting.

"Perhaps this private conversation would be amenable to everyone if Lady Eugenia accompanies me?" Cassia suggested.

"I would be happy to," Genie spoke up.

"Thank you, Lady Eugenia," Solia approved.

When Lio didn't protest, Cassia knew he understood her intent and trusted her judgment, no matter how much he was bristling at Ben. She rose and linked arms with Genie, and they accompanied Ben to an empty portion of the stands on Solia and the Ashes' other side.

Ben and Genie exchanged a charged look, as if she were warning or challenging him. Cassia stood between them, unsure whether she was flanked by allies or adversaries.

"Cassia…" Ben began.

The use of her name broke through her carefully mustered emotional defenses, and she realized just how much this conversation had the power to hurt her, after all.

"We have never shamed each other for what we didn't choose," he said. "My father's treason. Your father's dishonor toward your mother. Tell me you didn't choose this, and I will silence every tongue that insults you."

Cassia drew back. "What are you saying?"

"I know you are under no enchantments—the Semna has reassured me of that many times. But does the ambassador hold something else over you? Did he carry you away against your will last night?"

Oh, it did hurt. But her anger was far more powerful than her pain. "You'd rather I suffer coercion than lose my Tenebran morals, is that it? You would rather imagine he forced me than accept I might choose him?"

"I know your capacity for sacrifice. If his conversion is sincere, then he should choose to repent with or without your hand in marriage. You shouldn't have to become his wife to save his soul. It isn't right for anyone to demand that of you."

"It's not a sacrifice," Cassia tried to explain. "You of all people should understand impossible love."

He recoiled. "You love him? More than my lord and his family? More than your Kyrian sisters?"

"Ben!" Genie burst out. "How dare you invoke our family this way! There is no shame upon love in our household. Do you expect me to feel guilty about my parents?"

"That is another matter," he said.

"Why?" Genie demanded. "Because my father doesn't have fangs? He and my mother leave Tenebran morals outside their bedchamber door just the same."

Ben's cheeks flushed. "Don't talk that way."

"Don't be so innocent, Ben. We all know what Flavian does when he visits the Temple of Hedon with the Brotherhood. Don't tell me his girls haven't tried to convince you to open your breeches, too."

Ben's blush traveled up his forehead. "Genie!"

"Oh, don't worry, I know you would never dare loosen your laces. You've taken Flavian to task for it often enough. And yet you aren't threatening to stop defending him."

"That is another matter," he said once more.

"Oh, of course," Genie fumed. "Because Flavian is a man!"

"Because Cassia lied to me! You used me," Ben accused. "You told me you wanted out of your betrothal to serve the goddess, when all along, you wanted to marry a Hesperine."

"This confirms that I was right not to tell you the truth," Cassia said. "I knew you would only respond with judgment."

"I thought our shared past had created trust between us. I see now how wrong I was."

"You could always trust me. But I could never trust you with what was dearest to me. Yes, I chose to stay in Orthros for Lio. Yes, I love him. And I will not be ashamed of it."

"You were lying to us all this time."

"You think risking my life to avert war was a lie? Lio and I both nearly died to ensure our love never hurt anyone. If you still begrudge us our happiness, after everything we have done, then I think your sense of honor is broken beyond repair."

"You question my honor, after you let a Hesperine tarnish yours?"

Fury left Cassia cold from her head to her toes. She could try to tell him her bond with Lio was sacred in Hespera's eyes and valid under Hesperine law. She could explain how kind his family was, how much Zoe needed her, how Orthros was a much more principled land than Tenebra ever was.

But she knew it would fall on deaf ears. She would not lay her treasures before Ben, only for him to crush them under his heel.

"I have nothing else to say to you," Cassia told him.

His jaw set. "Genie, come with me."

"No," Genie said.

"Your own reputation is fragile enough. You cannot afford to associate with Cassia any longer."

Genie's arm tightened in Cassia's. "I will remain here and fulfill my duties as one of Princess Solia's ladies—and her sister's friend."

They turned their backs on Ben and left him standing there.

"Thank you," Cassia said. Genie might be a clever, budding politician, but Cassia did not believe any of her impassioned outburst just now had been an act.

Genie blinked back tears. "I'm so disappointed in him."

"So am I."

When they returned to their seats, Solia said, "He just lost the title I was planning to give him once I'm queen."

Lio brushed Cassia with his magic, and the fury inside her calmed. But she could feel his regret. "I am so sorry, my rose. I cost you a friend tonight."

She shook her head. "He was not a true friend, as it turns out."

Ben was gone, and where he had stood, vassals of Lord Hadrian filled the stands.

The herald's trumpet cut through the night, and the crowd went quiet. "Let the Full Council of Free Lords bear witness that Ambassador Deukalion Komnenos of Orthros has challenged Lord Flavian of Segetia to Trial by Combat, the prize to be Princess Cassia's hand."

Cassia could scarcely believe the words or the strange reality they were now living, in which they wore their secret for all to see, and her diplomat was about to raise his fists.

"Let the challengers and their seconds enter the field!" the herald declared.

Lio rose from his seat, and all eyes went to his tall figure.

Solia put a hand on Cassia's arm. "You can let Lio fight without appointing him your champion."

"That will make it seem he stole me from Flavian without my cooperation."

"Yes. It would mitigate the damage to your reputation."

"You know I cannot do that."

Solia released her. "I know. But I wouldn't be your elder sister if I didn't remind you of the option."

"I understand, Soli." Cassia stood and pulled a silk handkerchief out of her sleeve, a white one with Hespera's Rose embroidered on it in black silk. She let the crowd watch her tie it around Lio's wrist.

"This is the first handkerchief you gave me," she said, "the one I kept with me while we were apart. All those nights I shed tears over having to marry Flavian."

Lio pressed her hand to his lips. "No more tears after tonight, my Grace."

He descended the stands without magic, walking down with Lord Deverran and Eudias to meet Flavian and Benedict. Of course Ben would fight as Flavian's second. The sight of him there prodded Cassia's fresh pain, despite her resolve not to waste her grief on him.

The herald's voice rang out again, informing the crowd of the rules of the fight. *Sunfire Poison. Mortal strength. Fists only.*

Mak leaned toward her across Lio's empty seat. "Don't worry. This will be just like his fight with the Dexion."

Cassia nodded mutely, but her mind filled with visions of Lio's broken ribs and shattered ankle, of his desperate bite afterward, when he had needed her blood to heal. They had been in Orthros then, with help just a step away. This was Tenebra, where Hesperines were routinely run down by liegehounds, beheaded, immolated...and there were people in this crowd who would wish any of those fates upon her Grace.

Lio toed off his silk shoes and unfastened his elegant outer robe, handing them over to Lord Deverran. Underneath, Lio wore his Hesperine athletic tunic, paired with Imperial trousers as a nod to Tenebran standards of modesty. But Cassia dared anyone in the audience who appreciated male beauty not to stare. Lio ran through a quick stretch, his pale, lightly muscled forearms flexing in the torchlight, then stalked toward Flavian with immortal grace.

Flavian rolled up the sleeves of his tunic and said something to Eudias. The mage offered Lio a vial that must hold the Sunfire Poison. Lio raised the flask to Cassia as if toasting her, then drained it. When he handed it back to Eudias, his movements were studied and deliberate.

The whole crowd waited in silence for the potion to take effect. Her fingers closed over the arms of her chair.

Lio gave her mind a powerful, reassuring touch, before his magic began to fade.

Her heart started to pound, and before she could restrain the instinct, she reached for him with her aura. The resting current swelled to a tentative channel. But she felt as if she were reaching for his magic through thick cotton, and it responded sluggishly.

How disorienting must it feel for him to have his vast power dulled so? As someone who had yet to feel the full strength of her own magic, she hated every moment he must experience this.

He and Flavian raised their fists and faced one another. The herald's trumpet sounded. Lio smiled, his fangs flashing white in the night.

The first punch came from Flavian, and Cassia jumped in her seat. Lio dodged by leaning quickly to one side. She cursed herself for acting like a startled rabbit.

Flavian hurled his fists at Lio again, once and twice in quick succession, only for Lio to evade again. He made it look effortless.

Mak let out a low whistle. "Look at our scrollworm now."

Lyros leaned forward in his seat. "He's compensating for the poison based on his experience with the Dexion."

Cassia did not find the cool, collected determination on Flavian's face reassuring. He swung his fist toward Lio's face again, and she sucked in a breath, prepared to watch Flavian probe Lio's defenses.

Flavian's blow never landed. Lio's palm struck Flavian's wrist, then his long fingers closed, twisting Flavian's arm into an S-shape that made the man grimace and retreat. Lio let him go.

Cassia's cheer cut through the gasps from the crowd.

Mak laughed. "Lyros, we taught him well."

"Flavian's wrist won't be good for anything for a while." Lyros smirked.

Lio pursued Flavian with a grin and tossed a punch that landed lightly on the man's shoulder. A taunt. Flavian's calm demeanor dissolved into a scowl. Lio tapped his shoulder again, then his other one, his moves slow enough for even Cassia to follow.

"Brilliant," Mak said. "The poison has taken his speed, so he's relying on subtlety. See how still his body is before his fist moves? He isn't giving Flavian a clue where his attack will land before he strikes."

Lyros's eyes crinkled at Cassia. "He practiced this over and over again while you two were separated."

With a silent shout of triumph echoing through their Union, Cassia watched Lio enact justice on Flavian for every day she had spent betrothed to him.

Not a single one of Flavian's blows landed. Lio batted him aside with utter focus. With his tall, lean frame perfectly controlled, his fists leapt as if from nowhere and drove past Flavian's guard. The man could not escape Lio's longer reach. Lio's punches glanced Flavian's famous square jaw, his ballad-worthy cheekbones, and his battle-honed abdomen. Flavian's scowl became a snarl of effort, and Lio's fanged grin widened.

Lio embarrassed Flavian from his face to his torso and everywhere in between with blows too light to harm. Every time he landed one, he proved he had the upper hand.

Flavian had never had a chance to win this battle, Cassia realized, because he was fighting for politics. Lio was fighting for her.

Lio dragged out the spectacle, and Cassia sat back in the chair of a princess to relish it. She watched him wield his gentle, beloved body with careful force. Cotton and silk flexed with his strong shoulders and long legs as he pivoted and pursued. Muscles played along his arms. Even as his motions began to slow with exhaustion, he moved with beautiful power.

Flavian's tunic was drenched in sweat, his breath coming fast. Who would reach his limit first—the mortal, or the Hesperine with Sunfire in his veins?

When Lio's fangs lengthened, Cassia knew he was about to end it.

Lio propelled his fist from the center of his body and slammed it into Flavian's jaw. The sound of the impact disappeared under the crowd's shocked reaction. Cassia's own hand closed into a fist on her lap, and she felt as satisfied as if she'd landed the blow herself.

Lio hurled his left hand into Flavian's face, then came back with his right one again for good measure. The man's head snapped to one side, flinging drops of blood.

Solia let out a surprised laugh. "That's my favorite punch. The one I used on Lio in our duel."

Cassia grinned. "He landed a few for you, too."

Lio worked Flavian's torso over with a series of blows, ending with a jab to the man's gut that had him doubling over. All it took then was one more tap to his jaw, and Flavian landed on his back in the dirt with Lio looming over him.

Cassia surged to her feet, along with everyone in Solia's box. She didn't care if their cheers were fewer than the outraged cries of their opponents. She stamped her feet and called out Lio's name.

He lifted his hand to them, the one with her handkerchief around the wrist. He flicked his other fingers, shaking Flavian's blood from his knuckles.

Then he offered a hand to Flavian. The man groaned, spat a wad of blood onto the ground, and snarled something that Cassia suspected was a filthy curse.

Lio kept his hand out. At last, Flavian took it and, with as much dignity as such a battered man could muster, allowed Lio to help him up.

"Lord Flavian," the herald called, "do you hereby renounce Princess Cassia and acknowledge that no more betrothal promise binds you?"

Flavian inclined his head in Cassia's direction, giving her a sardonic look. "I release her."

A weight she had borne for a year finally lifted off of her. No mortal man had a claim on her any longer. She was free.

She locked eyes with her Grace. Her soon-to-be *husband*. She had always hated the notion. But looking at her Hesperine standing on the tournament field, the victor over Tenebran morals, she thought the title of husband could take on an entirely new meaning.

AN UNLIKELY UNION

PERITA GAVE CASSIA A bemused smile, arranging a sheer yellow veil over the length of her hair. "My lady, are you fidgeting?"

Cassia dropped the end of her golden girdle and folded her hands on the dressing table. She was! She, of all people, was fidgeting. "This is the first time a mortal courtship dance has ever…" She waved vaguely at her belly.

Perita giggled. "Given you that fluttery feeling?"

"Yes."

"Fidget all you like, my lady. Enjoy everything about your promise dance this time around." Perita stepped back to study her handiwork. "You look like a princess."

Cassia had to admit, Perita was right. They had discovered this piece of Tenebran high fashion hidden among the Hesperine robes in Cassia's travel trunk. She took it as a vote of confidence from Kassandra. The gown was the color of cinnamon and somehow made Cassia's complexion shine. She was afraid the texture of the velvet would attract dog hair terribly, though. Knight sat obediently out of range of her voluminous skirts.

Perita grinned. "I'm proud of your night owl for snatching his mouse from the hawk."

Now Cassia giggled. Instead of clapping her hand over the sound, she decided Perita was right, and she was entitled to enjoyment, even silly laughter.

"Now that's a man." Perita sighed. "Willing to do all of this so you can have your fangs and your sister, too."

"Perhaps I don't have to choose between the human and Hesperine worlds after all." Cassia clasped her friend's hand. "I'm not going to lose you."

"Lose me? Ha. It would take more than you leaving for a foreign land and turning into an immortal heretic for you to lose me. But I'm glad I'll be seeing more of you."

Cassia stood and embraced Perita, so grateful this would not be the last time.

"Now then." Perita drew back, dabbing at her eyes. "Let's get you to your promise dance—with the right suitor this time."

"You're coming too?"

"Miranda's keeping the babe tonight so Callen and I can have a dance. Lady Sabina and I will be right out."

"I thought Sabina was already down at the bonfire."

"She's running a bit late," Perita said with a conspiratorial smile. "While you were lying down, she sneaked into Flavian's chambers. To rub salt in his wounds or tend them, we can only guess."

"Well, well. Either way, I'm delighted to hear she's pressing her advantage."

After Perita left, there came a knock at Cassia's door. She sailed to answer it, her sleeves trailing luxuriously from her arms and her train sweeping behind her, her noble liegehound at her side. As Solia had said, they had all agreed to wear their costumes and play their roles. Surely there was no harm in feeling like a real princess for one night.

Even so, when she found Mak waiting in the corridor to be her escort, the sight of him in Stand regalia oriented her. Her hand went to her ambassador's medallion, hidden with Ebah's pendant under her gown.

Mak chuckled. "Don't worry. Putting on a Tenebran dress doesn't cover up the blinding glow of Hesperine magic all over you."

She blushed. "Lio and I decided we didn't need Nike's veil spells any longer."

"There will be no doubt in the mind of any mage within a vast radius that you and Lio are...well, I'll play along and say 'betrothed.'" Mak pulled her into a hug. "Congratulations."

She wrapped her arms around him and hugged him back. "I'm so glad we get to share this with you and Lyros, even if it is a stupid mortal tradition."

"It's not stupid. It's an adventure. Like the time Nike and Rudhira told us about, when the Blood Errant took on human guises to save a village from the lynx changer and his necromancer ally."

Cassia squared her shoulders. "Yes. If Nike can pretend to be a Tenebran lady, then so can I."

"Hm, I wonder if Lyros would fancy seeing me in a knight's armor?" Mak struck a chivalrous pose. "Probably not. He'd say it's too difficult to take off."

Cassia laughed. "You and Lyros will dance tonight, won't you?"

"No. We're on duty. A crowded dance, outside in the dark? Perfect place for unsavory types to cause trouble."

Her humor faded. "You're right, of course."

"Don't you worry. The Stand is trained for precisely these situations. How do you think my father survived sixteen hundred years of Equinox Summits?"

"Thank you for reassuring me. I wish you could relax and enjoy this, though."

"We'll get our chance to dance later. I may have let it slip to the Charge that you and Lio have something to celebrate. Now Lyros and I have strict orders to deliver you and any friends you'd like to invite to the Summit Sanctuary after the mortal festival is over."

"Oh, Mak. Of course you would think of that."

"What can I say? I am your favorite brother for a reason." He offered her his arm. "For now, I'll step you to the bonfire. No unnecessary risks, and no long walks for you either."

"Lio's orders?"

"Your bodyguards' orders, too."

A moment later, Sabina joined them in the corridor. Perita hurried along beside her, tucking tousled strands of Sabina's wavy brown hair under her headdress. Sabina appeared a bit flushed, and as pleased as a cat who had caught her mouse.

Cassia smiled and raised a brow at her. "Your hour of 'rest' was productive, I take it?"

"He still has much more groveling to do," Sabina replied, "but it's a start."

Callen clasped Mak's arm. "Do you need an extra pair of eyes on your patrol?"

"We're always glad to have your eyes," Mak said, "but tonight, you should dance. You and Perita have earned it."

"Stop being so dutiful and enjoy yourselves," Sabina agreed. "I insist."

"Yes, my lady." Callen smiled and took Perita's arm, his gaze softening, as if even that simple gesture was not something he took for granted.

Mak stepped them out of the dim corridor and onto the festival grounds, where the bonfire cast a brilliant glow over the men who stood ready for the dance. When Cassia saw who was at the head of the line, her belly fluttered again. Lio looked back at her with an almost tentative offer in his eyes.

His Tenebran attire put Flavian and all his fashionable friends to shame. The deep blue velvet tunic, trimmed in silver, flattered Lio's lithe build, the short hem stopping at his thighs. Snug-fitting black breeches showed off his runner's legs. He was not dancing in silk shoes tonight, but tall boots like Rudhira's.

She let her gaze slide down Lio's body, then back up again, and when their eyes locked this time, a smile spread across his face.

"I told Lio he should dress up like a cleric, the way Methu did," Mak said, "but he thought you'd like this better."

Cassia laughed and tried to swat his arm, but he dodged out the way. With a playful salute, he melted into the crowd. She spotted Lyros on the other side of the bonfire, a silent presence in the shadows.

Callen kissed Perita's cheek and went to line up with the men, while Valentia, Genie, and Nivalis came to Cassia's side. She found herself surrounded by the women who had watched her dance with Flavian last year, this time undivided by feuds or jealousy.

But Ben had been there that day, as well. Running her fingers through Knight's fur, Cassia scanned the line of dancers, then the crowd, but didn't see Ben. She checked herself, regretting that she had indulged her urge to look for him. He had made his position clear. She should stop wasting her thoughts on him.

The sting of his betrayal faded when Solia approached with Kella and Tilili. Kella said something in Azarqi, then translated into Divine, "'May he always bring strength and prosperity to your tent, and may your music always guide him through the sandstorms.' That's how my people offer well wishes upon a betrothal."

"That's beautiful, Standstill," said Cassia. "Thank you."

Solia stroked the top of Knight's head. "Would you like me to look after him while you dance?"

The question took Cassia by surprise, but seemed a peace offering. "Oh, yes, please. No banishment to the kennels for him this time."

"The kennels?" Solia asked with outrage. "That is no place for such a faithful friend. He can keep me company tonight."

"Thank you, Soli. And…thank you for being here, despite your reservations."

Solia pulled her close, and a sudden lump formed in Cassia's throat. Last year, she had danced in Solia's own Greeting dress, which had felt like a funerary gown. And yet here was her sister, alive and well. It was beyond belief. But it was real.

"I'm sorry I shouted," Solia said. "I want this to be a happy night for you."

"It is. I get to have you with me tonight." Cassia's breath hitched. "I didn't think you would be here for any of the important moments of my life."

Solia drew back, her eyes welling with tears. She waved a hand at her face and huffed. "Gods, I never imagined I would turn into one of those weeping mamas who wail through the entire Greeting dance."

"Well, I never imagined I would turn into a blushing bride, either," Cassia said.

"If it will make you feel better," Kella said, "I'll knock the tears and blushes out of both of you in the arena after this is over. Until then, I suggest you heed another Azarqi proverb. 'Eat the honey you find in the desert.'"

"Yes," Cassia said. "Tonight, life offers us something sweet. Let us enjoy it."

Buoyed by the women's well-wishes, she took her place across from Lio. His familiar smile reassured her, and yet took her breath away. His lips parted, as if he were about to say something, but the romantic moment was interrupted by the arrival of the mages. Master Gorgos supervised with a frown as Eudias came to stand beside Lio, and Ariadne by Cassia.

"Was dancing part of your diplomatic education?" Eudias murmured to Lio. "Do you know the steps of the Autumn Greeting?"

"Not to worry," Lio replied. "My parents taught me all the Tenebran dances. This one hasn't changed since my father's time."

Flavian approached them, his movements tired, carrying the sickle he had wielded in last year's Autumn Greeting rites.

"No, no, this cannot be," Master Gorgos blustered. "A Hesperine cannot wield the sacred sickle and become Anthros's champion in this dance!"

"I'm afraid I must agree," came the Semna's voice.

Ben escorted her forward, avoiding Cassia's gaze.

"Until Ambassador Deukalion undergoes his official conversion," the venerable mage said, "he cannot take on the role of Anthros. But he may certainly complete the promise dance, just like all the other young men every year who aren't selected to represent the god."

"Thank you for instructing me, Semna," Lio said with much more calm than Cassia felt.

She made an effort to keep her tone conciliatory, but gave Flavian a significant look. "As long as our dance is legally recognized as a betrothal promise, that is what matters."

"Allow me to preside as Anthros's champion from last year," Flavian replied. "No one can doubt this match if I bless it."

He would keep his end of the bargain, it seemed.

It took a few minutes of negotiation before a modification to the ritual was decided on, but at last the Semna gave them her blessing and let Ben escort her to a bench to watch. Master Gorgos made no further protests, but left Eudias to perform his role in the ritual. How politically convenient, to be able to claim or deny he had supported this union, depending on how the wind blew in the future.

Ariadne handed Cassia a sheaf of wheat, her eyes smiling. Cassia held it out to her Grace, and he took hold of it with her. Such a weak human symbol, compared to the bond that ran in their blood. But powerful for how it would protect them from their opponents.

Eudias raised his hands and said a prayer in Divine, ending in Vulgus, "With his Sickle, may Anthros bring his season of the sun to its end."

"With her generous hands," Ariadne finished the blessing, "may Kyria deliver unto us the season of her Bounty."

Flavian raised the sickle, and Cassia had a sudden vision of him taking revenge on Lio with that blade. But Flavian brought the scythe down without much force and cut cleanly through the wheat. Flavian surrendered his sickle to Eudias and joined the line of dancers.

Cassia and Lio joined hands and threw the two sheaves into the bonfire. Anthros's element crackled, while their friends cheered. Lio turned Cassia away from the flames, lifting their joined hands. The minstrels' tune floated up through the night, and he guided her into the first twirl of the age-old Autumn Greeting dance.

"You look so beautiful tonight," he said, when the steps brought him near.

"I see Kassandra sent a surprise along in your clothing trunks, as well."

"Is my attire appropriate for the occasion, Your Highness?"

"There is one very serious problem with it, my lord."

Doubt flickered across his face as they danced past each other. "What aspect of mortal clothes did I get wrong?"

She laughed, circling him. "Nothing. The problem is how much I want to take them off of you."

His smile returned, a bit wicked. "But I've been told that humans consummate their unions with their clothes on. I insist on taking part in all of these traditions."

"In that case, I will make sure to thoroughly enjoy keeping your clothes on you." She didn't care if the whole crowd could see the flush on her cheeks in the firelight.

There was a sly tilt to Lio's brow. "What did you and Flavian talk about when you danced?"

She giggled. "Not this, I assure you."

Lio was entitled to his smug expression. "Let me guess. Horses or hunting."

"Well, dogs, actually. In all fairness, he tried to set me at ease by talking about puppies."

"I can do better. Shall I get you a female liegehound as a wedding present?"

"Oh, Lio, would you consider it? I confess, I've been wanting to talk with you about it, but…they will make a terrible mess in the residence, I'm afraid. Are you sure you wouldn't object to me breeding Knight?"

His laughter was so full of affection it warmed her from head to toe. "You know I wouldn't object to anything that lights you up this way."

"Even multiplying my smelly dog?"

"Multiplying your happiness," he said.

"I love you so much."

"I love you, too." He spun her, and her awareness of him behind her sent gooseflesh over her skin.

Lio's immortal grace turned the decorous dance into something sensual. His magic filled the space between their bodies, making him feel big and powerful and close. Each time he wove past her, he pushed the boundary of how near the steps should bring him. Every chaste touch of his hand felt charged.

"How does it feel to dance these steps with me?" he asked.

"Effortless," she answered. "Life-changing."

"I don't want this to feel like a claim."

"It doesn't," she realized. "With you, it feels like…a promise."

"It is, Cassia. Whatever unknown steps we take into the future, we take them together."

A horn trilled, reminding her the rest of the world existed. It was time for her to dance with the other men, a symbol that they admitted defeat in pursuit of her.

Her first dancing partner held out his hand—Flavian. Lio hesitated an instant, a warning in his gaze. Flavian's mouth tilted in a humorless smile, and he offered Lio a slight bow, as if to say he wouldn't try anything. Cassia let him take her hand lightly.

At last, they repeated the steps of the Autumn Greeting, untying the betrothal that had entangled her all these months. Flavian danced stiffly, and Cassia was tempted to make a cutting remark about sore ribs, but decided his pride was already hurting enough.

"All this time," he said, "your plays didn't make sense to me. I couldn't understand your game. I was trying to explain it with politics, but none of the possibilities fit. It was him all along, wasn't it?"

"Yes."

"How long have you returned his affections, if I may ask?"

"Since the Equinox Summit."

"Before I began courting you."

"Did you think you and Sabina were the only ones having an affair?"

"Your sympathy for our cause does make more sense now." Flavian winced as he lifted his arm to turn her. "I would have understood. Why didn't you tell me?"

Cassia let out an incredulous laugh. "You were hardly understanding when you realized how Lio feels."

"I thought it was one-sided."

"Oh yes, you made that clear when you accused me of wrapping him around my finger."

His wince became a grimace. "You're so careful. I didn't imagine you would let any man near your heart, much less a Hesperine. But if *you* have finally given someone your devotion, then it is true and real."

"I have. It is."

"Then I will show you and Lio the same consideration you have shown Sabina and me."

"Thank you for that." She gave his hand a squeeze before releasing him to dance past him again. She might be able to forgive him after all.

"I was wrong about you. Again." Not just physical pain, but lingering temper made his steps taut. "Every time I believe I've figured you out, you take me down a notch."

"Is that why you're angry?"

"No." There was mockery in his tone. "I'm angry at the man who has most trampled on my pride today. Myself. You and Lio are braver than I. What have I ever sacrificed for love?"

"You are trying to make yourself king for Sabina, I'll grant you."

"Yes, my answer to our forbidden romance is to try to win more people's favor. And yet here you are, willing to lose everyone's good opinion just for the privilege of dancing together in public."

Cassia hesitated. "Have you considered asking Sabina to dance with you tonight?"

He was silent a moment, then shook his head. "One must choose the right moment to start a war. But this has certainly made me start planning a new campaign."

"I'm happy for you, Flavian. Truly. But I suppose it is too much to hope that this would inspire you to give up the kingship."

He sighed. "No. The lords must have a say in their people's future. The vote must go forward, for a greater cause than any one person here. We owe it to the kingdom to uphold the rule of law."

"I cannot fault you for that conviction."

"Whatever the outcome, Solia and I have the power to set a precedent of justice for Tenebra. Win or lose, we shall both respect the decision."

"And so will Orthros," Cassia promised.

"I know you speak for Orthros now." With that, Flavian surrendered her to Lio.

Her Grace took her hand, repeating the steps with her once more. "He appears to have behaved himself."

"I dare hope we've made our peace."

"If he forgets that, I can always make some more peace with him on the tournament field."

"I'm not sure he'd survive a second round, my love. Not to worry. He won't trouble us any longer."

One by one, Lio allowed the men of the Council a round of the Autumn Greeting with Cassia. Lord Adrogan tried to flatter his way into Blood Komnena's coffers, while Lord Deverran gave her a respite with heartfelt congratulations. But most of the lords were coldly formal, and some hesitated to take her hand, as if she were tainted.

She found her gaze darting through the crowd, then to the bonfire. It was all too easy for silent outrage to erupt into violence, and Mak was right. An event such as this was the perfect place for it.

Lio looked too exposed, standing before the fire at the front of the dance, awaiting her return.

When the last lord danced her back up the line and released her, she took Lio's hand with relief.

"Shhh," he soothed, sweeping her close to him again. "We made it. Now let me make your heart race for happier reasons."

Lio did not let his guard down until they stepped into the eternal wards of the Summit Sanctuary. Scarlet rose petals were scattered on the path through the tents and monuments, and cheerful spell lights lined the way. Music and familiar voices speaking Divine drifted from the direction of the pavilion.

"Do you need to go to our tent and rest before we celebrate?" he asked Cassia.

"No," she answered, "we should go to our tent after the Hesperine dances, and rest is not what I have in mind."

He smiled and gave her a kiss, trying to keep it appropriate for their mortal friends. As they all strolled along the path, Knight was finally at ease as well, trotting off to sniff at this and that. Mak took Lyros's hand, and Perita and Callen followed, their auras full of good spirits. Kella and Tilili padded alongside Solia with Sabina, Valentia, and Genie, who looked around in wonder and curiosity. Nivalis walked arm-in-arm with Deverran, while Hoyefe and Severin brought up the rear, the young lord standing closer to Hoyefe than he ever did at Council meetings.

Rudhira met them on the path and embraced Lio and Cassia. "I understand congratulations are in order—on your betrothal. Those are words I never imagined I would say to my Ritual children."

"You didn't have to hold a celebration here," Lio said.

Cassia shook her head. "This isn't even our avowal."

"This deserves to be celebrated," Rudhira said. "Do you know how long it has been since any Hespera worshiper took part in a marriage blessed by the mages of Kyria and Anthros?"

Lio raised his brows. "Since before the Ordering, I suppose."

"Sixteen hundred years." Rudhira shook his head. "This unprecedented union offers more hope to us all than you know. Besides, I welcome any excuse to lift my Chargers' spirits with a night of celebration."

Solia presented their companions to the First Prince, who welcomed them graciously. He led them through the vibrant red tents to the pavilion, where the aromas of mince pies and Notian red wine mingled with the fragrance of the roses that climbed the ancient stones.

Veil spells shifted, and there stood their Trial sisters, waiting for them in the pavilion beside the table. "Surprise!" Xandra called.

Cassia laughed and rushed forward to embrace them, Lio and their Trial brothers close behind. Knight's tail wagged with furious delight at the presence of not one, but two Hesperine royals. There was another flurry of introductions, embraces, and wrist clasps, before everyone began to circle the trestle table and fill their plates with delicacies from Orthros. Nearby, the sparring grounds had been cleared in anticipation of dancing, and a group of Chargers had brought out their flutes, lutes, drums, and harps.

Solia raised her wine goblet and called for everyone's attention. "I have seldom known anyone who fought as hard for their love as my sister and soon-to-be brother-in-law. Their courtship began here in Tenebra, but has spanned Orthros and the Empire as well—and left no one here unchanged. So join me in congratulating them in all our tongues."

"Congratulations," Kella and Hoyefe called in Tradewinds.

"Congratulations," said their Tenebran friends in Vulgus.

"May Hespera's Eyes gaze with joy upon your love," called the Hesperines in Divine.

They all raised their glasses and drank in Lio and Cassia's honor. She could scarcely believe their family and friends from Orthros, the Empire, and Tenebra were all gathered here in peace.

"Did it feel worth it?" Lio asked Cassia softly, under the applause. "Despite everything they're saying about us at court…do you regret anything?"

"I think it was worth this." She searched his gaze. "Do you?"

"Yes," he answered. "I would do it all again, just for this one night."

She stood on tiptoe and kissed him, resting her hand on his heart.

Everyone ate together without fear of poison and danced without worrying what people said. The steps of the Hesperine dances let Lio touch Cassia, and he sent magic pulsing into her with each beat of the music. She leapt and spun with him as if she would never tire.

Even the mortals let themselves be swept into Hespera's uninhibited pleasures. Xandra and Kia taught Sabina, Valentia, and Genie the steps for friends dancing together, which Solia appeared to have learned from Karege. Hoyefe and Severin danced the lovers' steps like Mak and Lyros. Kella joined Nodora and the Charge musicians, bringing out her imzad, and the Azarqi lute's haunting strains joined their songs. The moons seemed to pass slowly across the sky, and this night of equal length with the day felt long.

It was well after midnight when Lio finally pulled Cassia out of the dance and sat her down under the pavilion. Standing over her, he pressed a goblet of water into her hand.

Flushed and laughing, she leaned against him as she drank. "I feel marvelous, my love."

"I know. But you still need to sit down."

Her eyes sparkled with mischief. "Just remember I have no intention of swearing to obey you on our wedding day."

He propped his arm on the back of her chair and leaned over her. "I am far too persuasive to require vows of obedience, and you know it."

"What will you try to persuade me to do now, mind mage?"

Before he could persuade her back to their tent, their Trial circle joined them in the pavilion, raising veil spells once again. Lio straightened and rubbed his fangs.

"No sneaking off yet," Kia said.

Cassia set down her goblet. "No. We need to discuss Hesperine politics while you're here."

Solia and Kella joined them, followed by Rudhira. Just as they took their seats, Kalos slipped out of the shadows. He pulled out a chair and perched on it as if he might prowl off into the night again at any moment.

Trust Cassia to charge headfirst into the unpleasant topic. "Now that everyone is back in the north, when will the Firstblood Circle meet?"

Xandra reached for the wine flagon. "Night after tomorrow. Kona is first on the schedule, and she's planning to reopen the debate about the Departure."

Lio swore inwardly, although he was not surprised. "A debate though, not a vote?"

"The Circle will be watching the outcome of the Council," Xandra said, refilling her cup. "Once the lords vote, so will the Hesperines."

Solia accepted the flagon from Xandra. "I trust they will vote to keep the border open during my reign?"

"Oh, yes," said Xandra. "That isn't what we need to worry about."

A silence fell, punctuated only by the sound of the wine Solia poured calmly in her goblet.

Kia said, "What is your plan if Flavian wins?"

Lio could sense that Cassia feared Solia's answer. Would losing the crown be enough to convince her to go home with them? Or would she try to stay in some capacity, to protect her people against threats she believed Flavian was not strong enough to face? Lio and Cassia had already had many fraught midnight discussions with each other and their Trial brothers about what they would do in that eventuality.

"Let us cross that bridge if we come to it," Solia said.

"Do you know when the Council vote will happen?" Kia asked.

"Only two more lords have yet to raise their shields," Solia answered. "We expect them to declare soon. The vote could happen any day."

"Thorns," Kia said. "So no chance any of you can get away to come speak at the Circle."

Lio put his hand on Cassia's back. "I do not think it is wise for Cassia to leave Tenebra at all right now."

She shot him a regretful glance. "I think you're right. Remaining close to you is crucial, but proximity to the letting site—wherever it is—helps as well."

"I will attend the Circle," Rudhira said.

Hope and worry vied in Xandra's aura. "Can the Charge spare you?"

"I would prefer to be in Tenebra when the Full Council votes, in case anything goes wrong at Patria." Rudhira looked from Lio and Cassia to Mak and Lyros. "But the Charge will be on alert in case you need our aid. Do not hesitate to call upon them in my absence."

"Understood," the Stewards both replied.

"Thank you," said Cassia.

Lio nodded. "You must leave this duty in their hands and defend your mission as a whole. If Aunt Kona invokes the Departure, there will be no Charge."

"Yes, there will." Rudhira and Kalos exchanged a glance. "I have consulted with my officers, and we are all agreed. If the border with Orthros ever closes, the Charge will remain errant. Anyone who wishes to return home may do so without judgment, of course. But the leadership of the

Charge and any who wish to follow us will continue to defend Hespera's cause in these lands for as long as we live."

The revelation left Lio speechless.

"What?" Xandra leapt to her feet, dashing away sudden tears. "You can't! The Queen's won't allow it."

"I will stay, whether I am allowed or not."

"Nike tried that," Mak burst out. "You know what it did to all of us."

"I know," Rudhira said heavily. "But the Charge cannot abandon the people here who need our protection."

The Hesperites. Of course. The last remaining humans who worshiped Hespera would perish without the Charge's support. This was so like Rudhira, and yet it was unthinkable.

"We would never see you again," Xandra cried. "Forever."

He rose to his feet and pulled her into his arms. "I doubt it will come to that. When I appear before the Firstblood Circle and tell Kona she may choose between the Departure and me, I rather hope she will prefer her brother, hm?"

Xandra hung onto him. "I won't let either of you do this."

"This is also a bridge we should not cross unless we come to it."

So many possible futures lay before them, so many visions Lio could not bear to imagine. Only one thing was clear to him. Cassia must face that future with power.

"We are running out of time to find the letting site," Lio said. "Kalos, we need your help to search for it faster."

He leaned forward. "You know I'm willing, but do you think it's wise to risk it this close to the vote?"

"I agree," Cassia said. "We have pushed the Allied Lords to their limit, demanding that they accept my marriage to a Hesperine. Now is not the time to violate our terms with them by bringing a Charger to Patria."

"They cannot disapprove if they never find out," Lio said.

"If the Dexion detects me," Kalos pointed out, "he's sure to tell Flavian."

"And then Flavian can use that against Solia in Council," Cassia said.

Lio smiled. "That is why we must rid ourselves of the Dexion first."

Cassia's eyes widened. "This is the other part of the plan you mentioned?"

He took her hand. "Remember what I said. I need you to let me do this."

Her lips thinned. "I will not agree to anything until you tell us what you're planning."

Mak gave Lio a dubious look. "Bruising Flavian on the tournament field is one thing, but doing away with an Aithourian war mage?"

Rudhira glowered. "Lio, we have had this conversation about the Dexion before."

"Don't look so alarmed," Lio said. "I'm not planning an assassination. Merely a kidnapping."

Solia's eyes gleamed with interest. "When I tasked you with advising me, I was expecting boring cautionary tales. Now you have my attention."

But his most important ally did not appear convinced. He knew that stubborn set of Cassia's chin.

"Hear me out," Lio said. "We should quietly remove the Dexion from Flavian's custody and make him our own 'guest' in a location where he can't cause trouble. Then we'll spread the rumor that he escaped on Flavian's watch. Later, Solia can take credit for recapturing him."

Solia's brows rose. "You wish to give me credit for your plan?"

"All my satisfaction will come from carrying it out," Lio replied. "We should use it to your political advantage. This will weaken Flavian's position because the lords will see he's unable to hold his own against Cordium. It will also secure your hold over the Dexion, so you can later use him as leverage to avoid the Orders' retribution for being a fire mage. And in the immediate term, it will allow Kalos to come help us find the letting site."

Solia's soldier mask slipped, and an exasperated smile spread across her face. "My only complaint about this plan is that I can't help you with it. Succeed in this, and I'll consider your fourth labor complete."

"I'll soften the Dexion up for you, and you can finish the job once you're ready to reveal that you've returned."

"He and I will start with a conversation about reparations for the farmers he deprived of their only son."

Lio and Solia both looked to Cassia.

She pressed her lips together. "This is a dangerous, undiplomatic idea, and you both know it. Unfortunately, it's an excellent plan. And I shall enjoy it far too much."

Lio smiled and kissed her again.

That did not alleviate her scowl. "I will agree to support this on one condition. You must take me with you. The last time we broke the Dexion, it took both of us, together. And we regretted not having Mak and Lyros with us. The entire Hesperine delegation carries out this kidnapping, or not at all."

Mak crossed his arm. "Lio can't be trusted alone with the Dexion."

"You need at least two Stewards to help you safely transfer him," Lyros said.

Lio held up his hands. "I agree."

The fight drained out of Cassia. "I thought you would try to keep me safe in bed."

"That is precisely what I want to do." He brushed his fingers over her cheek. "But I know I can't."

"Good. You need me at your side for this."

"Yes. After our encounter with Lucis, we know how powerfully your channeling can aid us if anything goes wrong. And a liegehound can take a bite out of a war mage just like any man."

Cassia chuckled and leaned against his chest. "Knight and I will welcome this rematch."

Solia sighed. "I must agree with Lio about this, as well."

Kella nodded in approval. "Your Pup is fierce enough to fight her own battles."

"Thank you," Cassia said.

"This makes me want to go errant," Kia moaned. "Kidnapping an Aithourian war mage? Now there is some justice for our burned libraries."

"Don't you dare," Nodora said. "We need you rallying our partisans for the debate."

"Should we enlist Eudias's aid?" Mak asked.

Lio shook his head. "As much as I regret going behind his back, I believe it is better for him and his position if he can deny all knowledge of this plan."

"I agree," Cassia said. "He has worked hard to win the trust of the Allied Lords, and he has managed to maintain at least the appearance of neutrality in Solia and Flavian's contest for the throne. We don't want to jeopardize that."

"I have a question about your plan," Rudhira said mildly. "Where do you intend to keep the Dexion once you have stolen him from Flavian?"

"Does Castra Justa have a dungeon?" Lio asked.

Rudhira laughed and rubbed his face. "You sound like your father."

"Don't deny it, Rudhira," said Lio. "You would love to throw a war mage in your dungeon."

Rudhira's eyes glinted. "Don't tempt me. I think Castra Justa would be an unwise place to keep him."

"Hmm," said Mak, "the Stand could exile him under the midnight sun with Phaedros."

Kia sniffed. "Phaedros does not deserve that."

"He's also far too dangerous to let any mortal near him," Lyros added, "especially a war mage. No one wants revenge on the Aithourians more than Phaedros."

"Spoilsport," said Mak.

"What do you think, Kella?" Solia asked. "Shall we turn him over to the Empress?"

"Oh, I think exile and house arrest under the watchful eye of the Golden Shield would be a perfect solution. Her Imperial Majesty might also give my Ashes a bounty if we deliver such a valuable political prisoner to her."

"An excellent solution," Lio agreed.

"Yes," said Cassia, "and on your way back, you can pay a visit to Tuura."

"How is she?" Rudhira asked.

"According to her latest letter," Kella answered, "she's tired but out of danger. She and Karege are staying in Ukocha's village with...friends."

Specifically, a winged friend, as Lio had learned from his correspondence with Tendo. Judging by the sudden tension in Solia's posture, she had guessed this as well.

If fate robbed her of the crown she had expected to wear, just like Tendo, would she admit defeat and return to him? Tonight, celebrating his own unlikely betrothal to a Tenebran woman, Lio hoped for Tendo's sake that Solia might one day choose victory in love over victory in battle.

1

day after

AUTUMN EQUINOX

2 Kyria's Bounty, 1597 OT

WORTH SPARING

Guttering torches lit the landing at the top of Castra Patria's north tower. The heavy wooden door of the Dexion's prison was reinforced with iron and spells, but Lio could still sense the acrid aura of the fire mage inside.

Cassia pressed close to Lio on the cramped landing, her hand on her tense liegehound. "This does not appear sufficient to contain an elite war mage."

"It isn't," Mak said.

Lyros shook his head. "The Tenebran mages' wards are pathetic."

Lio tightened the weave of blood magic, illusions, and thelemancy that concealed them, but if the Dexion sensed anything out of the ordinary, one revelatory spell from him might betray their presence. "Hoyefe says the traversal cuff on the Dexion's ankle is what really keeps him here."

Mak snickered. "The kind of manacle his own Order uses on apostates to keep them from escaping with magic?"

Cassia covered her mouth with a hand. "How humiliating for him."

"But that won't prevent him from using other spells," Lio said.

Lyros closed his eyes. "I don't sense any battle wards against Hesperines."

Lio frowned. "He must know we're here. If Flavian didn't mention the arrival of a Hesperine delegation, the Dexion has surely sensed us nearby. I would expect him to take precautions against precisely the sort of visit we're about to pay him."

"A dangerous oversight," Mak said.

"Yes," Cassia mused, "he's fortunate our people are so self-controlled."

"Most of the time." The Dexion was indeed fortunate that Lio was not here for the sort of justice his father, Rudhira, and Nike had rained down on the war mages who had captured Methu.

Lyros opened his eyes again. "We should be careful. This feels too easy. I don't trust it."

"Wards up." Mak joined his bleeding palm with Lyros's.

Lio felt the weight of their wards settle over everyone. He pulled Cassia under the shelter of his arm. "Stay close."

"I will," she reassured him.

He cast his senses ahead of him, then stepped them through the door.

A flash of white-hot light blinded him, and warmth bathed his skin. Magefire. The explosion faded fast, but not before it seared away the wards.

Lio yanked Cassia tight against him and levitated, spinning to put his body between her and the Dexion. New shadow wards rose, and the second fire spell hit Mak and Lyros's defenses with a thud that rattled Lio's teeth. Paws pounded across the floor, and Knight snarled.

Lio jolted the Dexion's mind in warning. "Stand down! I'll disarm you with thelemancy if I must."

The Dexion gave a humorless laugh. "Of course. But you couldn't expect me to let you simply stroll in here without at least a slap on the wrist?"

The haze of firelight faded, leaving spots on Lio's vision, and the air cooled. He landed first, and feeling no traps, set Cassia on her feet as well. "All right?"

"Yes." She sounded a little breathless, but steady.

They turned to find the Dexion on his knees, Mak holding his arms behind him. The mage's black hair was tousled, his olive skin flushed, and his flame-red robes mussed. Knight snarled in his face, while Lyros held out two hands dripping with blood to feed the wards.

"Welcome to my humble abode," the Dexion drawled. "What brings you all to the Tenebran slums?"

Lio scanned the room with his gaze and his arcane senses, checking for other traps. But he noticed nothing more dangerous than the overturned chair and a desk covered in scrolls. A Kings and Mages game board sat on a table by the fire, and a sandbag hung in one corner. How like Chrysanthos to maintain his physique in captivity. "I see no cause for complaint. This is a far more pleasant prison than the crypt where you kept our Hesperine hostages."

"My traitorous colleague Skleros was responsible for their accommodations," the Dexion said. "One can't expect much better from a Gift Collector."

Mak hauled the fire mage into a chair. "Don't pretend you weren't complicit—and ready to immolate our people."

"Is revenge the reason you're here?" Chrysanthos arched a well-groomed brow. "How banal. I expected more sophisticated intrigue from you."

"No," Lio said. "You should be grateful we're above revenge."

"Excellent," the mage replied. "Torture and death are admittedly not how I would prefer for you to alleviate my boredom. I've been wondering when the Hesperine delegation would deign to seek out my company. You took long enough."

Cassia stood over the Dexion at her liegehound's flank. "As hard as it is for you to imagine, Florian," said Cassia, using his birth name, "we had more important matters to attend to than the all-mighty Dexion of the Aithourian circle."

"Oh, it's abundantly clear what has occupied you, 'Ambassador' Cassia. Could you at least have the decency to hide it? The amount of Deukalion's magic I can sense dripping off of you is nauseating."

Cassia bared her teeth, although she called Knight off. "Count yourself lucky I don't have my fangs yet."

"Which brings us to an interesting question. Why don't you? And what are all of you doing here, after you initially declined the Allied Lords' invitation to attend the Council?"

"We aren't here to indulge your curiosity." Lio began gathering up the papers on the desk.

"You won't find anything of interest in there," Chrysanthos said over his shoulder. "All I know about Skleros these days is what Lord Flavian has told me. I hear the Gift Collector is lurking, as his sort tend to do, but I know nothing of his plans."

"He is also not the reason we're here," Lio said. "You are."

The mage sat back in his chair, and Mak tightened his grip on the man's shoulder, making him wince. "Easy there. I'm not going anywhere." He stuck out his fine leather shoe to display the iron manacle around his ankle.

"You can throw fire spells from right here," Lyros said. "I advise against it."

"My fire traps were merely an obligatory friendly greeting between enemies. I also have no intention of torturing or murdering you, as tempting as it is. It seems we are all agreed that we are more advantageous to each other alive for the time being."

His words rang true. He hadn't put up as much of a fight as he might have. Lio tucked his nephew's letters into a satchel. "Hoping to keep us alive to stay in Flavian's good graces?"

"Naturally," the Dexion answered. "Killing my host's other guests would not encourage him to accept my bargain and release me."

"He won't be in a position to release you after tonight." Cassia dumped his Kings and Mages set into his clothing trunk.

It appeared to dawn on the Dexion that they were not ransacking his possessions. They were packing them.

"Gods," he said. "You can't be serious."

"We are taking you into our custody tonight," Lyros informed him. "You can make it easy on yourself, or more difficult."

Lio swung the pack full of scrolls onto the trunk, then helped Cassia search for any hidden compartments that might contain something informative or valuable.

The Dexion's gaze followed them, his eyes widening. "It is in your best interests to let Flavian take my bargain."

Cassia huffed. "You expect us to believe you will keep your promises to him? You and your Order have invested too much in Lucis to abandon him now."

"Lucis was always a means to an end. The harder he becomes for us to control, the less appealing he is as an ally. We can be persuaded to support Flavian—but not if he barters me to Orthros. What is the meaning of this?"

Lio yanked the blankets off the bed and ripped a seam on the mattress. How enjoyable it was to see the Magelands' foremost politician clueless about their plan.

"You are diplomats," Chrysanthos protested, "trying to prevent a war between my Order and your kind. I know you don't want to antagonize Cordium. It would be better for Orthros if Flavian remains on good terms with both of us."

Finding nothing of interest in the stuffing, Lio levitated the ruined mattress back onto the bed.

"Ready to go?" Mak asked.

"Yes, there's nothing else here." Cassia let a tapestry fall back over the wall.

"Wait." An edge of desperation had entered the Dexion's voice. "Flavian has nothing to gain from this."

Inwardly, Lio laughed. The Dexion was catching on, but they would not make it easy for him.

The mage's face froze. "You aren't helping Flavian."

"It took you remarkably long to realize that," Cassia said.

"Who are you working for?" the Dexion demanded.

"You should know better than to ask blunt questions," she returned.

"What happened to Hesperine compassion for children?" the Dexion spat. "I'll offer you the same bargain I offered Flavian—or a better one. Name your terms. As long as you will send me home to my nephew."

Cassia smiled. "Is he begging?"

"It sounds like begging to me," Mak agreed.

"Try not to enjoy it too much," Lyros advised.

Lio did not enjoy the thought of the boy missing his uncle. "You will survive your stay with our friends, and you can continue writing to your nephew."

"You have more to gain by letting me go," Chrysanthos said.

Cassia laughed.

"Listen to me." Raw emotion tore through the man's aura, unlike anything Lio had sensed in him before, except in that moment when he and Cassia had broken the Dexion in interrogation.

Lio shared a glance with Cassia. She touched her medallion, signaling that they should press their advantage.

"We're listening," Lio said.

"I've lost my taste for persecuting heretics," the Dexion burst out.

"There. Now you know the last secret you failed to pry out of me at the Summit. It was always my father and brother who thirsted for a glorious war with the Hesperines. I was never loyal to their cause...only to them."

Lio studied the pain in the man's aura.

Chrysanthos's lip curled. "Don't imagine for a moment that I have compassion for any of you. But provoking conflict with you has cost my family enough. Send me back to Cordium. Let me mitigate my father in his old age. Let me take over the Aithourian Circle when he dies and steer it in a different direction."

Mak raised his brows, and Lyros shot Lio and Cassia a questioning glance.

"I have nothing else to offer you but the truth," Chrysanthos said. "Take my bargain or leave it."

"If he tries to cast, stop him." Lio pulled Cassia aside and wrapped them in a veil spell.

"Do you believe him?" she asked.

Lio rubbed his chin. "I am wary, but his emotions ring true. This reminds me of when he confessed who his brother was."

Cassia nodded. "I'm thinking the same."

"He doesn't know our motivations, so he can't offer us anything we want. He's out of bargaining power. For him to drop his mask like this shows how desperate he is, don't you think?"

"Or it could be a political masquerade. He may want us to believe he's at our mercy so we'll let our guard down enough for him to escape."

"Yes, that could be true. But do you believe it is?"

She hesitated, her gaze thoughtful. "No. I believe he doesn't share his brother's religious zealotry against Hesperines. For why would Chrysanthos make an appeal to our hearts if he believed we had none?"

Lio looked at the Dexion. The man hung his head, awaiting his fate.

There would always be centuries of hatred between them, but this Aithourian believed Hesperines were, at least, a little human.

"The Summit worked," Lio breathed. "Even on him."

Cassia took his hand. "Yes, it did. And letting him take over the Aithourian Circle one day may truly be our best course of action. But not until Solia is ready."

"Yes. We can hope his time in the Empire may encourage him to continue on this path toward his better self."

Lio lowered his veils, and he and Cassia went to stand before Chrysanthos.

"Do not fear," Lio said. "You will find your new host more amenable than Flavian to your hopes for the future. We guarantee you will be treated with dignity and reunited with your nephew as soon as politics allow."

A hint of despair flashed in the man's gaze, and Lio felt its echo in the Blood Union. No, he did not enjoy this part of his plan in the least.

"When will politics allow?" Chrysanthos asked.

"I don't know," Lio said, "but all of us want this to be over as much as you do."

Heat flared behind Lio. He reached for the Dexion's mind even as Mak and Lyros tossed more shadow wards around the mage. But it was too late.

Flames had erupted at the base of the door, where a heptagram was now visible, glowing orange. The Dexion must have had a hidden flame trap in reserve. The Tenebran mages' wards shuddered with the impact of the magefire.

"Even Master Gorgos will sense that!" Cassia cried.

Lio cursed. "We have to get the Dexion out of here before they come to investigate."

Chrysanthos smirked, but the smug expression slipped from his face when Lio grasped his mind and drove him into unconsciousness. Mak and Lyros met Lio in the Union, and they all tried to step with the Dexion. But taking hold of the war mage was like trying to hold fire. Lio's veils wavered as he divided his focus.

Feet pounded up the stairs beyond the door. Magefire ate away at the wooden panel, warping the iron.

Cassia grasped Lio's hand. The channeling surged to life, and he felt her awareness join with his and their Trial brothers'. Chrysanthos's magic flowed toward her aura.

"Cassia, are you sure—" Lio began.

But the Dexion's magic bowed to her Will, subdued by the channeling. The world released him, and Lio, Mak, and Lyros's magic grasped him.

They stepped, the crash of the door and Master Gorgos's shouts echoing in their ears.

They landed hard at the sparring grounds in the Summit Sanctuary, Knight still snarling. The smell of magefire tainted the air. The Charge, Solia, and the Ashes gathered around, spells of every affinity at the ready.

Cassia staggered into Lio, and he caught her close. "Are you all right?"

She made a face and turned her head away to spit in the grass. "Ugh. I am never channeling Aithourian fire magic again."

"Did his magic hurt you?"

She shook her head. "No side effects except this foul taste in my mouth."

He cast a cleaning spell on her tongue and kissed her. All he tasted was blood magic, the Lustra, and Cassia.

Her fingers curled against his chest. When he pulled back, she sighed. "Much better."

He glanced around. They had made it with the Dexion and all of his possessions. Rudhira had rolled the man onto his back and stood over him, Thorn in his hands.

"I believe this one is worth sparing," Lio said.

Rudhira sheathed his sword and stepped back. "Whether he is worthy or not, we will spare him. It is for Hespera to judge his soul, not me. She will have to forgive me for how unwilling I am to let this one take Sanctuary here."

"It won't be for long," Kella said.

Solia extended her hand to Lio. "Well done, adviser. You managed to teach me something. Your fourth labor is complete."

He clasped her wrist. "What is to be my fifth?"

"For now, put all your effort toward getting Cassia to the letting site for your second labor. After that, we can discuss the fifth."

"Agreed."

Solia crossed her arms over the bodice of her gown, gazing down at the Dexion. "Well, the last time I saw one of his Order, they were chasing me across the docks of Cordium, bent on destroying the female fire witch. How satisfying to have one of them at my mercy now."

"Thank the Goddess they don't know that fire witch was you," Cassia said.

Solia tilted her head. "This one's aura doesn't feel as powerful as the men who almost killed me that day."

"What? He's one of the most powerful fire mages in the Order of Anthros." Lio probed the Dexion's aura with his thelemancy. "Hespera's Mercy. You're right. His magic is depleted."

Cassia stiffened. "You don't think I did that, do you?"

Lio hoped his own smirk didn't resemble the mage too much. "Your channeling weakened him."

Cassia flattened her hands on her skirts, as if to wipe them clean. "I don't care who he is, I don't want his magic in me, and I don't want to hurt him the way the Collector hurt Pakhne. Will he recover?"

"Don't worry." Lio let his own magic sink into her aura. "I sense no trace of his affinity in you. You didn't absorb it, merely redirected, I think."

"I was aiming to channel it back into his fire spell."

Lio chuckled. "Well, it will be interesting to see the state of the tower upon our return."

Rudhira's healing magic made a cursory pass over the Dexion. "He'll be back to his insufferable self all too soon. All you did was temporarily disarm him—for a good cause."

The Dexion stirred with a groan and squinted up at them all in the spell light.

Solia rested the tip of her sword on his sunstone medallion of office. "Dexion Chrysanthos, you are now my 'guest.' You will be treated fairly, but attempts to harm anyone will not be tolerated."

Very slowly, he lifted his hands in surrender. "May I ask who you are?"

"The rightful queen of Tenebra."

His jaw went slack, thoughts churning in his mind. "Solia Basilinna?"

Solia gave him a hard smile. "You catch on quickly."

His court mask fell back into place over his expression of pure astonishment. "Well played, Ambassadors. Well played indeed."

22

days after

AUTUMN EQUINOX

23 Kyria's Bounty, 1597 OT

LIFE'S WORK

LIO WATCHED FLAVIAN TAKE his seat in the great hall. The man was composed, for someone who had not recovered from the loss of his most valuable political hostage. His charade of confidence couldn't silence the gossip that thrived among the lords and ladies. It had been over a fortnight since the Dexion's so-called escape, but the whispers had only proliferated.

"...explosion woke me in the middle of the night...took every mage at Patria to put out the fire..."

"What of Lord Flavian's guarantee of protection?"

"If he cannot control one war mage, how is he to stand against all of Cordium as our king?"

Judging by Cassia's smile, she was enjoying what she read on the Council's lips tonight. But the political victory gave Lio little satisfaction. The only reason he could bear to sit in this chair while Cassia's life was in danger was because he had made way for Kalos. Even now, the scout was in the domain of Patria, searching for the letting site. Lio was counting the hours until he and Cassia could meet Kalos to hear if he had found anything.

As if sensing his troubled thoughts, Cassia reached over and rested her hand on his. Her soft touch sent a thrill through him. This was what it felt like to be allowed to touch her hand in front of the Tenebrans.

The doors banged shut, and Flavian rose from his chair. "Let the Council commence. No petitions will be heard tonight, as there is a matter of grave importance I must bring before you, my lords."

Lio narrowed his eyes at Flavian. What move would the man attempt this time in his ongoing efforts to save face and regain control?

"I object to this change to the proceedings," Solia called out. "It was agreed that both contenders would continue to respond to questions from the lords until the last two declare."

Flavian strode to the dais and turned to face the crowd. "We have no time for questions tonight. A grave danger threatens us all."

"And what of the danger of a war mage on the loose?" Solia challenged him.

"Yes," Lio spoke up, "the Hesperine delegation is still waiting for an explanation. How did the hostage we entrusted to you escape? You've had over a fortnight to investigate, and yet you have no answers for us or the Allied Lords who share our concerns."

There came murmurs of assent, and even some bold calls from the lords that their petitions be heard.

Flavian's expression hardened. "I might well ask you how a mage wearing a traversal cuff managed to magically disappear from the top of a locked tower."

"Be very careful what you are suggesting, Lord Flavian," Lio warned him.

"The time for caution is over," Flavian returned. "I have a serious accusation to make against an enemy in this very room."

Too late, Lio noticed that Flavian's guards had quietly moved into position at the ends of each row of chairs. Cassia's hand tightened on his. The Blood Union went taut with their companions' readiness for danger.

Lio had thought Flavian's investigation a sham, but had the man been gathering evidence against the Hesperine delegation? Through the flames that had engulfed the tower room that night, had someone caught a glimpse of them stepping away with the Dexion? Was Lio's plan about to shatter in their faces?

No diplomatic outcomes ran through Lio's mind. He felt only one conviction. His first duty was to get Cassia to the letting site. He could not let anything take him from her.

If Flavian's guards came for him, he would not go quietly.

"What is the meaning of this?" Cassia demanded.

Flavian did not answer, only nodded to his guards. The men closed in.

But not on Lio. They descended on Lord Severin and hauled him out of his father's Council seat.

Lio, Cassia, and Solia's allies leapt to their feet. Hoyefe's hand was already on his sword.

"Unhand me!" Severin tried to shrug off the guards, but they tightened their grasp. "You have no right!"

"How dare you assault a member of the Council?" Lord Gaius shouted.

"He has betrayed the Allied Lords," Flavian announced.

The guards brought Severin before Flavian. The blond lord held up his hands. "There is no need for violence. Let us discuss this like the honorable men we are. State your accusations against me, that I may defend myself."

"Lord Severinus the Younger," Flavian said, "you are under arrest for spying for the tyrant king and attempting to smuggle our secrets out of Patria. You have sought to undermine the rule of law and subvert the will of the Council of Free Lords. You will be held in my custody while you await your trial, which is to take place after the new monarch is crowned."

"This is a lie!" Severin backed away from Flavian, turning to face everyone else, his voice full of appeal. "The king tried to assassinate my father. He sent heart hunters to kill me. Why would I spy for him?"

"You wouldn't," Flavian said, "but your father would. We all know how hostile he is to Hesperines. I suspect that he chose Lucis, the specter he knows, over the foreign evil of Orthros. And when he demanded you spy for them, you had no choice but to obey, lest he disinherit you."

"I went to Orthros," Severin protested. "I signed the treaty, and I have been faithful to the Allied Lords, despite the risk to myself."

"But we all know where your ultimate loyalty lies." Flavian's tone softened, his aura full of regret. "With your people. For their sake, you would do anything to keep your position as your father's heir."

Severin straightened, mustering his dignity. "These are baseless accusations. You have no proof."

From his sleeve, Flavian withdrew a collection of small notes. The ciphers. "I found these in your chambers."

Shock numbed Severin's aura. "Someone else must have put them there."

"You may put forth that argument during your trial," Flavian said. "Until then, we cannot risk you remaining on the Council."

To Lio's surprise, it was Hoyefe who grasped Solia's arm, holding her in check. Her eyes flashed, the air around her heating. They watched in silence as Flavian's guards escorted Severin out of the great hall.

The whispers in the chamber had changed.

"...unmasked the spy the king planted among us...safer now..."

"Lord Severin must have plotted with the king to free the war mage..."

"...Severin was an ally of Princess Solia's..."

A chair creaked, and Free Lord Ennius stood. He lifted his Council Shield from his feet and hung it upon his chair. Then Lord Adrogan's brother also rose and raised his shield.

Flavian paced down the central aisle. "It appears no further petitions will be necessary. Every lord present has declared his readiness to choose a monarch." He halted in front of Sabina. "Except one."

Lord Hadrian's daughter raised her chin. "He will be here."

"So be it," Flavian said. "Tomorrow night, the Full Council of Free Lords will choose the next ruler of Tenebra."

Lio, Mak, and Lyros were waiting in the weaving room when Solia entered with Cassia and the Ashes. The door slammed behind them, and Lio felt the reverberation in his feet. Solia stalked forward and thrust her hands out. A ball of magefire shot into the hearth, reducing the logs to ash.

"This can't be true." Cassia hugged Knight to her. "I have always thought Severin a true ally."

Lio put his arm around her shoulders. "I did not sense that he was lying tonight."

Solia drew a deep breath, curling her hands into fists, then turned to Hoyefe. "Is he innocent?"

"Yes," Hoyefe said. "He has been framed. I say this not as Severin's lover, but as the Ashes' interrogator. If he were the king's spy, I would have discovered it long before now."

"Then Severin is innocent," Kella said simply.

Hoyefe nodded to her. "Thank you for your trust, First Blade."

Her mouth tilted. "Truth be told, you are better than any of us at not allowing your desires to guide your fortune blade."

Given Hoyefe's expertise in love and war, Lio believed that, but fear for one's lover was its own blade through the heart. "I am so sorry this is happening."

"Did you sense that Flavian was lying?" Hoyefe asked. "Did he knowingly accuse an innocent man?"

Lio shook his head. "He truly believes Severin is the spy. Despite my personal feelings toward Flavian, I must conclude he was trying to do the right thing tonight."

"To Hypnos with his good intentions," Solia said. "We will not let him do this to an innocent man."

"Leave this to me." Hoyefe pulled on a pair of dark leather gloves. "Severin will be out of his custody within the hour."

"What can we do to help?" Mak asked.

Hoyefe counted the enchanted lock picks hidden in the inner lining of his glove. "Thank you, but I owe it to Severin to take care of this myself."

Lyros handed Hoyefe his cloak. "At least let the Charge give him refuge at the Summit Sanctuary."

"Yes, that I would appreciate. But I will be responsible for his escape." Hoyefe drew his fortune blade, its deadly curved edge glinting in the firelight. "And for finding out who planted those ciphers in his rooms on my watch."

Tilili twitched her tail as Kella drew her nearer to Hoyefe. "Are you certain you don't want reinforcements, Lonesome?"

His smile returned briefly, but it was bleak. "Stay with Sunburn. I fear Patria will only become more dangerous in the next twenty-four hours."

"Yes. The king's real spy is still here. Until you find him, we must be prepared for anything." She clasped his forearm, then let him go.

Light wavered around Hoyefe, and he disappeared behind an invisibility spell. The door opened, then shut.

A moment of silence fell. Solia rested a hand on the mantle, her back to them.

This time tomorrow night, they would know if she had won or lost the throne.

Lio tallied the votes again in his mind. He had done it so often over the past weeks, it was a reflex. They had lost Severin's vote. Flavian had surely gained the support of the two lords who had raised their shields tonight. Lio counted the undecideds again.

"It could go either way." Solia voiced the same conclusion he had reached.

How much would the Dexion's loss weigh against Flavian, with Severin's arrest weighing in his favor? What would be stronger in the minds of the lords—how beloved Solia had been, or her sister's shocking betrothal to a Hesperine?

Would the blame for all of it, from the missing mage to Solia's tarnished associations, fall upon Lio and Cassia? They who ought to be her greatest defenders.

Lio might have come here out of necessity, not choice, but in these final hours, he found himself wondering how he would look his Gracesister in the eye if he was in some way to blame for her defeat.

When had he come to care so much whether she occupied the throne? Had it been when she had made him one of her exceptions? Perhaps it had happened much earlier, and he had not wanted to admit it—the night she had stood before his Queens and so passionately defended her vision for Tenebra. The same kingdom he had always intended to make his life's work.

Solia turned, her disciplined soldier's expression once more fixed on her face. "We have no choice but to divide our forces. I'll need one Steward with Sabina and me to escort Lord Hadrian back to Patria. We'll step him here under veils in the hope of not alerting the king or his spies."

"I can do that," Mak offered.

Kella fastened a saddlebag onto Tilili's back. "In that case, Lyros and I will patrol the perimeter. We should check our own defenses, even if Flavian is doubling his sentries and Master Gorgos is casting more wards."

"Such as they are," Lyros agreed. "Gorgos's wards will be sufficient to keep the king's mundane soldiers out and buy us time in case of a war mage attack. But we should strengthen the thelemantic ward with a libation in case the Collector tries anything."

Cassia stepped forward, taking Solia's hand. "Whatever happens to your banner tomorrow...don't forget there is a white rose for you, too."

Solia dropped her hand. "I want you and Lio to go meet with Kalos and join his search. We don't know what will happen tomorrow. This might be your best chance to find the letting site."

"Very well," Cassia said calmly, her aura in turmoil. "We'll return in time for the vote."

Solia was opaque beneath the spells on her scarf. "Don't concern yourself with the vote. Just get to the letting site."

"What?" Cassia demanded. "You think we've come this far to give up now? We are your advisers—we will see this through."

"I'm relieving you both of duty as my advisers," Solia told them. "I don't want you at the vote."

Lio should have expected it, but it came as a blow nonetheless, once to him and once to Cassia, doubled in their Union. As if burned, she stepped back from her sister.

He put his arms around her, his one certainty in all of this. "We must focus on your magic now."

THE EYES OF THE HAWK

HER SKIN STINGING FROM her sister's touch, Cassia held fast to Lio's cool hand. The castra slipped away, and they were standing in Mederi Village, where they were to meet Kalos.

The autumn wind cut across the deserted square, tangling their robes and casting a chill over her mortal body. Lio wrapped her in his cloak, and together, they stared at the statue of her sister. He held her in silence, sharing the weight of her despair.

"Come," Lio said at last. "Let us see what Kalos has found."

The scout waited just outside the village. Kneeling where they had found the undead crow, he studied the ground as if reading signs there. At the edge of the deserted fields, he had an air of confidence that he never displayed in the halls of Orthros.

He leapt the low wall, crossing the wards, and dusted off his tunic and breeches. Knight leaned in his direction, sniffing, but did not leave Cassia's side. His alert posture put her on edge, too.

"Good dog," Kalos said.

"What have you found?" Lio asked.

"There's no doubt the letting site is in the vicinity of Paradum. The Lustra magic is strong there. But finding it when it doesn't want to be found is another matter."

"We'll come with you to Paradum tonight," Lio said. "Perhaps together, you and Cassia can detect the letting site."

Kalos shook his head. "That's just it. I haven't found Castra Paradum either. How can an entire sunbound keep be so well hidden? But mark my words, no King of Tenebra is sneaky enough to keep me out of his keep."

Lio rubbed both hands over his face. "We're running out of time."

Cassia couldn't bear to see her Grace so despondent. "If Kalos can't find Paradum from this direction, we'll try a different approach. It's time to see if he can enter the passageways."

Lio let his hands fall. "Yes. I still think they could lead to the letting site."

"What passageways?" Kalos asked.

Cassia quickly explained the Changing Queen's hidden corridors inside Solorum and Patria.

"*Habuch joh Bero,*" Kalos breathed, and she wondered what Lustra beings he was swearing by. "You nature walked? That really is something out of tales."

"I don't know how to do it intentionally."

"I wish I could help, but that's a skill only the Silvicultrixes possessed."

"If only I could nature walk us to the letting site, we would have been spared all of this."

Lio put a reassuring hand on her back. "Within the corridors, the Lustra magic is so powerful that it almost seems to have a mind of its own. Perhaps there is some kind of tunnel or portal leading to Paradum."

Kalos's expression was solemn. "Are you sure you don't mind me entering?"

"Of course not," she said.

Lio stepped them back to his room, now empty, and showed Kalos behind the wardrobe. The scout ran his fingers over the stones and pressed his ear to the wall, but it held firm. "I can't sense anything."

Cassia lifted the Changing Queen's pendant off her head and offered it to him.

He held up his hands, shaking his head. "That's sacrilege."

"We're heretics," she said. "The Lustra had best be prepared for me to be as troublesome a Silvicultrix as I have been a lady."

"I think it has already received the message," said Lio, "judging by the moonflowers your magic spawned in place of the Anthros's fire."

Kalos's brows rose. "I'd like to see that."

Cassia pushed the pendant toward him.

With great hesitation, he put the pendant around his neck. The composed Hesperine visibly startled. "I've never touched an artifact this powerful."

Cassia put a hand on his shoulder and turned him to face the wall.

"Ebah," he said with reverence, extending his foot. The toe of his boot scuffed against the stone. He pressed the pendant hastily back into Cassia's hands. "See there? This isn't for the likes of me."

"Well, in that case, I will have to introduce you to my matriarchs, as I did Lio, and make it clear you are welcome." Cassia put the pendant back on and held out her hands.

Lio grasped one, while Kalos accepted the other, and Knight pressed against her robe. She led them through the wall.

These are my people. She focused her Will on the thought and sent it through the pathways of magic around her. *If I am to be yours, so must they.*

A howl echoed through the corridor, and they all jumped. Kalos's fangs unsheathed, his eyes wide and catching the glow of Lio's spell light. Something in his aura called back to that voice in the dark.

He followed Cassia and Lio through the corridors like someone in a dream. Occasionally he reached out to run his hand over the ivy. At a fork in the passage, he knelt, his nostrils flaring, and Cassia could feel his Hesperine senses calling out to the Lustra.

When they came to the copse of trees, Kalos halted on the threshold, staring at the moonflowers. A half smile crossed his face. "Looks like Hespera and the Lustra negotiated and reached amenable terms."

"That is our hope," Lio said.

"This is the farthest chamber we've reached," Cassia explained.

Kalos took the lead, and they ventured into the copse to search the area. Here, the masonry of the castra gave way to the natural stone walls of a cave. They had examined every nook and cranny of the walls, then Kalos and Lio levitated her to check the upper ledges and ceiling. They found no portal that would admit her.

They regrouped in the ring of trees, and Cassia cursed. "This feels just like the chamber with the red ivy. I can sense magical potential, but I don't know what to do with it."

"You say this chamber opened when your life was in danger?" Kalos asked.

"Yes." Lio's fangs flashed at the mention of that night.

"Beast magic responds to survival," Kalos reminded them. "Perhaps that's the affinity you need here."

"Excellent theory," Lio said.

"But how do I use whatever latent bit of beast magic I have?" Cassia asked.

"Try holding the pendant and focusing again." Kalos beckoned to Lio. "Give her some of your magic."

She cupped the ivy pendant in her palms and fixed her arcane senses on the complicated magic inside it. Lio rested his hands on her shoulders, and his rich well of power opened to her.

"What do you feel?" Kalos prompted. "Physically, I mean?"

"Pressure behind my eyes," Cassia replied.

"Focus on that," Kalos instructed. "Try to draw the magic there."

She Willed her power to build behind her eyes. As she drew on Lio's magic, the sense of fullness in her brow strengthened. Her vision blurred. She blinked hard.

"What do you feel now?" Lio asked.

"It's the strangest sensation in my eyes...as if they're..." She gasped. "Changing."

The room came into focus. She could see each delicate vein of the leaves and every curving petal of the moonflowers.

Lio looked into her face. "Goddess bless. Hawk eyes!"

Cassia clung to the pendant. "I shape-changed my eyes?"

Lio gave her an astonished smile. "This appears to have the same results as when Tendo shifts his eyes to his eagle form. He would be impressed."

She couldn't help laughing in wonder. "Thank you, Kalos."

He shrugged. "You did the hard work."

"You gave me the knowledge. But I don't know how long I can maintain this." She glanced quickly around the room, trying to see what the magic wanted to show her.

A glimmer caught her eye, guiding her to the back wall of the cave. There on the stone, traced in silver light, was an intricate design of intertwining lines and knots in the shape of a hawk.

"Hold on to my shoulders." She stepped forward.

The rune faded, leaving behind an open doorway. They forged ahead, deeper into the Changing Queen's realm.

They had taken a few steps into the passageway when her eyes began to ache, and her vision blurred again. She reached toward the wall for support. Her hand met Lio's chest instead, and he held her up as her knees buckled.

"It's all right." He poured more of his magic into her. "That was an excellent spell. Take a moment to catch your breath."

When her dizziness faded, the world looked…disappointing. She'd had a hawk's vision for mere moments, but her human eyes already felt limited by comparison. She sagged against Lio, trying to push away her sadness. There was no time for that now.

"This passage seems to go a long way," Kalos said from a few paces ahead, where he and Knight stood looking into the gloom. "Let's see where it leads."

Lio sent his spell light forward, and they walked on.

Cassia found it too easy to lose track of time down here. She wasn't sure how long they followed the tunnel, pausing to explore each and every fork they found. Lio marked their way in spell light, but Kalos also drew trail signs on the wall at every turn, in his own blood, as if making a libation.

At last they came to a stairway hewn from the rock and worn with time. It stopped at a solid ceiling, but Cassia succeeded in changing her eyes once more. She led them up through another silver-drawn portal.

Cold air hit them as they emerged from the ground. The sky was gray with predawn. She could see Castra Patria behind them, and ahead, the wooded hills of the east.

"We were right," Lio said. "There are tunnels leading a great distance under the keep. We could find one that goes all the way to the letting site."

Kalos gave Knight one more pat. "It's almost light. We need to take shelter for the Slumber, then keep searching."

"Don't you want to stay in the passageways with us?" Lio asked.

Kalos shook his head. "We should split up to cover more ground, then meet again at Mederi tomorrow night. Come nightfall, I'll scout for Paradum again. You two keep exploring the tunnels. Cassia knows what she needs to do now."

"Thank you for helping me understand," she said.

"Thank you for letting me walk here." Kalos bowed to her before slipping away into the night.

Cassia turned back to Lio, realizing too late that turning was not a good idea. He scooped her up in his arms before she fell.

"I've got you," he said, "and I've got as much magic as you need to open every portal in Tenebra. We won't give up."

She wrapped her arm around his neck, her other hand clutching her pendant. As he carried her down the stairs, back into the earth, she could only hope her own strength would last.

23

days after

AUTUMN EQUINOX

24 Kyria's Bounty, 1597 OT

HIGHER LOYALTIES

THE HOURS MELTED TOGETHER in the passageways, with only Lio's Slumber to prove that time had passed at all. When Cassia thought of what might be happening outside, anxiety gripped her. Had the vote begun? Was Solia already queen—or defeated? Without Cassia at her side. But there was little time for her to dwell on her sister's rejection.

Changing her eyes to find the portals demanded all her focus. She would have forgotten to eat or drink anything besides Lio's magic if he hadn't pushed water and provisions into her hands. But after a time, she felt too weary to eat. And finally, too tired to walk, even leaning on Knight. Lio carried her onward in his arms while she found the next portal, and the next.

"Turn left here," she said at a fork.

"Do you sense something that way?" he asked.

"Yes."

"You don't sound hopeful."

She cuddled closer to him, a sense of unease skittering over her. "I have a clear sense of direction that we should go that way. But also the feeling that nothing good awaits us."

He hesitated at the juncture, and his spell light floated in that direction, but it revealed only more stone and ivy. "Why would the Lustra want us to go that way if something dangerous lies there?"

"I don't know. There's simply a...wrongness...pulling me in that direction. As if the Lustra is trying to give us a warning."

"I'm not carrying you into danger. We need to keep searching for the letting—" He broke off with a sharp intake of breath.

"What's wrong?" she asked.

"A fire mage just crossed the thelemantic ward."

"This way." She pointed in the direction the Lustra was pulling her.

Lio hurried ahead, and they soon came to another stair. He levitated over the impassable tangle of ivy, Knight clearing it in one leap. They raced up through the next glowing portal.

When they emerged in a shallow gully sheltered by thickets, Cassia recognized the sentry tower on a nearby hill. This was an area of Flavian's guard perimeter they had searched on their rides.

Lio went as still as only a Hesperine could, and she felt his veil spells holding her tightly. Knight let out a low growl.

"*Baat,*" she whispered. "What do you see?"

Lio took a step higher along the side of the gully, and she peered over the top.

In the torchlight, she could see the bodies of Flavian's guards at the foot of the tower. A column of soldiers rode past with no regard for their victims. They were the hard men of the king's guard, dressed in Tenebran royal colors of sky blue and gold.

In the lead was King Lucis, his sword drawn and stained with blood. An image out of her nightmares.

"Master Gorgos's ward was supposed to stop them," Cassia cried.

"There's a gap in his spell," Lio said.

"The king used his magic? He blasted through it?"

"I sense no fire spells. There's an opening in the ward. A deliberate one that only the caster could have left."

"Master Gorgos framed Severin," Cassia realized. "He's the spy."

"He must have gotten word to the king that Lord Hadrian is here, then opened the ward after Lyros and Kella's last patrol."

"Oh, Goddess," Cassia said. "I should have known better than to underestimate him. Sometimes fools do the greatest harm."

"We have to get to the great hall and warn everyone."

"Let me down. I can stand."

He held her an instant longer as the soldiers rode past. Their horses' hooves sent pebbles skittering down the side of the gully. Lio looked into her eyes, worry etching his face. "Will you let me leave you safely in the tunnels and warn everyone myself?"

"No! I'm coming with you. Whatever happens, we face it together. We fight together for the people we love."

"I knew you'd say that. But I had to try." He kissed her forehead, sending a powerful surge of his magic into her, then set her on her feet. "Can you manage?"

"If I don't cast any more spells, your magic will keep me on my feet."

"Once we reach the great hall, I'll keep us veiled. We can split up and warn our allies throughout the room."

"Without alerting Master Gorgos," she agreed. "The warriors will know how best to mount a defense."

Pulling her close, his other hand on Knight's shoulder, Lio stepped them.

They arrived just inside the doors. Her gaze went to the dais, but no one yet occupied the Mage King's chair. Council Shields lay at the foot of each banner. The two piles appeared to be the same size. She couldn't tell who was winning, but saw the shield of Hadria below Solia's banner and Lord Hadrian in the chair beside Sabina.

Lio stepped left and appeared behind Eudias's chair. Master Gorgos sat next to him, observing the proceedings with his customary self-righteous expression, as if he had not sold out every soul in this room. Cassia darted right, heading for her sister. She dodged Lord Tyran, who strode up the central aisle with his Council Shield on his arm, oblivious to Knight's tail a hand's breadth from his leg.

To her horror, Lord Tyran turned to Solia's banner and placed his shield there amid the astonished outcries of the Council. With a sly smile, Lord Tyran bowed to Solia. She nodded back, her face impassive. He was certain to use this against her when she was queen—if any of them survived this night.

Cassia murmured near her sister's ear, "Soli, it's me. Don't react."

Solia had surely survived greater surprises than Cassia's disembodied voice, for she didn't even startle.

"The king is inside the perimeter and riding for the keep with a small army. Master Gorgos betrayed us and let him in. We must mount a defense. What do you want us to do?"

Solia ran her fingers over the Azarqi quiet charms in her hair. "Does he have other allies in the hall?"

"We don't know," Cassia said, "but only Master Gorgos could traverse and alert the king of what we know."

"Mak, Lyros," Solia murmured, "apprehend him with the Blood Shackles. Then we make our move."

"Understood," Mak said. "We need illusions."

Lio's ears must have picked up the request, for he nodded from across the chamber. Mak and Lyros stood, and images of them remained in their seats.

Flavian rose from his seat at the same time. "Princess Solia, all the votes are cast. Are you ready to count?"

Before she could speak, Ben's voice rang out. "Wait."

Mak and Lyros halted, remaining near Solia. Cassia watched, frozen, as Ben stood and raised his knightly shield. Genie leaned forward, her hands tight on the arms of her chair.

The sound of Ben's sword sliding out of his scabbard was far too loud a whisper in the quiet room.

"Ben?" Flavian said. "What is the meaning of this?"

Ben paused before his liege lord and dearest friend. "I owe you my life, and your family will always have my love. But I must now answer to a higher loyalty."

When he moved toward Solia, the command for Knight to attack hovered on Cassia's tongue. Solia's hand went to her hilt.

Ben knelt before her and placed his sword at her feet.

A breath rushed out of Cassia. Flavian had never looked so lost. But Genie's face shone.

"My father committed the ultimate betrayal," Ben said. "I am honor bound to right that wrong by remaining true to you, My Queen. I do not ask for his title or lands. I hope you will never make me a lord. Allow me to serve as your knight, come what may. My sword and shield are yours, if you will have me."

"Sir Benedict, let it be known that I do not hold you accountable for your father's crimes. You do not carry his shame. But I will gladly have you as my knight. I will need you. Rise, and keep your sword ready."

Mak and Lyros stepped behind the mages' chairs. The two Stewards' blood hit the floor before Master Gorgos could react. Wards far more powerful than his own sprang to life around him, and the feeling of that Hesperine magic gave Cassia hope.

Lio appeared at her side and took her hand. In another blink, they stood before the dais at the front of the hall. The Council members gasped, and every gaze landed on them.

"King Lucis is here," Cassia called out. "He's riding toward Castra Patria with enough soldiers to outnumber every warrior in the fortress. Master Gorgos let him through the wards and allowed him to slaughter Segetia's loyal men. We saw this with our own eyes."

"Madness!" Master Gorgos's jowls shook as he struggled against Mak and Lyros's grasp. The man's magic fluttered around him, batting against their wards. "These heretics dare accuse a holy man of betrayal?"

"Speak the truth." Lio's compelling voice rang through the hall and sent a shiver over Cassia's skin. As his spell swept past her, she wanted to spill all her darkest secrets to him.

Master Gorgos's eyes glazed under the effects of thelemancy. "Of course I allowed the king in. He'll slaughter all of you traitors and Hesperine sympathizers, and he will elevate me to royal mage at his side." A vacant smile came to his face. "How satisfying it was to frame that weakling Severin. What a pathetic excuse for a man, letting a foreigner into his bed. He belongs in prison."

All the color had drained from Flavian's face. In that moment, Cassia felt a throb of empathy for him. She knew how it felt to strive to do the right thing, only to ruin lives.

He strode toward the dais. As he closed his hand around the pole of his banner, he met Cassia's gaze for an instant.

Then he threw down his emblem upon the shields of Solia's supporters. "Your Majesty, I am at your command."

Solia ascended the dais with a quiet swish of her sky blue skirts. But once she stood before the Mage King's chair, she drew her golden sword and held it aloft. "Scion Angara, strengthen my heart with your holy fire and guide my blade for the protection of my people."

Cassia was the first to speak the words they had dreamed of all these years. "Long live the queen!"

"Long live the queen!" Lord Hadrian called out.

"Long live the queen!" rose from the lips of Solia's worshipful followers and unwilling subjects alike.

"The Empire is at your side," Kella cried.

"Orthros stands with you," Lio declared.

His magic swelled within Cassia, and on those currents, they shared this moment. They had done it. They had helped Solia seize her throne, if only for tonight.

There was no time for further ceremony before the doors banged open. One of Flavian's guard commanders rushed in, heaving for breath. "My lord, the king is approaching. He demands to speak with Princess Solia."

"Queen Solia," Flavian corrected. "It is her decision whether she will hear Lord Lucis's demands."

The guard's eyes widened, and he knelt before her. "Your Majesty."

The entire court seemed to hold their breath, waiting to see how she would answer the first challenge of her reign. Wondering if she dared stand between them and their former king.

"I will meet him." Solia smiled. "I want to see his face when I demand he kneel before me."

LORD LUCIS

Fifteen years before, Cassia had been a child at the foot of the fortress walls, powerless to stop the catapults that would spell doom for her sister. Now she stood at Solia's side on the battlements of a different castra and watched Lucis lead his army toward them.

"I count seven mages in flame-red robes," Lio said. "He's brought an entire war circle of Aithourians."

It was the trebuchets that made Cassia sick to her stomach. The magic on them had an arcane scent like burning flesh. "They have enchanted siege engines."

"Enhanced with fire magic," Lyros confirmed. "Designed by the Aithourian war mage Hephaestion, like the ones at the Siege of Sovereigns."

"Blatant," Mak said. "The Aithourians keep breaking their own religious laws against combining spells and weapons."

Flavian gave his head a shake. "Ben told me about the siege engines, but seeing this with my own eyes..."

"Now you know what I've watched happen to our kingdom all these years," Lord Hadrian rumbled.

"And what I lived with in Corona." Eudias looked down at his former colleagues with disdain.

Kella grimaced. "If those are half as destructive as what the Imperial army uses, a mundane fortress like this will crumple."

Cassia shuddered. "It's why the Siege of Sovereigns was the shortest in Tenebra's history. Not a living thing survived."

"Mak, Lyros," Solia asked, "how long will your wards hold against them?"

"Long enough for the Charge to get here," Lyros replied.

"We need one of you to step to the Sanctuary," Solia said. "Bring all the Hesperines errant you can."

"Stay here to help with siege strategy," Mak told Lyros, "and stay safe."

Lyros nodded, and they shared the long look of two Graces speaking in their Union. Then Mak stepped away.

Lucis's forces halted in the camp below, which was now a deserted ruin thanks to Ben's efforts. With astonishing speed, he and his men had gotten everyone to shelter inside the castra, leaving behind nothing the enemy could use against them. Lucis and the Aithourians split off from the army and galloped across the scorched festival grounds. Nearer. Nearer. They halted right below the gatehouse.

Despite the might he still wielded, Lucis looked so small sitting there below their vantage point.

He lifted his gaze. Cassia and her sister looked at the man who had sired them.

Lio's hand rested on her lower back, his presence even closer. She did not have to face this alone.

"Daughters," Lucis called up, "it is not too late for forgiveness. Return and swear your fealty to me once more, and I will pardon all those who were complicit in this treason. All within Patria will be spared."

What a laughable display for his Cordian allies. Cassia and Solia knew better than to believe his claims of clemency.

"Lord Lucis." Solia's tone was pure steel. "There are no traitors here. In accordance with the Free Charter, the Full Council of Free Lords has revoked their mandate from you."

"We stand united." Lord Hadrian's voice rang out over the battlements. "We no longer need a tyrant to stay our feuds. We have pledged ourselves to a strong and just monarch."

"You will be put on trial for your crimes," Solia declared. "Conspiring with Cordium against your own kingdom, the attempted assassination of the Council, the murder of Prisma Thalia, and countless other atrocities you have committed. I am your queen, and you will not be spared."

"Foolish girl," Lucis spat, his veneer of composure draining away. "I have held my throne against every man. I have buried every woman who dared call herself queen during my reign. How dare you presume to wield *my* power?"

"It is not your power any longer," Solia said.

"Such brave words," Lucis sneered, "but in truth, you are a frightened little bitch. You always were, just like your mother, cowering from me and staying out of my way. You've always known to fear your father."

"Now I know there are far more frightening things in this world. They fell before me. And so will you."

"Clearly, you need a new lesson in obedience. Has your sister been filling your ears with tales of her rebellion?" The king's attention fixed on Cassia. "You have not escaped me."

His empty taunts were a weak echo of her past. But this last declaration sent a chill down her spine. As if he knew something she did not.

She recalled the Collector's words to Lio. *Do not imagine she is bound to you more deeply than she is to me.*

Lio must have been thinking of the same, for his hand tightened, and he moved closer to her.

"I have escaped you." Cassia held her medallion. "The Queens of Orthros have given me Sanctuary and placed me beyond your power."

"The heretics will face punishment as well." Lucis drew his sword and raised it above his head. "I, the rightful King of Tenebra, and my allies, the Divine Mage Orders of Cordium, declare war on the rebels who threaten this land, and upon every Hesperine within the borders of this kingdom."

Mind magic made Lio's voice carry. "Orthros does not march to war. But Hespera's own will defend innocent mortals from the wrath of Anthros, as we always have."

"My campaign against you will not end as the Last War did," Lucis warned. "Unlike the Mage King, I will not allow Tenebra's enemies to flee. When I am finished, even immortals will cower before my might."

The Aithourians swiftly raised their hands. A torrent of magefire raced up toward the ramparts with a terrible roar. But the scent of blood magic filled the night, emanating from Lyros. The fire spells broke against a wall of shadows.

When Cassia's vision cleared, she saw the engineers loading the trebuchets. Their missiles burned with latent magefire.

On Lio and Cassia's watch, negotiations were at an end. The war had begun.

Ancient history was repeating itself before Lio's eyes. He knew how his uncle had felt sixteen hundred years ago, standing on the walls of his condemned temple. As the armies of Tenebra and Cordium had prepared to rain fire on everyone he loved, Argyros had faced the same decision Lio must make now.

Lio fingered the mortal minds below. He had mastered hundreds at once before. He had the power to turn this force away with sheer thelemancy, just as his uncle had done.

But what would be the cost? When they inevitably broke free of his control, where would they attack instead? It could be Mederi Village or Lord Hadrian's camp. They might rampage all the way back to Solorum to raze the Temple of Kyria. And while Lio lay recovering from the damage to his own mind, he would be powerless to protect Cassia.

Lyros took hold of his shoulders and looked him in the eyes. "I know what you're thinking."

"Tell me the truth," Lio said. "Strategically, is that what you need from me tonight?"

Lyros gave his shoulders a squeeze. "No. Tonight, you have what the Great Temples did not. Hesperine warriors. Let the enemy come."

"I want you and Cassia off the walls," Solia said.

"No," Cassia cried. "We belong at your side. Let us use our power to help you."

Solia faced her. "You know what those trebuchets can do. This won't be a long siege, and the fortress walls won't keep anyone safe. I need you and Lio to evacuate the non-combatants and animals."

"Don't send me away from you," Cassia pleaded. "Never again."

Solia didn't waver. "Lives depend on you doing as I ask."

Lio touched Cassia's arm. "Protecting the innocent is a worthy duty for Hesperine diplomats."

Her aura shook with her inner debate. But he felt her push down her fear, and her inner determination shone like adamas. "Yes. We will be their Sanctuary tonight."

"I can step everyone to safety," Lio said, "but with only one Hesperine, it will take time."

Cassia nodded. "We'll need somewhere for them to hide while you take them in groups. Let's bring them into the Lustra passageways. We'll use the portal in the great hall."

"Stay safe until the Charge gets here," Lyros told them. "Do you understand? Bodyguard's orders."

"We will be in the most secure parts of the castle—the inner keep and the passageways." Lio embraced his Trial brother. "You're the one who's facing magefire."

"This is what I trained for." Lyros gave Lio a Mak-worthy hug, then set Lio away from him.

"Wish us luck," said Eudias. "I've never fried catapults with lightning magic before."

"May your aim be true," Lio said, "and may you enjoy your poetic justice."

Eudias grinned. "I will."

"My Queen," said Lord Hadrian, "you must get down from the walls as well."

"I entrust our siege defenses to you." She fixed Flavian with a gaze. "I trust Segetia's soldiers will not hesitate to take orders from Hadria?"

"I will stand at Lord Hadrian's side," Flavian said, "and see to it that every man heeds his combat experience."

Lord Hadrian offered Flavian his hand. "We are all Tenebrans tonight."

Solia nodded her approval. "Lio, take Kella and me with you and Cassia."

As soon as Lio stepped the four of them down to the great hall, Solia and Kella began issuing orders like the commanders they were. Whenever one of the lords dared hesitated to heed the women, Lord Deverran and Lord Gaius encouraged obedience, and not gently. Soon the greatest warriors of Tenebra were deploying throughout the castra.

Sabina met Cassia and Lio with her handmaidens and Solia's ladies at her side. "What can we do?"

Perita had her son strapped to her chest and her sleeves rolled up. "We're ready for anything King Throneless tries to throw at us."

Callen stood beside her, his sword drawn. "Lord Hadrian has charged me with the defense of the great hall."

Lio clasped Callen's arm. "We will not allow any harm to befall our ladies."

Cassia pulled out the Changing Queen's pendant. "We must bring everyone who cannot fight here to the great hall. I have an artifact that will open secret passageways through the castle. They'll give us shelter from the siege engines while Lio steps everyone to safety in groups."

Sabina did not ask questions. "I'll clear the north wing. Nivalis and Valentia, take east and south, please. Genie, will you take the west and help Sir Benedict with the people he brought in from the camp?"

Lio cast his senses throughout the keep, sifting through the crowd of presences to bring these four ladies into focus. "If any of you encounter danger, focus your thoughts on your need. I will sense your distress call and step to you."

Genie gave him her curving smile. "The hens are in safe hands tonight."

Lio prayed she was right, and Pakhne would be the last one lost on his watch.

Ariadne joined them and gestured to where some of the guards were moving chairs for the Semna. "We're setting up our infirmary here."

"Good," Lio said. "Once Cassia and I finish evacuating everyone, we can help bring the wounded here. After the Charge arrives, they will place wards on the great hall, and the Hesperine healers will assist you."

"Where do you want me, my lady?" asked Perita.

"Right here with me," Cassia answered, "directing the evacuees as we bring them in."

"Where are we taking them?" Sabina asked.

"The Hesperine Sanctuary will welcome them," Lio offered.

Sabina shook her head. "Many will be too afraid to accept shelter there. I'm afraid some of our people still need convincing about Hesperines' good intentions."

"I understand," Lio said. "Where do you suggest?"

"Is there a keep nearby belonging to someone we can trust?" Cassia asked.

"I know a place."

They were the first words Miranda had spoken. Everyone looked at her.

"We can go to Paradum," she said.

Lio could scarcely believe his ears. After all this effort, Miranda might show them the way not only to refuge, but the letting site. She might save Cassia again.

Cassia's heartbeat had picked up. "Paradum? It is not under Lucis's control?"

Miranda shook her head. "He never gave it over to a new lord, after… my parents. He brought our tenants under direct royal control and let the castle fall into ruin. These days, it's abandoned. Except by me." She glanced around her, and Lio could smell her anxious sweat.

A boom came from outside, and the keep seemed to shudder. Or perhaps that was only Lio's Hesperine senses, responding on instinct to the first magefire that struck the walls.

Determination came over Miranda, and she said, "Paradum is protected by my spells. I've turned it into a haven of sorts, where I can hide from the authorities…or hide those in need."

"You aren't only a healer?" he asked gently. "A light mage too, perhaps?"

She raised her chin. "Yes. I swear to you, no one will find it under my illusions."

Goddess bless. Illusions powerful enough to fool Kalos would certainly keep out the enemy. If Miranda was telling the truth. Lio studied her aura and the thoughts drifting from her mind. He sensed none of the dissonance that occurred when someone was lying. He touched his medallion to signal Cassia.

"That's brilliant," she said. "Of course your old home is the last place anyone would expect to find you."

Miranda nodded. "The king always treated it like a place to stash useless things. Then he forgot about it all together. Now I've given it a purpose."

"How do we get there?" Lio asked.

Miranda hesitated. "Would you like me to traverse you? If I do that, can you step back there?"

"Yes, that would be ideal. We also have a Hesperine ally in the area who can help protect everyone, if you will let him in."

Miranda nodded. "I can reveal the castle to him."

"I should come too," Cassia said. "I'll check if there are portals."

"You go on," Perita encouraged. "Callen and I can have the first group ready when you get back."

Excitement and dread echoed between Lio and Cassia. Were they about to stumble into the letting site at Paradum? If her magic started to arrive, how would they manage an evacuation?

Another explosion came from outside, and this time, there was no doubt about the physical tremor under Lio's feet.

They had no choice but to go forward. And whatever happened, he must not allow anything to separate Cassia from him for even a moment during the siege. "Let's go."

Miranda held out her hands, and Lio took one, finding her grip strong for such a petite woman.

Cassia put her hand in Knight's ruff. "Would it be too much to ask for you to bring Knight with us?"

"We should keep him with us everywhere tonight," Miranda agreed. "He's good protection."

Cassia took her other hand. "Thank you for this. I want you to know I'm on your side."

"You've changed," Miranda said. "The Cassia I knew would never risk her life to save a castle full of people who mean nothing to her."

"Everyone here matters to me now."

Miranda squeezed her hand. "I know."

Her traversal spell took hold of them, a yanking sensation in Lio's sternum, so much more difficult than an intuitive step through the world. So much magic. The wild magic of an apostate, wielded with the force of a great mage. She was more powerful than he had imagined. How had she hidden this?

The world went still, and Lio reached out to steady Cassia. They were in a courtyard, surrounded by walls in disrepair. The trees were dead. Skeletal vines climbed the stones.

He had an instant to take this in before magic erupted around them. He tasted death in his mouth. Necromancy.

Cassia was torn from his grasp. A blast of manteia threw him onto his back. His head cracked against broken flagstones, but he barely felt the impact compared to the spell-pain clawing at the rest of his body.

He focused all his Will on Cassia's aura and tried to step them away. But his blood magic strained uselessly against arcane bindings. The harder he fought, the deeper the pain ripped into him.

A second blast of death magic sent him into oblivion.

24

days after

AUTUMN EQUINOX

25 Kyria's Bounty, 1597 OT

THE MASTER'S FAVORITE

Lio knew he was conscious when he felt pain again. On instinct, his thelemancy lashed out, reaching for Cassia.

His power collided with a chaos of Lustra magic. It circled her, howling, snarling. The Lustra caught him in its jaws and dragged his magic into her. He felt her heartbeat and heard her gasp for breath.

She was alive. *Oh merciful Goddess, thank you.*

The floor was hard under Lio's knees, his arms shackled above him against a wall. Dull agony coursed through his veins. So weary, to his bones.

What—who could do this to a Hesperine?

A Gift Collector.

The Old Master's Overseer must have been lying in wait at Paradum. What had he done to Miranda? Where was Knight?

Lio dragged his heavy eyelids open. He recognized this place. The small, shuttered windows. The bare stones of the ceiling Cassia had stared up at for days. He had seen this chamber in her memories and hated it as much as she did—the sickroom where she had nearly died of that fever eight years ago.

Where her bed had been, there was now a wooden table. He was chained to the wall alongside it, but out of reach, as if his captor wanted to taunt him with a perfect view of the person bound to the table's surface by thick leather straps.

Cassia. His Grace, trapped in this place out of her nightmares. Lio wanted to destroy this room, stone by stone.

"Cassia?" he called. "I'm here. You're not alone."

No answer. She lay still, her skin ashen.

The Lustra shared his fury. He had never felt magic this raw and powerful, not even in the halls of Orthros, soaked in sixteen centuries of immortal power. It crawled up the walls like parasitic ivy and prowled the room like a pack of half-mad beasts. It was in every stone and breath of air, crying out its claim. Its lament.

This had to be the letting site. But there was something horribly wrong with it—and Cassia.

Lio threw himself against his shackles, trying to break free and reach her, but pain pierced him under his manacles. He went still, drawing deep breaths in a fight to stay conscious. He twisted his head to look at one of his wrists. Blood seeped from under the shackle and ran down his arm in trails.

He found himself in one of the tales Hesperines errant told of their scrapes with death. He had heard of these shackles imbued with necromancy and forged with spikes on the inside. Gift Collectors tipped them with poison that could leave a Hesperine too weak to escape.

Lio bared his fangs. He was Apollon's son, trained by Argyros. He walked in Rudhira's footsteps and carried Methu's bloodborn legacy.

He was Cassia's Grace, the immortal the Goddess of Night had paired to the last Silvicultrix in an arcane union with the Lustra. And the magic here knew it.

If this Gift Collector thought he had bagged a soft, helpless young Hesperine, he was in for a deadly surprise. Lio was ready to teach the Old Master's Overseers to fear the name Glasstongue.

We will save her, he promised the Lustra.

The door creaked open. Boots trod in, their spurs jingling. A figure in a hooded black cloak entered Lio's vision and came to stand at the foot of the table.

The necromancer's aura was difficult to read in the chaos of magic, but he wasn't Skleros. This Gift Collector was too short to be the one who had sabotaged the Summit. Lio and Cassia were about to face a new enemy.

Small hands, one in a gauntlet, put back the black hood. Miranda smiled at Lio's reaction. She shook out her cropped hair, not covered by a demure kerchief now, and gave a delighted laugh. "Oh, the look on your face."

Goddess help him. How could he have been such a fool? He had held Cassia's hand and ushered her right into this trap.

Miranda pulled off her cloak, revealing a perfectly fitting set of leather armor over short necromancer robes. The Eye of Hypnos painted on her breastplate struck Lio with a familiar scent. Though dry and stale from a long-ago hurt, it was unmistakably his Grace's lifeblood. He nearly gagged.

"Did you think only men can be Gift Collectors?" Miranda approached a worktable in the corner and draped her cloak over a chair. "You come from Orthros, where women can be warriors and queens. And yet you failed to imagine that we can be assassins of Hesperines as well."

The worktable was covered with neatly organized tools of her trade. Mortars, pestles, and beakers for her poisonous alchemy; seamstress's needles and embalmers' scalpels appropriated for whatever torture she intended tonight. She picked up a kitchen knife and a shiny apple.

There came a tapping sound at one of the windows. Miranda waved her gloved hand, and the shutters swung open. A crow flew in to perch on her shoulder, the window slamming behind it. She cut off a bit of apple and fed it to the bird, stroking its breast where there was no heartbeat. It was a necromancer's bloodless familiar.

"We're just back from a patrol of my defenses," Miranda explained. "Your Hesperine friend lurking in the area will never be able to find us. And if he is unlucky enough to have the skill to get past my concealments, my traps will make short work of his immortality. No one is coming to rescue you."

Lio prayed she was underestimating Kalos's capabilities. But Lio should not depend on Kalos calling in the cavalry—or them arriving in time. It was up to him to save himself and Cassia.

Miranda popped a piece of apple in her mouth and strolled to stand over Cassia. Her savage enjoyment came through the powerful dream wards that guarded her thoughts and emotions.

Lio had no hope of bargaining with this enemy. It was clear all she wanted was revenge.

There was only one way to survive this. He would have to defeat her. But his magic was weakened by the poison, and a Gift Collector's dream wards were a challenge for a Hesperine thelemancer even at full strength.

It would take time to break down Miranda's mental defenses—time in which she could hurt Cassia.

"What do you plan to do to her?" he demanded.

"Ah, Lio the scrollworm. I hoped you would be the type to stay curious as you die." Miranda left the sliced apple next to Cassia's gardening satchel on the bedside table, and the crow hopped down to nibble at the fruit.

She walked over to stand in front of Lio and gently lifted his chin. He tried not to flinch at her touch. "This is my favorite part of the tales, when the villain explains his wicked plan to the hero. Then the hero escapes with all his secrets. Do you know why I like it so much?"

Could he catch her off guard if he bit her bare hand? No, her blood was probably poisoned, too. A common defense tactic among Gift Collectors.

Her grip tightened, bruising. "Are you curious or not, Lio?"

The longer he played along with her sick game, the more time he had to find a way out of this. "Why do you like that part of the tales?"

She leaned closer. "Because I love to mock the men in the stories. They're all fools. In my tale, the villain is a 'she,' and the heroes never escape her."

She let him go so abruptly that his head banged against the wall behind him. He felt pain and moisture where his skull had hit the ground in the courtyard. The poison was slowing down his healing.

"I am the best at what I do," she told him. "In only eight years, although I am the Master's youngest and newest Gift Collector, I have become his favorite. I've slain every colleague of mine who underestimated me. Don't make their mistake, hm?"

"I wouldn't dare." Never again.

A Gift Collector had been under his nose this entire time, and he had not known. All the power he possessed, all the knowledge he had gained when dueling the Old Master…none of it had been enough.

If he kept Miranda talking, would he learn something he could use against her? Or was every word she said merely another way to manipulate him?

He could only try, and pray that a Hesperine diplomat had what it took to stay one step ahead of a Gift Collector's poisonous tongue.

"What have you done to Cassia?" he asked.

"I never underestimate my enemies." Miranda circled the table again. When she reached toward Cassia, Lio's heart leapt into his throat. But all Miranda did was lift Cassia's eyelid, conjure a bright pinpoint of spell light, and peer into her eye. "I appreciate what a dangerous pair you are. I made sure you were both unconscious while I secured you. But I would hate for Cassia to miss this part. Let's wake her, shall we?"

Miranda moved her hand over Cassia's face, a finger's breadth from Cassia's skin. Cassia's lashes rose slowly.

Miranda leaned over her. "This is the part where I explain the grand plan to you. I watch as the realization dawns on you that you are just a little fly caught in the web. I enjoy the taste of your fear. You die afraid. But that knowledge is a gift. Most people die in complete ignorance, unaware they were pawns every moment of their lives. But you get to understand the meaning of your own existence. You get to glimpse the Masters' game that determines all our fates."

The whites of Cassia's eyes showed as she took in the sight of Miranda's armor.

"Cassia," Lio said. "I'm here. I'm with you."

Gritting her teeth, she struggled against the straps, her heartbeat racing. Her instinctive fear and misery tore at his heart.

"Cassia, look at me." Lio reached for her in their Union. Despite the poison in his blood, their Grace bond was strong and true. "Look at me."

She turned her head and met his gaze. A tiny sigh of relief escaped her.

"I'm here," he said again. "We'll get through this together."

"You want to be partners at my game board, I see. Very well. I accept your challenge, two against one." Miranda strode over to Lio again.

A dagger appeared in her hand as if out of nowhere. The stone weapon looked ancient, like something from a time before the arts of metallurgy. Lio held very still.

She touched the tip of the blade to his lips. "Play by the rules, or I will have to penalize you. If Lio resigns from the game or violates a rule, I punish you, Cassia. And if you stop playing or break a rule, I punish Lio. It will be hard for your partner to help you answer questions if I cut out his famous tongue."

"Do we learn the rules by playing," Lio asked, "as in Kings and Mages?"

"Now you are catching on." Miranda withdrew the knife and looked between them. "Will you play?"

Lio and Cassia both knew Miranda had offered them a choice that was no choice at all. They must take her deadly bargain.

"Whatever unknown steps we take," he reminded Cassia, "we take them together."

She gave a nod. "Glasstongue and the Brave Gardener."

At her mention of Zoe's name for her, it seemed she brought a blessing into this twisted place. A reminder of everything they were fighting for.

"We'll play your game," Lio said.

"Yes," Cassia agreed. "We are ready."

THE GAME OF THE EPOCHS

"We'll begin with an easy question." Miranda fitted her hand against Cassia's breastbone.

Cassia froze. Lio kept his mouth shut so Miranda would not see his fangs. The Lustra magic screamed, but through its noise, all Lio sensed from Miranda was healing magic flowing into Cassia.

"Am I really a healer?" Miranda asked.

A moment of silence ensued. The undead crow pecked at the apple.

Cassia said carefully, "Lio, I think we should take Karege's advice."

They waited. No retaliation from Miranda. Apparently it was not against the rules to consult each other.

"I agree," Lio said.

Cassia was better at questions about Miranda's past, so he let her answer for them. "I remember you standing over me in this room, using magic. But I don't actually recall you healing me. You took that affinity from Pakhne and used it at Mederi Village to make us believe you were an apostate healer, and I made an assumption to fill the gap in my memory."

"You were always too clever for your own good," Miranda said, "but I managed to outsmart you this time. I tore Pakhne's magic out of her right in front of you two while controlling my bloodless. When you examined my mind, Lio, why couldn't you tell I am a Gift Collector?"

How quickly they left the easy questions behind. Lio wracked his mind, but it was sluggish from the poison. He could not think of a single text on necromancy that gave him any hints.

"I can't deny it," Cassia said. "You are much cleverer than I am,

Miranda. You've learned so much about magic during these years, while I still know so little."

Miranda smirked. "Admissions of defeat are not against the rules."

Brilliant Lady Circumspect. With her well-chosen words, Cassia had given Lio a hint. The right answer was not necessarily correct information. Sometimes it was telling Miranda what she wanted to hear.

"Your arcane arts are beyond Hesperine comprehension," Lio said. "You knew I wouldn't be fooled by the trick the Collector used to enter Orthros within Eudias and Skleros. You must have used a more advanced tactic that is unknown even to scholars like me."

"Correct," said Miranda. "You understand so little about my bond with the Master. You see, the Collector did not possess Pakhne and me at the same time. I possessed Pakhne on his behalf. I displaced myself into her. And so my mind felt entirely as you expected, and I was able to wield my full power through her. She was a strong mount. She lasted longer than I expected."

Mount? Was that the word the Old Master used to describe those he possessed? Such a demeaning term for people like Eudias and Pakhne.

Miranda stepped back from Cassia and went to the worktable. "Am I a mount?"

"Of course not," Cassia answered.

"Clearly," Lio said, "Gift Collectors have a much higher status in the Master's game than mere mounts."

"You are learning quickly." Miranda picked up a mortar full of a crushed substance that smelled like apple peel and ash. "We Gift Collectors sacrifice our magic to the Master, and in return, he dwells within us. As long as he holds my affinity, I am as immortal as you, Lio. And he gives me the skill to fill myself with manifold magics."

Cup and thorns. Here was a mystery Rudhira had been trying to solve for hundreds of years—why Gift Collectors were nearly impossible to kill.

Miranda emptied the mortar into a dish of some liquid Lio had no desire to identify. While she worked, Cassia turned her head toward Lio again. "I hope Knight is all right."

"So do I," he said.

"I should punish you for that insinuation," Miranda snapped. "But I too will adhere to the rules. What do you take me for? Is your memory really so faulty that you've forgotten how much I love animals?"

Her crow flew to her, for all the world like a pet that sensed she needed comfort. Did an undead creature have such emotions? The crow ran its beak through her hair, and she stroked it.

"No," Cassia said. "I remember the time your father was beating his horse, and you tore the riding crop from his hand. Agata and I kept you out of his way for days, until his temper cooled."

Lio could imagine how a man who beat his animals might treat his daughter, too.

"Where is Knight?" was Miranda's next question.

"He's safe at Patria," Cassia answered. "You lied and told us you would bring him to give us a false sense of safety."

"Precisely. I take care of animals, and unlike you, I don't betray those who have been good to me. Did I hurt Perita or her child?"

"No," Cassia admitted, "but you gained her trust so you could use her to hurt me."

"She'll be better off without you."

There came a knock at the door. Lio jumped, and his manacles made him regret the small motion. Miranda set her concoction to heat over the small flame of a fire charm, then went to answer the door as if she had been expecting the visitor.

A woman in a simple gown and apron trundled in, carrying a tray. Her brown hair was streaked with gray and tied back in a messy knot under her kerchief. She had lines around her eyes and mouth, like someone who laughed often. But she had no heartbeat.

She gave Miranda a kind smile. "Here you are, my dear. Your favorite apple tarts, fresh out of the oven."

The scent of Cassia's tears was salty against the sweet aroma of the tarts. "Agata?"

The woman blinked at her, and then her face lit up. "Cassia? Why, it's been years! Kyria bless me, how wonderful to see you again." Agata crossed the room to set the tray on the bedside table. She patted Cassia's cheek as if oblivious to the leather straps and Lio bleeding a few paces away. "Oh, my dear girls, together again. You must come to the kitchen so we can have a nice long chat. I'll find a bone for Knight."

Miranda took her by the arm and guided her gently to the door. "Thank you, Agata. We'll be down later. I'll bring a bottle of that Cordian sherry you like."

"Oh, I really shouldn't indulge…"

"You've earned it."

"Well, I suppose a little sip would be all right." Agata left the room with a contented sigh, and her pleasant humming receded through the corridors.

Miranda shut the door. "I honored her by turning her into a greater bloodless, so she is still herself. Be grateful to me that she has no knowledge of your betrayal. I let her keep our happy memories."

Cassia shut her eyes, tears streaking her cheeks, and Lio wished he could hold her.

Miranda picked an apple tart off the tray. "I turned my parents into lesser bloodless, though. You should appreciate the poetry of it, Cassia. I have my father mucking out the stables. My mother cleans the castle, doing the work of the maids she used to terrorize. Do not imagine there is no justice in necromancy. Death is the ultimate balancer of the scales."

Miranda sat down and shared her pastry with her crow while she stirred her alchemical brew. "I would offer you tarts, but you'll have to forgive my poor hospitality. Cassia has a weak stomach, and I can't have her vomiting in the straps. As for you, Lio, poison is all I serve to Hesperines."

Picking up the dish in her gloved hand, she poured the steaming liquid into a goblet, then brought it over to Lio. "Remember that I'll punish Cassia if you break the rules."

"I'll take the punishment," Cassia said. "Don't drink it, Lio."

"What am I planning to do to you?" Miranda asked.

Lio met Miranda's gaze over the dark liquid. Her hard eyes were as opaque to him as her aura. But just like the knife and apple, gauntlet and crow, she had been leaving them clues.

"You need me alive," Cassia said, "so you aren't planning to kill me."

"I didn't ask what I am *not* going to do to you." Miranda dug her fingers into Lio's hair and tilted his head back.

"Cassia is necessary to your master's plans," Lio bit out, "but I cannot understand why, Miranda. Your brilliant plot eludes me. My most educated guess is that you wish to ransom her to influence Solia."

Miranda swirled the poison in the goblet. "Your training in diplomacy has prepared you well for the game. But in this case, don't bother playing innocent. We all know Cassia's magical value outweighs her political value. I know more about how her magic works than you do. I am rather an expert on feeding off of others' power, after all."

"Then you must know Lio's magic is keeping me alive," Cassia broke in, "and if you kill him, I will not survive to be useful to you."

"Unfortunately for Lio," Miranda said. "No quick death awaits him, I'm afraid."

She forced his head back with astonishing strength. He braced himself and didn't resist. The poison hit his throat, tasting of apples, honey, and burning rot. She kept holding his head until he swallowed and managed not to gag.

Within moments, magic tingled through Lio's limbs and swelled in his chest. His magic. But it seemed to have a mind of its own, rising to the surface, uncontrolled and flowing freely.

Miranda stood back and tilted her head with a smile. "Excellent. It seems I have succeeded in adapting this drug for use on Hesperines. It strengthens your magic but weakens your control. It will make your power easier for me to work with—and impossible for you to use against me."

No. Using his thelemancy against her dream wards was their only hope of escape. He could not sit here, full of power and yet powerless, with Cassia at her mercy.

Miranda set the goblet back on the table. "You haven't finished answering my question. What am I planning to do to you?"

Lio swayed on his knees. "Hesperines are immune to possession...we must be immune to essential displacement too." He blinked hard. "You aren't planning to take my magic."

But she might as well have. It wouldn't save Cassia now.

Miranda sighed. "It's a shame. I would love to add your thelemancy to my collection of affinities. Mind magic is one of my favorites to displace.

It's the darkness in your affinity, you know. The power. The temptation to control others. And the challenge. I enjoy hunting dangerous prey." She looked him up and down with a voracious glint in her eyes.

"You are not going to make him your prey," Cassia cried. "It's my magic you want."

"Ha. Correct."

"That's why you lured us to the letting site," Cassia said, "so my magic will awaken and you can take it from me for the Old Master to use."

Lio wanted to hurl every drop of magic inside him at Miranda. But it was beyond his control. Spots danced on his vision as the poison advanced through his body, stirring his power and shredding his focus.

Miranda circled the table, checking the security of the straps. "You, Cassia, are what we call a leech. Empty of magic for so long that you've started sucking it out of others. How the mighty have fallen. You could have been a Gift Collector like me, but now you are reduced to this. It is the most demeaning fate. Worse than being a mount. You are the bottom feeder of the Master's hierarchy." Miranda smiled. "And it is I who have become his favorite. I, whom you betrayed and discarded. Who is in control of our destinies now?"

Cassia studied the ceiling, her expression neutral, all her outrage hidden behind it. Lio knew another person might have snapped at Miranda's baiting, but not his Lady Circumspect. Her self control was all that stood between him and Miranda's punishment, and he hated Miranda for putting Cassia in that position, as much as he loved Cassia for protecting him.

"There is just one problem," Miranda went on. "You couldn't feed off any mage like a proper leech, could you? That would have been so much easier, if I could simply let you run through a few idiots like Master Gorgos to keep you alive until I'm done with you. But you had to fasten onto a Hesperine of all things."

Not much of a Hesperine errant now. Lio had never felt so helpless and unable to defend his Grace.

"Last question," Miranda said. "What am I waiting for while I play with you?"

Lio drew in a breath, shuddering. "You're waiting…for the poison…to work."

"Well done. You two answered all my questions correctly without breaking any rules. That is a first."

Miranda let a moment of silence fall. Her reverence was so great that Lio felt it through her dream wards. The whole room filled with her sense that this was a moment both sacred and profane.

"You survived a match with an Overseer," she said. "You may progress to the Masters' Game. And once you proceed, there is no going back."

She drew her stone dagger again and slid the flat of her blade up the inside of his arm, coaxing his poisoned blood into a bowl. "Epochs ago, the Diviner Queen brought her magical knowledge to this realm. The Six Old Masters became greater than their teacher, and she was fearful of them surpassing her power. She sought to destroy them, but they banished her from their domain."

Miranda strode to the wall at his right, which he and Cassia could both see. With Lio's blood as her ink and the dagger as her brush, she drew a hexagram on the wall. "The Old Masters reign supreme over life and death, magic and fate. Their power is beyond imagining. When they go to war against each other, civilizations rise and fall. We all live upon the graves of their past games."

She painted an Eye of Hypnos on the wall, then another, and another, until there were six.

Miranda's voice seemed to crawl over Lio's skin. "Akanthia is their game board. To prevent each other from destroying the world, they have established rules to which all six adhere. In each epoch, there are different rules and a new winner."

Lio wanted to dismiss all of this as Miranda's mad ravings. But he had read the hints about the Old Masters in the scrolls. Cassia had beheld the ruins at Btana Ayal.

Lio could imagine it, this twisted contest that had reduced the shadowlands to ruins again and again and left Tenebra a stunted child compared to the thriving Empire.

Lio believed Miranda.

She smeared the remaining blood onto her hand. With a loving caress, she left her handprint on the Eye at the top of the hex. "In every epoch, the Masters choose new followers, and only the strong survive until the next game. I will fight for the Collector in every game, from now until the end of time."

She faced them. "In this time, the rules of the game are that the Masters must not reveal themselves to their playing pieces. It is one of the greatest challenges they have ever devised for themselves. This contest of subtlety and manipulation, of strategy and patience is the Collector's element. This is his epoch to win."

She stood still, lifting her face toward her master's glyph. "You have stayed on the board long enough to earn this privilege: you may know his name."

She scrawled Divine script on the wall in Lio's blood.

"Cassia is such a slow reader," Miranda said. "Lio, read it aloud for her and tell her what it means."

"Kallikrates." The name sent a pall over him, as if he were invoking a dangerous god. "It means 'beautiful power' in the Divine Tongue."

Cassia shot Lio a look. From the mocking tilt of her brow, he could imagine what she wanted to say. *Impressed with himself, isn't he?*

Lio recalled her words after their battle with the Collector at the Summit. *I don't care who he is. He'll get no respect from me. He's just another man with too much magic trying to take what he wants. That is as old as the world, and they're all the same.*

In the middle of Miranda's deadly sermon, Lio almost laughed.

Then his magic cresting under his skin. It finally broke free. The poison had done its work.

His power crashed along the current between him and Cassia. She gasped, her body levitating against the straps. Miranda stood between them, watching with an expression of concentration. Her necromancy coiled around them. Was she *studying* them?

"Hypnos's nails," she cursed. "This is the most unnatural magical interaction I've ever seen. What did you do to her, Lio? I won't be able to displace her magic until I unfasten her from you."

Hespera's Grace. In this hour, as always, that was his and Cassia's hope. Miranda could not understand how their Grace bond interacted with Cassia's magic.

"I will find out," Miranda warned them, "and once I discover how a leech is managing to feed off of a Hesperine, I will use it to discover how I can perform essential displacement on your kind."

An empty threat, Lio hoped. Surely the only reason he and Cassia were able to defy the laws of magic was because they were Graced.

Miranda's lip curled. "You Hesperines have always violated the rules of the game. You shouldn't exist. It is one of my most important duties—making you extinct. I'll enjoy stealing your magic, once I discover how. And I will relish every moment of killing you slowly after I'm done. Just imagine me outliving you, using your mind magic against all the people you left behind."

That didn't frighten Lio. But what did was the thought that Miranda might extract the secret of Grace from them. Hesperines had managed to conceal it from their enemies for sixteen hundred years so the Gift Collectors could not use the Craving against Graced pairs. He and Cassia had to find a way out of this without revealing the nature of their bond.

"Your lesson is over," Miranda announced. "Now it is time for me to get to work."

She spun toward Lio and plunged her dagger into his chest.

THE GRAND DESIGN

Cassia screamed his name. The torrent of his magic stopped all at once and hurled her back against the table. He slumped, dangling from his shackles.

"You need him alive!" Cassia cried. The Lustra roared with her.

"Don't be so dramatic," Miranda said. "It takes more than a dagger to kill a Hesperine. Think of that as a stopper in his magic."

"Lio?" Cassia called. "Lio, can you hear me?"

His eyes came open, and he lifted his head.

"I'm here," she said. It was all she could do for him. Remind him, as he had done for her, that he did not suffer alone.

"I know," he said hoarsely.

Why must Lio endure this? Kind Lio, who had never harmed a soul in his life. Why had Hespera paired him to Cassia and let him be dragged into the Collector's plans for her?

Footfalls told Cassia the Gift Collector was coming to her side again. She kept her eyes on Lio.

Miranda's voice came from the opposite side of the table. "Let's try the most straightforward solution first. I'll put some magic back into you, so you'll no longer need to leech. Perhaps then your aura will release Lio." Miranda chuckled. "I love seeing you try to be brave as I explain what's about to happen to you. But I can smell your fear, Cassia. What affinity shall we use for this experiment? Why don't I give you Pakhne's magic? You'll hate that."

"None of this is your fault, Cassia," Lio said.

His voice was the last thing she heard before Miranda's fist made impact with her chest. Cassia's ears roared, and stars exploded on her vision. She tried to suck air into her hollow chest, but a crushing weight seemed to collapse her lungs. Pain tore into her throat.

But worst of all, she felt consciousness slipping away. No, she had to stay awake, despite the pain…had to protect Lio…

She fell into darkness.

When she came to, she heard Lio saying her name. "I'm here. Come back to me, Cassia."

Cassia coughed. "Are you all right?"

"She hasn't done anything else to me," Lio reassured her. "You were only out for a few minutes. The displacement didn't work."

Cassia opened her eyes in time to see Miranda yank the dagger out of Lio's chest. His face twisted with pain, and a spot of blood bloomed on his robes. His magic slammed into Cassia, numbing her pain and filling the hollowness inside her.

So much power. If only they could turn it against Miranda somehow. But Cassia was helpless in its flow, the straps biting into her skin as her body arched.

Lio grunted in pain, and the channeling ceased. The dagger was back in his chest. Miranda unrolled a scroll on her work table, running a finger down the gore-stained page with her lips pursed.

Could she feel the way the Lustra magic snapped its jaws around her? If so, she gave no sign.

Cassia focused on the wild magic that was rooted deep beneath Paradum. The Lustra reached back, and a whine sounded in her arcane senses. It was trying to help her somehow, but it seemed unable to.

It was nothing like the magic in the passageways at Patria. Here at Paradum, the Lustra seemed to be a wounded animal. She felt like a damaged creature herself, crumpled just out of the Lustra's grasp.

She couldn't understand why her own magic was not coming to her as it should. There was something wrong with her and the letting site.

Was her starvation for magic harming it in return somehow?

Would feeding it Lio's magic help the Lustra as well?

The idea took hold of Cassia, and she felt sure it was their only chance. They had a powerful ally in this room—the Lustra itself. If they enlisted its aid against Miranda, there was hope they could defeat her.

"Lio," Cassia said softly.

He lifted his head slowly, his eyelids heavy. And yet she could see his love for her in his eyes. "Yes, my rose?"

Tears pricked her eyes. He had a Gift Collector's dagger in his chest because of her, and he still called her his rose.

"Do you remember the time you cast a veil spell over the Font of the Changing Queen to hide me from a war mage?"

A smile ghosted across his face. "You didn't stay put inside it. You sneaked away on your own instead. Self-reliant as always."

"If the situation had been reversed, would you have trusted my magic to keep you safe?"

She hoped he would recall how she had referred to this event to send him a subtle message before. That night during the Solstice Summit, he had been about to duel a war mage, and he had needed to know she trusted him. Tonight, they were about to duel a Gift Collector, and he had to trust Cassia.

Lio's gaze sharpened with understanding. "Yes. I trust you unconditionally."

Her throat tightened. "Even after everything you've been through because of me?"

"I would do it all again," he said, "just for that moment when you first trusted me."

Miranda snapped her scroll shut. "This is why you make such interesting opponents. Your partnership is both your greatest strength and your greatest weakness. You are more powerful together—and yet I can use your love against you."

Not if they used it against Miranda first.

Miranda touched the Eye of Hypnos on her breastplate. "But you see, my partner in this is much more powerful than either of you, and my loyalty to him in the game will withstand the test of time, long after even your eternal love is dust."

She returned to Cassia's side. "I met the Master the day the temple mages came to take me away. The ones who found out about my magic because of *you*. The Master was in the area, you see, keeping an eye on you. My spells impressed him." She closed her fingers around Cassia's throat.

"No Hesperines rescued me, Cassia. The Master did. And he has made me far more powerful than you ever would have been, even with fangs."

Cassia looked into Miranda's eyes. The friend she had scorned. The monster her own choices had created.

"You deserved so much better," Cassia said.

"I am better than you now, don't you see? You're just an empty creature that must be filled with someone else's magic to survive. A leech, living on borrowed time from one feeding to the next. A slave to your appetites. I bet you fuck him while you feed on him, don't you? Disgusting. You have no control. Not over yourself or others. Not over your fate. And certainly not over the magic you devour. You are powerless."

Cassia kept her expression of regret frozen on her face. She mustn't let on that Miranda had just revealed something important. She didn't know Cassia had control over the magic she absorbed. Was it a side effect of Grace? Or because her magic belonged to a channeling paradigm? Whatever the reason, it seemed Cassia was not just a leech like the others.

"Look at you," Miranda said, "reduced to this. Just think. If you had made different choices, you could have become me."

The words made Cassia ill, because they were true. "I meant everything I said about how much I regret my past. I am so sorry I hurt you, Miranda."

"Don't be." Miranda's hand tightened on Cassia's throat. "Our battles with pain are how we win our true power. You are nothing but another of the wounds I have survived."

Healing magic jolted into Cassia's throat. Pakhne's magic, once again putting Cassia back together so Miranda could try to tear her apart.

"This experiment will be your next battle with pain," Miranda said. "I'll try displacing Lio's magic through you. You're coming up in the world, leech. Now you'll become a channel. You are familiar with that, are you not? I believe you saw Skleros displace the Dexion's magic through a channel—the son of those farmers."

Cassia suppressed a shiver at the memory of the poor man writhing on the ground. Could Miranda really access Lio's magic through Cassia? They could not afford to risk it and find out. When Miranda took the dagger out again, Cassia must be ready. She would have only one chance to give his magic to the Lustra instead.

Miranda walked over to Lio once more. Her fingers closed around the dagger.

Cassia held Lio's gaze, mustering confidence she didn't feel, so he might find hope in her eyes. He gave her the slightest nod.

The dagger tore from Lio's chest, and his magic tore through the channeling. Cassia was ready for it this time. She breathed, bringing herself into the rhythm of the current buffeting her.

Miranda walked toward her.

Cassia guided the current of Lio's magic down through her body, down into the stones beneath them, down to the hungry maw of the Lustra.

That untamed presence threw off Lio's magic so hard that Cassia's neck snapped back.

Goddess help her. It hadn't worked.

Miranda's hand curled into a fist on the front of Cassia's robes.

It hadn't worked yet. Cassia would not give up so easily.

Miranda pulled.

Lio's magic shuddered under Cassia's ribcage. She bared her teeth at Miranda. No Gift Collector would take her Grace from her.

Miranda's fist tightened. "If you fight me, this will only hurt you more."

Holding fast to Lio's magic, Cassia focused all her Will on the Lustra. It was too ancient a presence to understand words, but Will was the oldest and most universal language.

He is my Grace, she told it. *My mate. He is bound to me. He is part of you.*

She let Lio's magic wash over the keening wilds. They quieted.

Miranda's eyes widened. "What do you think you're doing?"

Her next pull made Cassia's teeth ache and her bones grind. But Lio's magic receded deeper below them.

"How dare you," Miranda spat. "That's impossible!"

His magic is a gift to us, she called to the Lustra. *He keeps us free and makes us strong. Take his power.*

The letting site bloomed open and wrapped around Cassia like an embrace. She could hear Lio's thelemancy in the Lustra's call, feel his light in its teeth and claws. His blood magic poured deep into its roots.

The shutters snapped open, and thorned vines crawled inside the windows. They raced over the sill, and the stones crumbled beneath their strength, until the wall collapsed.

Beyond lay the ruins of Cassia's garden. Amid the weeds and nettles that choked the once-tidy rows, Hespera's thorns tore from the soil.

"No!" Miranda screamed. She closed both hands around Cassia's throat, and her necromancy scored Cassia's chest as if it sought to carve out her heart.

Then pale hands closed around Miranda's, prying her off of Cassia. The Gift Collector was hurled across the room. She crashed into her worktable and staggered.

Lio stood over Cassia, his fangs fully extended and his wrists covered in blood. She glanced from him to the wall where he had been chained. His manacles lay broken and twisted, their fragments and Miranda's dagger in the grasp of the vines.

Lio leaned heavily on the table with one hand and rifled through her gardening satchel. He yanked out her spade. With its sharp edge, he sawed at the leather strap around her wrist. She could feel the necromancy in her bonds, but with a flare of blood and Lustra magic, her spade began to split the leather.

Behind Lio, Miranda found her feet. Before Cassia could call out a warning, a vine of thorns twisted around Miranda's ankle and dragged her to the ground.

Lio gave the spade a heave, slicing through the cuff. The bloodstain on his robes widened.

"Drink." Cassia held up her wrist.

He bent over her and bit into her vein. His body jerked, and he made a sound of surprise in his throat.

"What's wrong?" she rasped.

But even as she said it, she realized nothing was wrong. She felt the channeling crack open inside her and let out a cry. The wildness of the letting site raced through her veins and into his mouth.

His magic was not only flowing into the Lustra. The Lustra's power was flowing into him, through her blood.

Behind Lio, Miranda strained against the vines, reaching toward a cleaver that had fallen from her worktable.

"She's going to break free," Cassia cried.

With a gasp, Lio sealed her vein and rose, his mouth stained with her blood. She took the spade from him and began cutting through the strap across her chest. "I can do this. Focus on Miranda."

"I have to break her dream wards."

"The Lustra will protect you while you cast."

Miranda's hand closed around the cleaver. She hacked at the vines, and they shriveled, falling dead around her, blighted with necromancy.

Every glass beaker shattered as Lio turned to face the Gift Collector.

Cassia's cleansing blood pounded through Lio's veins, driving away the lethargy of the poison. The magic of the letting site throbbed through him. He had never felt so powerful.

With another blast of levitation, Lio sent Miranda flying across the room. Her cleaver clattered out of reach. She hit the wall where she had imprisoned him, and the Lustra's vines coiled around her, pinning her in place. Lio advanced on her.

Miranda lifted her chin. "Do your worst. I'm trained to withstand tortures that would make your Hesperine sensibilities writhe. You cannot hurt me."

"I don't want to hurt you, Miranda. But I promise you, I will find a way to deal your Master pain as no one ever has in his epochs of existence."

Lio gripped her temples and struck her mind with his full power.

The poison in her thoughts wafted away, and he barely felt the prick of her mental daggers. Layer upon layer of dreams wards crumpled under his thelemancy, empowered by the Lustra.

At last he saw fear in her eyes. She whimpered in his hold like a frightened child. The girl she had once been.

Cassia could have become this. But Miranda could also have become Cassia.

Lio cradled her head in his hands and gently unfolded the deepest reaches of her mind.

What he saw made him want to retreat. It was all laid out in her thoughts in neat, complex patterns, like a game board with each move planned and labeled. The Master's design in this time.

"Do you see it?" she whispered. "Isn't it beautiful?"

He beheld a vision of Tenebra in flames. War mages hurled fire at Hesperines errant, whose shadow wards shattered before the onslaught. The blood of his people soaked the soil before their bodies disappeared in flashes of light.

"It's one of the requirements." Miranda smiled. "The Orders and the Hesperines must fight a war on Tenebran soil."

"That will never happen again," Lio said. "The Last War is over."

"But the next one has already begun. You started it for us."

"We have always striven for peace!"

"Your negotiations ended in a siege, didn't they? Why do you think Lucis waited until that precise moment to attack? We could have crushed your little council anytime we wished, but the Master wanted Solia to win."

"No." It couldn't be. Everything they had worked for…it could not have been part of the Master's plot all along. Could it?

"Solia is a gift to our game," Miranda said. "We have tried to lure your kind to war for so long, to no avail. But now, at last, Tenebra has a queen the Hesperines will fight for."

Hespera help them. Miranda was right.

Her logic carried him deeper into the plot, and he saw the second prerequisite. Thalia waited in a bedchamber in Solorum Palace, while Lucis entered and shut the door behind him. Lio shied away from the vision.

"The Master bred Thalia and Lucis to produce Cassia," Miranda said, "a Silvicultrix of the reigning line."

The third requirement flashed before Lio. Cassia strapped to the table, with the Gift Collector dragging her three magics out of her. Cassia's screams echoed in Lio's head.

"Why?" Lio demanded. "What will he gain from toying with all our lives?"

"Oh, that's the important secret. I can't tell you that. No—no please, the Master will never forgive me if you find out—please, Lio…"

Lio drove deeper into Miranda's mind, knowing her begging would haunt him.

Her thoughts took him through the Lustra passages inside Solorum Palace. A great stone door waited there, sealed tight. He aimed a blast of thelemancy at the final defenses in Miranda's mind.

The pleading faded from her gaze. Her begging ceased. From her lips emerged the deep, masculine voice of the Collector. "If you want that secret, you will have to duel me for it."

Lio heard a snap behind him. He glanced over his shoulder to see that Cassia was free. But the moment her feet touched the floor, she crumpled. Her spade slipped from her hand and hit the stone floor of her sickroom, and her precious artifact shattered into pieces.

The Lustra keened, and Lio knew its Will.

It couldn't save Cassia. He didn't understand why, but he understood what he must do.

Lio looked into the Collector's eyes. "Keep your secrets. I'm taking your queen."

He struck Miranda's mind once more, sending her deep into unconsciousness. As he turned away from her, her crow flew over to perch on her shoulder again, nibbling fretfully at her hair.

Lio lifted Cassia in his arms. The channeling realigned, and he swayed on his feet as the Lustra gave them back his magic, pouring all of it into his fading Grace.

He tried to step. But the letting site held him as surely as the passageways did. He had to get out of Paradum to step her to safety.

He levitated through the broken wall and over the thorns. Seeing who awaited him above the garden, he froze midair.

Skleros stood atop a crumbling wall, a crossbow resting in the crook of his arm. His scarred face pulled into a smile. "Did you think the Master would let you escape with his queen so easily?"

At the edges of Lio's vision, a swish of a cloak and a gleam of moonlight on a spur told him other Gift Collectors were traversing in.

Lio reached for the Lustra's power, but the connection was gone. It had fastened all his magic onto Cassia again to keep her alive.

By the time his power broke the dream wards of this many Gift Collectors, Cassia would be out of time.

Skleros was still smiling when a blade swept through the air and sent his severed head tumbling into the courtyard below. His crossbow and his body fell after him into the thorns.

Rudhira stood on the wall with Thorn in hand, his adamas sword gleaming red with the Gift Collector's blood. The sounds of battle erupted all around Lio as more Chargers appeared, descending on the Gift Collectors.

Lio stared at his Ritual father. "I thought you were at the Firstblood Circle."

"I was. Orthros voted against the Departure. Our people have not abandoned Tenebra—or my Charge." Rudhira levitated down to hover before Lio, and the prince's healing magic surged into Cassia.

"It can't be too late," Lio said. "Tell me I can save her."

"Yes." Rudhira tucked Cassia's limp hand closer against Lio's chest. "The Gift can still save her, if you hurry. She is beyond my power, but not Hespera's."

Another necromancer's body crashed through the garden gate, and Mak and Lyros levitated over him to Lio's side.

"Thank the Goddess," Lio said. "How did you all get here?"

Kalos appeared out of the shadows with blood on his knuckles. "I told you no one could hide a castle from me."

"The rest of the Charge is at Patria," Lyros said quickly. "With their wards, the fortress is holding out against Lucis."

"Get Lio and Cassia out of here," Rudhira ordered. "Leave this nest of death to me."

"We'll get you home safely," Mak promised.

"I'll lead you out. Come with me." Kalos beckoned.

Lio followed the scout with Mak and Lyros's wards surrounding them. Kalos raced through the garden gate and through the kitchens, where Agata was taking another batch of tarts out of her oven, singing a Tenebran lullaby.

They emerged among the skeletal trees of what had once been the apple orchard, where three more Gift Collectors waited. Their crossbow bolts ricocheted off of Mak and Lyros's wards. More near-immortal enemies, standing between them and safety, slowing them down while Cassia's life slipped away.

Mak and Lyros darted forward, but before they reached the necromancers, the Gift Collectors went up in flames. They staggered to the side to reveal Solia standing between the trees, her elegant skirts smeared with blood and ash, her sword in hand. Knight was at her side, snarling like the Lustra beneath their feet.

Over the Gift Collectors' screams, Solia called, "Leave them to burn."

Lio heaved a sigh of relief and raced toward her.

With her magefire and Knight's snapping jaws, his Trial brothers' wards and Kalos's guidance, they fought their way through Castra Paradum. They left maimed Gift Collectors behind and dodged the undead archers on the walls. Miranda's bloodless servants cowered in corners, and the undead horses in the stables whinnied in fear.

At a postern in the outer bailey, Solia blasted through the door with another fireball. Mak and Lyros tore the warped iron and wood away to clear the exit. They followed Lio through, and Solia collapsed the door behind them.

Beyond the castle walls, the fields were strangely peaceful. Solia brushed Cassia's hair back from her forehead with a sooty hand.

"Your Majesty," Lio said, "you left your siege for your sister."

"I was her sister first. What happened here, Lio?"

"The letting site is broken," Kalos said. "I've never felt anything like it. Something evil happened here."

"Can we take her to another one?" Solia demanded, as if she longed to shake her fist at the gods or burn a hole in the laws of the world.

"She doesn't have time for us to find it. She's..." Lio didn't want to say the word, but they deserved to know. "She's dying. I failed her."

"No, Lio." Mak put a bracing hand on his shoulder. "You're the one who can save her."

"Get her home," Lyros said.

"She won't have her magic." Lio's voice broke.

Solia touched his face. "She'll have her fangs. This is your fifth labor, Lio. Give my sister the Gift. It's what she would want. And for what it's worth, you have my blessing."

"That is worth more than you know, Grace-Sister."

"Tell her I never wanted to send her away. But you two are so selfless,

I knew you wouldn't go to the letting site if I asked. I had to drive you off. Tell her I want her at my side always. . . forever."

That word *forever* hung in the air between them, daring him to hope. "I'll make sure she knows."

Solia let them go. "We will stay and fight."

"Stay safe," Lio said, his throat tight. "She'll want to show you her new fangs."

But he knew the greatest challenge was still before them. Her transformation. Lio cradled Cassia against his chest and stepped them away from Tenebra.

GIFT NIGHTS

33 Eidon, 1597 IS

PARTAKING

THE RITUAL CIRCLE OF House Komnena pulled Lio home. When he felt the power of their bloodline under his feet again, he slid to his knees. Blood still dripped from some injury on him, making a libation on the marble mosaic of Hespera's rose.

Goddess, let Cassia survive.

Coffee cups slammed onto the table, and his family sprang from their seats to crowd around. Their familiar voices washed over him, their fury and empathy filling the Union until it shook.

"Get Annassa Soteira," he pleaded.

His mother stepped away. His father pressed his wrist to his mouth. Lio drank deeply, feeling his chest knit together and more of the poison fade from his blood. His magic revived and flowed into the channeling, and Cassia's heartbeat grew louder. He would need all his bloodline's strength for her tonight.

Uncle Argyros's magic touched Lio's mind, the gentle probe of a thelemancer checking for damage. He could surely sense the ghosts of tonight's duels.

"Where is the battle?" Aunt Lyta demanded.

Patria. Paradum. None of that was Lio's focus now. "Inside of Cassia. The letting site didn't awaken her magic. The Lustra asked me to save her."

Queen Soteira's presence filled House Komnena up to its vaulted ceilings. As she touched Cassia's head, the warmth of her healing enveloped her and Lio both. "So it has come to this."

"Is she strong enough for her Gifting?" Lio asked.

"I will make her as strong as I can. You and Hespera must do the rest. Drink from your mother."

Lio accepted his mother's wrist. She stroked Cassia's anxious dog with her free hand, her voice calm as always in a crisis. "The sucklings are with Kadi and Javed at House Argyros tonight. I'll take Knight to them."

"Thank you," Lio said, when he had completed the Ritual Drink.

"Your crates are in your residence," she said. "There are sheets on the bed, and the spell lights are on."

Goddess bless his mother for thinking of such things at a time like this.

His father clasped his wrist. "You know what to do, Lio. Everything Cassia needs is within you. Go and do what Hespera has meant for you two all along."

His uncle embraced him, touching a hand to Cassia's medallion. "Send up a spell light when she comes through safely, hm?"

"We will pray through the night," Aunt Lyta promised.

"May the Goddess's Eyes light your path," said Queen Soteira, "and may her darkness keep you in Sanctuary."

With that benediction from one of their Queens, he stepped Cassia to their residence. The Sanctuary ward over their bedchamber closed around him. That, at last, convinced him they had escaped.

Their Sanctuary was still here. The four stained glass panels in the peaked windows filled the room with color. Beyond the empty window frames, the waxing crescents of the two moons shone their portents over Cassia's Gift Night.

"Stay with me, Cassia," he said. "You have to stay to see the moonflower window I want to make you next."

Moving quickly, he lay her down on their big, round bed. The roses growing up the bed posts shivered and turned their faces toward Cassia, as if sensing that their Lustra mage was in distress. So did the moonflower that had bloomed early, which someone had set on the beside table.

"Stay with me. I want to see your face when you wake and look at these flowers." Lio pricked his hand and clutched at the glyph stone set in the wrought iron headboard. The Sanctuary ward pulsed with renewed power. They would need it.

He had no idea what her magic, or lack of it, was about to do when he gave her his blood.

"Don't be afraid." He peeled her out of her ruined clothes. "I'll give you a cleaning spell to calm your nerves. I know you need to feel clean when you're frightened."

He banished the odor of death from them both. He would not let any foul remnants of Miranda pollute their Sanctuary—or risk getting poison residue into Cassia's bloodstream as he transformed her.

Remembering his warded earring, he flicked it off, then tossed his tattered robes onto the floor. With levitation, he threw back the crimson bedspread and settled them on the black silk sheets. Such foolish, romantic luxuries he had chosen for this room, when he had thought they would spend her Gift Night in peace.

"I won't let the Collector take that from us. I swear to you, I will make this the best night of our lives."

Even if it was her last.

No, he could not allow any doubts within himself. She needed his faith.

At last he pulled off their ambassador medallions and her ivy pendant. There was no artifact that could guide them through this. All the magic must come from within themselves.

Lio ran through each stage of the Gifting in his mind, reciting them in a logical order. *One step at a time. Take one challenge at a time, and give it everything you have.*

First, he had to rouse her enough to swallow his blood. Leaning against the headboard, he pulled Cassia onto his lap, resting her face against his shoulder. He reached for her mind. She felt more distant than she had just moments ago.

"Stay with me, Cassia!" He sent his magic deep into the mind ward and jolted her consciousness.

Still she lay limp in his arms.

"No," he said, "it is not too late."

Lio slashed his wrist with his fangs and pressed his bleeding veins to Cassia's mouth. With his free hand, he massaged her throat. "Drink, my Grace. This is what you've always wanted. I can finally give it to you. Drink for me."

He felt her swallow under his touch. *Oh Goddess, thank you.*

Cassia's Gifting had begun.

She closed her hands over his wrist. Holding him to her, she dug her dull mortal canines into the wounds he had made.

"That's the best thing I've ever felt in my life, Cassia."

She mewed in her throat and sucked. He looked into her beautiful hazel eyes as she drank from him for the first time.

The world seemed to stop. His entire being focused on the sensation of his blood flowing out of his wrist and into her mouth. He felt the pull on his veins, an exquisite ache. The texture of her tongue on his skin. The pleasure-pain of her blunt teeth fighting his healing power to keep his flesh open for her.

"Oh my Goddess," he breathed.

Cassia curled closer, her nostrils flaring, and moaned.

"Do I taste so good, my Grace?"

She sucked harder and rubbed her hip against his groin. With his free hand, he reached around to hold her still. "Not yet, my rose. The time for that is later, and it will be…" His breath hitched in his throat. "…everything you dreamed. I promise."

But she must survive this first.

He watched her Partaking, giving herself over to the innocent instinct to take her Grace's blood. He wished this pure moment could last forever. But his blood would hurt her before it healed her.

Her visions were about to begin.

DIVINING

EVERYTHING CEASED TO MATTER except his blood.

She must get the next swallow into her. And the next.

He tasted like home. Deep, cold snows and warm, tender laughter. Like happiness. Ink, moonflowers, starry skies. Like lust and love and rage so powerful he could tear open the substance of creation to protect her.

She tasted their whole lives in his blood, every moment that had healed her and every century that lay ahead.

She bit down harder, clinging to the lives they could still have.

"Yes," she heard him say, "fight with me."

He held her hip, but she shifted in his grip, unable to lie still. Every swallow sent hot, liquid desire pooling between her legs. She had never imagined. Nothing else would ever taste this good. She forgot the flavor of food and wine. She curled her toes, her krana tensing on the verge of release from his flavor alone.

He looked down at her, his gaze riveted on her face. "Oh, Cassia. That is…incredibly flattering. Thank you."

She dragged in another swallow, and the taste of him sent a decadent climax rolling through her.

"You're always beautiful when you climax," he said, "but the sight of you with my blood running down your chin…"

Her body calmed, and a sweet languor came over her. The warmth in her belly began to spread. It was a strange sensation, a tingle traveling down her limbs to her fingertips. She shivered.

He held her closer. "It's all right, my Grace. This is exactly what's supposed to happen. Blood magic will spread throughout your body so it can change you. Your starved aura will be very glad to have it."

The warmth blossomed into heat that raced through her veins. Something vast and far more powerful than her was taking control of her. Fear flashed through her.

"I know it's always difficult for you to relinquish control," Lio said, "but I'm here to guide you through. Surrender to the Gift, Cassia Komnena."

She knew this power. The magic overtaking her was so familiar. It had kept her safe and given her hope on all the worst nights of her life. Hesperine power. Blood magic.

And now it was inside her.

Lio's blood and Hespera's magic were inside her body. There was no turning back now.

When the magic reached her eyes, her vision blurred. Lio's face above her began to fade.

"I'm here." His voice was so sure and steady. "Your Divining is starting. I will experience the visions with you in Grace Union, and my thelemancy will enable me to help you even more. We'll do this together."

The fear sank in and did not let her go. Her past was coming for her, and she must face it.

Please, Hespera. Forgive me. Redeem me.

That prayer was her last coherent thought before her memories rose up to drown her.

CASSIA STOOD UP, HER spade in hand, and surveyed the rows of pea seedlings. The sun shone on their little green leaves and warmed her aching muscles. Knight lay stretched on his side, sunning himself at the edge of the garden.

She was proud of this, she realized. People all over Paradum would eat her peas. And they would know she had grown them. For the first time in her life, she had...created something. Something that mattered to others.

She wasn't sure what this feeling was, tiny and new, poking up out of her like the little plants out of the soil.

"You were happy." Lio stood beside her in his veil hours robe, his bare toes digging into her soil. He held up a hand to shade his eyes. He looked so handsome in the sunlight.

"I'm glad you're here," she said. "You should get to see my good memories, too."

Cassia knelt down again, measuring a pea seedling with her hand. She would grow the people of Paradum the best vegetables they had ever tasted. She was determined. That sense of purpose filled her.

It seemed to build into a force of its own and flow out of her. Something else she couldn't see swelled up from the ground to meet her. The world shifted, and she dug her spade into the ground to steady herself, clinging to the handle.

An exhilaration she had never known coursed through her. Before her eyes, the pea seedlings began to grow. She watched in frozen wonder as her vegetables sprang up to her shoulders.

She was still staring at them in astonishment when motion in the kitchen doorway caught her eye. Miranda was standing there, a knife in her hand and a slice of apple halfway to her mouth.

The strength rushed out of Cassia suddenly. Lio caught her as she tumbled over onto her side.

He rested her head on his lap. "Cassia, what just happened? Did you use magic at Paradum when you were fourteen?"

"I don't know. I don't remember."

"The Gifting is restoring your missing memories. Your visions will reveal to us what really happened."

Miranda rushed to Cassia's side and helped her up. She put Cassia's arm around her shoulders and guided her to the kitchen door. "Don't worry. We'll tell Agata. She'll know what to do."

The memory blurred. Cassia found herself sitting at the kitchen table with Lio and Miranda on either side of her.

Agata was across from them, her eyes shining. "Kyria bless, my girl. Do you know what this means?"

"I...I have magic." If Cassia kept saying it aloud, perhaps she would believe it.

Agata smiled. "Garden magic, to be sure."

Cassia clutched her spade on her lap. "Does this mean I must go into a temple?"

"Is that what you want?" Agata asked.

No one had ever asked Cassia what she wanted, not since Solia had died. Cassia made a point not to think too hard about what she wanted. It only led to disappointment.

Miranda scratched Knight's ears, his head resting on the bench between her and Cassia. "That's not what I would want. Being trapped in veils and walls? All those rules and praying on a schedule? That's even worse than here."

"Are there any temples nearby?" Cassia asked. "Could I still visit Paradum?"

"Of course, my dear," said Agata. "I'm good friends with the mages at the Patrian temple. As soon as I tell them about you, they'll want to snatch you up before another temple can. If you take the veil there, we would see each other often."

That new feeling began to shake up inside of Cassia, more powerful than ever.

"Would they let me in, even though I'm a bastard?" she asked.

Agata patted her hand. "That won't matter, sweetling. They'll let you in because of your magic. And respect you for it, I dare say. You'll learn all about how it works, and you'll get to work in their gardens every day."

Miranda touched her arm. "If that's what you want, Cassia, you should do it."

"It's the only way I won't get sent away from Paradum. We wouldn't have to say goodbye…as long as my father will allow it."

Agata's expression became more serious. "It's the law. If he wants to keep in the good graces of the Orders, he'll have no choice but to dedicate you to the temple. You will belong to the mages of Kyria, not him."

A future Cassia had never imagined opened before her.

Freedom.

She *wanted* it. She ached for it. And she would not let him take it from her.

"I'm a mage," she breathed. "I'm going to enter the temple."

The king would never be able to hurt her again.

Lio of the present held out his hand to Cassia of the past. "I wish you could have had that."

She clutched his fingers. "What if I had? What if I'd been in a temple instead of at the Equinox Summit, and I had never met you?"

"You would have, I'm sure of it. Hespera would have found a way. I wish you could have had an easier path to me." Pain filled his eyes. "Do you realize what this means?"

The happiness of the memory began to fade, replaced by her dread of what must come next.

"That...that was my plant magic," she said. "The letting site gave it to me. Eight years ago."

Shouting from outside the kitchen pulled Cassia back onto the path of memory. She and Miranda leapt up to look out the door to the orchard. But Miranda hung back where she couldn't be seen.

The lord of the castle was disrupting the peace under the apple trees, brandishing his hunting bow. His ale-belly heaved over the edge of his belt as he cursed. "Filthy scavengers, always stealing what's mine!"

"Come back inside," Agata murmured. "When he's in his cups, he doesn't care where his arrows land."

Miranda's father took aim at a small black form sitting on a branch. Cassia recognized the bird Miranda had been feeding at her window.

"No!" Miranda raced outside. "That's my crow."

Cassia hurried after her with Knight barking a warning. But her present mind could have told her past self it was too late.

The crow fell to the ground, an arrow through its breast. Miranda went down on her knees beside it, her hands hovering over it helplessly. She lifted her tear-streaked face to her father.

Cassia could feel the scream of rage about to come out of Miranda. It was the same scream Cassia held in every time she looked at the king.

But the empathy Cassia had felt that day in the past now waxed under her breastbone. Her heart thundered in her chest, and her blood seemed to carry Miranda's grief through her every vein. Her friend's rage became a part of her flesh and bones.

In her present voice, Cassia screamed at the memory of Miranda's father, although he could not hear.

"How could you? That bird is the one thing that comforts her after the cruelties you deal her every day. And you don't even comprehend. You'll forget this happened when you're sober tomorrow. How can you so carelessly destroy your own child?"

Lio enfolded her in his arms. His voice echoed in her mind and blood. "Your Blood Union has awoken."

The unbearable pain flowed into him, and with both of them holding it, she felt she would not break. But still she wept. "I can't stop what's going to happen. I can't help her."

"You tried to help her that day, didn't you? Show me what you did."

Cassia hurried to her friend's side, fearing what would happen if Miranda lashed out at her father. All she could envision was the next arrow going through her friend's heart.

She knelt beside Miranda and pulled her friend's head against her shoulder to stifle her outburst. "It's not worth it," she whispered in Miranda's ear. "Don't give him the satisfaction. I won't let him hurt you."

Miranda clung to her, shaking with quiet sobs.

"Stupid bitch," her father said. "Crying over vermin. Why didn't the gods give me a son?"

His emotions struck Cassia in the Union like foul breath. Derision. Bitterness. Lust for his next mug of ale. He stalked away and left them alone.

Dusk had fallen by the time Miranda's tears were spent. In the fading light, she carefully snapped the arrow and removed it from the crow's body.

When she gathered the broken creature on her lap, there came a flash like what Cassia had felt in her garden, a dark mirror of the power she had poured into the soil. The force swept out of Miranda, leaving her gasping.

The crow spread its wings and took flight. Its happy chatter filled the orchard as it circled their heads, then returned to perch on Miranda's lap again.

With shaking hands, she touched its breast. "Its heart isn't beating. Cassia, what have I done?"

Just like Miranda had for her in the garden, Cassia kept her tone calm and without judgment, putting an arm around her friend for support. "I believe you are a mage, as well. There's only one kind of magic I know of that can bring a creature back like this."

"Necromancy." Miranda held the bird against her chest, rubbing her face in its feathers. Her emotions washed over Cassia in powerful waves, awe and fear and horror and joy.

"You can't tell anyone!" she begged. "Not even Agata. I don't want the mages to punish her for keeping a secret like this… Cassia, I can't be sent to a temple. I'm my parents' only child. What will my people do if I can't inherit Paradum?"

Cassia knew what would happen. Her own father would install a new lord as wretched as Miranda's father. Like Tenebra without Solia, Paradum would lose any hope of a better future.

"I will keep your secret," Cassia said. "I swear it. Temple life is for me, but not for you. We'll do everything in our power to make sure no one ever learns of this."

The promises tasted like ash in Cassia's mouth, for she already knew she would break them.

"How could I do this to her?" she whispered to Lio.

"I know this next part will be most difficult of all," he said, "but I'm here."

RECKONING

Now Miranda stood in the shelter of the garden wall. "I'll go to my grandmother's."

"Is she kinder than your parents?" Cassia wiped her spade clean on a rag.

Miranda snorted. "Hardly. She's the woman who made my mother. But she'll be all too eager for me to stay with her for a few weeks so she can treat me like a servant."

"I'm sorry."

"Don't be. It's a small price to pay to ensure I won't be here when the mages come to test you for your magic."

"When do you leave?" Cassia asked.

"In four days, to make sure I'm gone before the Kyrians get here."

"By the time you get back, I'll be in the temple. But the moment you return, I'll come visit."

Miranda embraced her. "I'm so happy this goodbye will only be temporary."

Miranda's mother called to her, the lady's shrill voice carrying through the bright afternoon. Miranda rolled her eyes. "I'd best go see what that witch wants, before she sends father to look for me."

Cassia let her go, but before she could return to her gardening, Agata rushed out of the kitchen. "A royal messenger just arrived. I overheard everything when I took Miranda's father his midday meal. Someone sent word to the king about your magic, and the king sent back that the Kyrians are not to take you."

"Who told him?" Lio broke in.

"I had no idea then," Cassia said, "but now I suspect it was the Collector, wherever he was hiding at Paradum. He told the king my magic was coming in so they could make their move."

Her gut clenched as her past self protested to Agata. "But it's the law. He must let me go."

Agata's indignation felt like the hum of angry bees in the Union. "He's demanding we keep your magic a secret. He'll be here the day after tomorrow."

"The king is coming for me?" Cassia's hand tightened in Knight's ruff, her heart racing. The king had not shown this much interest in her in years. What was he planning to do to her? "I can't let him take me away from here. I can't go back to him. Oh, Agata, please—there must be something we can do—"

Agata radiated hope and confidence. Her intent was so pure, and for an instant, past and present Cassia both took comfort in it. "There, there, my girl. It's hardly treason if some mages visiting the kitchens accidentally sense some magic in your aura. I'll send two of the maids over to the temple. The Kyrians can come back with them tomorrow, instead of next week. By the time the king gets here, the Prisma will have evidence of your magic."

A new horror came over Cassia. "You said the Prisma is so powerful that she can detect the tiniest whiff of any affinity, anywhere in the castle."

"Oh, yes, her tests will be definitive. The king will not be able to deny that you belong in a temple."

Miranda would never have time to escape by then.

Cassia's voice came out small. "Agata, I…I can't take the tests tomorrow."

Agata frowned. "Now is not the time for a case of nerves about your magic test, my dear. This is your chance. Your *only* chance to escape the king. If he gets here before the mages do, I'm afraid of what he'll do. And it will be too late for a common spinster from the kitchens to protect you."

"The mages mustn't come."

"Do not let your fear of the king stop you. You must go through with this, Cassia. I will not stand by and watch you give up your entire life."

Cassia looked into her future as she had seen it in that moment.

Endless years in silent rooms, punctuated by audiences with the king that made her shake with fear. Unless he sent her on a short journey to meet her sister.

She had not known there would be Hesperines in her future.

Her fourteen-year-old heart hardened into certainty. It was her or Miranda.

Cassia opened her mouth to speak. She fought the motion, trying to change the words she had said. But her tongue obeyed her past choices.

"I will take the tests," she said, sealing their fates. "Bring the mages."

Her memories dissolved in a haze. Then they were in the main hall of Castra Paradum. Among the mages of Kyria, there now stood a mage of Chera. She held up a cage. Inside, Miranda's row screamed, rattling the door.

"Her magic is great—and very dangerous." The Cheran mage's voice drifted from within the linen that wrapped her from head to toe. "She must don the shroud and remain within the confines of the temple until she learns to control her power over life and death. Once it is certain she will not harm anyone, we can allow her out to assist with embalming and burials."

Across the room from Cassia, Miranda struggled against the grasp of her father's guards.

"Be still, girl," her father hissed. "Don't cause me even more trouble, not now."

Miranda lifted her face. Her emotions struck Cassia like a blow to the chest on that table in the sickroom. No revenge of Miranda's could hurt more than this—to experience this moment in Union with her.

Together, they felt Miranda's future closing around her. She couldn't breathe. She stared down into her own grave, but long before she reached it, she knew her spirit would die.

An open wound gaped inside her where her first and only friend had been stripped away.

Her gaze condemned Cassia. "How could you do this to me?"

"I'm so sorry," Cassia whispered.

"I don't want your apologies. I want my life." Miranda raised her voice. "Kallikrates! I accept your bargain!"

The magic that descended upon the room made Cassia stagger and fall to her knees. The others around her went still. Every person in the room opened their mouths and spoke with the same man's voice. "Miranda. Welcome to my game board. We will accomplish great things together, you and I."

The mage of Chera flicked open the cage and set the crow free. It flew to Miranda, and she held it against her chest. The mage walked forward, extending a shrouded hand to stroke Miranda's face.

"Now I will make you mine," the Collector said.

As Miranda fell, the Collector caught her against him. He held his hand above her mouth and made a beckoning motion. Her head fell back, and her lips parted.

A long sigh escaped her, and with it, her magic. The Collector held her to his breast as a shudder went through her. The crow struggled in her embrace, even as her power fluttered against the Collector's grasp. But he drew it into himself on an inexorable current. That pull seemed to scream through the entire room, and Cassia's vision began to darken.

But she saw Miranda lift her head. She looked at Cassia with a gaze not her own. The Collector's voice came from Miranda's mouth. "It is a pleasure to meet you, Cassia."

Cassia could no longer feel Miranda's emotions in the Blood Union.

Although everything within her recoiled, she pushed her senses open, tapping into the new and powerful awareness flowing through her with Lio's blood. She reached for Miranda.

"Don't look," Lio warned her. "I've seen inside him. It's not—"

But Cassia looked. Miranda was a void. All Cassia could sense within her friend was him. Kallikrates felt like the moment of death, everlasting.

Lio caught her as she slipped into unconsciousness. His helpless rage roared through their Blood Union. He could not stop what was to come.

WHEN CASSIA SURFACED, SHE was lying in her bed at Paradum. Knight was nowhere to be found. But Lio was holding her hand.

"I thought I had escaped this place," she said.

"You have," Lio replied. "This is only a memory. You're safe in our residence with me."

She tightened her hold on his hand. "I think I know what's about to happen. What he did to me."

When Lio didn't answer, she looked at him.

Tears slid down his cheeks. "I don't want you to have to go through this."

Miranda approached the bed, the stone dagger in her hand. She now wore a necromancer's robe, her hair long and unbound. She looked so young and vulnerable.

Until the Collector spoke through her. "You now face the most important decision of your existence, Cassia. You see, I am the reason you exist, and one day, I will be the reason you die. Unless you choose to change your fate tonight."

Betraying no fear, Cassia put on the stony expression she always showed the king. She asked the question that might give her leverage. "What do you want?"

"You," he said simply. "You are already mine. I hold you in the palm of my hand. I am called the Collector for a reason. But you have great potential. You could be more to me than a tool in my collection, if you wish."

"I'm listening."

"Your father is not the most powerful being in your world, Cassia. I am. And I can make you more powerful than the king, as well."

Cassia resisted the urge to wet her dry lips. "What are you?"

"Your people would call me a necromancer," he answered, "but my colleagues and I are more than that. We have existed since before any of the kings or mages who believe they rule this world. I am one of the six Old Masters, known as the Master of Dreams. I can destroy your dreams—or make them come true."

"I only want to disappear into the Temple of Kyria and stay out of the king's way. What do you want in exchange for making him forget about me?"

"That is the trouble, my dear. He has let you believe you are useless and unwanted, when in fact, you are required. We made you to our specifications. What I want from you is your magic."

Before she could stop herself, she shrank back. "No."

"I can understand your attachment to it. But a quiet life in the temple is a small dream. Give your magic to me, and I will give you other magics. So much power that you can accomplish any dream."

"Will I become like Miranda?"

The Collector smoothed Miranda's hands down her robe. "She is a magnificent piece, isn't she? Just think what you and your dearest friend could achieve together. She will forgive you if you join our cause. I can make you sisters for eternity."

"What would we be expected to do for you?" Cassia asked.

"What you excel at already. Subtlety. Manipulation. You can be my voice, wielding influence with carefully chosen words. My hand, adjusting outcomes. Of course, there may be times when I call upon you to act more directly. I will let you kill the king once we are done with him."

"You want me to assassinate my father?"

"Eventually. But your destiny will not end there. You can have any life you wish after he is gone."

Even as Cassia's present mind shied away from the memory, repulsed, the lure she had felt in her past pulled her back.

Not garden magic and a peaceful escape into the temple. Powerful, deadly magic. Revenge.

She could make her father pay for what he had done to Solia.

The Collector's smile spread across Miranda's face. "I knew we would understand one another."

Cassia had thought betraying Miranda would be her Reckoning, when Hespera would deem her worthy of immortality—or unworthy to survive her Gifting. How wrong she had been.

This was her most unforgivable act. She looked into the Collector's eyes and imagined the future he could give her. And she was tempted.

"I'm so ashamed," she whispered.

Lio kept holding her hand. "I'm here."

He neither excused nor condemned her. Just as he had promised, he saw her as she was, and he remained. And she realized that this was the real reason why the Gifting was an act of love.

She turned her face away from the Collector and looked into Lio's eyes. "Surely I refused him! It can't be...I have not been his Overseer all this time. Have I?"

Cassia waited for her Gifting to reveal what her answer had been and issue its verdict on her heart.

THE END

"TAKE SOME TIME TO consider," the Collector said, "while Miranda and I prepare. But don't keep us waiting too long."

Miranda opened the wardrobe and donned leather armor over her necromancer robes. She strapped on an array of mundane tools turned into arcane weapons. Cassia recognized that attire. She had seen it on the Order of Hypnos's assassins who sometimes paid visits to her father.

Cassia was no longer holding Lio's hand. She reached for her own makeshift weapon, pulling her spade out of her gardening satchel and under the bedclothes.

"Miranda has become a Gift Collector?" Cassia asked.

Miranda turned and gestured to her blank breastplate, speaking in the Collector's voice again. "Tonight is her initiation. You get to be a part of it."

"You want us to kill Hesperines for you?"

"That will be one of your most important duties. You and Miranda can train together. I know how the thought of killing the king excites you. Imagine how powerful you will feel once you can slay immortals."

"You're right," Cassia said. "I understand you so well."

The Collector sat down beside her on the bed and caressed her hair with Miranda's hand. Lio bared his fangs.

"I understand you have Hesperine blood on your hands." Cassia yanked her spade from under the bedclothes and took a desperate swing at the necromancer's face. "I'll never help you!"

The Collector caught her wrist in an iron grip and forced her hand back down to the bed. "Where did you develop such a loyalty to the Hesperines? This is a very unfortunate position for you to hold."

She struggled with all her might against his grasp. "I won't tell you anything, no matter what you do to me."

He laughed softly. "You need not tell me. I am a mage of dreams. I can see into your thoughts."

Lio slid his hand behind Cassia's head. His presence filled her mind and memories. He was everywhere, even in this moment in the past when she had not had his mind ward to protect her.

"No," Cassia cried. "No!"

"I will handle you with caution," the Collector assured her. "You are far too valuable for me to be careless with you. I am not like your father, who wasted your mother in a petty fit of temper."

Cassia faltered. "He what?"

"He is the fire mage who killed your mother, I'm afraid. I had nothing to do with that, I assure you. Thalia was very valuable, and she could have borne other valuable daughters like you. You can make Lucis regret his mistake. What are the Hesperines to you, compared to your mother's life? Don't you want revenge on your father for her death? Would killing a few heretics be too high a price to pay?"

"I will not give you information on the Hesperines." But she knew her protests were in vain. He was a mind mage of Hypnos. He could take anything he wanted from her.

"I'm with you, Cassia," Lio said. "He can never hurt you again. You're safe with me. This is only a memory."

She turned her face away from Miranda, resting her cheek on Lio's palm. He kept talking, his familiar voice soothing, quoting the verse from their window seat at home. "Awaken unto me, to my certain embrace, under the wing of darkness, where together we find shelter..."

She focused on his voice, his touch, as the Collector clawed into her mind and plucked her most precious secret from her thoughts.

"The Hesperines saved your life and disposed of your sister's remains?" The Collector's voice was icy with rage. "There is rarely a complication I fail to predict. And when there is, the Hesperines are always to blame. They will regret this."

Lio's mind magic rended Cassia's memories, staining her visions of Paradum red. His voice split the Collector into fragments. "No. You will regret that you did this to her. No matter how many epochs it takes me, I will punish you for daring to lay a hand on her thoughts."

The Old Master's words snapped back together slowly, in disjointed pieces. "I can see that your loyalty to the Hesperines is very strong. But life debts are meaningless compared to the forces of death. I will give you one more chance to change your mind."

"Never. No matter what you do to me, I won't betray them."

"Allow me to explain why you should." He traced Miranda's finger down Cassia's breastbone. "Your Lustra magic is the most difficult of all paradigms to tame. It has taken me centuries to devise a process for displacing your affinities, and my experiments severely reduced the number of surviving Silvicultrixes. If you give me your magic willingly, it will be much less painful for you."

"You think pain is enough to make me surrender? Every day of my life has caused me pain you cannot imagine."

"Not pain like this. I will not be able to render you unconscious for the experience. Once I begin displacing you, I must not use my mind magic on you again. If I so much as touch your thoughts, your magic will use the connection to escape me and return to you. Do you understand, Cassia? You will be awake through it all. You will feel everything."

Fear seized her, more powerful than any she had felt in the king's presence. But she looked the Collector in the eye. "I will fight you for everything you try to take from me."

"What a pity. You would have made an excellent Overseer. But perhaps your love for the Hesperines will be of use in the long game."

Miranda's hand flicked, and Cassia's spade flew across the room. The leather straps seemed to come from nowhere, snaking over her. She thrashed against her bonds, but to no avail.

Miranda grasped Cassia's hand and slashed her palm with the knife. Cassia hissed in pain as Miranda squeezed the wound over a bowl. Dipping her knife into Cassia's blood, she painted an eye of Hypnos on her breastplate.

When Miranda spoke again, it was in her own voice. She was hoarse, as if the Collector had ruined her throat when he had torn her magic out of her. "You are my first task for him. Let us see how you feel without that precious magic of yours."

"No," Cassia pleaded. "Please, Miranda, don't do this. I never wanted any of this to happen. Give me a chance to earn your forgiveness."

"It's too late. I've made my choice, and so have you."

"Please! There are other ways to escape the temple than serving him. He is not offering you freedom. He has only put you in his cage."

"You don't understand. You can't feel the power that's flowing through me even now. And you never will. I'll leave you just enough magic to keep you alive and sane. And then I'll take your memories. You'll never even know you were a mage."

Miranda's hand curled into a fist, aimed at Cassia's heart.

"No." Lio's words cut through the memory. "You will not relive *this*."

His thelemancy blasted outward all around her, pushing back the fabric of her past reality. The sound of her own screams receded. He took her in his arms, lifting her out of the shredded straps, and slid her spade into her hand.

He carried her out of the sickroom and knelt in her garden, holding her on his lap. She was too weak to move, her throat in agony. There was nothing inside her. No magic. No emotion. No Cassia.

"He took it from me." She sounded as hoarse as Miranda. "It's been gone all this time."

Lio rocked her, pressing his forehead to hers. "My Grace. Your grief runs in my veins."

She lay limp in his arms and let him mourn. She had no tears left. He stroked her face, her hair, as if trying to put her back together. But she was broken beyond repair.

"I remember the bodies now," she said. "The epidemic never happened. Essential displacement requires human sacrifice. And I had so much magic that it took every soul at Paradum. Every person here died because of me."

"Oh, Cassia."

"If I'd chosen to serve him, I could have saved them. But he would have made me harm Hesperines."

"You've done nothing wrong, my Grace. You made the only heroic choice you could. You fought him until the last."

She looked around her at her garden. It was nothing but barren soil. Pulling breath into her chest took so much effort.

"I am no hero," she said.

"Don't you dare give up now!" Lio cupped her face in his hand and held her gaze. His fangs were fully unsheathed and tipped with his own blood. He held his wrist out before her. "Drink."

The aroma of his lifeblood banished her numbness. Her belly burned with hunger. But with the return of feeling came her shame. "Your blood is so pure. Don't sully it on me."

"You think I'm a hero, Cassia? I couldn't save Pakhne. But I will save you. Drink!"

Castra Paradum was crumbling around them, her memories turning to rubble and fog. The power in her blood was fading. If she didn't drink more now, it would be too late.

Lio could feel it approaching. The End. The moment in her Gifting when her visions would break—or she would die.

It couldn't end like this.

After everything they had survived together, Lio could not let his Grace slip away in his arms, when the Gift was right here in his blood.

She reached up and touched his face. "Lio. I don't want to do this to you."

He wanted to beg her to Drink for his sake. If he pleaded for his own life, she might ignore her guilt and grief. But he knew that was wrong. "You can't stay for me. You must stay for you. If you can't bear to live without your magic, then I will understand. And I'll still be with you every step, all the way to Sanctuary."

She trailed her finger down his bloody fang. "I don't deserve you."

"You deserve *everything*. Nights around the Ritual circle with family who love you. Greenhouses full of flowers to make you smile. Real freedom to choose your path. Real immortality. You deserve to feel safe and whole forever."

She slid her hand down his chest, her touch so weak he could barely feel it. "I wanted all of that so much."

"That is what you chose, Cassia! Not the Collector. You chose Hespera."

"I tried so hard to do the right thing. Why did that only hurt more people?"

"It's not your fault. You have to forgive yourself."

She searched his face. "I don't know how. How do I forgive myself, after everything that's happened?"

Lio opened his mouth, ready to find the most persuasive speech of his life, if talking her back from death was what it took. But no words came to him.

He didn't know. He still had not learned how to forgive himself, either.

But Cassia needed him to learn how, right here, right now.

He hadn't been able to save Pakhne. And now the prophecy in his nightmares was coming true. He was failing to save Cassia with each moment that passed, each heartbeat that came slower and quieter in her chest.

Pakhne was beyond his reach now, just like everyone else the Collector had destroyed. But Cassia was here in his arms. There was still hope for her.

She was his hope. She was his answer.

"You save the people you can," he said. "And everyone else...you must let them go."

She clung to the front of his robes, but her grip was loosening. "How can I let Miranda go?"

Lio held Cassia's hand against his chest. "You are responsible for her hurt, but not her choices. And you have already done the brave, difficult thing—you've faced your own deeds and taken action to make them right."

"No action I take can save Agata. She didn't deserve this fate."

"You are not to blame for her death, any more than I am to blame for Pakhne's suffering. We must recognize that we are not responsible for the Collector's abuses."

"But he did it to them because of us."

"*He* did it. He harmed them and us. All of us...Agata, Pakhne, Eudias, you, me...we are all alike."

"But admitting that...means admitting he controls us all."

"No. He might call us his playing pieces, but we are not. We are all players in our own right, making the best moves we can."

"What about when we play into his strategy? There is no escaping his evil. It's too easy to become part of it and never know we're hurting others."

"But Hesperines have always violated the rules of the game. We are the complication he fails to predict. We are living proof that it isn't futile to resist him."

He sensed the moment when his words sank in, and she did not merely think they were true—she felt their truth. She tightened her fingers around her spade. "You're right. The only heroic choice is to resist."

He wrapped his hand around hers. "You made a promise in that room, the night you chose our side. You told the Collector you would fight him."

"But I don't feel strong enough. Not without my magic."

"Cassia, look."

She followed his gaze. There in the dead ground beside them grew one tiny moonflower seedling. A fragile thing, and yet it did not sway in the howling wind of her collapsing memories.

"Do you feel it?" he asked.

She sucked in a breath. "There's Lustra magic in it."

"It's your magic, Cassia. That little reserve of it that Miranda and the Collector had to let you keep, so you would survive. It's still there inside you."

She reached out and touched the delicate leaves with one finger. "This is the magic I've been using. You gave me enough power that I could wield what's left of mine."

He held out his wrist to her once more. "Try. That's all I ask. Don't give up until you find out what the Gift will do to your magic. Let me have this chance to give you back what he took from you."

Cassia's fragile hand closed around his wrist. She stared at his blood with that broken girl's longing in her eyes.

With her other hand, she lifted her spade.

"Yes, Cassia. Open my vein. Everything I have within me is yours. Take my Gift."

She slashed the sharp edge across his wrist and covered his bleeding vein with her mouth.

A tremor went through the ground. The moonflower burst from the soil, blossoms unfurling along its strong new vines. The green tendrils coiled around Lio and Cassia.

Sanctuary magic shone around them, closing them off from Paradum.

The fragrance of moonflowers and Hespera's roses drenched the air, driving away the stench of death. The moonflowers had spread all over their bed, entangled with the roses that now trailed down from the bedposts.

Cassia's lashes rose, and her eyes focused on the moons shining through the empty window frame meant for his moonflower panel. She was back with him in this place and time. Her visions had broken.

Lio. Her voice came from within his mind, as near as his own thoughts. Their Grace Union had awoken. And this time, it would never end.

She would live through her Gifting.

FANGS

LIO SENT REASSURANCE ALONG the eternal cord that now held them in Union. He had promised to guide her through the harrowing changes in her body. Now he didn't need spoken words.

You're going to be all right, he said in her mind. *The flowers are growing. See what the Gift is doing to your magic.*

But she didn't look at the roses and moonflowers. Her aura, swelling with awakening power, reached out to him.

Yes, my Grace. Keep reaching. We're so close. Just a little longer, and you'll have your fangs. He lay her back in the sheets, careful not to dislodge her mouth from his wrist. *This is unlike any other Gifting. You will need more blood than other Hesperines to finish your transformation. We'll heal your magic together, all right?*

She parted her mouth from his vein and licked his blood from her lips. The erotic vision made him forget his next calm, reassuring words.

More. I need more of you. She lifted her hand, but it seemed a struggle for her. She let her arms fall back to the bed on either side of her head.

It's all right, he said. *Your strength will ebb and flow until your transformation is complete. We'll get you all the way there, my Grace.*

He brought his mouth down to hers. She kissed him as if he were her last meal. In her desperation, she scraped her tongue on his fang.

The flavor of his blood and hers mingled in his mouth, and it tasted *right.*

She kissed her way down his jaw, then bit at his throat with a whimper of frustration. Her dull canines still couldn't pierce his skin.

Not yet. He rested her head back onto the mattress and positioned himself over her. *I promised I would make love to you as you change. Do you want me inside you now?*

Yes. Her legs slid apart. *I need all of you.*

I need to watch you transform.

He pressed his hand between them and found her wet. Her Craving had primed her for her first feast. At the scent of her hunger, his instincts took hold of him, honing his body and magic to meet her need. His power surged, unleashed by the pure elixir of blood magic. His rhabdos throbbed with sudden, hard lust, and his thoughts pounded with the imperative of getting inside her.

He stopped breathing her scent and tried to think through his over-eager Grace instincts. She needed him gentle and alert.

And Goddess help him, he wanted to be coherent enough to savor this moment.

Look at me, he said.

Her heavy-lidded eyes focused on him. He held her gaze and entered her mortal body for the last time.

When he bit down on his wrist, her nostrils flared. He opened the strong flow of blood she needed and quickly pressed it to her lips. Catching the stream in her mouth, she began to suck.

As he matched his rhythm to her swallows, the intensity made him groan. He had known it would enhance the experience, but nothing could have prepared him. And she was only drinking from his wrist yet.

The tower shook. Lio's magic burst up through his heart and trailed along his veins into Cassia's mouth. He felt his life flowing out of him and putting down roots in her.

She threw her head back, letting out a clear, exultant cry against his skin. And then magic burst from her. It tangled around him and drove down deep through the tower. Her power took hold in the frozen soil of Orthros, and he sensed a new presence on the polar wind. Lustra magic.

She lifted her mouth from his wrist with a gasp.

Her last human breath. Before Lio's eyes, her top canines lengthened. They narrowed to sharp tips and extended from her gums, while the lower pair honed to fine points.

With a sudden burst of strength, she flipped him onto his back and pinned him down. He stared up at his Grace's petite, vicious fangs, fully unsheathed with hunger for him.

A tendril of moonflowers snaked across his chest to hold him against the pillows, while a vine of their roses lifted his chin to expose his throat to her. Cassia's pupils dilated, catching the light of his stained glass windows, and her eyes began to glow.

He lay still beneath her, throbbing where she gripped him inside her. *Oh my Goddess. You're divine.*

Her incandescent gaze fixed on the rose thorn a finger's breadth from his jugular. He could see her fighting for focus amid her delirium. Her Will flared through their Union and echoed in the Lustra magic growing through their tower. *Release him.*

The flowers slid away to tangle in a wild arbor around their bed.

The light of her eyes winked out for an instant as she blinked hard. *This will be your first feast. You've never made love with anyone's fangs in you.*

A smile came to his face. *You've always been my first and only.*

She brushed her fingers down his neck. *Are you ready? Do you want my bite?*

He would never forget those words or how she looked in this moment. His hands tightened on her hips, and he didn't dare move inside her. *I've wanted this since…the night we met. No…for my whole immortal existence. I want it to be everything you imagined.*

It already is, he said, as he watched her lower her newborn fangs to his throat.

She positioned her lips in the place he had shown her when they had longingly practiced for this in bed. Her careful approach reminded him of the first time he had bitten her…of their tentative touches on the floor of their shrine when they had first made love… Oh Goddess, her fangs were so close. If she made him wait another instant, he would lose his head.

She closed her fingers around her Grace braid encircling his neck. At last, her canines pricked him. Her fangs sank tenderly through his skin, into his flesh. The lower pair anchored her, while her top canines sought his vein. She caressed his face, her touch reverent.

He dragged his hands down her back and felt her muscles straining for control. *I want you to lose control.*

As if his words set her free, she pulled her head back. Then her fangs came down, and she clamped onto him. Flecks of crimson spattered onto the white petals of the moonflowers by his head.

The blood surged from his vein. The magic of his deepest soul released. His shout echoed around them, his back arching, as his climax tapped him and spilled him inside her. Better than channeling. Better than anything.

Now, at last. She feasted on his blood and body and magic. He was her everything.

There came a wrenching sensation in his chest that knocked the breath from his lungs, even as power and pleasure kept pounding through him. As if his own body were changing somehow. He gave himself over to the ecstatic pain.

When he surfaced, his body spent and yet exhilarated, it seemed mere moments or a century might have gone by. She still gripped him between her thighs, suckling his vein as if she would never get enough. The wet strokes of her tongue and the tight pressure of her mouth sent new lust pulsing through him.

They throbbed together in a single rhythm, he realized. Their hearts were beating in unison.

Her bite had changed him. And now there was a fully Hesperine heart beating in her chest, with the power to see the rest of her body through the transformation.

He let his head fall back as she began the next course of her feast. Tears coursed down his face. This was what it felt like. They had survived for him to find out.

The worst was over. They had won.

RENEWAL

ONCE WOULD NEVER BE enough. She had to make him climax again.

Cassia pulled back to lick an escaping trail of blood from his throat, greedy for every drop that held the lingering flavor of his release. Then she covered his bleeding vein with her mouth once more.

She had the power to make him come apart again and again. Strength was spreading outward from her heart, driving back the weakness in her limbs. Lio's blood pumped into the void inside her, flowing along every carved-out arcane path to soothe and fill her.

There had once been a world beyond this. Hadn't there? She didn't remember it. Nothing divided her attention from him, not even breathing, for her lungs no longer demanded air. She was immersed in a sea of blood and emotion and sensation, and she never needed to surface again. Their Union was her world.

She slid her hand lightly over his nipple, fascinated with the twin sensations of his skin against her palm and the flare of his desire in their Union.

You feel my response, then I feel your vicarious pleasure. His mind-voice was as rich as his blood. *It cycles between us until it's too much for us to hold.*

She shifted on him and felt him already hardening inside her again. Suckling his vein, she swiveled her hips, coaxing his erection. Soon he was so thick and hard that she had to withdraw, then sink down on him again to reseat herself. As she covered him to the base of his shaft, his response felt like an erotic groan in their Union, and she groaned aloud.

Neither of us needs time to recover. His tone was a wicked tease in her thoughts. *I no longer have to worry about tiring you, and I intend to enjoy it.*

He was right. She wasn't tired. She had more energy than when they had begun. She realized what they both wanted now. She could bite the other side of his neck. Another vein to give her more blood. A part of him she hadn't tasted yet.

But she mustn't leave his precious blood flowing out on this side. She began to lap at his vein.

He sighed. *You take such good care of me, my Grace.*

Why isn't my tongue healing you?

Don't be distressed. He stroked her back again. *We're still healing you. Your body needs all that power for yourself. Let my own Gift see to me for now.* His amusement warmed their Union. *But for your bite to close, you have to pull your fangs out of me first.*

Oh. Her face heated. She still had her canines in his neck. The pressure felt so good.

His smile felt like the soft gleam of spell light. *Even with my blood in your veins, I can still make you blush.*

Her flush deepened.

This is your Renewal, he said, *when you require more blood so you can continue to heal and transform. Your body knows what you need. Don't be embarrassed if you lose control.*

But right now, she needed control if she was to enjoy his other vein.

He cupped her face in his hand. *Take a breath. Your first Hesperine breath.*

His suggestion awoke some new instinct, and she flared her nostrils, drawing in air. She discovered what her lungs were for. A thousand scents struck her. Through the chaos, she recognized the glory of Hespera's Roses and the vitality of moonflowers.

At last she released him from her bite so she could gasp. She tilted her head back, closing her eyes, while his blood ran down her throat and his scent filled her head. Mortal life had cheated her. He smelled like so much more than moonflowers and sandalwood and books.

His body emanated a musk that made her want to put her mouth all over him. Masculine arousal.

He bucked his hips under her and pulled her face to the other side of his neck. She couldn't think. All she could do was sink her fangs into her throat. When his blood rushed onto her tongue again, her new sense of smell made his flavor so bold that she moaned. The fullness of his blood in her mouth and his hard length in her core were perfect.

The scent of male lust grew thicker in the air. It shuttered her coherent mind and unleashed some primal part of her. She mated him like a wild thing, devouring his blood. She lived for his growl in her ear and the dig of his fingers into her hips. Her body flew out of her control, and he unleashed himself with her. With a snarl against his throat, she panted through the spasms of their release.

New flavor notes bloomed in her mouth, so intense her head spun. Richer than chocolate, bolder than coffee, sweeter than wine. Oh. Goddess. How could he taste *better*?

Everything is better with a Hesperine tongue, he said. *Your sense of taste has awoken.*

Her hungry whimpers gave way to a cry of ecstasy as the flavor of him drove her over the edge again. She would be drunk on him forever.

No need for temperance, he purred.

When her thoughts came together again, they fixed on one thing. *I have to taste you everywhere.*

Bleeding thorns, yes. I've been waiting for this.

The lure of the rest of his body gave her the willpower to slide her teeth out of his neck. She pressed her tongue to his vein while his own Gift healed him, then lifted her head.

Her ears roared. Sound came crashing in on her. The rasp of their skin against the sheets. The cacophony of the flowers and leaves rustling around them. And above all, their matching pulses, like a heartbeat at the center of the world, pounding through everything.

Lio covered her ears with his hands and held her face against his chest. She lay against him, grateful for the relief.

After a long moment, he lifted his hands, and she found the overwhelming noise had settled. The sounds around her were crystal clear, more beautiful and vivid than any her mortal ears had ever heard.

She looked into his eyes. *I want your voice to be the first I hear.*

He spoke to her in the Divine Tongue. "I love you, Cassia."

This was what Glasstongue's voice truly sounded like. Deep enough to drown in, smooth enough to make her moan. So full of love she could weep.

"Lio," she breathed, trying her new voice. "I love you, too."

She looked down at him, bracing her hands on his shoulders to steady herself. There were bloodstains and flower petals everywhere. Beyond the haze of her hunger, some part of her mind was appalled that she had done this to him, when he had always been so gentle with her.

But he reached into their Grace Union and gave her a caress as carnal as it was arcane. "I told you I want you to lose control."

He could have discussed the weather in that tone of voice, and it would still have made her curl her toes.

"Don't resist," he said. "Tell me how it makes you feel."

Her gaze traveled over the red splashes on the pale skin of his neck, the darker smears over his rosy mouth. She bit her lip, only to taste his blood there, too. "Just the sight of your blood arouses me."

"That's natural for us."

"You enjoy it too."

"Of course. Seeing my blood on your breasts…you can feel in our Union what that does to me."

Her nipples pebbled, and she looked down. Flecks of crimson were spattered all over her brown freckles. But he was right. What she felt in their Grace Union could melt the snow swirling outside the windows.

Her doubts banished, she lowered her mouth to his throat again, but not to bite. She licked the smears of his blood from his neck, then along his collarbone, savoring the combined flavor of his blood and skin. She could lie here for hours, just relishing this. But there was more.

She pried their slick bodies apart and kissed her way down his chest. The light dusting of hair on his chest changed the taste of his skin. And the rough peak of his nipple had yet another flavor. She indulged her need to suck, and the rise of his arousal in their Union urged her on.

She let her instincts take over again. She drew one fang over his pectoral, a little deeper than she had meant to. He hissed.

Am I hurting you? It took all her strength to yank herself back.

His canines were straining in his mouth. He cupped her head and pulled her back down to him. "I want to feel your fangs everywhere."

She couldn't have resisted that voice of his if she had wanted to. And she didn't. She reopened the quickly healing cut on his chest. Laving at his blood, she spread it over his nipple to discover how this combination tasted.

She got lost in his contours and flavors, experimenting down his torso and along the insides of his thighs. With nips and grazes, she learned how complex he was. She waited with bated breath for every crest of pleasure in their Union to tell her what he most enjoyed.

At last she paused with her mouth above his erection. This was what her fangs had done to him. He was beautiful, standing proud and massive within reach of her mouth. Her tongue darted out to wet her lips, but she hesitated.

He put a finger under chin and tilted her face to look at him. "If you want to know what this tastes like, too, go ahead."

Her new fangs felt like clumsy spikes in her mouth. "I'm afraid I'll hurt you."

His laughter seemed to dance over her skin and touch the shameless parts of her mind. "I'm not worried. But if it will reassure you, we can save it for another night. We have the rest of eternity to explore."

They would never run out of time? It didn't seem real. She felt like devouring all of him before someone took him away from her. She was already shaking with need again. No, that tremble in her limbs was exhaustion.

Why was she feeling weak, when the Gift should be making her strong?

COMPLETION

HE GATHERED HER INTO his arms and rolled them onto their sides. "Remember, this is normal. Your strength will surge and fade until your Gifting is finished."

"I don't want to be tired," she protested.

"I know. But while you rest, would you like me to take control for a little while?"

Feeling his erection resting against the inside of her thigh, she nodded, her hair falling in her eyes with the motion.

He brushed her tousled hair away from her face. "We can expect structural transformation next. Bones, muscles, tendons. The rest of your organs. Your new strength will become permanent."

"I want to be strong."

"You will be so powerful. But this part can be uncomfortable. The slower you go through it, the harder it will be. If we cycle your blood more quickly, it will be much easier for you."

"This is the part where you need to drink my blood." She swallowed.

"Yes, Cassia. It will make you a little dizzy. But you'll enjoy it."

"I'll feel your fangs in me. With my fangs in you."

A slow smile curved his beautiful mouth. "Yes. Are you ready?"

"Yes," she pleaded.

He eased her back onto the pillows, sliding one under her head and another on each side of her. He spread her trembling legs to lean against the pillows, then slid between her thighs. "Just rest under me."

She nodded again. He fitted his rhabdos to her and sank in slowly. She felt it in her fangs, her gums aching.

"Have I told you your fangs are perfect?" He increased the pressure of his hips, gliding deeper. "I love watching them respond to me."

She couldn't speak. Not with her fangs like this and him impaling her in the cocoon of the pillows. He leaned down over her, closer, closer. Her heart raced, and she heard his heart quicken. Because of her.

"I'm going to bite you hard," she gasped. "I'm not in control."

"That's why I'm in control right now. So you don't have to be."

"My hunger is in control."

"That's all right. I can pull back if I want you to stop. But I won't want you to stop for anything."

At last his jugular was within reach of her fangs. As if her muscles obeyed only her Craving, she struck his throat. She barely recognized the feral sound she made.

"Yes," he grunted. "That's what I want to hear."

Her reflexes made her swallow over and over. She felt a spasm in her jaw, and then the joint locked, holding her onto him without effort.

"Your jaw changed," he gritted in her ear. "It's starting. I need to drink from you now."

Yes. Yes. Yes. It was all she could think with each pound of their hearts.

"Do you want me to bite you gently or hard?" he asked.

Hard, she begged.

His hand slid into her hair, and he tilted her head, holding her more firmly to his vein. His smooth cheek slid along hers.

And then two spikes of pleasure drove into her neck. His familiar bite, as she had never imagined it could feel.

Their beings flowed together. The cycle was complete, body to body, blood to blood. Power exploded through their Grace Union, and she heard thorns scrape iron. Petals fluttered across her skin.

She had surrendered to this cycle long ago, and now lay pliant beneath him, locked on his vein. But she was no longer afraid.

She trusted the force penetrating and shaping her. Trusted the strong, reassuring hands that grasped her knees, holding her in position for the changes about to take hold. She trusted her hunger, ravishing his throat for her.

His long, hard draughts at her vein made her head rush and more liquid heat slick her channel to ease his thrusts and withdrawals. She lay still on the bed, but the world seemed to be spinning around her, just as he'd warned.

He stopped moving inside her, pinning her to the bed with irresistible strength. His shaft anchored her amid the vertigo. *I've got you.*

Her bones felt heavy. Then her spine popped, releasing tension she'd carried there all her life. Other joints began to align, easing countless tiny pinches of pain. Groups of muscles tightened, then released, granting her a relaxation she had never known.

Through each spasm, he held her. She found the strength to lift her arms and dig her nails into his back. She wrapped her legs around him and held him close. Her body reshaped itself around his, which had been made to fit hers all along.

He began to move inside her again, teaching her shifting frame their familiar rhythm. He built the next cycle of pleasure in their Union, coaxing her toward her next change. She could sense what was to come, and she quivered.

Her inner muscles squeezed hard around him, then they too released, transforming in convulsions that left her speechless. His thrusts into her erratic rhythm were hard and sure, guiding her through the climax.

She was still shaking when he pinned her on the bed once more and surged into her. The taste of his release made her claw at his back and clamp her thighs around him.

His shout rang in her ears, and his words were triumphant in their Union. *Feel how strong you are.*

Strong enough to hold him. To fight for him. To keep him safe.

We're both safe. You need to let go of me for now. I shouldn't be inside you for the final change.

She didn't understand, but she trusted him. She found the Will to untangle herself from him. He slid his fangs out of her neck and pulled out of her swiftly, leaving a rush of wetness trickling out of her. Her teeth tightened on his throat. She wasn't sure she could stop biting.

That's all right. Keep drinking.

He lowered himself over her again, this time only holding her under his weight. She began to see why when her skin prickled. Her every nerve tingled. And then sensation inundated her.

She screamed against his throat.

Her skin felt raw. Only the smoothness of his Hesperine skin and the pressure of his body gave her relief. Thank the Goddess the sheets were Orthros silk, perfectly smooth against her tortured sense of touch. She lay there without moving or uttering a sound, she knew not how long, hiding from stimulation.

His voice in her mind soothed her. *Your sense of touch is the last change. It's too much now, but when you grow used to it…it will be incredible.*

The last change? It is finished?

He massaged her jaw with deft fingers. The joint unlocked, and he eased her head back onto the pillow.

He looked down at her with emotions in his eyes that would take her centuries to name. *You have reached Completion. You are Hesperine, inside and out. My Hesperine.*

Gratitude filled their Union. It was built into her new bones and her regrown heart.

My Grace, he murmured in her mind. *Rest now. Spend your first Slumber in my arms.*

She slipped into the deepest sleep she had ever known.

Lio heard her new heart ease into the steady rhythm of the Slumber, and his own heart calmed in his chest. Silence fell over their Sanctuary, unbroken by mortal breath.

Her body felt small under his, but her aura emanated power. He couldn't begin to understand what he sensed within her—and welling up from beneath their tower. Blood magic. Lustra magic.

All he knew right now was that she would live. Forever. They had time to learn her new nature. They had eternity.

She was immortal.

He rolled onto his side and looked at her. She was a work of art, her hair wild, her transformation painted across her olive skin in the deep maroon of their drying blood. Her fangs, barely tamed, peeked out at him between her slightly parted lips.

He had never beheld anything so beautiful as her lying there, sleeping off all her ordeals, as still as only a Hesperine could be. After everything she had endured in her life, he had never seen her so at peace.

Rolling onto his back, he rested her Slumbering form on top of him. He pulled the bedclothes over her to give her the smoothness and weight her new senses would want upon waking. She would need more care. More blood. He would make sure everything she required was ready before her Awakening.

But for now, he needed this. To rest with her in his arms. To feel every moment of her first Slumber easing past, knowing there would be so many more.

He listened to his blood flowing through her veins. Their mingled life force, thriving inside both of them. They had grown together, entangled for all time.

That force swelled in his changed heart, and he let it flare out of him in a spell light, bright and beautiful. He sent that beacon flying up through the ceiling to hover above their tower like one of the Goddess's stars. Now all of Orthros would know.

A new Hesperine had been born tonight.

AWAKENING

SLEEP, COMPLETE AND DREAMLESS, released her slowly. She surfaced gently toward his voice, his presence. Yes. She wanted to wake and be closer to him.

Don't be afraid of your hunger, he said. *I'm right here.*

She felt the gnawing fire in her belly first. Then the ravenous ache in her veins. Finally, her parched throat.

She wanted to scream, but couldn't speak. She needed to touch him, but couldn't move.

You're safe, he soothed. *Your mind has awoken, but the rest of you needs more time. Be patient with your body.*

Her mind. Yes. She reached for him with the only thing that would obey her. *Lio?*

I'm here, Cassia.

So hungry.

I know, and I will give you all the blood you want.

Blood. You.

Yes. All of me.

She felt his hands on her cheeks, moving her head. His throat met her lips.

Yes, she cried out to him. *Your vein.*

Don't worry. Your fangs will wake first.

Her canines shot out of her gums, her whole mouth aching with the need to bite. With one hand tangled in her hair and his other on her chin, he guided her mouth open and helped her press her fangs into his flesh.

His blood hit her tongue, driving back her panic. Yes. This. Nothing mattered but this. She fastened onto him and began her next feast.

His deep groan met her ears. His voice was gravelly with desire. "It feels so good, my Grace."

She heard his heart racing, pumping blood into hers. She gulped him down.

"That's right, Cassia. You're a natural, just as I knew you would be."

Sensation returned. The gentle pressure of his arms around her. His lap under her. The warm bath water that enclosed their bodies. The magic everywhere, immersing her.

She could move. She wrapped her arms around his neck, releasing him from her bite so she could sink her fangs into him again.

"*Goddess*," he ground out. "I'll never get enough of this feeling."

Neither would she. Thrilling energy rushed through her. She had never felt so strong. Was she holding him too tight?

"You can't hurt me," he said. "We're both immortal now."

Immortal. She was immortal. She was a Hesperine.

At last, his blood sharpened her mind, and coherent thought returned. Memories came crashing back to her. Her first taste of his blood. Her body changing in his arms. Hours of ecstasy that had remade her into *this*.

Her new senses told her the truth. She could hear every sparkling droplet of water they stirred. She could smell every flower petal that floated around them. Replete with his blood, she lifted her head and opened her eyes.

They were home. Safe in Orthros Boreou, deep under their tower. He had brought her down into the bathing pool and surrounded her with soft veil spells that muffled the echoes. Dim, diffuse spell light showed her their reflection in the mirrors that lined the walls and ceiling.

Her own gaze glowed back at her, green-gold. Her jaw dropped, and she beheld her fangs.

"Look how magnificent you are," he said.

She opened her mouth wider and tilted her head from side to side to admire her new canines. She had never felt more beautiful.

"This is your true self," he told her.

She looked into his face, really looked at him with her new eyes for the first time. She trailed her hand through his hair, fascinated by the feel of him. She traced his brow, then ran her finger along his cheekbone, down to discover the contours of his lips. She felt his sigh on her fingertips.

Now she could see him as he truly was. Their Grace Union showed her the soul behind the windows of his eyes. She sank through the layers inside him, more complex even than the myriad flavors of his blood. "Now I understand what you mean whenever you tell me it will take you centuries to know me."

"We have millennia now."

She held onto him, enfolded in his embrace, knowing it was finally true.

She had the Gift.

Long moments passed by, she knew not how many. Her sense of time had altered. Even the city bells of Selas that counted the hours were not to be heard in this veiled realm of their own. The world they had left behind in flames felt like another life.

"I know you have questions," he said, "but right now, you need blood and time. I'll tell you anything necessary for your peace of mind, and then I want you to focus on your own needs, all right?"

Already, his seductive voice was all she could hear. But he was right. There were things she should ask him before she slipped back into the delirium of bloodlust. "Just tell me if Solia is all right."

"Yes. When I brought you home, she was holding her own. The Charge will keep her and everyone else safe. Knight is with Zoe." His expression softened. "You should know that your sister gave us her blessing."

"On our love?" Cassia asked, scarcely daring to hope.

"On your Gifting."

Cassia gasped.

"Can you let that be enough for now?" Lio asked. "There will be time to deal with the rest of the world later. Will you forget with me that anything beyond our tower exists?"

Her sacred choice had not cost her Solia's love. Yes, that was enough.

"I can scarcely see beyond you and me," Cassia confessed.

"Good. Nothing matters to me right now except taking care of you. Will you let me do that?"

"Have you not yet realized, my Grace? You no longer share me with the rest of the world. Nothing matters to me except you."

He framed her face in his hands, stroking her. "I cannot tell you what that means to me."

"You needn't tell me. I can feel it in our Union. I can smell it on you."

Scents hung in the air, as heavy as the clouds of steam blanketing her new skin. Amid the fragrance of roses and moonflowers, her nose picked out his musk.

"Let me introduce you to your new form," he said. "There are things I want to show you about your body...and your magic."

At that invitation, her fangs sprang to their full length in an instant, and she groaned in surprise.

He tilted her head back to look at her mouth. "I'll never tire of watching that."

"I just drank from you." Her words slurred around her fangs. "How can I need more blood already?"

"You'll be hungry all the time at first. That's why we're naked in a locked tower covered in veil spells."

Laughter bubbled out of her.

He beamed at her. "Not that I would mind if all of Selas heard my screams and envied me for my Grace's appetite."

She let out another peal of laughter.

He gazed down at her as if he truly were the most fortunate person in the world. "That's the first time I've heard you laugh as a Hesperine."

"Everything feels new."

"Fall in love with me all over again," he invited.

He cradled her face in his hand and touched his lips to hers. She went still, riveted to the feeling, as new and wondrous as their first kiss.

He brushed his lips carefully over hers, giving her time to absorb the thrilling sensations. Overwhelming. And yet she needed more.

She parted her lips for him. He slid his tongue gently in to play against hers, and she experienced his mouth with her Hesperine sense of taste. Stars seemed to skitter across her skin.

Just when she could scarcely bear the delicious feeling any longer, he pulled back. Her eyes focused on his fangs, and her hearing attuned to the pulse of his blood under his skin.

"I brought you here to ease the inundation on your new senses," he said. "Let's stay in the bath until you feel comfortable in your own skin."

She realized how grateful she was for the water around her. "Thank you."

"I will start touching you. If it feels like too much, tell me to stop. Is that all right?"

His voice warmed her in indecent places. But no places were indecent to Hesperines. "Yes."

"It will be less intense without direct eye contact."

She wanted to look into his eyes, but he was right. "I suppose so."

"Would it feel good if I turn you over?"

She saw the image in their Union. Her clinging to the side of the bath with him standing behind her, entering her fully transformed body for the first time. Even as an immortal, she discovered he could still make her go weak in the knees. "Yes. That's what I want."

He smiled. "It is the favorite position for one's first time as a Hesperine. It will reduce stimulation of your kalux and allow me to guide you. And you can easily drink from my wrist."

"I can tell you studied this, Sir Scholar."

He raised a brow, as if to say, *of course I did my research.* "The 'Discourse on the Gift' is the longest section in the *Discourses on Love.*"

He slid them off of the bench built into the side of the bath. Standing on the bottom of the pool, he turned her around in the water to face the mirrors. They showed her the fantasy she had seen in his mind a moment ago. Her Grace behind her, ready to show her what Hesperine pleasure truly felt like.

"I don't know how it can be more intense than our Feast during my transformation," she said.

"Your sense of touch had not awoken then."

Gooseflesh spread across her skin. Right. He had withdrawn before that final change.

He draped her hair over her shoulder and pressed his cheek to hers. "Aren't you glad I shaved?"

She moaned in frustration. "By the time your beard grows back in, I will be ready for it."

"Challenge accepted."

He began to massage her, starting at her shoulders. With firm hands, he explored her, and they learned her new shape together. In the mirror, she watched her fangs respond to his touch.

When he lifted both of her breasts in his palms, she let her head fall back to rest on his shoulder. In the mirrors on the ceiling, she watched him fondle her under the water. "Is it my imagination…or is there…a little bit more of those than before?"

His enjoyment heated their Union. "They are undoubtedly bigger. But still small enough to be a perfect mouthful."

Cassia might be short and skinny for eternity, but she finally had breasts.

"And hips." His hands slid down and squeezed her buttocks. "Just the right amount for me to hold on to while you feast on me. This is your natural shape when you're healthy."

Once his massage and the bath lulled her into ease, he lightened his touch, showing her what his caresses felt like. His palm slid down her throat, then across the sensitive top of her shoulder. She couldn't have borne callouses on his palms, but his smooth scholar's hands were a delight to her skin. He slipped his hand along the lower curve of her breast, the water making his skin glide over hers, and she bit her lip at how sensitive she was there. He paused.

She shook her head. "More."

He stroked her stomach. Lower. He swirled his fingers in circles below her navel, and her muscles shivered under his touch.

His hand swept along the outside of her hip. "I won't touch your most sensitive place. Not until you make it very clear you want that."

She could not imagine what that bud of nerves felt like now. "I…am not ready for that."

He swept his hand along her inner thigh. "How is this?"

She squeezed her legs together.

"Mmm," he said in her ear, "you have a strong grip. I will enjoy that."

"I can finally please you the way I've always wanted to."

He eased closer to her, making the water ripple around them. The hard ridge that came to rest lightly at the crease of her buttocks made her clench her thighs tighter. "See how much you please me, without even trying?"

She needed that inside her. It would be too much. But she needed it.

He positioned her hands on the smooth tiles at the rim of the bath. She fixed her gaze on the pattern of deep blue and cerulean instead of his hungry gaze in the mirror.

"Stretch," he said. "Feel how powerful your new body is."

She stretched luxuriously in the water. There were no pockets of tension in her muscles. She was so limber.

"We'll enjoy that, too." Resting one hand on her hip, he slid his other hand between her legs from behind.

He cupped her curls in his long fingers. In the bath, she hadn't realized how wet she was. Of all the power her new body granted her, right now it seemed ruled by her most basic appetites.

"You can always tell me no," he reminded her, "and you can even tell your own hunger no, if you're not ready. If you want me to stop, Will it, and I will know, even before you say a word."

The anticipation in her was more powerful than her apprehension. "Touch me."

He slipped one finger in the shallows of her channel, and she hissed at the frisson that traveled through her.

"Bleeding thorns," she swore. "Are you this sensitive all the time?"

"Now you know how I feel whenever you touch me."

"Oh my Goddess. I had no idea...what I was doing to you..."

He slid deeper and stroked her with just that one finger, in and out, in and out, accustoming her to the feeling. His familiar touch felt new and strange and wonderful, and her greedy body knew only one way to respond. His single finger brought her right up to the edge, and she floated there, caught between temptation and trepidation.

"I don't think you're ready for that yet, either." He withdrew his hand.

She sighed, then gasped at the feeling of his two fingers easing inside her.

"How does this feel?" he asked.

She gritted her teeth, even as she spread her thighs farther apart for him in the water.

He smiled at her in the mirror, and the sight of his fangs made her want more than could handle. She shut her eyes. But robbing herself of that sense made all the others more acute somehow. Her entire awareness focused on the gentle invasions of his two fingers. He pushed her to her limit again and held her there.

The throbbing in her fangs seemed to pound away her thoughts. "I'm so hungry."

"I think we need to stretch you more before you're ready."

"I need your blood."

He withdrew his fingers again. "Mm. No need to wait for that."

His chest molded to her back as he leaned down over her, and his arm wrapped around her waist. When she scented his blood under her nose, she opened her eyes. His wrist was before her, his veins delicate blue under pale skin.

She lowered her head, her hands tightening on the tiles. He held her feast to her lips so she could bite down. The sound of her own licks and sucks filled her keen ears.

Then his voice. "I love the way you feast on me. You're beautiful when you're ravenous. It drives me wild, too."

She arched in his hold, instinctively seeking his body to feast on.

"I am so hard," he warned in her ear, "and you are very, very tight."

She tilted her hips up against him, demanding more.

"If you're certain. But I'll need both hands to work you onto me."

I want your wrist again, when you're inside me.

"How I enjoy your demands, my Grace. You're even more vocal about what you want than when you were human."

Flushed with another dose of his blood and the feeling of her own power, she released his vein.

He eased off of her and grasped both her hips in his hands, adjusting her position in the bath. "This will take some time."

He rested the tip of his rhabdos at the entrance of her krana. Oh Goddess. She knew his size and shape well, but he was right. She had never been this tight, and he had never seemed so big.

What would they feel like together now? Would he overwhelm her again, a high like they had shared during her Gifting? She needed to know. "I want everything."

"Then I'll give it to you," he said.

His head nudged into her, and she couldn't hold back a soft cry. Not only because of the deluge of sensation.

It was the intimacy. The most private parts of their bodies touching, joining, when Grace Union already bound their hearts and minds so close.

He pushed another inch inside her and waited, giving her time to adjust. She marveled at his control. She was in such good hands for her initiation into eternity.

His lust and affection warmed their Union. *I was made for this, just as you were.*

He eased deeper inside. Deeper. He massaged her buttocks, his immortal strength pushing through her Hesperine body's equally powerful resistance. As he stretched her apart, her head grew light. She felt every texture and contour of his erection gliding against her inner walls, sending cascade after cascade of pleasure through her.

Fitting his pelvis against her buttocks, he stopped. She floated there in his grip, panting and crying out with every breath. She didn't dare move. She felt herself sinking toward unconsciousness. But the darkness never came.

Very few things can make a Hesperine faint, he explained. *Pleasure is not one of them.*

She would not miss a single moment of what he was about to do to her. "Don't stop."

He adjusted their position, leaning down over her back again. Her body flexed for him effortlessly, but the movement drew another cry out of her, the angle stretching her in new ways.

His arm closed around her abdomen, holding her securely on his shaft. He opened his mouth on her neck and kissed her there. "Are you ready to have all of me inside your new body?"

She was unprepared, and yet, she had never been more ready. "Yes."

"That word is even more arousing to me in your immortal voice."

He sank his canines into her as gradually and gently as he had penetrated her between her legs. With a scream, she bared her fangs.

He held his wrist before her mouth. *Now complete our Union.*

She bit down on his wrist with all the strength and hunger she possessed. The cycle that had destroyed and recreated her in her Gifting took hold of them again. But this time, she could experience pleasure as he did. This time, she was powerful enough to ride it.

Now I'd like to give you your first magic lesson, he said.

What? she cried out in his mind. She couldn't think of magic when her nerves were consumed by nothing but *him*. She couldn't think at all.

You don't need to think. And I don't need to explain. I can show you in our Union, if you will allow me.

It will bring you closer?

As close as I can get.

I want it.

He hesitated, reminding her, *If it feels like too much, I'll stop.*

But it felt as natural and easy as their heartbeats for him to slide into her thoughts. He was already there. His focus deepened their connection as his body pressed heavier over hers, sinking her lower in the water. He delved into her arcane pathways with her, stretching her senses, opening her, guiding her toward what would sate her hunger.

When she tapped into the power under the tower, magic jolted through her. She thrashed in the water, but he held her steady amid the torrent.

This magic…feels like us. It feels so good. What's happening?

Let me show you.

He began to move inside her. She saw a whole starry sky behind her eyelids. His thrusts and his pulls at her vein awoke her instinct to suckle his wrist to the same rhythm. And she realized what she wanted the magic to do.

It obeyed her desire. The magic surrendered to the cycle between her and her Grace. Power poured through her with every undulation of their bodies, rising higher each time.

When there was too much inside her for even her Hesperine form to hold, she overflowed. Pleasure tore through the endless channels between them, into him, and back into her.

When that climax ebbed, he said, *More.*

She pulled more from his vein and more of that mysterious power up from the earth. He set a new pace, and they pleasured themselves on blood and magic again.

There was no reason to ever lift her mouth from his vein. But sometime in the endless night, he eased their fangs and bodies apart to care for her. He floated her on her back in the center of the pool with a gentle levitation spell, one hand under her head. "Rest your senses."

Flowers drifted against her, as if drawn to her. The petals had bloomed into fully grown roses and moonflowers, thriving in the bath like water lilies.

"Impossible," she breathed.

"Nothing is impossible anymore," he said.

Lio, always telling her to hope her dreams would come true. Always making them a reality.

"This is my plant magic," she said. "All of it. But I can feel the blood magic in it, too."

"You now possess an affinity unlike any other," Lio said. "A perfect Union of *haima* and *hulaia*."

Hespera had taken that stunted remnant of her power and made it grow into this boundless garden. She had made Cassia's Lustra magic her own. This magic did not belong to that desperate girl in the kitchen garden. It belonged to Cassia Komnena.

And this new sorceress she had become understood what she sensed below them.

"Lio...the magic under our tower is a letting site."

"That was my theory." His whole aura was alight. "But I needed my Silvicultrix to confirm it. This means you are the first to create a new letting site in untold centuries—and the first in history to open one in the soil of Orthros."

"I don't understand how I did it, but there is no doubt."

"It seems to have been an intuitive act of Will during a singular magical phenomenon—the precise moment of your transformation, when your fangs first unsheathed, and your own magic was changed by the Gift. Clearly, your letting site is as unique as your affinity, for it is imbued with both Lustra magic and blood magic."

"It will take us centuries to study it," she said, just to feel his delight at the prospect.

"Most importantly, it will allow you to draw power from the wilds. Right here in our Sanctuary, while you draw blood from me." A satisfied smile curved his lips. "As we have already tested rather extensively."

She savored the arcane flavor that lingered in her mouth. "I can taste you in my wilds. My magic knew what to do. It infused my letting site with your power, just like my Gifting infused me with you."

"I feel my bond with your Lustra. Your transformation changed me, too."

Tears slipped from the corners of her eyes. He caught one on his finger and lifted it to his lips. With a sigh, he closed his eyes. "Your first Hesperine tears. I was so afraid you would be disappointed. But I can taste your joy."

"*Disappointed?* How could you imagine I would feel *disappointed* after everything we just did together?"

His quiet pain filled their refuge, and she could scarcely bear it. "Not even your letting site has given you your beast magic and soothsaying. I will understand if you mourn the loss of your other affinities."

She turned herself upright and took hold of his shoulders. "Look at me, Lio."

He met her gaze as she asked, holding her close in their Union.

At last, she could hold him back. "I don't need more and more affinities in order to be happy. Garden magic is what I yearned for my whole life. I realize now, I was missing what I didn't know I had lost."

Her past felt distant, a burden she had left behind in the ruins of the sickroom. Hespera had carved all of that away, letting the real Cassia emerge. She had been shaped by it, yes. But now she was free.

"My Gifting healed me," she said. "Do you still carry wounds from it, my Grace?"

He shook his head. "I feel the same. As if your Divining cleansed us of what Kallikrates has done to us."

The name had no power here.

"But there is one wrong that must still be righted," Lio said. "I want you to have all of your magic."

She wrapped her arms around his waist, resting her face on his heart. "My list of wants has grown so long, my Grace. But my needs are still simple. My garden magic, my Gift, and you. I have all of that in my arms right now."

"I can sense that you are truly satisfied. But I am not."

He held her against him, and she met a new layer of him in their Grace Union. She had always known it was there, under his placid surface.

When he made up his mind, he was unbreakable.

"If it takes me a thousand years," he swore, "I will find a way for you to complete your magic. We'll study your letting site. We'll scour Tenebra for another one. We'll learn how a Hesperine Silvicultrix can acquire the rest of her power."

"I don't want to scour anywhere. I want to stay right here. Who knows? Perhaps in another hundred years, my immortal life will meet the conditions, and my other magics will rise up out of my letting site without strife."

"I make no promises to be so patient. But do not misunderstand me, my rose—you are perfect as you are."

"Thank you, my love. I think my mother would be proud of who I've become. But even if she weren't, I would be. We are heretics. We make our own path. This is mine."

"Then you have no regrets."

"None. Do you?"

"You don't need me to answer," he said. "You can sense it. Reach into our Union and tell me what I feel."

She let go of all her inner defenses and opened herself to her Grace, letting his emotions become her own.

Grief. Gratitude. Anger. Relief. Pain. Joy.

At last she realized they were all different flavors of one emotion, which imbued his every thought of her.

Love.

His love for her would survive every epoch, and now she could love him in return until the end of time.

Are you ready for Cassia's adventures as a Hesperine? Her new life with Lio continues in Blood Grace Book 8, *Blood Feast*...

vroth.co/feast

GLOSSARY

Abroad: Hesperine term for lands outside of Orthros where Hesperines errant roam, meaning Tenebra and Cordium. See **Orthros Abroad**

acacia: see **Battle of Souls**

adamas: strongest metal in the world, so heavy only Hesperines can wield it. Invented in secret by Nike.

Adrogan: ambitious Tenebran lord, a younger son who traveled to Orthros to make his fortune. Once one of Cassia's unwanted suitors, now betrothed to Biata.

affinity: the type of magic for which a person has an aptitude, such as light magic, warding, or healing.

Agata: the cook at Paradum, who was kind to Cassia.

Aithourian Circle: the war mages of the Order of Anthros, sworn enemies of the Hesperines, who have specialized spells for finding and destroying Hespera worshipers. Founded by Aithouros in ancient times, this circle was responsible for most of the destruction of Hespera's temples during the Last War. Oversees the training of all war mages from Tenebra and Cordium to ensure their lifelong loyalty to the Order.

Akanthia: the world comprising Tenebra, Cordium, Orthros, and the Empire.

Alea: one of the two Queens of Orthros, who has ruled the Hesperines for nearly sixteen hundred years with her Grace, Queen Soteira. A mage of Hespera in her mortal life, she is the only Prisma of a temple of Hespera who survived the Ordering.

Alexandra: royal firstblood and Eighth Princess of Orthros, the youngest of the Queens' family. Solaced from Tenebra as a child. She raises silkworms for her craft. Lio's childhood sweetheart.

Alkaios: one of the three Hesperines errant who saved Cassia as a child. He retrieved the ivy pendant from Solia's body for her. He and his Grace, Nephalea, recently settled in Orthros after years as Hesperines errant with his Gifter, Nike.

Anastasios: Ritual Firstblood who Gifted Apollon, founder of Lio's bloodline. He was a powerful healer and Prismos of Hagia Boreia, who sacrificed his life to help Alea protect their Great Temple from the Order of Anthros's onslaught.

ancestors: forebears who have passed into the spirit phase. Imperial mages can commune with them to channel their power into spells and rituals. Hesperines cannot contact the ancestors or wield ancestral magic because their immortality prevents them from entering the spirit phase.

Andragathos: god of male virtue and righteous warfare in the Tenebran and Cordian pantheon. The seventh scion and youngest son of Kyria and Anthros. A lesser deity alongside his brothers and sisters, the Fourteen Scions. See **Knightly Order of Andragathos**

Anesu: the current Sandira King, brother of Tendeso.

Angara: goddess in the Tenebran and Cordian pantheon who blesses warriors with morale in battle. Often portrayed wearing golden armor and bearing a sword. The second scion and eldest daughter of Kyria and Anthros, a lesser deity alongside her brothers and sisters, the Fourteen Scions.

Annassa: honorific for the Queens of Orthros.

Anthros: god of war, order, and fire. Supreme deity of the Tenebran and Cordian pantheon and ruler of summer. The sun is said to be Anthros riding his chariot across the sky. According to myth, he is the husband of Kyria and brother of Hypnos and Hespera.

Anthros's fire: a flower commonly grown in Tenebra, used by humans in combination with the herb sunsword to ward off Hesperines.

Apollon: Lio's father, an elder firstblood and founder of Orthros. In his mortal life before the Ordering, he was a mage of Demergos. Transformed by Anastasios, he was the first Hesperine ever to receive the Gift from one of the Ritual firstbloods. Renowned for his powerful stone magic and prowess in battle, he once roamed Abroad as one of the Blood Errant. Known as the Lion of Orthros. Now retired to live peacefully in Orthros with his Grace, Komnena.

apostate: rogue mage who illegally practices magic outside of the Orders.

arcane: of or related to magic, as opposed to mundane.

Archipelagos: land to the west of the Empire comprising a series of islands, which maintains strict isolation from the rest of the world. See **Menodora**

Argyros: Lio's uncle and mentor in diplomacy and mind magic. Elder firstblood and founder of Orthros from Hagia Anatela, Gifted by Eidon. Graced to Lyta, father of Nike, Kadi, and Mak. An elder firstblood and founder of Orthros like Apollon, his brother by mortal birth. Attended the first Equinox Summit and every one since as the Queens' Master Ambassador. One of the most powerful thelemancers in history, known as Silvertongue for his legendary abilities as a negotiator.

Ariadne: an apprentice mage of Kyria who accompanied the Semna and Pakhne to Orthros. One of the mages who helped the Hesperine embassy take Zoe and the other Eriphite children to safety.

Arkadia: Lio's cousin, daughter of Argyros and Lyta. Solaced from Tenebra as a child. With her mother's affinity for warding and aptitude for the battle arts, she serves as a Master Steward in Hippolyta's Stand.

Ashes: band of mercenaries renowned for their great deeds in the Empire. Hoyefe, Karege, and Tuura are the current members under Kella's command.

Retired members include Ukocha, their former leader; Solia; and Tendeso.

Athena: three-year-old Eriphite child Solaced by Javed and Kadi. Younger sister of Boskos by birth and blood. The severe case of frost fever she suffered as a mortal damaged her brain. While the Gift has healed her, she is still recovering lost development.

Autumn Greeting: ancient courtship festival of Tenebra. When a woman shares this dance with a man, it is considered a promise of betrothal, after which their fathers will arrange their marriage.

avowal: Hesperine ceremony in which Graces profess their bond before their people; legally binding and an occasion of great celebration.

Ayur: Azarqi goddess of the moons.

Azarqi: nomads of the Maaqul Desert who control trade routes between Vardara and the rest of the Empire. Known for their complex politics, the Azarqi were te original negotiators of the Desert Accord with the jinn.

Bamaayo: word for "mother" in Queen Soteira's first language.

Basileus: title of the King of Tenebra, appended to the name of every monarch who takes the throne.

Basilinna: title of a princess of Tenebra.

Basilis: title of a non-royal female relative of the king, outside of the line of succession.

Basir: Hesperine thelemancer and one of the two spymasters of Orthros, alongside his Grace, Kumeta. From the Empire in his mortal life. His official title is "Queens' Master Envoy" to conceal the nature of their work.

Battle of Souls: the most prestigious tournament in the Empire, held once every eight years. The winner, known as the Victor of Souls, receives a boon from the Empress and an acacia branch, as well as the right to display the acacia symbol for the rest of their lives.

beast magic: type of Lustra magic that gives those with this affinity the power to influence animals and, if very powerful, to change into animal forms. See **changer**

Bellator: Tenebran free lord who kidnapped Solia and held her for ransom inside Castra Roborra. Led the short-lived rebellion that ended there with the Siege of Sovereigns. Father of Benedict.

Benedict: First Knight of Segetia, Flavian's best friend, who harbors unrequited love for Genie. Cassia trusts him and considers him a friend. Traveled to Orthros as Lord Titus's representative during the Solstice Summit. The son of Bellator, he carries guilt over his father's treason.

Blood Errant: group of four ancient and powerful Hesperine warriors who went errant together for eight centuries. See **Apollon, Ioustinianos, Pherenike, Prometheus**

blood magic: type of magic practiced by worshipers of Hespera, from which the power of the Gift stems. All Hesperines possess innate blood magic.

Blood Moon: Hesperine name for one of the two moons, which appears red with a liquid texture to the naked eye. Believed to be an eye of the Goddess Hespera, potent with her blood magic.

blood shackles: warding spell cast with blood magic, which compels a person to not take a particular action. Persists until they are released by a key, a magical condition determined by the caster.

Blood Union: magical empathic connection that allows Hesperines to sense the emotions of any living thing that has blood.

Blood-Red Prince: see **Ioustinianos**

bloodborn: Hesperine born with the Gift because their mother was transformed during pregnancy.

bloodless: undead; a corpse reanimated by a necromancer, so called because blood no longer flows through its veins, although it has a semblance of life. Often used as an insult by Hesperines.

Bosko *or* **Boskos**: eleven-year-old Eriphite child Solaced by Javed and Kadi. Elder brother of Athena by birth and blood. Zoe's best friend. Harbors anger over what the children suffered. Training to become a Steward is helping him adjust to life in Orthros.

Brotherhood of Hedon: secret society of highborn men dedicated to the god Hedon, who engage in indulgences such as gambling, drinking, magical drugs, and sex with prostitutes in their god's temples.

Btana Ayal: "Shattered Hope"; the ruins of an ancient city that flourished in the Maaqul Desert during the Hulaic Epochs. Under the leadership of the Diviner Queen, the people of Btana Ayal traveled to Tenebra via a spirit gate. Their encounter with the other continent ended in tragedy, when the Diviner Queen had to collapse the gate to prevent the Old Masters from invading the Empire, destroying the city in the process.

Caelum: Solia and Cassia's fourteen-year-old half-brother, only son of King Lucis, crown prince of Tenebra.

Callen: Perita's loving husband and Cassia's bodyguard in the royal household who accompanied her to the Solstice Summit. Has since returned to Tenebra.

Cassia: newgift awaiting her transformation into a Hesperine so she can spend eternity with Lio, her Grace. Once a Tenebran lady who secretly supported the Hesperines and helped Lio secure peace during the Solstice Summit. Born the illegitimate daughter of King Lucis and his concubine, Thalia.

Castra Justa: the stronghold of the First Prince and base of operations for the Prince's Charge.

Castra Patria: the ancient fortress at Patria, dating from the Mage King's time, where the Council of Free Lords convenes.

Castra Roborra: fortress in Tenebra belonging to Lord Bellator, where he held Solia captive. Site of the Siege of Sovereigns.

Chalice of Stars: Nike's legendary round shield, which she uses along with the Stand's hand-to-hand combat techniques.

changer: practitioner of Lustra magic with the power to take on animal form.

Changing Queen: Queen Hedera of Tenebra, the Mage King's wife and co-ruler during the Last War. As a Silvicultrix, she was a powerful mage in her own right. Her own people knew her as Ebah. Also known as the Hawk of the Lustra and associated with her plant symbol, ivy. Cassia's ancestor through her mother, Thalia.

channeling: when a mage draws power from a source greater than themselves, instead of from an innate store of magical power. Progonaia and hulaia rely on channeling.

the Charge: see **Prince's Charge**

Charge Law: legal code of Orthros Abroad, named for the Prince's Charge. An evolving body of laws established and enforced by the First Prince, based on the Equinox Oath and Hespera's sacred tenets.

charm: physical object imbued with a mage's spell, usually crafted of botanicals or other materials with their own magical properties. Offers a mild beneficial effect to an area or the holder of the charm, even if that person is not a mage.

Chera: goddess of rain and spinning in the Tenebran and Cordian pantheon, known as the Mourning Goddess and the Widow. According to myth, she was the Bride of Spring before Anthros destroyed her god-husband, Demergos, for disobedience.

Chief Diviner of the High Court: the highest-ranking theramancer in the Empire, who advises the Empress.

Chrysanthos: war mage from Cordium with an affinity for fire. As the Dexion of the Aithourian Circle, he is one of the elites in the Order of Anthros. During the Solstice Summit, he tried to sabotage peace talks with hostage negotiations.

Chuma: daughter of Ukocha, beloved and protected by all the Ashes.

Cifwani Matriarchate: powerful sister-state in the Empire bordering the Sandira Kingdom. Ruled by matriarchal clans and known for their craftswomen and warriors. The Cifwani are the present-day descendants of Queen Soteira's ancient culture.

the Collector: one of the Old Masters, both a necromancer and mage of dreams, who uses his power to possess his victims and force them to do his bidding. He has used essential displacement to amass unnatural amounts of magic of various affinities. The Gift Collectors are his willing servants, helping him carry out a far-reaching conspiracy to achieve his mysterious ends in alliance with King Lucis. With the help of Skleros and by exploiting Eudias, he entered Orthros during the Solstice Summit and would have caused terrible suffering and destruction if Lio and Cassia had not stopped him.

Cordium: land to the south of Tenebra where the Mage Orders hold sway. Its once-mighty principalities and city-states have now lost power to the magical and religious authorities. Wealthy and cultured, but prone to deadly politics. Also known as the Magelands.

Corona: capital city of Cordium and holy seat of the Mage Orders, where the main temples of each god are located.

Council of Free Lords: a body of Tenebran lords who have the hereditary authority to convey or revoke the nobility's mandate upon a reigning monarch. Their rights and privileges were established in the Free Charter.

Council Shield: a free lord's ceremonial armament passed down through the generations of his line, which he uses at the Council to declare his support for his chosen monarch.

Court of Claws: exclusive sparring area at the Sandira Court where gold roster mercenaries and royal guards challenge each other.

the Craving: a Hesperine's addiction to their Grace's blood. When deprived of each other, Graces suffer agonizing withdrawal symptoms and fatal illness.

Dakkoul: leader of the Rezayal, who befriended Cassia, only to betray he rand take her captive in Btana Ayal. A theramancer who has weaponized his mind healing.

Dawn Slumber: deep sleep Hesperines fall into when the sun rises. Although the sunlight causes them no harm, they're unable to awaken until nightfall, leaving them vulnerable during daylight hours.

Departure: contingency plan that dates from the founding of Orthros, when Hesperines feared the Last War might break out again at any time. If the Queens invoked the Departure, all Hesperines errant would return home, and the border between Orthros and Tenebra would be closed forever.

Deukalion: bloodborn firstgift of Apollon and Komnena, Ambassador in Orthros's diplomatic service who has devoted his career to improving relations between Orthros and Tenebra. He and Cassia, his Grace, succeeded in securing a treaty with the free lords during the Solstice Summit.

Deverran: Tenebran free lord who was betrothed to Caelum's mother before Lucis married her. Now betrothed to Nivalis.

Dexion: second highest ranking mage in the Aithourian Circle.

Discourses on Love: Orthros's canon of erotic texts.

Divine City: see **Corona**

Divine Tongue: language spoken by Hesperines and mages, used for spells, rituals, and magical texts. The common tongue of Orthros, spoken freely by all Hesperines. In Tenebra and Cordium, the mages keep it a secret and disallow non-mages from learning it.

diviner: Imperial theramancer trained in ancient traditions who protects their people from necromancy and communicates with the ancestors. Their ancestral magic enables them to open passages through the spirit phase.

Diviner Queen: theramancer who founded Btana Ayal and the surrounding civilization in the Hulaic Epochs. When she led her people to the shadowlands through a spirit gate, they taught the people of what would later become Tenebra and Cordium how to use magic. When the Old Masters began to abuse the power they had learned from her, she made the ultimate sacrifice and destroyed everything she had built to contain their evil.

the Drink: when a Hesperine drinks blood from a human or animal; a nonsexual act, considered sacred, which should be carried out with respect for the donor. It's forbidden to take the Drink from an unwilling person. Or Hesperine sacred tenet, the commitment to thriving without the death of other living things.

eastern Tenebrae: wilderness east of the settled regions of Tenebra, sparsely populated by homesteads under the leadership of hold lords. Officially under the king's rule, but prone to lawlessness. Hesperines roam freely here.

Ebah: see **Changing Queen**

Eighth Circle: Lio and Cassia's Trial circle. See **Alexandra, Eudokia, Lysandros, Menodora, Telemakhos**

elder firstbloods: the ancient Hesperine founders of Orthros. Gifted by the Ritual firstbloods. See **Apollon, Argyros, Hypatia, Kassandra**

the Empire: vast and prosperous human lands located far to the west, across an ocean from Tenebra. Comprises many different languages and cultures united under the Empress. Allied with Orthros and welcoming to Hesperines, many of whom began their mortal lives as Imperial citizens. Maintains a strict policy of isolation toward Tenebra and Cordium to guard against the Mage Orders.

the Empress: the ruler of the Empire, admired by her citizens. The Imperial throne has passed down through the female line for many generations.

the Empress's privateers: pirates who sail with the sanction of the Empress, granted by a letter of marque, which authorizes them to rob her enemies. They make voyages to Cordium to secretly pillage the Mage Orders' ships.

enchantment: a spell anchored to a power source, which can last indefinitely without a mage's attention.

envoy: according to common knowledge, a messenger attached to the Hesperine diplomatic service. In fact, envoys are the Queens' spies who gather information from the mortal world to protect Orthros and Hesperines errant. See **Basir, Kumeta**

Equinox Oath: ancient treaty between Orthros and Tenebra, which prescribes the conduct of Hesperines errant and grants them protection from humans.

Equinox Summit: peace talks in which the Hesperines send ambassadors from Orthros to meet with the King of Tenebra and renew the Equinox Oath. Each mortal king is expected to convene it once upon his accession to the throne.

Eriphites: worshipers of the pastoral god Eriphon, branded heretics by the Order of Anthros. The last surviving members of their cult are twenty-four orphaned children recently brought to safety in Orthros thanks to Cassia and Lio. See **Zosime, Boskos, Athena**

errant: a Hesperine who has left Orthros to travel through Tenebra doing good deeds for mortals

essential displacement: process by which necromancers can transfer the magic of one person, the source, into another person, the vessel, through a third person called the channel. The vessel must die for the source to reclaim their power.

Eudias: young war mage from Cordium with an affinity for weather, including lightning. Compelled to join the Aithourian circle due to his magic, he defected during the Solstice Summit, aiding the Hesperines and the Tenebran embassy against Chrysanthos and Skleros. He and Lio faced the Collector in a mage duel, in which Lio helped him free himself from the Old Master's possession.

Eudokia: Hesperine youngblood, one of Lio's Trial sisters in Orthros. Solaced from Tenebra as a child. An initiate mathematician, calligrapher, and accomplished scholar. Daughter of Hypatia.

Eugenia: young Tenebran lady, believed to be Flavian's cousin and heir of his late uncle, Lord Eugenius. In fact she is his sister, the daughter of Titus and his concubine Risara.

Evander: son and heir of Evandrus the Elder, who was with him at Castra Roborra during the Siege of Sovereigns.

familiar: the animal companion of a Hesperine, bound to them by blood.

the Fangs: Prometheus's famous twin swords.

the Feast: Hesperine term for drinking blood while making love.

feuds: bitter conflicts that have raged between the free lords of Tenebra for centuries, which cause widespread destruction and suffering.

fire charm: a charm created by a fire mage that those without the affinity for fire can use to light a flame.

First Prince: see **Ioustinianos**

firstblood: the first Hesperine in a bloodline, who founds the family and passes the Gift to their children.

Firstblood Circle: the governing body of Orthros. Every firstblood has a vote on behalf of their bloodline, while non-voting Hesperines can attempt to influence policy by displays of partisanship. The Queens retain veto power, but use it sparingly.

firstgift: the eldest child of a Hesperine bloodline, first to receive the gift from their parents.

Flavian: Tenebran lord, son of Free Lord Titus and heir to Segetia's seat on the Council. Despite his family's feud with Hadria, he is admired by both sides and is a unifying figure for the fractured nobility. Cassia has prepared the way for him to take the throne from Lucis in a peaceful transfer of power.

Florian: see **Chrysanthos**

Font of the Changing Queen: stone fountain on the grounds of Solorum Palace that dates from the time of the Changing Queen. This historical monument is a subject of legends, which say it ran with blood the day the Mage King died. Lio and Cassia first met here in a forbidden nocturnal encounter.

fortune blade: dagger issued to mercenaries by the Empress's administration, which shows they are professionally recognized and may fight for profit, and that they abide by the Empress's code of conduct.

fortune name: name given to an Imperial mercenary, by which they are professionally known. Traditionally, they take the name of something they wish to avoid in order to ward off that evil.

the Fourteen Scions: see **Scions**

Free Charter: founding document of the kingdom of Tenebra, an agreement between the Mage King and the lords regarding the rights and privileges of the nobility. Grants the free lords influence over the royal succession.

free lord: highest noble rank in Tenebra. Has a seat on the Council of Free Lords and heredity authority to vote on whether a king should receive the nobility's mandate.

frost fever: contagious illness that is dangerous for adults but especially deadly to children. Tenebra suffers periodic epidemics of frost fever due to poor sanitation and nutrition.

Gaius: aging Tenebran lord loyal to Free Lord Hadrian who traveled to Orthros to represent him during the Solstice Summit.

Galanthian: Tenebran free lord with lands in the cold northern region of the kingdom. Father of Nivalis.

Genie: see **Eugenia**

the Gift: Hesperines' immortality and magical abilities, which they regard as a blessing from the goddess Hespera. The practice of offering the Gift to all is a Hesperine sacred tenet.

Gift Collector: mage-assassin and bounty hunter who hunts down Hesperines for the Order of Hypnos using necromancy, alchemy, and fighting tactics. Known for adapting common items into weapons to skirt the Orders' religious laws against mages arming themselves. They secretly have a higher loyalty to the Collector, the founder of their profession.

Gift Night: the night of a person's transformation into a Hesperine, usually marked by great celebration.

Gifter: the Hesperine who transforms another, conveying Hespera's Gift to the new immortal. For Hesperines transformed as children, their Gifters are their parents. For adults, their Gifter remains a lifelong mentor and usually becomes their Ritual parent.

Gifting: the transformation from human into Hesperine.

Glasstongue: see **Deukalion**

glyph: sacred symbol of a deity. Each god or goddess in the pantheon has a unique glyph. Often used as a pattern in spell casting or carved on shrines and temples.

glyph stone: the capstone of the doorway of a shrine, inscribed with the glyph of the deity worshiped there, where any spells over the structure are usually seated.

the Goddess's Eyes: the two moons, the red Blood Moon and the white Light Moon; associated with Hespera and regarded as her gaze by Hesperines.

gold roster: list maintained by the Empress's administrators of the mercenaries who have received the most gold in service to the Empire's interests. A measure of a mercenary's prowess, wealth, and how many contracts they have completed to benefit the common good.

Golden Shield: the Empress's personal guard, who answer only to her, an order of highly skill woman warriors with access to powerful magic. They give up their identities to devote their lives to the Empress's protection, and their families must live in seclusion so their loved ones cannot be used to gain an advantage against them.

Gorgos: master mage from the Sun Temple of Anthros at Solorum who aspires to become royal mage.

Grace: Hesperine sacred tenet, a magical bond between two Hesperine lovers. Frees them from the need for human blood and enables them to sustain each other, but comes at the cost of the Craving. A fated bond that happens when their love is true. It is believed every Hesperine has a Grace just waiting to be found. See **Craving**

Grace braids: thin braids of one another's hair that Graces exchange. They may wear them privately after professing their bond to one another, then exchange them publicly at their avowal and thereafter wear them for all to see to signify their commitment.

Grace Union: the particularly powerful and intimate Blood Union between two Hesperines who are Graced; enables them to communicate telepathically and empathically.

Grace-family (Grace-son, Grace-father, Grace-sister, etc.): the family members of a Hesperine's Grace; compare with human in-laws.

Great Temple Epoch: the historical period when the Great Temples of every cult flourished across Tenebra and Cordium, and all mages cooperated. Came to a cataclysmic end due to the Ordering and the Last War.

greater sand cat: species of large predator with special adaptations for surviving the Maaqul Desert. With specialized magic and great effort, they can be bonded to humans and ridden as mounts. See **Tilili**

Guardian of Orthros: see **Hippolyta**

Hadria: domain of Free Lord Hadrian, located on Tenebra's rocky western coast, where the seas are treacherous.

Lady Hadrian: Lord Hadrian's wife, a mature lady above reproach in the court of Tenebra, admired for her graces and respected for her political acumen.

Lord Hadrian: one of the two most powerful free lords in Tenebra, who commands the fealty of many other free lords and lesser nobles. His family has been feuding with Segetia for generations. Known for his loyalty to the throne, but also for honor superior to the king's.

Haima: capital city of Orthros Notou.

haima: blood magic. It is a subject of debate whether it is its own paradigm of magic or a blend of mageia and manteia.

Hammer of the Sun: Apollon's famous battle hammer, which he wielded while Abroad with the Blood Errant. He left it in Tenebra when he brought Komnena to Orthros.

Healing Sanctuary: infirmary in Orthros founded and run by Queen Soteira, where humans are given care and Hesperines are trained in the healing arts.

heart bow: traditional gesture of devotion to the Queens of Orthros, a deep bow with one hand over the heart.

heart hunters: warbands of Tenebrans who hunt down Hesperines, regarded by their countrymen as protectors of humanity. They patrol the northern borders of Tenebra with packs of liegehounds, waiting to attack Hesperines who leave Orthros.

Hedera: see **Changing Queen**

Hedon: god of pleasure and chance in the Tenebran and Cordian pantheon, patron of sexual acts and gambling. Styled as the god of fertility and prosperity by the Order of Anthros in their attempts to promote morality.

Hephaestion: a mage of the Aithourian Circle during the Last War, the war mages' most brilliant military strategist and inventor of magical siege engines.

Hespera: goddess of night cast from the Tenebran and Cordian pantheon. The Mage Orders have declared her worship heresy punishable by death.

Hesperines keep her cult alive and continue to revere her as the goddess of the moons, Sanctuary, and Mercy. Associated with roses, thorns, and fanged creatures. According to myth, she is the sister of Anthros and Hypnos.

Hespera's Gift: Hesperines' immortality and magical abilities, which they regard as a blessing from the goddess Hespera. The practice of offering the Gift to all is a Hesperine sacred tenet.

Hespera's Rose: the most sacred symbol of the Hesperines, a rose with five petals and five thorns representing Hespera's sacred tenets. Frequently embroidered on clothing or represented on stained glass windows. Based on real roses, which are the Goddess's sacred flower and beloved by Hesperines. The mages uproot them wherever they're found in Tenebra or Cordium and punish those who grow them for heresy.

Hesperine: nocturnal immortal being with fangs who gains nourishment from drinking blood. Tenebrans and Cordians believe them to be monsters bent on humanity's destruction. In truth, they follow a strict moral code in the name of their goddess, Hespera, and wish only to ease humankind's suffering.

Hesperite: human worshiper of Hespera, persecuted as a heretic by the Orders.

Hesperite settlement: community of Hesperites living in secret in the wilds of Tenebra. Reliant on the Prince's Charge to help them survive the hostile territory.

hex: a circle of six necromancers who exchange magical secrets and punish any who betray them.

Hinan: Queen Mother who represents the Azarqi on the Empire's council, queen of an influential nomad clan with great influence on desert politics and trade. Mother of Kella.

Hippolyta: Lio's aunt, Graced to Argyros, mother of Nike, Kadi, and Mak. Greatest and most ancient Hesperine warrior, a founder of Orthros. Known as the Guardian of Orthros for her deeds in Tenebra during the Last War and for establishing the Stand.

Hippolyta's Arena: arena in Orthros Notou where Hesperine athletes and warriors train with Hippolyta.

Hippolyta's Gymnasium: gymnasium in Orthros Boreou founded by Hippolyta, where she trains the Stand and Orthros's athletes compete.

Hippolyta's Stand: Orthros's standing army, founded by Hippolyta. Under her leadership, they patrol the border with Tenebra as Stewards of the Queens' ward. So few of the peaceful Hesperines take up the battle arts that the only Stewards are Nike, Kadi, Alkaios, Nephalea, Mak, and Lyros.

hold lord: Tenebran lord who holds a homestead in the eastern Tenebrae.

House Annassa: the residence of the Queens of Orthros, the Hesperine counterpart to a royal palace.

House Komnena: Lio's family home in Orthros, seat of his bloodline, named for his mother.

Hoyefe: mercenary illusionist and master fencer, member of the Ashes. Of Owia descent, he is an alumnus of Imperial University's School of Fine Arts and a playwright favored by the Empress.

hulaia: lustra magic, the paradigm of magic that channels from nature. Includes affinities such as plant magic, beast magic, and soothsaying.

Hulaic Epochs: eras of pre-history before the Great Temple Epoch, known only through oral traditions.

the Hunger: a combination of sexual desire and the need for blood, which Hesperines experience with their lovers.

Huru: Ziara's first mate and lover, a knife expert and theramancer.

Hypatia: an elder firstblood and founder of Orthros from Hagia Anatela, mother of Kia. Orthros's greatest astronomer, who invented the Hesperine calendar.

Hypnos: god of death and dreams in the Tenebran and Cordian pantheon. Winter is considered his season. Humans unworthy of going to Anthros's Hall are believed to spend the afterlife in Hypnos's realm of the dead. According to myth, he is the brother of Anthros and Hespera.

Imperial University: illustrious university in the Empire. Only students with wealth and the best references gain entry, usually those of noble or royal blood. Known for traditionalism and conservative approaches to research.

In Sanctuary: Hesperine term for the current historical era, marked from the date of Orthros's founding.

initiate: Hesperine who has achieved initiate rank in their craft or service, more advanced than a student but not yet of full rank. Attained after the young Hesperine completes a significant crafting project or research treatise that meets with their mentor's approval.

Initiation: see **Trial**

Ioustin *or* **Ioustinianos**: First Prince of the Hesperines, eldest child of the Queens of Orthros. Lio's Ritual father. Solaced from Tenebra as a child. Once a warrior in the Blood Errant known as the Blood-Red Prince, he now leads the Charge. Young Hesperines call him Rudhira, an affectionate name given to him by Methu.

Irene: mage expelled from the Temple of Kyria at Solorum after betraying them to Dalos. Sister of Lord Tyran, she is scheming to regain her status in the nobility.

Iris: Tenebran lady, Solia's handmaiden and closest companion, who sacrificed her life for Solia at the Siege of Sovereigns.

ivy pendant: wooden pendant carved with a triquetra of ivy. An artifact of the Changing Queen secretly passed down by the women of her line. Thalia entrusted it to Solia to give to Cassia.

Javed: Lio's Grace-cousin, avowed to Kadi, father of Bosko and Thenie. From the Empire in his mortal life. Has an affinity for healing and now serves in Orthros's Healing Sanctuary.

Jinn: immortal beings that dwell in the Maaqul Desert. Unlike Hesperines, they were never human. Endowed with powerful magic drawn from elements of nature, they also have a connection with the spirit phase. A long history of conflict between jinn and Imperial humans culminated in the Thousand Fires War and ended with the Desert Accord.

Justinian: see **Ioustinianos**

Kadi: see **Arkadia**

Kalos: the Charge's best scout, who uses his tracking skills to find Hesperines errant who are missing in action.

kalux: Hesperine word in the Divine Tongue for clitoris.

Karege: Hesperine warrior and member of the Ashes. Offered Sanctuary by Princess Konstantina five centuries ago, he prefers to spend his immortality adventuring and earning gold in the Empire, rather than fulfilling his duties as an elder in Orthros.

Kassandra: Lio's Ritual mother, an elder firstblood and founder of Orthros. Ritual sister to the Queens, who Gifted her, and mother of Prometheus. A princess in her mortal life, she abdicated during a dynastic dispute and became the first Hesperine from the Empire, securing her homeland's alliance with Orthros. Now the Queens' Master Economist who oversees Orthros's trade. Has the gift of foresight and as Orthros's oracle, guides the Hesperines with her prophecies.

Kella: Azarqi princess, daughter of Hinan, and Ukocha's successor as first blade of the Ashes. A fierce warrior with a preference for daggers, as well as a water mage skilled at desert survival. Bonded to her greater sand cat mount, Tilili, after her legs were amputated above the knee due to a combat injury.

Kia: see **Eudokia**

King of Tenebra: see **Lucis**

Kings and Mages: Tenebran and Cordian name for the game Hesperines call Prince and Diplomat.

Knight: Cassia's beloved liegehound. Solia gave him to Cassia as a puppy so Cassia would have protection and companionship.

Knightly Order of Andragathos: holy warriors who adhere to a strict moral code and persecute Hesperines in the name of their patron god. See **Andragathos**

Komnena: Lio's mother, still rather young by Hesperines standards. Fled a life of squalor as a Tenebran farmwife and ran away to Orthros with Apollon, who Gifted her while she was pregnant and raised her son as his own. Now a respected mind healer. As the Queens' Chamberlain, she is responsible for helping newcomers to Orthros settle and adjust.

Kona *or* **Konstantina**: royal firstblood, Second Princess of Orthros, the second child and eldest daughter of the Queens. From the Empire in her mortal life. As the Royal Master Magistrate, she is the author of Orthros's legal code and an influential politician who oversees the proceedings of the Firstblood Circle.

krana: Hesperine term in the Divine Tongue for vagina.

Kumeta: Hesperine light mage and one of the two spymasters of Orthros, alongside her Grace, Basir. From the Empire in her mortal life. Her official title is "Queens' Master Envoy" to conceal the nature of their work.

Kyria: goddess of weaving and the harvest in the Tenebran and Cordian pantheon, known as the Mother Goddess or the Wife. Her season is autumn. According to myth, she is married to Anthros.

the Last War: the cataclysmic violence sparked by the Ordering sixteen hundred years ago. When the Order of Anthros sought to suppress all resistance to their authority, magical and armed conflict ravaged Tenebra and Cordium, destroying the civilization of the Great Temple Epoch. Peace came at the cost of the Hesperines' exile and the Order of Anthros's victory, while the Mage King secured his rule in Tenebra.

letting site: a location where Lustra mages can channel the most power from the wilds. These ritual sites were created by the Silvicultrixes in ancient times to release magic from nature for their use.

liegehound: war dogs bred and trained by Tenebrans to track, hunt, and slay Hesperines. Veil spells do not throw them off the scent, and they can leap high enough to pull a levitating Hesperine from the air. The only animals that do not trust Hesperines. They live longer than other canines and can withstand poison and disease.

Light Moon: Hesperine name for one of the two moons, which appears white with a smooth texture. Believed to be an eye of the Goddess Hespera, shining with her light.

Lio: see **Deukalion**

Lion of Orthros: see **Apollon**

Lonesome: Hoyefe's fortune name.

Lucian: see **Mage King**

Lucis: current King of Tenebra, who reigns with ruthlessness and brutality. Born a lord, he secured the crown by might and political schemes, and he upholds his authority by any means necessary. Cassia has never forgiven him for his cruelty to her, Solia, and Thalia.

the Lustra: the wilds of Tenebra, source of Lustra magic.

Lustra magic: The old nature magic of Tenebra practiced in ancient times by the Changing Queen. The Orders have never been able to understand or control it, and most knowledge of it is now lost. See **hulaia**

Lustri: the ancient peoples of Tenebra who practiced Lustra magic, led by priestess-queens known as Silvictulrixes, such as the Changing Queen.

Lyros *or* **Lysandros**: Lio's Trial brother and Grace-cousin, avowed to Mak, Solaced as a child from Tenebra. Also a warder and warrior serving in the Stand.

Lyta: see **Hippolyta**

Maaqul Desert: a vast and treacherous desert the size of several states in the Empire. Few besides the jinn and the Azarqi nomads can survive here.

Mage King: King Lucian of Tenebra, who reigned sixteen hundred years ago, widely considered by Hesperines and mortals to have been a great monarch. He and his wife, the Changing Queen, made the original Equinox Oath with the Queens of Orthros. A fire mage and warrior, he ruled before the Mage Orders mandated that men must choose between wielding spells or weapons.

mage of dreams: mage of Hypnos with an affinity for thelemancy.

Mage Orders: the magical and religious authorities in Cordium, which also dictate sacred law to Tenebran temples. Responsible for training and governing mages and punishing heretics.

mageia: magery, the paradigm of magic that affects the physical world. Includes elemental affinities such as fire, water, and stone magic.

Magelands: see **Cordium**

Mak: see **Telemakhos**

manteia: sorcery, the paradigm of magic that affects the thought, emotion, and life force. Includes affinities such as mind magic and necromancy.

Martyrs' Pass: the only known passage to Orthros through the Umbral Mountains. When an army of heart hunters possessed by the Collector ambushed the Tenebran embassy here, Lio defeated them with his mind magic and rescued Cassia.

Master of Dreams: see **the Collector**

Mederi Village: a small farming village near Patria, known for its loyalty to Solia's memory.

Menodora: Hesperine youngblood, one of Lio's Trial sisters. Daughter of Kitharos and Dakarai. An initiate musician, admired vocalist, and crafter of musical instruments. She is one of only two Hesperines from the Archipelagos and the immortal expert on the music of her mortal homeland.

Mercy: Hesperine sacred tenet, the practice of caring for dead or dying humans.

Methu: see **Prometheus**

Midnight Moonbeam: black-and-white dwarf goat kid, one of Zoe's two familiars.

Migration Night: event twice a year when Hesperines travel between hemispheres to avoid longer hours of daylight. The night after Spring Equinox, they vacate Orthros Boreou in the northern hemisphere and migrate to Orthros Notou in the southern hemisphere. The night before Autumn Equinox, they change residence again, leaving Orthros Notou and returning to Orthros Boreou.

mind healer: see **theramancer**

mind mage: see **thelemancer**

mind ward: mental defense cast by a thelemancer, which protects a person's mind from mages seeking to invade their thoughts or subdue their Will.

Miranda: one of Lady Sabina's handmaidens and a close friend of Perita's.

Monsoon: Tendeso's fortune name.

moon hours: by the Hesperine clock, the hours corresponding to night, when Hesperines pursue public activities.

Moon Market: hidden bazaar on the island of Marijani, where the Empress's privateers sell their spoils.

moskos: Hesperine term in the Divine Tongue meaning testicles.

mundane: unmagical, as opposed to arcane.

Mweya: winged Sandira deity who blessed his descendants with the ability to shapeshift.

natural phase: the physical world where living creatures exist, as opposed to the afterlife. See **spirit phase**

Natural Union: Hesperine term for sexual intercourse

Nephalea: one of the three Hesperines errant who saved Cassia as a child. She and her Grace, Alkaios, recently settled in Orthros after years as Hesperines errant with his Gifter, Nike.

newgift: a newly transformed Hesperine, or a person who has decided to become immortal and awaits their Gifting.

Night Call: magical summons a Hesperine elder can perform on a less powerful Hesperine to prematurely break them out of the Dawn Slumber.

Nike: see **Pherenike**

Nivalis: young Tenebran lady, one of Lady Hadrian's followers who frequents her weaving room. Daughter of Lord and Lady Galanthian. Her three younger siblings died in a past epidemic of frost fever. Sister of Pakhne and betrothed to Deverran.

Nodora: see **Menodora**

Noon Watch: Karege's fortune name.

the Oath: see **Equinox Oath**

the Old Masters: the oldest known hex of necromancers in Tenebran and Cordian record. Little is known about them from legends and surviving ancient texts, but their influence is linked to catastrophic events and suffering throughout history. They extend their lives and hoard power using abusive magic such as essential displacement. See **the Collector**

ora: strong Sandira liquor.

Order of Anthros: Mage Order dedicated to the god Anthros, which holds the ultimate religious and magical authority over all other Orders and temples. Bent on destroying Hesperines. War mages, light mages, and warders serve in this Order, as do agricultural and stone mages.

Order of Hypnos: Mage Order devoted to Hypnos, which holds authority over necromancers, mind mages, and illusionists. Oversees rites for the dead, purportedly to prevent Hesperine grave robbing, but in practice to stop rogue necromancers from raising the dead. The Order of Anthros's closest ally in their effort to destroy Hesperines.

Ordered Time: Tenbran and Cordian term for the current historical era, which they mark from the Ordering.

the Ordering: historical event over sixteen hundred years ago, when the Order of Anthros came to prominence and enforced its doctrines upon all other cults, who had previously worshiped and practiced magic freely. New mandates forbade warriors from practicing magic and required all mages to enter temples and remain celibate. The war mages also branded all Hespera worshipers heretics and destroyed their temples. The Ordering caused the Last War and the end of the Great Temple Epoch.

the Orders: see **Mage Orders**

Orthros: homeland of the Hesperines, ruled by the Queens. The Mage Orders describe it as a horrific place where no human can survive, but in reality, it is a land of peace, prosperity, and culture.

Orthros Abroad: the population of Hesperines who are errant in Tenebra at any given time. Under the jurisdiction of the First Prince, who is the Queens' regent outside their ward.

Orthros Boreou: Hesperine homeland in the northern hemisphere, located north of and sharing a border with Tenebra.

Orthros Notou: Hesperine homeland in the southern hemisphere, located across the sea to the southeast of the Empire.

Orthros Warmbloods: unique breed of horses originated by Hippolyta. Hesperine blood magic gives them intelligence, strength, and longevity superior to mundane horses.

Owia: the dynasty that currently holds the throne of the Empire.

Pakhne: eldest daughter of Free Lord Galanthian, sister to Nivalis. Happily left her life as a lady to become a mage of Kyria. Travels to Orthros as one of the Semna's attendants during the Solstice Summit.

paradigm: a major pattern of magic, consisting of a set of affinities that follow the same rules and affect related aspects of reality. See **haima, hulaia, mageia, manteia, progonaia.**

Paradum: a hunting estate of the King of Tenebra, located near Patria. The king sent Cassia to live there for a brief time when she was fourteen.

Patria: a domain in Tenebra, the traditional location for the Council of Free Lords to gather each time they must grant their mandate to a new monarch.

Peanut: Tuura's fortune name.

Perita: Cassia's handmaiden and dearest friend who accompanied her to Orthros for the Solstice Summit and assisted with all her schemes. Has now returned to Tenebra with her husband, Callen.

Phaedros: mage of Hespera and brilliant scholar from ancient times. The only survivor of his Great Temple's destruction by the Aithourian Circle. After he took revenge against the mortals, he lost his status as an elder firstblood. Now lives in eternal exile under the midnight sun.

Pherenike: Lio's cousin, a warder and warrior second only to her mother Lyta in strength, a thelemancer second only to her father Argyros in power. Solaced from Tenebra as a child. Known as the Victory Star, one of the Blood Errant alongside her uncle, Apollon, and her Trial brothers Rudhira and Methu. After the surviving Blood Errant's campaign to avenge Methu, she remained Abroad alone, missing in action for over ninety years. Recently returned to Orthros to once again serve in the Stand.

plant magic: type of Lustra magic that grants the power to make plants grow.

Prince and Diplomat: board game and beloved Hesperine pastime; requires strategy and practice to master.

Prince's Charge: the force of Hesperines errant who serve under the First Prince.

Prisma: highest ranking female mage in a temple.

privateers: see **Empress's Privateers**

progonaia: ancestral magic, the paradigm of magic that is channeled from the spirit phase. Includes Imperial affinities such as divination.

Prometheus: legendary Hesperine warrior and martyr. Bloodborn to Kassandra and descendant of Imperial royalty. Known as the Midnight Champion, he was a member of the Blood Errant with his comrades Nike, Rudhira, and

Apollon. Captured by the Aithourian Circle before Lio's birth. Orthros still mourns his death.

Pup: Solia's childhood nickname for Cassia.

pyromagus: mage with an affinity for fire.

Queen Mothers: matriarchs from each sister state within the Empire who possess the sacred artifacts that symbolize power to their particular people. Each Imperial dynasty must secure their blessings in order to reign.

the Queens: the Hesperine monarchs of Orthros. See **Alea, Soteira**

the Queens' Couriers: young Hesperines who serve Orthros as messengers, delivering correspondence and packages throughout Selas.

the Queens' ward: the powerful Sanctuary ward cast by the Queens, which spans the borders of Orthros, protecting Hesperines from human threats.

Rainbow Aurora: brown-and-white dwarf goat kid, one of Zoe's two familiars.

resonance: when a mage draws power from magical reserves within themselves, which resonate with certain aspects of the spiritual or physical, such as the mind or fire. Manteia and mageia rely on resonance.

revelatory spell: one of the Anthrian mages' specialized spells for revealing hidden Hesperines.

Rezayal: "Hope's Fragments"; a fanatical secret society of diviners based in the ruins of Btana Ayal, who believe only they can protect the Empire from the Old Masters. They use any means necessary to preserve the Empire's isolation and to persecute shadowlanders. Sometimes known as the Broken Hands due to their tattoo. Their members were deeply embedded at every level of Imperial society and government until the Empress recently broken their influence over her lands.

rhabdos: Hesperine term in the Divine Tongue meaning penis.

rimelace: flowering herb that requires extremely cold conditions. Difficult to grow in Tenebra, even with the aid of magic, but thrives in Orthros. The only known treatment for frost fever.

Risara: Titus's charismatic, beloved concubine of thirty years, adept at navigating the nobility's personal and political foibles.

Ritual: Hesperine sacred tenet. A ceremony in which Hesperines share blood, but in a broader sense, the whole of their religious beliefs.

Ritual circle: area where Hesperines gather to perform Ritual, usually marked with sacred symbols on the floor.

Ritual Drink: the Drink given by one Hesperine to another for healing or sustenance, without intimacy or invoking a family bond.

Ritual hall: central chamber in Hesperine homes where the bloodline's Ritual circle is located.

Ritual parents: Hesperines who attend a new suckling's first Ritual or who give the Gift to a mortal becoming a Hesperine as an adult. They remain mentors and trusted guides for eternity. Comparable to Tenebran temple parents.

royal firstbloods: the Queens' children, who are to establish their own bloodlines in order to share the Annassa's power with their people.

Rudhira: see **Ioustinianos**

Sabina: Tenebran lady, eldest daughter of Lord and Lady Hadrian. With no brothers, she is the heir of Hadria and runs the estate while her parents are at court.

Sanctuary: Hesperine sacred tenet, the practice of offering refuge to anyone in need. Or Hesperine refuge in hostile territory, concealed and protected from humans by Sanctuary magic.

Sanctuary mage: a mage with a rare dual affinity for warding and light magic, who can create powerful protections that also conceal. Queen Alea of Orthros is the only mage with this affinity who survived the Orders' persecution of Hespera worshipers.

Sanctuary Rose: a variety of white rose that originated in the Great Temples of Hespera. The only vine that survived the Last War now grows in Princess Konstantina's greenhouse, and she has propagated it throughout Orthros. Traditionally, each person who requests Sanctuary is given one of these blooms in welcome.

Sanctuary ward: ward created by a Sanctuary mage, which can both protect and hide those within it. Strong Sanctuary wards require the caster to remain inside the boundaries of the spell. Should the mage die there, their sacrifice will increase the ward's power and sustain it indefinitely.

Sandira Court: capital city and royal seat of the Sandira Kingdom, one of the most populous cities in the world. Known for its magnificent stone architecture. Mercenaries congregate in this metropolis seeking contracts with trade caravans in need of protection.

Sandira King: eagle shifter and monarch of the Sandira Kingdom known for showing no leniency. He rules with a strong hand to meet the challenges faced by his rapidly expanding people.

Sandira Kingdom: powerful sister state that controls the flow of gold, ivory, and copper between the Kwatzi City-States and the Empire's interior. Ruled by hereditary shifters whose animal forms signify their status within the hierarchy of warriors, nobility, or royalty.

Scions: lesser deities in the Tenebran and Cordian pantheon, the fourteen children of Anthros and Kyria, comprising seven sons and seven daughters. Each has their own cult and mages. See **Angara, Andragathos**

Segetia: domain of Free Lord Titus, landlocked and known for its fertile hills.

Selas: capital city of Orthros Boreou.

Semna: elderly retired Prisma of the Temple of Kyria at Solorum, who travels to Orthros for the Equinox Summit to spread her goddess's teachings to the Hesperines.

Severin *or* **Severinus the Younger**: son and heir of Severinus the Elder, who tries to mitigate his father's abuses against their people.

Severinus the Elder: Tenebran free lord with deeply held prejudices against Hesperines and close ties with heart hunters. His domain occupies Tenebra's border with Orthros.

Severitas: domain of Free Lord Severinus

shadowlander: Imperial term for a person from Tenebra or Cordium

shadowlands: Imperial term for Tenebra and Cordium, sometimes used with pity or disdain.

shifter: a person of Sandira descent who is blessed by their ancestors with the ability to shapeshift. Sandira shifters take on the form of a particular animal with which their clan has cultivated a sacred bond over many generations.

Siege of Sovereigns: King Lucis's assault on Castra Roborra, where rebel free lords held Solia for ransom. Ended the rebellion and resulted in the death of every living thing in the fortress.

Silvertongue: see **Argyros**

Silvicultrix: a Lustra sorceress with the triune affinity for beast magic, plant magic, and soothsaying. They ruled the Lustri as priestess-queens in ancient times, and the Changing Queen was known to be a powerful Silvicultrix. They have nearly died out, and Silvicultrixes like Thalia and Cassia are extraordinarily rare in the present day.

sister states: independent lands within the Empire ruled by their own monarchs, all owing allegiance to the Empress. She is seen as their eldest sister, and they are symbolically members of her clan.

Sisters' Port: harbor in Orthros Notou that is the hub of sea traffic between the Empire and Orthros.

Skleros: master necromancer and Gift Collector who holds the Order of Hypnos's record for completing the most bounties on Hesperines. Expert in essential displacement. Helped the Old Master known as the Collector cause devastation during the Solstice Summit.

Slumber: see **Dawn Slumber**

Solace: Hesperine sacred tenet, the practice of rescuing and Gifting abandoned children.

Solia: Princess of Tenebra, King Lucis's legitimate daughter and heir before the birth of his son. When she was seventeen, rebel lords kidnapped her. Lucis refused to ransom her and ensured all witnesses perished in the ensuing Siege of Sovereigns. Nobles and commoners alike still mourn her, not knowing she survived. After escaping to the Empire thanks to the privateers, she fought with the Ashes for several years under the name Sunburn. She won the Battle of Souls, earning a commission in the Golden Shield and the Empress's support for her overthrow of King Lucis. The love of Tendeso's life, Solia broke his heart when she chose her duty to Tenebra above their relationship.

Solorum: ancestral capital of Tenebra, royal seat of the king.

Solorum Palace: oldest palace in Tenebra, built by the Mage King, still the most important royal residence for the King of Tenebra.

Solstice Oath: new treaty between Orthros and the Tenebran nobility, secured thanks to Lio and Cassia's efforts during the Solstice Summit.

Solstice Summit: diplomatic negotiations between Tenebra and Orthros that marked the first time a mortal embassy from Tenebra ever entered Hesperine lands. An unprecedented event proposed by Lio in an effort to prevent war and make it possible for Cassia to stay with him.

soothsayer: Lustra mage with the affinity for soothsaying, which gives them the power to influence others' thoughts and choices with their words.

sophia: title of a Hesperine whose service is teaching and scholarship.

Soteira: one of the two Queens of Orthros, who has ruled the Hesperines for nearly sixteen hundred years with her Grace, Alea. Originally from the Empire, she was a powerful mortal mage with an affinity for healing before leaving to found Orthros alongside Alea.

speires: symbolic hair ties Lyta gives to trainees when they begin learning the battle arts. Stewards wear them as part of their Stand regalia.

spirit gate: a portal that allows magical travel by opening a passage through the spirit phase. Imperial diviners maintain regulated spirit gates throughout the Empire and Orthros Notou.

spirit phase: the spiritual plane of existence where the ancestors dwell, where living souls originate and to which they return in the afterlife.

spirit walk: ability of Imperial mages, who can walk through the spirit phase to travel between locations in the natural phase. Spirit walking is only possible in the territory of their own ancestors, and they must use spirit gates in other regions.

the Stand: see **Hippolyta's Stand**

Standstill: Kella's fortune name

stepping: innate Hesperine ability to teleport instantly from one place to another with little magical effort.

Steward: see **Hippolyta's Stand**

suckling: Hesperine child.

Summit Sanctuary: Hesperine Sanctuary located near Patria. Built by the Hesperine founders during the Equinox Summit as a safe place to stay while negotiating with the Mage King. Now an important outpost for the Prince's Charge.

sunbound: mild Hesperine curse word.

Sunburn: Solia's fortune name.

Sunfire Poison: alchemical poison concocted from sunsword and Anthros's fire. Lethal to Hesperines at the right dose, in smaller amounts it can reduce them to mortal strength and ability.

Telemakhos: Lio's cousin and best friend. Exposed as a child in Tenebra due to his club foot, Solaced by Argyros and Lyta. A warrior by profession and warder by affinity, he serves in the Stand. He and his Grace, Lyros, are newly avowed.

temple day: the day a Tenebran or Cordian child is presented to the gods in a temple for the first time at fourteen days old. Celebrated every year for the rest of their lives.

Tendeso: Prince of the Sandira Kingdom and brother of King Anesu. After the ancestors passed over him and gave his brother the throne, he fought with the Ashes for several years under the name Monsoon. Solia's lover for eight years until she defeated him in the Battle of Souls and chose her duty to Tenebra over him.

Tenebra: human kingdom south of Orthros and north of Cordium. Agrarian, feudal society ruled by a king, prone to instability due to rivalries between lords. Land of the Hesperines' origin, where they are now persecuted.

Thalia: Cassia's mother, believed to be merely Lucis's concubine. In truth, a Silvicultrix descended from the Changing Queen. Born in Cordium, where she became a powerful mage of Kyria, she was forced out of her temple when her triune affinity manifested. She chose to join Lucis in Tenebra to escape the Mage Orders and make her own secret bid for the throne.

thelemancer: a mage with an affinity for thelemancy, or mind magic, which gives them the power to manipulate others' thoughts and control their Wills.

Thenie: see **Athena**

theramancer: a person with an affinity for theramancy, or mind healing, who can use magic to treat mental illness.

the Thirst: a Hesperine's need to drink blood, a non-sexual urge like a human's need to drink water or eat food.

Thorn: Rudhira's two-handed sword, which he carried as one of the Blood Errant and now wields as he leads the Charge.

Tilili: greater sand cat bonded to Kella who serves as her mount and partner in combat.

Titus: free lord of Segetia, one of the most powerful men in Tenebra, who commands the fealty of many other free lords and lesser nobles. Segetia has been feuding with Hadria for generations.

Tradewinds: language used to conduct commerce across the multilingual Empire.

traversal: teleportation ability of Tenebran and Cordian mages; requires a great expense of magic and usually leaves the mortal mage seriously ill.

Trial circle: age set of Hesperines who go through the Trial of Initiation together. They consider each other Trial sisters and brothers for the rest of their immortal lives. Although not related by birth or blood, they maintain strong bonds of loyalty and friendship for eternity.

Trial *or* **Trial of Initiation**: Hesperine rite of passage marking an immortal's transition into adulthood.

triune affinity: the combination of three powerful types of Lustra magic: plant magic, beast magic, and soothsaying. See **Silvicultrix**

Tuura: mercenary theramancer, the Ashes' diviner and alchemist.

Twice-Seven Scions: see **Scions**

Tychon: young war mage with an affinity for fire, Chrysanthos's apprentice. Zealous in his devotion to his master and the Aithourian Circle's cause.

Tyran: ambitious free lord of Tenebra, loyal to Flavian and eager to stoke Segetia's feud with Hadria. Known for his and his soldiers' misconduct toward commoners, especially women.

Ukocha: retired leader of the Ashes, a swordswoman and fire mage who inspires awe among mercenaries. Mother of Chuma.

Union: Hesperine sacred tenet, the principle of living with empathy and compassion for all. See **Blood Union**

Valentia: Tenebran lady who fell into disgrace after her family supported Lord

Bellator's rebellion. Known for her excellent personal character. Loyal to Flavian's faction, unhappily betrothed to Tyran.

Vardara: now one of the mightiest sister states, once a sovereign land that fought wars with the Empire throughout history. The conflict ended sixteen hundred years ago when the Empress and a royal from the Silklands had a child together, Kassandra. Their union joined Vardara to the Empire.

veil hours: by the Hesperine clock, the hours corresponding to day, when Hesperines Slumber or devote their private time to friends, family, and lovers.

veil hours robe: Hesperine garment worn during veil hours, only in the presence of those with whom a Hesperine has a close relationship.

veil spell: innate Hesperine ability to cast magical concealments that hide their presence and activities from humans or fellow immortals.

Victor of Souls: see **Battle of Souls**

Victory Star: see **Pherenike**

Vulgus *or* **the vulgar tongue**: common language of all non-mages in Tenebra and Cordium.

war mage: person with an affinity for fire, lightning, or other type of magic that can be weaponized. The Order of Anthros requires them to dedicate their lives to the Aithourian Circle.

warder: mage with an affinity for warding, the power to create magical protections that block spells or physical attacks.

Will: free will, willpower. Or Hesperine sacred tenet, the principle of guarding the sanctity of each person's freedom of choice.

Winter Solstice: the most sacred time of the Hesperine year, when they celebrate Hespera with the sacred Festival of the Rose and Vigil of Thorns.

Xandra: see **Alexandra**

youngblood: young adult Hesperine who has recently reached their majority by passing the Trial of Initiation.

Zalele: supreme goddess of the Imperial pantheon, the deity of the sun and sky who is revered as the maker and nurturer of all creation. Believed to be too great and powerful to trouble herself with day-to-day mortal affairs, which she leaves to lesser deities and the ancestors.

Ziara: one of the most accomplished of the Empress's Privateers, famed for her powerful wind magic and daring voyages to Cordium. Captain of the Wanted, which she sails with Huru and their all-woman crew.

Zoe *or* **Zosime**: Lio's little sister, an eight-year-old Eriphite child Solaced by Apollon and Komnena. Loves her new family and idolizes her brother for his role in saving her from Tenebra. Has yet to heal from the emotional wounds she suffered as a mortal.

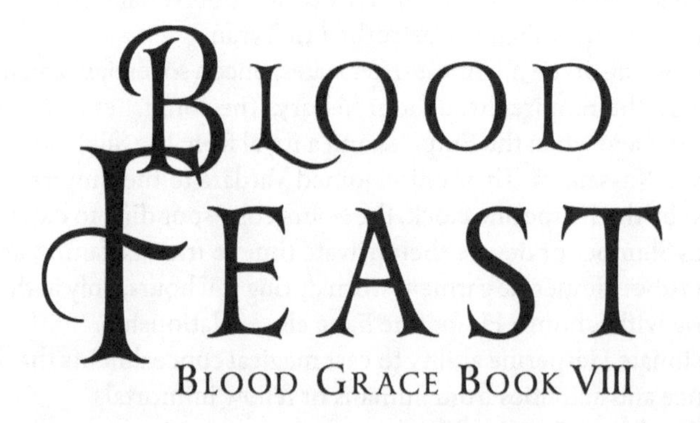

Her Grace is in danger - and her fangs are ready for battle.

Cassia has risen from the ashes of her human life as a Hesperine with magic the world has never seen. The Gift of immortality from Lio seals their fated Grace bond and frees her from the ancient necromancer known as the Collector. But she won't leave everyone they love, Hesperines and humans alike, as pawns in his schemes.

Lio fears their hard-won alliances only played into the necromancer's plots. With their warrior brothers Mak and Lyros, Lio and Cassia embark on a quest to uncover the conspiracy he's been brewing for centuries. Lio must duel the mage for his secrets on the most dangerous battlefield of all - the minds of the assassins who serve him.

As the four Hesperines face off with the Collector's deadliest playing pieces, he's intent on punishing Lio for stealing Cassia from him. Can her new power protect her Grace from their enemy's revenge?

Steamy romance meets classic fantasy worldbuilding in Blood Grace. Follow fated mates Lio and Cassia through their epic love story for a guaranteed series HEA.

Are you ready for Cassia's adventures as a Hesperine? Her new life with Lio continues in Blood Grace Book 8, *Blood Feast*...

vroth.co/feast

Get free books about characters from the world of Blood Grace!

Are you excited to read more books about the Hesperines - for free? Get bonus stories about Cassia and Lio as well as other characters from their world when you sign up for Vela's newsletter!

From dangerous adventures with Hesperines errant to cozy coffee dates on the docks of Orthros, new and familiar couples find Grace or fall deeper in love in these spicy reads.

Some stories are only available for a limited time, so be sure to check out the current selection of freebies before they're gone.

Read the free books here:
vroth.co/free

Vela Roth manifested unstable writing powers at a young age, and many of her early experiments had unintended results. As she grew, a curriculum of fantasy novels with strong heroines helped her learn to control and wield her abilities.

Eventually she dared pursue the knowledge inside the most forbidden tomes: romance novels. She's been practicing the dark arts of fantasy romance ever since, but strives to use her noveling powers only for good.

She lives in a solar-powered writer's garret at the foot of the mountains with her familiar, a rescue cat with a missing fang and a huge heart.

Vela loves hearing from readers and hopes you'll visit her at velaroth.com, where you can find her social media links or get signed books and swag at her shop, the Moon Market.

Made in United States
Troutdale, OR
11/24/2023